Dictionary of Literary Biography • Volume Eight

Twentieth-Century American Science-Fiction Writers

Part 1: A-L

Dictionary of Literary Biography

Twentieth-Century American Science-Fiction Writers

Part 1: A-L

Edited by
David Cowart
University of South Carolina
and
Thomas L. Wymer
Bowling Green State University

Foreword by Thomas M. Disch

A Bruccoli Clark Book
Gale Research Company • Book Tower • Detroit, Michigan 48226
1981

Planning Board for
DICTIONARY OF LITERARY BIOGRAPHY

John Baker
William Emerson
A. Walton Litz
Orville Prescott
William Targ
Alden Whitman

Matthew J. Bruccoli, *Editorial Director*
C. E. Frazer Clark, Jr., *Managing Editor*
Richard Layman, *Project Editor*

Manufactured by Braun-Brumfield, Inc.
Ann Arbor, Michigan
Printed in the United States of America

Library of Congress Cataloging in Publication Data

Main entry under title:

Twentieth-century American science-fiction writers.

   (Dictionary of literary biography ; v. 8)
   "A Bruccoli Clark book."
   1. Science fiction, American--History and criticism.
2. Science fiction, American--Bio-bibliography.
3. Authors, American--20th century--Biography.
I. Cowart, David, 1947- . II. Wymer, Thomas L.
III. Series: Dictionary of literary biography ; 8.
PS374.S35T88   813'.0876'09   81-4182
ISBN 0-8103-0918-1   AACR2

Contents

Foreword

SCIENCE FICTION: THE STATE OF THE ART TODAY

Virtually all science fiction of significant literary merit was written within the lifetimes of all but the two or three youngest writers treated in this volume. Like other arrivistes, the field of science fiction has been anxious to establish a pedigree, but between the scientific romances of H. G. Wells and Jules Verne and the emergence in the postwar years of such writers as Isaac Asimov, Robert A. Heinlein, and Theodore Sturgeon, most of our ancestral voices have dimmed to a deserved extinction. We are all contemporaries; thus, to speak of the state of the art "today" is to make a somewhat nugatory distinction, if that "today" describes as broad a span of time as it does in other literary chronicles. This essential contemporaneity of all science fiction, while a boon to its writers, who may merrily cross-fertilize in the living present, offers difficulties to literary chroniclers, who are inclined to view generations as successive and to speak in the past tense.

This is not to suggest that the last thirty-five years have not witnessed notable and rapid development; rather, that in science fiction ontogeny recapitulates phylogeny on an almost instant replay basis. An evolutionary model, however, is liable to evoke too linear a sense of the progress of the field and needs to be qualified by some sense of the ecological diversification that has led to today's many-niched pluralism. Aboriginal space opera continues to be written by established and by aspiring hacks, while the other niches of the imitable—High Tech, Clarkean engineering specs, fanciful chocolate boxes in the tradition of Charles Harness and Cordwainer Smith, sociological extrapolation a la C. M. Kornbluth and Frederik Pohl, satirical japes in the Sheckley manner—continue to be filled, more or less amply, by the descendants and epigones of those great originals.

In a field in which the short story has maintained aesthetic parity with the novel, magazine editors have played an especially significant role in the development of science fiction. (Awards in the field are named after editors, not writers.) These influential editors (e.g., John W. Campbell, Jr., Horace Gold, Michael Moorcock, Ben Bova) have often taken an active, demiurgic role in the creative process. It is as though (pursuing the ecological analogy) each editor had staked out certain generic possibilities—rodents, insectivores, proboscidians—which were then developed and diversified under his guidance till they had reached the farthest extent of their territorial range; i.e., till the market had been glutted. Commercial considerations generally bulk large in genre writing, and genre writers are usually prepared to defer to what they are told are the market's demands, for the sufficient reason that the possibility exists for the genre writer to earn a living from his work *without* having to pick a winning number in the lottery of the best-seller list. As it is the editor who mediates between the writer and the market place, inevitably it is the editor who presides over the transformation of imagination and originality into formular production. Few writers, adequately tempted, will refuse to write a sequel (or a tetralogy of them) or to duplicate an established success, their own or someone else's. This is not invariably unfortunate: some first-rate works have been inspired by the challenge to produce the ultimate story of a certain type or to out-Herod Herod. Samuel R. Delany's *Nova* (1968) was conceived as the space opera to end all space operas, and it was so received by its critics. Philip K. Dick's early novels owe a considerable debt to those of A. E. van Vogt, while Ursula K. Le Guin's *The Lathe of Heaven* (1971) is a third generation work in the direct line of descent. Throughout the last thirty years, while mainstream critics and writers have mourned the death of the novel and bemoaned the exhaustion of its subject matter, science-fiction writers have celebrated the plenum of possibilities still unrealized within the genre. One early critic expressed this sense of nascent expansiveness when he compared our situation to that of the Elizabethan dramatists—with the significant proviso that science fiction has yet to find its Shakespeare, a writer who can encompass in his own oeuvre all a genre's latent excellences. A quarter century later we continue to await our Shakespeare.

The years from 1945 through 1965, during which today's best-known professionals established and consolidated their reputations, also witnessed the appearance of certain singular creations, each by itself a rather lonely eminence, but, viewed together, constituting what may be regarded as an alternate tradition to that which grew out of the pulp magazines—an anti-science fiction, we might call it—for its admirers (and usually its writers) were anxious to disavow the genre label. The two most notable examples of this anti-science fiction are the classic dystopian novels of Aldous Huxley and George Orwell, but many science-fiction novels by Americans have contributed to the tradition: George R. Stewart's *Earth Abides* (1949); Kurt Vonnegut, Jr.'s *Slaughterhouse-Five* (1969; written after he had abjured the field), William S. Burroughs's *The Naked Lunch* (1959), Don DeLillo's *Ratner's Star* (1976). One might also cite the work of those science-fiction writers whose output has been characterized by similar "elitist" values of literacy, high ambition, and a refusal to write to a formula—such writers as Walter M. Miller, Algis Budrys, and Alfred Bester.

It was these writers of the countertradition who were most honored and emulated by the generation of writers who began publishing in the 1960s. The pulp tradition continued to survive and, indeed, to flourish, but even there standards of performance were rising. Most of the early pulp writers were as innocent of and inept at the crafts of storytelling, as distinct from the arts of enchantment, as movie serials of the same era. The essential difference between *Star Wars* of 1977 and *Buck Rogers* of 1939 may be very small, but the difference with regard to entertainment technology is vast. Similarly, in science fiction the hoisting gear that suspends disbelief has generally become more sophisticated and efficient. This in itself would not have constituted a revolution. However, the art of science fiction has evolved in a manner that parallels its development as a craft. The possibility had always existed, and sometimes been realized, that science fiction might transcend the intellectual limits of vicarious adventure stories directed toward a juvenile or naive audience, but the expectation persisted, until very recently, that formular hackwork would be the standard and that departures from this standard were to be regarded as happy exceptions to the rule.

It was against this background that the so-called New Wave science fiction of the mid-1960s and early 1970s emerged. Immediately that epithet is mentioned, one must qualify it by insisting that the New Wave never constituted a unified phenomenon. Its most characteristic writers—Brian Aldiss, J. G. Ballard, Harlan Ellison, Le Guin, Delany, Norman Spinrad—have also been, by virtue of their talent, the most idiosyncratic. As a group they can be seen to share a diminished regard for the consensual High Tech future of hard-core, technocratic science-fiction writers (e.g., Poul Anderson, Bova, Larry Niven), but in this they mirrored prevailing intellectual currents. Of course, countercultural proclivities are no guarantee of literary accomplishment, for any ideology can be adapted to the market's insatiable demands for hackwork. In the later 1970s some of the genre's most popular productions—Robert Silverberg's *Lord Valentine's Castle* (1980), the stories of John Varley and Vonda N. McIntyre—have been capable syntheses of countercultural advocacy (especially of those values associated with consciousness raising and sexual therapeutics) and formula pulp adventure. Today most science-fiction writers of the second and third rank follow this pattern, while the remainder emulate those hard-core writers who employ formula pulp adventure to celebrate a future of triumphant technocracy and (interstellar) imperialism.

The loyalties of readers tend to follow their politics, and if the political content of a work is too overtly partisan, its audience will be polarized on strictly political lines. Almost all the controversy associated with the New Wave or with the School of Heinlein has been of an ideological tendency. Art can go far, however, to depolarize partisan responses, and those science-fiction writers who have produced bodies of work of consistent aesthetic distinction have generally achieved recognition (critically, at least) proportioned to their merits. The last decade and a half has witnessed works as varied in their (high) distinction as Le Guin's *The Dispossessed* (1974), Delany's *Dhalgren* (1975), Gregory Benford's *Timescape* (1980), John Crowley's *Engine Summer* (1979), and the short stories of Ellison, Gene Wolfe, Spinrad, and many others.

As a genre literature, science fiction is commonly defined by its subject matter, and its commonest subject matter has been the future, near and far. This, however, is a much less specific directive than those governing other genres, and the range of concerns it may encompass is correspondingly greater. Already in the 1950s and increasingly through the 1960s, the exploration of space had ceded its supremacy as the defining image of science fiction to extrapolations more rooted in immediate social concerns, albeit concerns of a more macroscopic order than conventional mainstream fiction generally treats of: the imminence and dread of war (Miller's *A Canticle for Liebowitz*, 1960, Vonnegut's *Slaughterhouse-Five*); overpopulation and ecological catastrophe (Harry Harrison's *Make Room! Make Room!*, 1966, Ballard's *The Burning World*, 1964); investigations, often of an allegorical nature, into the foundations of the social order (Robert E. Sheckley's *Journey Beyond Tomorrow*, 1962, Delany's *Dhalgren*, Joanna Russ's *The Female Man*, 1975); and (displacing the exploration of space as the locus of that sense of optimism once more characteristic of the genre as a whole) the evolution of the human species through psychic metamorphosis or biological engineering. If there is, indeed, a characteristic theme in science fiction today, it is the last of these. From Arthur C. Clarke's and Sturgeon's milestone novels of 1953 (*Childhood's End* and *More Than Human*) the theme of transcendental evolution has yielded such classic works as Anderson's *Brain Wave* (1954), Daniel Keyes's *Flowers for Algernon* (1966), James Blish's *The Seedling Stars* (1957), and Pohl's *Man Plus* (1976). In recent years (following the lead, once again, of Clarke in his seminal movie and novel, *2001: A Space Odyssey*, 1968) the emphasis of this theme shifted from that of species-wide evolution to personal transcendence, often with strongly religious overtones.

If there has been a single writer whose work can be said to draw together all these diverse themes into a coherent and unified prophetic vision, a vision to rival the High Tech future of early science fiction, that writer is arguably Philip K. Dick. Though he has yet to win public recognition on a scale commensurate with his merits (possibly because of the unevenness of his large oeuvre), Dick is regarded by very many of his peers, especially those of a New Wave sensibility, as the foremost science-fiction writer of our time. His best work combines those qualities of inventiveness and vision specific to the proverbial sense of wonder with an acute and deeply humane sensitivity to everyday life.

Needless to say, Dick is not alone in striking that balance between the macroscopically amazing and human-scaled verisimilitude. Indeed, science fiction might well be characterized as a field, if not invariably in its published productions, at least in its Platonic form, where obtaining such a balance has been the main aesthetic ambition of its writers.

—Thomas M. Disch

Preface

Twentieth-Century American Science-Fiction Writers contains critical/biographical studies of ninety authors who began writing after 1900 and before 1970. Their work represents the best and most significant of what Americans have written in science fiction so far this century. During this period American science fiction has grown from a minor subgenre of popular fiction paying struggling writers a half cent a word—or less—into a major division of fiction, accounting in the 1970s for over one-quarter of all fiction book titles published and earning sizable incomes for its better writers. It is now almost common for paperback rights to a science-fiction novel to sell for over $50,000, and several advances for over $100,000 were made during the 1970s; the record so far is the $500,000 guaranteed to Robert A. Heinlein for *The Number of the Beast* (1980). It is also significant that in 1979 one of a half-dozen sales of paperback rights for over $50,000 was for a science-fiction collection of short fiction. During this century science fiction, with its specialized magazines beginning in the 1920s, with its proliferation of reprint anthologies beginning in the 1950s, and with the appearance of numerous original short-story anthologies beginning in the 1960s, has increasingly attracted more and better writers of short fiction, a form which has otherwise received little support this century from the public, the publishing industry, or academics.

Along with financial success, science fiction has over this period come to attract considerable critical attention. Some sort of science-fiction course is now taught in most colleges and universities in the nation. Three scholarly journals regularly publish articles and reviews: *Extrapolation: A Journal of Science Fiction and Fantasy*, which began as a newsletter for the Modern Language Association seminar on science fiction in 1959, *Science-Fiction Studies*, which began in 1973, and *Alternative Futures: The Journal of Utopian Studies*, which began in 1978. In addition to its affiliations with scholarly organizations such as MLA, the Popular Culture Association, and the American Culture Association, science fiction has its own such organization, founded in 1970, the Science Fiction Research Association. Scholarly books on science fiction have been published by a number of major university presses, including Oxford, Princeton, Yale, and Notre Dame, adding to the already substantial body of scholarship contributed, especially during the last thirty years, by nonacademic experts in the field. Indeed, this volume, its editors and contributors, and all students of science fiction are indebted to the important foundations provided by the encyclopedias and bibliographies of scholars such as L. W. Currey, Peter Nicholls, R. Reginald, Donald H. Tuck, and many more who like them are not academics.

This volume, with its combination of biography and criticism, both synthesizes the best of the existing body of scholarship and breaks new ground by providing original critical assessments of a group of authors who have made significant contributions to twentieth-century fiction but about many of whom little or no criticism exists beyond book reviews in specialty magazines. At the beginning of each entry a bibliography of the author's books is provided, including work in other genres unless indicated by the heading *Selected Books*. Primary bibliographies at the ends of entries are selected to include works other than original book-length writings, such as screenplays, translations, books edited, and, when they are items of special significance not available in the author's published collections, contributions to books and periodicals. The most useful books and articles about the authors are selected for the secondary bibliographies. If there are significant public collections of an author's papers, the information is listed at the end of the entry. A bibliography of general studies useful to the student of science fiction is provided at the end of the volume.

—Thomas L. Wymer

Permissions

The following generously permitted the reproduction of photographs: Jay Kay Klein, pp. 5, 26, 37, 44, 59, 78, 84, 98, 102, 110, 115, 131, 143, 156, 172, 175, 199, 201, 207, 213, 253, 258, 282; Elizabeth S. Hill, p. 106; Richard Todd, pp. 163, 166; Phil H. Webber, pp. 235, 236; University of Southern California, p. 247; Lisa Kroeber, p. 266; Gordon Grant, p. 277.

Acknowledgments

This book was produced by BC Research.
Nadia Rasheed was the in-house editor.
The production staff included Janet E. Black, Anita Dunn, Joyce Fowler, Robert H. Griffin, Chad W. Helms, Patricia S. Hicks, Sharon K. Kirkland, Inge Kutt, Cynthia D. Lybrand, Karen L. Rood, Shirley A. Ross, Walter W. Ross, Robin A. Sumner, Cheryl A. Swartzentruber, Margaret A. Van Antwerp, Carol J. Wilson, and Lynne C. Zeigler.

The editors would like to acknowledge the assistance of the staff at the Bowling Green State University Libraries and, especially, the staff at the Popular Culture Library. Bill Blackbeard and M. Harvey Gernsback were helpful in providing illustration materials. Anne Dixon and Jacquelyn Price did the necessary library research with the aid of the following librarians at the Thomas Cooper Library, University of South Carolina: Michael Havener, Donna Nance, Harriet Oglesbee, Jean Rhyne, Paula Swope, Jane Thesing, Ellen Tillett, Gary Treadway, and Beth Woodard. Photographic copy work for this volume was done by Pat Crawford of Imagery, Columbia, South Carolina, and Colorsep Graphics, Columbia, South Carolina.

Finally, grateful acknowledgment is due the subjects of entries in this book who were kind enough to read their entries for accuracy.

Dictionary of Literary Biography • Volume Eight

Twentieth-Century American Science-Fiction Writers

Part 1: A-L

Dictionary of Literary Biography

Poul Anderson

Michael W. McClintock
University of Montana

BIRTH: Bristol, Pennsylvania, 25 November 1926, to Anton William and Astrid Hertz Anderson.

EDUCATION: B.S., University of Minnesota, 1948.

MARRIAGE: 12 December 1953 to Karen Kruse; children: Astrid.

AWARDS: Hugo Award for "The Longest Voyage," 1961; Hugo Award for "No Truce With Kings," 1964; Hugo Award for "The Sharing of Flesh," 1969; Nebula and Hugo awards for "The Queen of Air and Darkness," 1971, 1972; Nebula and Hugo awards for "Goat Song," 1972, 1973.

SELECTED BOOKS: *Vault of the Ages* (Philadelphia: Winston, 1952);

Brain Wave (New York: Ballantine, 1954; London: Heinemann, 1955);

No World of Their Own (New York: Ace, 1955); revised as *The Long Way Home* (New York: Ace, 1978);

Planet of No Return (New York: Ace, 1956; London: Dobson, 1966); republished as *Question and Answer* (New York: Ace, 1978);

Star Ways (New York: Avalon, 1956); republished as *The Peregrine* (New York: Ace, 1978);

Earthman's Burden, by Anderson and Gordon R. Dickson (New York: Gnome Press, 1957);

The Snows of Ganymede (New York: Ace, 1958);

War of the Wing-Men (New York: Ace, 1958; London: Sphere, 1976); republished as *The Man Who Counts* (New York: Ace, 1978);

The Enemy Stars (Philadelphia: Lippincott, 1959; London: Coronet, 1972);

Virgin Planet (New York: Avalon, 1959; London: Warner, 1977);

The War of Two Worlds (New York: Ace, 1959; London: Dobson, 1970);

We Claim These Stars! (New York: Ace, 1959; London: Dobson, 1976);

Earthman, Go Home! (New York: Ace, 1960);

Guardians of Time (New York: Ballantine, 1960; London: Gollancz, 1961);

The High Crusade (Garden City: Doubleday, 1960);

Mayday Orbit (New York: Ace, 1961);

Orbit Unlimited (New York: Pyramid, 1961; St. Albans, U.K.: Panther, 1976);

Strangers from Earth (New York: Ballantine, 1961);

Three Hearts and Three Lions (Garden City: Doubleday, 1961; London: Sphere, 1974);

Twilight World (New York: Torquil, 1961; London: Gollancz, 1962);

After Doomsday (New York: Ballantine, 1962; London: Gollancz, 1963);

The Makeshift Rocket (New York: Ace, 1962; London: Dobson, 1969);

Un-Man and Other Novellas (New York: Ace, 1962; London: Dobson, 1972);

Let the Spacemen Beware! (New York: Ace, 1963; London: Dobson, 1970); republished as *The Night Face* (New York: Ace, 1978);

Shield (New York: Berkley, 1963; London: Dobson, 1965);

Three Worlds to Conquer (New York: Pyramid, 1964; London: Mayflower, 1966);

Time and Stars (Garden City: Doubleday, 1964; London: Gollancz, 1964);

Trader to the Stars (Garden City: Doubleday, 1964; London: Gollancz, 1965);

Agent of the Terran Empire (Philadelphia: Chilton, 1965; London: Coronet, 1977);

The Corridors of Time (Garden City: Doubleday, 1965; London: Gollancz, 1966);

Flandry of Terra (Philadelphia: Chilton, 1965; London: Coronet, 1976);

The Star Fox (Garden City: Doubleday, 1965; London: Gollancz, 1966);

Ensign Flandry (Philadelphia: Chilton, 1966; London: Coronet, 1976);

The Trouble Twisters (Garden City: Doubleday, 1966; London: Gollancz, 1967);

World Without Stars (New York: Ace, 1966; London: Dobson, 1975);

The Horn of Time (New York: New American Library, 1968);

Beyond the Beyond (New York: New American Library, 1969; London: Gollancz, 1970);

The Rebel Worlds (New York: New American Library, 1969; London: Coronet, 1972);

Satan's World (Garden City: Doubleday, 1969; London: Gollancz, 1970);

Seven Conquests (New York: Macmillan, 1969; London: Collier-Macmillan, 1969);

A Circus of Hells (New York: New American Library, 1970; London: Sphere, 1978);

Tales of the Flying Mountains (New York: Macmillan, 1970);

Tau Zero (Garden City: Doubleday, 1970; London: Gollancz, 1971);

The Byworlder (New York: New American Library, 1971; London: Gollancz, 1972);

The Dancer from Atlantis (Garden City: Doubleday, 1971; London: Sphere, 1977);

There Will Be Time (Garden City: Doubleday, 1972; London: Sphere, 1979);

The Day of Their Return (Garden City: Doubleday, 1973; London: Corgi, 1978);

The People of the Wind (New York: New American Library, 1973; London: Sphere, 1977);

The Queen of Air and Darkness and Other Stories (New York: New American Library, 1973; London: New English Library, 1977);

Fire Time (Garden City: Doubleday, 1974; St. Albans, U.K.: Panther, 1977);

The Many Worlds of Poul Anderson, ed. Roger Elwood (Radnor, Pa.: Chilton, 1974);

A Knight of Ghosts and Shadows (Garden City: Doubleday, 1974; London: Sphere, 1978);

Homeward and Beyond (Garden City: Doubleday, 1975);

The Winter of the World (Garden City: Doubleday, 1975);

Star Prince Charlie, by Anderson and Gordon R. Dickson (New York: Berkley, 1975);

The Best of Poul Anderson (New York: Pocket Books, 1976);

Homebrew (Cambridge, Mass.: NESFA Press, 1976);

Mirkheim (New York: Berkley / Putnam's, 1977; London: Sphere, 1978);

The Avatar (New York: Berkley / Putnam's, 1978);

The Earth Book of Stormgate (New York: Berkley / Putnam's, 1978);

The Merman's Children (New York: Berkley, 1979);

A Stone in Heaven (New York: Ace, 1979);

Conan the Rebel #6 (New York: Bantam, 1980);

The Dark Between the Stars (New York: Berkley, 1980);

The Demon of Scattery, by Anderson and Mildred D. Broxon (New York: Ace, 1980).

Shortly after Poul Anderson's birth, his father, an engineer, moved the family to Texas, where they lived for over ten years. Following Anton Anderson's death his widow took her children to Denmark but returned with them to the United States after the outbreak of World War II, settling eventually on a Minnesota farm. Although he earned his baccalaureate degree with honors, Anderson seems to have made no serious attempt to work as a physicist; his first story was published in 1947 while he was still an undergraduate at the University of Minnesota, and he has been a free-lance writer since 1948. After his marriage to Karen Kruse in 1953 he moved with her to the San Francisco Bay area. A daughter, Astrid, was born in 1954. For over twenty years the Andersons have lived in Orinda, California, near Berkeley.

Until the publication of *Tau Zero* in 1970, "The Queen of Air and Darkness" in 1971, and "Goat Song" in 1972, readers of science fiction tended to regard Anderson, somewhat lightly, as a journeyman fabricator of interstellar adventures and an occasional heroic fantasy. He is a journeyman, and he would find no disgrace in the term; he does write interstellar adventures, and no one has written them better. But it is increasingly clear that he is one of the five or six most important writers to appear during the science-fiction publishing boom of the decade following the end of World War II. Although he still has not quite the prominence of Frank Herbert or Philip K. Dick, much less of Arthur C. Clarke or Kurt Vonnegut, Jr., both the quantity and quality of his work are more than sufficient to place him in their company.

In Anderson's best work an extrapolative intelligence and a mythic sensibility combine with occasionally florid but more often powerful rhetoric to generate structures of imagery, setting, character, event, and metaphor that both claim and reward serious attention. In all of his work he is careful about science, or, if science does not, as such, figure in the story, he is consistent and logical in constructing background. This is not, in itself, remarkable. But particularly since the mid-1950s Anderson has employed his knowledge of science to construct in his fiction planets that meet rigorous standards of plausibility and, at the same time, figure as critical elements in the signification of the work. Anderson's planets, like Thomas Hardy's landscapes, are not just settings but aspects of meaning. Like Hardy's fiction, too, Anderson's often signifies more than the interpreter may easily reduce to statement. Anderson is not precisely mythopoeic, but his sensibility is mythic and strongly influenced by the Nordic *Edda* and sagas that are part of his heritage. He is inclined to regard the world from their elemental, sometimes manic, sometimes grim perspective. Thus Anderson's stories take place in settings splendid in themselves, that chasten the wildest action. Yet the human action does not lose its significance, for in Anderson's fiction value resides in the mind and the spirit, not in the mechanical operations of the universe. At his best Anderson evokes responses not unlike those appropriate to *Beowulf* or the *Volsungasaga*. He is committed to rational understanding but vulnerable to the resonances of ancient and deep feeling.

Anderson's first published story, "Tomorrow's Children" (*Astounding Science-Fiction*, March 1947), expresses his characteristic preoccupations and displays, if modestly, some of the strengths that have sustained a long career. The setting is that commonplace of post-Hiroshima science fiction, the world following an atomic war. An epigraph from *Siegfried* establishes the tone: "On the world's loom / Weave the Norns doom, / Nor may they guide it nor change." The doom seen by Hugh Drummond is less apocalyptic than many nuclear holocaust speculations. Drummond finds that no place on Earth is free from the radioactive dusts and gases that are causing a catastrophic increase in mutations. There is no way for the human race to escape the consequences of its folly. But the high rate of mutant births does not necessarily mean the end of life: the child born at the end of the story with tentacles instead of arms and legs may "get along all right," Drummond says, if he can use the odd appendages. The human race must live with things as they are, not attempt vain evasions. "Tomorrow's Children" was combined with Anderson's story "Logic" and a

new ending to form the novel *Twilight World* (1961); although F. N. Waldrop was the author with Anderson of the original *Astounding* story, Waldrop is not listed as a coauthor of *Twilight World*.

Six years later in "Sam Hall" (1953) Anderson presented a triumphant account of a brave man turning evil against itself. Again the setting is a common one of the period: a repressively bureaucratized future United States in which the government keeps close accounts of all citizens by means of a prodigious computer. Thornberg, the chief of the Technical Division of Central Records, uses his position and expertise to construct Sam Hall, a brilliant and elusive rebel against totalitarian authority who exists solely in the data banks. Eventually Sam Hall exists, too, in the imaginations of the oppressed and in the fears of the oppressors. The old ballad of defiance runs as a motif through the novelette: "Oh, my name it is Sam Hall, / And I hate you one and all, / . . . God damn your eyes." The optimism of this story, in which the apparent security investigator is revealed to be a member of the ultimately victorious libertarian underground, is no less characteristic of Anderson than the grimness of "Tomorrow's Children." The rebel victory is an entirely human and social victory. Furthermore, the

Poul Anderson

1

The Gate of the Flying Knives — 29

ladyless,

Again penniless, houseless, and ~~in/sweetheartless~~ Cappen Varra
~~justxthexxx~~ made a brave sight just the same as he ~~twisted~~ wove his
~~wayxamongxthexfe~~ way ~~aeroxamong~~ amidst through the bazaar throng. After all,
until ~~only~~ yesterday he had for some weeks been in, if not quite of,
the household of Molin Torchholder, as much as he and ancilla
Danlis could contrive; and the priest-engineer had rewarded him well
whenever he sang a song or composed a poem. That situation had
changed with ~~terrible~~ suddenness and terror, but he still had a
bright green tunic, scarlet cloak, canary hose, ~~softxha~~ soft half-boots
trimmed in silver, and a plumed cap to wear. Though naturally
heartsick at what had happened, full of dread for his darling, he
saw no reason to sell the garb yet. He could raise enough money to
live on, one way or another -- if need be, as often before, by pawning
his harp -- while he searched for her.

If that quest had not succeeded by the time he was reduced to
rags, then he ~~feared~~ would have to suppose ~~it was hopeless, that~~
Danlis and the Lady Rosanda were forever lost. But he had never been
one to grieve over future sorrows.

Beneath a westering sun, the bazaar ~~brawledxand~~ surged and clamored.
Merchants, artisans, porters, servants, slaves, wives, nomads,
courtesans, entertainers, beggars, thieves, magicians, acolytes,
soldiers, and who knew what else mingled, chattered, chaffered,
~~drankyxatex~~ quarreled, plotted, sang, drank, ate, and who knew what
else. ~~Now and then a~~ Horseman, cameldriver, ~~or~~ wagoner pushed through,
raising ~~A~~ waves of ~~obscenities~~ curses. Music tinkled and tweedled from
wineshops, vendors proclaimed the wonders of their wares from booths,

"The Gate of the Flying Knives," revised typescript

problem the libertarians and Thornberg face provides to the reasoning intellect the means of its own solution.

The enemy in the heroic fantasy *Three Hearts and Three Lions* (1961) is more primitive than bureaucracy, and the response to the threat is mythic, not rational. An examination of the conflict between law and chaos, the novel concerns the adventures of Holger Danske in a world of Carolingian romance. The sentiment of the novel is on the side of law, for Anderson sees law as the context that gives meaning to liberty. Thus the fundamental threat posed by chaos is the voiding of the significance of any act. The climax of Holger's adventures is not his destruction of the hosts of chaos but his remembrance of his own identity and the consequent understanding of the purpose of his errantry. This moment of knowledge is the "turn" of which J. R. R. Tolkien writes in his essay "On Fairy-Stories," the moment in which peril and promise join. It is, moreover, the first fully developed expression of the complexity of Anderson's vision. Though Holger's triumph is the triumph of law, and though a victory for chaos would be a comprehensive disaster, the glamour of Faerie, the chaotic realm, is real, and the charm of Morgan le Fay is genuine. The beauty of the Wild Hunt that runs after Holger in the climactic chapter is no less authentic than the beauty of the recognition with which the chapter ends.

Anderson's first two science-fiction novels, *Vault of the Ages* (1952) and "Silent Victory" (1953, in book form as *The War of Two Worlds*, 1959), were clearly apprentice pieces, far less accomplished than *Three Hearts and Three Lions*. *Brain Wave*, the second of his novels to be published as a book, appeared in 1954. It seems to be the only significant work in which Anderson has followed the instruction of H. G. Wells to employ but a single "marvel" in a story and work out the logical consequences of the innovation. Anderson supposes that for one hundred million years or so the solar system has been passing through a force field that has inhibited the functioning of certain types of neurones. When the Earth emerges from the field, brains begin to work much more quickly and efficiently: everything with a brain becomes more intelligent. The novel is an episodic consideration of the effects of this fundamental alteration of the human condition. Arthur C. Clarke's roughly contemporary *Childhood's End* (1953), which features a more radical but less ingenious alteration, has proven to be in several ways the more important novel, but Anderson more poignantly examines the human consequences of such change, showing,

together with the new triumphs and new possibilities, how those whom increased intelligence has only made more conscious of their unhappy limitations nevertheless survive with grace and dignity.

In the winter 1954 issue of *Startling Stories* Anderson published a time chart for a future history series. Robert A. Heinlein had introduced this concept to American science fiction, perhaps borrowing it from Olaf Stapledon, but Anderson has utilized it more extensively—and arguably to better advantage—than any other writer. Anderson produced at least nineteen works in this series before abandoning it toward the end of 1957. By then he had begun a second future history, the so-called Technic Civilization series, which comprises about fifty novels and shorter works so far. The most notable work in the first series is *Star Ways* (1956), which like many another of Anderson's works has a plot constructed around a puzzle or mystery: Nomad starships have been disappearing in a certain stellar region, and both Joachim Henry of the Nomad ship *Peregrine* and Trevelyan Micah of the Stellar Union Coordination Service want to learn why. The answer they find poses an early form of a moral conundrum to which Anderson has often returned. The holistic, organic Alori culture insists upon a totally harmonious order; whatever cannot be made to blend gracefully with the rest must be eliminated. The Alori are philosophic totalitarians, and they are implacably antimechanical, thus implacably hostile to human civilization. But they are not evil, and their achievements are of great value. In the end, with great pain, the humans reject the attractions of the Alori culture, not because they believe that their own is morally superior, but because they know it is their own. "This isn't a matter of ethics," Trevelyan says. "We're going to stay free—and that's that."

Freedom is the central concern of the novella "Call Me Joe" (1957), a work sharing certain concerns and certain conclusions with Clifford D. Simak's short story "Desertion" (1944). The setting of both works is Jupiter, and the plot motive of both works is the supernal attraction to some humans of living on the Jovian surface. Anderson's use of science (or, in these cases, pseudoscience) is more sophisticated than Simak's, but their points are similar: life on Jupiter, in artificially developed bodies superior to natural human ones, may well be superior to life on Earth. Simak, the most pastoral of science-fiction writers, emphasizes the beauties of the Jovian environment; Anderson emphasizes its challenges; both show how splendid it is to encounter that alien place in a body perfectly suited to meet it. Edward Anglesey, the central character of "Call Me Joe," has been reduced by an accident to "a head [and] pair of arms" atop a machine. By means of a telepathy machine his mind can occupy the brain of Joe, the synthetic creature sent as a human surrogate to explore the Jovian surface. When Anglesey permanently transfers his personality into the body of his living puppet, he is escaping not only the prison of his own flesh but also the prison of the ordinary human world.

In 1958 the two most important novels of the first half of Anderson's career appeared: "The Man Who Counts" (serialized in *Astounding*, 1958; first published as a book under the title *War of the Wing-Men*, 1958) and "We Have Fed Our Sea" (serialized in *Astounding*, 1958; in book form as *The Enemy Stars*, 1959). Both feature vividly realized settings, as his readers had come by then to expect in Anderson's work. Both utilize to good effect elements of the most current scientific thought then available to Anderson. The fundamental distinction between these highly accomplished, virtually simultaneous works is that *War of the Wing-Men* is political, while *The Enemy Stars* is mythic. By the mid-1950s Anderson had become a practiced and confident artificer. "The Man Who Counts" was his 128th professional publication, "We Have Fed Our Sea" his 135th. He had become adept at the use of conventions of popular (chiefly magazine) science fiction in the service of significant themes. If he has regularly denied, in essays, introductions, and occasional published letters, any consistent purpose beyond entertaining as many readers as he can, he has just as regularly devised entertainments that repay thought.

The man who counts when three humans are shipwrecked far from the nearest human station on Diomedes is Nicholas van Rijn, bon vivant and owner of Solar Spice and Liquors. Van Rijn figures in more than a dozen stories and novels set during the earlier, Polesotechnic League period of Technic Civilization; this relatively early novel is, however, the most extended consideration of his abilities. The problem he and his companions face is straightforward: they must somehow reach or contact the human station before their food runs out, because all the proteins indigenous to Diomedes are poisonous to humans. There are intelligent natives who, under normal circumstances, might be helpful, but the two groups between whom the humans have fallen are at war with each other. The corpulent and sybaritic van Rijn sets out to use the means at hand— the warring natives—to save himself, Lady Sandra, and Eric Wace. The second man is ostensibly better

suited to the hero's role, but in the end it is Lady Sandra who must explain for Wace how van Rijn has not only saved them but also has brought about an accommodation between the native groups. Van Rijn's methods are flamboyant, sometimes violent, and often unethical, but he saves more lives than he sacrifices. He is, in this and other works, Anderson's model of the entrepreneur who, in a laissez-faire system, must also be an effective leader. Motivated by greed, sensuality, and egoism, his character is also formed by intelligence, knowledge, and the capacity, if not the taste, for self-discipline. The climactic scene of the novel approaches slapstick, but it is also metaphoric. Having determined that only cultural patterns, not racial differences, account for the sharply divergent breeding patterns that have led each group to abominate the other, van Rijn contrives to bring the leaders together for a truce meeting. His own rhetoric persuades all but one fanatic, who, unfortunately, is the absolute ruler of the more powerful group. But van Rijn, insulting the fanatic past endurance, provokes him to bite van Rijn on the buttock. The Diomedean soon dies of a massive allergic reaction to van Rijn's flesh. Leadership, van Rijn has at one point told Wace, is not a matter of doing but of getting others to do what is necessary.

The motivations for action in *The Enemy Stars* vary among the four main characters, and none seems particularly admirable. But the tone of the novel's brief prologue, which somewhat cryptically introduces a spaceship before any character is introduced, suggests for the spaceship some drive or purpose worthier than any of those which bring the ship's crew aboard her: "They named her *Southern Cross* and launched her on the road whose end they would never see. . . . They manned her by turns, and dreamed other ships, and launched them, and saw how a few of the shortest journeys ended. Then they died." *Southern Cross* is one among a fleet of interstellar exploration vessels, each carrying one unit of a linked pair of matter transmitters, the other unit of which is on the Moon. For this novel Anderson makes the respectable assumption that gravitation is instantaneous across any distance, and he speculates somewhat less respectably that gravity can be modulated to carry signals that are sufficiently complex to represent a human being— neural circuitry and all. Thus the crews of the interstellar ships, which must travel more slowly than light, are transmitted to and from their watches. *Southern Cross*, aimed for Alpha Crucis, has gone farther than any of her sisters, but she has been diverted to inspect a burned-out star. Four men go on the mission. Terangi Maclaren, an excellent physicist, is slightly bored at home and amused by the political maneuvering required to authorize the diversion of the ship from her planned course. David Ryerson is forced to go by his father, who wants him to be a spaceman as all the Ryerson men have been. Seiichi Nakamura feels guilt for his brother's death, fear of the void, and a compulsion to confront both emotions. Chang Sverdlov goes because his political underground orders him to. Only Maclaren returns, to learn finally from Ryerson's father that such ventures have a significance that transcends individual motives: it is the nature of humans to explore. Here Anderson reaches, as he occasionally does elsewhere, the edge of a species of mysticism, and thus the limits of paraphrasable meaning.

A similar approach toward the mystic, more blithely expressed, informs *The High Crusade* (1960). In this jeu d'esprit an alien spaceship lands in medieval England and is captured by Sir Roger de Tourneville. Thinking to defeat France and liberate the Holy Land, Sir Roger loads his army and his village aboard the vessel but ends up among the stars instead of among the paynim. He founds a feudal and Christian interstellar empire which, by the end of the tale, is expanding lustily toward the center of the galaxy. This is a tale, rather than a novel, with simple characters and lively action. It is also vigorous, witty, and clever in its display of the advantages a band of feudal warriors might have over an excessively technological military machine. Like *The Enemy Stars*, it is a celebration of human courage, intelligence, and the ability to meet the unimaginable with fortitude and high style.

If novels like *The Enemy Stars* and *The High Crusade* show Anderson at his most effectively spirited, certain other works, such as *The Star Fox* (1965), represent him at his most argumentative and problematic. Published as a series of related novellas during the period when the national debate on Vietnam was growing rancorous, *The Star Fox* is its author's most overt attempt to solicit his reader's assent to a political position. Described by Gordon R. Dickson as "an eighteenth century liberal," Anderson has sometimes announced his sympathies for contemporary libertarianism. He might be expected to sympathize with a small nation beset by a larger, richer one, and, indeed, such novels as *The People of the Wind* (1973) and *The Winter of the World* (1975) appear to express at least the fictional analogue of such sympathy. But Anderson has also announced his beliefs that patriotism remains a virtue and that collectivism is wrong, a social evil. The patriotic individualist speaks in *The Star Fox*.

The political situation of the novel is roughly modeled on that of the later 1930s, with a considerable admixture of the 1960s. A disorganized and weak-willed World Federation is confronted by an intelligent and aggressive enemy. The Aleriona have captured the planet New Europe, and few on Earth can see or will admit that this is only the first step in the Aleriona expansion. Gunnar Heim sees it. He seeks to rouse humankind to its peril by proving that Alerion has lied about what happened on New Europe. Eventually, after getting himself declared a privateer and defeating the Aleriona forces on New Europe, he is successful. Baldly summarized, the novel sounds crudely jingoistic. But the Aleriona are not analogues of either Nazis or Communists. Ancient, cultured, graceful, and ritualistic, they are more reminiscent, perhaps, of the Japanese. But their motive for war is neither to seize territory nor to seize power; it is to ensure their own endless peace. They are appalled by the human potential for growth. They cannot "trust a race without bounds to its hope."

Yet just this boundless hope is the saving grace for the marooned spacemen in "The Ancient Gods" (in book form as *World Without Stars*, 1966). Anderson wrote the novel to match a painting by Chesley Bonestell of the galaxy as seen from a planet outside it. The setting of the novel, where the spaceship crashes, is such a planet, and its detachment from the main body of this island universe (as galaxies were once called) becomes emblematic of the novel's theme. Human science has developed both a means of traveling faster than light and an inoculum against aging. Thus liberated from the constraints of space and time, people have grown unaccustomed to urgency. But Hugh Valland matured before the antithanatic drug was developed, and he has not had his memories of that time edited away. In his maturity he has no need, no ambition, to be more than a crewman. Yet in the strength of his age, his maturity, and his fidelity to a single woman, to whom he intends to return, he is the man best suited to deal with the problem of how to get home. The basic necessity, besides day-to-day survival, is to build a ship with which to reach a race of spacefaring aliens on another planet of this extragalactic system. In order to do that the humans must help the aliens of the planet on which they crashed to develop science and engineering. They must also help these aliens overthrow the parasitic tyranny of a third group of aliens. Clearly the project requires patience and a firm sense of purpose. Valland possesses these characteristics. Only after they have returned safely to Earth does the narrator learn the final cause of

Valland's indomitability: the woman whom Valland refuses to stop loving, the anchor of his immortality, has been dead for three thousand years.

Perhaps Anderson's most impressive accomplishment to date in the invention of planets and aliens occurs in *Satan's World* (1969). The planet that David Falkayn names Satan is a rogue, formed independently of any star, passing nearly all of its existence in the nearly perfect cold and dark of interstellar space. The novel's plot hinges on the planet's passage near a star, the blue-white giant Beta Crucis. The specific conditions brought about on Satan on this occasion will turn it into the perfect site for the large-scale transmutation of elements. Falkayn and his team, in the employ of Nicholas van Rijn, set out to claim the prize but encounter most peculiar rivals in a race of killer herbivores. The plot of *Satan's World* is somewhat rambling and less than elegant, but it serves well enough to establish the connection between the odd planet and the strange race and to present the compound to Falkayn, van Rijn, and their friends as a challenge representative of a profoundly complex and surprising universe. Since both planet and race are rational extrapolations from the known, they serve also as representatives of the surprises the universe may really hold in store. In a sense, such surprises are gifts: although they threaten and may destroy man, without them life tends to be dull, insipid, and tedious.

Tau Zero first appeared as a magazine serial entitled "To Outlive Eternity"; in 1971 it finished second to Larry Niven's *Ringworld* in the balloting for the Hugo Award. Certain comparisons of the two are instructive. All of Anderson's characters are human; Niven features some aliens in central roles. Both novels extrapolate, but Niven pays more attention to engineering concepts, Anderson to scientific ones. Both novels are fabulous, but *Ringworld* is an elegant game, and *Tau Zero* is something like a philosophic credo. When James Blish, a man not given to rash enthusiasms, reviewed *Tau Zero*, he called it "the ultimate 'hard science fiction' novel." The story is based on a peculiarity of special relativity: although the velocity of light may not be exceeded, it may be approached. You may not achieve 100 percent light speed, but if you can achieve, say, 99.999 percent, there is no theoretical reason not to add as many nines to the right of the decimal point as you choose. Anderson describes a spaceship capable of adding those nines and devises an accident that forces her to keep adding them indefinitely. As more nines are added, time moves more slowly aboard the ship relative to the rest of the universe. Before the *Leonora Christine* concludes her wild career, she has not only circumnavigated the universe, she has outlived its collapse and reexpansion.

The notion can be stated but hardly described. Anderson states what happens and struggles to render what his characters experience; the inadequacy of the prose becomes, in the end, simply the inadequacy of human perceptions. The people aboard the *Leonora Christine* survive, and what they earn for their accomplishment is an index to the significance of it: after they have repaired their ship and begun to search the reborn galaxies for a suitable planet, Charles Reymont says, "Let's make this . . . a human galaxy, in the widest sense of the word 'human.' Maybe even a human universe." Reymont, who has been the key to survival through this fantastic passage, may be the most difficult element of the novel for some readers to accept, partly because Anderson does not allow him to make any important mistakes. Embarking as the constable of the ship, he becomes the chief authority figure and the center of psychological stability for everyone else after the accident. He perhaps too closely resembles some of Robert Heinlein's "competent men" and John Wayne's heroes. But the context demands a hero. No group of people has ever been—in life or in fiction— so sundered from all that has given it meaning. Who could win through but someone for whom meaning derives preeminently from acts of the individual will? Reymont is difficult to accept, but not so difficult as the end of all conceivable things.

The mythic dimension of *Tau Zero* is implicit, an apparent but unspecified response to the extremity reason has generated. In "The Queen of Air and Darkness," the novella that won Anderson his first Nebula Award, he explicitly puts reason and myth in contention. The setting is one of Anderson's ingenious planets, a world that provides by astrophysics the twilight appropriate for legends. Throughout much of the story, indeed, it appears that on Roland, legends walk. Backcountry settlers speak guardedly of Outlings dancing like faerie-folk under the moons and sing a ballad of a darkling queen; whatever kidnapped Barbro Cullen's son flew and was not human. But Sherrinford, the rational detective, discovers the rational truth: a secretive, alien race with certain telepathic powers has employed the archetypes of the human imagination in an attempt to conquer the human invaders. Armed with the knowledge that the enemy's only weapon is myth, technological culture reasserts its superiority. That superiority is not only a matter of power. The goal of the aborigines, demonstrated by their treatment of their human captives, is the enslavement of all the human settlers on Roland. All the Outling captives live amidst what they perceive to be beauty and believe themselves to be free, but the beauty is deceptive, the freedom fraudulent. Anderson chooses genuine freedom, even if the price is the glamour of all legend. The choice is less easy than it appears, for however deceptive the queen, the beauties she creates are given an authenticity by Anderson's text. At the end of the story, after Sherrinford at somewhat tedious length has explained the solution of the mystery, Anderson gives the last lines to one of the defeated queen's people: "Likely none would meet here again for loving or magic. . . . He stood and trilled: 'Out of her breast / a blossom ascended. / The summer burned it. / The song is ended.' " Anderson implies that even if man is better off to lose the ancient gods, the loss is real.

Anderson's next important compounding of rational intellect and mythic sensibility, "Goat Song," is still more problematic than "The Queen of Air and Darkness." The later work borrows its plot and characters directly from myth but, Anderson claims, uses "no concept that the most conservative scientist could say is theoretically impossible." The mythic source is the Orpheus story; the scientific concept is the ruling computer. SUM keeps the human world in order, "stable, just, and sane," but therefore also determined and therefore necessarily unfree. Harper, the story's Orpheus, does not at first understand that he desires freedom. He petitions SUM to restore to life the woman he loves, who has died of an adder's bite. As an element of its stabilizing policies, SUM has promised that every individual personality—each soul—will be recorded in its data banks, to be restored someday to life in a regenerated body. Harper wants SUM to give back his beloved now. If it will do this, he will be its prophet, an attractive bargain for SUM, since Harper is the last man who knows song and poetry. But SUM gives Harper the Orphic test, and Harper fails it: he looks back toward his beloved, and she is carried back to the subterranean halls. After he masters his grief and rage at this second loss, Harper comes to understand that SUM must be destroyed, that people who live in the promise of assured immortality can have no meaning in their lives. He goes finally to his death at the hands of the wild women, to complete his release of Dionysus upon an Apollonian world.

Read in the context of Anderson's other work,

"Goat Song" is an unusual story. The association of the giant computer with death and dominance is a common trope in science fiction (Harlan Ellison's 1967 short story "I Have No Mouth, and I Must Scream" is an unsettling counterpoint to "Goat Song"), and Anderson had previously employed it, quite realistically, in "Sam Hall." But Anderson generally associates technology with liberty; by extending the potential of human action, machines extend the limits of human freedom. "Goat Song," coming so soon after "The Queen of Air and Darkness," demonstrates the intensity with which Anderson continues to examine the balance between science and myth, reason and feeling.

A Knight of Ghosts and Shadows (1974), Anderson's most important novel between *Tau Zero* and *The Avatar* (1978), displays another aspect of that continuing examination. The background of the novel is the later, Terran Empire period of Technic Civilization, and the central figure is Anderson's longest-lived series character, Dominic Flandry. Introduced in "Tiger by the Tail" (1951) as a stereotype, a cynical adventurer working in the intelligence service of a decadent empire, Flandry has grown to become one of Anderson's preferred points of view for moral concerns. *A Knight of Ghosts and Shadows* draws its title from the last stanza of "Tom o' Bedlam's Song" (it is also the song that Harper sings in his madness after the second loss of his beloved). The wilderness in which Flandry wanders is a moral wilderness where judging right action is difficult. Anderson constructs a situation in which Flandry must act in the certain knowledge that his own feelings make suspect his capacity for rational judgment. At the outset of the novel Flandry is just becoming acquainted with the son he did not know he had and is discovering friendship as well as paternal affection. Soon thereafter Flandry becomes involved in a complicated affair on the Imperial marches. The two plots—of the novel and against the Empire—are deceptively conventional. The plot against the Empire has been devised by an old adversary, the enigmatic Aycharaych. In defeating the plot, Flandry discovers the location of Aycharaych's home planet. The plot of the novel complicates Flandry's response to this knowledge. The woman he loves has been killed during the action, and his son, revealed as an agent of the Merseian enemy (who also employ Aycharaych), has been reduced to drooling idiocy by hypnoprobing. Yet Aycharaych, the architect of all this agony, has a claim on any civilized intelligence: he is the last survivor of an ancient race whose machinery still maintains intact the art, the science, and the wisdom of their splendid culture. When Flandry orders the obliteration of this world, he knows he cannot be sure either of his own motivation or of the justness of his choice.

The ambition of *The Avatar*, one of Anderson's most recent novels, suggests that he has become more self-conscious as a literary artist. His work has grown in popularity, so that now most of his novels and many collections of his shorter fiction are in print; he is beginning to gain the critical attention worthy of his work. Although his attempt in *The Avatar* to make sexual passion and an interstellar adventure somehow metaphoric of each other may present insuperable difficulties to many of his readers, it is impressive evidence of his courage as a writer. His readers may hope and expect yet more challenging work to come.

Other:

Christian Molbech, *The Fox, the Dog, and the Griffin*, adapted by Anderson (Garden City: Doubleday, 1966);

"The Creation of Imaginary Worlds," in *Science Fiction, Today and Tomorrow*, ed. Reginald Bretnor (New York: Harper & Row, 1974), pp. 235-257;

"On Thud and Blunder," in *Swords Against Darkness III*, ed. Andrew J. Offutt (New York: Zebra Books, 1978), pp. 271-288.

Periodical Publications:

FICTION:
"Tomorrow's Children," by Anderson and F. N. Waldrop, *Astounding Science-Fiction*, 39 (March 1947): 56-79;

"Tiger by the Tail," *Planet Stories*, 4 (January 1951): 38-55;

"Sam Hall," *Astounding Science-Fiction*, 51 (August 1953): 9-36;

"Call Me Joe," *Astounding Science-Fiction*, 59 (April 1957): 8-40;

"Trader Team," *Analog Science Fiction/Science Fact*, 75 (July 1965): 8-48; (August 1965): 107-149;

"Supernova," *Analog Science Fiction/Science Fact*, 78 (January 1967): 10-49;

"Starfog," *Analog Science Fiction/Science Fact*, 79 (August 1967): 8-61;

"The Sharing of Flesh," *Galaxy*, 27 (December 1968): 7-41;

"The Queen of Air and Darkness," *Magazine of Fantasy and Science Fiction*, 40 (April 1971): 5-45;

"Goat Song," *Magazine of Fantasy and Science Fiction*, 42 (February 1972): 5-35;

"The Problem of Pain," *Magazine of Fantasy and Science Fiction*, 44 (February 1973): 5-24;

"The Bitter Bread," *Analog Science Fiction/Science Fact*, 95 (December 1975): 10-36;

"Joelle," *Isaac Asimov's Science Fiction Magazine*, 1 (Fall 1977): 148-186.

NONFICTION:
"The Profession of Science Fiction: VI / Entertainment, Instruction or Both?," *Foundation: The Review of Science Fiction*, no. 5 (January 1974): 44-50;

"Poul Anderson Talar Om Science Fiction," *Algol*, 15 (Summer-Fall 1978): 11-19.

Interviews:

Paul Walker, "An Interview with Poul Anderson," *Luna Monthly*, no. 37 (June 1972): 1-7, 17;

Elton T. Elliot, "An Interview with Poul Anderson," *Science Fiction Review*, 7 (May 1978): 32-37;

"An Interview with Poul Anderson," phonotape-cassette, released by The Center for Cassette Studies, number 32911.

References:

Charles N. Brown, "Poul Anderson and War of the Wing-Men," in *War of the Wing-Men* (Boston: Gregg Press, 1976), pp. v-ix;

Patrick L. McGuire, " 'Her Strong Enchantments Failing,' " in *The Book of Poul Anderson*, ed. Roger Elwood (New York: DAW, 1975), pp. 81-105;

Sandra Miesel, *Against Time's Arrow: The High Crusade of Poul Anderson* (San Bernardino, Cal.: Borgo Press, 1978);

Miesel, "Challenge and Response," in *The Book of Poul Anderson*, pp. 184-203;

Miesel, *"War of the Wing-Men* and the Technic Civilization Series," in *War of the Wing-Men* (Boston: Gregg Press, 1976), pp. xi-xvii.

PIERS ANTHONY
(PIERS ANTHONY DILLINGHAM JACOB)
(6 August 1934-   )

BOOKS: *Chthon* (New York: Ballantine, 1967; London: Macdonald, 1970);

Omnivore (New York: Ballantine, 1968; London: Faber & Faber, 1969);

The Ring, by Anthony and Robert E. Margroff (New York: Ace, 1968; London: Macdonald, 1969);

Sos the Rope (New York: Pyramid, 1968; London: Faber & Faber, 1970);

Macroscope (New York: Avon, 1969; London: Sphere, 1972);

Orn (Garden City: Doubleday, 1970; London: Corgi, 1977);

The E. S. P. Worm, by Anthony and Margroff (New York: Paperback Library, 1970);

Prostho Plus (London: Gollancz, 1971; New York: Berkley, 1973);

Var the Stick (London: Faber & Faber, 1972);

Race Against Time (New York: Hawthorn Books, 1973; London: Sidgwick & Jackson, 1974);

The Bamboo Bloodbath, by Anthony and Robert O. Fuentes (New York: Berkley, 1974);

Rings of Ice (New York: Avon, 1974; London: Millington, 1975);

Triple Detente (New York: DAW, 1974; London: Sphere, 1975);

Phthor (New York: Berkley, 1975; St. Albans, U.K.: Panther, 1978);

Neq the Sword (London: Corgi, 1975);

Ninja's Revenge, by Anthony and Fuentes (New York: Berkley, 1975);

Ox (New York: Avon, 1976; London: Corgi, 1977);

Amazon Slaughter, by Anthony and Fuentes (New York: Berkley, 1976);

Steppe (London: Millington, 1976);

Hasan (San Bernardino, Cal.: Borgo Press, 1977);

A Spell for Chameleon (New York: Ballantine, 1977);

Battle Circle (New York: Avon, 1978);

The Cluster (New York: Avon, 1978; St. Albans, U.K.: Panther, 1979);

Chaining the Lady (New York: Avon, 1978; St. Albans, U.K.: Panther, 1979);

Kirlian Quest (New York: Avon, 1978; St. Albans, U.K.: Panther, 1979);

The Source of Magic (New York: Ballantine, 1979);

Pretender, by Anthony and Frances Hall (San Bernardino, Cal.: Borgo Press, 1979);

God of Tarot (New York: Harcourt Brace Jovanovich, 1979);

Castle Roogna (New York: Ballantine, 1979);

Vision of Tarot (New York: Berkley, 1980);

Faith of Tarot (New York: Berkley, 1980);

Split Infinity (New York: Ballantine, 1980).

Piers Anthony is the pen name of Piers Anthony Dillingham Jacob, an Englishman who became an American citizen in 1958. "My major motivation as a writer," he observes, "has been my inability to quit writing, and my dissatisfaction with all other modes of employment." As a result of this focusing of energies, Anthony has been a veritable writing machine in recent years, authoring or coauthoring twenty-four novels since 1967. Born in Oxford, England, Anthony was brought to the United States as a child, celebrating his sixth birthday on board a ship. He found his early schooling in this country unpleasant, but he thoroughly enjoyed college. In 1956 he earned his B.A. from Goddard College, submitting as his creative writing thesis his first science-fiction novel. He married Carol Marble on 23 June 1956 and later served in the army from 1957 to 1959. Anthony's moral convictions made military service difficult for him, and, as he says, he "barely made it through basic," being a "pacifistically inclined vegetarian." He continued to write without success until the publication in 1962 of "Possible to Rue" in the April 1963 *Fantastic*. After receiving a teaching certificate from the University of South Florida in 1964, he pursued a variety of occupations, including those of English teacher, technical writer, and free-lance writer. But none of these satisfied him, and he began to devote his entire energy to writing. In 1967 he published his first novel, *Chthon*, the story of young Anton Five and his fellow prisoners in the garnet mines on the planet Chthon. Their plight is symbolically that of humanity in general, but the hero's initiation and escape adumbrate possibilities for human redemption. During this same year Anthony's *Sos the Rope*, a revised segment of his B.A. thesis, won the $5000 prize jointly sponsored by Pyramid Books, the *Magazine of Fantasy and Science Fiction*, and Kent Productions.

Publication became easier at this point in Anthony's career, and *Sos the Rope* was only one of three books published in 1968. In *The Ring* he again makes use of the youthful hero in quest of justice and vengeance, this time on an Earth ruled by the morally questionable "Ultra Conscience." The enslaving Ring of the novel's title introduces an important moral question in Anthony's fiction, for the Ring "makes a man a pacifist when the world is a battlefield." For Anthony, the will to moral activism

Piers Anthony

dissolved, but the innermost recesses of the individual consciousness are revealed. The novel focuses on the effect such a machine could have on a humanity that finds itself diminished in relation to the vastness of the universe; in doing so, it becomes an allegory on the fate of the individual diminished and possibly destroyed by mass society.

In *Orn* (1970) the heroes of *Omnivore* reappear and are transported to a prehistoric world in an age similar to the Paleozoic on Earth. Although constantly threatened by shifting land masses, erupting volcanoes, and massive tidal waves, they come to prefer the honest wildness of this world, which they call Paleo, to the deviousness of their own. The symbol of the innocent wildness of this world is Orn, a great noble bird doomed to extinction at the hands of the governmental agents who will follow the three explorers. Moved by what they see, the three protagonists decide to protect Paleo, and though ultimately unavailing, their attempts to do so establish them as ecologically humane, linked with the natural universe. It is in this novel that the predatory habits of man and animals are explored and differentiated most fully. The phrase "man as omnivore" becomes a motif in the novel, and man is eventually defined as more dangerous in his wanton destruction of nature than the less calculating beast who kills in moderation and out of necessity.

The thematic concerns of Anthony's fiction are often reflections of his own ardent vegetarianism. His contribution to Harlan Ellison's *Again, Dangerous Visions* (1972), for example, was a story entitled "In the Barn," in which female humans on an alien planet are kept as animals, as "cows" for giving milk. The story makes its point through a device that is hardly original (man is to alien as beast is to man), but the collapsing of the distance between human and nonhuman, between sentient and beastly, is nevertheless effective.

In 1972 and 1975 respectively, *Var the Stick* and *Neq the Sword* appeared to complete the trilogy begun with *Sos the Rope*. Collectively titled *Battle Circle* (1978), these books are set in a postholocaust America reduced to nomadic barbarians and an isolated underground vestige of the once powerful technological society.

In *Ox* (1976), Anthony returned to the adventures of Cal, Veg, and Aquilon, who are this time trapped in alternate dimensions of time and space along with their friends the Mantas from Nacre and a superwoman government agent, Tamme. This book reads a bit more slowly than its predecessors, and the sections featuring the creature Ox are a bit dense. But

is one of the distinctive marks of being human, and pacifism can be a negative quality when it is used as a facade for moral complacency, be it in speculative fiction or international politics. In Anthony's best fiction, questions of man's place in the ecology of the natural universe blend with considerations of the individual's role in providing satisfactory and humane answers. Thus in *Omnivore*, the third of the novels published in 1968, the reader is introduced to the trio of Cal (a superintellectual type), Veg (a strongman vegetarian), and Aquilon (a beautiful female artist). Sent to the planet Nacre to explore a jungle of multiform mushrooms, the group establishes contact with sentient fungoid life forms, the Mantas, which become a threat to Earth when the trio returns with them. The adventures on Nacre are set within the frame of an official investigation of the group by the superhuman government agent Subble, and the emotional ties among the heroes evolve along with their growing awareness of the cold viciousness of an Earth government that would sacrifice human lives in the paranoid attempt to destroy the imported aliens.

Anthony's next novel, considered his best by many readers, was *Macroscope* (1969). The mechanical invention of the title is a device that permits man to see the entire continuum of space and time. Not only are the secrets of the universe the novel is thematically tied to Anthony's other works by its concern with man's role in the natural world. Anthony places more emphasis on the fantastic in *A Spell for Chameleon* (1977) and *The Source of Magic* (1979), works that are basically adolescent fare, complete with witches, magicians, and evil spells. Such work does, however, prove Anthony's ability to entertain on the strength of his vivid imagination.

The Cluster, Chaining the Lady, and *Kirlian Quest* all appeared in 1978. Together they compose the Cluster trilogy, a space opera of galactic conquest on a grand scale, which seems to lead into the more recent Tarot trilogy, *God of Tarot* (1979), *Vision of Tarot* (1980), and *Face of Tarot* (1980). But whereas the Cluster trilogy is galactic in scale, *God of Tarot* takes as its theme questions of individual belief. Much of the quest here is an internal one as Brother Paul of the secular Holy Order of Vision is sent to the planet Tarot to investigate the strange tarot animations which may represent manifestations of the deity. The question becomes complex as Brother Paul reaches the planet and realizes that the colonists are religiously fragmented, segregated into many sects, each of which professes worship of a different god. Paul's journey is both inward and outward as he finds companions in his quest, confronts temptations, fails and recovers, and finally faces his own personal hell.

By Anthony's own admission, the Tarot trilogy is complex and a bit confusing, "and some scenes may be offensive to certain readers." Yet Anthony is not the author to sacrifice his artistic purpose to arbitrary convention; that would be literary pacifism. There is a rationale for this complexity and the offensiveness: "It is difficult," says Anthony, "to appreciate the meaning of the heights without first experiencing the depths." With the Tarot trilogy, it seems, Anthony has again returned to the serious science fiction grounded in personal conviction that has always been his forte, and readers may expect much from works to come.

—*Stephen Buccleugh and Beverly Rush*

Other:

"In the Barn," in *Again, Dangerous Visions,* ed. Harlan Ellison (Garden City: Doubleday, 1972).

Periodical Publication:

"Possible to Rue," *Fantastic* (April 1963).

Isaac Asimov

Stephen H. Goldman
University of Kansas

BIRTH: Petrovichi, U.S.S.R., 2 January 1920, to Judah and Anna Rachel Berman Asimov.

EDUCATION: B.S., 1939, M.A., 1941, Ph.D., 1948, Columbia University.

MARRIAGE: 26 July 1942 to Gertrude Blugerman, divorced; children: David, Robyn Joan. 30 November 1973 to Janet Jeppson.

AWARDS: Hugo Award for the Foundation Series, 1966; Hugo Award for Distinguished Contributions to the Field, 1963; Nebula and Hugo awards for *The Gods Themselves,* 1972, 1973; Nebula Award for "The Bicentennial Man," 1976; Hugo Award for "The Bicentennial Man," 1977.

SELECTED BOOKS: *I, Robot* (New York: Gnome Press, 1950; London: Grayson, 1952);

Pebble in the Sky (Garden City: Doubleday, 1950; London: Transworld, 1958);

The Stars Like Dust (Garden City: Doubleday, 1951; St. Albans, U.K.: Panther, 1958);

Foundation (New York: Gnome Press, 1951; London: Weidenfeld & Nicolson, 1953);

Foundation and Empire (New York: Gnome Press, 1952; St. Albans, U.K.: Panther, 1962);

David Starr: Space Ranger, as Paul French (Garden City: Doubleday, 1952; London: World's Work, 1953);

The Currents of Space (Garden City: Doubleday, 1952; London: Boardman, 1955);

Second Foundation (New York: Gnome Press, 1953; London: Digit, 1958);

Lucky Starr and the Pirates of the Asteroids, as French (Garden City: Doubleday, 1953; London: World's Work, 1953);

The Caves of Steel (Garden City: Doubleday, 1954; London: Boardman, 1954);

Lucky Starr and the Oceans of Venus, as French (Garden City: Doubleday, 1954);

The End of Eternity (Garden City: Doubleday, 1955; St. Albans, U.K.: Panther, 1959);

The Martian Way, and Other Stories (Garden City: Doubleday, 1955; London: Dobson, 1964);

Lucky Starr and the Big Sun of Mercury, as French (Garden City: Doubleday, 1956);

Earth Is Room Enough (Garden City: Doubleday, 1957; St. Albans, U.K.: Panther, 1960);

The Naked Sun (Garden City: Doubleday, 1957; London: M. Joseph, 1958);

Lucky Starr and the Moons of Jupiter, as French (Garden City: Doubleday, 1957);

Lucky Starr and the Rings of Saturn, as French (Garden City: Doubleday, 1958);

Nine Tomorrows: Tales of the Near Future (Garden City: Doubleday, 1959; London: Dobson, 1963);

The Rest of the Robots (Garden City: Doubleday, 1964; London: Dobson, 1967);

Fantastic Voyage (Boston: Houghton Mifflin, 1966; London: Dobson, 1966);

Through a Glass, Clearly (London: Four Square Books, 1967);

Asimov's Mysteries (Garden City: Doubleday, 1968; London: Rapp & Whiting, 1968);

Nightfall and Other Stories (Garden City: Doubleday, 1969; St. Albans, U.K.: Panther, 1971);

Opus 100 (Boston: Houghton Mifflin, 1969);

The Best New Thing (New York: World, 1971);

The Early Asimov (Garden City: Doubleday, 1972; London: Gollancz, 1973);

The Gods Themselves (Garden City: Doubleday, 1972; London: Gollancz, 1972);

The Best of Isaac Asimov (Garden City: Doubleday, 1973; London: Sidgwick & Jackson, 1973);

Buy Jupiter and Other Stories (Garden City: Doubleday, 1975; London: Gollancz, 1976);

The Bicentennial Man and Other Stories (Garden City: Doubleday, 1976; London: Gollancz, 1977);

The Dream, Benjamin's Dream, Benjamin's Bicentennial Blast (New York: Privately printed, 1976);

In Memory Yet Green: The Autobiography of Isaac Asimov, 1920-1954 (Garden City: Doubleday, 1979);

In Joy Still Felt: The Autobiography of Isaac Asimov, 1954-1978 (Garden City: Doubleday, 1980).

While Isaac Asimov officially celebrates his birthday as 2 January 1920, his birth date is uncertain. Records were not well kept in the U.S.S.R. in the period between World War I and World War II, particularly if the records concerned Jews. By the time Asimov was three, his family had immigrated to the United States and taken up residence in Brooklyn, New York. Asimov's father tried a number of jobs but finally owned and operated a candy store, continuing in that business through a number of family moves. As a family operation, the candy store soon became the center of Asimov's life. His out-of-school hours were devoted to the store, and he ascribes many of his personal habits and traits—eating quickly, careful use of time, shyness—to his early responsibility. Certainly, it left little time for more than school work until he started to attend college, and even then he continued to work in the store.

The candy store, however, did eventually offer Asimov one distinct advantage. Its newspaper stand always contained the latest issues of the popular pulp magazines. Thus, the new science-fiction magazines were readily available to him. His only problem was that his father clearly did not approve of such reading material; he saw all pulp magazines no matter what their genre as mind rotting, and he had a healthy respect for his son's intelligence. It was years before Asimov was able to convince his father that he should be allowed to read the magazines, and then his father gave in with reluctance and a sense of frustration.

Asimov's thirst for science fiction followed a pattern that is typical of most fans: he read anything that held the barest promise of being science fiction. In his case, however, it must be added that he read almost anything, period. While Asimov's formal education extends to a Ph.D. in biochemistry, he is extensively self-educated as well. His broad reading has extended his knowledge far beyond that of most men—however well educated—and prevented him from a narrowness of mind that often accompanies specialized degrees.

On 18 September 1938 Asimov attended his first meeting of the Futurians, one of the most celebrated of the early science-fiction fan clubs. According to Damon Knight,

> The Futurians were apparently not much
> impressed by Asimov at this time. Pohl
> remembers him as small, skinny and pimpled,

and says that his conversation did not sparkle; he seemed to have absorbed a lot of information without thinking much about it. Wollheim says that later on, when he came to visit the Futurians, he often had to be ejected because he was noisy. "After about half an hour we couldn't take him. Dirk [Harry Dockweiler] and myself, or Dick Wilson and Bob Lowndes would simply take him and heave him through the door. We couldn't stand him, you know. You can't really offend Ike, he always came back."

While Asimov insists that he has no memory of any such incident, it is not difficult to accept Wollheim's words as only a slight exaggeration. Any reader of Asimov's prefaces to his own works and others' would agree that he is hardly laconic.

On 21 June 1938, a few months earlier than his first encounter with the Futurians, Asimov first met John W. Campbell, Jr., the new editor of *Astounding Science-Fiction*. Asimov had just finished his first science-fiction story and had decided to show it to Campbell. From that first meeting there developed the most fruitful collaboration between editor and writer ever established in science fiction. John Campbell was the most important editor of science fiction in the late 1930s and throughout the 1940s, and he found in Asimov a promising writer who might eventually produce the kinds of fiction that he, Campbell, most wanted to see published in *Astounding*.

James Gunn, in an unpublished interview with Asimov (April 1979), called him "the quintessential Campbell writer." Asimov is always ready to agree to such a description and, in fact, seems to glory in it:

> Well, in a way, I suppose I was the perfect foil for John Campbell. On the one hand I was close to him. I lived right in town and I could see him every week. And, for another, I could endure him. That is, I imagine that a great many other writers found him too rich for their blood—at least to sit there and listen to him hour after hour. But I was fortunate in the sense that he was in some ways a lot like my father. And I had grown up listening to my father pontificate in much the same way that John did, and so I was at home and I listened to probably—I suppose if you took all the time that I sat there listening to John and put it all together, it was easily a week's worth of just listening to him talk. Day and night. One hundred and sixty-eight hours. . . . And I remember everything he said and how he thought and I did my best because I

desperately wanted to sell stories to him. I did my best to incorporate his method of thinking into my stories, which, of course, also had my method of thinking, with the result that somehow I caught the Campbell flavor.

But if Asimov did, indeed, catch the Campbell flavor, it is his successful translation of that flavor into concrete examples of exciting science fiction that has made his work such a force in the genre. The stories and novels of Asimov came to represent science fiction during its Golden Age, and it is no accident that Campbell was his editor.

Asimov's first short story accepted for publication was "Marooned Off Vesta" (1939; collected in *The Best of Isaac Asimov*, 1973). The story concerns the destruction of a starship, the *Silver Queen*, by an asteroid that leaves three survivors to maneuver their tiny, sealed-off section of the ship to a safe landing on Vesta, a tiny outpost used for astronomical observation. Thus, "Marooned Off Vesta" follows a common plot in science fiction: the unexpected happens; the characters must resist panic; they must comprehend their situation; and they must use their full physical and mental resources to overcome this situation.

The three marooned men are typical science-fiction characters. Mark Brandon is a young, inexperienced man who panics in the face of slow suffocation. Warren Moore is the coolheaded man of experience who uses common sense and scientific know-how to solve their dilemma. And Michael Shea is a calm but very worried foil for Moore. Shea is a competent but slow thinker who is in possession of the same basic information as Moore. He knows that their sealed compartment contains a water tank filled with a year's supply of water, and he also knows that the tank's back wall is also one of the outside walls of the compartment. But it is Moore, not Shea, who puts all this information together, applies the law that for every action there is an equal and opposite reaction, punctures the outside wall, and starts the ship on its way to Vesta. Shea is in the story to outline the resources. Moore is in the story to show how an intelligent, enlightened thinker can use the information. And it is Brandon's function to illustrate how not to act in such cases.

Even though "Marooned Off Vesta" was rejected by Campbell, it clearly shows Asimov's desire to follow the Campbell line. Man can overcome the unexpected if he remains calm, uses his intelligence, and adds just the right amount of creative thinking. Ignorance and uncontrollable emotion, not the immediate danger that characters find themselves in, lead to defeat and death. But if the short story does follow a Campbell line, it is still not difficult to see why he rejected it. Asimov had not yet learned how to handle background information or dialogue among his characters. The result is a very stiff and awkward story that never quite engages the reader. *The Early Asimov* (1972) contains many of his stories from this period and illustrates how Asimov continually grappled with the problems of needed exposition and dialogue.

In his interview with Asimov, Gunn characterized the early stories as "inferior . . . , they didn't live up to what you hoped them to be." Gunn further suggested that it was when the "stories began to incorporate not just detective elements, but also a kind of mystery to be discovered" that Asimov became pleased with his work and started to consider it successful. Asimov's reaction to Gunn's description of his earlier stories and the reasons for his later success identifies one of the more significant features of his writings:

> Certainly the very first stories that really satisfied me and made me feel good about my writing were my robot stories, and the robot stories, of course, virtually every one of them, has a situation in which robots—which couldn't go wrong—*did* go wrong. And we had to find out what had gone wrong, how to correct it—within the three laws of robotics. This was just the sort of thing I loved to do.

Starting in 1940 with "Robbie" (first published as "Strange Playfellow," 1940) and extending through 1950 with the publication of "The Evitable Conflict" (1950), Asimov wrote a series of highly successful short stories on robots with positronic brains. Besides "Robbie" and "The Evitable Conflict," seven more of these stories were collected and published under the title *I, Robot* (1950): "Reason" (1941), "Liar!" (1941), "Runaround" (1942), "Catch the Rabbit" (1944), "Escape" (1945), "Evidence" (1946), and "Little Lost Robot" (1947). Most of these stories concern malfunctions on the part of the robots and the ways the human characters explain the malfunctions and correct them. In "Runaround," for example, two troubleshooters for U.S. Robot and Mechanical Men, Inc., Gregory Powell and Mike Donovan, are confronted with a problem caused by a conflict between two of the three prime directives, programmed into all robots. These prime directives, known as The Three Laws of Robotics, state: 1) A robot may not injure a human being, or, through inaction, allow a human being to

come to harm; 2) A robot must obey the orders given it by human beings except where such orders would conflict with the First Law; 3) A robot must protect its own existence as long as such protection does not conflict with the First or Second Law.

In "Runaround" the conflict involves the Second and Third laws. Powell and Donovan have been sent to Mercury with a new model robot, Speedy, to determine its ability to handle the mining of selenium. Selenium is used as the major element in power cells, including those that protect the Mercury mining camp from the vast heat of the sun. When the two men land on Mercury, their first task is to send out Speedy to one of the nearer pools of selenium to gather a sufficient amount for the power cells that protect the humans. However, the order to Speedy is given in a rather casual manner by Donovan, and as Speedy approaches the pool, the robot senses the presence of dangerous fumes being emitted from a volcanic fissure. The fumes are capable of destroying the metallic body of the robot. Confronted with an immediate and sure threat to its existence and a rather low-order command from a human, Speedy continually circles the pool from a safe distance, trying to protect itself and, at the same time, carry out the command. In effect the overload created by the conflict between the second and third laws has caused in Speedy the robot equivalent of drunkenness.

Since Powell and Donovan face the probability of being roasted by the heat, a solution must be found to pull Speedy out of this state. Powell manages a solution by invoking the First Law. Since it must be observed by all robots to the exclusion of the second and third laws, it is Powell's plan to place himself in immediate danger so that Speedy must respond or allow a human being to come to harm through its own inaction. And, of course, Powell's plan works. So strong is the force of the First Law that Speedy snaps out of its electronic drunkenness and saves Powell. The robot is then sent on to another selenium pool that has no volcanic fissure near it.

While many of the robot stories are concerned with similar problems, it would be an oversimplification to state that this is the pattern for all the stories. Often Asimov deals with an entirely different issue: the relationship of man to the technology that the robots symbolize. The way the stories in *I, Robot* are arranged (departing from the order in which they were written) implies an increasing concern with exactly this relationship.

"Robbie," the first story, can be seen as an introduction to this concern. Robbie is a very early model robot that functions as a nursemaid to little

Gloria Weston. But Gloria's mother is having second thoughts: "I won't have my daughter entrusted to a machine—I don't care how clever it is. It has no soul, and no one knows what it may be thinking." Mr. Weston tries to defend Robbie from these charges and through him the reader learns how capable, friendly, and trustworthy a robot Robbie is. Mrs. Weston, however, will have none of this, and when in sheer frustration her husband asks her why she now feels so strongly against Robbie when she wanted him to buy the robot in the first place, she replies: "It was different at first. It was a novelty; it took a load off me, and—and it was a fashionable thing to do. But now I don't know. The neighbors...."

The point here is that Asimov makes the chief opponent against robots a shallow, fashion-conscious woman who first allowed Robbie into her house because it took "a load off" her. Now that the neighbors feel that robots are out of fashion, she has had second thoughts about Robbie. Asimov has, in effect, equated antirobot or antitechnology feelings with shallowness.

Robbie, moreover, has all of the reader's sympathy. The robot obviously misses Gloria, and when it rescues the girl from certain death, Mr. Weston's characterization of robots is amply proven. Obviously, if robots have no soul, they possess something else that functions as one.

That quality is identified in "Runaround," the story that follows "Robbie." Between "Robbie" and "Runaround," Asimov, with considerable help from John Campbell, invented The Three Laws of Robotics. While these laws control robot behavior, it is not too difficult to see that they are also the basis for moral human behavior as well, a point that Asimov makes clear in a later story. Human morality, in other words, has been reduced to essentials, and the robots have been programmed accordingly. In "Runaround," "Reason," and "Catch the Rabbit," as the robots become progressively more complex, the stories become more concerned with the basic morality of the robots. In each story the conflicts that arise can be seen as the problems humans have in dealing with creatures that so faithfully follow moral imperatives.

The fifth of the nine stories, "Liar!," is central not only by position but also by theme. In this story human characters allow harm to come to a robot. The robot Herbie is accidentally given the ability to read minds. The scientists do not know why or how this ability was gained, and they cannot duplicate it in other robots. It is this ability to read minds that gets Herbie into trouble. He is able to read the mind of Susan Calvin, and he finds out that she is in love

with Dr. Lanning. Herbie also knows that Lanning is not in love with her. Yet when Susan asks Herbie whether or not Lanning loves her, the robot answers that he does. According to the First Law, a robot cannot harm a human being, and Herbie knows that the truth would cause Susan great pain. The plot is further complicated by the fact that both Dr. Lanning and another scientist named Bogart are arguing over the answer to a difficult problem. Herbie knows the right answer, but if he tells them, he will be revealing their ignorance to them and that will cause harm to humans as well. Eventually Susan Calvin finds out that Lanning does not love her, and Lanning and Bogart learn that Herbie knows the answer to their problem. Angry and frustrated, Susan deliberately drives Herbie insane by taunting him with the paradox: " 'You must tell them, but if you do you hurt, so you mustn't; but if you don't, you hurt, so you must; but—' And Herbie screamed! ... It was like the whistling of a piccolo many times magnified—shrill and shriller till it keened with a terror of a lost soul. . . . And when it died into nothingness, Herbie collapsed into a huddled heap of motionless metal." No robot is capable of doing

Astounding Science-Fiction, *September 1941 cover*

what Susan Calvin does to Herbie. In fact, in the story "Evidence," which follows "Liar!," Susan Calvin characterizes robots as creatures simply motivated by "the essential guiding principles of a good many of the world's ethical systems." It is impossible to tell a robot from "a very good man."

Herbie had to follow the First Law, and, as a robot psychologist, Susan Calvin should be fully aware of the dilemma the robot faced. But, as a human being, she needs to fix the blame for her own frustration, and Herbie is available. It is at this point in *I, Robot* that the machines become the moral superior of man himself. Humans are, after all, guided by their emotions more often than not; robots, on the other hand, are guided only by the three laws.

In the next three stories in the book ("Little Lost Robot," "Escape!," and "Evidence") the robots become more and more complex and finally develop into a vast stationary "brain" that carries out all administrative functions for human civilization. In "The Evitable Conflict," the final story, this brain has complete charge of the economic life of the planet. The story opens with a series of investigations into some minor problems that have caused missed deadlines, mechanical failures, and lost production. In each case a supervisor is blamed and transferred to some less demanding position.

However, this obvious answer is not the correct one, and it is left to Susan Calvin, now a thorough advocate of machine intelligences, to identify the real cause: the brain is systematically removing from positions of importance those people who are still superstitiously fighting against it. She sees such action on the part of the brain as mankind's best hope for the future. Stephen Byerley, the politician in "Evidence" who is strongly suspected of being a robot and is the current World Coordinator in "The Evitable Conflict," wants to stop the brain because it threatens human freedom. But Susan replies that only the machine, with its vast knowledge, can now determine what is best for mankind. Moreover, it is simply an illusion to talk of human freedom. Mankind has always been "at the mercy of economic and sociological forces it did not understand." But with the machines in control "for all time, all conflicts are finally evitable."

Susan's optimism is, quite naturally, not shared by a significant number of readers of "The Evitable Conflict." Mrs. Weston is now far behind them, and what would appear to be superficial shallowness on her part becomes a serious philosophical question in the face of a society controlled by machines. In the work credited with the first coining of the term "robot," Karel Capek's *R.U.R.*, the robots also take

control of the world, but there it is meant to horrify the reader. Asimov has no such intention in mind. He wants Susan Calvin's optimism to be taken seriously. As Joseph F. Patrouch points out in *The Science Fiction of Isaac Asimov* (1974), the "mature placidity and confidence" that she displays throughout the story allow the reader to empathize with her far more than with most characters in Asimov's earlier fiction. But Asimov wants the reader to empathize with Susan Calvin because he wants the reader to believe in her words.

It is important to remember that the machines are, after all, robots, and that they have been programmed with Asimov's version of moral imperatives. They are not monsters, but creations that will allow man to remain man, with all his faults. The only difference is that now, while man will remain something less than perfectly moral, the moral machines will not allow man's imperfections to destroy the race.

In *I, Robot* Asimov gives the reader the robots and The Three Laws of Robotics as images of the moral ideal. He measures twentieth-century man against the robots and finds man wanting. But finally Asimov accepts man for what he is, refuses to damn mankind for what it is not, and credits the human race with the ability to create through its technology those inventions that will make up for human shortcomings. Many readers and critics of science fiction simply do not share this faith.

Two and a half years after the publication of "Marooned Off Vesta," Asimov wrote "Nightfall" (1941; collected in *Nightfall and Other Stories*, 1969), one of the most anthologized of all science-fiction stories. "Nightfall," as in so many other cases, was suggested to Asimov by Campbell during one of their frequent conversations. Campbell had been reading Ralph Waldo Emerson's *Nature*, and a passage in chapter eight of that book suggested to Campbell an interesting premise for a story. Asimov describes the conversation in which Campbell proposed the story in part one of his autobiography, *In Memory Yet Green* (1979):

> Campbell asked me to read it and said, "What do you think would happen, Asimov, if men were to see the stars for the first time in a thousand years?"
>
> I thought, and drew a blank. I said, "I don't know."
>
> Campbell said, "I think they would go mad. I want you to write a story about that."
>
> We talked about various things, thereafter, with Campbell seeming to circle the idea and occasionally asking me questions such as,

"Why should the stars be invisible at other times?" and listened to me as I tried to improvise answers. Finally, he shooed me out with, "Go home and write the story."

In order to explain why the stars appear only once in a thousand years, Asimov creates a planet, Lagash, that orbits among six suns. Scientists there have made two important discoveries. First, there is evidence that at least nine prior civilizations had flourished on Lagash, "all of which, without exception, were destroyed by fire at the very height of their culture." Second, astronomers discovered that the orbit of Lagash is not in accord with its predicted motion based on the Universal Law of Gravitation. This observation led to the postulation of another planetary body that would account for Lagash's orbit, a moon that, given the perpetual light that bathes Lagash, had been obscured by the six suns. Only one sun, Beta, lies in the plane of revolution of the moon, and after calculating the motions of all the heavenly bodies, the scientists have found, only two months before the next disaster, the answer to the rise and fall of the earlier, highly developed civilizations. Every 2049 years the moon eclipses Beta when Beta is alone in its hemisphere; and the eclipse lasts long enough for the entire planet to experience the darkness. The story opens just before the coming of one of these eclipses.

Asimov gives the reader all this background information through the device of an interview between one of the scientists, Aton 77, and a reporter. The scientists of Saro University have predicted the coming catastrophe and, as a result, have been ridiculed by the press and government. Now that the predicted disaster is less than an hour away, a reporter has decided to record the scientist's reaction when the moment of danger comes and harmlessly passes. In the reporter's opinion Aton is as foolish as the Cultists and their *Book of Revelations*, which also mentions periodic darkness and mysterious things called "stars."

In the course of "Nightfall" Asimov is able to accomplish many things that are characteristic of the best science-fiction stories. He is able to explain the conditions under which the stars can be seen only once in 2049 years; he illustrates the consequences of one such climacteric; he portrays credible technology, or lack of it, in a world used to constant light; he describes a religious cult that has some knowledge of previous eclipses; and finally he presents science as the only hope for progress. Ignorance does have its disastrous results, which is demonstrated when the shock of recognition of the vastness has also

established a "Hideout," a cave provided with enough oil-and-rag torches to last through the eclipse, where a group of scientists, their families, and the records and knowledge of their scientific breakthroughs have a chance of surviving while the rest of the planet goes mad. Asimov offers no guarantees, but he does make it clear that science offers the only hope that the cycle of rise and fall of civilization on Lagash can be broken.

From 1942 to 1951 Asimov produced five novelettes and four novellas now known as the Foundation trilogy. There is, perhaps, no more influential work in all of science fiction. Its concept of a galactic empire filled with some twenty-five million worlds, all inhabited by humans, and the invention of the science of psychohistory have become part of the mythos of the genre. Many science-fiction writers have assumed as the background for their own works the universe described in the trilogy. Asimov, moreover, has described this collection as the very foundation of his success as a writer and believes that it assured his later works easier acceptance from both editors and readers.

The Foundation series is not without its detractors. Charles Elkins, writing in Olander and Greenberg's *Isaac Asimov*, has been particularly harsh in his description of its literary shortcomings:

> From just about any formal perspective, the *Foundation* trilogy is seriously flawed. The characters are undifferentiated and one-dimensional. Stylistically, the novels are disasters, and Asimov's ear for dialogue is simply atrocious. The characters speak with a monotonous rhythm and impoverished vocabulary characteristic of American teenagers' popular reading in the Forties and Fifties.

Such criticisms are widespread among academic circles. Other critics of the Foundation trilogy point out the numerous inconsistencies among different parts of the narrative. Nevertheless, the trilogy presents a very special challenge to literary critics for two reasons. First, as Asimov himself has stated, his works do not easily lend themselves to traditional literary criticism because he has the habit of centering his fiction on plot and clearly stating to his reader, in rather direct terms, what is happening in his stories and why it is happening. In fact, most of the dialogue in an Asimov story, particularly in the trilogy, is devoted to such exposition. Stories that clearly state what they mean in unambiguous language are the most difficult for a scholar to deal with because there is little to be interpreted.

The second characteristic of the Foundation trilogy that frustrates critics is that it is very much a product of its medium: the science-fiction magazine. While *Foundation* (1951), *Foundation and Empire* (1952), and *Second Foundation* (1953) were each published in novel form and then collected as a trilogy under one cover in 1963, it is too often forgotten that the component parts were produced separately to appear in *Astounding Science-Fiction* over an eight-year period. As Gunn points out, literary critics refuse to admit the importance of magazine publication or the fact that the trilogy does not represent a single unified text. Asimov did not write the novelettes and novellas in the series with the thought that they would some day be collected so as to appear to be three unified novels.

How then should the trilogy be viewed? First, account must be taken of the drawn-out serial publication of the whole while the author was a part-time writer working with a rather strong-minded editor. Second, they should be seen as definitive examples of the strengths of magazine science fiction. In narration, plot, and technological invention, these stories are very strong indeed. Third, in aggregate they present a view of sheer galactic magnitude and multiplicity unsurpassed by any science-fiction work yet produced. Asimov did this so well that later writers simply built upon his "Foundation."

The first part of the trilogy, *Foundation*, consists of five novelettes, the first of which, "The Psychohistorians," was written by Asimov for the publication of *Foundation* in 1951. The other four novelettes were all published earlier in *Astounding*: "The Encyclopedists" (as "Foundation," 1942), "The Mayors" (as "Bridle and Saddle," 1942), "The Traders" (as "The Big and the Little," 1944), and "The Merchant Princes" (as "The Wedge," 1944).

"The Psychohistorians" is an introduction to the concept of psychohistory and an explanation of how the first foundation was set up on Terminus, a planet on the outer fringes of a decaying galactic empire in the last stages of its glory. The administrative center of this empire is Trantor, a planet of over forty billion bureaucrats and their families. So developed is the bureaucracy necessary to run the Empire that the administration buildings cover the planet's entire surface and extend far below the surface as well. Into this center of bureaucratic activity comes Gaal Dornick, a young man trained in the new science of psychohistory. As defined by Hari Seldon, the psychologist who created this new science, psychohistory is a mathematical science for predicting mass behavior. As Gaal Dornick puts it later, psychohistory is

> that branch of mathematics which deals with the reactions of human conglomerates to fixed social and economic stimuli. . . .
>
> . . . Implicit in all these definitions is the assumption that the human conglomerate being dealt with is sufficiently large for valid statistical treatment. The necessary size of such a conglomerate may be determined by Seldon's First Theorem. . . . A further necessary assumption is that the human conglomerate be itself unaware of psycho-historic analysis in order that its reactions be truly random. . . .

Through the use of psychohistory, Seldon has seen that the Empire is coming to an end and will be followed by thirty thousand years of anarchy. Seldon hopes to shorten that period to only a thousand years by creating two foundations of scientists, one of physical science and one devoted to psychology, "at opposite ends" of the galaxy. As a result of the crisis created by psychohistorical predictions, the government is happy to send Seldon and his physical scientists to the planet Terminus to work on their task of preserving knowledge for the future.

The four novelettes that follow this introduction are concerned with how the foundation of physical scientists establishes itself and then manages to survive threats from its neighboring worlds. Beyond psychohistory itself two elements dominate these stories and the two books that follow them. The first is plot. While very little action takes place in any single story, each of the threats to the Foundation and to Seldon's plan is well presented. Whether or not psychohistory has already predicted the crises and their consequences, the reader becomes involved in their immediacy for the humans who must live through them.

The second dominant element in *Foundation* is the portrayal of the many worlds that make up the Empire. Asimov's description of Trantor, for instance, is a fine example of what science fiction does best:

> He could not see the ground. It was lost in the ever increasing complexities of man-made structures. He could see no horizon other than that of metal against sky, stretching out to almost uniform grayness, and he knew it was so over all the land-surface of the planet. There was scarcely any motion to be seen—a few pleasure-craft lazed against the sky—but

all the busy traffic of billions of men were going on, he knew, beneath the metal skin of the world.

There was no green to be seen; no green, no soil, no life other than man. Somewhere on the world, he realized vaguely, was the Emperor's palace, set amid one hundred square miles of natural soil, green with trees, rainbowed with flowers. It was a small island amid an ocean of steel, but it wasn't visible from where he stood.

In *Foundation*, whether Asimov is describing the physical aspects of one of the more than twenty-five million worlds or the social, political, or economic systems of that world, he successfully convinces the reader of the utter vastness of the universe. Only in such an arena could psychohistory take place. The fact that the validity of psychohistory itself depends on staggeringly large numbers of people increases the reader's sense of the enormity of the universe.

By the end of *Foundation* Terminus has established itself as the dominant power in its sector of the Empire. In the two novellas that make up part two of the trilogy, *Foundation and Empire*, Terminus must deal with far greater forces than those that could be directed against it by some local world in this fringe area. In "The General" (first published as "Dead Hand," 1945) the force to be reckoned with is a young and brilliant general of the dying Empire who is carving out a new empire for himself. In "The Mule" (1945), which takes place over one hundred years after the Foundation has survived the threat posed by the general, a new threat to the Foundation arrives in the person of the Mule— a mutant who has successfully conquered the remnants of the old Empire and is steadily moving toward Terminus. The crisis presented by the Mule is Asimov's answer to the question: what happens if something occurs that is not predicted by psychohistory? The Mule is a genetic accident that Hari Seldon could not predict by psychohistory. While for most of the novella it appears that Seldon's plan will finally be defeated by a unique individual, the Mule has within himself the seeds of his own defeat.

Having reintroduced the Second Foundation (the one composed of psychologists and located at "Star's End") in the second volume, Asimov devotes part three of the trilogy, *Second Foundation*, to the search for this enigmatic entity, which is perceived as a threat by both the Mule and, after his demise, by the First Foundation. The problem is that the activity of the Second Foundation is increasingly noticeable— as individuals are mentally tampered with or

"adjusted" by their agents. In "Search by the Mule" (first published as "Now You See It . . . ," 1948) the mutant makes a desperate attempt to run the Second Foundation to ground, but the resourceful psychologists win the psychic duel and their antagonist is himself adjusted. In "Search by the Foundation" (first published as ". . . And Now You Don't," 1949-1950), which takes place seventy years after the Mule's defeat, the resurgent First Foundation inherits the task of seeking its shadowy sister-organization, which is strongly suspected of continuing to adjust people. The implied limitation of the First Foundation's freedom of action is as objectionable to that organization's leaders as to the Mule. At the end of the book the First Foundation believes it has defeated the Second Foundation, a necessary belief if Seldon's plan is to succeed. Psychohistory only works if the subjects are not aware that it is being used. But Asimov leaves unanswered his own attitudes toward the Second Foundation. Thus, as in "The Evitable Conflict," Asimov raises once again the whole issue of human freedom in an age when possibilities for control are manifold. It is the old question of free will versus determinism. Can the individual retain any shred of control over his personal destiny, or must it be surrendered to some select group of individuals or to some other force? Unfortunately Asimov never really answers this question; he seems unwilling to confront the paradoxes of freedom and responsibility that proliferate toward the end of this third volume.

Having worked on the Foundation series for eight years, it is not surprising that Asimov reports in his autobiography that while working on the final story he became tired of the series:

> I had gone through too much trauma on "—And Now You Don't" to continue the series. I had spent too much time, far too much, on working out the twists in the plot that would fit what had gone before. I think by this time even Campbell realized that I had had enough, though I'm sure that if he could have had his way, he would have had me work on the Foundation forever, since there is no question that the stories were crowd pleasers.

Two subsequent novels, however, do make use of Foundation background material. Both *Pebble in the Sky* (1950) and *The Stars Like Dust* (1951) use the growing Empire as their settings. *The Stars Like Dust* returns to the pattern of the Foundation stories with the only difference being that the action takes place during the Empire instead of the First

Foundation. A group of planets not yet part of the Empire are threatened by a warlike world that has managed to enslave a number of worlds and exact a heavy tribute. In addition these tributary worlds have their economic and technological growth managed for them—just as colonies on Earth have been controlled by imperialistic nations. The plot of the novel concerns a future war for independence with the Constitution of the United States playing a prominent role.

In *Pebble in the Sky* Asimov takes advantage of one of the most significant features of science fiction to examine racial prejudice. He creates a future Earth that is shunned by the other worlds of the Empire. The setting is so far in the future that a major nuclear war that had devastated the Earth is no longer even remembered. Earth is a moderately radioactive world that is considered a backwash of the Empire unfit for habitation by any intelligent person. And the "natives" of this Earth are considered to be every bit as undesirable as the planet. As one of the officers of the garrison stationed by the Empire on Earth says, "I don't like Earthies . . . I never liked them. They're the scum of the Galaxy. They're diseased, superstitious, and lazy. They're degenerate and stupid. But, by the Stars, most of them know their place."

Asimov has developed a world that exactly fits the specifications for his theme. He wants to present the character of racial prejudice as strongly as possible without singling out one particular ethnic group. Thus all Earthmen are the subject of this prejudice, not because a nuclear war has ruined their planet sometime in the distant past but because other humans from other planets simply do not like the Earth. While Asimov makes clear that Earth was the original home planet for all humans, that point is no longer known by the inhabitants of the other worlds of the Empire, and when an Earthman suggests such a possibility, it is met with ridicule. The reaction is that Earthies are just trying to find some reason to make their planet seem more respectable than it really is.

Given such a place in the scheme of things, it is not surprising to learn that the leaders of Earth have developed a plan to strike back at the rest of the galaxy. The Presidium of the Society of Ancients and, in particular, its High Minister and his private secretary, Balkis, have gathered a group of people who have developed a mutated virus to which Earthmen are immune, but which is capable of affecting all other humans. As a physicist named Affret Shekt warns, once the virus is delivered to a number of worlds, "millions will die each day, and nothing will stop it." The result of racial prejudice, Asimov implies, is further prejudice. The shunned Earthmen wish to strike back at the outsiders who have relegated them to the role of exiles from the human race.

Asimov makes use of two outsiders as major characters in the novel. The first of these is actually from Earth's far distant past. One day in the summer of 1949 Joseph Schwartz steps into the path of a stray beam of nuclear origin and is whisked into the future. Treated by an intelligence-heightening machine developed by Shekt, he develops an unexpected telepathic talent. The other outsider who plays a significant role in the novel is Bel Arvardan, an archaeologist from Sirius. The Sirius Sector of the Empire is particularly strong in anti-terrestrialism, but Arvardan claims that "I have as little intolerance in me as any man living. I believe in the oneness of humanity to my very scientific core, and that includes even Earth." But Arvardan is a familiar type of liberal: "Of course even tolerance must draw the line somewhere. Intermarriage, for instance, was quite unthinkable."

Eventually, Schwartz and Arvardan join forces to stop Balkis's plan, but first they must arrive at an understanding. This understanding is brought about by Shekt and his daughter Pola, both of whom are also trying to stop the spread of the disease. At one point Arvardan, Schwartz, Pola, and Shekt are captured by Balkis, and it appears as if the Earth will succeed in starting germ warfare. Arvardan, Pola, and Shekt try to escape, but Schwartz does not care. He is sickened by the treatment Earth has received, and now he sides with the fanatics. When Arvardan tries to convince him to help stop the plot, Schwartz turns on him, denouncing his superficial tolerance and exposing his unconscious racism. Since he is telepathic, he knows of the hypocritical shame Arvardan feels over his growing involvement with Pola. While Arvardan is shocked by this reading of his emotions and hotly tries to deny them, the truth of Schwartz's statement is clear. Yet it is Pola who teaches both Arvardan and Schwartz the real meaning of such emotions: "He's looking below the surface to the residue of your childhood. He would see the same if he looked into mine. He would see things similar if he could look into his own in as ungentlemanly a fashion as he probes ours." It is not what one has been conditioned to feel that is important, but how one rationally handles these feelings and acts. Thus both Schwartz and Arvardan are taught a lesson in what makes a man good. They will now work together, and Balkis will be stopped. The novel ends with the hope that the Empire will soon acknowledge its debt to Earth and accept its responsibilities for its inhabitants.

In *Pebble in the Sky* it is Pola's appeal to reason that finally assures success, and, as Gunn points out, Asimov's works are filled with "the triumph of reason or the struggle of reason to triumph over various kinds of circumstances, including emotional reactions, to situations that are existing" as the story begins. More often than not, Asimov's stories are explicitly concerned with how the right use of reason will solve problems while its abuse or defeat by the emotions will create problems. In the short story "C-Chute" (1951; collected in *Nightfall and Other Stories*) Earth is at war with an alien species, the Kloros, out of simple patriotic stupidity on the part of both races. The Kloros breathe chlorine and, therefore, the very different life-chemistries of humans and Kloros should lead to a peaceful cooperation: "There is no way we could maintain permanent hostility. Our races just don't coincide. Is there reason to fight then because both races want to dig iron out of the same airless planetoids when there are millions like them in the Galaxy?" Asimov does not focus on the war between the two races in "C-Chute." Instead he tells the story of how a group of humans traveling on a spaceship are taken prisoner by the Kloros. He examines each man's emotional reaction to the capture and describes his lack of ability to react effectively to the situation. All but one of the humans are frozen by private psychological problems or blind prejudices. One human, however, an accountant named Randolf Fluellen Mullen, thinks of a possible way of recapturing the ship and then logically goes about putting his plan into effect.

In order to succeed, Mullen must kill the two Kloros on board the ship, and Asimov describes one of the killings in unusually graphic terms:

> The Kloro threw its hands up. The little beak on its head-nodule opened alarmingly but noiselessly. It staggered and fell, writhed for a moment, then lay still. Mullen approached and played the oxygen-stream upon the body as though he were extinguishing a fire. And then he raised his heavy foot and brought it down upon the center of the neck-stalk and crushed it on the floor.

Mullen, however, does not glory in what he does. Reason dictated his actions because of the situation he was in. Other people's stupidity had forced his brutality, and Mullen is heartily sick afterward.

Asimov constantly resisted Campbell's requests for more man-versus-alien stories. He claims to have had a natural sympathy for aliens and clearly any situation in which humans fought aliens would cloud one of his basic messages: never fight when

reason will do as well. Thus, in "The Martian Way" (1952; collected in *The Martian Way, and Other Stories,* 1955) the potential for war exists between Earth and her colonies on Mars. Earth seeks to control her colonies and restrict their movement. In particular, the people of Earth unjustifiably believe that the Martians' use of water from Earth will endanger Earth. In a series of McCarthy-like hearings Earth politicians move to reduce greatly the accessibility of water to the Martians. As a result, many of the Martians are ready to go to war. Cooler heads, Martian heads, prevail, and the colonies develop an alternate source of water from the ice in the rings of Saturn. There is no need for war because the humans on Mars were able to look beyond a personal battle with Earth to a future that would exploit the full resources of the solar system.

Asimov's interest in finding reasonable solutions to unique and pressing problems finally led him to combine the mystery novel with the science-fiction novel. In April 1952 Horace Gold, the editor of *Galaxy Science Fiction,* suggested that Asimov put a murder into one of his science-fiction novels and then have it solved by a human detective of the future working with a robot partner. From this suggestion came *The Caves of Steel* (1954). In this novel Earth is an outcast in the solar system. Other planets and their moons have been colonized and have developed into independent worlds that take a rather superior view of themselves. These "Outer Worlds" frown upon an Earth that is now a series of burrows under the surface of the planet. All inhabitants live below the ground, acclimated to a life of artificial light and crowded space. Thus, the human detective, Elijah Baley, fears open spaces. The Outer Worlds have established an area on Earth, Spacetown, which is basically for members of these worlds only. It is a sort of colony on the mother planet itself, and when an important robot designer is murdered there, the Spacers, in what appears to be a plan to embarrass Earth government, insist that an Earth detective be assigned to the case. Since the central government's Terrestrial Bureau of Investigation wishes to avoid any appearance of failure in the complicated case, it ends up in the lap of Baley, a New York City detective.

Baley must balance the political overtones of the murder investigation with the difficult police work needed to solve the case. Even worse, however, is the fact that the Spacers insist Baley work with an Outer-World detective, one R. Daneel Olivaw. The problem with working with R. Daneel is that he is a robot and Earthmen utterly despise robots. Only the most basic models are used on the planet, and even

Samuel R. Delany and Isaac Asimov

then there seems to be a constant fear that somehow robots can do things better: "He [Baley] could feel R. Daneel's nearness and he wondered if R. Daneel could not replace an ordinary plainclothesman C-5." Thus, for the first half of the novel, Baley must learn simply to coexist with R. Daneel. Not until he loses his self-consciousness around the robot does he really start to devote his attention to the case at hand. As a result, in the early part of the investigation Baley's fears that the robot detective is more able than he is seem to be all too well founded.

But Baley does finally adjust to his new partner, and they function as an excellent team. Using Baley's intuitions on human nature and R. Daneel's ability to absorb and produce objective facts, the two detectives are able to solve the case without any embarrassment to Baley or the Earth. And, moreover, they solve the case despite political roadblocks that are constantly put in their way. A reasonable human detective is able to overcome his childhood conditioning, much like Arvardan in *Pebble in the Sky*, and come up with the right solution to a murder that has as many political implications as it has criminal ones.

One of the major reasons for the success of *The Caves of Steel* is the way Asimov presents Earth three thousand years from now. His descriptions are every bit as effective as those in the Foundation series, and

they convince the reader that he is indeed seeing a world that has undergone great change and adapted to that change. The people of this future Earth have made their adjustments to underground life and crowded conditions, and Asimov shows these adjustments with no undertone of contempt or condemnation. Typical is a description of Baley's visit to the communal bathroom for his section of apartments:

> Baley paused before the large double door on which there glowed in large letters PERSONAL—MEN. In small letters were written SUBSECTION 1A—1E. In still smaller letters, just above the key slit, it stated: "In case of loss of key, communicate at once with 27-101-51."
> A man inched past them, inserted an aluminum sliver into the key slit, and walked in. He closed the door behind him, making no attempt to hold it open for Baley. Had he done so, Baley would have been seriously offended. By strong custom men disregarded one another's presence entirely either within or just outside the Personals.

Critic Joseph Patrouch finds such descriptions objectionable because he sees Asimov's "cheerfully optimistic" assumptions that man will overcome present problems in such science-fiction works as

The Caves of Steel as running counter to the assumptions implicit in his nonfiction, where he seems "pessimistic about our civilization surviving this century. Where in his fiction do we find an emphasis on the things he is really concerned about?" Asimov himself, however, answers Patrouch's question in his interview with Gunn. The difference between fiction and factual writing accounts for the contrasting tones of each work: "in my public statements I have to deal with the world as it is— which is a world in which irrationality is predominant; whereas in my fiction I create a world, and in my world, my created worlds, things are rational." The world of *The Caves of Steel* is based on the hope, the conviction even, that rational men will find rational solutions. Asimov creates rational characters whose accomplishments exemplify what can be achieved by people who use reason. Such an approach addresses the present world as effectively as one that harps upon the irrational and its ultimate destructive power. A novel need not be pessimistic to be considered relevant.

Asimov brings Baley and R. Daneel together in one other novel, *The Naked Sun* (1957), which again succeeds in combining a good detective plot with a science-fiction world, and a short story, "Mirror Image" (1972; collected in *The Best of Isaac Asimov*) which centers on Baley's intuitive understanding of the human character more than on any created world. Asimov introduced another detective, Wendell Urth, in a series of stories published in *The Magazine of Fantasy and Science Fiction*. Professor of Extraterrology Urth is a classic armchair detective, overweight, disorganized, and afraid of almost any means of mechanical transportation, yet he is also the acknowledged expert on life forms on other worlds and a brilliant thinker. In "The Singing Bell" (1955), "The Talking Stone" (1955), "The Dying Night" (1956), and "The Key" (1966; all collected in *Asimov's Mysteries*, 1968), Urth combines humor, a sound knowledge of the physical laws of the universe, an acute understanding of human nature, and common sense to solve a series of mysteries that appear to have no easy solution. And Urth does this with information immediately available to all the other characters in the story and to the reader as well. Thus by 1957 Asimov's interest in solving complex situations through the clear application of reason had produced a formidable group of works that prove that science fiction, particularly Asimov's, mixes well with the mystery genre.

It would be wrong to assume, however, that all of Asimov's fiction is concerned with the triumph of reason. "The Dead Past" (1956; collected in *Earth Is Room Enough*, 1957) shows the consequences when a historian becomes so obsessed with his research concerning Carthage that he accidentally leaks information to an unsuspecting world that will change the entire fabric of society. And in "The Last Question" (1956; collected in *Nine Tomorrows*, 1959) Asimov leaves the theme of the struggle of reason and produces a computer reworking of Genesis. Finally in "The Ugly Little Boy" (first published as "Lastborn," 1958; collected in *Nine Tomorrows*), Asimov seems to point out that reason is not the only part of the human character that is needed. Sometimes a woman's concern and love for a child is far more important. Certainly, in this particular story Edith Fellowes's decision to return to a prehistoric age so that a Neanderthal boy, plucked from that age and now about to be dumped back into it, will have an adult to care for him is far more admirable than any voice of reason. The final scene, in which she holds the boy as they both start back into time, is one of the most moving, and least typical, of any passage written by Asimov.

Two additional works by Asimov, written in the 1970s, deserve mention because of their particular accomplishments. The first, *The Gods Themselves* (1972), is the only science-fiction novel Asimov has written since his novelization of the screenplay for *Fantastic Voyage* in 1966. *The Gods Themselves* is notable for two reasons. First, its development is a good example of how a writer goes about creating a science-fiction world. Asimov describes the origin of the novel in his introduction: at a science-fiction convention, Asimov attended a discussion in which Robert Silverberg illustrated a point he was making on chemical isotopes by inventing "plutonium-186":

> Naturally, when the dialogue was over, I accosted Bob, in order to tell him (with considerable glee) that there was no such thing as plutonium-186 and could not be. Bob did not, however, wilt under this demonstration of his scientific illiteracy but said, stolidly, "So what!"
>
> "So this," said I. "Just to show you what real ingenuity is, I will write a story about Plutonium-186."

The result was the first part of *The Gods Themselves*—"Against Stupidity . . ."—a story in which a quantity of plutonium-186 is found. Since the existence of this isotope defies all known laws of the physical universe, one of the scientists, Frederick Hallem, applies Occam's razor to the problem and reasons that if plutonium cannot be of this universe it must come from a parallel universe that is ordered by chemical laws that would allow such an isotope to exist. Hallem discovers an interface between our universe and the parallel one and then develops a use for this discovery: by means of the Electron Pump, an invention of his utilizing plutonium-186, he creates an unlimited source of power for his own world.

The problem is that the Electron Pump poses a danger to the entire solar system. A young scientist named Peter Lamont learns that Hallem was only able to develop the Pump after he received instructions from the aliens in the parauniverse and, upon further examination, that the mechanics of the Electron Pump make it likely that its continued use will trigger nuclear reactions in the suns of both Earth and the aliens' planet. Lamont, therefore, tackles the entire scientific and political establishment in an effort to turn off the Electron Pumps. However, Hallem is jealous of his now established reputation as "Father of the Electron Pump" and will not listen to a challenge from a young Turk. The politicians, moreover, choose to ignore Lamont because any such decision would be politically disastrous.

As a final bid to stop the Pumps, Lamont sends a message across to the parauniverse in hopes that the aliens will realize the danger and stop the Pumps from their end. He actually contacts a sympathetic alien who agrees with his predictions, but the alien is as helpless as Lamont in trying to convince the authorities to take the necessary step. "Against Stupidity . . ." ends as a friend of Lamont's quotes Schiller to him as an explanation of why he has failed to convince people of the danger threatening them: "Against stupidity, the gods themselves contend in vain."

In this way Asimov has given a reasonable explanation for the existence of an impossible isotope and then traced the significance of its discovery from its initial appearance to its practical application. Asimov has defined science fiction as "that branch of literature which deals with a fictitious society, differing from our own chiefly in the nature and extent of its technological development." Within science fiction, moreover, Asimov sees a subgenre he calls social science fiction that he defines as that branch of science fiction "which is concerned with the impact of scientific advance upon human beings." In "Against Stupidity . . ." Asimov supplies the reader with a classic example of social science fiction.

The second section of *The Gods Themselves*—"... The Gods Themselves..."—centers on the parauniverse and its inhabitants, and in so doing treats the readers to an almost prototypal example of how a good science-fiction writer is able to create a totally alien world. The parauniverse is not only described in detail but its entire structure is thoroughly consistent. It *is* a world that would naturally produce an isotope such as plutonium-186. The aliens, too, are described in terms that make them very much a product of their universe. Their physical structure, their mental habits, their social institutions, their science, and their very views of themselves and the Earthmen all fit neatly into the environment that has shaped them.

Given such successful accomplishments in the first two parts, the reader is doomed to disappointment when he turns to the third and final section, ". . . Contend in Vain?" As the question mark added by Asimov to the Schiller quotation hints, a solution to the problem will be presented in this section, but it is a rather unhappy solution in terms of the unity of the novel. A third parauniverse is discovered and an equilibrium is established that allows for the continued use of the Electron Pumps. As Patrouch points out:

> the men of the para-universe are never brought on-stage again. They are slipped into the background as a permanent but impersonal threat which is finally neutralized. . . . The para-men deserve far better handling than to be so abruptly dropped because there is simply too much preparation in the second part for their continued use.

In a more recent story, "The Bicentennial Man" (in *The Bicentennial Man and Other Stories*, 1976), Asimov returns once again to his positronic robots and directly addresses an issue that had been implicit in such earlier works as "Evidence," "The Evitable Conflict," and *The Caves of Steel*: what is man's relationship to his finest technological creation, the robots? In "The Bicentennial Man" the robot Andrew seeks to break down the barriers that separate him from the human race. He starts as a robot designed to be the perfect household servant, but Andrew, like Herbie in "Liar!," is a mutant: he has artistic and creative talent. The Martins, his owners, encourage his creativity, and slowly Andrew starts his evolution toward humanity. But it is an evolution that is constantly thwarted by humans who refuse to accept Andrew as anything more than a "soulless machine." The Mrs. Westons exist in great number in this world. Eventually, however, using arguments worthy of Susan Calvin's own final belief in the ultimate goodness of robots, the Martins and Andrew succeed in winning for him the right to live independent of human masters.

Still Andrew is constantly harassed by people. He once again returns to the courts that had freed him from servitude and succeeds in having a decision rendered that gives him the same protection from people that they have from him. Ironically, while the Three Laws of Robotics are sufficient to guarantee Andrew's moral behavior, a law is necessary to insure that of humans.

Andrew then continues his fight to be considered human at least under the law, but is stopped by a decision from the World Court that makes a fixed differentiation between robots and humans. Andrew reasons that the prime factor in the decision is that the makeup of his brain promises him immortality. Therefore, he undergoes an operation that restructures his positronic brain so that it will slowly die. When one of his friends asks Andrew how he could allow himself to undergo such an operation when the third law forbids a robot to place itself in known danger, Andrew answers: "I have chosen between the death of my body and the death of my aspirations and desires. To have let my body live at the cost of the greater death is what would have violated the Third Law." Andrew's sacrifice quickly captures the imagination of the population. Now mortal, Andrew is declared a human being. In the final scene Asimov presents Andrew's gentle and contented death in a manner which he admits was "deliberately . . . reaching for the pocket handkerchief." In effect, after years of being characterized as cheerfully optimistic about his machines and their potential good for humanity, Asimov has turned the tables and asked man if he can measure up to one of his robots. "The Bicentennial Man" is not primarily a reasoned statement about the moral goodness of the robot controlled by the Three Laws. It still makes such a statement, but the primary strategy appeals directly to the readers' emotions. If they will not believe Susan Calvin's measured words, perhaps they will believe their own feelings as they read of Andrew's death.

Since the late 1950s Asimov's production in science fiction has markedly declined. He presently spends more of his time writing mysteries and nonfiction than ever before. While he does occasionally mention the possibility of a fourth Foundation book, his science fiction since 1972 has been restricted to fewer and fewer short stories, and his public statements seem to indicate that this will be the case for some time to come. Yet Asimov cannot refuse a challenge. It was in answer to a challenge that he wrote *The Gods Themselves*, and, one

suspects, there will be yet another challenge that will so intrigue him that he will not be able to resist returning to science fiction for yet another time.

Other:

"Social Science Fiction," in *Modern Science Fiction*, ed. Reginald Bretnor (New York: Coward-McCann, 1953), pp. 157-196;

The Hugo Winners, Vol. I, edited by Asimov (Garden City: Doubleday, 1962; London: Dobson, 1963);

Tomorrow's Children, edited by Asimov (Garden City: Doubleday, 1966);

The Hugo Winners, Vol. II, edited by Asimov (Garden City: Doubleday, 1971; London: Sphere, 1973);

Where Do We Go From Here, edited by Asimov (Garden City: Doubleday, 1971);

Nebula Award Stories Eight, edited by Asimov (New York: Harper & Row, 1973);

Before the Golden Age; A Science Fiction Anthology of the 1930's, edited by Asimov (Garden City: Doubleday, 1974; London: Dobson, 1974);

The Hugo Winners, Vol. III, edited by Asimov (Garden City: Doubleday, 1977);

100 Great Science Fiction Short Stories, edited by Asimov, Martin Harry Greenberg, and Joseph D. Olander (Garden City: Doubleday, 1978).

Interviews:

Darrell Schweitzer, "Algol Interview: Isaac Asimov," *Algol*, 14 (Fall-Winter 1977): 22-26;

Paul Walker, "Isaac Asimov" in *Speaking of Science Fiction: The Paul Walker Interviews* (Oradell, N.J.: Luna, 1978), pp. 121-127.

References:

Paul A. Carter, *The Creation of Tomorrow: Fifty Years of Magazine Science Fiction* (New York: Columbia University Press, 1977);

Damon Knight, *The Futurians* (New York: John Day, 1977);

Marjorie Miller, *Isaac Asimov: A Checklist* (Kent, Ohio: Kent State University Press, 1972);

Joseph D. Olander and Martin Harry Greenberg, eds., *Isaac Asimov* (New York: Taplinger, 1977);

Jospeh F. Patrouch, *The Science Fiction of Isaac Asimov* (Garden City: Doubleday, 1974).

ALFRED BESTER
(18 December 1913-   )

BOOKS: *The Demolished Man* (Chicago: Shasta, 1953; London: Sidgwick & Jackson, 1953);

Who He? (New York: Dial, 1953); republished as *The Rat Race* (St. Albans, U.K.: Panther, 1959);

The Stars My Destination (New York: New American Library, 1956); republished as *Tiger! Tiger!* (London: Sidgwick & Jackson, 1956);

Starburst (New York: New American Library, 1958; London: Sphere, 1968);

The Dark Side of the Earth (New York: Signet, 1964; London: Pan, 1969);

The Life and Death of a Satellite (Boston: Little, Brown, 1966; London: Sidgwick & Jackson, 1967);

An Alfred Bester Omnibus (London: Sidgwick & Jackson, 1967);

The Computer Connection (New York: Berkley, 1975); republished as *Extro* (London: Eyre Methuen, 1975);

The Light Fantastic (New York: Berkley, 1976; London: Gollancz, 1977);

Star Light, Star Bright (New York: Berkley, 1976; London: Gollancz, 1978);

The Great Short Fiction of Alfred Bester, 2 volumes (New York: Berkley, 1977);

Golem[100], illustrated by Jack Gaughan (New York: Simon & Schuster, 1980).

Alfred Bester has published little science fiction, but his impact on the genre has been enormous. Robert Scholes and Eric Rabkin have aptly commented that in the 1950s Bester "pumped new life into that hallowed American form of science fiction, the space opera. In two books [*The Demolished Man* and *The Stars My Destination*] first serialized in *Galaxy* during the early fifties, Bester made his reputation and then fell silent for almost twenty years, but these two books are still very much alive, and have been influential on a younger generation of writers. . . . Bester brought the Gosh-Wow! back into science fiction, but accompanied by a knowing wink, and he almost started an American New Wave all by himself. It is not surprising that his third novel, *The Computer Connection* (1975), which appeared in *Analog* as *The Indian Giver* in 1974, fits in beautifully with what is presently going on in science fiction—since a lot of what is going on is what Bester started in the early fifties." Scholes and Rabkin adequately testify to the high reputation Bester enjoys today.

Bester was born in New York City, the son of James J. Bester and Belle Silverman Bester. As Bester describes it, the family was hardworking and middle class, and his home life, liberal and iconoclastic: "I was born a Jew but the family had a *laisser faire* attitude toward religion and let me pick my own faith for myself. I picked Natural Law." From the University of Pennsylvania, where he studied a wide variety of subjects, he received his B.A. in 1935 and was a postgraduate student at Columbia University and New York University, where he studied law and protozoology. After winning the *Thrilling Wonder Stories* amateur contest in 1939 with "The Broken Axiom," he became a professional writer, turning out a series of science-fiction stories in the early 1940s. In addition to scenarios for comics, radio, and television, he has produced English libretti for Verdi's *La Traviata* and Moussorgsky's *The Fair at Sorochinsk*. He has also written a satirical novel about television, *Who He?* (1953), and reported on NASA satellites in *The Life and Death of a Satellite* (1966). As senior editor of *Holiday*, he was the magazine's most prolific contributor. "*Holiday* failed after a robust twenty-five years," Bester comments, "my eyes failed, like poor Congreve's; and here I am, here I am, back in my workshop again, immured and alone, and so turning to my first love, my original love, science fiction."

Bester is not reticent about defining himself as a writer: "Call me an *Hommes libre* writer. Look, I write about Man, contemporary Man, subjected to wild, free, unusual stresses and conflicts. For the unusual I'm forced to use sf. Back in the 19th century authors of the Richard Harding Davis type sent their characters to Africa, Asia, or South America in order to confront them with the unusual. Today we send them into the future or out into space to do the same thing. Think for a moment . . . *The Short Happy Life of Francis Macomber* could easily be transformed into my kind of sf." Bester does not write technically oriented science fiction; his scientific gadgetry is often not explained, and scientific developments—such as the terraforming of Venus and Mars—are left to the reader's imagination. These are the givens of his fiction, and little is made of them. "I'm bored to tears," he writes, "by stories about hard heavy water or marauding alien leucocytes or how to make a cyclone spin counter-clockwise, thus making the earth safe for Scientology." A more important assumption of his fictive world is that man can develop unusual powers—telepathy, teleportation, and physical immortality—under unusual stress, and that once developed, these powers can be taught to others. Perhaps following Cuvier, Bester emphasizes transformation through crisis, evolution through catastrophe. Moreover his novels may generally be classified as science-fiction mystery stories, in which the protagonist as a detective, official or unofficial, tries to solve a mystery or series of mysteries. These quest stories are filled with exotic locales as well as a mature and cultured allusiveness. As Bester acknowledges, his mind is filled with "books, music, travels, cultures, education, writings, experiences. . . . Think of me as one of the composers of the High Baroque who cheerfully borrowed and adapted from each other and themselves." His finest work is characterized by a serious playfulness.

His first novel, *The Demolished Man* (1953), won the Hugo Award in 1953. The protagonist, Lincoln Powell, Prefect of Police and one of Earth's most perceptive telepaths, must combat the evil machinations of Ben Reich, one of the most powerful businessmen in the solar system. Reich kills Craye D'Courtney, apparently to take over his commercial conglomerate, though early in the novel D'Courtney has actually agreed to a merger and harbors no ill will for Reich. The murder seems pointless, and Powell, though he has broken through Reich's mental blocks and knows that he is the murderer, can establish no plausible motive for the crime. The quest for that motive leads Powell from the colorful slums of New York to the deserts of

Alfred Bester

Venus and the playgrounds of the asteroids into the very depths of Ben Reich's mind. Powell and Reich are stark and mighty opposites. The search for D'Courtney's missing daughter—deranged by witnessing her father's murder at the hands of Reich—becomes personally more important to Powell. In fact the two quests turn out to be parallel, as Powell works to bring Barbara D'Courtney back to normal maturity as well as to learn the secrets of her psyche—that is, an eyewitness vision of the murder. Likewise Powell must bring Reich to Mass Cathexis (the ultimate mental duel) and Demolition (psychological destruction and reconstruction under clinical conditions). Love is equally balanced with hate, and ironically Powell ends up giving to Reich the box of candy he buys at the end of the novel for Barbara. The two quests are intricately balanced, linked, and contrasted—not without a sense of humor.

The novel is heavily psychological. Reich is recurrently tormented in his dreams by The Man With No Face, who always frustrates his fantasy desires. After the murder of D'Courtney this shadowy figure emerges from Reich's mind and sets a series of booby traps to murder him. During the Mass Cathexis, Powell probes deeply into Reich's mind to find that this faceless creature is in fact a double-faced man—Ben Reich and Craye D'Courtney. Reich's natural father, D'Courtney had abandoned both mother and son and had been driven by his subsequent guilt to desire his own death. On the other hand, Reich was driven by more than normal oedipal hatred to murder his father, whom Reich unconsciously recognized as D'Courtney. The Man With No Face is a symbol of Reich's relationship with D'Courtney; the figure has no face because Reich cannot accept the fact of his paternity. As Reich contemplates the murder of D'Courtney, the faceless figure begins to appear in his dreams, a figure of threatened punishment. After the murder the figure becomes the suicidal punishment itself. In the depths of his mind, Reich cannot reject his father completely, nor can he bring himself to murder Barbara D'Courtney to save himself from Demolition. She is his half sister, to whom he is psychologically linked. Powell finds that deep in Barbara's disturbed mind is the "half-twin image" of herself and Reich. Apparently the mind is able to intuit family connections even where obscured, and the disintegrated family is held together by bonds of hate and love far stronger than the appearances of everyday reality. Neither Reich nor D'Courtney is governed by the rationalities of economics, but by the primordial feelings of guilt, hate, and love—feelings that apparently are not susceptible to psychotherapy even in a society where telepathic psychiatry is a developed art. Bester underlines the limits of conventional rationality and the power of instinctual passions. ·

Powell's relationships with Reich and Barbara are equally interesting. He is strangely attracted to Reich, seeing him as "tall, broad-shouldered, determined, exuding a tremendous aura of charm and power. There was a kindliness in that power, but it was corroded by the habit of tyranny." For Powell, Reich is two men—half saint, half killer—and Powell promises him, "I'm going to strangle the lousy killer in you, because I admire the saint." Reich is the great man who pits himself against society, "*a Galactic focal point . . . A crucial link between the positive past and the probable future.*" He is one of those "rare World-Shakers" who, if not stopped, could have recreated society in "his own psychotic pattern." The problem is not Reich's great power but the psychosis that accompanies that power. Powell admires in Reich qualities that they both share, for Powell is also charming, powerful, and deceptive. The basic difference between them is a matter of mental health and cultural values.

When Powell thinks of his lover, Mary Snow, he thinks of mint, tulips, and taffeta—highly improbable images of passion. In the course of the action Powell unconsciously rejects Mary and falls in love with Barbara D'Courtney. Exploring Barbara's mind for clues of her father's murder, he finds the image of himself, an image associated with "Father," but "nude, powerful; its outlines haloed with an aura of love and desire." Unfortunately, because of the rules of his Esper Guild, Powell can marry only a telepath, and Barbara does not seem to be one—until the final segment of the mystery is solved: how was Barbara able to hear her father, ridden with severe throat cancer, call for help the night of his murder?

In the last scene the lovers are brought face to face with the demolished Reich: "A naked thing . . . gibbering, screaming, twitching . . . crying and jerking as though a steady stream of voltage was pouring through its nervous system." Reich topples over the edge of a terrace, crashes through a flower bed, and lands on the lawn at their feet. The scene may be disconcerting, but it is perfectly apt for this novel of strange juxtapositions. Powell and his telepathic friends play at intellectual gymnastics, a game of psychic patterns; Maria Beaumont and her debauched friends play the licentious game of Sardines. Chooka Frood's Rainbow House, a confusing maze of half-ruined architecture and splattered color, is a West Side gaming house for the most arcane of entertainment, while Spaceland—"a

patchwork quilt worked in silver and gold"—is a series of pleasure domes in the asteroid belt, containing, among other things, a wildlife preserve. This juxtaposing of the most outrageous locales proves Bester's fertile imagination and emphasizes the completeness of his fictive world where all contraries meet.

In *The Demolished Man* Bester comes close to fantasy, as he does in much of his science fiction. However, Bester writes, "I hate fantasy because it's undisciplined, without parameters, ideal for the lazy, unstructured writer. Have you got a conflict which you can't resolve? Not to worry. Just ring in a witch or a magic spell or an enchanted sword or a princess with spectral powers." But in Bester's work the fantasy is of a different order, used for the sake of realism, variety, and, most of all, play. For the most distinctive quality of Bester's prose is its playful fertility, where the sophisticated reader is continually amazed and amused by the next juxtaposition.

"Millions for nonsense but not one cent for entropy" is the slogan of Geoffrey Fourmyle, alias Gulliver Foyle, the protagonist of *The Stars My Destination* (1956). The novel is considered, as Samuel Delany notes, "by many readers and writers, both in and outside of the field, to be the greatest single sf novel"; it is packed with "verbal wit, psychological and sociological sophistication, typographical inventiveness, structural cleverness, color, dash," writes Norman Spinrad. It grew out of Bester's desire to build a story on the pattern of *The Count of Monte Cristo*, for, he says, "I'd always preferred the anti-hero and I'd always found high drama in compulsive types." Gully Foyle is the "stereotyped Common Man," trapped in the wreckage of the spaceship *Nomad*, alone for 170 days. During that time the spaceship *Vorga* passes the wreckage but refuses to rescue him. Foyle is thus given a compulsive mission—revenge—and a mystery to solve—who ordered him to be passed by? Saved by the culturally primitive Scientific People of the Sargasso asteroid, Foyle's face is tattooed with a symbolic, devilish tiger's mask, and the name *Nomad* is printed across his brow. After his daring return to Earth, Foyle is driven by his quest for revenge; the common man within him is energized, and he is now ready for a series of amazing transformations, each marked by a visit to the Scientific People and each associated with a woman—Moira, Jisbella, Robin, and Olivia.

Linked with the epigraph to book one (William Blake's "Tiger! Tiger! burning bright / In the forests of the night, / What immortal hand or eye / Could frame thy fearful symmetry?"), Foyle's tiger mask forces the reader to consider the nature of Foyle's progress, as well as the ultimate sources of his story. His forename, Gulliver, leads the reader to think of Lemuel Gulliver, a man who never seems to learn a great deal from his incredible travels and experiences. Will Gulliver Foyle also be a figure of satiric laughter? The juxtaposition of Jonathan Swift and Blake, in any case, points the reader toward the two major thrusts of the work: on the one hand, social satire, and on the other, personal growth and responsibility. As Foyle analyzes the problem, human society is governed by tiger men like himself: "Tiger men who can't help lashing the world before them." But, Foyle asks, "Who the hell are we to make decisions for the world because we are compulsive? Let the world make its own choice between life and death. Why should we be saddled with the responsibility?" Foyle brings his challenge to the common man—PyrE, a substance that may destroy the world in a fiery holocaust and that can be ignited by human Will and Idea. As he says in his final passionate moments on Earth: "Die or live and be great. Blow yourselves to Christ gone or come and find me, Gully Foyle, and I make you men. I make you great. I give you the stars." Oligarchy, he implies, may be transformed into true democracy by personal responsibility.

The element of crisis evolution in the novel is teleportation, called jaunting after Charles Fort Jaunte, who saves himself from burning (a recurrent image in the story) by teleporting to a fire extinguisher. After Jaunte's first effort society "learned to teach man to recognize, discipline, and exploit yet another resource of his limitless mind." However, one type of teleportation, the space-jaunte, seems to be impossible since a jaunting man must know beforehand the coordinates of his landing stage in relation to his departure area. But, during the course of the novel, the reader comes to understand that Foyle has space-jaunted during his stay on the wrecked *Nomad*, and later Foyle learns the incredible feat of time-jaunting. The recurring figure of the mysterious Burning Man is Foyle himself, caught, near the end of the novel, in a raging fire of PyrE in old St. Patrick's Cathedral. In this desperate situation Foyle time-jauntes in a supreme effort to escape. The action comes full circle, for it had begun with Jaunte's escape from burning and his discovery of teleportation. As the novel ends, Foyle space-jauntes back to the Sargasso asteroid and the Scientific People. "He is dreaming," their priest surmises. "Presently he will awaken and read to us . . . his thoughts." Like Jaunte, Foyle will awaken to be a teacher, but the reader suspects, given Foyle's

tigerish, fiery temperament, that he will not be the same kind of teacher as the bland Jaunte, who, at the age of fifty-seven, was "immortalized, and ashamed to admit that he had never dared jaunte again." Foyle is made of sterner stuff.

The world of *The Stars My Destination* is a world of freaks. In Trenton Dr. Harley Baker runs a Freak Factory creating monstrosities such as bird men, mermaids, hermaphrodites, two-headed twins, centaurs, and even a mewling sphinx. Foyle's hideous tiger mask is matched by Saul Dagenham's "death's head" caused by radioactivity. Foyle's beloved Olivia Presteign is a Snow Maiden, an Ice Princess, with coral eyes and lips, who can see only heat patterns. Robin Wednesbury is a telesend who cannot help communicating mentally to others but who hears nothing in return. When Foyle returns in disguise after breaking prison, he comes appropriately as Geoffrey Fourmyle with a "grotesque entourage," a circus. As the action nears its end Foyle admits, "I'm a freak of the universe . . . a thinking animal" and asks the most important of questions: "Am I to teach the world to space-jaunte and let us spread our freak show from galaxy to galaxy through the universe? What's the answer?" The only acceptible answer that Foyle receives is from a broken robot who says, "You're all freaks. . . . Life is a freak. That's its hope and glory." But all the same, the novel ends with Foyle spreading the potentially devastating PyrE throughout the Earth and then space-jaunting to Sargasso. PyrE is the final test; if it is used wisely, if its challenge is met, the human freak show will be given the chance to populate the universe.

A new departure for Bester, *The Computer Connection* is a first-person narrative dictated to a diary-computer by Edward Curzon, called Guig (for "Grand Guignol") by his friends. Curzon died in the Krakatoa explosion of 1883 but revived to find that his physical body was now virtually immortal and that a rather large group of survivors from different crises had experienced similar deaths and subsequent physical immortality. Lethal cellular secretions cause aging and normal death. "Each of us knew we were going to die," Guig explains, "and received a psychogalvanic shock that wiped out our lethal cell products and turned us into Molecular Men; Molemen for short. . . . It's a sort of updating of Cuvier's 'Catastrophism' theory of evolution." As the Grand Guignol, Curzon periodically murders important people in the most ghastly manner to see if he can create more Molemen. Until his meeting with the Indian chief Sequoia Guess, a cryonic expert, Guig's dubiously charitable murders have been failures. To bring Sequoia out of a postepileptic delirium, Dr. Lucretia Borgia poisons him and then brings him back to life, making him a Moleman and at the same time inadvertently connecting his brain to a giant Extrocomputer. "The Extro set up a one-to-one relationship with him—its bits and his brain cells. He is the Extro and the Extro is him. It's a fantastic interface." In one sense this astonishing symbiotic relationship is "a giant forward step in evolution." But this evolutionary step proves disastrous as the Extro, with the help of Sequoia, begins an undeclared war on mankind. The mystery to be solved is why and how the computer has become malicious.

Transformation is the central theme of the novel. Molecular Man is defined as "an organism that can transform any molecule into an anabolic buildup." The one disease to which Molemen are susceptible is Lepcer—a variation and combination of nodular and anesthetic leprosy—which in its final stage transforms the diseased Moleman into a lionlike creature. Sequoia's cryonauts are transformed from ordinary men into "naked rats" ("cryology recycles ontogeny") and finally into strange hermaphrodites who have extraordinary powers, communicate musically, and look like "seven-foot termites." The point is also made that people can be internally transformed, especially through love. Guig sees that Fee-5's love for Sequoia has caused her to grow up overnight; she has "made a quantum jump." And Guig's own love for Sequoia's sister, he says, "made me love and understand the whole damn lunatic world." Although transformation is not constantly positive, it is inevitable. Even the relatively stable Molemen are subject to the degenerating effects of Lepcer and the elevation of love. But the final puzzle of transformation is embodied in the cryonic hermaphrodites with their flowerlike genitals who now control the Extrocomputer from anywhere. "We've programmed it to respond to our electronic valence," they tell Guig. When Guig suggests that they will have godlike power, they tell him that God is neither man nor woman: "God is Friend." The enigmatic statement is not explained, and the significance of the hermaphrodites is left to the reader's judgment.

The impetus for change in this society does not come from its mainstream, but from the Indians and the Group of Molemen. The Indians and the Group live outside the modern society of brutal contradictions, giant computers, and terrible decay—a bewildering welter of madness. Among the outsiders traditions and values are preserved. The Molemen speak twentieth-century English in contradistinction to the Black Spanglish of the semiliterate society. In the marriage of Guig to Natoma Guess, the emphasis is

on ritual and ceremony. Ironically, change—be it negative or positive—comes from these traditionally oriented outsiders. The whole mystery of Sequoia's connection to the computer becomes "a monumental challenge of much fascination," and Guig admits that he is unable to resist the challenge. Again, as in Bester's earlier novels, the emphasis is on crisis, mystery, transformation, and a successful solution by an extraordinary protagonist. These are themes to which he returns again in his next novel.

An experimental novel, Golem[100] (1980), attempts to explode the parameters of print by combining words, musical scores, and graphics in order to create a new technique of synesthetic visio-narration. The experiment is successful because Bester carefully links new techniques with traditional form. The musical scores are part of the bee-ladies' diabolical ritual; the first sequence of Jack Gaughan's surreal graphics is explained in the novel by one of the most perceptive characters, Ind'dni; and, for the longtime reader of Bester, the graphic techniques developed here were already incipient in The Stars My Destination. Bester is careful to keep his signposts clear.

Golem[100] is a sardonic novel about diabolic possession, where the devil is not external, but a manifestation of the id. The characters agree to call this monstrous projection Golem-one-hundred because it is "a polymorph and can assume a hundred different shapes." The Golem is a personification of the human polymorphous perverse urges seeking to break out of the dark into the full light of consciousness. The failure of the superego—in the person of Subadar Ind'dni—to repress or destroy the brutal and lascivious id in its attempt to dominate society can lead only to the collapse of civilization. The final chapter of the novel, set one hundred and five years in the future, makes this collapse clear. An unnamed lady is awakened from cryonic freeze to be told "how oletypus mans go aus-out, exstink like dinnersours, and N*E*W breed primal poisons like us we make quantum jump & replace her." The decline of language and the pun on poisons/persons alert the reader to what has happened to the world of the novel. The awakened lady very aptly wishes to return to her coffin.

Initially three characters—Subadar Ind'dni, Gretchen Nunn, and Blaise Shima—claim the reader's attention and sympathy. Each, through the agency of Promethium, which is found to be a drug that can release the libido, passes over into the Phasmaworld of the id, and each is ultimately captured by the deadly forces of that world. Shima murders Droney Lafferty in cold blood; Gretchen,

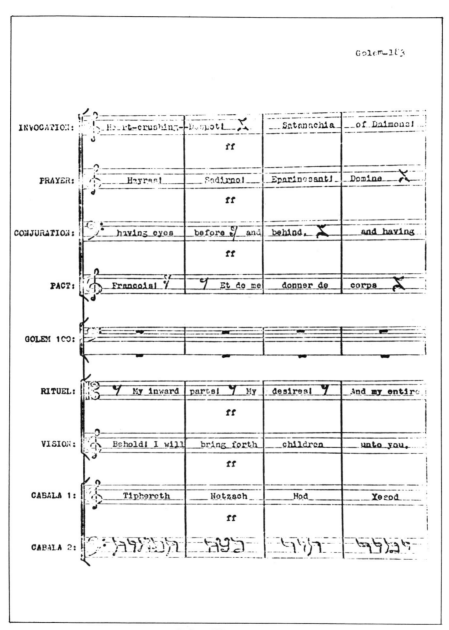

Golem[100], *typescript*

"getting back to Nature's basics," tears Shima's penis off and leaves him to bleed to death, then murders her rivals as the new queen of the bee-ladies; and Ind'dni actually becomes the Golem itself. The initial sympathy for these characters is lost as the reader watches them degenerate.

Unity becomes a central issue in the novel. After Shima's murder of Lafferty, Ind'dni comments with horrible clarity: "You have just joined the pieces of yourself together at a frightful cost." The reader is left wondering if the unification is worth the cost in human life. In fact, the major impression of the novel is disunity, polymorphism. Bester gives us this impression by returning again and again to series of disconnected events, especially scenes of violence and perverse sexuality. The world of the novel, as well as its characters, is literally falling apart.

Once again Bester uses the idea of the evolutionary breakthrough. Shima comments, "Gretchen's a fantastic mutation, a quantum jump toward the primal pinnacle. And if I believed in God, I'd pray this genetic change is favorable and inheritable." Ironically, the change appears to be unfavorable and inheritable. Gretchen's physical blindness, at first seen as an interesting psychic phenomenon since she can see through the eyes of others, is ultimately perceived as a symbol of her lack of moral insight. If we are puzzled about the meaning of the hermaphrodites in *The Computer Connection*, Bester leaves us in no doubt here. By giving themselves to the powers of the id, the characters lose their humanity, becoming the creatures of darkness and death. The world of *Golem*[100] is death obsessed, a necro culture. As Gretchen herself observes, "Most of us are Golems, one way or another." In this novel, there is no successful solution by an extraordinary protagonist. We are left finally with a sense of horrific failure.

The Great Short Fiction of Alfred Bester (1977) collects some stories from *Starburst* (1958) and *The Dark Side of the Earth* (1964) with new additions such as "The Four-Hour Fugue" and "Isaac Asimov." Originally published in two volumes, *The Light Fantastic* (1976) and *Star Light, Star Bright* (1976), it contains the most complete selection of Bester's short fiction along with authorial introductions, commentary, and the autobiographical "My Affair with Science Fiction." Though Bester is not at his finest in the short story, the collection clearly reveals the author's romantic turn of mind, as well as his ability to use a wide variety of subject and genre. Here the reader finds satire, time-travel, abnormal psychology, parallel universes, and surreal confessions. One of the most interesting

stories is "They Don't Make Life Like They Used To," which chronicles the meeting of the last woman on Earth with the last man, their attempts to preserve order and tradition, and their final failure when confronted with an unknown but terrifying enemy. Faced with possible death, the two characters assault each other sexually, succumbing to their own animality. "Galatea Gallante" (1979) is an updating of the Pygmalion myth, where, in a world of freaks and unusual mental powers, the bioengineer Dominie Regis Manwright falls in love with his own unusually beautiful, but highly unmarketable, creation.

Thematically Bester has remained constant in his concern with the basics of human passion and personal change. Technically he is an experimenter, and his influence can be charted in the works of such writers as John Brunner, Robert Silverberg, Clifford D. Simak, and Kurt Vonnegut, Jr. With readers he has always been popular. At present Bester is planning a work in which the *anima mundi*, the world soul, acts as the narrative voice in a totally animated universe, and the female protagonist is a polymorphic creature from outer space. As always Bester is playfully struggling against the limits of established form. —*William L. Godshalk*

Periodical Publication:

"Galatea Gallante," *Omni*, 1 (April 1979): 42-46, 124-132.

References:

Samuel R. Delany, "About Five Thousand One Hundred and Seventy Five Words," in *SF: The Other Side of Realism*, ed. Thomas D. Clareson (Bowling Green, Ohio: Bowling Green University Popular Press, 1971), pp. 130-146;

William L. Godshalk, "Alfred Bester: Science Fiction or Fantasy?," *Extrapolation*, 16 (May 1975): 149-155;

Jeff Riggenbach, "Science Fiction as Will and Idea: The World of Alfred Bester," *Riverside Quarterly*, 5 (August 1972): 168-177;

Robert Scholes and Eric S. Rabkin, *Science Fiction: History, Science, Vision* (New York: Oxford University Press, 1977), pp. 67-69;

Norman Spinrad, ed., *Modern Science Fiction* (Garden City: Anchor Press, 1974), pp. 191-193, 228-267;

Paul Williams, Introduction to *The Stars My Destination* (Boston: Gregg Press, 1975), pp. v-xv.

LLOYD BIGGLE, JR.
(17 April 1923-   )

BOOKS: *The Angry Espers* (New York: Ace, 1961; London: Hale, 1968);

All the Colors of Darkness (Garden City: Doubleday, 1963; London: Dobson, 1964);

The Fury Out of Time (Garden City: Doubleday, 1965; London: Dobson, 1966);

Watchers of the Dark (Garden City: Doubleday, 1966; London: Rapp & Whiting, 1968);

The Rule of the Door (Garden City: Doubleday, 1967); republished as *Out of the Silent Sky* (New York: Belmont Books, 1977);

The Still, Small Voice of Trumpets (Garden City: Doubleday, 1968; London: Rapp & Whiting, 1969);

The World Menders (Garden City: Doubleday, 1971; Yorkshire: Elmfield Press, 1974);

The Metallic Muse (Garden City: Doubleday, 1972);

The Light That Never Was (Garden City: Doubleday, 1972; Yorkshire: Elmfield Press, 1975);

Monument (Garden City: Doubleday, 1974; London: New English Library, 1975);

This Darkening Universe (Garden City: Doubleday, 1975);

A Galaxy of Strangers (Garden City: Doubleday, 1976);

Silence is Deadly (Garden City: Doubleday, 1977);

The Whirligig of Time (Garden City: Doubleday, 1979).

Lloyd Biggle, Jr., was born in Waterloo, Iowa. After winning a Purple Heart with oak-leaf cluster in World War II, he took an A.B. with high distinction at Wayne University (now Wayne State) in 1947 and a Ph.D. in music at the University of Michigan in 1953. He taught the literature and history of music there from 1948 to 1951 and has been self-employed since then. He married Hedwig Janiszewski, a violin teacher, in 1947; they now live in Ypsilanti, Michigan.

Biggle has contributed over fifty stories to science-fiction and mystery magazines; many of his books have been republished in Europe. Theodore Sturgeon has praised his work, and *The Metallic Muse* (1972) and *Monument* (1974) are included in Pfeiffer and de Bolt's list of basic science-fiction titles in Barron's *Anatomy of Wonder*. Frequently a science-fiction convention participant, Biggle has promoted the scholarly study of science fiction and attacked the superficial treatment it sometimes receives from academics.

Lloyd Biggle, Jr.

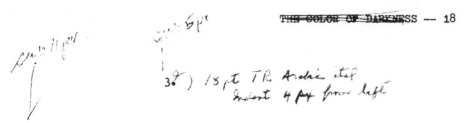

THE COLOR OF DARKNESS -- 18

Only one New York paper gave the Universal Transmitting Company's opening front-page coverage. Other papers across the country treated the announcement as a filler, usually under the terse heading, "AGAIN?" There was little editorial comment. Even the newspaper editors were tired of pointing out, with suitably cutting sarcasm, that Universal Trans was merely making propaganda to gain itself a temporary respite from the troubles that plagued it.

The average citizen was thoroughly fed up with Universal Trans. He was not just unenthusiastic, he was uncurious to the point of indifference. As a result, the hour of the opening found the Universal Trans terminals everywhere deserted except for employees.

The swank, half-finished New York terminal on Eighth Avenue south of the Pennsylvania Station was no exception. Ron Walker entered at 8:01 that Monday morning, and looked about with the sinking feeling that he'd been had. Getting the assignment had been a problem, not because anyone else wanted it, but because his boss wanted no time wasted on Universal Trans, then or ever.   The only thing that kept Walker from turning around and walking out was the knowledge that he had wasted twenty minutes of his editor's time in arguing about the newsworthiness of Universal Trans, and he damned well had to produce some kind of story.

Walker stopped at the information desk and was directed to the mezzanine, where he found a row of ticket windows backed up by ticket agents. He asked for a ticket to Philadelphia. He was sold a ticket to Philadelphia, presented with an artistically printed pamphlet on the joys of transmitting, issued a free fifty-thousand-dollar insurance policy, and directed to a

"The Color of Darkness," typescript

Biggle imagines a galaxy of diverse sentient species, united by commerce but sometimes divided by xenophobia. He has become increasingly sophisticated in creating situations that allow an individual's heroism or creative imagination to save the day for humanistic values. Biggle combines elements of science fiction and detective fiction in an early character, Jan Darzek, an Earthling private eye. In *All the Colors of Darkness* (1963) Darzek discovers the pangalactic government of Supreme, a world-sized computer. Although Earth has not evolved morally to the level required for admission to Supreme's Galactic Synthesis, Darzek becomes a high ranking agent for this enlightened government in *Watchers of the Dark* (1966), *This Darkening Universe* (1975), and *Silence is Deadly* (1977). In *Watchers of the Dark* (nominated for a Nebula Award) Darzek masquerades as an interplanetary entrepreneur to investigate an epidemic of xenophobia—the moral "darkness" most dangerous to Supreme's government. The plot resolution rather simplistically indicts demagoguery, but the story is enlivened by witty portraits of alien businessmen, such as the many-tentacled patriarch E-Wusk, who are surprisingly tolerant and genial by human standards. In the later books Darzek comes to resemble the cultural exchange officers in Biggle's Interplanetary Relations Bureau stories. These officers visit alien worlds that are technologically primitive, despotically governed, but aesthetically sophisticated. In *The Still, Small Voice of Trumpets* (1968) cultural survey officer Jef Forzon must foment revolution on Gurnil, in Kurr, tyrannized by King Rovva. Tor, a stringed instrument virtuoso, has had one arm cut off by the cruel king, and Forzon prompts him to lead a rebellion of others who have suffered a similar punishment by providing them with a new instrument that can be played with one hand: the trumpet. In spite of treachery among the Interplanetary Relations Bureau staff and Forzon's own misgivings about changing a contented and culturally rich, if "backward," society, the rebellion succeeds in clearing the way for democracy. Among other Interplanetary Relations Bureau books, *The World Menders* (1971) is notable. *The Light That Never Was* (1972)—the title is an allusion to Wordsworth's "Peele Castle"—treats the xenophobia confronting nonhuman painters but never defines an alien perspective in art and lamely resolves the plot by unmasking an individual villain.

Biggle's most sophisticated treatment of intercultural relations, and his best novel, is *Monument*, from a story nominated for a Hugo Award in 1962. Here Biggle combines a light-handed critique of profit-oriented social priorities with deft manipulation of science-fiction conventions. The hero, Cerne Obrien, is not an agent for a pangalactic government, but a space bum who crashlands on a paradise planet where the humanoid natives specialize in culinary art. He protects them from exploitation by entrusting a secret plan to the young leader, Fornri. Soon after Obrien's death Federation ships arrive, and bloated entrepreneur Wembling builds a huge resort hotel; a predictable destruction of the native culture begins, despite protests from Wembling's niece, medical student Talitha Warr, and Aric Hort, an anthropologist. Yet no really brutal crimes are committed (unlike Ursula K. Le Guin's 1972 novella, "The Word for World Is Forest"), and the fatal illness of a native child makes the reader feel that medical innovations, at least, might be an unmixed blessing. Meanwhile, the natives doggedly pursue Obrien's plan and save themselves with civilized finesse in a surprise ending, in which they prove to be quick learners in exploiting the power of money. Biggle plays neatly on the reader's expectations, making *Monument* intriguing at first reading, but absolutely delightful in retrospect.

Yet whatever its charm, psychological and philosophical depths are not probed in Biggle's science fiction, and his later works have not shown the literary sophistication of *Monument*. His strengths lie in a commonsense portrayal of human motivation and in an ability to exploit the obvious for clever plot twists, as in *Silence is Deadly*, where the natives' lack of hearing organs—their most striking characteristic—becomes a vital clue to the nature of the "death ray" found on their primitive planet, Kamm. Biggle's science fiction never errs through excess in intention or design and is altogether engaging and entertaining.

—*Patricia Bizzell*

Other:

Nebula Award Stories Seven, edited by Biggle (New York: Harper, 1972; London: Gollancz, 1972).

James Blish

Raymond J. Wilson III
Kearney State College

BIRTH: East Orange, New Jersey, 23 May 1921, to Asa Rhodes and Dorothea Schneewind Blish.

EDUCATION: B.S., Rutgers University, 1942; Columbia University, 1945-1946.

MARRIAGE: 23 May 1947 to Mildred Virginia Kidd Emden, divorced; 1964 to Judith Ann Lawrence; children: Elizabeth, Charles Benjamin.

AWARDS: Hugo Award for *A Case of Conscience*, 1959; guest of honor, 18th World Science-Fiction Convention, 1960.

DEATH: London, England, 30 July 1975.

BOOKS: *Jack of Eagles* (New York: Greenberg, 1952; London: Nova, 1955); republished as *ESPer* (New York: Avon, 1958);
The Warriors of Day (New York: Galaxy, 1953);
Earthman, Come Home (New York: Putnam's, 1955; London: Faber & Faber, 1956);
They Shall Have Stars (London: Faber & Faber, 1956; New York: Avon, 1966); revised as *Year 2018* (New York: Avon, 1957; London: Four Square Books, 1964);
The Seedling Stars (New York: Gnome Press, 1957; London: Faber & Faber, 1967);
The Frozen Year (New York: Ballantine, 1957); republished as *The Fallen Star* (London: Faber & Faber, 1957);
The Triumph of Time (New York: Avon, 1958); republished as *A Clash of Cymbals* (London: Faber & Faber, 1959);
A Case of Conscience (New York: Ballantine, 1958; London: Faber & Faber, 1959);
VOR (New York: Avon, 1958; London: Corgi, 1959);
Galactic Cluster (New York: Signet, 1959; London: Faber & Faber, 1960);
The Duplicated Man, by Blish and Robert W. Lowndes (New York: Avalon, 1959);

The Star Dwellers (New York: Putnam's, 1961; London: Faber & Faber, 1962);
So Close to Home (New York: Ballantine, 1961);
Titan's Daughter (New York: Berkley, 1961; London: Four Square Books, 1963);
The Night Shapes (New York: Ballantine, 1962; London: Four Square Books, 1963);
A Life For the Stars (New York: Putnam's, 1962; London: Faber & Faber, 1964);
Doctor Mirabilis (London: Faber & Faber, 1964; New York: Dodd, Mead, 1971);
The Issue at Hand, as William Atheling (Chicago: Advent, 1964);
Mission to the Heart Stars (New York: Putnam's, 1965; London: Faber & Faber, 1965);
Best Science Fiction Stories of James Blish (London: Faber & Faber, 1965; revised, 1973);
New Dreams This Morning (New York: Ballantine, 1966);
Star Trek (New York: Bantam, 1967);
Welcome to Mars! (London: Faber & Faber, 1967; New York: Putnam's, 1968);
A Torrent of Faces, by Blish and Norman L. Knight (Garden City: Doubleday, 1967; London: Faber & Faber, 1968);
The Vanished Jet (New York: Weybright & Talley, 1968);
Black Easter (Garden City: Doubleday, 1968; London: Faber & Faber, 1969);
Star Trek 2 (New York: Bantam, 1968; London: Corgi, 1969);
Star Trek 3 (New York: Bantam, 1969; London: Corgi, 1969);
Cities in Flight (New York: Avon, 1970);
Anywhen (Garden City: Doubleday, 1970; London: Faber & Faber, 1971);
Spock Must Die! (New York: Bantam, 1970);
More Issues at Hand, as William Atheling (Chicago: Advent, 1970);
The Day After Judgment (Garden City: Doubleday, 1971; London: Faber & Faber, 1972);

Star Trek 4 (New York: Bantam, 1971);

. . . *And All the Stars a Stage* (Garden City: Doubleday, 1971; London: Faber & Faber, 1972);

Midsummer Century (Garden City: Doubleday, 1972; London: Faber & Faber, 1973);

Star Trek 5 (New York: Bantam, 1972; London: Corgi, 1972);

Star Trek 6 (New York: Bantam, 1972; London: Corgi, 1972);

Star Trek 7 (New York: Bantam, 1972; London: Corgi, 1973);

Star Trek 8 (New York: Bantam, 1972);

The Quincunx of Time (New York: Dell, 1973; London: Faber & Faber, 1975);

Star Trek 9 (New York: Bantam, 1973);

Star Trek 10 (New York: Bantam, 1974; London: Corgi, 1974);

Star Trek 11 (New York: Bantam, 1975; London: Corgi, 1975);

Star Trek 12 (New York: Bantam, 1977).

James Benjamin Blish began writing stories for the specialized science-fiction magazines during the 1940s while he was an editor of a trade newspaper in New York. Although he had published dozens of books, mostly science fiction, it was not until Blish moved to England in 1968 that he permanently became a full-time author. From 1951 until that time, he worked mostly as a public relations counselor in New York and Washington, D.C., writing advertising copy. After 1968 Blish spent a considerable amount of time on contract work for the *Star Trek* novels, work that was apparently congenial though hardly challenging. He also published a contemporary novel, an extensively researched historical novel, two witchcraft novels, and two books of essays; in addition he edited numerous volumes of others' work. In spite of these demands on his time, Blish produced more than twenty original science-fiction novels and four collections of original short stories—a remarkable production for a lifetime that lasted only fifty-four years.

Blish was born in East Orange, New Jersey, the son of Asa Rhodes and Dorothea Schneewind Blish. After completing a B.S. in zoology at Rutgers University in 1942, he spent two years in the army as a medical laboratory technician. Discharged before the end of World War II, he did graduate work in zoology at Columbia University, but soon came to see literature as his real interest. On 23 May 1947 he married author and literary agent Mildred Virginia Kidd Emden. Divorced in 1963, he was remarried the

following year to Judith Ann Lawrence. From the beginning Blish used autobiographical material in his science fiction. He set his first novel, *Jack of Eagles* (1952), in New York, where the main character has a job with a trade newspaper; similarly, a certain type of narrow military personality that recurs frequently in his work probably reflects his own service in the army during World War II. The novel *VOR* (1958) and an excellent short story called "Tomb Tapper" (1956; collected in *Galactic Cluster*, 1959) both occur in the context of the Civil Air Patrol, a volunteer civilian adjunct to the air force. This setting no doubt reflects Blish's own membership in the C.A.P. (which must have put further demands on his time). *VOR* also depicts a character, again like Blish, in the midst of a failing marriage.

While the quality of Blish's work is uneven, his best stories are genuine masterpieces. *Jack of Eagles* is an astonishingly good first novel. *Earthman, Come Home* (1955) will remain a science-fiction classic because of Blish's originality and imaginative sweep, and few novels sustain the high level of invention and clarity that Blish achieves in *The Seedling Stars* (1957), a novel composed of stories that follow the history of human genetic engineering for colonizing un-Earthlike planets. In the excellent thinkpieces *Midsummer Century* (1972) and *The Quincunx of Time* (1973), Blish makes full use of science fiction as a forum to pose interesting questions, and *A Case of Conscience* (1958) combines the virtues found in all of these novels. But not all of Blish's science fiction reaches these heights. *VOR* and *A Torrent of Faces* (1967) are not more than solid, respectable examples of the genre. *The Duplicated Man* (1959) contains a truly excellent idea that the novel fails to exploit. Such books as *The Star Dwellers* (1961), *Titan's Daughter* (1961), and . . . *And All the Stars a Stage* (1971) are formula works that compare poorly to Blish's best writing, while *Welcome to Mars!* (1967) and *The Vanished Jet* (1968) are even more disappointing.

Blish's most consistent strength in his serious books is his ability to produce close-knit structures. Even *Cities in Flight* (1970), a two-thousand-year future history consisting of four novels written over the course of a decade, is remarkably coherent. The tetralogy does have inconsistencies among novels, but Blish leaves few major questions unanswered. Moreover, in his best plots, such as *Jack of Eagles*, Blish approaches an ideal of literary economy: nearly every word is necessary. If the reader skips any part, even a page or two, he will miss some element needed to comprehend a later section of the book.

Jack of Eagles describes the development of psychic powers by Danny Caiden, "a normal guy" according to his own estimation and a battery of psychological tests. He first hears voices and then begins inadvertently predicting the future and levitating furniture. He draws all sorts of attention: his boss fires him from his newspaper job for accidentally writing something as fact which was really one of his predictions; the Securities and Exchange Commission and the FBI want to know how he is predicting, or influencing, the stock market; gamblers want to know how he has predicted the outcome of so many horse races; a beautiful gypsy girl wants to know his tricks as a magician so she can work out a similar act. As Danny comes into ever greater control of his psychic repertoire—ESP, telekinesis, teleportation, etc.—he becomes the center of conflict between two rival groups. One, the Psychic Research Society, or PRS, whose members wear hooded robes and sponsor a mumbo jumbo ritual, want to keep the existence of such powers a secret in order eventually to create a dominant elite. Most of the members have freakishly developed only one of the many possible psychic talents. The other group, members of which simply refer to themselves as the real psi-men, wants to bring psi powers into the open, seeing them as the potential heritage of all humanity. Danny favors the real psi-men and helps them with the aid of machinery set up by a conventional scientist from a university. The novel's main point is that psychic powers are not supernatural powers but natural forces which have not been sufficiently explored as yet, but which are potentially as comprehensible as anything so far discovered by conventional science.

Extraordinary mental properties also figure in *The Warriors of Day* (1953), which opens with a crude Freudian appeal. Tipton Bond poises with a knife "between his thighs" and, in the embrace of a Kodiac bear, "heaved the knife up from his groin with all his strength. . . . Blood gushed warmly over his whipcords, soaked through, filled his boots." After the animal dies with orgiastic heavings, trembling weakness washes over the hero. The rest of the novel might be described as William Blake's Orc-Albion symbolism, interpreted by a naive Jungian, applied to a planet of telepaths, and retold in imitation of Edgar Rice Burroughs. Tipton Bond, like John Carter of Burroughs's Barsoom tales, appears to be a supernatural human, with no memory of his childhood, who is teleported mysteriously to another planet. As Carter was a great soldier, Bond is a great hunter. The planet Xota, where Bond mysteriously appears, resembles Barsoom

in social structure and some culturally produced physical details, such as tunnels under its cities. The main female character is named Deje, reminding one of Burroughs's Dejah Thoris.

Xota is under attack from giant warriors, giving Bond the chance to play Gulliver to their Brobdingnagians. Then, in events that evoke Blake's image of a sleeping Albion, Bond's mind merges with that of an enormous reclining statue and animates it, becoming much bigger than the giant warriors. Blish thus lets his hero play Brobdingnagian in his own right. It turns out that the statue is part of the personification of Xota's telepathic collective unconscious. Bond is the emanation, split from the personality of the giant statue, which arises when Bond returns and merges with it again. The statue/Bond then saves Xota—and Earth as well—from conquest by the giant Warriors of Day. The novel reveals its author's powers of imagination and his sensitivity to the literary work of others, some of which he assimilates, but its slightness becomes immediately apparent when it is compared to a real masterpiece such as *The Seedling Stars*.

The four stories that make up *The Seedling Stars* trace the development of the Adapted Man—man that has been genetically engineered—in human history. Book one, "The Seeding Program," surveys the origin of genetic engineering of human beings for settlement of planets that do not fit the narrow range of temperature, atmosphere, and gravity in which human life can survive on Earth. As in *They Shall Have Stars* (1956), a courageous individual creates a scientific advance by first deceiving and then challenging the authorities who are shortsightedly trying to limit the development of mankind. The men in power want massively expensive but economically "exploitable" projects such as "terraforming" a planet to make it more like Earth. These authorities see genetic engineering or "pantropy" as a threat, because it will not stimulate the solar system's economy. The hero of the story, Don Sweeny, enters the Adapted Man base on Ganymede, a moon of Jupiter, with the firm intention of spying for the Earth government. Little by little he is won over to support the rebels, and in the end he is instrumental in helping a rebel spaceship escape to found the first interstellar colony and perpetuate the pantropic seeding program.

Book two, "The Thing in the Attic," describes one of the pantropic communities on a planet where the swampy and dangerous surface is swarming with dinosaurs and saber-toothed cats. The humans, long out of touch with the truth about their origins, are adapted to live a treetop existence, and only criminals are expected to try to survive on the forest floor. Honath, the story's main character, is sentenced to Hell, the culture's name for the planet's surface, for refusing to believe the somewhat mythologized version of the race's origin found in its holy writ. Honath and Mathild learn the basic techniques for survival on the planet's surface just as the Earthmen return to check on the colony's progress. As it happens, movement from the trees to the surface is the required next step for this "attic" race, and Honath and Mathild will be the new leaders of the movement.

Book three, "Surface Tension," proposes a more specialized situation: a spaceship with its crew and seeding team has crash-landed on a rocky, watery planet. Before they die, they use their own body cells to seed the planet's freshwater ponds, where a microscopic race of men develops. It is a superb tale if one can forget that complex intellectual behavior requires a certain minimum brain size. It is a minor point, and in fact the reader does suspend disbelief, but it is worth noting that in the critical essays written under the pseudonym of William Atheling—collected in *The Issue at Hand* (1964) and *More Issues at Hand* (1970)—Blish expresses disapproval of just this kind of cavalier treatment of scientific fact. Further sections of the tale relate mankind's successful battle against the microscopic eaters of the pond and the subsequent development of a means of getting from pond to pond, the primitive equivalent of a spaceship, a two-inch-long watertight wooden vehicle capable of rolling along the sand to the next water hole. The final judgment is a possible motto for the entire book: ". . . what Man can dream, Man can do."

Book four, "Watershed," makes a neat circle for *The Seedling Stars*. The story occurs on a spaceship going to a planet whose ecology has been so ruined that it cannot support its original inhabitants. The crew, made up of basic-form humans, is prejudiced against the adapted seeding team, much as the Earthmen had been toward the Adapted Men on Ganymede in book one. The irony of the story is that the ecologically devastated planet they are going to seed is Earth—where the basic-form humans would die in minutes if they tried to step out, unprotected, on its surface. The race, and the novel, has come full cycle, and the closing of this last link of the circle makes a satisfying ending.

Blish always referred to *The Frozen Year* (1957) as "a contemporary novel" apparently to distinguish it from his science fiction. However, the novel presents a special case; it has the same relationship to science fiction as Henry James's *The Turn of the Screw* has to the ghost story. In James's book a woman claims to see ghosts, but the reader suspects she may merely be insane. Similarly, in *The Frozen Year* an Arctic expedition has discovered evidence that there was once a planet where the asteroid belt now circles the sun, and that there had once been life on that world—a familiar science-fiction theme. A member of the expedition claims to be a Martian who must kill all the other members because the Martians had destroyed the asteroid-belt planet fifteen thousand years ago, and the expedition's discovery might lead Earthlings to discover the Martians' guilt. The other members of the research group immediately assume that the man who claims to be a Martian is crazy, but in an atmosphere of increasing cabin fever, they begin to suspect that his claim might be the truth. Though they try to save themselves, only two of the dozen members return alive. Back in the sane atmosphere of civilization, the survivors feel virtually certain that the killer was crazy. Yet in the last chapter the narrator expresses his lingering suspicion that the man might have been what he had claimed to be. Blish leaves the reader to decipher the ambiguity.

The ambiguities proliferate in *A Case of Conscience*, in which Blish presents Lithia, a many-threaded puzzle of a planet. A four-man investigating team has little trouble determining the outward facts of this strange world; their difficulty comes in the interpretation of the facts. Each of the three main members interprets the details of the planet according to his own personality. Cleaver, a bullheaded human chauvinist, feels that Lithia's high content of bomb-making metals provides an excellent nuclear bomb laboratory. He thinks of the Lithians, a race of intelligent saurians, as potential cheap labor, by which he means slaves. Michelis, a humane man and liberal scientist, sees an admirably balanced rational community—a society that permits individuality because it operates in harmony with nature. There is no crime or poverty, and consequently there is not even a government to repress such ills. Michelis wants men to learn from these admirable creatures. Father Ruiz-Sanchez, the expedition's third member, is a Jesuit priest who accompanies this voyage of exploration just as members of his order once participated in the opening of North America. Father Ruiz-Sanchez at first suspects that Lithia is Eden, and that the Lithians, not being descended from Adam and Eve, are living in the unfallen state of natural harmony with their environment. Jo Allen Bradham, in an article in *Extrapolation*, explicates the elaborate symbolism that buttresses this position. The priest discovers that the Lithians recapitulate their evolution in their life cycle space through the stages of egg, tadpole, lungfish, amphibian, wild reptile, and warm-blooded intelligent creature. To the priest this can mean only that Lithia is a trap prepared by Satan, which "seems to show us evolution in action on an inarguable scale. It is supposed to settle the question once and for all, to rule God out of the picture." Bradham insists that this is blindness on the priest's part, but the novel admits both theological and scientific interpretations, and Blish has indicated that he intended to be ambiguous.

the usual intuitive moral sense of the Lithians. He becomes an outlaw and his presence becomes a catalyst for a breakdown of the strained, fragile "shelter economy" of Earth. The authorities insist on returning him to Lithia, escorted by Michelis and Ruiz-Sanchez. These two stand before the returning spaceship's viewscreen, watching their approach to the planet. Michelis is worried about Cleaver's scheduled bomb test, which may destroy the entire planet. Ruiz-Sanchez must decide whether Lithia is Eden or Hell. If it is Eden, he feels that Egtverchi, corrupted by Earth, may be returning to fill the role

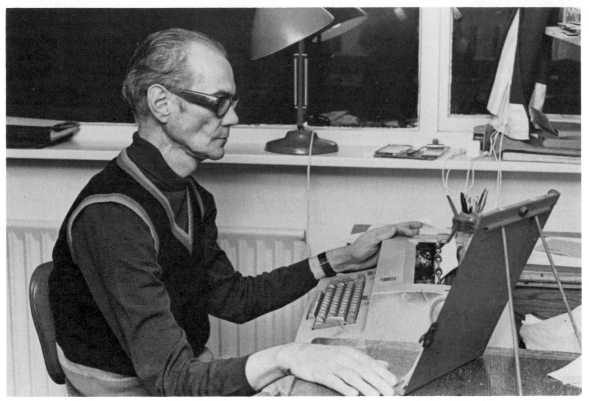

James Blish

Allusions in the book extend the ambiguity. The planet sounds like Eden when described in terms of Genesis, but it sounds hellish when the author invokes Dante or James Joyce's *Finnegans Wake*, "a book which to all intents and purposes might have been dictated by the Adversary himself."

The Earth government ignores Ruiz-Sanchez and secretly agrees with Cleaver, sending the fanatic back to Lithia to set up a bomb-testing facility. Michelis is put in charge of raising Egtverchi, a Lithian who came to Earth as a zygote floating in a jar of fluid. Egtverchi has all the intelligence and attractive personality of his race, but having been raised on Earth in abnormal circumstances, he lacks

that the serpent had played with Adam and Eve. However, the priest says the words of exorcism, and, as he finishes, the planet explodes. Did the planet only exist by the power of the devil and explode when that power departed? Or did it explode because Cleaver went stupidly ahead with his nuclear testing? Again, Blish leaves the reader in doubt, but the literary allusions, the sharp contrast between the Earth and Lithian societies, and especially the carefully controlled ambiguity, give *A Case of Conscience* a value not only as science fiction, but as literature.

Another extraordinary extraterrestrial visits Earth in Blish's 1958 novel *VOR*. In this novel Marty

Petrucelli, an unhappy husband and a decorated combat pilot who is now afraid even to enter an airplane, must deal with the dangerous alien named VOR. The alien turns out to be a robot created by an unknown race to survey star systems. But something has gone wrong. VOR is virtually indestructable and immortal, but he *wants* death and so travels from one star system to another demanding to be destroyed. When those he talks to do not kill him, VOR destroys *them*; consequently, Earth is in great danger. The military bombards VOR futilely, and there seems no hope. At the crucial moment, however, a scientist thinks that he can convince VOR to destroy himself. Naturally he must fly to VOR, and the only pilot available is Marty. In Earth's moment of need, the hero overcomes his fear of flying, and the scientist succeeds with VOR, who speeds away, presumably to throw himself into the sun. But Marty does not succeed in mending his marriage. This antiromantic note combines with the unusual twist of the alien's demand for death and with Blish's general emphasis on a human relationship to make *VOR* above average science fiction.

In both *VOR* and "Tomb Tapper," a story in Blish's 1959 collection *Galactic Cluster*, Civil Air Patrol pilots investigate a downed aircraft on the theory that it might be a Soviet missile or aircraft; details fail to confirm that theory, and a character decides that the downed craft is an alien spacecraft. In "Tomb Tapper" the clinching details are the pilot's small size and a strangely colored pastoral image picked up on a special mind-reading device, which is the story's only true science-fiction element. But the pilot turns out to be a Russian child trained for combat, and the image is a coloring-book memory. Other stories in the collection feature similar surprise endings. "Common Time" (1953), which Brian Aldiss praised highly in *Extrapolation*, and "Nor Iron Bars" (1957) speculate on the time effects of faster-than-light travel. "Beep" (1954) later became important as the basis for Blish's novel *The Quincunx of Time*. "A Work of Art" (1956) imagines Richard Strauss seemingly brought back to life in the body of a volunteer by a hypnotic "mind sculptor" of 2161. Strauss writes an opera but realizes as it plays that it is not something fresh and new, not a master work. His old habits were too strong, and he feels like an old man, dreading the fifty years his young body may survive. The audience applauds madly, and Strauss turns condescendingly toward them only to find that they are not applauding him but the mind sculptor, who congratulates himself for evoking a work of genius from a personality that previously had no musical talent—the volunteer whose body Strauss inhabits. At a word from the mind sculptor the Richard Strauss personality will disappear and the donor's personality will reemerge. This will be a second death for Strauss, but he smiles grimly at the irony of the mind sculptor's true failure: "No, he need not tell Dr. Kris that the 'Strauss' he had created was as empty of genius as a hollow gourd. The joke would always be on the sculptor, who was incapable of hearing the hollowness of the music. . . ."

If "A Work of Art" represents Blish at his best, *The Duplicated Man*, written with Robert Lowndes, is one of Blish's weaker efforts. In a war between Earth and its Venus colony each of the planets has a prowar central government and an outlawed antiwar political party, which in each case has been penetrated by agents of the government but allowed to continue to act. The novel's title character, Paul Danton, is duplicated by a machine that produces not identical copies but variations that reflect aspects of the original colored by the machine-operator's opinion of the person duplicated. The process gives Danton a unique opportunity to gain self-insight and to understand what various operators think of him. The novel concentrates on the spy-thriller adventures of the original and his copies, for it turns out that a key figure in the government of each planet has been working in concert with his counterpart to keep the war going, because only thus can the use of atomic weapons be avoided. Danton works with both to resolve the deadly and destructive impasse. Unfortunately the tortuous logic involved in the beliefs and actions of the two pacifist warmongers is hastily explained in the last few pages rather than worked out in the novel's structure. In one way the novel appears, for a while, to be ahead of its time. The President of the Security Council, which has become a true world government, is a woman, but in the epilogue she resigns to be "nothing more than Mrs. Paul Danton, from here on out."

The Star Dwellers contains a similar bias. A lightweight but pleasant book, *The Star Dwellers* is a novella based on the premise of an adult society that trusts its teenagers. Jack Loftus is a seventeen-year-old cadet in the Space Diplomatic Service, and Sylvia McCrary, also seventeen, is an apprentice reporter for a major news agency. As the novel develops, Jack becomes the principal negotiator of a treaty with the Angels—pure energy life forms who have perfectly charming personalities—and Sylvia becomes instrumental in getting the misguided adults back on Earth to do the wise thing and accept the treaty. The novel does not, as one might expect, contrast childlike innocence with adult corruption.

Rather, it expresses the adolescent yearning for adult competence in an important job and for the concomitant respect competence earns from the adult world. Real competence, however, is evinced only by the males. Jack succeeds by outperforming his adult supervisors at their own jobs, but Sylvia gets into a position to report the treaty by using her father's influence, and her contribution to the treaty's acceptance comes not through her professional position as a journalist but through her feminine wiles by which she outwits adult males.

Titan's Daughter, which like *The Seedling Stars* investigates the social consequences of genetic engineering, is somewhat more serious than *The Star Dwellers*. Dr. Fred's manipulation of genes has produced "tetraploids," nine-foot human giants who have unusually high intelligence, great physical strength and toughness, and extra long lives. Their single shortcoming is their low fertility. They are the objects of prejudice on the part of the normal populace, and there has even been one pogrom in which many ploids died. Maurice, the most intelligent of the giants, wants to respond with violence. Dr. Fred, Sam, and Sena want to work for their ends peacefully. Maurice discovers that Dr. Fred does not intend to set up a new species of giants but wants to breed the best traits of the tetraploids back into the mainstream of Homo sapiens. The intelligence, longer life span, and physical toughness would be common, but the extra size would be recessive for many generations and then would break out as a variation common enough to preclude prejudiced reaction. Maurice cannot accept Dr. Fred's plan. Becoming more and more clearly insane, he murders the scientist who formed him and kidnaps Sena. The story ends as Sam rescues Sena with the help of her lovable tetraploid dog, but the story's serious message remains: martyrdom such as that of Dr. Fred is often the price of human advancement.

His sacrifice is similar to that of Bliss Wagoner of *They Shall Have Stars*, the first volume of Blish's *Cities in Flight* series. *Cities in Flight* is a tetralogy which, in addition to *They Shall Have Stars*, includes *A Life For the Stars* (1962), *Earthman, Come Home*, and *The Triumph of Time* (1958). The series embodies a theory of history broadly influenced by Oswald Spengler's *The Decline of the West* (1918). Spengler posits a universal progression from "culture" to "civilization"; the feudal order that arises out of precultural chaos gives way to breakdown and interregnum, followed by the aristocratic states, which dissolve in revolution and Napoleonism (the rule of the dynamic individual), which is followed by

Caesarism or institutional absolutism. In the final stage a living "culture" fossilizes into "civilization," the forms of which may last for centuries but which ultimately become mere loot for a young culture.

Blish accepts this formulation most closely for the Western culture of the late twentieth and early twenty-first centuries, dramatized in *They Shall Have Stars*; he drifts further away from Spengler as the series progresses in time. In the later stages of his two-thousand-year history, Blish's system resembles Spengler's in little more than the notion of cyclic empires, an idea which far antedates Spengler. Furthermore, Blish ends his epic, in *The Triumph of Time*, with cosmic concepts that dwarf theories of history.

Even where the history most closely follows Spengler, Blish uses the Spengler cycles as a backdrop and emphasizes the resourceful individual struggling against the prevailing current of the cycle. *They Shall Have Stars* shows the United States of 2013 sinking inevitably into Spengler's final stage of absolute rule. Director MacHinery, a cross between J. Edgar Hoover and Joseph McCarthy, is moving toward the presidency and the irreversible establishment of Caesarism. Western science has fallen into doldrums with enormous, costly projects yielding minuscule returns, but continuing to receive funding if they are seen as weapons research. In the person of Senator Bliss Wagoner, *They Shall Have Stars* dramatizes the counterforce that works against this historical process. A single human being pitted against his era's historical current, Wagoner uses the society's crazes for secrecy and for weapons projects to set up the two scientific research programs that will make interstellar travel a reality: the "bridge" and the "drug." Though it costs hundreds of lives, the bridge on Jupiter is an invaluable study of the relationship between gravity and magnetism necessary to faster-than-light travel. The drug research requires experiments on human infants, but supplies the medicine that will give interstellar travelers the longevity they will need. The novel is mainly structured on a series of conflicts: the bridge builders vie against the cold and wind on Jupiter and against their own nerves as they make terrible sacrifices for a project that appears meaningless to them; Wagoner fends off MacHinery; Colonel Paige Russell, who approves of Wagoner's goals, must decide whether these goals justify Wagoner's means. The most crucial conflict occurs within Bliss Wagoner. His conscience wrestles with itself over the loss of human lives on his projects, weighing this cost against the boon of the stars. Though the projects succeed in opening the universe to the human spirit, Wagoner stays behind to face the wrath of MacHinery, for apparently he can believe in the justice of his ordering others to their deaths only if he sacrifices his own life. Wagoner's death provides a moving conclusion to the novel.

A Life For the Stars begins several centuries after the end of *They Shall Have Stars*. Earth, in the grip of the moribund bureaucratic state, has fallen into stagnation, while its vigorous, chaotic colonies have annihilated the alien Vegan civilization with unbelievable ferocity. A feudal empire of humans has already risen and fallen. Whole cities on Earth have one by one equipped themselves with "spindizzies," as the antigravity devices which power them are called, and gone out to the stars to wander, the tramps and hoboes of the interstellar economy. Blish fondly calls these cities "The Okies."

Chris deFord, a young boy at the novel's opening, loves Earth and wants only to help his brother support their ailing father, but he is impressed onto Scranton, one of the last cities to scrape together the funds for a couple of spindizzies and go Okie. Chris must learn to survive and win a place in the ferociously restrictive Okie society. He must earn citizenship and the right to the long-life drugs by proving his worth to the city, for passengers, actually a large percentage of city residents, are not entitled to the valuable treatments. The mayor of an Okie city is more akin to a starship captain than to a twentieth-century elected official. On New York, to which Chris's services are sold, Mayor Amalfi is a benevolent dictator, his rule moderated by the City Fathers, a group of computers wired in series, who see to it that decisions are made for the city's good.

At the opening of *Earthman, Come Home*, it is casually mentioned that the City Fathers have ordered "shot" a man named deFord for breaching a contract and thus endangering the city. *Earthman, Come Home* was written seven years before *A Life For the Stars*, so the reference was probably made before Chris became a distinct personality in Blish's imagination, but the reference certainly emphasizes the desperate quality of Okie life. *Earthman, Come Home* takes New York through adventures with colony planets and other Okies, similar to those in *A Life For the Stars*. As it becomes harder and harder for Okies to make it, Mayor Amalfi organizes two hundred Okie cities for a march on Earth, which has been transformed from the exhausted backwater of *A Life For the Stars* to a capital planet commanding a powerful fleet with galaxy-wide influence. Although Mayor Amalfi is instrumental in defeating an alien warship threatening Earth, he is obliged to flee the

galaxy with his city. He escapes toward the Magellanic Clouds. The novel thus belies its title. The Earthmen do not come home but range farther afield than ever. If there is a moral here, it is that the galactic human culture has committed suicide by creating so many difficulties for the Okie cities which were its lifeblood.

In *The Triumph of Time* New York gets to the Magellanic Clouds by rigging a planet with spindizzies. Planets, as New York had discovered in *Earthman, Come Home*, fly much faster than cities because of their greater mass. But when they arrive in the Cloud, they find it already occupied by the Interstellar Master Traders, a hated outlaw city that has gone to seed as a planet-bound city. Realizing the IMT, however effete, will have to be reckoned with sooner or later, Amalfi seeks and wins a confrontation by setting down on the very place where IMT is involved in small-time domination of a preindustrial peasant society. With IMT taken care of, the novel appears to be describing simply the conflict between the old Okies-in-retirement, who have been deprived of their accustomed duties, and the new generation, who were born with the relaxation of fertility restrictions that comes as the city establishes itself permanently on a planet. But a problem to dwarf all others now arises, for it is discovered that "the triumph of time" is at hand. The universe will soon come to an end. All will die, but they can hope to influence the character of the next universe; to do this they must be at the center of collapse when it occurs. They rig another planet, select a crew, proceed to their destination, fight and win a battle with aliens who have the same idea of influencing the new universe's course, and do, indeed, experience the end of time. Each of four Earth people can influence a universe that forms in each of the four quadrants of reality. Scientists have determined an exact sequence of actions that will create a new universe much like the old one. On a whim Amalfi decides to deviate from the sequence: his dying act is to insure that the new universe will be something altogether different from its predecessor. In a sense his death parallels that of Wagoner in *They Shall Have Stars*. Wagoner died that man might inherit the stars, but Amalfi dies that something different and possibly even vaster might be inherited.

After his labors on *Cities in Flight*, Blish rested by producing some juvenile science fiction and the distinguished historical novel *Doctor Mirabilis* (1964), based on the life of Roger Bacon. The juvenile *Mission to the Heart Stars* (1965) begins with the situation at the end of *The Star Dwellers*: two of its primary characters are teenage cadets of the

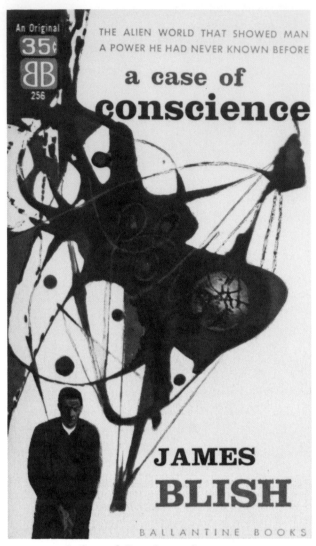

THE ALIEN WORLD THAT SHOWED MAN
A POWER HE HAD NEVER KNOWN BEFORE

a case of
conscience

JAMES
BLISH

BALLANTINE BOOKS

A Case of Conscience, front wrapper

Space Diplomatic Service. The Hegemony of Malis, a confederacy of the "heart stars" in the galaxy's central cluster, has put Earth on fifty-thousand-year probation for membership, and the Earth government has ordered the diplomatic service to try to intimidate the confederacy into allowing Earth to enter immediately, using a threat of Earth's alliance with the Angels, the pure energy beings described in *The Star Dwellers*. The diplomats and their cadets see this as foolhardy, dangerous to both the negotiators and to the Earth, and contrary to the spirit of the alliance with the Angels, but they follow orders and proceed on their mission. The Hegemony makes them prisoner and decides to bring Earth into its confederacy, not as a partner but as a subject world. Furthermore, the heroes discover that it would not be desirable for Earth to join the confederacy, even as a partner, because the

confederacy's strong emphasis on the value of stability has resulted in stagnation. The Angels intervene to save the situation both for the negotiators and for Earth. Deciding that they like humanity's spunk, the Angels plan a new coalition of themselves, the Earth, and several of the more vigorous new races.

In the foreword Blish says that he wrote the novel to explore "the future of individual human freedom in a high-energy culture like ours." Toward the end of the novel a character claims that "an unstable culture and a short lifetime" lead to personal freedom and creativity "such as mankind has been pouring out in torrents for most of his recorded history." The dramatic lesson is complementary: obeying orders, even when doing so will result in political aggression, will senselessly threaten humanity with extermination or slavery and will endanger one's own life. The serious handling of ideas does not, however, extend to Blish's next juvenile, *Welcome to Mars!*, which tells the highly unbelievable story of Dolph Haertel, a seventeen-year-old boy who discovers antigravity and flies to Mars in a homemade spaceship disguised as a treehouse. Blish does create an interesting catlike Mars creature, but this is not nearly enough to move the novel out of the juvenile category.

The same year saw the appearance of *A Torrent of Faces*, a collaboration with Norman Knight. This novel studies the effect of unchecked population growth in the twenty-eighth century, when Earth's population has reached six hundred billion and is still growing. Blish convincingly depicts a world very delicately balanced, able to keep everyone in the comparative luxury of a twentieth-century apartment dweller, but only by allowing no other living creatures, not even insects, to live in the world-city. Roof-garden forests replenish the oxygen, and specimens of the animals and insects that once roamed the world are maintained in special reserves. Genetic engineering has produced the Tritons, human beings who can breathe both air and water, to exploit the food-production capacity of the oceans. Part of the novel explores the conflict between Tritons and Drylanders, as "normal" humans are called. There is some intermarriage, however, which produces hybrid children with secret psychic power. Such matters at first seem to be digressions from the main point of the novel, the precarious balance of civilization with such an enormous burden of numbers. However, their relevance becomes clear when an asteroid striking the Earth breaches one of the wildlife preserves, spreads insects over hundreds of miles, and destroys the fragile balance of the world-city. The novel's main characters intend to retreat to an island and begin an entirely new mode of existence based on the sea and on the psychic powers of the hybrids, while countless billions die on the overpopulated continents. The novel's thesis is a piece of classic extrapolation: from the high-energy, growth-oriented trends of contemporary civilization it projects an overpopulated world and its terrible fate.

Blish's 1968 novels present an odd contrast in subject matter and quality. *The Vanished Jet*, a juvenile of little thematic or literary interest, traces the efforts of a fifteen-year-old boy to locate his parents, who were aboard a jet that disappeared. The novel touches the science-fiction field only in that the vanished craft of the title is an experimental Sub-Orbital Transport plane. One suspects that this was a manuscript that Blish had on hand unpublished since early in his career. It is simply beyond belief that the mature Blish could have written this even as a quick money-maker. *Black Easter* (1968) is a novel of black and white magic that assumes the existence of demons, angels, and God. It is not, strictly speaking, a science-fiction novel. But Blish does try to make his religious assumptions compatible with natural law, and he includes an episode in which his black magician explains the evil laboratory to Dr. Adolph Hess, a scientist who finds himself unwillingly impressed. The novel depicts the terrible miscalculation by which the human characters release all the demons from Hell. The infernal war with Heaven is thus expedited, and the last words of the novel, spoken by a devil, are "God is dead." In a sequel, *The Day After Judgment* (1971), the scientific elements figure more prominently. American troops are thrown into combat with the devils, and nuclear bombs cause the minions of Hell to be "seriously inconvenienced." A scientist at Strategic Air Command headquarters works out a partial equation to express the dynamics of eternal life, and the novel ends ironically with Satan chafing under the burden of playing God and predicting that humanity will someday suffer under that burden.

Blish had not exhausted the overpopulation theme of *A Torrent of Faces*, and in 1969 he contributed *We All Die Naked* to *Three For Tomorrow*, which was composed of Blish's novella as well as Robert Silverberg's *How It was When the Past Went Away* and Roger Zelazny's *The Eve of Rumoko*. Based on Arthur C. Clarke's dictum that "With increasing technology goes increasing vulnerability," this novella combines several familiar elements of the end-of-the-world story: the escape to space of a limited number of refugees, the man who plays God by deciding who gets a place on the escape ships, and the rioting of the people left behind. The main character, Alex D., is not particularly attractive at first. Chubby in a world of hunger, he keeps a set of sycophants to flatter him in exchange for a free meal, but in his gentle, protective relationship with his mistress and in his rising to the occasion when he must choose potential survivors, the reader sees his better side. What makes *We All Die Naked* noteworthy in addition to the ability of its author to reinvigorate a hackneyed plot, is the technical detail in the rendering of the final cataclysm. The immediate cause of the catastrophe is the overburdening of the Earth's fragile ecology by mankind's waste materials. When the south polar ice melts, momentum formerly existing in the Antarctic ice pack goes into the Earth's crust and causes enormous earthquakes. In a final twist the main characters decide to stay with the old Earth rather than try to escape.

The year following the appearance of *We All Die Naked*, Blish also published *Anywhen* (1970), a collection of seven sparely-written and witty stories. The first of these, *A Style in Treason* (1970), is a novella that answers the question: what if there were

Vanguard Science Fiction, *June 1958 cover*

a society where traitor was a highly respected profession and all governments employed traitors to betray the governments? From that premise the story extrapolates a colorful and varied political universe of planets, nation states, and empires of humans and aliens. A second highly original story explains the accidental introduction of bisexuality to a barren satellite's energy-field life form. Other stories in the collection center on more familiar themes: chauvinistic colonists mistreating native Martians, a race force-feeding its own evolution by encouraging pandemic disease, medical rescue teams trying to undo the harm done by early contamination of native planets. The Martian story is set in the same universe as *Welcome to Mars!*, and the evolution story is set in the universe of *The Star Dwellers*. The stories make better use of their settings than the earlier novels.

Perhaps the most extraordinary story of the collection is "Writing of the Rat" (1956), in which humanity encounters a race of squat, gray-furred, sharp-toothed beings that resemble rats. They live anywhere and everywhere that it is possible to live, even on unpromising rocks. Even more suspiciously, they have radically different social systems and languages on each planet where they are established, and their buildings often seem designed for some other species. All this looked to some Earthmen as if the "rats" had overrun a series of civilizations and ousted or exterminated the creators of each culture. John, the story's hero, cannot fault the logic of this guess, but emotionally he finds it hard to believe since he had never met a "rat" whose personal characteristics he does not admire; they are honest, dignified, proud, and intelligent. Eventually it is revealed that the "rats" were preserving the cultures of people who had been dragged away into slavery to distant stars. The "rats" were preserving the cultures the only possible way—by living them. This act of stunning generosity and responsibility explains the facts just as well as the more negative assumptions, assumptions that might not have been made if the race's physical form had not, purely by chance, resembled the rodent that man so abhors. The story is thus a clever attack on prejudice, teaching the fallibility of first impressions.

Where "Writing of the Rat" explores racial stereotypes, . . . *And All the Stars a Stage*, Blish's next novel, explores sexual ones. On a planet in the system of a prenova sun, society is matriarchal and polyandrous, but during a transgalactic exodus aboard the starship *Javelin*, society becomes male dominated and monogamous. One at first takes the doomed planet for Earth in the distant future, but gradually Blish introduces evidence to the contrary.

Most of the novel is devoted to the *Javelin*'s voyage from system to system in search of a planet to settle on. The third system visited turns out to be Earth's, in 3900 B.C.

From Earth's distant past, Blish turns again to the future in *Midsummer Century*. Named for a warm period in the Earth's future, this superb short novel "was conceived," according to Brian Aldiss, as "a quickie novella for a vanished magazine back in the 1940's." The novel builds elements of fantasy and mystery on a firm science-fiction base. Martels, a twentieth-century scientist-engineer, accidentally propels his personality into the far future of Rebirth IV, a jungle-village culture. Civilization has fallen and been reborn four times, but mankind's end seems near. Birds have evolved to threaten humanity, which is further hampered by its own resignation to death. After an epic journey in the mind of a villager named Tlam, Martels reaches a computer cared for by a few survivors of Rebirth III, a technological culture more like his own. Martels learns that, anticipating the end of their cycle, scientists of Rebirth III had set up the Qvant, a human brain connected to the computer. The combination was intended to store all the knowledge of Rebirth III until little by little the people of Rebirth IV could use it. But the Qvant discovered the pathways open to him through meditation and drifted into solipsism. As a Rebirth III technician describes it, "The Qvant became so immersed in this mental pilgrimage that he lost all interest in leadership, allowed the Birds to evolve and develop without any interference, and eventually began to impede many of our own practical, day-to-day uses of the computer." So they cut the Qvant off from the computer. Now the human race is rapidly losing its war with the birds. Martels brings knowledge of human twentieth-century warfare—especially germ warfare—but more importantly, he brings a fierce will to live, a commitment to the future of his species, which makes mankind the victor and ends the novel with the dawning of Rebirth V. With its disembodied brain—for Martels encounters the Qvant as a bizarre village oracle—and its crepuscular humanity, the novel explores questions of identity and mortality in terms of the individual and of the species. It is also a cautionary tale of Darwinian alternatives. Evolution, Blish says, has not been magically arrested, and man must be prepared to compete against new species with a fierce will to survive and dominate.

Blish's next major novel reveals a similar thoughtful expansion of earlier material, in this case, the short story "Beep." *The Quincunx of Time* is a short novel about the ramifications of a remarkable piece of technology. "The Service" has discovered an instrument, called the Dirac, for instantaneous transmission and reception of messages throughout the galaxy. The Dirac has an extra-ordinary side feature—it sends and receives messages across time as well as space. Obviously, the Dirac transmissions provide insight into the future; the twist is that the Service must act to assure that everything reported on the Dirac does indeed occur: "Everything, good or bad. . . . If an event is mentioned in the Dirac beep, then by God we rush there and *make* it happen." They even make sure that the parents of every single person mentioned in the Dirac meet. This policy involves a difficult moral judgment. Suppose a faulty part in a spaceship's engine shorts out causing an explosion that kills two-thirds of the crew and passengers. The survivors call for help on the Dirac. Knowing of the tragedy in advance, the Service will have rescue craft on the spot to pick up the survivors. But would it not have been better to replace the faulty part and avoid the tragedy completely? The appropriate crewman could then send a fake report at the appropriate moment. The Service is afraid to tamper in this way—especially as the results, on the whole, benefit the Service and the government it represents.

A woman character thinks otherwise. Dana, the heroine, hears the name of her future husband on the Dirac transmitter. She decides that what will happen, will happen and that she should fall in love with the man. Her theory is that motivation, wanting something to happen, and trying to make it happen are mere rationalizations having nothing to do with causing it to happen—that such motivations are mere illusions. A scientist tries to suggest that the explanation lies in a definition of the universe in at least five dimensions, giving rise to the word *quincunx* in the title. Dana decides to stick with her explanation and to keep her man. To do so she makes a special transmission on the Dirac to assure that she will know the answers several months ahead. Dealing with such a subject, the novel is wonderfully paradoxical and complicated. There is a frame story in which an apprentice agent suspects that The Service has some sort of access to the future; this is followed by the main story, which explains the Dirac—but even within the principal tale there are a mystery subplot and a love subplot and plenty of time-travel/foreknowledge paradoxes. The characters are thin but no more so than most science-fiction characters, and the book is interestingly anchored in speculative physics and the author's knowledge of the classic philosophical problems of free will and determinism.

"Originality," said James Blish, "is valued more highly in science fiction than in any other branch of literature." Yet between 1967 and his death in 1975 Blish turned out twelve books containing adaptations of *Star Trek* television scripts and one original *Star Trek* novel, *Spock Must Die!* (1970). Why did he spend so much of his own time on a project so little his own? Blish's friend Brian Aldiss said he did so "to guard against the slings and arrows of outrageous economic circumstance." And in the preface to *Star Trek 12* (1977), Blish himself says, "A number of you have asked me how I came to write these adaptations in the first place. The answer is simple and unglamorous: Bantam Books asked me to, out of the blue as it were. . . . I took on the job to see if I would like it, for one book. I did; and, furthermore, your letters convinced me that you made up a huge new audience for science fiction, one that had never been reached by the specialized magazines." Blish obviously enjoyed getting letters from *Star Trek* fans, and, in his prefaces, he would encourage them to write more. He claimed they helped him to decide which episodes to choose for adaptation and even to make the adaptations better. In his prefaces, Blish tried to answer his most common questions from the fan mail and would specifically refer to some of the letters. One particularly intrigued him, and he printed a large section of it in the preface to *Star Trek 6* (1972). It was from a Captain Pierre D. Kirk of the U.S. Army, whose troops, while stationed in Vietnam, had taken his name as an excuse to set up an elaborate "organization within an organization" paralleling their company to the *Enterprise* crew. Encountering an apparent ambush, this real life Captain Kirk had taken the microphone of his jeep radio and announced, "Attention Viet Cong. We are the Federation Starship *Enterprise*, and you are now in deep trouble. Phaser banks—charge your phasers and fire on the enemy." Kirk meant the comment as a morale booster for his own men, but after a short flurry of excited radio talk in Vietnamese, the sniping ceased and the convoy proceeded without molestation. Whatever the explanation for this event, it is easy to see that Blish felt he was participating in a project that was reaching many people. He once said about the series, "Idealism lasts, if you love it; and these books would have been impossible without it, just like the show itself."

In *Star Trek 12* Blish explained that he worked with final drafts of the scripts and that he tried to be "as faithful to their texts as length permits." Admitting that he once changed the conclusion of an episode, he apologizes: "I did this only once, and long ago; it's not a privilege I mean to abuse." He had more latitude, of course, in *Spock Must Die!*, in which a machine has apparently duplicated Spock, giving Kirk the task of deciding which is the original and which the duplicate. The second Spock is a mirror image who reverses all motives, morals, and loyalties, making him a vital threat to the *Enterprise*. Yet even though *Spock Must Die!* is theoretically an original *Star Trek* novel, the characters, setting, and many thematic matters, such as the rationale for the *Enterprise*'s mission, were already created for Blish. Even in the material he supplied, he borrowed from one of the weaker of his own novels, *The Duplicated Man*.

Blish should not be judged harshly for the *Star Trek* books. Before contracting for them he had mostly held a regular job while writing on his own time; he may, therefore, have considered them only a more congenial and useful method of supporting himself while he worked on more original projects. At any rate, his best work is distinguished in terms of both themes and style. Of the small body of writers to treat religious topics positively in science fiction, he was one of the most sensitive and profound, especially in *A Case of Conscience, Black Easter,* and *The Day After Judgment.* He was perhaps the first to realize that an antigravity, faster-than-light drive would provide lifting power to make the shape and size of a load irrelevant. Future space travelers would not have to travel enclosed by a thin shell of metal in the cramped confines of ships. His *Cities in Flight* series makes impressive use of this insight, sending the Okie cities of Earth to the far corners of the galaxy. Here, too, Blish uses science fiction to predict the consequences of current trends and to propose alternatives, to speculate on the ability of individual humans to influence vast political systems, and even to oppose impersonal currents in the affairs of men. Many science-fiction writers have done this; Blish did it particularly well. He was also one of the first writers to think out the consequences of genetic engineering in *Titan's Daughter* and the pantropy stories of *The Seedling Stars.*

Blish was also an important critic of science fiction. His essays—many of them under the pen name William Atheling—reviews, and speeches always insisted on applying the same standard of literary construction to science fiction that is applied to any other form of public writing. Blish did not always live up to his own highest standards; William Atheling would certainly have ripped into *Welcome to Mars!* and *The Vanished Jet.* Yet when Blish seriously applied himself, which was most of the time, he produced an extremely well-made product:

self-consistent, rationally constructed, with neatly tied ends. By this example, Blish may have raised the standards of science-fiction writing more effectively than he did in his essays.

Other:

New Dreams This Morning, edited by Blish (New York: Ballantine, 1966);

We All Die Naked, in *Three For Tomorrow* (New York: Meredith, 1969; London: Gollancz, 1970);

Nebula Award Stories Five, edited by Blish (Garden City: Doubleday, 1970; London: Gollancz, 1970).

Periodical Publication:

"Probapossible Prolegomena to Ideareal History," as William Atheling, *Foundation,* no. 13 (1978): 6-12.

References:

Brian Aldiss, *Billion Year Spree* (Garden City: Doubleday, 1973), pp. 251-252, 310;

Aldiss, "In Memoriam: James Blish," *Extrapolation,* 17 (December 1975): 5-7;

Aldiss, "James Blish: The Mathematics of Behavior," *Foundation,* no. 13 (1978): 43-50;

Brian Ash, *Faces of the Future—the Lessons Of Science Fiction* (London: Elek/Pemberton, 1975), pp. 185-187;

Harold L. Berger, *Science Fiction and the New Dark Age* (Bowling Green, Ohio: Bowling Green University Popular Press, 1976), pp. 130, 131-132, 156-158, 188;

Jo Allen Bradham, "The Case in James Blish's *A Case of Conscience,*" *Extrapolation,* 16 (December 1974): 81-95;

Paul Carter, *The Creation of Tomorrow* (New York: Columbia University Press, 1977), pp. 19, 86-87, 222, 297;

Grace Eckley, *"Finnegan's Wake* in the Work of James Blish," *Extrapolation* 20 (Winter 1979): 330-342;

Damon Knight, *The Futurians* (New York: John Day, 1977), pp. 151-158, 209-213, 251;

Knight, *In Search Of Wonder,* revised edition (Chicago: Advent, 1967), pp. 168-174;

Robert W. Lowndes, "James Blish: Profile," *Magazine of Fantasy and Science Fiction,* 42 (April 1972): 66-71;

Sam Moscowitz, *Seekers of Tomorrow: Masters of*

Modern Science Fiction (New York: World, 1966), pp. 412-413;

Moskowitz, *Strange Horizons: The Spectrum Of Science Fiction* (New York: Scribners, 1972), pp. 14-15, 17-18;

Mark Owings, "James Blish: Bibliography," *Magazine of Fantasy and Science Fiction*, 42 (April 1972) 78-83;

Alva Rogers, *A Requiem For Astounding* (Chicago: Advent, 1964), pp. 188, 189, 195, 198, 200, 202, 203, 204, 206, 207;

Brian Stableford, "The Science Fiction of James Blish," *Foundation*, no. 13 (1978): 12-42;

Paul Walker, "An Interview with James Blish," in *Speaking of Science Fiction: The Paul Walker Interviews* (Oradell, N.J.: Luna, 1978), pp. 229-241.

ANTHONY BOUCHER
(WILLIAM ANTHONY PARKER WHITE)
(21 August 1911-29 April 1968)

SELECTED BOOKS: *The Case of the Seven of Calvary* (New York: Simon & Schuster, 1937; London: Hamish Hamilton, 1937);

Rocket to the Morgue, as H. H. Holmes (New York: Duell, Sloan & Pearce, 1942);

Far and Away: Eleven Fantasy and Science Fiction Stories (New York: Ballantine, 1955);

The Compleat Werewolf and Other Stories of Fantasy and Science Fiction (New York: Simon & Schuster, 1969).

Anthony Boucher may not have been quite the first to bring the civilizing touch of the knowledgeable bookman and tasteful literary critic to pulp science fiction (actually, that quixotic deed was performed by A. Langley Searles with his *Fantasy Commentator* of 1943-1958), but he was certainly paramount in initiating the broad dissemination of that touch through his long-lived *Magazine of Fantasy and Science Fiction*. Under Boucher's editorial direction the *Magazine of Fantasy and Science Fiction* became a publication that successfully emulated the donnish style of the pre-1960 *Ellery Queen's Mystery Magazine* in an arena of magazines hitherto best typified by the lurid superlatives of their titles, such as *Astounding*, *Startling*, *Astonishing*, and (perhaps most ambitiously) *Cosmic*. Launching the *Magazine of Fantasy and Science Fiction* in the fall of 1949 (initially as the

Magazine of Fantasy) with close friend and bibliophile J. Francis McComas as coeditor, Boucher wrote a story for the first issue under his alternate pen name of H. H. Holmes that typified the approach of both the *Magazine of Fantasy and Science Fiction* and Boucher himself to the science-fiction field: light, literate, and good humored. Called "Review Copy," the semi-autobiographical story deals with the revenge of a writer who, savaged by a San Francisco newspaper book reviewer, arranges for the reviewer to receive a satanically cursed copy of his latest book. Boucher had shortly before been a noted reviewer of mystery fiction for the *San Francisco Chronicle*.

Anthony Boucher was the main pen name for William Anthony Parker White. He was born in Oakland, California; his parents, both physicians, were James Taylor and Mary Ellen Parker White. He attended Pasadena Junior College from 1928 to 1930 and earned a B.A. from the University of Southern California in 1932 and an M.A. from the University of California, Berkeley, in 1934. He married Phyllis Mary Price on 19 May 1938; they had two children. In 1937 Boucher published his first novel, an ingenious detective story called *The Case of the Seven of Calvary*. Encouraged by sales and reviews, he continued to write, producing five more crime novels under the Boucher name and two (about his nun-detective, Sister Ursula) as H. H. Holmes. One of the Sister Ursula books, the now classic *Rocket to the Morgue* of 1942, dealt intimately with the Southern California science-fiction author and fan community of the period; portraying under thin disguise such personalities as John W. Campbell, Jr., Edmond Hamilton, Robert A. Heinlein, and L. Ron Hubbard, it reflected Boucher's amused interest at his initial exposure to the science-fiction world in the early 1940s. As a book reviewer for such papers as the *Chicago Sun-Times* and the *New York Times* as well as the *San Francisco Chronicle*, Boucher undertook to cover science fiction together with mysteries and entered the fantastic-fiction field himself with the short story "Snulbug" for Campbell's *Unknown* of December 1941. Although all of Boucher's widely acclaimed book-length fiction was in the detective genre, several of his shorter works for the science-fiction and fantasy magazines proved equally notable, principally the *Astounding Science-Fiction* titles "The Barrier" (September 1942), "Q. U. R." (March 1943), and "The Chronokinesis of Jonathan Hull" (June 1946); and the *Unknown* novella "The Incompleat Werewolf" (April 1942). Eleven of his other early stories were collected in his first science-fiction book, *Far and Away: Eleven Fantasy and Science Fiction*

Stories, published simultaneously as a hardcover and paperback book by Ballantine in 1955. Included are "Snulbug" and "Review Copy," but the best of Boucher's fantastic fiction is to be found in the posthumous anthology of 1969, *The Compleat Werewolf and Other Stories of Fantasy and Science Fiction*. These two titles, unfortunately, comprise the only book collections of Boucher's science fiction and fantasy to date; a number of memorable but uncollected stories must still be sought in separate anthologies or in the original magazines.

Moving his newspaper science-fiction and fantasy reviews to the pages of the *Magazine of Fantasy and Science Fiction* in 1950, Boucher shared with Damon Knight the honors of bringing consistently literate and perceptive criticism to the science-fiction magazine field. As coeditor of the *Magazine of Fantasy and Science Fiction* (and as sole editor after September 1954), Boucher encouraged, imaginatively edited, and published works by such developing talents as Richard Matheson, Philip José Farmer, Alfred Bester, Damon Knight, Gore Vidal, and J. T. McIntosh, as well as obtaining offbeat material of now classic stature by such established writers as Heinlein, Ray Bradbury, Theodore Sturgeon, Arthur C. Clarke, Isaac Asimov, and others. By April 1958, however, Boucher was forced to resign his editorship of the *Magazine of Fantasy and Science Fiction* due to ill health; he had also to abandon prolonged writing of virtually any kind at this time. Nevertheless, so individual was the stamp he placed on the *Magazine of Fantasy and Science Fiction*, and so firmly shored had he left its circulation and reputation, that the magazine has continued profitable monthly publication through the subsequent two decades virtually unchanged in layout or editorial orientation by Boucher's editorial successors, and it is now regarded as one of the three basic science-fiction magazines of the postwar era, together with *Galaxy* and *Analog Science Fiction / Science Fact*.

A noted anthologist in the detective-fiction field, Boucher worked the same vein memorably in science fiction, editing the superb two-volume *A Treasury of Great Science Fiction* in 1959, as well as the first eight of the annual *Best From Fantasy and Science Fiction* series (1952-1959). A founding director of the Mystery Writers of America organization, Boucher first invented (as a fictional group in *Rocket to the Morgue*) then helped found in real life the Manana Literary Society, a semiformal group of professional California science-fiction writers active in the 1950s and later, which has included in its roster such luminaries as Heinlein, Henry Kuttner, C. L. Moore, and Cleve Cartmill. Regrettably, there is no collected edition of Boucher's literary criticism in the science-fiction field (he was too modest to include any of it in his annual *Best From Fantasy and Science Fiction* volumes), nor has any full assessment of his work in the field and of the development and impact of the *Magazine of Fantasy and Science Fiction* been written to date. His death at age fifty-seven, at his Dana Street home in Berkeley, California, left a void of humor, gentle critical perception, literary encouragement, and quiet, bookish imagination in the crime and fantasy-fiction fields that is not likely to be filled again. —*Bill Blackbeard*

Other:

Best From Fantasy and Science Fiction, edited by Boucher, first and second series (Boston: Little, Brown, 1952, 1953); third through eighth series (Garden City: Doubleday, 1954-1959);

A Treasury of Great Science Fiction, edited by Boucher (Garden City: Doubleday, 1959).

Reference:

Lenore Glen Offord, comp., *A Boucher Portrait: Anthony Boucher as Seen by his Friends and Colleagues . . . And a Boucher Bibliography Compiled by J. R. Christopher with D. W. Dickensheet and R. E. Briney* (White Bear Lake, Minn.: The Armchair Detective, n.d.).

JOHN BOYD
(BOYD B. UPCHURCH)
(3 October 1919-   )

BOOKS: *The Last Starship from Earth* (New York: Weybright & Talley, 1968; London: Gollancz, 1969);

The Slave Stealer, as Boyd Upchurch (New York: Weybright & Talley, 1968; London: Jenkins, 1968);

The Pollinators of Eden (New York: Weybright & Talley, 1969; London: Gollancz, 1970);

The Rakehells of Heaven (New York: Weybright & Talley, 1969; London: Gollancz, 1971);

Sex and the High Command (New York: Weybright & Talley, 1970);

The Organ Bank Farm (New York: Weybright & Talley, 1970);

The Gorgon Festival (New York: Weybright & Talley, 1972);

The I.Q. Merchant (New York: Weybright & Talley, 1972);

The Doomsday Gene (New York: Weybright & Talley, 1973);

Andromeda Gun (New York: Berkley, 1974);

Barnard's Planet (New York: Berkley, 1975);

Scarborough Hall, as Boyd Upchurch (New York: Berkley, 1976);

The Girl with the Jade Green Eyes (New York: Viking, 1977; Harmondsworth, U.K.: Penguin, 1979).

John Boyd was born Boyd Bradfield Upchurch in Atlanta, Georgia. Commissioned into the U.S. Navy in 1940, he served in the Philippines, Russia, Japan, and England. On 26 January 1944 he married Fern Gillaspy, and he took a degree in history and journalism from the University of Southern California in 1947. Boyd is a salesman of photoengravings and lives in Los Angeles.

Publishing his science fiction under a pseudonym, Boyd has signed his legal name to two novels that can be described as Southern Gothic romance, *The Slave Stealer* (1968) and *Scarborough Hall* (1976). Perhaps because of a reluctance to identify himself as a science-fiction writer, Boyd's critical reputation has not advanced appreciably since the enthusiastic reviews of his first novel, *The Last Starship from Earth* (1968), which Robert A. Heinlein endorsed highly.

As well as employing an element of humor—often satiric—and demonstrating a fondness for literary allusion, Boyd's fiction explores the dangers of man's inability to keep morally and emotionally abreast of his exploding technology. The subsequent perversion of humanity is what Haldane IV, a theoretical mathematician who turns to literature, must endure in *The Last Starship from Earth*. The novel is the first of what he considers a trilogy based on myths; in his preface to the 1978 Penguin edition, Boyd says, "Insofar as a writer plans for the marketing of his books, I chose mythic themes in hope of sounding echoes in the racial memory of readers."

Originally written as a radio drama called *The Fairweather Syndrome*, *The Last Starship from Earth* describes the destructive force of sociology's glorification of the conditioned response; in fact, the idea for the story came to Boyd as he listened to what he calls "the involved, obfuscating, and nonsubstantive jargon" of a sociology professor—language that was "a fitting subject for satire." By consorting with the poetess Helix, mathematician Haldane defies computer-established professional mating boundaries and suggests, heretically, that man is more than his particular social function. He is, therefore, exiled to the planet Hell, tantamount to a paradise since it is inhabited by men who have escaped the rigidity of a computerized world. In this and other of Boyd's works, man's fall from grace is the negation of his individual genius by social behaviorism.

Though not as successful as their precursor, the other two novels in the trilogy are also loosely based on myth: *The Pollinators of Eden* (1969) on the story of Phaedra and *The Rakehells of Heaven* (1969) on that of Prometheus. In her article on Boyd's first novel, Jane Hipolito points to a premise that reasserts itself in his later work: "the human mind must forever return to its primitive beginnings for inspiration." Dr. Freda Caron, the Phaedra figure, does just that as she is converted from objective empiricism to personal love for nature; her physical and emotional union with a plant introduces a recurrent theme in Boyd's work—that of human reconciliation with nature surpassing mere subject-object distinctions. In *The Rakehells of Heaven*, however, Adams and O'Hara are the atavistically passionate protagonists who discover that man's ancestors were the defective beings expelled from Harlech, a society that has evolved to technical and moral superiority. In their bumbling efforts to discipline the Harlechians to the restrictions of Earthly vision, Adams and O'Hara demonstrate that, although man's beginnings provide inspiration, a

A WARM AND LOVING WOMAN

By

BOYD UPCHURCH   161.

OR John Boyd — HAVEN'T DECIDED WHICH.

man, and Casper Duncan's father was a chemist, so Casper, with no other tradition to follow, chose her from a comic strip character.

"Karl, I'm honored, maybe. Of course I'll talk to Alex Hawkins, but only in the afternoon. My morning's are TAKEN, spent writing, and Since I'm so intelligent and imaginative, though, I'm sure I can think of a good reason for turning Alex down. After all, mothers of cubs are bears, and I don't have claws. Also, I don't have loads of time."

"It'd only be about an hour every Sunday afternoon, Mrs. Ashley. We could meet at Stokes Poges. Mama says we ought to use that building for something, or the San Jacinto - ATLANTIC Pacific people might take a notion to tear it down."

There was an eagerness in the child's voice she could not dampen outright, so, rising, she said, "You tell Alex he may call on me, but you can tell him, too, also, that at the first blush his idea doesn't appeal to me. Anyhow, Alex may not be so eager to have me, once he sees me with clothes on."

Duncan was who found her holding her a place in the shuffled line, standing next to and talking only to Percy Duncan. As we approached them it occurred to her that any man named Percy should be more sensitive to his playmate...

"A Warm and Loving Woman," revised typescript

precarious balance must be maintained to insure that primitive responses do not obscure spiritual potential.

Boyd's next three novels give rein to his penchant for satire. Again borrowing from the Greeks, he recasts Aristophanes' *Lysistrata* in *Sex and the High Command* (1970) and makes sport of both the bureaucratic military's lack of compassion and imagination and of feminist violations of personal relationships to foster peace. In *The Organ Bank Farm* (1970) society's attempts at perfection in Paradise Valley result in a cryonic morgue that simulates the circles of Dante's *Inferno*. Man's overreaching science of brain transplants and musico-therapy is epitomized by his futile efforts to make an angel. Ironically, the madness of an inmate offers a glimpse of salvation: she accepts guilt for man's past disasters and, because she exists mentally in her imagined Middle Ages, embodies the past in the present. Boyd reserves his most savage satire, though, for the hip culture of contemporary Southern California in *The Gorgon Festival* (1972). Physical perfection is again man's goal, but the prize he wins is an awareness and acceptance of his limitations.

A lack of such awareness precipitates the crisis in *The I.Q. Merchant* (1972). Aiming his barbs at modern consumerism and its attendant advertising empire, Boyd probes the perhaps insoluble conflict between individual rights and man's purely logical control of his environment. A pill to increase intelligence redirects and accelerates human evolution and creates new social classes: many are killed by the pill, some remain unaffected, and some develop a detached brilliance that designates them as a new species devoid of sentiment. Boyd tempers the bleak prospects, however, with his constant faith in the well-integrated man—he who rises from the ranks of the supposedly unaffected with inklings of new intelligence but, more importantly, with his basic humanity intact.

The Doomsday Gene (1973) continues the fictive depiction of the individual's struggle against scientific manipulation in an overcrowded world. The Thanatos Syndrome, designed for early intellectual productivity and early death, is genetically imposed on Amal Severn, a young seismologist whose best efforts to escape his fate miscarry. Moreover, the gene's deadly effectiveness defies and devastates even its ambitious creators. The distance between the cold, scientific hierarchy and the needs of its human protectorate reflects both the Cartesian split of the modern sensibility and the fallacy of complete devotion to the altar of science.

The clash between biological determinism and free will takes its most original guise in Boyd's ninth science-fiction novel, *Andromeda Gun* (1974), in which he draws not on classic myth but on angelology and on the Christian concept of conflict between flesh and spirit. True to the stock science-fiction device of explaining all phenomena in objective, rational terms, Boyd describes the evolutionary origins of creatures of pure spirit and light who search the galaxies for host bodies because they miss physical sensation and, more to the point, because they wish to improve the universe. Johnny Loco, a gunslinger in the Old Wild West, is selected for sainthood by his possessor, G-7. In a reversal of the traditional idealistic triumph of spirit, however, G-7 becomes so enamored of human senses that he is the second of his kind to defect—to abandon his light-bearing spirit to Loco's flesh; even angels fall from their Eden to the temptation of Earthly delights. But man's spiritual aspirations, as assessed by G-7, are firmly rooted in and must be educated by his mortal state. *Scarborough Hall* presents a similar possession of the modern mind by ancient forces—a possession that may enrich the present, but only if controlled and balanced with contemporary reality.

Barnard's Planet (1975) and *The Girl with the Jade Green Eyes* (1977) celebrate acceptance of the order

John Boyd

of nature, an order that seems chaotic to man's limited perception. After again dramatizing a reciprocal awareness between plants and animals in *Barnard's Planet*, in his latest novel Boyd reconciles such an awareness in the alien character Kyra. Kyra and her small band of compatriots, the lone remnants of a world that sought union with nature to survive, endanger man's diverse society with their resulting biological efficiency. Unlike many of Boyd's characters, Kyra escapes the threat posed by the suspicions of Earthmen and grants forest ranger Breedlove a transcendent vision that surpasses not only man's science, but also his imagination.

Boyd's faith in that imagination, however, has not been exhausted in his thirteen books—although most of his fictional concerns appear as early as his first, widely acclaimed novel. His satiric humor maintains as its object any social contrivance that impedes man's goal of being spiritually and intellectually whole. In describing the ideal reader of one of his early novels, Boyd offers a description that serves as well for appreciation of any of his books: the reader "should have the mentality of a Southern stock-car racer, be a Baptist with a sense of detachment, have a well-developed sense of the absurd, and be fascinated with the quirks and accomplishments of the human animal."

—*Tyler Smith*

References:

Jane Hipolito, "The Last *and First* Starship from Earth," in *SF: The Other Side of Realism*, ed. Thomas D. Clareson (Bowling Green, Ohio: Bowling Green University Popular Press, 1971), pp. 186-192;

Willis E. McNelly, "The Science Fiction Novel in 1978," in *Nebula Award Stories Four*, ed. Poul Anderson (Garden City: Doubleday, 1969), pp. xiii-xxv.

LEIGH BRACKETT
(7 December 1915-18 March 1978)

BOOKS: *No Good from a Corpse* (New York: Coward-McCann, 1944);

Shadow Over Mars (Manchester, U.K.: S. Pemberton, 1951); republished as *The Nemesis from Terra* (New York: Ace, 1961);

The Starmen (New York: Gnome Press, 1952; London: Museum Press, 1954); republished as *The Galactic Breed* (New York: Ace, 1952); republished again as *The Starmen of Llyrdis* (New York: Ballantine, 1976);

The Sword of Rhiannon (New York: Ace, 1952; London: Boardman, 1955);

The Big Jump (New York: Ace, 1955);

The Long Tomorrow (Garden City: Doubleday, 1955; London: Mayflower, 1962);

An Eye for an Eye (Garden City: Doubleday, 1957; London: Boardman, 1958);

The Tiger Among Us (Garden City: Doubleday, 1957; London: Boardman, 1958); republished as *Fear No Evil* (London: Transworld, 1960);

Rio Bravo (New York: Bantam, 1959);

13 West Street (New York: Bantam, 1962; London: Transworld, 1962);

Alpha Centauri—or Die! (New York: Ace, 1963);

Follow the Free Wind (Garden City: Doubleday, 1963);

The Secret of Sinharat and *People of the Talisman* (New York: Ace, 1964);

The Coming of the Terrans (New York: Ace, 1967);

Silent Partner (New York: Putnam's, 1969);

The Halfling and Other Stories (New York: Ace, 1973);

The Ginger Star (New York: Ballantine, 1974; London: Sphere, 1977);

The Hounds of Skaith (New York: Ballantine, 1974; London: Sphere, 1976);

The Reavers of Skaith (New York: Ballantine, 1976);

The Best of Leigh Brackett, ed. Edmond Hamilton (New York: Ballantine, 1977).

Leigh Douglass Brackett was born in Los Angeles, California, the daughter of William Franklin and Margaret Douglass Brackett. On 31 December 1946 she married science-fiction writer Edmond Hamilton. During the later years of their marriage, which was childless, they lived in Kinsman, Ohio, maintaining a winter residence in Lancaster, California, where Brackett died in 1978. Edmond Hamilton had died one year before on 1 February 1977. Although Brackett's first love was science fiction, her first full-length novel was a suspense thriller, *No Good from a Corpse*, published in 1944, the same year in which she collaborated with Jules Furthman and William Faulkner on the screenplay of Raymond Chandler's *The Big Sleep* (1946). She wrote only three more suspense novels during her career: *An Eye for an Eye*,

The Tiger Among Us, both appearing in 1957, and *Silent Partner*, published in 1969. But between 1944 and 1977 she produced fourteen volumes of science fiction. In 1957 Brackett won the Jules Verne Fantasy Award and in 1964 the Western Writers of America Award for *Follow the Free Wind* (1963).

Brackett was first attracted to science fiction after reading Edgar Rice Burroughs's *The Gods of Mars* (1918), and she is best known for her novels of adventure fantasy in the Burroughs tradition. Her first science-fiction novel, *Shadow Over Mars*, appeared in *Startling Stories* in 1944. Published as a book in England in 1951, it was republished in the United States as *The Nemesis from Terra* (1961). In this novel the author paints a Mars at once similar to and distinct from Burroughs's Barsoom. Brackett's red planet is a slowly dying world inhabited by ancient races who have lost the technology of their progenitors and who are more given to swordplay and intrigue than to the scientific advances of the space-age Earthmen who colonize the planet. In *The Sword of Rhiannon* (originally in the June 1949 *Thrilling Wonder Stories* as "Sea-Kings of Mars" and published in book form in 1952) Brackett gives the planetary legends depth as Matt Carse, archaeologist turned thief, is involuntarily transported to an era in the Martian past when the lost oceans and many of the ancient sciences still flourished. *The Sword of Rhiannon* is as fine a space-age swashbuckler as one could ask for.

Brackett's next two novels were not published in book form until they appeared in an Ace double volume in 1964. *The Secret of Sinharat* had appeared originally in *Planet Stories* (Summer 1949) as "Queen of the Martian Catacombs." *People of the Talisman* is a revised version of "Black Amazon of Mars," which had also appeared originally in *Planet Stories* (March 1951). These stories introduce a soldier of fortune on Mars named Eric John Stark, a human born in the Twilight Belt of Mercury and raised by the subhuman aborigines of that planet, who give him the name of N'Chaka. Stark was one of Brackett's favorite characters, and toward the end of her life she made him the hero of her last and longest work, the Skaith trilogy (1974-1976).

Her first science-fiction novel to take place outside of the Martian setting, *The Starmen* (1952), combines intergalactic travel with a murder-mystery plot. Michael Trehearne, part Earthman, part Vardda, arouses the jealousy of Kerrel, a policeman on Llyrdis, the Vardda's home planet. Because Trehearne can withstand the rigors of interstellar flight, for which only true-bred Vardda have been genetically prepared, he threatens not only Kerrel's

Leigh Brackett

one-sided romance with the rich and beautiful Shairn, but the Vardda's monopoly on intergalactic travel as well. *The Starmen* establishes one of Brackett's most common themes: what it means to be human in a universe full of alien beings.

The Big Jump (1955), a second science-fiction murder mystery, places Arch Comyn on the Edenic world of the Transuranae, beings made of the energy of life itself. To those who come to them, the Transuranae impart the primal innocence and beauty of life at its very source, a gift that carries with it the consequent unfitness for and indifference to the mundane concerns of Earth. The novel escapes the lotus-eaters theme to which it seems bound by presenting the gift of the Transuranae as actually superior to the rewards of ordinary civilization. In a novel where the characters are thinly drawn and the dialogue labored, it is to Brackett's credit that Comyn's last-minute deliverance from the spell of the Transuranae is as much an occasion for despair as it is for rejoicing. His final acceptance of his own imperfect humanity is presented as inevitable, not laudable.

Alpha Centauri—or Die! (1963) restates this theme of human imperfection, but with a variation. Kirby, an ex-spaceman, defies the government in order to lead a reluctant, half-hearted crew on the first manned space flight since robot ships eliminated the need for human operators. Ironically, their colony is saved from the pursuing robot ship by creatures without rational mentality, but gifted with psi powers. Although much of the narrative is ultimately unexciting, one feels that Brackett saves a good part of the novel by her refusal to present human mentality as superior to the peaceful, mindless, but nearly omnipotent psi creatures.

The tension between alternate modes of life is a characteristic of Brackett's best works. In *The Long Tomorrow* (1955), her finest novel, cities have been banned, and the people have turned to fundamentalist religion in the aftermath of a nuclear war. Len Coulter and his cousin Essau, two teenage boys, are driven by their curiosity about the past to leave home and seek Bartorstown, the legendary outlaw remainder of prewar civilization. The dramatic tension between the two boys is one of Brackett's highest achievements. The product of kinship and a common goal, their friendship is at best tenuous. Young Len, sensitive as well as adventurous, cannot accept what he finds in Bartorstown as easily as the older, wilder Essau. Although less exciting than some of Brackett's interplanetary fantasies, *The Long Tomorrow* is nonetheless suspenseful, and in its depiction of the blighting effects of superstition and of the fundamental conflict between destructive science and blind faith, it has a depth that her other works lack.

If *The Long Tomorrow* is Brackett's most successful novel, the Skaith trilogy (*The Ginger Star*, 1974; *The Hounds of Skaith*, 1974; and *The Reavers of Skaith*, 1976) is a comparative failure. Eric John Stark, a character praised by Ray Bradbury, may be memorable, but the novels in which he makes his final appearance are not. Stark comes to Skaith, a planet orbiting a dying sun, to rescue his mentor Simon Ashton. Ashton had come to Skaith earlier to facilitate emigration and was taken prisoner by the Wandsmen. The Wandsmen and their superiors, the Lords Protector, do not fear losing their power so much as losing the traditions that have evolved on Skaith over untold centuries. Nevertheless, one of

those traditions, though begun in good faith, now enslaves over one-third of the population.

The excitement and the imaginative variety of the novels in the trilogy are simply overdone. Narrow escapes (some of them handled rather unconvincingly) multiply until they become boring rather than exciting. The variety of life forms, though imaginative, is too artificially balanced. Unlike the Mars and Venus she developed through the years, the relatively small area of the planet, which is presented as a somewhat cohesive unit in itself, does not bear the profusion of forms and customs with which Brackett invests it. There is material here for one good, exciting novel, but not for three.

Leigh Brackett's best works are those in which she places her protagonist in a moral rather than a physical dilemma, though her reputation rests on the latter kind of fiction. Only in *The Sword of Rhiannon*, however, does she really sustain the swashbuckling excitement that she achieves in her short stories. Although she is at times capable of refreshing creations and exciting plots, her execution is not always what one would like. She has a small following among the devotees of adventure fantasy, including Ray Bradbury and Lester del Rey, but her work is uneven at best. —*Alex Batman*

Screenplays:

The Big Sleep, by Brackett, Jules Furthman, and William Faulkner, Warner, 1946;
Rio Bravo, by Brackett and Furthman, Warner, 1949;
Hatari, Paramount, 1962;
El Dorado, Paramount, 1966;
Rio Lobo, by Brackett and Burton Wahl, Cinema Center, 1970;
The Long Goodbye, United Artists, 1973.

Other:

Best of Planet Stories No. 1: Strange Adventures on Other Worlds, edited by Brackett (New York: Ballantine, 1975);
The Best of Edmond Hamilton, edited by Brackett (New York: Ballantine, 1975).

Ray Bradbury

Gary K. Wolfe
Roosevelt University

BIRTH: Waukegan, Illinois, 22 August 1920, to Leonard Spaulding and Esther Moberg Bradbury.

MARRIAGE: 27 September 1947 to Marguerite McClure; children: Susan, Ramona, Bettina, Alexandra.

AWARDS: Selected best author of 1949 by National Fantasy Fan Federation; Benjamin Franklin Magazine Award for "Sun and Shadow," 1954; National Institute of Arts and Letters Award in Literature, 1954; Boys Club of America Junior Book Award for *Switch on the Night*, 1956; Academy Award nomination and Golden Eagle Film Award for *Icarus Montgolfier Wright* (screenplay), 1963; Writers' Guild of America West Valentine Davies Award, 1974.

BOOKS: *Dark Carnival* (Sauk City, Wis.: Arkham, 1947; abridged edition, London: Hamish Hamilton, 1948);
The Martian Chronicles (Garden City: Doubleday, 1950); revised as *The Silver Locusts* (London: Rupert Hart-Davis, 1951);
The Illustrated Man (Garden City: Doubleday, 1951; revised edition, London: Rupert Hart-Davis, 1952);
The Golden Apples of the Sun (Garden City: Doubleday, 1953; revised edition, London: Rupert Hart-Davis, 1953);
Fahrenheit 451 (New York: Ballantine, 1953; abridged edition, London: Rupert Hart-Davis, 1954);
Switch on the Night (New York: Pantheon, 1955; London: Rupert Hart-Davis, 1955);
The October Country (New York: Ballantine, 1955; London: Rupert Hart-Davis, 1956);
Dandelion Wine (Garden City: Doubleday, 1957; London: Rupert Hart-Davis, 1957);
A Medicine for Melancholy (Garden City: Doubleday, 1959); revised as *The Day It Rained Forever* (London: Rupert Hart-Davis, 1959);

The Small Assassin (London: New English Library, 1962);
Something Wicked This Way Comes (New York: Simon & Schuster, 1962; London: Rupert Hart-Davis, 1963);
R is for Rocket (Garden City: Doubleday, 1962; London: Rupert Hart-Davis, 1968);
The Anthem Sprinters and Other Antics (New York: Dial, 1963);
The Machineries of Joy (New York: Simon & Schuster, 1964; abridged edition, London: Rupert Hart-Davis, 1964);
The Vintage Bradbury (New York: Vintage, 1965);
The Autumn People (New York: Ballantine, 1965);
Twice 22 (Garden City: Doubleday, 1966);
Tomorrow Midnight (New York: Ballantine, 1966);
S is for Space (Garden City: Doubleday, 1966; London: Rupert Hart-Davis, 1968);
I Sing the Body Electric! (New York: Knopf, 1969; London: Rupert Hart-Davis, 1970);
The Wonderful Ice Cream Suit and Other Plays (New York: Bantam, 1972; London: Hart-Davis, MacGibbon, 1973);
The Halloween Tree (New York: Knopf, 1972; London: Hart-Davis, MacGibbon, 1973);
Zen and the Art of Writing and the Joy of Writing (Santa Barbara, Cal.: Capra Press, 1973);
When Elephants Last in the Dooryard Bloomed (New York: Knopf, 1973; London: Hart-Davis, MacGibbon, 1975);
Pillar of Fire and Other Plays (New York: Bantam, 1975);
Long After Midnight (New York: Knopf, 1976);
Where Robot Mice and Robot Men Run Round in Robot Towns (New York: Knopf, 1977; London: Hart-Davis, MacGibbon, 1979).

Although Ray Bradbury remains perhaps the best known of all science-fiction writers, and although his stories and themes have permeated all areas of American culture as have those of no other science-fiction writer—through more than five hundred stories, poems, essays, plays, films, television plays, radio, music, and even comic books—Bradbury is still something of an anomaly in the genre. In a field that thrives on the fantastic and the marvelous, Bradbury's best stories celebrate the mundane; in a field preoccupied with the future, Bradbury's vision is firmly rooted in the past—both his own personal past and the past of America. In a popular genre where reputations, until recently, have been made through ingenious plotting and the exposition of scientific and technological ideas, Bradbury built an enormous reputation virtually on style alone—and then, when the rest of the writers in the genre began to discover the uses of stylistic experimentation, turned ever more toward self-imitation and the recapitulation of earlier themes. When science fiction seemed almost exclusively a literature of technophiles, Bradbury became a lone symbol of the dangers of technology, even to the point of refusing to drive an automobile or fly in an airplane. But when science fiction came increasingly to adopt an ambivalent attitude toward unchecked technological progress, Bradbury became an international spokesman for the virtues of spaceflight and technological achievement. Clearly Bradbury cannot be accused of following the dominant trends in science fiction or even of literature in general. He is his own most important referent, and despite his widely avowed love of earlier writers from Poe to Thomas Wolfe to Hemingway, it is in Bradbury's own Midwestern background that one finds the most important sources for his fiction.

Bradbury is perhaps the most autobiographical of science-fiction writers, and this, too, seems anomalous: how, after all, can one construct meaningful future worlds from so much reference to the past and so little to the present? One answer, of course, is that Bradbury's science fiction is, in fact, seldom extrapolative, for the values Bradbury seeks to express are the values he associates with his own past. Bradbury was born and spent most of his childhood in Waukegan, Illinois, a small community on the western shore of Lake Michigan, which was to become the "Green Town" of many later stories. Early in life he was introduced to the world of fantasy and the supernatural. By the time he was six, he had seen a number of horror movies—notably *The Cat and the Canary*, Lon Chaney's *The Hunchback of Notre Dame* and *The Phantom of the Opera*—and had developed a morbid fear of the dark. (His 1955 children's book, *Switch on the Night*, was based on these memories and designed to allay the fear of darkness for his own children.) His Aunt

Neva, whose name was given to a character in a few stories and who received the dedication of the 1953 collection *The Golden Apples of the Sun*, introduced him to fairy tales and to the Oz books of L. Frank Baum, whom Bradbury later counted among his chief influences. Bradbury's father, Leonard Spaulding Bradbury, worked as a lineman for the Waukegan Bureau of Power and Light. Not only did "Leonard Spaulding" later become a Bradbury pseudonym, but even his father's mundane occupation was transformed into romance in the 1948 story "Powerhouse," collected in *The Golden Apples of the Sun*.

Numerous Bradbury stories, including several in his 1947 collection, *Dark Carnival*, can be traced back to specific events in his childhood. Even his earliest memories would later become raw material for his fiction: "The Small Assassin" (1946; collected in *Dark Carnival*), about a newborn infant who murders his parents, was supposedly drawn from the author's memories of his first two years of life. "The Lake" (1944; collected in *Dark Carnival*) is based on the experience of a cousin's near drowning in Lake Michigan when Bradbury was seven. The shadowy character called The Lonely One who is said to inhabit a ravine in *Dandelion Wine* (1957) is drawn from the author's own fears of such a character when he was eight. The preoccupation with libraries most evident in *Something Wicked This Way Comes* (1962) is certainly related to the ten-year-old Bradbury's spending each Monday evening with his brother at the Waukegan Public Library. His fascination with circuses and carnivals may be related to the traveling shows of his youth, and in particular to a day in 1931 when he appeared onstage as an audience volunteer with Blackstone the Magician. The stories "Uncle Einar" (1947) and "Homecoming" (1946), also collected in *Dark Carnival*, feature a character based on a favorite uncle named Einar, who moved away when Bradbury was fourteen. An early interest in science fiction and the future is indicated by Bradbury's discovery of the pulp magazine *Amazing Stories* in 1928, his discovery of Edgar Rice Burroughs's Martian stories in 1929, and Jules Verne in 1932, and his visit with his Aunt Neva to the Century of Progress exposition at the 1933 Chicago World's Fair.

Twice during his childhood, in 1926-1927 and again in 1932-1933, Bradbury lived with his family in Arizona, where his father hoped to find work after being laid off during the Depression. It is possible that these early impressions of the desert affected his later visions of Mars, and perhaps his sensitive views of Mexican Americans as well. But both moves were abortive, and in both cases the family returned to Waukegan. The Bradburys did not move west permanently until their 1934 move to Los Angeles. Bradbury dates his career choice from about this time: at the age of fifteen, he began submitting short stories to major national magazines, hoping ultimately for a sale to the *Saturday Evening Post* but receiving no acceptance. Encouraged by sympathetic high school literature teachers, however, he became active in his school's drama classes and wrote for school publications.

In 1937 Bradbury's first real connection with the world of science fiction began when he joined the Los Angeles Science Fiction League. Here he met Henry Kuttner, a budding professional writer whose first story was published that same year and who would become something of a mentor to the younger writer. The league's fanzine, *Imagination!*, printed Bradbury's first published short story, "Hollerbochen's Dilemma," in 1938, and his increasing involvement as a science-fiction fan led him, in 1939, to begin his own mimeographed publication, *Futuria Fantasia*. That same year he attended the World Science Fiction convention in New York and visited the New York World's Fair.

At the age of twenty Bradbury was still living with his family and selling newspapers for income, but by this time a career as a writer seemed a real possibility. Bradbury had been listed in a national directory of fans of science fiction, and his letters were becoming familiar features of the letter columns of the professional pulp magazines. *Futuria Fantasia* lasted for only four issues, but in the last issue in 1940, Bradbury published a story called "The Piper," which gave early evidence of the central themes of *The Martian Chronicles* (1950). Aided by such professional writers as Robert Heinlein, Leigh Brackett, Jack Williamson, Edmond Hamilton, Ross Rocklynne, and Henry Hasse, he was finally able to break into professional markets in 1941 with "Pendulum," a story written in collaboration with Hasse that appeared in the November *Super Science Stories*. The following year he began selling stories to *Weird Tales*, which, though not a science-fiction pulp in the strictest sense, would prove during the next few years to be the most natural home for the fantasy and horror stories that would go to make up Bradbury's first collection, *Dark Carnival*. Bradbury soon discovered that his distinctive poetic style would be more readily welcomed by *Weird Tales*, a few detective magazines,

and eventually the "slicks" such as *American Mercury*, *Charm*, and *Mademoiselle*, than by the science-fiction magazines he had so avidly read as a teenager.

By 1944 Bradbury, exempt from the draft because of his eyes, seemed aware that style was his strong point and became more conscious of developing it. As a teenager he had been briefly infatuated with Thomas Wolfe; now he began to read writers whose work was more spare, more controlled, such as Jessamyn West, Sherwood Anderson, Eudora Welty, and Katherine Anne Porter. He was at the same time discovering new sources of material for his fiction. While selling newspapers in 1940, Bradbury had kept an office in a tenement inhabited largely by Mexican Americans (whom he would feature prominently in several later stories). In 1945 his interest in Mexican culture deepened during a two-month-long automobile trip to Mexico when Bradbury accompanied an artist friend to collect masks for the Los Angeles County Museum. Bradbury was increasingly impressed with the growing sense of an alien culture whose values were different from those of the United States, a sense of alienation later captured in stories such as "The Highway" (1950; collected in *The Illustrated Man*,

Ray Bradbury, age 25

1951) and "And the Rock Cried Out" (1953; collected in *A Medicine for Melancholy*, 1959), both of which concern the plight of North Americans trapped in Mexican villages while nuclear war devastates the United States. Bradbury would draw more optimistic portraits of Mexican culture in other stories. "En La Noche" (1952) and the award-winning "Sun and Shadow" (1953), two of the stories collected in *The Golden Apples of the Sun*, emphasize what he took to be the uninhibited sensuality of Mexicans. In "Sun and Shadow," for example, a poor Mexican, tired of being treated as a "local," deliberately exposes himself to foil a North American fashion photographer on location; whenever the photographer attempts to take a picture, the Mexican appears and drops his pants.

What most impressed Bradbury about this trip to Mexico was the preoccupation with death that seemed to permeate much of the culture. The trip eventually led to Guanajuato, northwest of Mexico City, where Bradbury was horrified and fascinated by the underground catacombs with their upright rows of mummified remains. In 1978 Bradbury provided the text for a photographic essay on these mummies. This text was "The Next in Line" (1947), another of the stories in *Dark Carnival*. The longest of Bradbury's Mexican stories, it portrays the profound, immobilizing horror a young North American wife feels at the idea of being placed in such a crypt or dying in such a country. Besides the mummies, the most affecting of Bradbury's experiences in Mexico was probably the Day of the Dead celebration, which also figures prominently in "The Next in Line" and is the focus of "El Dia De Muerte" (1947). Whether or not this first real experience with an alien culture influenced other aspects of Bradbury's writing, such as his portrayal of the Martians in his many Martian stories, is a matter of conjecture; much of what Bradbury seemed to find attractive about the Mexicans—their respect for the past and their uncomfortably easy union of religion, sensuality, and death—is reflected in his rather sketchy portrayal of the ancient Martian civilization in *The Martian Chronicles*.

Bradbury's reputation as a short-story writer had by the mid-1940s reached the point where book publication began to seem a logical next step. August Derleth, the Wisconsin author who had established the small fantasy press Arkham House primarily to publish in book form the fiction of H. P. Lovecraft and his circle, accepted "The Lake" for his 1945 anthology *Who Knocks?* and suggested that Bradbury might prepare a whole volume of fantasy and horror stories for Arkham House. Don Congdon,

a New York editor and agent who in 1947 became Bradbury's agent, also began to explore the idea of a collection. His career clearly on the upswing, Bradbury was so confident of his own future output that on the eve of his wedding to Marguerite McClure in 1947, he claims he burned more than a million words of his earlier writing that he felt did not meet his current standards.

Bradbury's career also seemed to be moving rapidly in several directions at once. His first book, *Dark Carnival*, published by Arkham House in 1947, would bolster his reputation as a writer of weird fiction, but that was a kind of fiction that Bradbury was coming to write less and less frequently. From *Weird Tales* he had moved increasingly into such markets as *American Mercury*, *Mademoiselle*, *Charm*, *Harper's*, and the *New Yorker*, and his fiction was beginning to appear with some regularity in such mainstream collections as *The Best American Short Stories* and the *Prize Stories: O. Henry Awards*. Even though many of his stories were fantasy and science fiction, Bradbury was gaining a reputation as a sensitive stylist who tackled the contemporary social issues of racism and illegal immigration of Mexicans into this country. At the same time the first of the *Martian Chronicles* stories, "The Million-Year Picnic," appeared in *Planet Stories* in 1946, and by 1949 Bradbury had won such wide acceptance among the legions of science-fiction fans from whom he had sprung that he was voted best science-fiction author of the year by the National Fantasy Fan Federation. With the assistance of shrewd editors and careful packaging of his stories in book form, Bradbury was able to exploit his range as a writer during the next twenty years.

One of Bradbury's most consistent themes in this early fiction was that of alienation—alienation from technology, from a culture, even from the body itself—and while this theme is most readily apparent in the stories dealing with Mexicans in America and Americans in Mexico, it permeates other stories in *Dark Carnival* at an even more fundamental level. "The Next in Line" concerns not only the young wife's fear of the strange Mexican society she finds herself in, but also her growing rejection of her own body as she comes to realize that it, too, could become like the mummies of Guanajuato. The story is replete with sensual images of the wife's body, and as she begins to withdraw, she ceases eating, begins to sleep in the nude, and finally seems to abandon any possibility of physical action at all. Other stories in the collection reflect even more directly this discomfort with a fragile physical frame. "Skeleton"

(1945) concerns a man so disgusted with his aching bones that he is persuaded by a mysterious little man to have his skeleton removed entirely. "There Was an Old Woman" (1944) portrays a reclusive old woman, literally separated from her body at death, whose passion for life is such that, in a reversal of the usual pattern in these stories of rejecting the body, she visits the mortuary and reclaims her corpse by melding back into it. In "The Crowd" (1943) a man finds that the same crowds seem to gather at all accidents—victims of earlier accidents, again separated from their too fragile bodies. "The Lake" concerns a little girl, drowned in Lake Michigan, whose childish body is washed up on the shore ten years later, just when her childhood boyfriend, now grown, revisits the site: she is preserved in death, while he has grown older. In "The Man Upstairs" (1947) a young boy becomes fascinated with the anatomy of a mysterious boarder, to the point of dissecting him and revealing him to be some sort of alien or vampire: it is the vampire's body, not his actions, that betrays him. Two stories that deal with a supernatural family, "Uncle Einar" and "Homecoming," focus on characters whose physical bodies alienate them from their surroundings. Uncle Einar is a friendly vampire, but he must stay hidden until he discovers that he can fly disguised as a kite. In a clever reversal on the same theme "Homecoming" depicts a boy who is out of place at his vampire family reunion simply because he *is* ordinary and has no supernatural powers or physical abnormalities. "The Small Assassin" initially focuses on the fear and alienation a mother feels for her newborn infant, but the infant's own homicidal impulses are later explained in terms of the fierce sense of rejection and hostility a newborn baby must feel at being thrust from the womb at birth. Alienation from children is also the theme of "Let's Play 'Poison' " (1946), which concerns a teacher ultimately murdered by his pupils.

Other stories in *Dark Carnival* concern different kinds of outcasts. "The Handler" (1947) is a maladjusted mortician, disliked by his community, who wreaks vengeance on the citizens by playing practical jokes on them after they are dead (such as embalming a racist with black ink). In "The Jar" (1944) a hillbilly gains the respect of his community by purchasing from a traveling circus a jar containing what appears to be an unidentifiable mass of animal matter, only to be threatened with exposure by his unfaithful wife, whom he kills and places piecemeal into the jar. Still other stories touch upon mythical themes and suggest the hostility of elemental nature. In "The Scythe" (1943) a man

takes over an abandoned wheat farm in the Midwest, only to find he has also taken on the task of the Grim Reaper. A character in "The Wind" (1943) discovers a hidden valley said to be the source of the world's winds and is pursued and eventually killed by winds.

While many of these tales are firmly connected to the *Weird Tales* tradition by their grotesque imagery and morbid preoccupation with decay and disintegration (many, in fact, would later be adapted with remarkable faithfulness by the horror comic books of Albert Feldstein), many are also compelling prose poems on themes of nature and mortality, slightly plotted and stripped of all but essentials of character and setting. Printed in an edition of only 3,000 copies, *Dark Carnival* quickly became a collector's item among science-fiction and fantasy aficionados. It established clearly the curious mix of stories that was to become a trademark of later Bradbury collections, and it may have the distinction of having been the first book by a popular fantasy author to include stories from sources as diverse as *Harper's*, *Mademoiselle*, and *Weird Tales*.

Although it was significant in demarcating the first stage of Bradbury's professional career, *Dark Carnival*, available in such a limited edition from a specialty press, could not give Bradbury the wide public he eventually achieved. As always, the book market for fantastic literature was more receptive to novels than to short-story collections. When Walter Bradbury, a Doubleday editor, suggested in 1949 that Bradbury put together a book with at least a semblance of narrative continuity, the author's response was almost immediate; he had already published nearly a dozen stories depicting episodes in the colonization of Mars by Earthmen. He quickly produced an outline and began arranging stories and writing connective passages to give the book an appearance of unity.

Not all of the Martian stories Bradbury had written lent themselves easily to a common narrative. "The Naming of Names" (1949), for example, presents the Martian landscape as exerting such a powerful influence on the colonists from Earth that they are eventually physically transformed into Martians. "The One Who Waits" (1949) depicts a Martian as a troll-like creature living at the bottom of a well, waiting to absorb the personalities of the Earthmen who visit. Stories such as these, which could not easily be made consistent with the larger group of Martian stories that portrayed the colonization of Mars in terms of the colonization of North America in the nineteenth century, were omitted from *The Martian Chronicles* to appear in later Bradbury collections. (Though the title "The

Naming of Names" appeared as a bridge passage in *The Martian Chronicles*, the story itself was not collected until *A Medicine for Melancholy*, where it was retitled "Dark They Were, and Golden-Eyed"; "The One Who Waits" appeared in the 1964 collection, *The Machineries of Joy*.) Inappropriate though they may have been in terms of narrative consistency, however, these stories neatly encapsulate one of the most important themes of *The Martian Chronicles*: the theme that the environment transforms and finally absorbs the settler. While this theme was evident even in some of the stories in *Dark Carnival*, *The Martian Chronicles* gave full range to this and other Bradbury themes. The book was the first opportunity for readers to explore Bradbury's vision in a sustained narrative.

Published in May of 1950, *The Martian Chronicles* was a seminal event in the history of science fiction's growing respectability. The book was widely reviewed by a critical community that extended well beyond the science-fiction subculture, most notably by Christopher Isherwood, who praised it lavishly in the journal *Tomorrow*. Impressed by Bradbury's poetic language and unconcerned by his lack of even a semblance of scientific verisimilitude, many readers found in the book a profound exploration of the state of America in 1950 with its fears of nuclear war, its problems with racism and growing book censorship, its confused values, and its yearning for a simpler life. By November 1952 the book had gone through six printings and had appeared in England as *The Silver Locusts*; during the next several years it would remain constantly in print in paperback and be translated into more than thirty foreign language editions, one of which (1955) featured an introduction by Jorge Luis Borges.

Science-fiction readers have criticized *The Martian Chronicles* on the grounds that the Martian colonies of the book are little more than transplanted small towns from the American Midwest of the 1920s. But Bradbury was certainly conscious of this and has repeatedly maintained that his Mars is not a projection of the future but rather a mirror of American life. Indeed the subject matter of the book is more history than science, and what technology the book features is largely technology in the service of exploring new frontiers. Bradbury does not dwell on making his machines believable any more than he dwells on making his Mars astronomically accurate; his real concern, it may be argued, is to explore some of the key issues in American history—capitalism, technology, the family, the role of imagination—in a context free of historical constraints. The central

myth of the book is the myth of the frontier, and the chronology that Bradbury has imposed upon his stories and bridge passages makes this clear.

After a brief prologue that presents the rocket ship as a harbinger of summer to a Midwestern community locked in winter, the narrative begins with the story "Ylla" (1950), which establishes the purely fanciful Martian setting of crystal houses and wine trees and introduces the Martians, who telepathically sense the impending arrival of Earthmen and react with both wonder and fear. Ylla, a Martian wife, is romantically transported by her dream-images of the tall, strange aliens, but her husband senses danger and participates in the murder of these first arrivals. A second expedition from Earth, in the story "The Earth Men" (1948), is also quickly dispatched in a tale that deliberately parodies the notion of triumphant explorers arriving in a new world. In this case the explorers are regarded as hallucinations by the Martians, who attempt a cure by destroying them. "The Third Expedition" (1948), originally titled "Mars Is Heaven," which recalls Bradbury's earlier horror stories, makes fuller use of the Martians' telepathic abilities to introduce one of the major themes of the book: that of the past as a trap. This time the Earthmen find on Mars what appears to be a community made up of their own memories of childhood and family. Seduced by this telepathic hallucination, they too are destroyed, unable until it is too late to overcome the powerful pull of their own past lives. To survive in the new environment, one must be willing to forgo the past entirely.

Unwittingly, however, the Earthmen have already begun the conquest of Mars. By the time of the fourth expedition, in "—And the Moon Be Still as Bright" (1948), virtually all the Martians have died from chicken pox brought by the earlier explorers. Suddenly the perspective on the Martians shifts. No longer are they viewed as the monsters of "The Third Expedition" or the middle class burghers of "Ylla"; instead, they are seen as the last scions of a civilization that had united art and technology and religion into the kind of stable society that Earthmen seem unable to maintain. In this story the focus is on the different kinds of Earthmen who come to Mars: Spender, sensitive to the fragile Martian environment and cynical about the inevitable destruction of it by future immigrants, who becomes the first American to be transformed by the new environment and comes to think of himself as the last Martian, even to the point of plotting to kill all future arrivals; Parkhill, the small-minded exploiter who seeks to make the planet over in the image of Earth; and

Captain Wilder, the man of reason who shares Spender's fears but also realizes the inevitability of men such as Parkhill and the futility of trying to preserve Mars as it is.

A short bridge passage titled "The Settlers" (1950) introduces the second major section of the book, which deals with the colonization of Mars by a wide variety of Americans. (Except for the involvement of one or two Mexicans, Bradbury sees the expansion to Mars as a peculiarly American project. He offers the excuse that other nations were too preoccupied with warmongering to devote energy to settling new planets.) The following story, "The Green Morning," makes the emerging parallel with American history clear. Little more than a vignette, it tells of Benjamin Driscoll, who goes about seeding Mars with trees in the fashion of Johnny Appleseed. By the time of "Night Meeting" (1950) the settlement of Mars is well underway. This story, which comes as something of an interlude in the ongoing narrative of Martian colonization, reemphasizes the theme of "The Third Expedition": that one must live in the present. But "the present," the reader learns, is subjective: on a lonely road at night Tomás Gomez encounters a Martian, only to find that the Martian sees the world differently. For the Martian, the ancient civilization of Mars thrives, while for Tomás, it lies in ruins, and the new Earth society thrives. Though this apparent time warp is not explained, the story serves as a reminder that the new society on Mars is built in the shadow of an earlier civilization, just as America was built in the shadow of Indian civilizations. This story, which proclaims the integrity of the vanished Martian society, is ironically contrasted later in the volume by "The Martian" (1949), in which a surviving Martian seeks to win acceptance among Earthmen by transforming himself into whatever human form is most acceptable to them. By now the Americans are firmly in control, and it is the Martians who must conform.

This section of the book also explores some of the reasons why people go to Mars. In "Way in the Middle of the Air" (1950) blacks emigrate to escape the oppression of the American South. In "Usher II" (1950) a character named Stendahl builds a mechanized monument to Edgar Allan Poe in defiance of a growing trend toward censorship of all forms of imaginative literature on Earth. (An earlier story, "The Exiles" (1949) in the 1951 collection, *The Illustrated Man*, had even depicted Mars as a haven for the ghosts of imaginative writers whose books were banned on Earth.) The father in "The Million-Year Picnic" (1946) flees the hectic rat race of American life and the impending nuclear war. For

these characters, Mars represents less an opportunity for exploitation than freedom from an oppressive past and from a society which is rapidly tending toward self-destruction.

The final section of *The Martian Chronicles* concerns the effect of a massive nuclear war on Earth upon the Martian settlers. As with his stories that deal with Americans trapped in Mexico during nuclear war, Bradbury's premise is that Americans will flock home at the first sign of war. The exploitation of Mars thus comes to an abrupt halt, and in "The Off Season" (1948) those who had greedily sought to acquire land and wealth, such as Sam Parkhill from "—And the Moon Be Still as Bright," find their wealth without meaning. "The Silent Towns" (1949) depicts the loneliness and alienation felt by the few who remain on Mars; the loneliness is so great that in "The Long Years" (1948) a man builds a whole family of robots to keep him company. The robots outlive the man and continue the meaningless charade of family life long after he has died. This idea of technology surviving its makers is also the subject of "There Will Come Soft Rains" (1950), which details the gradual destruction of a mechanized house on Earth which continues to function long after the family that had lived in it dies in the atomic war.

"The Million-Year Picnic," the final story in the book, synthesizes many of the themes of the earlier stories into what remains one of Bradbury's most memorable short stories. A family escapes the nuclear devastation on Earth by migrating to Mars in a family rocket, which the father promptly destroys shortly after their arrival. The rocket is only the first of many reminders of the old civilization to be abandoned. Soon, as Earth civilization dies, the radio becomes useless, and as the family explores the dead Martian cities in search of a place in which to settle, the father ceremoniously buries stocks, bonds, and other documents symbolic of the way of life he has chosen to reject (in clear contrast to earlier, unsuccessful settlers who sought to transfer that way of life to Mars). Throughout the story Bradbury gradually builds a pattern of imagery in which the family—particularly the father—is described in terms of features of the Martian landscape, and this invites the reader to come more and more to think of them as somehow natural to this environment. Without the dramatic physical transformation of "Dark They Were, and Golden-Eyed," or the pathological rejection of humanity by Spender in "—And the Moon Be Still as Bright," Bradbury presents a convincing parable of the need to adapt to the new environment. When the father promises to

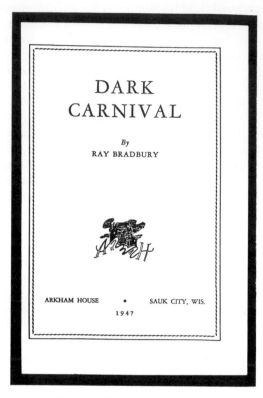

Title page of Bradbury's first book

burning that would be a central feature of *Fahrenheit 451* (1953). A third Martian story, "The Fire Balloons" (1951), seems unconnected with *The Martian Chronicles* except in setting, but this thoughtful parable on whether a benign alien life form can be said to have achieved Christian salvation represents an unusual early treatment of a serious religious theme in science fiction. A second religious story in this collection, "The Man" (1949), is considerably less successful with its portrait of an obsessed rocket captain who travels around the galaxy in search of the Messiah after narrowly missing His advent on an alien planet.

"The Concrete Mixer" (1949), though not set on Mars, manages successfully to capture the social criticism implicit in *The Martian Chronicles* in a much more direct and satirical way: a planned Martian invasion of Earth is foiled not by military might, but by the corruption of the Martians themselves in the face of America's relentlessly materialistic culture. Other stories in *The Illustrated Man* return to familiar Bradbury subjects. In "The Veldt" (1950) children murder their parents in an automated playroom, and in "Zero Hour" (1947) children spearhead an alien invasion. "The Highway" (1950) concerns a Mexican peasant whose way of life is undisturbed by the atomic war to the north, while in "The Fox and the Forest" (1950) time-travelers escape a dystopian future by hiding in the Mexico of 1938. "The City" (1950) is an automated monstrosity that waits twenty thousand years for the opportunity to chop up some representatives of humanity who had abandoned it so long ago.

Several of the stories dwell on various aspects of Bradbury's continuing fascination with the romance of space travel. In the simplest of these, "The Rocket" (1950), a poor Italian manages to save enough to buy a rocket simply to give his children a view of outer space. "The Rocket Man" (1951) clearly views the rocket pilot as a romantic hero who dies a romantic death by falling into the sun. Bradbury undercuts the glamour of this by telling the story from the point of view of the son of the rocket man and dealing with the anguish of the wife, for whom the sun will always be a reminder of her husband's death. "No Particular Night or Morning" (1951) is a kind of epistemological fable of a spaceman who, freed of all referents of time and space, comes to doubt the reality of his own past and finally his own surroundings. "Kaleidoscope" (1949), which Bradbury later dramatized, describes the radio conversations of survivors of an exploded spaceship as they drift apart toward certain death. In

show his children some real Martians, it comes as little surprise that what he shows them is their own reflections in the still waters of a canal.

Less than a year after *The Martian Chronicles* Bradbury brought out a second Doubleday collection, *The Illustrated Man*. Again Bradbury tried to connect the stories by means of a framing device. In this case each story acts out one of a myriad of illustrations on the skin of an ominous character whom a young man meets on a country road in Wisconsin, but here the frame is much slighter, and there is no attempt to connect the various stories into any kind of an overall narrative. Four of the stories are set on Mars, and two of these have clear connections to *The Martian Chronicles* stories. "The Other Foot" (1951), perhaps a sequel to "Way in the Middle of the Air," concerns a Mars settled mostly by blacks, who see the coming of white men in the wake of a devastating atomic war as an opportunity to reverse the pattern of racism they had suffered on Earth; in the end their compassion gets the better of them. "The Exiles" reiterates the theme of "Usher II" by depicting ghosts of imaginative writers surviving on Mars until the last copies of their books are burned. Thematically, this fantasy also anticipates the growing concern with book the most romantic of these deaths, one of the spacemen falls to Earth as a flaming meteor.

By 1952 Bradbury's reputation was firmly established, and *The Ray Bradbury Review*, a fanzine, was devoted exclusively to his work. Bradbury began his involvement with Hollywood by providing an original screen story for a film that would eventually be released as *It Came From Outer Space* (1953). For Bantam Books he edited an anthology of fantasy fiction, *Timeless Stories for Today and Tomorrow* (1952), that clearly revealed his predilection for psychological symbolism over scientific extrapolation as a basis for fantastic fiction. His early horror fiction began to reappear in comic books. In August 1953 film director John Huston invited him to Ireland to work on the screenplay for *Moby Dick* (1956), and Bradbury's experiences with the Irish later proved a rich mine of material for stories and plays, just as his experiences with Mexicans had been eight years earlier.

Also in 1953 Bradbury's fourth collection of short stories was published. Drawing on stories originally published between 1945 and 1953, *The Golden Apples of the Sun* abandoned the frame narrative linking the stories of his two previous collections and freely mixed stories of all genres— fantasy, crime, science fiction, humor, and realism. It was the first of Bradbury's collections to be clearly addressed to a nonspecialty market; fewer than half the stories could be labeled fantasy or science fiction, and only two of them came from the science-fiction magazines (a market Bradbury had understandably moved away from as he began regularly selling to more prestigious markets, but which he never abandoned entirely).

Of the handful of science-fiction stories in the book, one, "The Wilderness," almost serves as a gloss on *The Martian Chronicles*. First published in 1952, the story is little more than a plotless sketch of the anxieties of women preparing to join their husbands on Mars. But the rocket is leaving from Independence, Missouri, and the obvious parallels with the westward movement of the nineteenth century give Bradbury a chance to make this frontier aspect of his Martian stories more explicit than in any of his previous stories. The other science fiction in the book shows Bradbury moving in other directions. Both "The Fog Horn" (1951), which became the barely recognizable basis of the 1953 film *The Beast from 20,000 Fathoms* and "A Sound of Thunder" (1952) reveal an emerging interest in dinosaurs, and "A Sound of Thunder" reiterates the favorite Bradbury theme of the profound effect of the past on the present by depicting a time-travel safari

that inadvertently changes the modern world when a hunter steps on a prehistoric butterfly. The title story, written apparently to illustrate a line from Yeats's "Song of Wandering Aengus," achieves some poetic power at the expense of the outlandish premise that a rocket might deliberately fly into the sun to scoop up "solar matter" for use as an energy source on Earth. But the most effective of Bradbury's science fiction in this collection is thematically related to *Fahrenheit 451* and is indirectly alluded to in that novel. "The Pedestrian" (1951) is a chilling satire of a future society when addiction to television has become such a norm that a man can be arrested for antisocial behavior merely for taking a walk. This growing fear of the impact of technology on daily life is also expressed in "The Murderer" (1953), which concerns a rebellious technophobe who "murders" the automatic appliances and gadgets in his house and is promptly arrested, and in "The Flying Machine" (1953), in which a wise emperor in ancient China executes a man who invents a flying machine when the emperor realizes the device's potential use as a weapon.

The collection also contains some of Bradbury's more sensitive nonfantastic portrayals of Mexicans and Mexican-Americans in "I See You Never" (1947), "En La Noche" (1952), and "Sun and Shadow"; and it reprints for the first time some of his stories concerning the loneliness and isolation of small towns and rural areas: "The April Witch" (1952), "Invisible Boy" (1945), "The Great Fire" (1949), and "The Great Wide World Over There" (1952). It also includes Bradbury's story of racism in a small town, "The Big Black and White Game" (1945). "The Meadow" (1953), about a night watchman who persuades a movie producer not to destroy the sets of old movies, reveals Bradbury's growing fascination with the details of moviemaking. While *The Golden Apples of the Sun* may be of limited interest to the reader interested in Bradbury's contributions to science fiction, it nevertheless was the first of his books to reveal his breadth and variety as a writer of short stories.

Later in 1953 Bradbury published what would become his only work to approach *The Martian Chronicles* in popularity and influence. *Fahrenheit 451* had been germinating as early as 1947 when Bradbury wrote a short story, "Bright Phoenix," about a small town whose residents foil government book burnings by each memorizing one of the censored texts. (Bradbury eventually published this, in a slightly revised form, in the May 1963 issue of the *Magazine of Fantasy and Science Fiction*.) In 1951 this basic premise involving government book burners was expanded to novella length as *The Fireman*, which appeared in the February issue of *Galaxy*. Expanded again to twice the length of *The Fireman*, *Fahrenheit 451* became Bradbury's first and best novel.

Although hindsight invites the reader to view *Fahrenheit 451* as a passionate attack on censorship and perhaps on the McCarthyism of the early 1950s as well, the book is equally an attack on the growing power of a mass culture, particularly television, whose dynamics disallow complexity of thought and which consistently falls prey to the demands of special interest groups. Above all, the book-burning firemen of the novel are concerned that culture be made inoffensive, unthreatening, and universally accessible. Books, they feel, confuse citizens with contradictory values and ambivalent portrayals of human behavior. Beatty, the fireman supervisor who explains this to the protagonist Montag (who has begun to exhibit an unhealthy interest in the books he is burning), traces this tradition of book burning throughout American history; Benjamin Franklin, according to the history of the firemen, became America's first "fireman" in this new sense when he sought to limit the distribution of Royalist pamphlets in the colonies. The history is not as distorted as it may seem: one of the strengths of Bradbury's argument in the novel is that he sees book burning as not simply a totalitarian phenomenon, but one that has at least some roots in the process of democratization that led to the rise of American mass culture in the first place.

As with his other science-fiction settings, Bradbury makes little effort to paint a convincing portrait of a possible future society; instead, he strips the story of all but essential details, characters, and images that are needed to make his point. The novel takes place in what appears to be a totalitarian state, but the only real feature of this totalitarianism that the reader sees is the book burning, and even that does not seem to be in the service of any particular political philosophy. In fact, it is suggested that the totalitarianism of this state is simply mass culture enforced by law. Nor is there much evidence of technological advance in this future society: the chief image of technology is the Mechanical Hound, a rather baroque robot version of the traditional firemen's mascot, which is programmed to detect anomalous variations in body chemistry—presumably this is a hint of possible antisocial behavior—and to track down criminals like a real hound. Why a society given to the abolition of imagination would choose to cast its technology in such a bizarrely imaginative form as this is not explained, but as an

image of the replacement by an ominous piece of machinery of a tradition of middle-class society the Hound is effective.

The novel ends when Montag, who has finally come to reject his role as a book burner and has murdered his supervisor Beatty, escapes a massive manhunt and joins a rural community of individuals who seek to preserve books by memorizing them. Whereas the society from which Montag has escaped is associated with the image of the salamander—the destructive fire-lizard—this new society associates itself instead with the image of the phoenix, rising from the ashes of the burning books. Culture, Bradbury says, periodically undergoes such self-destructive convulsions as the book burning represents and can only be preserved by the self-sacrificing efforts of a few individuals. The individuals in this communal society literally give up their identities to become the books they have memorized: ironically, this new culture seems to care as little for the individual as the mass culture from which Montag has escaped. The difference is that the new society allows for a multiplicity of viewpoints and hence holds out some hope for the eventual revival of the human imagination.

Throughout the first part of 1954 Bradbury remained in Ireland working on the screenplay for *Moby Dick*, toured Europe, and met such luminaries as Bernard Berenson and Bertrand Russell. In 1955, after returning to the United States, he became involved in television writing (primarily for the "Alfred Hitchcock Show," later for Rod Serling's "The Twilight Zone") and collected many of the stories from *Dark Carnival* in a new anthology, *The October Country* (1955). Of the four new stories included in the collection, "The Dwarf" (1954) is closest to the earlier *Dark Carnival* stories in spirit, and "Touched with Fire" (1954) is clearly in the tradition of the crime stories that Bradbury had earlier sold to detective magazines. The other two indicate an emerging interest, perhaps sparked by the European trip, in literary and artistic culture. "The Watchful Poker Chip of H. Matisse" (1954) parodies bohemian artists and is surprisingly prescient in its delineation of what would later become known as "camp." In the story a man becomes an artists' hero by virtue simply of his appalling middle-class dullness, until he begins to replace parts of his body with works of art produced by masters. (Matisse's poker chip, for example, becomes a monocle.) "The Wonderful Death of Dudley Stone" (1954) concerns a brilliant writer who, under a murder threat from a jealous competitor, abandons his career on the eve of his

9:15 TO 9:20 A.M.

january 26th, 1978 / r.b *Ray Bradbury*

REVISIONS
FEB. 5, 1979

"THE ~~AUTUMN~~ POET CONSIDERS HIS RESOURCES"
~~THE AUTUMN SEA, OCTOBER SEA~~
— Ray Bradbury

The autumn sea, October sea

It tears dark seams inconstantly

And stitches clouds with rain and fire

And charcoals hearths with dead desire

And turns old souls on burning spit

Forget all good, because of it,

Because of traveling night and shrouds

Which bury moon in winding clouds

The heart is buried, blood turned ice

And all the fruit jams, teas and spice

Are pantry poisoned, forced to change

By weathers that incline to strange,

So what was health now is an ill

ANd light itself dies on the sill

And what was dead now sits upright

TO KNOCK its head on lid's midnight,

And while all cold things jump and start,

Antarctica floes in warm heart,

And tropic seas of ;blood are purged

NIGHTMARE By ~~Panics~~ iceburgs ~~until now~~ ONCE submerged

Which ^NOW raise ~~with~~ blizzard brows to seize   NOW RAISE

Sane room, sane door, sane locks, sane keys,

And ~~shake~~ SHRIEK the tumblers, ~~melt~~ WARP the walls

With ~~panic~~ PANIC -colored storms and squalls,

And all of it, both live and dead?

Trapped in circumference of ~~mere~~ MY head,

* * * *

"The Poet Considers His Resources," revised typescript

greatest success, destroying his new novel, only to reveal later that he felt he had lost his talent and needed a graceful way to retire anyway.

A second collection edited by Bradbury for Bantam, *The Circus of Dr. Lao and Other Improbable Stories*, appeared in 1956 and is notable chiefly for the title story by Charles G. Finney—a tale of a bizarre carnival that visits a small town and a clear influence on Bradbury's later novel on a similar theme, *Something Wicked This Way Comes*. The following year Bradbury's first book with no pretensions to being either science fiction or fantasy, *Dandelion Wine*, appeared. Essentially a series of sketches based on Bradbury's childhood in Waukegan, *Dandelion Wine* is distinguished primarily for its evocative style; its only real theme is that, through a series of experiences in a single summer, young Douglas Spaulding (a name compounded from Bradbury's own middle name and that of his father) comes to realize that he is alive. Although most of the contents of *Dandelion Wine* had been published previously as individual short stories and sketches, Bradbury made his greatest effort so far to create the impression of a unified book, revising the stories, writing bridge passages, and dropping individual titles and the table of contents. The result is a highly impressionistic, often moving, but essentially plotless series of episodes of value not only for their collective portrait of budding adolescence and small-town life, but also for the ways in which they reveal the sources of much of Bradbury's other fiction. While none of the new episodes are quite fantastic, many of them capture the fear and wonder of childhood that, transmogrified into the grotesque and the marvelous, provide the basis of Bradbury's science fiction and fantasy. The roots of his horror fiction, for example, can be seen in the episode originally titled "The Night" (1946), which concerns the fears of a family when a young boy is late returning at the end of a day (and which is based on Bradbury's own childhood fears of the neighborhood ravine and the "Lonely One" who reputedly lurked there). Another episode, "The Happiness Machine" (1957), presents a telling childhood view of technology in which machines can magically influence human behavior in ways not to be fully understood. The machine turns out to be more of a wish-fulfillment fantasy than a real invention, as are most of Bradbury's machines. More than any other single book, perhaps, *Dandelion Wine* consolidated Bradbury's reputation as a poet of small-town nostalgia and provided the clearest perspective to date on the essential sources of his overall vision.

By 1958 Bradbury had become one of the most

financially successful of American writers and moved his family (now with four daughters) to the Cheviot Hills address in West Los Angeles where he now lives. Deeply involved in various film projects (most of which were never produced), he began to take an increasing interest in the adaptation of his works to other media, particularly the stage. But his reputation remained essentially that of a short-story writer, and another collection, *A Medicine for Melancholy*, including stories originally published between 1948 and 1959, appeared in February 1959. With half of the twenty-two stories either fantasy or science fiction, the collection represented the largest sampling of Bradbury's fantastic writing to appear in print (except for *The October Country*) since *The Illustrated Man* in 1951. But while the collection included samples of the now familiar Martian stories ("Dark They Were, and Golden Eyed," "The Strawberry Window," 1954), horror stories ("Fever Dream," 1948), Mexican and Mexican-American stories ("The Wonderful Ice Cream Suit," 1958, "The Little Mice," 1955), and romantic views of space travel ("The End of the Beginning," 1956, "The Gift," 1952), it revealed few new directions in Bradbury's fiction. Most notable was the first appearance in book form of two stories based on Bradbury's experiences in Ireland, "The First Night of Lent" (1956) and "The Great Collision of Monday Last" (1958). Both are built around specific aspects of what he took to be the Irish character, such as their legendary drinking and their bicycle-riding habits. Two other stories in the collection later provided the basis for films: "Icarus Montgolfier Wright" (1956) for the animated short of the same title that was nominated for an Academy Award in 1963 and "In a Season of Calm Weather" (1957) for the feature *The Picasso Summer* (1972). Perhaps the most notable story in the collection, "All Summer in a Day" (1954), concerns a group of school children on a rain-soaked Venus who get their first view of the sun, which emerges only once every seven years when the clouds part.

Except for *Fahrenheit 451* Bradbury had not yet produced a truly unified, sustained work of fiction, and readers and publishers alike looked forward to a major novel, not made up of previously published stories, that would realize the narrative promise so long held out by Bradbury's short fiction. This novel turned out to be *Something Wicked This Way Comes*. A highly self-conscious work, full of allusions to such early Bradbury stories as "The Dwarf" and "The Skeleton," the novel suffers from an artificially inflated style and a barely controlled wealth of imagery and incident. Its theme—the

Ray Bradbury

struggle between the power of love and the power of evil—is handled in such a way that the main characters are reduced to symbolic archetypes. The strong point of the novel is the character of Charles Halloway—perhaps Bradbury's first true hero—whose melancholy and isolation are presented as foreshadowings of his final, lonely confrontation with the forces of evil represented by a traveling carnival.

Halloway's thirteen-year-old son Will is essentially Douglas Spaulding from *Dandelion Wine*—innocent, open, and optimistic. But Will's close friend Jim Nightshade is, as his name suggests, Will's antithesis. Warned by a traveling lightning rod salesman of an impending storm, the boys find that, instead of the storm, a mysterious carnival arrives in town in the dead of night—"Cooger and Dark's Pandemonium Shadow Show"—which features a playerless calliope that screams perverted versions of hymns and funeral marches. As in much of Bradbury's earlier fiction, the carnival represents not only present evil, but also the vulnerability of the human form and the seductive dangers of the past. Two of its main attractions, the mirror maze and the carousel, involve returning to a past self (the mirror maze shows reflections of a younger self; the carousel

runs backwards and actually makes a person younger), and its featured performers are grotesque transformations of familiar characters. (The dwarf, for example, turns out to be the lightning rod salesman from the opening scene, shrunken and deformed.) Characters undergo endless transformations: one of the show's proprietors, Mr. Dark, turns out to be the Illustrated Man; the other, Mr. Cooger, becomes a twelve-year-old boy and later a wizened old man named "Mr. Electrico" (a name taken from an actual circus performer of Bradbury's youth). Miss Foley, the local schoolteacher, becomes a wailing little girl, and both Will and Jim are threatened with being transformed into wax dummies.

Charles Halloway, who works in a library, discovers that this carnival is a continuing source of evil in the world, returning every thirty or forty years to wreak havoc on a local population, and perhaps dating back to medieval Europe or before. Cooger and Dark, aided by a balloon-riding witch, engage Halloway in a struggle for the souls of the two boys, particularly Jim's, whose dark personality naturally attracts him to this evil. In a final showdown during a performance in which the witch is to catch a bullet in her teeth, Halloway wins his victory, his ultimate weapon nothing more than the power of laughter. The carnival is vanquished, but in the closing scene Halloway explains that it will return, that it ultimately resides in each individual, and that the struggle never really ends.

Despite the occasional power generated by the sheer wealth of invention in *Something Wicked This Way Comes*, the work failed to establish Bradbury as a significant novelist, and Bradbury began to focus more and more on dramatic writing. His first collection of published plays, *The Anthem Sprinters and Other Antics*, appeared in 1963. These four comic one-act plays all draw upon Bradbury's experiences as an American innocent in Ireland and somewhat make up in language what they lack in dramatic form. All set in a mythical pub called Heeber Finn's (and with Finn a continuing character), three of the plays—"The Great Collision of Monday Last," "The First Night of Lent," and "The Anthem Sprinters"—are adaptations of previously published short stories, and all deal with the comic recalcitrance and imagination of the Irish as displayed in relatively trivial episodes such as bicycle collisions and attempts to escape movie theaters before the national anthem is played.

The Machineries of Joy appeared in 1964, containing the now predictable mix of stories dealing with Mars, Mexico, Ireland, childhood, and show business, but with little that was new or different. "The Vacation" (1963) offers an Earthbound variant on "The Million-Year Picnic," with its family abroad on an endless vacation in a depopulated United States; and "Almost the End of the World" (1957) provides a neat counter to the television-addicted world of "The Pedestrian" and *Fahrenheit 451* in a tale of sunspots wiping out all television and radio signals and forcing people to rediscover each other. With "The Drummer Boy of Shiloh" (1960) and "Perhaps We Are Going Away" (1962) Bradbury turns to historical fiction to depict worlds on the verge of imminent change, and "A Flight of Ravens" (1952) offers a more cynical view of the sophisticated literary life than the author had essayed thus far. "To the Chicago Abyss" (1963) provided the basis for one of Bradbury's more successful science-fiction plays with its depiction of a character in a postnuclear war age who goes about reminding people of life before the war.

By the mid-1960s Bradbury was devoting much of his time to drama. *The World of Ray Bradbury* opened in Los Angeles in 1964 and New York in 1965, and *The Wonderful Ice Cream Suit* opened as a musical in 1965. During this time publishers began repackaging much of Bradbury's earlier material in various forms. *R is for Rocket* (1962) and *S is for Space* (1966) consist mostly of previously anthologized stories repackaged for a teenage market, though *S is for Space* is significant for the first appearance in a Bradbury anthology of "Pillar of Fire," a 1948 story concerning a man resurrected in a future world where he finds he is the last remnant of literary culture and imagination. *Twice 22* (1966) combined in one omnibus volume *The Golden Apples of the Sun* and *A Medicine for Melancholy*; and *The Autumn People* (1965) and *Tomorrow Midnight* (1966) are collections of comic-book adaptations of Bradbury stories from the early 1950s. *The Vintage Bradbury* (1965), a representative selection by Bradbury of his own best works, established the author for the first time in a quality paperback format.

The next new collection of Bradbury's fiction did not appear until *I Sing the Body Electric!* in 1969, which followed the almost formulaic mix of stories of his previous collections. The dangers of the past are again made apparent in a number of ways. "Night Call, Collect" (1949) concerns a man alone on the deserted post-*Chronicles* Mars who is haunted by prerecorded phone calls planted by himself decades earlier. The only other Martian story in the book, "The Lost City of Mars" (1967), portrays a hidden, automated Martian city that seduces all who visit it with images drawn from their memories and

fantasies; both stories are variations on stories published earlier in *The Martian Chronicles*. Two other stories deal with robots and how they can be used to preserve the past. In "Downwind from Gettysburg" (1969) the assassination of Lincoln is reenacted by a demented man named Booth who shoots a robot Lincoln obviously modeled on the Disneyland exhibit. "I Sing the Body Electric!" (1969), is a sentimental tale of a robot grandmother who raises a motherless family. "The Haunting of the New" (1969) is about a sumptuous mansion destroyed by fire and meticulously reconstructed— only to be haunted by memories of its previous reality. The book memorizers who preserve the past in earlier Bradbury stories are transformed into a failed writer who assumes the identity of Dickens by memorizing his works in "Any Friend of Nicholas Nickleby's is a Friend of Mine" (1966).

I Sing the Body Electric! also included the first appearance in a Bradbury anthology of one of his poems, "Christus Apollo," a Christmas cantata celebrating the Apollo space program in Christian terms. Bradbury's poetry, often characterized by an inflated diction that calls to mind an uncomfortable blend of Whitman and Genesis, came to constitute an increasing amount of his creative output. His first volume of poetry, *When Elephants Last in the Dooryard Bloomed* (an obvious homage to Whitman), appeared in 1973.

During the 1970s Bradbury continued to concentrate on drama and poetry, producing relatively little new fiction. His 1976 collection *Long After Midnight* drew heavily on his earlier stories. Nearly half of the twenty-two stories collected dated from before 1955, the earliest from 1946. While the collection had the virtue of bringing back into print some of Bradbury's more unusual stories, such as the effective horror piece "The October Game" (1948) and his homage to Thomas Wolfe, "Forever and the Earth" (1950), its chief value may lie in the focus it places on a kind of Bradbury story that had long been characteristic, but infrequently collected: the story that depicts an epiphanic discovery of love between two people. "One Timeless Spring" (1946), perhaps the simplest of these stories, is a short evocation of the onset of puberty in a young boy as he first comes to realize the love he feels for a girl. A more complex story is "Interval in Sunlight" (1954), which portrays a bickering couple on vacation in Mexico who gradually come to appreciate their dependence on one another. "A Story of Love" (1976) concerns the growing mutual love of a teenage boy and his youthful teacher; "The Wish" (1973) deals with the realization a boy comes to of his love for his father.

Deeply felt and sensitively written, albeit with occasional overtones of melodrama, it is in these stories that the most basic theme of all of Bradbury's fiction becomes apparent: the power of love to make permanent a valued moment from the past, to overcome evil, or simply to provide the communicative link that draws people together in trying circumstances.

Stories such as these assure Bradbury a permanent place in the history of the American short story, just as his introduction of stylistic sophistication and metaphorical use of science-fiction concepts in the late 1940s earn him a significant place in the history of science fiction. It does not seem at this time that he will attain a comparable stature as a poet or playwright. Much of the early criticism of his science fiction for its scientific unsoundness has abated as the genre broadens its scope to make room for metaphor and poetry, but it is increasingly being replaced by a feeling on the part of many readers that Bradbury's best work remains his early work, that he no longer tests and experiments with his storytelling powers as he once did, and that he has increasingly turned away from the areas of his greatest strength in favor of forms in which he is less comfortable. At the same time, it would be unfair to expect Bradbury either to return to these earlier forms or, as his own character Dudley Stone did in "The Wonderful Death of Dudley Stone," suddenly to abandon writing altogether in the face of the too great expectations of his public. Bradbury has always been a resourceful artist, and any final conclusions about the value or direction of his later work would be premature. Of his earlier work, however, there can be little doubt: for all its eclecticism and occasional stylistic excesses—perhaps even because of these—it stands as one of the most interesting and significant bodies of short fiction in modern American literature.

Plays:

The Meadow, Hollywood, Huntington Hartford Theatre, March 1960;

Way in the Middle of the Air, Hollywood, Desilu Gower Studios, August 1962;

Yesterday, Today, and Tomorrow, Hollywood, Desilu Gower Studios, June 1963;

The World of Ray Bradbury, Hollywood, Coronet Theater, October 1964;

The Wonderful Ice Cream Suit, Hollywood, Coronet Theater, February 1965;

Dandelion Wine, New York, Lincoln Center, April 1967;

The Anthem Sprinters, Beverly Hills, Beverly Hills Playhouse, October 1967;

Any Friend of Nicholas Nickleby's is a Friend of Mine, Hollywood, Actor's Studio West, August 1968;

Christus Apollo (cantata), by Jerry Goldsmith, text by Bradbury, Los Angeles, Royce Hall, University of California, December 1969;

Leviathan '99, Hollywood, Samuel Goldwyn Studio, Stage 9 Theater, November 1972;

Madrigals for the Space Age, by Lalo Schifrin, text by Bradbury, Los Angeles, Dorothy Chandler Pavilion, February 1973;

Pillar of Fire, Fullerton, California State College, Little Theatre, December 1973.

Screenplays:

Moby Dick, by Bradbury and John Huston, Warner Brothers, 1956;

Icarus Montgolfier Wright, by Bradbury and George C. Johnson, Format Films, 1963;

An American Journey, U.S. Government, 1964;

Picasso Summer, by Bradbury and Ed Weinberger, Warner Brothers / Seven Arts, 1972.

Other:

Timeless Stories for Today and Tomorrow, edited by Bradbury (New York: Bantam, 1952);

The Circus of Dr. Lao and Other Improbable Stories, edited by Bradbury (New York: Bantam, 1956).

Periodical Publications:

FICTION:

"Hollerbochen's Dilemma," *Imagination!* (1938);

"The Piper," *Futuria Fantasia*, No. 4 (1940);

"Pendulum," *Super Science Stories*, 3 (November 1941);

"Bright Phoenix," *Magazine of Fantasy and Science Fiction*, 24 (May 1963): 23-27.

NONFICTION:

"Day After Tomorrow: Why Science Fiction," *Nation*, 176 (2 May 1953): 364-367;

"Marvels and Miracles—Pass It On!," *New York Times Magazine*, 20 March 1955, pp. 26-27, 56-57;

"The Joy of Writing," *Writer*, 69 (October 1956): 293-295;

"A Serious Search for Weird Worlds," *Life*, 49 (24 October 1960): 116-130;

"How to Keep and Feed a Muse," *Writer*, 74 (July 1961): 7-12;

"Cry the Cosmos," *Life*, 53 (14 September 1962): 86-94;

"Remembrances of Things Future," *Playboy*, 12 (January 1965): 99, 102, 191;

"The Secret Mind," *Writer*, 78 (November 1965): 13-16;

"How, Instead of Being Educated in College, I was Graduated from Libraries or Thoughts from a Chap Who Landed on the Moon in 1932," *Wilson Library Bulletin*, 45 (May 1971): 843-851;

"From Stonehenge to Tranquillity Base," *Playboy*, 19 (December 1972): 149, 322-324.

Interviews:

R. Walton Willems, "The Market is Not the Story," *Writers' Markets and Methods*, (March 1948);

Harvey Breit, "A Talk with Mr. Bradbury," *New York Times Book Review*, 5 August 1951, p. 11;

Everett T. Moore, "A Rationale for Bookburners: A Further Word from Ray Bradbury," *American Library Association Bulletin*, May 1961, pp. 403-404;

F. A. Rockwell, "Ray Bradbury Speaks of Writing as Self-Discovery," *Author and Journalist*, 47 (February 1962);

Frank Roberts, "An Exclusive Interview with Ray Bradbury," *Writer's Digest*, 47 (February 1967): 40-44, 94-96; 47 (March 1967): 41-44, 87;

Pierre Berton, "Ray Bradbury: Cassandra on a Bicycle," in *Voices from the Sixties* (Garden City: Doubleday, 1967), pp. 1-10;

Paul Turner and Dorothy Simon, "Interview with Ray Bradbury," *Vertex*, (April 1973): 24-27, 92-94;

Arnold Kunert, "Ray Bradbury: On Hitchcock and Other Magic of the Screen," *Journal of Popular Culture*, 7 (Summer 1973): 227-248;

Robert Jacobs, "The Writer's Digest Interview: Bradbury," *Writer's Digest*, 56 (February 1976): 18-25.

References:

Kingsley Amis, *New Maps of Hell* (New York: Ballantine, 1960), pp. 90-97;

Kent Forrester, "The Dangers of Being Earnest: Ray Bradbury and *The Martian Chronicles*," *Journal of General Education*, 28 (1976): 50-54;

Jose Luis Garci, *Ray Bradbury, Humanista del Futuro* (Madrid: Helios, 1971);

Martin H. Greenberg and Joseph D. Olander, eds., *Ray Bradbury* (New York: Taplinger, 1980);

David Ketterer, *New Worlds for Old: The Apocalyptic Imagination, Science Fiction, and American Literature* (Bloomington: Indiana University Press, 1974), pp. 31-34;

Damon Knight, *In Search of Wonder: Essays on Modern Science Fiction*, second edition (Chicago: Advent, 1967), pp. 108-113;

Sam Moskowitz, *Seekers of Tomorrow: Masters of Modern Science Fiction* (New York: Ballantine, 1967), pp. 351-370;

William F. Nolan, *The Ray Bradbury Companion* (Detroit: Gale Research, 1975);

Nolan, "Ray Bradbury: Prose Poet in the Age of Space," *Magazine of Fantasy and Science Fiction*, 24 (May 1963): 7-22;

Robert Reilly, "The Artistry of Ray Bradbury," *Extrapolation*, 13 (December 1971): 64-74;

Peter Sisario, "A Study of Allusions in Bradbury's *Fahrenheit 451*," *English Journal*, 59 (February 1970): 201-205;

George Edgar Slusser, *The Bradbury Chronicles* (San Bernardino, Cal.: Borgo Press, 1977);

Anita T. Sullivan, "Ray Bradbury and Fantasy," *English Journal*, 61 (December 1972): 1309-1314;

Donald J. Watt, "Hearth or Salamander: Uses of Fire in Bradbury's *Fahrenheit 451*," *Notes on Contemporary Literature*, 1 (1971): 13-14.

Papers:

A collection of Bradbury's manuscripts is located at the University Library at the University of California, Los Angeles.

MARION ZIMMER BRADLEY
(3 June 1930-   )

SELECTED BOOKS: *The Door Through Space*
(New York: Ace, 1961);

Seven from the Stars (New York: Ace, 1962);

The Planet Savers and *The Sword of Aldones* (New
York: Ace, 1962); republished separately as *The
Planet Savers* (London: G. Prior, 1979) and *The
Sword of Aldones* (London: Arrow, 1979);

The Colors of Space (New York: Monarch, 1963);

The Bloody Sun (New York: Ace, 1964; London:
Arrow, 1978);

Falcons of Narabedla and *The Dark Intruder and
Other Stories* (New York: Ace, 1964);

Star of Danger (New York: Ace, 1965; London:
Arrow, 1978);

The Brass Dragon (New York: Ace, 1969; London:
Methuen, 1978);

The Winds of Darkover (New York: Ace, 1970;
London: Arrow, 1978);

The World Wreckers (New York: Ace, 1971);

Darkover Landfall (New York: DAW, 1972; London:
Arrow, 1978);

Hunters of the Red Moon (New York: DAW, 1973);

The Spell Sword (New York: DAW, 1974; London:
Arrow, 1978);

The Heritage of Hastur (New York: DAW, 1975;
London: Arrow, 1979);

Endless Voyage (New York: Ace, 1975);

The Shattered Chain (New York: DAW, 1976;
London: Arrow, 1978);

The Forbidden Tower (New York: DAW, 1977;
London: G. Prior, 1979);

Stormqueen (New York: DAW, 1978);

The Ruins of Isis (Virginia Beach: Donning,
1978);

The Survivors, by Bradley and Paul E. Zimmer (New
York: DAW, 1979);

The Catch Trap (New York: Ballantine, 1979);

House Between the Worlds (Garden City: Doubleday, 1980);

Two to Conquer (New York: DAW, 1980);

The Keeper's Prices and Other Stories, by Bradley
and the friends of Darkover (New York: DAW,
1980).

Marion Zimmer Bradley is a prolific writer of
science fiction and fantasy. Born in Albany, New
York, she attended New York State College for
Teachers from 1946 to 1948 and Hardin-Simmons
College, where she took a B.A. in 1964. She has also
done graduate work at the University of California at

Berkeley. In 1949 she married R. A. Bradley. After
their divorce in 1964, she married Walter Breen. She
has one child by her first husband and two by her
second. Bradley has been actively involved in science
fiction since adolescence, first as a fervent fan and
then, gradually, as an author. Though she began
publishing short stories in 1953, she did not begin
writing professionally until the early 1960s. Early
stylistic influences were Henry Kuttner, Theodore
Sturgeon, Catherine L. Moore, and Jack Vance.
From the beginning her works were reviewed,
usually with favor, by the science-fiction press, but it
was not until the 1970s that she began to receive
attention from outside that narrow critical sphere.
Since then she has been widely recognized as a
capable and imaginative writer.

Although she has received neither of the two
major science-fiction awards, she was nominated for
the Nebula Award in 1964 for *The Sword of Aldones*
(1962) and in 1978 for *The Forbidden Tower* (1977).
Her works have sold well, but a self-imposed
limitation to the paperback format and to primarily
one publisher has until recently made them
inaccessible to a large audience. The fact that Gregg
Press has, since 1977, begun to reissue her books in
hardback attests to an increasing popularity and
marketability. Many Bradley novels have been
published in England as well, primarily under the
Arrow imprint. Her productivity has steadily
increased in the last few years, and the interest in the
Darkover series has become almost a cult phenomenon.

Two major themes may be identified in
Bradley's works. The first is the reconciliation of
conflicting or opposing forces—whether such forces are
represented by different cultures or by different facets of
a single personality. The second, closely related to the
first, is alienation or exile from a dominant group.
These features are readily seen in Bradley's Darkover
novels, a loosely connected series dealing with the
perpetual opposition between the citizens of the Terran
Empire and those of the planet Darkover. The Darkover
books were not, however, written in the order that their
own gradually emerging internal chronology would
seem to dictate. It was not, in fact, the author's original
design to construct a series; each novel was written as a
self-contained work.

The Sword of Aldones, the first Darkover novel,
introduces Lew Alton, the most classically alienated of
all Bradley heroes. A Darkovan on his father's side and a
Terran on his mother's, he is a metaphor for the uneasy
union between the two cultures. A hideous facial scar
and the loss of one hand, tokens of previous discord on
Darkover, are both the symbol and the cause of his

Marion Zimmer Bradley

isolation. Central to the novel is the friction between Alton and a renegade, Kadarin, who has unleashed the unutterably destructive power of the starstone weapon Sharra. Alton is urgently recalled to Darkover by the Regent of the Comyn, Darkover's aristocratic governing body, to quell that power. With Alton in command the Comyn forces are triumphant and Sharra is destroyed. Alton is still not reconciled to life on Darkover, however. He abhors the violence of the planet and the Darkovans' growing tendency to embrace Terran technology. Moreover he cannot love a world which has never accepted him. The end of the novel finds him en route to some other planet. *The Sword of Aldones* is unlike other Bradley novels in that no permanent reconciliation occurs between the protagonist and that which he opposes. Although the plot tends to be disconnected and the pace frenetic, the depth of characterization and the degree of suspense that Bradley achieves make *The Sword of Aldones* ultimately a successful novel.

In the character of Jason Allison, protagonist of *The Planet Savers* (1962), Bradley's two major themes are intertwined. Opposing forces in the novel are represented by the two opposing selves of Allison, who suffers from a dissociative personality disorder. Jason's dominant personality is cold and

introverted. Jay, his subordinate self, is adventurous, willful, warm, and generous. Neither self is entirely satisfactory. It is the Jay part of Jason who succeeds in procuring a serum for Trailmen's fever, an epidemic which had threatened to decimate the Darkovan population. Finally Jason's two personalities become integrated. The successful joining of his two selves is followed by another union, a romantic one between Jason and Free Amazon Kyla Raineách.

The relationship between two adolescent boys provides the context for Darkovan/Terran conflict and reconciliation in *Star of Danger* (1965). Larry Mantray, son of a Terran Empire civil servant, and Kennard Alton, son of a Comyn lord, become friends in spite of their fathers' misgivings. En route to the Alton country estate, Larry and the Altons discuss the difference between Darkovan reliance on the self and the Terran idea of community purpose and a society based on rules and laws. The antitechnological, antibureaucratic Darkovans are spared untold destruction when Larry's knowledge of cloudseeding techniques, in combination with Darkovan telekinesis, subdues an immense forest fire. The theme of complementarity is explored further when Larry is rescued from kidnappers by Kennard. As they head for safety they use both Darkovan and Terran knowledge to overcome the several obstacles they encounter. Near the end they learn that it was the Terrans who first settled on Darkover; from that settlement came the succeeding generations, the self-styled "natives" of Darkover.

Another Terran comes to the aid of Darkovans in *The Winds of Darkover* (1970) but not, this time, by choice. Storn, the rightful lord of Storn Castle, seeks redress for the appropriation of his household by Brynat Scarface. Storn, who is blind, takes over the mind of Earthman Dan Barron. With his mind controlling Barron's physical strength, Storn and his sister Melitta seek help from kinsmen. Even though the telepathic bond that has made it possible for Storn to control Barron is broken, Barron becomes committed to saving Storn Castle. He also falls in love with Melitta. Having felt himself a misfit on Earth, he finds a niche on Darkover and looks forward to the future with Melitta in "this curiously divided world." Thus one more alienated hero achieves fulfillment; one more union is made between Darkover and Terra.

The events leading up to the settlement of Darkover are narrated in *Darkover Landfall* (1972), set in the twenty-first century. The characters are members of an Earth expeditionary force and the crew of the spaceship that is transporting them. Marooned on a strange planet, they begin to organize in two opposing factions represented by Leicester, captain of the ship, and Moray, chief of the colonizers. Leicester argues for reconstructing the ship and returning home. Moray argues for abandoning that futile attempt and founding an agrarian, nontechnological settlement on Darkover. Thus the conflict between technology and its antithesis, the conflict which dominates all relations between Terra and Darkover, is given a historical background. *Darkover Landfall* is less a work of science fiction than it is a conventional novel with an extraterrestrial setting. Few traditional science-fiction elements are employed. There are no identity switches, horrific creatures, battles between human beings and aliens, or time warps, few parapsychological elements, and little suspense. Greater emphasis is placed on the psychological workings of the characters than is usually found in Bradley's works.

In Bradley's next novel, *The Spell Sword* (1974), the Darkovan lady Callista is rescued from savage catmen by Earthman Andrew Carr. Surprisingly Carr possesses telepathic powers identical to those of Comyn men and women. Eventually he resolves to join his future with Callista's and, like Dan Barron

in *The Winds of Darkover*, to make his place among the Darkovans. In *The Heritage of Hastur* (1975) Lew Alton reappears. The events of the story, however, antedate those in *The Sword of Aldones*. Both Alton and fellow protagonist Regis Hastur feel somewhat alienated from Darkover, Alton because of his mixed parentage and Hastur because he apparently lacks telepathic powers and so feels unfit for leadership. Hastur gradually discovers his telepathic powers and decides to assume his responsibility as Regent-heir to the Comyn Council. Alton, on the other hand, horribly injured and embittered, vows to leave Darkover forever.

It is not the conflict between Darkover and the Terran Empire that Bradley investigates in *The Shattered Chain* (1976) but that between men and women. In this novel three women from widely different backgrounds come to terms with their own lives and set about realizing their potential as women equal to, and not in opposition with, men. There is the necessary admixture of Darkovan and Terran characters, although the terms of conflict are sexual and not cultural. Typically for a Bradley novel, a marriage between a Terran man and a Darkovan woman closes the work. In *The Shattered Chain* Bradley begins consciously to work out some of the issues raised by the feminist movement. The theme of women's equality, which is central also to *The Ruins of Isis* (1978), becomes an increasingly important element in her work.

Stormqueen (1978) depicts life on Darkover before the arrival of the Terrans and before the establishment of the code which forbids use of any weapon capable of widespread destruction. The lack of personal freedom for both men and women in an autocratic, strife-ridden world is the dominant theme of the novel. By combining both masculine and feminine traits in each of the principal figures, Bradley creates more fully realized characters than ever before.

Not all of Bradley's work has been part of the Darkover series, but the reader who is acquainted with the thematic concerns of the Darkover books is well equipped to encounter the other fiction. Her first novel, for example, *The Door Through Space* (1961), is set on the planet Wolf, which in all particulars, including its resistance to the Terran Empire, is identical to the planet Darkover. Like Lew Alton, Cargill, the hero of this novel, is badly scarred, disaffected, and anxious to begin another life on another planet. Summoned by the chief of the secret service, Cargill stays on Wolf to help locate his missing niece. In the process he quashes a scheme by which control of the planet Wolf would have been turned over to evil forces. A reconciliation occurs between Cargill and his archenemy and brother-in-law, Rakhal Sensar. Ultimately Cargill decides to remain on Wolf; his story, in effect, is Lew Alton's with a happy ending.

Published twenty years after it was written, *Falcons of Narabedla* (1964) is juvenilia now disclaimed by the author; its central concern—one person's mind inhabiting another's body—was later handled more successfully in *The Winds of Darkover*. *Hunters of the Red Moon* (1973), on the other hand, is one of the most compelling of Bradley's novels. Five people are kidnapped and become the prey in a ritual hunt on an alien world. Of the few who have survived the hunt, not one has ever seen the Hunters. The Hunt, then, is a desperate struggle against absolutely unknown forces. Each of the principal characters represents a positive human trait. Alone, none could survive. Together, complementing each other, they are nearly indomitable. In Aratak, the philosophical "protosaurian" who quotes fluently and often humorously from the divine egg, Bradley has created her most memorable character.

Not a single person but a whole race—the Explorers—suffers from alienation in *Endless Voyage* (1975). The Explorers are a group, distinct from planetmen, whose destiny is to open up new worlds for colonization. Bleached white by years of radiation contact, their difference from other human beings is dramatically apparent. Because they cannot breed among themselves, they must buy babies for fosterage. For this "baby stealing" they are universally reviled. Even when the occasional emotional link is made between a planet person and an Explorer, it cannot be sustained because the nature of Explorer work dictates dissociation from places and people. Their anomie is heightened when newly discovered territory proves uninhabitable, and their ranks are depleted. Resolution comes when they find a planet that accepts them and that they can use henceforth as home base.

Aratak, Dane Marsh, and Rianna from *Hunters of the Red Moon* are also the principal characters of *The Survivors* (1979). Assigned to investigate mysterious happenings on Belsar, they discover an ancient race of protosaurians who, having survived one nuclear holocaust, live underground in a highly developed, zealously separatist and pacific society. Above ground a separate culture exists, rife with superstition and ignorance. Dane, Rianna, and Aratak are catalysts for what promises to be fruitful future contact between the two cultures. Aratak remains on Belsar to help achieve harmony between the two groups. Joda, a young Belsar native who has been hopelessly out of step with his own world, joins Rianna and Dane on their return home.

In many of these later works Bradley has shown a tendency to more careful delineation of character, greater attention to human relationships, particularly those between men and women, and more logical plot progression. Though her interest in women's rights is strong, her works do not reduce to mere polemic. If popularity were an index of caliber, her stature would be undeniable. It seems likely that the apparent neglect shown her works by many science-fiction scholars will be short-lived.

—*Laura Murphy*

Other:

"Experiment Perilous: The Art and Science in Science Fiction," *Algol* No. 19 (November 1972);

Men, Haflings, and Hero Worship (Baltimore: T-K Graphics, 1973);

The Necessity for Beauty: Robert W. Chambers and the Romantic Tradition (Baltimore: T-K Graphics, 1974).

References:

Walter Breen, *The Gemini Problem: A Study in Darkover* (Baltimore: T-K Graphics, 1976);

Linda Leith, "Marion Zimmer Bradley and Darkover," *Science-Fiction Studies*, 7 (March 1980): 28-35;

S. Wise, *The Darkover Dilemma: Problems of the Darkover Series* (Baltimore: T-K Graphics, 1976).

FREDRIC BROWN
(29 October 1906-11 March 1972)

SELECTED BOOKS: *What Mad Universe* (New York: Dutton, 1949; London: Boardman, 1951);

Space on My Hands (Chicago: Shasta, 1951; London: Corgi, 1953);

The Lights in the Sky Are Stars (New York: Dutton, 1953); republished as *Project Jupiter* (London: Boardman, 1954);

Angels and Spaceships (New York: Dutton, 1954; London: Gollancz, 1955); republished as *Star Shine* (New York: Bantam, 1956);

Martians, Go Home (New York: Dutton, 1955);

Rogue in Space (New York: Dutton, 1957);

Honeymoon in Hell (New York: Bantam, 1958; London: Bantam, 1965);

The Mind Thing (New York: Bantam, 1961; London: Transworld, 1961);

Nightmares and Geezenstacks (New York: Bantam, 1961; London: Corgi, 1962);

Daymares (New York: Lancer, 1968);

Paradox Lost (New York: Random House, 1973; London: Hale, 1975);

The Best of Fredric Brown, ed. Robert Bloch (Garden City: Doubleday, 1976; London: Futura, 1977).

Fredric Brown was one of the most versatile writers of science fiction, producing more than one hundred short stories and five novels, in addition to a large body of detective fiction. Fellow writers mention him with respect and affection, remembering the inventiveness of his plots and the humor he displayed in person as well as in his works.

Born in Cincinnati, Fredric William Brown spent a year at Hanover College in Indiana and another year at the University of Cincinnati. In 1929 he married Helen Ruth, by whom he had two sons. In 1936, after some years as an office worker, he began a career in journalism by becoming a proofreader for the *Milwaukee Journal*. Several of his early works reflect his knowledge of the printing industry. He began writing science fiction in 1941, and in 1947, after a divorce, he became a full-time writer. The following year he married Elizabeth Charlier. For health reasons he moved to Taos, New Mexico, and then to California, where he worked briefly and unsuccessfully on screenplays for Hollywood producers. Brown eventually settled in Tucson, Arizona, where he died in 1972. His last collection, *Paradox Lost* (1973), was published posthumously. In 1976, Robert Bloch edited a retrospective volume, *The Best of Fredric Brown*.

Using many of the conventions of science fiction, including bug-eyed monsters, time-travel, and alternate worlds, Brown created situations in which he could probe human foibles with a humorous or ironic twist. His progress as a writer of short stories reflects the development of science fiction over three decades, from the early 1940s to the late 1960s, from space opera through dystopia to absurdist fantasies. Brown's novels show a similar progression, from the satire of *What Mad Universe* (1949) to the horror of *The Mind Thing* (1961), but they are usually more conventional and less intense than his short stories and vignettes.

Although the point of a typical Brown story sometimes seems to be a simple joke, often the works are more complex. While a reader may find that the bewildering array of Brown's plots resists easy categorization, he often finds a fascination with the workings of the human mind under stress, serious or playful considerations of the question "what is reality," romantic wish fulfillment, and (especially in the later work) exploitation of the absurd for effects of black humor and horror. Yet even in the latter period of his work when horror and the absurd predominate, Brown continued to produce light humor in such stories as "Cartoonist" (a 1961 collaboration with Mack Reynolds; collected in *Nightmares and Geezenstacks*, 1961) and "Puppet Show" (1962; collected in *Paradox Lost*).

Brown's protagonists, who are seldom figures of eminence or power, tend to triumph through sheer plodding. Thus the physical strength of the outlaw Crag in *Rogue in Space* (1957) is as rare as the mental prowess of Doc Staunton, who brilliantly solves the mystery posed by the alien in *The Mind Thing*. A small, bright-eyed man fond of beer and poker, Staunton resembles Brown himself. Though Brown did most of his work in the period when science fiction was being criticized for weakness of characterization, his interest in the human psyche produced convincing portraits, especially in his novels and in those short stories dealing with the mind and its perception of reality. Brown succeeded in imparting personality even to inanimate objects such as game pieces and ball bearings, but most notably to the linotype machine in "Etaoin Shrdlu" (1942). The machine, a substitute for the usual bug-eyed monster, is defeated only by being converted to Buddhism and achieving nirvana.

Among the best of Brown's early stories, "Etaoin Shrdlu" is collected in *Angels and Spaceships* (1954), along with "Placet is a Crazy Place" (1946), a love story set on a planet whose orbit in a binary system causes multiple perceptual aberrations. Other notable stories from Brown's early period are "Arena" (1944; collected in *Honeymoon in Hell*, 1958) and "Come and Go Mad" (1949; collected in *Space on My Hands*, 1951). In the former, a simple, compassionate human is pitted against a vicious alien to decide a war. The latter is based on the premise that one may not be able to face truth and remain sane.

Brown's approach to mind, reality, and madness is simple: reality is outside human control, and the mind has a limited tolerance for incongruity. Presented with a reality that is too strange or too painful, the mind retreats. "Come and Go Mad" is the most serious of Brown's tales using the reality-madness theme. Napoleon Bonaparte, translated to modern times in the guise of George Vine, conceals the truth about himself by pretending to be an amnesiac, but he is troubled by the phrase "the brightly shining," which keeps cropping up in his mind. Eventually he discovers that the Earth is sentient and that "the Brightly Shining" is the name of Earth's intelligence. The revelation of the true status of man on such a world drives him to madness—which ironically takes the form of his becoming convinced that he really *is* George Vine, instead of Napoleon Bonaparte. Only thus is the truth concealed by the entities that rule the Earth and the other sentient worlds. Brown returns to this theme in other works, such as *Martians, Go Home* (1955), but nowhere with the clarity and balance of "Come and Go Mad."

What Mad Universe, Brown's first science-fiction novel and one of his most popular works, is an extended parody of space opera. Keith Winton, editor of a pulp science-fiction magazine, is blasted into a parallel world that is the replica of one in a science-fiction tale conceived by one of the magazine's adolescent enthusiasts. The world is real, nevertheless, and he must eventually act out a heroic role before being returned to his own world. *What Mad Universe* transforms parody into satire, since Winton gradually realizes that he is himself responsible for his presence in the new universe, which actually represents *his* conception of the fantastic world a reader would invent. Thus, the new world stands as a criticism of his prejudices: if it is improbable, the improbabilities are his alone. Brown provides further irony in Winton's minor alteration of the world into which he returns, for he comes back not as an editor but as the owner of a chain of popular publications.

The 1950s represent a rich and diverse phase for Brown. In this period he wrote *The Lights in the Sky Are Stars* (1953; republished as *Project Jupiter*, 1954), which best represents all of his qualities as an author: the probing of motivation, concealed hints of the true story, and the depiction of human love, determination, and belief in the stars as man's destiny. Max Andrews, a rocket mechanic and former space cadet, passionately wants to reach the stars despite the handicap that disqualifies him for space duty. He manipulates his way into a position of power as director of the Jupiter project but loses his chance to pilot the rocket. His failure comes as a surprise to the reader, but upon reconsideration, it becomes clear that here, more than any other place in Brown's science fiction, the hand of the mystery writer is most evident. Andrews's motives are all-

important, and subtle hints, provided by characterization, render the climax not a gratuitous alteration of circumstances, but the true and proper result of what has gone before.

Martians, Go Home, another novel of this period, is a parody of the tale of the menace from beyond and a variation on the reality-madness theme. Brown's Martians are not the malevolent, maleficent creatures of H.G. Wells's work, but are impudent, contemptuous nuisances who delight in practical jokes, such as swimming in people's soup, and verbal abuse. For the writer Luke Devereaux, they become an obstacle to sanity. He retreats into catatonia and then turns to solipsism as his only defense against the invaders: "if the universe and everything and everybody in it were simply figments of [his] imagination," then he had invented the Martians and they were not real. Brown's point is that absurdity can be just as dangerous as outright violence. Part of the absurdity of this invasion comes from the absence of any reason for the Martians' presence and the assortment of possible reasons for their departure, ranging from Luke's solipsistic efforts to uninvent the Martians to the juju of an African witch doctor. Although Brown sustains the comic tension between serious form and ridiculous content that is the heart of this parody, the disparity between Devereaux's distress and the silliness of the

Fredric Brown

Martians is an unresolved weakness in the novel.

The last ten years of Brown's work in science fiction are dominated by absurdist fantasies and gothic horror. Typical, though not the most powerful expression of this literary trend, is *The Mind Thing*, his only novel of this period. *The Mind Thing* is the tale of an exiled alien who can assume mental control of any entity, but who can be freed only by the host's death, generally suicide. The mind thing is totally emotionless and amoral; its desire to return home with news of a new planet of hosts is pragmatic, not malicious. Despite the creature's repellent deeds, Brown's impassive narration avoids mere sensationalism. Although it is nearly impossible to sympathize with the mind thing, the reader is compelled to recognize it as a rational being with its own instincts for self-preservation. Within the novel the focus on the mind thing is so exclusive that the human figures are almost caricatures.

In the 1960s Brown for the most part exploited the horrific potential of the commonplace. Notable in this series are the tales collected in *Nightmares and Geezenstacks*, especially "Nightmare in Gray" (1961), a moving vignette of the psychological frailties of old age. "The House" (1960) is more deeply absurdist: a man roams through a house which, with its inescapable, reserved rooms, is reminiscent of the grave. The reader is never sure whether the man has died; the horror of the story comes from its subtle imagery of being buried alive.

The absurdist trend continues in "It Didn't Happen" (1963; collected in *Paradox Lost*), one of the last of Brown's stories. Lorenz Kane, the caddish protagonist of this play on solipsism, accidentally discovers the unreality of most of the human race and takes this as a license for murder. There is, however, an agency that guards reality, and these "real-estate" agents remove him from the file of real people, eliminating him and obliterating his deeds. Puns and solipsism are hallmarks of Brown's science fiction, but "It Didn't Happen" is an effective character study as well, with its subtle presentation of the moneyed, self-indulgent Kane.

There is inevitably repetition in so extensive a canon as Brown's, but each return to a favorite theme takes a fresh approach. One must look to the best of Brown's short fiction for evidence of his development as a writer; there, not in the relative consistency of his novels, one finds intensity, psychological perception, and a true grasp of the fantasic mode with a leavening of humor. —*Amelia A. Rutledge*

Other:

Science Fiction Carnival, edited by Brown and Mack Reynolds (Chicago: Shasta, 1953).

References:

Robert Bloch, "A Brown Study," in his *The Best of Fredric Brown* (Garden City: Doubleday, 1976; London: Futura, 1977);
Philip Klass, Introduction to *What Mad Universe* (New York: Dutton, 1949).

A. J. BUDRYS
(9 January 1931-   )

BOOKS: *False Night* (New York: Lion Books, 1954); expanded as *Some Will Not Die* (Evanston, Ill.: Regency, 1961; London: Mayflower, 1964);
Man of Earth (New York: Ballantine, 1958);
Who? (New York: Pyramid, 1958; London: Gollancz, 1962);
The Falling Torch (New York: Pyramid, 1959);
Rogue Moon (Greenwich, Conn.: Fawcett, 1960; London: Muller, 1962);
The Unexpected Dimension (New York: Ballantine, 1960; London: Gollancz, 1962);
Budrys' Inferno (New York: Berkley, 1963); republished as *The Furious Future* (London: Gollancz, 1964);

The Amsirs and the Iron Thorn (Greenwich, Conn.: Fawcett, 1967); republished as *The Iron Thorn* (London: Gollancz, 1968);
Michaelmas (New York: Berkley, 1977; London: Gollancz, 1977);
Blood and Burning (New York: Berkley, 1978);
The Life Machine (New York: Berkley, 1979).

In a little over twenty-five years, A. J. Budrys has produced eight novels, over one hundred short stories under eight known pen names (including "Algis"), and three collections of selected stories. He has been praised by Poul Anderson as "one of our best" science-fiction authors, even though, oddly enough, he has never been honored with either the Hugo or Nebula award. Budrys's major work is characterized by an international flavor, the result of

A. J. Budrys

the author's European background. The son of Jonas and Regina Kashuba Budrys, he was born in Königsberg, East Prussia, in a time that was to witness the rise of Adolf Hitler, a man whom Budrys was later to call the "great maniac." Budrys's family fled Nazism, and the young man spent the war years in what was supposed to be temporary exile. His father was the United States representative of the Lithuanian government-in-exile, a situation similar to the galling exiles-from-Earth story dramatized in *The Falling Torch* (1959). Unfortunately, after the war part of East Prussia was absorbed by Russia, and Königsberg became Kaliningrad. Budrys's homeland was lost. The question of one's proper identity and the means by which one might cope with an intolerable situation became major themes in his work.

Budrys attended the University of Miami from 1947 to 1949 and Columbia University from 1951 to 1952, with a year as an investigations clerk for American Express in between. In 1952 he became assistant editor at Gnome Press, and in 1953 he moved to *Galaxy* in the same capacity. He was married to Edna F. Duna, with whom he would have four sons, on 24 July 1954, the year he began a stint of free-lancing that lasted until 1957. He returned to editing in 1958 and worked for Royal Publications

for three years. From 1961 to 1963 he was editor-in-chief at Regency Books, after which he became editorial director at Playboy Press.

Budrys is a master of the dramatic realization of theme and the use of scientific detail. More important, he creates worlds of subtle psychological conflict in which individuals are caught in problems of identity and the traumas of growth and change. *Who?* (1958) typifies this approach in his early fiction. In an undesignated near future, the East and the West are locked in familiar camps of tension and hostility. There are security forces, shrewd secret agents on both sides, and top-secret projects to be protected. In short, all the elements of an international spy thriller are present.

But *Who?* is different in a way that is symptomatic of Budrys's approach to science fiction. Lucas Martino, a top Western scientist, is the survivor of an explosion. He lands, barely alive, in enemy hands and is rebuilt into something more metal than human. He is not a "bionic man," nor is he superhuman. He is a man whose identity has been lost, a man so altered in the process of rebuilding that when he is returned to the West, it is impossible for anyone to tell if he is the real Martino, a brainwashed Martino, or an enemy operative pretending to be Martino. There is cold-war rhetoric in *Who?*, but there is also concern for the psychological impact of such a change on the man who is something new, both physically and mentally. The physical and psychological changes are, however, mirror opposites. While he remains a physical freak, at the end of the novel Martino is, paradoxically, more of a man than he had ever been. As a youth, he had been intellectually brilliant but emotionally sterile. As a result of his new body and the fear and loathing it causes in others, Martino becomes, psychologically, someone else. In response to the question "Are you the *real* Lucas Martino?"—a question put to him for years by baffled Western security men—Martino finally answers no. But the reader later learns that he is Martino and that the Russians had been unable either to brainwash him or place a substitute for him inside a metal disguise. Martino's denial of his old identity is indicative of the real change.

In *The Falling Torch*, using the props of "ultradrive" and galactic colonization, Budrys sets up another psychological drama surrounding the recapture of the mother planet Earth after its seizure by Invaders ('Vaders). In the twenty-fifth century, Michael Wireman, the young son of Earth's last president before the fall, returns secretly to Earth on a seemingly hopeless mission to free Earthmen. Like Lucas Martino, Wireman finds himself caught between two forces—the polished, military Invaders and the commercial, expansion-minded Centaurians, descendants of Earth pioneers. Neither can figure him out or predict what he will do. And both offer Wireman something attractive, posing a dilemma for him which thickens the plot.

But *The Falling Torch* is also the story of a boy trying to grow up. Through strife and experience, his uncertainty, vain hopes, and personal doubts are transformed by Wireman into a mature knowledge of human relationships. His particular insight is that men are all alike. He assumes the burden of living realistically, accepting himself for what he is, and eschewing the grandiose role of a great man. He can lead others successfully only after he recognizes that "treachery is as much a part of the human soul as faith. And . . . [a man] must learn to live with that, and that's all." Wireman frees Earth and does what he can for others because he can now "see them as they are"; that is, like him, they can be alternately weak and strong, good and evil, and cynical and hopeful. It is a realistic appraisal of human nature.

In *The Falling Torch* there are also traces of Budrys's attempts to rise above the merely businesslike prose usually found in science fiction. For example, at the end of the novel the former president of Earth returns to cheer his son's victory. He wonders at the

irony of his having a still active mind in a frail body: "Is that why . . . the old are so outwardly stolid . . . because if they permitted themselves to express the storm of their feelings, they would shake their frail bodies apart?"

Budrys has never been good at choosing captivating titles for his novels. *Rogue Moon* (1960), for example, is distinguished by a quality of craftsmanship and ideas one would hardly expect from a book so titled. In this novel, to account for an alien formation found on the moon, one man must systematically have killed or driven mad a number of other men. The agony this might afford the man in charge is skillfully drawn. The theme and conflict are good ones: something strange is found on the moon. What is it? Who left it there? What will have to be done to find out? What does it all mean? As the protagonist, Edward Hawks, comments on the problems involved, he also suggests the problem science fiction faces: "We have to make a new language for describing [the alien thing], and a new way of thinking in order to be able to understand it." Creating a new language and a new way of thinking is not easy.

In *Rogue Moon* Budrys tries to set up at least a new way of thinking about problems that could arise. He shows that he knows how to handle the science of science fiction. He uses just enough technical knowledge, just enough hardware, to make the reader believe that what transpires could conceivably transpire, but not enough to lose his interest in the novel's narrative flow. Hawks, one of the many brilliant scientists who people science fiction, discusses in some detail how a man can die and be resurrected. The reader learns the basic nature of Hawks's matter-duplicating machine, how a man is prepared for entry into it, how it works, what the result will be, and how it will affect the men involved. This kind of balanced storytelling— utilizing action, suspense, science, and philosophy— is of course vital to all good science fiction. In terms of philosophy, *Rogue Moon* is central for under- standing Budrys's work. In it he dramatizes his belief that man exists without prior knowledge or supernatural sanction, and that this puts a burden of self-determination on man. Hawks comments that a man's "brain is only a complex of stored memories. There is no other mind like it. In a sense, a man is his own creation."

The odd formation in *Rogue Moon* has been on the moon for over a million years; it anticipates the later, better-known alien objects of Arthur C. Clarke's *2001: A Space Odyssey* (1968) or his *Rendezvous with Rama* (1973). With Budrys's object a man can enter at one point and be killed in many different ways, depending on the route taken. To find the proper route, to go successfully from beginning to end, requires the same man to die repeatedly and so learn from his mistakes. The resurrections are accomplished through Hawks's matter-reproduction machine coupled with a proper sender on the Earth and a receiver on the moon. Copies of the man are made; one is kept safely on Earth, the other is sent to the alien labyrinth. The result is a captivating map of bloody horror leading to self-knowledge.

The alien structure is itself a metaphor for what Budrys calls the "undisguised face of the unknown universe" that has "resources of death which we have barely begun to pick at." In a universe like that, it is necessary to explore all the resources of both life and death. In a relatively optimistic conclusion Hawks comes to believe that death will be conquered: "Some day I, or another man, will hold [death] in his hand." Hawks knows what it is like to die, to enter into the vexing ambiguities of radical change, and to be resurrected as something else.

There is a ten-year gap between the story of a man who tries to find his rightful heritage on Mars, *The Amsirs and the Iron Thorn* (1967), and the publication of *Michaelmas* (1977). It is almost as if Budrys felt compelled to bypass completely the years of the much-publicized New Wave science fiction of the late 1960s and early 1970s, or preferred to write critical assessments of the genre. But whatever the reason for the silence, *Michaelmas* broke it. It has been hailed as a triumphant return for Budrys, and the basic Budrys techniques are all there: the well-laid plot, the narrative hooks, the intelligent dialogue, the interesting characters, the still straightforward, if more interesting, prose.

What is new, and topical, is the way in which his concern with the search for identity is handled. In *Michaelmas* Budrys displays a firm grasp of both the jargon and the implications of the mass media and the variety of ways they can govern reality. At one point Laurent Michaelmas ("Mikkelmoss"), a popular newsman who is also a benevolent manipulator and force for good in the uncertain forum of human affairs, remarks on the necessity of his own existence: "What accounts for the steady exposure of conniving politicians, for increasingly rational social planning, and reasonably effective execution of the plans? I *must* exist!" In effect Michaelmas and his trusty computer sidekick, Domino, rule the world.

The plot of *Michaelmas* revolves around a

possible counter to such rational planning, a possibly evil, irrational force at work against the two. And indeed there is. An alien, a "Fermierla," has made contact with Earthmen who wish to be manipulators themselves. The alien must use a "probability coherence device" to communicate since it believes that the men it talks to are only "chance occurrences" or "demonstration" models, something created by its own desire to prove that within an infinity of time and space anything is possible. The alien can duplicate anything if it is suitably described. It creates world tensions by resurrecting an astronaut thought dead. Since the seating on an upcoming space shot is consequently imperiled and the true nature of the astronaut is in some question, Michaelmas, the man who is in oblique control of mankind, sets out to discover the truth of things. The Fermierla is strong enough to be a match for Michaelmas and Domino; but Michaelmas wins alone, and he does so in the way heroes have typically defeated their foes: through guile, cunning, and a good aim. It seems appropriate, given Budrys's major theme, that the threat to Earth is extinguished after Michaelmas comes literally face to face with himself—or rather with an inchoate version of himself, for the alien has nearly succeeded in twinning him. The real Michaelmas knows himself, however, and the world is saved for rational planning. A hint of the dystopian aspects of media manipulation—however benevolent—comes from Domino when it wonders "what the world might be like when a completely even tenor had settled over all its policies, and there was nothing left for the news to talk about but the incessant, persistent, perhaps rising sound of individual people demanding to assert their existence."

Budrys believes that very good science-fiction writers are those who set trends. In reading through the best of Budrys's work and recognizing ideas and themes that seem to have been used even by those in the so-called New Wave—for example, the exploration of psychological "inner space" in science-fiction terms—one can understand the basis of Poul Anderson's admiration. In the hope that he will continue to live up to his own standards, readers should give careful attention to A. J. Budrys's work in the years to come. —*William C. Barnwell*

Papers:

The Spencer Library, University of Kansas, has a hand-corrected typed draft of *Who?*

EDGAR RICE BURROUGHS
(1 September 1875-19 March 1950)

SELECTED BOOKS: *Tarzan of the Apes* (Chicago: McClurg, 1914; London: Methuen, 1917);

The Return of Tarzan (Chicago: McClurg, 1915; London: Cazenove, 1915);

The Beasts of Tarzan (Chicago: McClurg, 1916; London: Cazenove, 1916);

The Son of Tarzan (Chicago: McClurg, 1917; London: Methuen, 1919);

A Princess of Mars (Chicago: McClurg, 1917; London: Methuen, 1919);

Tarzan and the Jewels of Opar (Chicago: McClurg, 1918; London: Methuen, 1919);

The Gods of Mars (Chicago: McClurg, 1918; London: Methuen, 1920);

Jungle Tales of Tarzan (Chicago: McClurg, 1919; London: Methuen, 1919);

The Warlord of Mars (Chicago: McClurg, 1919; London: Methuen, 1920);

Tarzan the Untamed (Chicago: McClurg, 1920; London: Methuen, 1920);

Thuvia, Maid of Mars (Chicago: McClurg, 1920; London: Methuen, 1921);

Tarzan the Terrible (Chicago: McClurg, 1921; London: Methuen, 1921);

At the Earth's Core (Chicago: McClurg, 1922; London: Methuen, 1923);

The Chessmen of Mars (Chicago: McClurg, 1922; London: Methuen, 1923);

Tarzan and the Golden Lion (Chicago: McClurg, 1923; London: Methuen, 1924);

Pellucidar (Chicago: McClurg, 1923; London: Methuen, 1924);

The Land that Time Forgot (Chicago: McClurg, 1924; London: Methuen, 1925); republished in three volumes as *The Land that Time Forgot, The People that Time Forgot,* and *Out of Time's Abyss* (New York: Ace, 1963);

Tarzan and the Ant Men (Chicago & London: McClurg, 1924);

The Cave Girl (Chicago: McClurg, 1925; London: Methuen, 1927);

The Eternal Lover (Chicago: McClurg, 1925; London: Methuen, 1927);

The Moon Maid (Chicago: McClurg, 1926);

The Tarzan Twins (Joliet, Ill. & New York: Volland, 1927; London & Glasgow: Collins, 1930);

The Master Mind of Mars (Chicago: McClurg, 1928; London: Methuen, 1939);

Tarzan, Lord of the Jungle (Chicago: McClurg, 1928; London: Cassell, 1928);

Tarzan and the Lost Empire (New York: Metropolitan, 1929; London: Cassell, 1931);

Tanar of Pellucidar (New York: Metropolitan, 1930; London: Methuen, 1939);

Tarzan at the Earth's Core (New York: Metropolitan, 1930; London: Methuen, 1938);

Tarzan the Invincible (Tarzana, Cal.: Burroughs, 1931; London: John Lane, 1933);

A Fighting Man of Mars (New York: Metropolitan, 1931; London: John Lane, 1932);

Jungle Girl (Tarzana, Cal.: Burroughs, 1932; London: Odhams, 1934);

Tarzan Triumphant (Tarzana, Cal.: Burroughs, 1932; London: John Lane, 1934);

Tarzan and the City of Gold (Tarzana, Cal.: Burroughs, 1933; London: John Lane, 1936);

Pirates of Venus (Tarzana, Cal.: Burroughs, 1934; London: John Lane, 1935);

Tarzan and the Lion Man (Tarzana, Cal.: Burroughs, 1934);

Lost on Venus (Tarzana, Cal.: Burroughs, 1935; London: Methuen, 1937);

Tarzan and the Leopard Men (Tarzana, Cal.: Burroughs, 1935; London: John Lane, 1936);

Swords of Mars (Tarzana, Cal.: Burroughs, 1936);

Tarzan and the Tarzan Twins, with Jad-bal-ja the Golden Lion (Racine, Wis.: Whitman, 1936);

Tarzan's Quest (Tarzana, Cal.: Burroughs, 1936; London: Methuen, 1938);

Back to the Stone Age (Tarzana, Cal.: Burroughs, 1937);

Tarzan and the Forbidden City (Tarzana, Cal.: Burroughs, 1938);

Carson of Venus (Tarzana, Cal.: Burroughs, 1939);

Tarzan the Magnificent (Tarzana, Cal.: Burroughs, 1939; London: Methuen, 1940);

Synthetic Men of Mars (Tarzana, Cal.: Burroughs, 1940; London: Methuen, 1941);

Land of Terror (Tarzana, Cal.: Burroughs, 1944);

Escape on Venus (Tarzana, Cal.: Burroughs, 1946);

Tarzan and "The Foreign Legion" (Tarzana, Cal.: Burroughs, 1947; London: Allen, 1949);

Llana of Gathol (Tarzana, Cal.: Burroughs, 1948);

Savage Pellucidar (New York: Canaveral, 1963);

Tales of Three Planets (New York: Canaveral, 1964);

Tarzan and the Madman (New York: Canaveral, 1964);

John Carter of Mars (New York: Canaveral, 1964);

Tarzan and the Castaways (New York: Canaveral, 1965);

The Wizard of Venus (New York: Ace, 1970).

It is probably not surprising that a man nearly forty years of age, with a wife and children to support but no real taste for the pedestrian routines of business, should dream of being carried away to another planet or of being born in the jungle, free of civilization and its entanglements. What is surprising is that so much of the world should have found in his daydreams mythological figures.

Burroughs was born in Chicago, but he seems to have spent much of his young manhood yearning for the wide open freedom and independence of the West. In the vacations between his years at private schools (including a year at Phillips Academy) he joined his older brothers, who were trying to make a go of a ranch in Idaho; and after his graduation from the Michigan Military Academy he enlisted for a tour with the Seventh Cavalry in Arizona. The latter adventure, however, proved to be a great disappointment, and Burroughs's father was obliged to use political influence and the excuse of his son's youth and ill health to buy the young man's way out of his enlistment.

Even after his marriage Burroughs continued to seek his fortune in the far West, dredging for gold in the Snake River and working at various jobs in Idaho and Utah. But his dreams of wealth and independence failed to materialize, and he regularly found himself back in Chicago, working for his father or for some other relative. It was only after a series of selling jobs, which were attempts to start his own business, and a successful but intolerable period with Sears, Roebuck and Company, that he began to dream in prose, on the back of letterhead stationery from his failed projects, the dream that became *Under the Moons of Mars*, which ran in *All-Story Magazine* in 1912 and was the first of what would become the Mars series (as a separately published novel, it was retitled *A Princess of Mars*). Burroughs finally settled in California and even lived for a while in Hawaii, but he found his escape from the confines of lifeless and mercantile culture not in the land west of the Mississippi, but in the grandeur of his vision of mankind struggling to continue to exist in a universe where not only every individual but every species dies.

The theme of the struggle for survival is obvious enough in the stories for which Burroughs is best known, the Tarzan series, comprising twenty-four novels about an English lord's son who was raised in the jungle by apes. But the Tarzan stories, measured in modern terms, are not, strictly speaking, science fiction; measured in nineteenth-century terms, however, when darkest Africa and lost races were among the major settings and motifs of the scientific

romance, they are at least marginal science fiction. Nevertheless, it is most appropriate here to concentrate on Burroughs's series which are less ambiguously science fiction. Most notable among these are the five-volume Venus series (*Pirates of Venus*, 1934; *Lost on Venus*, 1935; *Carson of Venus*, 1939; *Escape on Venus*, 1946; and *The Wizard of Venus*, 1970); the seven-volume Pellucidar series, set at the center of the Earth (*At the Earth's Core*, 1922; *Pellucidar*, 1923; *Tanar of Pellucidar*, 1930; *Tarzan at the Earth's Core*, 1930; *Back to the Stone Age*, 1937; *Land of Terror*, 1944; and *Savage Pellucidar*, 1963); and, best known to readers of science fiction and the stories that started it all for Burroughs, the Mars series (*A Princess of Mars*, 1917; *The Gods of Mars*, 1918; *The Warlord of Mars*, 1919; *Thuvia, Maid of Mars*, 1920; *The Chessmen of Mars*, 1922; *The Master Mind of Mars*, 1928; *A Fighting Man of Mars*, 1931; *Swords of Mars*, 1936; *Synthetic Men of Mars*, 1940; *Llana of Gathol*, 1948; and *John Carter of Mars*, 1964). Most representative of Burroughs's science fiction is the Mars series, which details the adventures of John Carter, a Virginia gentleman transplanted to the red planet. One can get an excellent idea of Burroughs's themes and plot patterns as well as of the coherence of his imagination from just the first three novels of this

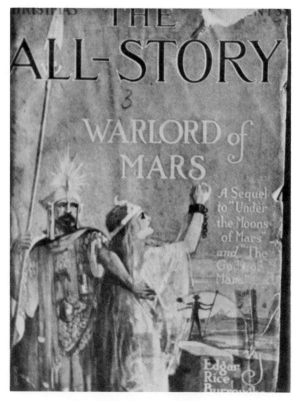

Warlord of Mars, *dust jacket*

Edgar Rice Burroughs

series, *A Princess of Mars, The Gods of Mars,* and *The Warlord of Mars.*

In the archetypal Burroughs novel, it has often been noted, an incredibly strong man saves an incredibly beautiful woman from rape by incredible villains. However, if one looks more closely at these novels, what emerges from behind the threat of rape is the far more universal threat of death. Burroughs's original Martian trilogy is a particularly fine instance of science fiction's attempt to cope with what Burroughs himself called "the stern and unalterable cosmic laws," the certainty that both individuals and whole races grow old and die.

The importance of the threat of rape in a Burroughs plot should not be underestimated: it is certainly true that, in each of these early John Carter novels, the hero encounters adventure on the way to rescuing "the incomparable Dejah Thoris" from the unwanted attentions of the villains. It is also true that Princess Dejah's role is minimal: in none of the novels does she have much to do except flee, always nearly nude and always threatened. Throughout the series, even though John Carter does win her, Dejah Thoris remains at a distance, seen but not touched, never any more clothed or any more human. She is, of course, a sex object. The threat of rape may be directed at her, and may even be aroused by her beauty, but finally the novels do not dwell on the threat of rape as endured by a captive woman; they dwell instead on the rape as an attack on John Carter. "Earth man," screams one of the villains, "that the death you die tonight may be doubly bitter, know you that when you have passed, your widow becomes the wife of Matai Shang, Hekkador of the Holy Therns." Significantly, the beautiful woman is identified with the beauty of being alive; long after John Carter is dead—according to this threat—Dejah Thoris will still be possessed by his enemies. The beautiful woman, in other words, becomes the symbol of the life the hero preserves; and although Burroughs's novels feature insufficiently clad ladies fleeing from rapacious villains, the books are really about men who are strong enough to survive regular and repeated attempts on their lives.

"I cannot go on living forever," John Carter says in the opening sentence of *A Princess of Mars*; "someday I shall die the real death from which there is no resurrection." He has to say so, because he has already died a kind of death at least twice, once in an Arizona cave, from which he awoke to find himself on Mars, and again at the end of his first adventures on the red planet, when he had to die on Mars to return to Earth. "I do not know why I should fear death, I who have died twice and am still alive," he continues; "but yet I have the same horror of it as you who have never died, and it is because of this terror of death, I believe, that I am so convinced of my mortality."

At first it seems as if Burroughs has written himself into a corner; needing a way to get his hero to Mars and back, and at the same time requiring a hero who is vulnerable enough to be human, he has to make a distinction between "death" and "real death." But even if Burroughs did not realize it, in these stories John Carter comes to embody one of science fiction's more optimistic visions, that of mankind triumphant. Carter becomes the hope that if any species can put off ending as individuals must end, as other species have ended, surely it is mankind—not because man is favored by the gods, but because men can work together to stay a step or two ahead of racial extinction.

Afraid of death as he may be, John Carter does not, as do those less venturesome, avoid its probable occasions. Instead, he seeks them out. He is a professional soldier, most alive in the midst of battle, ankle deep in the blood of his foes. Life, as these novels present it, is a struggle, and blessed is the hero who has the strength to resist death for as long as possible. John Carter, who cannot remember his childhood (or even if he ever had one), who has no idea of how old he is (as far as he can remember, he has always been a fighting man of about thirty years of age), becomes the spirit of struggle itself. He is allowed a little more individuality than the nearly naked Dejah Thoris, but he too becomes more symbol than person; he becomes the spirit of man fighting, of the continual struggle to stay alive in a universe of death.

Burroughs's Mars is, as is usual for Mars in science fiction, a planet past its prime. It is further evolved toward the inevitable end of life than is Earth; a once dominant white race has long since passed, the oceans all are dry, and the atmosphere itself would disappear were it not for the pumping station run by Dejah Thoris's now dominant red race. In such circumstances, where life is more clearly a struggle, it becomes obvious that just as one day John Carter must die, so one day all life on Mars must end.

As John Carter's strength helps him to put off his own end, however, so he is able, over the course of these three novels, to postpone the end of life on Mars by enlisting the various races in his cause and by persuading them to share the planet's dwindling resources. Dejah Thoris is not the only Martian he rescues; he saves Sola, who alone among the green Martians has gentle human feelings; Tars Tarkas, in whose fierce bosom he reawakens the feelings of friendship; Kantos Kan, the red Martian who becomes his faithful lieutenant; Thuvia, the beautiful courtesan who learns from the love between John Carter and Dejah Thoris "what true love may be"; and many others, including Xodar, the prince of the black Martians, and Talu, the prince of the yellow Martians, both of whom he helps to their thrones and thus to the eventual unification of Mars. That John Carter regularly has his skin dyed the color of the Martians with whom he is dealing and that he illustrates the truth that all Martians are alike under the skin are interesting comments on the racism of which Burroughs has been accused.

John Carter, then, is a deliverer: the first novel ends with his "dying" to save the Martian pumping station, and the third novel ends with the gathered rulers hailing him as savior. Certainly Carter is godlike. He comes to Mars from out of the heavens, and he saves the whole of his adopted world; his initials are even those of Jesus Christ. It seems likely, however, that there is a contrast between Carter and Christ. The message of Burroughs's hero, for example, is hardly that the meek shall inherit the red planet; what John Carter preaches is the Darwinian

gospel that, in a universe of death, only the fit survive.

The most important contrast between John Carter and Jesus Christ is that Burroughs's hero comes to destroy religion altogether. Although in the first book Burroughs did not do much with the mythology he gave his Martians, in *The Gods of Mars* and *The Warlord of Mars* the whole planet is dominated by a religion that teaches that, for Martians willing to give up the world, there is at the end of the river Iss in "the valley known as Dor" "by the shores of the lost Sea of Korus" both an earthly paradise and eternal life. What John Carter finds out, as he must in any novel that emphasizes life as a struggle, is that the river of life leads to the valley of the grave, to the door of the tomb. The Goddess of Being herself, Issus, turns out to be mortal.

The novels are surprisingly coherent. On the level of plot the two Martian priest classes, the Holy Therns and the self-called First Born, themselves victims of the desire for eternal life in an earthly paradise, selfishly prevent the other Martians from sharing the still abundant water supplies at the planet's poles. On a larger level the religion which promises that the good life will one day be made eternal turns out to be a lie; the truth is that life is a struggle for existence. In one sense, Burroughs's antireligious stance is a fairly predictable proevolutionary position. In another sense, however, such consistency is more than one expects; more serious thinkers than Burroughs have argued that religion's focus on a paradise can cause the neglect of the dying worlds in this universe.

But the real center of Burroughs's Martian novels is not the rescue of Dejah Thoris, nor the salvation of Mars, nor even the destruction of the false religion. The real center is those days, months, almost years, that John Carter spends in various pits, prisons, and dark mazes. The situation is always the same: John Carter has ventured too far, has not been careful enough; and as he loses his way in the labyrinth, as he tries to guess what path to take, the trapdoor drops, the lock clicks behind him, or he is outnumbered, overwhelmed, and carried off to a dark prison. There is always the sound of laughter, sometimes hollow, sometimes fiendish, just as the trap is sprung. This image, man lost in a maze and finally trapped, is the real center of Burroughs's imagination. The laughter is not just the laughter of John Carter's enemies: it is the cackle of a malicious, or at least uncaring, universe.

John Carter, of course, always escapes. Sometimes he is freed by others, more often he frees himself, but the point is that he fights and wins his way back from such graves. That, clearly, is what Burroughs hopes is the truth about mankind; his John Carter embodies the hope that the species, unlike its individuals, will continue to escape the end.

There is, in this regard, an interesting preface to the last of the Martian books published in Burroughs's lifetime, a collection of stories called *Llana of Gathol.* In it Burroughs pictures himself sitting late one evening on a beach in Hawaii, thinking almost aloud that the sound of the trade wind in the coconut palms might well be taken to be the ghosts of the savage kings who ruled the islands "long before the sea captains brought strange diseases or the missionaries brought mother-hubbards." So musing, he has a sudden vision of one of the greatest of those kings, Kamehameha, striding down from the mountains, stepping over fields and houses, leaving a lake at every step; the hem of the king's great feather cape catches on a church spire and topples it to the ground. Burroughs wakes, not to our reality, but to see John Carter standing before him; and the parallel is appropriate, for not only does Burroughs's hero deny the religion of the missionaries, he also embodies the ancient warrior spirit of man, that which is of more use in this universe of death than any promise of a paradise.

John Carter announces that he has returned to Earth for one last visit with Burroughs before the author has to die. He will himself live on, not only because men live longer on Mars, but also because it is in the nature even of popular literature for the creature to outlive the creator. Burroughs ends by asking that the Martian hero visit the Burroughs children sometimes; they are, after all, the only part of the future of the species that he as an individual can claim.

Burroughs died not quite two years later, in 1950. Ironically for the creator of both John Carter and Tarzan, he died in bed of a heart attack on a Sunday morning while reading the comic strips.

—*John Hollow*

References:

Brian W. Aldiss, *Billion Year Spree* (Garden City: Doubleday, 1973), pp. 156-180;

Thomas D. Clareson, "Lost Lands, Lost Races: A Pagan Princess of Their Very Own," in his *Many Futures, Many Worlds: Theme and Form in Science Fiction* (Kent, Ohio: Kent State University Press, 1977);

David Cowart, "The Tarzan Myth and Jung's Genesis of the Self," *Journal of American Culture*, 2 (Summer 1979): 220-230;

Philip José Farmer, *Tarzan Alive* (Garden City: Doubleday, 1972);

Robert W. Fenton, *The Big Swingers* (Englewood Cliffs, N.J.: Prentice-Hall, 1967);

John T. Flautz, "An American Demagogue in Barsoom," *Journal of Popular Culture*, 1 (Winter 1967): 263-275;

John Harwood, *The Literature of Burroughsiana* (Baton Rouge: Cazadessus, 1963);

Henry Hardy Heins, *A Golden Anniversary Bibliography of Edgar Rice Burroughs* (West Kingston, R.I.: Donald M. Grant, 1964);

Tom Henighan, "Tarzan and Rima, the Myth and the Message," *Riverside Quarterly*, 3 (March 1969): 256-265;

Mark Hillegas, "Martians and Mythmakers: 1877-1938," in *Challenges in American Culture*, ed. Ray B. Browne, Larry N. Landrum, and William K. Bottorff (Bowling Green, Ohio: Bowling Green University Popular Press, 1970), pp. 150-177;

John Hollow, "Rereading *Tarzan of the Apes*; or, 'What Is It,' Lady Alice Whispered, 'a Man?,' " *Dalhousie Review*, 56 (Spring 1976): 83-92;

Robert R. Kudlay and Joan Leiby, *Burroughs' Science Fiction* (Geneseo, N.Y.: School of Library and Information Science, State University College of Arts and Science, 1973);

Richard Kyle, "Out of Time's Abyss: The Martian Stories of Edgar Rice Burroughs," *Riverside Quarterly*, 4 (January 1970): 110-122;

Francis Lacassin, *Tarzan ou le Chevalier crispé* (Paris: Union Générale d'Editions, 1971);

Richard A. Lupoff, *Barsoom: Edgar Rice Burroughs and the Martian Vision* (Baltimore: Mirage, 1976);

Lupoff, *Edgar Rice Burroughs: Master of Adventure*, revised edition (New York: Ace, 1975);

Robert E. Morsberger, "Edgar Rice Burroughs' Apache Epic," *Journal of Popular Culture*, 7 (Fall 1973): 280-287;

Sam Moskowitz, *Explorers of the Infinite* (New York: World, 1963);

Richard D. Mullen, "Edgar Rice Burroughs and the Fate Worse than Death," *Riverside Quarterly*, 4 (June 1970): 186-191;

Mullen, "The Prudish Prurience of H. Rider Haggard and Edgar Rice Burroughs," *Riverside Quarterly*, 5 (August 1973): 14-19; 6 (April 1974): 134-146;

Mullen, "The Undisciplined Imagination: Edgar Rice Burroughs and Lowellian Mars," in *SF: The Other Side of Realism*, ed. Clareson (Bowling Green, Ohio: Bowling Green University Popular Press, 1971), pp. 229-247;

Irwin Porges, *Edgar Rice Burroughs* (Provo, Utah: Brigham Young University Press, 1975);

John F. Roy, *A Guide to Barsoom* (New York: Ballantine, 1976);

Tom Slate, "Edgar Rice Burroughs and the Heroic Epic," *Riverside Quarterly*, 2 (March 1968): 118-123.

WILLIAM S. BURROUGHS
(5 February 1914-   )

SELECTED BOOKS: *Junkie*, as William Lee (with *Narcotic Agent* by Maurice Helbrant) (New York: Ace, 1953; London: Digit, 1957); as William S. Burroughs (New York: Ace, 1964; London: Olympia/New English Library, 1966); unexpurgated edition, *Junky* (New York: Penguin, 1977);

The Naked Lunch (Paris: Olympia, 1959); republished as *Naked Lunch* (New York: Grove, 1962; London: Calder/Olympia, 1964);

Minutes to Go, by Burroughs, Sinclair Beiles, Gregory Corso, and Brion Gysin (Paris: Two Cities Editions, 1960; San Francisco: Beach Books, 1968);

The Exterminator, by Burroughs and Gysin (San Francisco: Auerhahn Press, 1960);

The Soft Machine (Paris: Olympia, 1961; revised and enlarged edition, New York: Grove, 1966; revised and enlarged again, London: Calder & Boyars, 1968);

The Ticket That Exploded (Paris: Olympia, 1962; revised and enlarged edition, New York: Grove, 1967; London: Calder & Boyars, 1968);

Dead Fingers Talk (London: Calder/Olympia, 1963);

The Yage Letters, by Burroughs and Allen Ginsberg (San Francisco: City Lights Books, 1963);

Nova Express (New York: Grove, 1964; London: Cape, 1966);

Time (New York: "C" Press, 1965; University of Sussex, U. K.: Urgency Press Rip-Off, 1972);

Health Bulletin: APO-33: A Metabolic Regulator (New York: Fuck You Press, 1965); republished as *APO-33: A Report on the Synthesis of the Apomorphine Formula* (San Francisco: Beach Books, 1966);

The Last Words of Dutch Schultz (London: Cape Goliard, 1970; (New York: Viking/Seaver, 1975);

The Wild Boys: A Book of the Dead (New York: Grove, 1971; London: Calder & Boyars, 1972);

Exterminator! (New York: Viking/Seaver, 1973; London: Calder & Boyars, 1975);

The Book of Breeething (Ingatestone, Essex, U. K.: OU, 1974; Berkeley: Blue Wind Press, 1975);

Oeuvre Croisee, by Burroughs and Gysin (Paris: Flammarion, 1976); republished as *The Third Mind* (New York: Viking/Seaver, 1978);

Blade Runner: A Movie (Berkeley: Blue Wind Press, 1979).

William Seward Burroughs was born in Saint Louis, Missouri, to Perry Mortimer Burroughs, son of the industrialist who invented the cylinder that made the modern adding machine possible, and Laura Lee, a direct descendant of Robert E. Lee, Civil War general and commander in chief of the Confederate army. Dominated by his mother's obsessive Victorian prudery and haunted by vivid nightmares and hallucinations, Burroughs led a restlesss childhood. He was educated in private schools in Saint Louis and Los Alamos, New Mexico, where he developed seemingly disparate fascinations with literature and crime, and later studied literature (for lack of interest in any other subject) and anthropology at Harvard University, where he encountered a set of wealthy homosexuals. He graduated with an A.B. in 1936. Subsequently Burroughs traveled to Europe, briefly studied medicine in Vienna, and returned to the United States and Harvard to resume his study of anthropology, which he soon abandoned due to his conviction that academic life is little more than a series of intrigues broken by teas. Although he attempted to use family connections to acquire a position with the Office of Strategic Services, Burroughs was rejected after he deliberately cut off the first joint of one finger in a Van Gogh-like attempt to impress a friend. Moving to New York City, he worked in an advertising agency for a year and underwent psychoanalysis. He entered the army in 1942, engineered his discharge for psychological reasons six months later, and then moved to Chicago, where he easily found work as an exterminator and a private detective, among other odd jobs.

In 1943 Burroughs returned to New York City and met Jean Vollmer, a student at Columbia University whom he married on 17 January 1945. She introduced Burroughs to Jack Kerouac, who in turn introduced him to Allen Ginsberg. The Beat generation was born in Burroughs's 115th Street apartment after Burroughs acquainted Kerouac and Ginsberg with the experimental writings of Blake, Rimbaud, and others; and the three friends soon emerged as leaders of the movement. *The Yage Letters* (1963), collected correspondence between Ginsberg and Burroughs written during Burroughs's 1952 expedition to South America in search of Yage, a legendary hallucinogenic potion, clearly reveals that Burroughs was Govinda, the master, to Ginsberg's Siddhartha, the disciple.

Late in 1944 Herbert Huncke, a Times-Square hustler involved in criminal activity to support his drug habit, introduced Burroughs to the use of morphine and its derivatives. Burroughs was for most of the next thirteen years a heroin addict who frequently altered his place of residence to evade the police. In 1946 he moved to Waverly, Texas, where he tried farming, and in 1948 he voluntarily entered a drug rehabilitation center at Lexington, Kentucky. Returning to Waverly and already back on drugs, Burroughs was hounded by the police until he moved to Algiers, Louisiana. To avoid prosecution for illegal possession of drugs and firearms after his Algiers farm was raided, he relocated to Mexico City, where he became involved in the violence of the Aleman regime. He continued his archaeological studies at Mexico City University, pursuing an interest in the Mayan codices. On 7 September 1951 Burroughs accidentally killed his wife while allegedly attempting to shoot a champagne glass off her head while playing "William Tell," a version of the incident he later denied. Although Mexican authorities let the matter drop, Burroughs moved to Tangier and soon thereafter traveled to the jungles of Colombia in his search for yage.

He returned again to New York City in 1953, lived for a while with Ginsberg, and then returned to Tangier, where from 1955 to 1958 he was frequently visited by other Beat writers and worked on the manuscript that would develop into his quartet of science fiction-like novels: *The Naked Lunch* (1959), *The Soft Machine* (1961), *Nova Express* (third book in the series, although it was not published until 1964), and *The Ticket That Exploded* (1962), his most serious works and, with *The Wild Boys: A Book of the Dead* (1971), his major literary successes. In 1957 Burroughs again sought treatment for his heroin addiction. This time he placed himself in the care of John Yerby Dent, an English physician who treated drug addicts with apomorphine, a crystalline alkaloid derivative of morphine and a drug Burroughs praises and mythologizes in his writings.

The following year, cured of his addiction, Burroughs moved to Paris, home of Olympia Press (for the next several years his primary publisher), and by the mid-1960s he had settled in London, where he is still an active writer.

Burroughs did not begin writing seriously until 1950, although he had unsuccessfully submitted a story titled "Twilight's Last Gleaming" to *Esquire* as early as 1938. His first novelistic effort, "Queer," which deals with homosexuality, also remains unpublished. Ginsberg finally persuaded Ace Books to publish Burroughs's first novel, *Junkie* (1953), which originally appeared under the pseudonym William Lee, as half of an Ace double paperback. (It was bound with Maurice Helbront's *Narcotic Agent*.) While strictly objective and conventional in style, *Junkie* is a luridly hyperbolic, quasi-autobiographical first-person account of the horrors of drug addiction. It contains such absurdities as a scene in which the desperate protagonist gouges a hole in his arm with a fragment of broken glass so that he can mainline heroin with an eyedropper. Of little literary merit in itself, this first novel is interesting in that it introduces not only the main character, Lee, but also several of the major motifs that appear in Burroughs's subsequent works: the central metaphor of drug addiction, the related image of man reduced to a subhuman, usually insectlike creature by his drug and other lusts, and the suggestion of concomitant and pervasive sexual aberration.

Burroughs's next novel, *The Naked Lunch*, first published in Paris, reached the United States, according to *Newsweek*, "carrying a heavier burden of literary laudations than any piece of fiction since *Ulysses*." The Grove Press edition (1962) became a national best-seller. Like James Joyce's *Ulysses*, it also successfully withstood American censorship attempts; it was cleared of obscenity charges in Los Angeles in 1965. The Supreme Court of Massachusetts handed down a decision in 1966 that reversed an earlier decision of the Superior Court of Boston that had threatened a state-wide ban on the book. Ginsberg and Norman Mailer, who asserted that Burroughs is "the only American novelist living today who may conceivably be possessed by genius," were among those who testified in the book's defense. Actually, while it does detail with exceptional brutality the ugly, revolting, and perverse, *The Naked Lunch* is at bottom a strikingly moral as well as richly but darkly comic work that employs irony and allegory, among more unconventional techniques, to satirize much that is false and defective in modern American life in particular and in human nature in general. *The Naked Lunch* as satire has been compared to the works of Jonathan Swift, who also wrote with "a moral view design'd to cure the vices of mankind." It is especially effective as a subliminal argument against the specific vice of heroin abuse, and its successful publication in America elevated its heretofore practically unknown author to membership in the literary elite.

In *The Naked Lunch* and its three less celebrated sequels, *The Soft Machine, Nova Express,* and *The Ticket That Exploded,* Burroughs weaves an intricate and horrible allegory of human greed, corruption, and debasement. Like Orwell's *1984* and Huxley's *Brave New World,* these four works, taken collectively, seize on the evils or tendencies toward a certain type of evil that the author sees as being particularly malignant in his contemporary world and project them into a dystopian future, where, magnified, they grow monstrous and take on an exaggerated and fantastic shape. And like these classics of dystopian fiction, Burroughs's works are more like novels of ideas that cleverly utilize the trappings of science fiction than what most people would consider pure science fiction.

While progressively clarifying and developing Burroughs's thought, these novels share themes, metaphorical images, characters, and stylistic approach. All contribute to a single plot; or rather they combine to suggest the elements of what little plot there is. In them Burroughs utilizes a "cut-up" and "fold-in" style that has its closest analogue in the cinematic technique of montage, although that technique is here more radically employed. He juxtaposes one scene with another without regard to plot, character, or, in the short view, theme to promote an association of the reader's emotional reaction to the content of certain scenes (sexual perversion, drug abuse, senseless violence) with the implied narrative content of others (examples of "addictions": to drugs, money, sex, power). The theory is that if such juxtapositions recur often enough, the feeling of revulsion strategically created by the first set of images will form the reader's negative attitude toward the second set of examples.

Surely, as many critics, such as John Ciardi, have recognized, "What Burroughs has written is a many leveled vision of horror." He has constructed a science fiction-like fantasy wherein, on a literal level, the Earth and its human inhabitants have been taken over by the Nova Mob, an assortment of extraterrestrial, non-three-dimensional entities who live parasitically on the reality of other organisms. In these novels exploitation of the Earth has reached such

proportions that the intergalactic Nova Police have been alerted. The Nova Police are attempting to thwart the Nova Mob without so alarming them that they will detonate the planet in an attempt to destroy the evidence while trying to make what escape they can. The most direct form of Nova control, control that enables the Nova Mob to carry on its parasitic activity with impunity, is thought control of the human population through control of the mass communication media. Since the middle of *Nova Express* the reader has been in the midst of a science fiction-like war of images in which the weapons are cameras and tape recorders. The Nova Police and the inhabitants of earth have discovered how to combat the Nova Mob with similar techniques (of which these novels are examples) and engage in a guerrilla war with the Nova Criminals, who are desperately trying to cut and run. The ending of *The Ticket That Exploded* is optimistic for Earth but inconclusive. It is not known if the Earth will be rid of the Nova Mob before the criminals succeed in destroying it.

The Naked Lunch is the complex of impressions and sensations experienced by William Lee (Burroughs's pseudonym in *Junkie*), here revealed as an agent of the Nova Police. Lee has assumed the cover of a human homosexual heroin addict because with such a cover he is most likely to encounter Nova Criminals, who are all addicts of one sort or another and who, therefore, prefer to operate through addicted human collaborators. Consequently, *The Naked Lunch* is on one level, as Ciardi expresses it, "a monumental descent into the hell of narcotic addiction." It is only toward the conclusion of the novel that we discover Lee is some sort of an agent "clawing at a not-yet of Telepathic Bureaucracies, Time Monopolies, Control Drugs, Heavy Fluid Addicts."

The "naked lunch" of the title is the reality seen by Lee, what Burroughs describes as that "frozen moment when everyone sees what is on the end of every fork." From the bleak homosexual encounters and desperate scrambles to make drug connections, two ideas emerge: the concept of addiction, the central motif of these novels, and the concept of "the algebra of need." The latter states simply that when an addict is faced with absolute need (as a junkie is for heroin or a control addict for power) he will do anything to satisfy that need. The Nova Criminals are nonhuman personifications of various addictions. The Uranians, addicted to Heavy Metal Fluid, are types of drug addicts. Dr. Benway, Mr. Bradley Mr. Martin, and the insect people of Minraud—all control addicts—are types of the human addiction to power. The green boy-girls of Venus, addicted to Venusian sexual practices, exemplify the human addiction to sensual pleasure, which Burroughs portrays essentially in homosexual terms. The Death Dwarf, addicted to concentrated words and images, is the analog of the human addiction to various cultural myths and beliefs. He is the most pathetic of these depraved creatures. As Ciardi notes, "Only after the first shock does one realize that what Burroughs is writing about is not only the destruction of depraved men by their drug lust, but the destruction of all men by their consuming addictions, whether the addiction be drugs or over-righteous propriety or sixteen-year-old girls."

Burroughs sees *The Soft Machine* as "a sequel to *The Naked Lunch,* a mathematical extension of the Algebra of Need beyond the Junk virus." Here the consuming addiction, displayed again in juxta-position with scenes of drug abuse and sexual perversion and through a number of shifting narrators, is the addiction to power over others. The central episode concerns a time-traveling agent's destruction of the control apparatus of the ancient Mayan theocracy (Burroughs's primary archaeologi-cal interest), which exercises its control through the manipulation of myths; this is the prototype of the struggle between the Nova Police and the Nova Mob that breaks into the open in the subsequent two novels. The "soft machine" is both the "wounded galaxy," the Milky Way seen as a biological organism diseased by the virus-like Nova Mob, and the human body, riddled with parasites and addictions and programmed with the "ticket" (that is, obsolete myths and dreams) written on the "soft typewriter" of culture and civilization. Burroughs contends that any addiction dehumanizes its victims. The Mayan priests in the novel, for example, tend to become half-men/half-crab creatures who eventually change into giant centipedes and exude an erogenous green slime. And Bradley the Buyer, who reappears as Mr. Bradley Mr. Martin, Mr. and Mrs. D., and the Ugly Spirit, has a farcical habit of turning into a bloblike creature who is addicted to and absorbs drug addicts.

Nova Express and *The Ticket That Exploded,* in which there are many instances of metamorpho-sis, most clearly reveal the plot situation of the entire quartet of novels and explore the Nova Mob's exploitation of media, especially the addiction to language. As Stephen Koch argues, here "The 'moralist' in Burroughs addresses himself to . . . the freedom or bondage of consciousness, insofar as consciousness is a function of language. . . . Consciousness is addicted . . . to what sustains it and gives it definition: in particular, it is addicted to the word, the structures of language that define meaning and thus reality itself." Thus, contemporary existence is seen here as a film that is forever rerun, trapping the human soul like an insect imprisoned in amber, negating any possibility of choice.

Burroughs meant for his works to be the most vicious of allegorical satires, in his own words, "necessarily brutal, obscene and disgusting," as are the situations from which he drew his images and metaphors. On one level of interpretation Burroughs's satire is directed at those men addicted to pleasure or power in any form; these men, obeying the dictates of "the algebra of need," will stop at nothing to fulfill their desires. They have "lost their human citizenship." They are the Nova Mob, nonhuman parasites feeding on the essences of others; they shamelessly lie, cheat, and manipulate to attain what has come to be equated in the reader's mind with excrement, perversion, and death. Burroughs's satire goes deeper than this, however. He attacks not only the men, but also the structure of the culture that enables their practices to continue. He attacks the myths that imprison all men, that limit vision and action through stone walls of patriotism and religion, for example, while distracting thought through dreams of romantic love. Burroughs calls for nothing less than a revolution of consciousness. He demands that man free himself from these "word and image addictions." He insists that everyone heed the last words of Hassan I Sabbah (cribbed out of context from Dostoyevsky's *The Brothers Karamazov*): "Nothing is True—Everything is Permitted."

Burroughs's other notably science-fiction-like novel, *The Wild Boys,* is also composed of scenes linked more by associated images than by any clearly linear narrative framework. Here the author posits a bizarre alternative to the problematical apocalypse-in-progress depicted in his earlier quartet. In a world wrecked by famine and controlled by police, the wild boys, a homosexual tribe of hashish smokers, have withdrawn themselves from space and time through indifference and have developed into a counter-culture complete with its own language, rituals, and economy. The existence of this counterculture, of course, poses a threat to those who create the false images upon which the larger, repressive, external society is based; but the wild boys cannot be tamed because their cold indifference to the mass culture entails a savagery that refuses to submit to control. Burroughs's thinking clearly becomes more political in *The Wild Boys* and in the book that followed it, *Exterminator!* (1973), a collection of short stories and poems that revolve around the common theme of death through sinister forces. But his primary concern for freedom from the controllers and manipulators—chemical, political, sexual, or cultural—has remained constant from the beginning of his literary career.

Burroughs's literary reputation was firmly established with the American publication of *Naked Lunch* in 1962. Many reviewers, however, some seemingly oblivious to the irony of his work, have not been responsive or sympathetic to Burroughs's themes and techniques; and none of his novels since *Naked Lunch*, with the exception of *The Wild Boys*, has received comparable critical acclaim. While *Naked Lunch* was lauded by Terry Southern, Mary McCarthy, Karl Shapiro, and Marshall McLuhan, as well as by Ginsberg and Mailer, the subsequent novels were considered by some critics, not totally inaccurately, as "language without content" and "the world's greatest put-on." But Burroughs himself admits that *"Naked Lunch* demands silence from the reader. Otherwise he is taking his own pulse." He warns that this and his other similar novels do not present their "content" in the manner in which the reader ordinarily expects. One of the triumphs of Burroughs's unique style is that he has created the low-content form or the narrative near-vacuum upon which the unwary reader is tempted to project his own psyche, personal myths, or forgotten dreams. While they do have their own message to convey, his works also encourage the reader to develop or invent his private fictions and to append them to the skeletal narrative structure provided by the author. The reader is thus invited to create the work as he reads it. And in place of the easily perceived, clearly coherent story the reader might have expected, Burroughs's best works keep one reading through the very hypnotic fascination of the author's incantatory prose. —*Donald Palumbo*

Bibliographies:

Michael B. Goodman, *William S. Burroughs: An Annotated Bibliography of His Works and Criticism* (New York: Garland, 1975);

Joe Maynard and Barry Miles, *William Burroughs:*

A Bibliography (Charlottesville: University Press of Virginia, 1977).

References:

John Ciardi, "Book Burners and Sweet Sixteen," *Saturday Review*, 42 (27 June 1959): 22;

Gerard Cordesse, "The Science Fiction of William Burroughs," *Caliban*, 12 (1975): 33-43;

Ihab Hassan, "The Subtracting Machine: The Work of William Burroughs," *Critique*, 6,1 (Spring 1963): 4-23;

Conrad Knickerbocker, "William Burroughs," *Paris Review*, 35 (Fall 1965): 13-49;

Stephen Koch, "Images of Loathing," *Nation*, 203 (25 January 1965): 25-26;

Marshall McLuhan, "Notes on Burroughs," *Nation*, 199 (28 December 1964): 517-519;

Robert Mertz, "The Virus Visions of William Burroughs," *Itinerary 3: Criticism* (Bowling Green, Ohio: Bowling Green University Popular Press, 1977), pp. 11-18;

Miles Associates, comp., *A Descriptive Catalogue of the William S. Burroughs Archive* (London: Covent Garden Press, 1973);

E. Mottram, *William Burroughs: The Algebra of Need* (Buffalo, N.Y.: Intrepid Press, 1971);

Daniel Odier, *The Job: An Interview with William Burroughs* (New York: Grove, 1970);

Neal Oxenhandler, "Listening to Burroughs' Voice," *Surfiction: Fiction Now . . . and Tomorrow* (Chicago: Swallow, 1975), pp. 181-201;

Donald Palumbo, "William Burroughs' Quartet of Science Fiction Novels as Dystopian Social Satire," *Extrapolation*, 20 (Winter 1979): 321-329;

William L. Stull, "The Quest and the Question: Cosmology and Myth in the Work of William S. Burroughs, 1953-1960," *Twentieth Century Literature*, 24 (1978): 225-42;

Tony Tanner, *City of Words: American Fiction, 1950-1970* (New York: Harper & Row, 1971), pp. 109-140.

JOHN W. CAMPBELL, JR.
(8 June 1910-11 July 1971)

BOOKS: *The Mightiest Machine* (Providence, R. I.: Hadley, 1947);

The Atomic Story (New York: Holt, 1947);

Who Goes There? (Chicago: Shasta, 1948); republished as *The Thing and Other Stories* (London: Fantasy Books, 1952);

The Incredible Planet (Reading, Pa.: Fantasy Press, 1949);

The Moon is Hell! (Reading, Pa.: Fantasy Press, 1951; London: New English Library, 1975);

Cloak of Aesir (Chicago: Shasta, 1952);

The Black Star Passes (Reading, Pa.: Fantasy Press, 1953);

Who Goes There? and Other Stories (New York: Dell, 1955);

Islands of Space (Reading, Pa.: Fantasy Press, 1956);

Invaders from the Infinite (Hicksville, N.Y.: Gnome Press, 1961);

The Ultimate Weapon and *The Planeteers* (New York: Ace, 1966);

Collected Editorials From Analog (Garden City: Doubleday, 1966);

John W. Campbell Anthology (Garden City: Doubleday, 1973);

The Best of John W. Campbell (London: Sidgwick & Jackson, 1973);

The Best of John W. Campbell (Garden City: Doubleday, 1976);

The Space Beyond (New York: Pyramid, 1976).

John W. Campbell, Jr., has been called perhaps the first writer to devote his life deliberately to science fiction, and certainly an examination of a career begun at the age of eighteen and continued until his death at sixty-one bears out this statement. Campbell believed strongly in the worth of science fiction; he is said to have dismissed mainstream fiction as a mere subheading in his chosen area of concentration. He devoted himself to helping the genre find what he considered to be its proper direction, its full potential. As a writer his work inspired wide imitation. It was, however, as editor of the dominant *Astounding Science Fiction* (originally *Astounding Stories*, later *Analog*) that Campbell's concepts became a major influence, creating much of the genre's Golden Age and establishing a tradition of science fiction which today bears his name.

John Wood Campbell, Jr., was born in Newark, New Jersey, the son of an electrical engineer for Bell Telephone. There are indications that an unhappy home life soon turned his attention from family concerns to other interests: the repairing of bicycles and small electrical appliances, and reading. His literary exposures varied from Jules Verne and Edgar Rice Burroughs to astronomy texts and works by physicists Sir James Jeans and Sir Arthur Stanley Eddington. These disparate influences—unbound flights of imagination and coldly factual science— would later contend and seek a balance with each other in his writing.

At fourteen he was sent to Blair Academy, a boarding school. His work there was uneven, and despite good marks in physics and Spanish, he never received a diploma. In 1928 he entered M.I.T.; at that time he was strongly influenced by the *Skylark of Space* series by E. E. Smith. A year later he began his writing career with "Invaders from the Infinite," a short story accepted by *Amazing Stories* but never published because the manuscript was lost. (Subsequently, Campbell used the title for a novel published in 1961.) In 1931 a failing grade in German forced him to leave M.I.T. Later that year he married Dona Stuart. Supported by his father, he completed his education at Duke University, taking a B.S. in 1932. He continued to write stories, but following graduation his relations with editors were strained; uncertain payments from pulp magazines made it impossible, during the worst of the Depression, to support himself and his wife by his writing, and he was forced to work at a variety of jobs. Finally he found his real calling when, in September 1937, he joined the editorial staff of Street and Smith, the pulp chain which owned *Astounding Stories*. In October he became editor of this highly influential publication, the title of which was changed, in March 1938, to *Astounding Science-Fiction*. He devoted himself to *Astounding*, which became *Analog* in 1960, until his death on 11 July 1971.

There is a paradoxical quality to Campbell's fiction. Most often criticized for the dehumanized, impersonal, and technology oriented content of his stories, he is nonetheless credited with opening the field for exploration of sociological themes. His earlier works may be faulted for their unvarying presentation of a world view that is essentially white, Anglo-Saxon, and Protestant. His plots center not on human conflict but on conflicts between man and impersonal alien races. He expresses his conceptions of the higher human values through his heroes, who are most often dedicated, lone scientists who function as the driving force behind human progress. They are the creators of the Machine, which in all of its many incarnations is the focal point of the plots, carefully and elaborately delineated in terms of the science of the day. Literary finesse may suffer; it is more than overbalanced by the sheer enthusiasm Campbell's technological visions are capable of generating. The Machine becomes the vehicle for Campbell's personal view of man as a race driven toward greatness by the still active force of evolution, forced into competition with other races by a hostile universe. The race shaped by tools is still being shaped by ever more sophisticated tools.

These earlier works come under the common label of space opera and as such were quite successful, giving Campbell a preeminence in the field even over the legendary E. E. Smith. In the middle and late 1930s, however, he began to work toward a different style and content. While continuing to write in the old style under his own name, he began to produce under a variety of pseudonyms (primarily Don A. Stuart) stories that sought a greater balance between science, mood, and character. Still focused on a theme of evolution, Campbell's vision expanded to view this force as an inexorable series of waxing and waning cycles; man has been driven upward to the pinnacle and now, inevitably, must descend into the darkness again. The time in the crest of the cycle may be prolonged temporarily, but once twilight has come, night must surely follow. Campbell most often expresses this theme through the image of the dying city, a place of assembled greatness that now lies forgotten and decaying. Dark, largely pessimistic, with an oppressively dreamlike atmosphere, these works may have taken both mood and imagery from the Depression years which spawned them.

"When the Atoms Failed" (1930), Campbell's first published story, sets the tone and establishes the conventions of his earlier style. Scientist Steve Waterson's revolutionary new devices are completed just in time to engineer the defeat of an attempted Martian invasion of Earth. Having done so, Waterson uses the same weaponry to force the nations of Earth to discard their mutual animosity and unite with the Martians under a "Supreme Council of Solar System Scientists" headed by Waterson. The technological advances that are immediately converted to weaponry, the casually described, devastating space battles, and the lone scientist who triumphs where inefficient humans en masse fail (and thus gains the right to control mankind's destiny) are all recurring devices in the early stories. They reappear in "The Metal Horde"

John W. Campbell, Jr.

(1930) along with the character of Waterson.

Campbell made use of the same devices in a series of novelettes of the early 1930s, centering on the characters of Arcot, Wade, and Morey, physicist-heroes cut from the same basic cloth as Campbell's other early protagonists. *The Black Star Passes* (1930), *Islands of Space* (1931), and *Invaders from the Infinite* (1932), which did not appear in book form until 1953, 1956, and 1961, respectively (all reprinted in the one-volume *John W. Campbell Anthology*, 1973), take their impetus, as usual, from the rapid scientific breakthroughs of the three heroes. Their discoveries progressively propel them from Venus to other stars to other galaxies, cataloguing the wonders of the universe and firmly establishing man's place in it. Although their actions determine the destiny of the race they represent, Campbell's heroes are curiously isolated from their fellows. They are in essence a law unto themselves, determining the fate of their own and other races by their own standards.

With his reputation as a writer of superscience epics firmly established, Campbell began to move toward a new style with "The Last Evolution" (1932; collected in *The Best of John W. Campbell*, 1976). Here, the final act of two scientists, the last survivors of a devastated Earth, is to create man's successor, a machine that is better equipped to survive in a hostile universe. It is just as well, Campbell is saying: man's time is at best limited, but he can justify his existence by creating a worthy heir. Essentially pessimistic, as is characteristic of the stories he was soon to write and publish under the pen name Don A. Stuart, "The Last Evolution" is still linked to the earlier works by the suggestion, typical of Campbell, that so long as progress is continued by someone, all is well with the cosmos.

Campbell returned to the space-epic style in 1934 to write *The Mightiest Machine*, his most successful novel. Serialized in *Astounding Stories* beginning in December 1934, it was published as a book in 1947. The story concerns a group of Earthmen who are accidentally embroiled in a space war between the human Magyans and the devillike Tefflans, both descendants of races originally from Earth. The Earthmen, led by physicist Aarn Munro, are reluctant to succumb to the irrational "racial hatred" that exists within them, but eventually they side with the Magyans and destroy their enemies' planet with Munro's "mightiest machine." Though written at the height of Campbell's earlier style and thematically related to the early superscience stories, *The Mightiest Machine* also has elements of the bleaker world picture associated with the contemporaneous Stuart stories. The Magyans and Tefflans have ridden the wave of evolution from crest to trough to new crest without resolving their conflict; now the universe intervenes through the agency of the Earthmen to send the two races to their proper destinies: the Magyans (humans) onward, the Tefflans back into darkness. Campbell's plot may have come from his fear of a night about to envelop his own time; he firmly believed in the inevitability of United States intervention to curtail the emerging fascist threat.

According to Sam Moscowitz, Campbell began publishing under the Don A. Stuart pen name when the enthusiastic F. Orlin Tremaine, then editor of *Astounding Stories*, could not resist publishing the story "Twilight" (1934) at a time when its wholly different style and mood would clash with the other Campbell works readers had encountered and would encounter in the magazine. Widely anthologized, "Twilight" was collected, along with its sequel, "Night" (1935), in *Who Goes There?* (1948); it concerns a time-traveler who journeys to Earth's far future to find that the human race has almost died out due to the loss of the essential racial trait of curiosity. He remedies the situation by creating a "curious" machine which will take man's place in the movement upward. An extension of the theme of "The Last Evolution," "Twilight" is a story both darker in mood and more evocative in its image of an empty and dying world where machines, the ultimate superiors of man, still labor uselessly for his benefit. Oddly, Campbell chooses to negate even the left-handed optimism of the story's ending; in the sequel, "Night," the time-traveler journeys even farther into the future to find that he has only prolonged the inevitable. Now the universe itself is dying, succumbing to its own entropy, and there is no place for even the machines to escape. Once the cycle is complete, the end can only be prolonged, not avoided. Nonetheless, Campbell's essential optimism seems briefly to reassert itself and reverse the process in "The Machine" (1935; collected in *Cloak of Aesir*, 1952). Here, the master computer which has turned Earth into a technological utopia voluntarily turns itself off in order to force the humans to retake control of their own destiny and avoid the fatal loss of curiosity. This trend continues with "Forgetfulness" (1937; collected in *Cloak of Aesir*), in which a band of alien colonists land on Earth in the midst of a human race apparently sunk into gentle apathy, the use of the still functioning machines surrounding them forgotten. By the end of the story the aliens have found that the end of one cycle of development has only presaged the beginning of another, one which has brought man to a height from which the Machine, with all its magic, is only an abandoned toy.

One of Campbell's last pieces of fiction, the novelette *Who Goes There?* (published under the pseudonym Don A. Stuart in *Astounding Science-Fiction* in 1938; published in the collection with the same name) is perhaps best known as the basis of the seminal 1951 film *The Thing*, although the movie little resembled its source. A departure from his earlier thematic material, the story concentrates to a much greater degree on mood and characterization. A group of scientists isolated at an Arctic installation find themselves confronted with an alien invader capable of duplicating any living thing it comes into contact with. Perhaps the apogee of Campbell's literary achievement, the story effectively portrays an alien whose motivations are completely removed from human understanding. The use of the contained Arctic environment allows a mood of near-suffocating claustrophobia and inescapable mounting tension. With *Who Goes There?* Campbell unquestionably achieves his goal of a balance between the engendering idea and the literary devices that allow the idea to be effectively communicated.

Campbell's fiction writing almost ceased with

his assumption of the editorship of *Astounding Stories* in 1937. "When I write," he once said, "I write only my own stories. As editor, I write the stories that a hundred people write." And indeed, Campbell labored ceaselessly to place his imprint on every page of *Astounding* and thus on all of science fiction. He began by attempting to upgrade the image of science fiction, compiling endless lists of statistics to prove the relatively high social, professional, and educational status of his readers, and striving to lift *Astounding* from its pulp magazine image.

The great thrust of his efforts, however, was turned toward the improvement of the magazine's content. With a clear idea of the type of story he wanted, he began to assemble a stable of writers whose work, under his tutelage, reflected his concepts. He sought, as in his own writing, a balance between the *science* and the *fiction*, through writers who could postulate reasonable scientific advances, in light of current knowledge, and then intuit their effects on society and the individual. He heavily emphasized the quality of believability of science, plot, and characterization.

His influence on his highly talented group of writers—which included Robert Heinlein, Isaac Asimov, Theodore Sturgeon, and A. E. van Vogt—is virtually incalculable. He was apparently a rich source of ideas; Asimov attributes both the plot of "Nightfall" (1940) and much of the outline of the Foundation trilogy (1951-1953) to him. At the same time Campbell expounded his firmly held notions on theme and approach, and almost all of his writers, consciously or not, began to work along these lines. Campbell has been accused of imposing crippling limitations on the genre's development—by rejecting the use of sex as a character's motivation, for example—but at the time, the guidelines he created resulted in a quality of science fiction unequalled in the field. His talent as an instructor in the *Astounding* format and his payment of the highest rates in the business assured the maintenance of that quality. He sustained reader interest by printing the lively responses stimulated by his own editorials. He was an indefatigable writer both of fiction and of work on virtually every sociopolitical subject that could be connected with science, and his point of view—highly conservative, technocratic elitist—provoked his readers to prolonged and endlessly varied discussions. In the 1950s and 1960s these editorial debates began to concern themselves increasingly with Campbell's own growing preoccupation with the more outré branches of science, and *Astounding/Analog*'s fictional content began to

turn to the old technological emphasis. Campbell's former fondness for the primacy of scientific idea was perhaps overcoming the successful formula of balance between science and imagination. The New Wave was arriving and would eventually challenge his magazine's accustomed dominance.

If Campbell's influence on science fiction has in fact waned to a degree, it still remains very strong, stronger perhaps than any other in the field. His writing remains as an example, and his editorial policies are still to be seen shaping some of the best writers' work. The greatest testimony of his place in the history of science fiction is surely the title of the Hugo Award for best new writer: the "John W. Campbell Memorial Award." —*Gerald W. Conley*

Other:

From Unknown Worlds, edited by Campbell (New York: Street & Smith, 1948);

The Astounding Science Fiction Anthology, edited by Campbell (New York: Simon & Schuster, 1952); republished in part as *The First Astounding Science Fiction Anthology* (London: Grayson, 1954) and *The Second Astounding Science Fiction Anthology* (London: Grayson, 1954);

Prologue to Analog, edited by Campbell (Garden City: Doubleday, 1962; St. Albans, U.K.: Panther, 1967);

Analog One, edited by Campbell (Garden City: Doubleday, 1963; St. Albans, U.K.: Panther, 1967);

Analog Two, edited by Campbell (Garden City: Doubleday, 1964; St. Albans, U.K.: Panther, 1967);

Analog Three, edited by Campbell (Garden City: Doubleday, 1965; London: Dobson, 1966);

Analog Four, edited by Campbell (Garden City: Doubleday, 1966; London: Dobson, 1968);

Analog Five, edited by Campbell (Garden City: Doubleday, 1967; London: Dobson, 1968);

Analog Six, edited by Campbell (Garden City: Doubleday, 1968; London: Dobson, 1969);

Analog Seven, edited by Campbell (Garden City: Doubleday, 1969; London: Dobson, 1975);

Analog Eight, edited by Campbell (Garden City: Doubleday, 1971; London: Dobson, 1976).

Periodical Publications:

"When the Atoms Failed," *Amazing Stories* (January 1930);

"The Metal Horde," *Amazing Stories* (August 1930);

"Science Fiction We Can Buy," *The Writer*, 81 (September 1968): 37.

References:

John Bangsund, ed., *John W. Campbell: An Australian Tribute* (Canberra: Ronald E. Graham & John Bangsund, 1972);

Albert I. Berger, "*The* Magic That Works: John W. Campbell and the American Response to Technology," *Journal of Popular Culture*, 5 (Spring 1972): 868-942;

William Johnson, "John W. Campbell," interview in his *Focus on the Science Fiction Film* (Englewood Cliffs, N.J.: Prentice-Hall, 1972), pp. 153-154;

Sam Moskowitz, "John W. Campbell," in his *Seekers of Tomorrow* (Cleveland: World, 1966), pp. 27-46.

HAL CLEMENT
(HARRY CLEMENT STUBBS)
(30 May 1922-   )

BOOKS: *Needle* (Garden City: Doubleday, 1950; London: Gollancz, 1961); republished as *From Outer Space* (New York: Avon, 1957);

Iceworld (New York: Gnome Press, 1953);

Mission of Gravity (Garden City: Doubleday, 1954; Harmondsworth, U.K.: Penguin, 1963);

The Ranger Boys in Space (Boston: L. C. Page, 1956);

Cycle of Fire (New York: Ballantine, 1957);

Close to Critical (New York: Ballantine, 1964; London: Gollancz, 1966);

Natives of Space (New York: Ballantine, 1965);

Small Changes (Garden City: Doubleday, 1969; London: Hale, 1969); republished as *Space Lash* (New York: Dell, 1969);

Star Light (New York: Ballantine, 1971);

Ocean on Top (New York: DAW, 1973; London: Sphere, 1976);

Through the Eye of a Needle (New York: Ballantine, 1978);

The Best of Hal Clement, ed. Lester del Rey (New York: Ballantine, 1979).

Hal Clement is the pen name of Harry Clement Stubbs, one of the most exactingly scientific of science-fiction writers. Most of his novels and stories work out in minute detail the physical conditions for life on other worlds, from the astrophysical characteristics of the planet and its system to the chemical composition of its seas and atmosphere and the physiological adaptations of its inhabitants.

Stubbs was born in Somerville, Massachusetts. His interest in science and technically accurate science fiction dates from about 1930, when a *Buck Rogers* panel referred to a race to Mars, "forty-seven million miles away," and young Hal went to the library to check the reference. He took a B.S. in astronomy at Harvard in 1943, a master's degree in education at Boston University in 1947, and an M.S. in chemistry at Simmons College in 1963. His first published story, "Proof," appeared in *Astounding Science-Fiction* in June 1942, when he was a junior in college. Since 1949 Stubbs has taught science at Milton Academy in Milton, Massachusetts. His professional interest in teaching is as evident in the structure of his fiction as his wide range of scientific knowledge is in his subjects and method.

Hal Clement's science fiction is unabashedly didactic. The ideal reader of his books is very likely a science buff who would be moved to verify the astronomical accuracy of Buck Rogers's adventures. Each novel is a puzzle that requires lessons in physical science and in scientific method for its solution. The special quality of Clement's fiction is its combination of serious scientific accuracy with a clear sense of the need for scientific imagination. Empirical information, Clement shows, is only part of knowledge. Method and perspective can hide or reveal the significant facts, and perspective always determines interpretation. Clement's young heroes must learn how to learn.

Needle (1950), Clement's first novel, is the story of a symbiotic relationship between intelligent life forms. The host is fifteen-year-old Bob Kinnaird; the "guest" ("parasite" would be misleading though correct) is an alien, known only as the Hunter, who has chased a criminal of his own species to Earth. The Hunter lives in the interstices of his host's tissues and shares his sense organs. To a certain extent he can control Bob's metabolism and protect him from infection and some kinds of physical injury. With some difficulty and a considerable shock, he makes his presence known to Bob, and together they search for the criminal, whose crime is maltreatment of his hosts on his home planet.

Needle is a detective story; indeed, it is the only Clement novel with a real plot. But the success of *Needle* is due as much to Clement's ability to control details of character and setting as it is to the continuity of the plot. The detection consists mainly

Hal Clement

of a process of elimination in the effort to find the criminal's host. But Bob's home, a Pacific island that supports a limited population and a remarkable kind of industry, is abundantly detailed and fully imagined. The tantalizing possibilities and problems of the symbiotic relationship are Clement's chief concerns, but the possibilities are examined as functions of a fully dramatized story. Clement's later works do not reach so complete a state of integration.

The opening of *Iceworld* (1953) is an exemplary instance of science fiction's affinity for beginning in medias res. Sallman Ken, a high-school science teacher, is asked to help in some space police work involving a drug ring. Ken is hesitant but agrees. Shortly thereafter he is on his way to the planet— presumably inhabited—that produces the drug. But the planet is terribly cold, far from its sun, and Ken cannot imagine what sort of life could exist there. The planet is Earth, as the reader should have guessed from the clue that the planet's surface is "cold enough to freeze potassium," and Ken is not, after all, human. This joke is even better if the reader knows that the author, like Ken, is a high-school science teacher with an interest in space travel.

Iceworld announces the premise of the rest of Clement's fiction: cosmology implies geology, which implies topography and meteorology, which

imply biochemistry and physiology. This chain has a weak link to society and psychology—Clement's aliens tend to be human inside—but the rest of the links are quite well forged. By taking the Earth-as-Iceworld perspective, Clement very neatly demonstrates the flaws of perspective—the prejudice of logic and the inadequacy of unassimilated empirical evidence. Ken attempts to make the chain of connections, but his logic, based on his experience of his own world, Sarr, leads him into many errors that readers easily detect.

Meanwhile, on Earth, Mr. Wing, the alien drug traders' contact, tries to teach his children about the logic-and-evidence relationship in his own way. He supplies the drug that Ken has come to investigate, but Wing has no way of knowing that the innocuous substance that he trades for platinum is used in an unethical way. His decision to keep the alien contact secret and to enrich himself by it is certainly questionable—Clement's inability to deal with this problem is a serious flaw in the novel—but his method of trading with the aliens is a stroke of genius. Wing is a model teacher-father who initiates his family into the scientific method. He stresses logic, problem solving, and analysis, in addition to the observation and identification required for his lessons in natural history. The cleverness that

HOOK---Clement   1.

As usual, it was hard to decide whether or not to be sorry

for Bob. He ~~knxxknxxx~~ *knows* perfectly well that I can't do anything

about motion sickness, *except put him to sleep* but had insisted just the same on making

the flight that afternoon. To that extent, his trouble was his

own fault.

On the other hand, he had some pretty strong reasons for

getting back to Ell as quickly as possible, and most of those

reasons ~~were my fault~~ *could be blamed on me*. There are human beings, just as there are

people of my own races, who have no trouble convincing themselves

that someone else is always to blame, but I don't think any of

them could have talked himself out of my corner.

Nope On the whole, *therefore,* I was feeling both (guilty) and (sorry). Bob

was sitting beside the pilot, with ~~his~~ the jice sloshing around

in his ear canals, ~~and~~ the tension on his seat belt changing

and his nervous system trying to reconcile the conflicting data, and taking its frustration out on his stomach reflexes. Fortunately the stomach was empty.

randomly, We were bothing looking ahead for the first sign of

the island, but so far the fair-weather cumulus clouds which

topped so many of the afternoon convection cells were too

thickly scattered to let us see that far. Long-range visibility

would have been better below their bottoms, but the riding would

have been worse--we were above at least some of their tops--

and I didn't expect my friend to ask our driver to go any lower.

He had ~~asked~~ suggested getting above all the ~~tops~~ *convection*, but the pilot--

a fellow in his thirties named Dulac, whom we had met a couple

of times before--had given a long speech about fuel economy and

held his altitude.

It seemed a little silly to me. Ell is less than two hours

from Papeete even in this machine, which ~~was~~ *I had heard* called a Dumbo with

definite tones of contempt in its ~~driver~~ *operator's*'s voice, and I knew

309

"Hook," revised typescript

enables him to maintain contact with the drug traders helps his children establish even better contact with Ken and the Sarrian police. Once the Wings understand more about Ken, they cooperate with him. By this time, however, Wing has made his fortune and the ethical questions are buried rather than resolved. The problem, perhaps, is that Wing is the novel's authoritative voice, so the novel implicitly approves his decisions, as it approves his mode of fatherhood.

The joys of *Iceworld* are in the informational and educational themes: learning about life on the hot planet Sarr; discovering how the Sarrians learn about Earth and communicate with the Wings; and watching the young Wings learn from their father (their mother defers to her husband), who is a Mr. Wizard, full of teaching tricks to explain math, optics, Newtonian mechanics, chemistry, and biology. The plot is much looser than in *Needle*, but the puzzle-solving method absorbs most of the reader's attention.

In *Mission of Gravity* (1954), his best-known novel, Clement abandons the detective-story structure of *Needle* and *Iceworld* to concentrate entirely on the cosmology-physiology chain. A simple quest replaces plot, and the puzzles consist entirely of working out links in the chain of implications, based on observations made during the quest. But the planet Mesklin is so brilliantly conceived that it completely justifies Clement's choice of a loose structure for the novel. Mesklin is an enormous planet, spinning furiously around its axis, elongated around the equator and flattened at the poles. The main effect of its structure is that gravity increases from three Earth gravities at the equator to over six hundred at the poles.

The Mesklinites undertake a quest from equator to pole to recover an Earth space probe. Humans, of course, can barely move even at Mesklin's equator, so once an agreement is reached, the humans repair to their spaceships and remain in radio and television contact only. The Mesklinites are physiologically adapted to the extreme conditions of their world— they are like large caterpillars with claws and tough exoskeletons—but inside they are rather too human. On their journey they meet some interesting creatures. The humans teach them enough science to explain the strange qualities of Mesklin's geochemistry. The Mesklinite leader, Barlennan, emerges as the hero, with a distinct personality.

In "Whirligig World," the afterword to *Mission of Gravity*, Clement reveals the calculations and speculations that resulted in the world that is examined in the novel. Here, too, Clement announces his theory of science fiction as a game between writer and reader. The writer attempts accurate extrapolations according to the best available knowledge, and the reader tries to catch him in mistakes. Although that seems a limited theory of authorship, it works for *Mission of Gravity*. Mesklin is so rich an idea that it meshes perfectly with the part of his theory that Clement does not mention—his imaginative didacticism. *Mission of Gravity* is very much a joyful science-class romp. How better to teach and learn physics, chemistry, and astronomy than to wander through the vast conceptual laboratory of Mesklin, with its methane seas, hydrogen atmosphere, varying gravity, and bizarre but logically consistent life forms? Clement provides an explanation for each startling event or circumstance, but not until the reader has had time to guess or work it out.

Cycle of Fire (1957) demonstrates one of the flaws of Clement's method: the world he chooses to explore is at once too complex and too simple for the method. Abyormen is a planet in a double-star system, and the planet's chief oddity is a function of the double-star orbits: during "double summer" the planet's entire ecology changes. The pattern of change is not, however, apparent, and a stranger to the planet must adapt to and seek to anticipate the changes in order to survive. For two-thirds of the novel Clement tries to build clues, and he produces an interesting tale. Again, instead of a plot there is a quest, undertaken by an alien and a stranded human space cadet of sixteen. But Clement has no outlet for an authoritative voice to make sure the clues are correctly interpreted. And instead of leaving it to the reader to figure out, or writing a separate article of explanation, Clement depends on a spaceship load of scientists to explain everything. The reader must pick through the dry informative portion for remnants of the story.

Star Light (1971), a sequel to *Mission of Gravity*, shares the flaws of *Cycle of Fire*. Barlennan returns, troubleshooting for his human friends on the heavy-gravity planet Dhrawn. Clement uses the *Mission of Gravity* structure, but Dhrawn is not as interesting a planet as Mesklin. Perhaps to compensate, Clement multiplies the number of characters and quests and puts a version of the Wing family into the orbiting spaceship (writing in the 1970s here, the author makes the mother dominant). The result is a satisfyingly long stay in Clement's conceptual laboratory, but a cumbersome and often dull novel. *Star Light* was nominated for a Hugo Award but lost to Larry Niven's *Ringworld*.

Through the Eye of a Needle (1978) is a sequel to *Needle*. It is delightful to return to the island, to old and some new friends, and of course to Bob and the Hunter, who has no way to get back to his own planet. Unfortunately there is only the shadow of a detective story here, and the end of the novel drifts uncomfortably. Bob has graduated from college and returned to the island, but after eight years in residence it seems that the Hunter has unwittingly debilitated Bob's metabolism. The Hunter has kept Bob healthy, but Bob has lost his own reserves and defenses against injury and infection. This ingenious development leads to a number of touchy situations as Bob and the Hunter search for some way to signal the rescue party that the Hunter assumes is out searching for him. A mild love interest develops for Bob; there is a hint that the criminal from *Needle* was not after all dispatched; and several other checks and encouragements punctuate their efforts in this pleasant, occasionally exciting return to one of Clement's best settings.

Clement's style, from first to last, is direct and well controlled. The didactic structure of his novels rarely affects the tone: except for parts of *Cycle of Fire*, there is no lecturing in Clement's fiction. With a less technically expert writer, the game of best extrapolation means "what has the author sacrificed in science for the sake of the fiction?" or "how is the story flawed by illogic or misinformation?" In *Mission of Gravity* Clement wins the game by eliminating the gap between story and logic: the novel is the vehicle of its own explanation. If in *Star Light* this amounts to sacrificing the story to the explanation, it is nonetheless a distinctive achievement in scientific fiction and a style that refuses to be satisfied with sloppy thinking. —*Bruce Herzberg*

Other:

First Flights to the Moon, edited by Stubbs (Garden City: Doubleday, 1970);

George Gamow, *The Moon*, revised by Stubbs (New York & London: Abelard-Schuman, 1971).

Reference:

Poul Anderson, Introduction to *Mission of Gravity* (Boston: Gregg Press, 1978).

RAY CUMMINGS
(30 August 1887-23 January 1957)

BOOKS: *The Girl in the Golden Atom* (London: Methuen, 1922; New York: Harper, 1923);

The Man Who Mastered Time (Chicago: McClurg, 1929);

The Sea Girl (Chicago: McClurg, 1930);

Tarrano the Conqueror (Chicago: McClurg, 1930);

Brigands of the Moon (Chicago: McClurg, 1931);

Into the Fourth Dimension (London: Swan, 1943);

The Shadow Girl (London: Swan, 1946; New York: Ace, 1962);

The Princess of the Atom (New York: Avon, 1950; London: Boardman, 1951);

The Man on the Meteor (London: Swan, 1952?);

Beyond the Vanishing Point (New York: Ace, 1958);

Wandl the Invader (New York: Ace, 1961);

Beyond the Stars (New York: Ace, 1963);

A Brand New World (New York: Ace, 1964);

The Exile of Time (New York: Avalon, 1964);

Explorers Into Infinity (New York: Avalon, 1965);

Tama of the Light Country (New York: Ace, 1965);

Tama, Princess of Mercury (New York: Ace, 1966);

The Insect Invasion (New York: Avalon, 1967).

Ray Cummings was one of the most prolific authors science fiction has ever produced. In a career that spanned five decades—from 1919 into the 1950s—Cummings wrote approximately one thousand stories, and he has had in print, at one time or another, over a score of novels and novellas. Today, however, few of his stories are generally available. Most have yellowed with age in the hands of collectors and fans of the pulp magazines for which he mainly wrote. Only a handful of his novels are currently in print, and the amount of critical attention he has received has been scant indeed. The reasons for Cummings's relative neglect are not hard to find: he was one of those pioneers who helped pave the way for others while winning for himself few of the rewards his efforts deserved. Serious science fiction has generally moved away from the kind of romantic adventure story—space opera as it is contemptuously called today—which Cummings helped perfect. And yet, had it not been for pioneers like Cummings writing in the early decades of the century and helping to popularize this new genre, it is doubtful whether science fiction would have achieved the success it now enjoys.

Raymond King Cummings was born near New

York City's Times Square in 1887 when a triangular green park occupied the center of the square and the area was still quite fashionable. Years later Cummings would frequent Toffenetti's Restaurant on Forty-third Street and Broadway and sit at a table situated directly over the spot where he was born. Cummings came from an extremely well-to-do family, and after attending Princeton for two months when he was sixteen, he moved with his family to Puerto Rico. There his father and two brothers bought land and planted orange groves. His father sold the oranges in New York for a handsome profit. His family engaged a special tutor for Cummings, but his education was spotty, as he and his tutor spent less time on their studies and more on the entertainments offered by San Juan.

Cummings later boasted that the only regular job he ever held was with Thomas Alva Edison. For five years he edited house organs and wrote copy; in fact, some of the early Edison phonograph records still bear the facsimile of Cummings's signature. The story that Cummings was Edison's personal secretary was apparently the work of overeager press agents trying to lend the science-fiction writer a more scientific air. Likewise, family excursions to oil wells in Wyoming and gold mines in Alaska—remarkable enough in those days—were romanticized and exploited by the

Ray Cummings, portrait by his daughter, Elizabeth S. Hill

blurb writers for his books, who often tried to make Cummings seem like the adventurers who so often populate his novels.

He left Edison in 1919, and from that time until his death he remained a full-time writer. In addition to his science fiction, he also wrote detective and horror stories, almost all of which appeared in pulp magazines. Cummings died of a stroke in Mount Vernon, New York, on 23 January 1957. He was survived by his wife Gabrielle, who had written several stories with Cummings under the joint pseudonym Gabriel Wilson, and his daughter, also a successful writer, who had published her first story in *Liberty* at the age of thirteen.

Cummings's success with a 22,000-word novelette called *The Girl in the Golden Atom* allowed him to leave his position with Edison. The story was first published on 15 March 1919 in *All-Story Weekly*, a Frank Munsey general-fiction magazine (science-fiction stories such as Cummings's were called "different stories" when they appeared), and was an overwhelming popular success. Although Cummings was paid only two hundred dollars for the story (about average—the going rate was a penny a word), the demand for a sequel was obvious. Cummings soon complied with a full-length novel, *The People of the Golden Atom*, which ran in *All-Story Weekly* in six installments from 24 January to 28 February 1920.

Cummings had suddenly and brilliantly arrived on the scene. The editor of *All-Story Weekly*, Bob Davis, headlined Cummings in one issue as "A Jules Verne returned, and an H. G. Wells going forward." This was high praise indeed, and Davis was quite perceptive in pointing out Cummings's connections—both in theme and technique—with those two giants. One measure of Cummings's early success was that his work soon appeared in hardcover: his first two stories about the "realm of the infinitely small" were spliced together and published as one novel, *The Girl in the Golden Atom*, in 1922. It was extremely rare for the work of a pulp writer to be published in hardcover, and the fact that Cummings continued to have some of his magazine pieces published in book form—A. C. McClurg published four novels by Cummings in the next decade—indicates his status as a best-selling novelist.

Cummings said later that *The Girl in the Golden Atom* was inspired by an ad for Quaker Oats showing an endless series of identical labels dwindling into nothingness. Actually, a more probable source for the idea was a story by Fitz-James O'Brien, "The Diamond Lens," which appeared in the *Atlantic Monthly* in January 1858. It was about a man who sees a girl living in a drop of water on a slide in his microscope. The beginning of Cummings's 1922 novel closely parallels this story. While looking into an atom of his mother's gold wedding ring with a new and infinitely powerful microscope, the protagonist happens to see Lylda, a "fragile beauty." Immediately falling in love with her, Rogers invents a drug which allows him to decrease and enlarge his size. He enters the subatomic world, meets Lylda (who immediately falls in love with him), and becomes involved in some standard pulp adventures: Lylda's peaceful but indolent civilization is set upon by a barbaric and warlike race. Rogers, with the aid of his size-altering drugs, helps defeat the barbarians and marries Lylda. After five years Rogers's friend, called only the Very Young Man, follows him and immediately falls in love with Lylda's sister Aura. There ensues a second rebellion by the barbarians, which, despite the ability of the two men to become giants, succeeds. The heroes and heroines are forced to enlarge their size and flee to the normal world.

Cummings followed his successful first novel with what became a seemingly interminable series of sequels and variations on the theme of infinite smallness (and infinite largeness as well). Some of his best novels on this theme are: *Explorers Into Infinity* (1965; first published in *Weird Tales* as two separate stories in 1927 and 1928); *Beyond the Stars* (1963; first published in *Argosy*, 1928); *The Princess of the Atom* (1950; first published in *Argosy*, 1929); and *Beyond the Vanishing Point* (1958; first published in *Astounding Stories*, 1931). As Sam Moskowitz says, Cummings reworked the theme until he had "divested it of all novelty, and the advance of scientific knowledge further divested it of all probability." Nonetheless, Cummings had hit upon a surefire pulp formula. The idea of infinite smallness was clearly material for fantastic adventure, and it also possesses a kind of logical aptness. The idea of the atom as a miniature solar system— with electrons circling the nucleus in the same way that our planet revolves around the sun—provides a mechanistic view of existence that is reassuring in its orderliness and comprehensibility. To be sure, the microcosmic and macrocosmic universes always pose an immediate threat in Cummings's fiction (a villain usually acquires a size-altering drug and tries to conquer the Earth); yet, like the Elizabethan notion of correspondence, the concept of a series of universes infinitely larger and smaller than our own is an inherently appealing one. Though modern atomic theory has exploded Cummings's notions of

subatomic worlds, his stories still provide a great deal of pleasure and interest, even for contemporary readers.

The Girl in the Golden Atom is central to Cummings's work, not only because it was always Cummings's personal favorite and the most highly regarded of all his novels, but also because it is an example of his work at its freshest and most innovative. One of the occupational hazards of writing almost exclusively for the pulp magazines as Cummings did was that they rarely demanded a writer's best. Innovation was not always highly prized; in fact, as with most subliterary genres, the pulp magazines tended to settle for, even demand, formula writing. The money, moreover, was never particularly good. Even a popular and successful writer such as Cummings—receiving double what lesser talents might make on a story—still had to scramble to make money. Thus, it was not unusual for Cummings to have two or three stories a month in different magazines. With such an output, combined with an unsophisticated, undemanding, and in some cases barely literate readership, it is little wonder that Cummings fell into bad habits, endlessly repeating himself, writing carelessly, and often getting by with the most threadbare cliches.

In *Beyond the Vanishing Point*, for instance, the hero, upon learning that his friend's sister has been kidnapped by a misshapen villain intent on conquering a subatomic world, can only "shudder with a nameless horror." Cummings's novels abound with the flattest kind of writing: "indescribable scene of ruin"; "Ah, the futile plans of men"; "if I had only known then." Indeed, one of the secret pleasures of reading Cummings's work is coming upon one of these absolute clunkers. In *The Shadow Girl* (1946; first published in *Argosy*, 1929), the narrator describes a battle fought in a domed New York City, five hundred years in the future: "A hundred thousand personal combats. Inconceivable sanguinary warfare this! All indoors!" Sometimes the writing is merely pretentious: "Sixty minutes! A very little time! Yet it can be an eternity."

Cummings's earlier work tends to display his best writing: it is often clear, spare, and straightforward. Only when Cummings loses interest in his subject does he resort to the flowery, overblown language that so often characterizes his work. A good example of Cummings at his best is his first time-travel story, *The Man Who Mastered Time* (1929; first published in *Argosy*, 1924). The novel contains many of the characters who appeared in *The Girl in the Golden Atom*; Rogers's son Loto is now the hero. As in the earlier novel, Rogers has invented a device which allows him to see the incredible—this time into the far distant future. Rogers and Loto spy a beautiful girl, Azeela, who is obviously a captive. Immediately falling in love with Azeela, Loto decides to rescue her with the aid of a time-travel machine his father has recently invented. The novel follows the typical Cummings formula: the Earth, twenty-eight thousand years in the future, is in a second ice age; an advanced but indolent civilization ("not barbarism but decadence") is threatened by a horde of barbarians, who have managed to steal a time machine and travel into the past to obtain superior weapons.

The novel is memorable for several reasons. The action is compelling and exciting, and as in *The Girl in the Golden Atom*, Cummings is interested enough in this story to invest the kind of attention necessary to achieve the vividness his fiction so often lacks. He provides some interesting theories about time, carefully builds up suspense, and wonderfully describes Loto's journey into the future.

Subsequent time-travel stories, such as *The Shadow Girl* and the popular *The Exile of Time* (1964; first published in *Astounding Stories*, 1931), suffer from an obvious lack of attention: Cummings leaves them sketchy and undernourished. Even though Cummings never made any claims for the scientific plausibility of his fiction (he usually employs some meaningless mumbo jumbo to explain the workings of a particular scientific innovation, or shamelessly pleads ignorance), it is obvious that his stories work best when they are tied to a scientific interest. His best novels, such as *Explorers Into Infinity*, are adventure stories, but they are always balanced by a larger scientific curiosity. It is this balance which distinguishes Cummings's superior brand of space opera.

Cummings also wrote numerous space operas that are not particularly distinguished. These novels, curiously enough, still appeal to readers, perhaps because of their charming lack of literary sophistication. Nonetheless, Cummings was an innovator here as well, dealing with what were to become such standard pulp themes as space pirates in *Brigands of the Moon* (1931; first published in *Astounding Stories*); invaders from other plants in *A Brand New World* (1964; first published in *Argosy*, 1928); *Wandl the Invader* (1961; first published in *Astounding Stories*, 1932); *Tarrano the Conqueror* (1930; first published in *Science and Invention*, 1925); and

journeys into other dimensions in *Into the Fourth Dimension* (1943; first published in *Science and Invention*, 1926).

It would be easy to sneer at Cummings's work today. Even the best of it is, after all, merely space opera. His science is frequently faulty; his language is dated and sometimes preposterous; and his themes and plots are maddeningly repetitious. And yet, before finally judging Cummings's significance, two facts should be considered: first, Cummings began writing science fiction before that term had been coined; second, no matter what readers may think of his work today, his original audience loved it. Cummings had obviously struck a responsive chord in his readers, for hardly a month went by in the 1920s and 1930s when one of his stories did not appear in a pulp magazine somewhere.

It is doubtful whether Cummings will ever again achieve even a fraction of the popularity he once enjoyed. But at the time he was writing, at least, he provided his readers with something they wanted and needed. Almost every story is the expression of some fairly common adolescent fantasies. In fact, the general outline of a typical Cummings story sounds like a juvenile daydream: the hero is a young man who is suddenly presented with the spectacle of a beautiful (often "frail" or "slight") young woman in distress. Somehow getting to the girl, who often is an impossible distance away, the hero meets her, and they fall immediately in love. The hero must invariably protect the girl from a cruel, almost subhuman villain, whom he defeats in a climactic battle. The hero and heroine, hopelessly in love, are headed for marriage as the story ends.

One might accuse Cummings of pandering to his readers' escapist fantasies. Perhaps he did, but while doing so he also helped create a much needed audience for science fiction. Many of these young "escapists" became the talented writers and devoted readers of science fiction's next generation.

—*Erich S. Rupprecht*

References:

Sam Moskowitz, *Under the Moons of Mars* (New York: Holt, Rinehart & Winston, 1970), pp. 175-176, 421-422;

Donald Wollheim, *The Universe Makers* (New York: Harper & Row, 1971), pp. 23-30.

AVRAM DAVIDSON
(23 April 1923-   )

SELECTED BOOKS: *Or All the Seas With Oysters*
(New York: Berkley, 1962; London: White Lion,
1976);

Joyleg, by Davidson and Ward Moore (New York:
Walker, 1962);

Mutiny in Space (New York: Pyramid, 1964;
London: White Lion, 1973);

Masters of the Maze (New York: Pyramid, 1965;
London: White Lion, 1974);

Rogue Dragon (New York: Ace, 1965);

What Strange Stars and Skies (New York: Ace, 1965);

Rork! (New York: Berkley, 1965; London: Rapp &
Whiting, 1968);

Clash of Star-Kings (New York: Ace, 1966);

The Enemy of My Enemy (New York: Berkley, 1966);

The Kar-Chee Reign (New York: Ace, 1966);

The Island Under the Earth (New York: Ace, 1969;
London: Mayflower, 1975);

The Phoenix and the Mirror (Garden City:
Doubleday, 1969; London: Mayflower, 1975);

Strange Seas and Shores (Garden City: Doubleday,
1971);

Peregrine Primus (New York: Walker, 1971);

The Enquiries of Doctor Esterhazy (New York:
Warner, 1975);

The Redward Edward Papers (Garden City:
Doubleday, 1978);

The Best of Avram Davidson, ed. Michael Kurland
(Garden City: Doubleday, 1979).

Though for years a successful and respected
science-fiction writer, Avram Davidson has never
been entirely at home in the genre and has largely
forsaken it for fantasy and mystery writing. Even his
science-fiction stories have seldom emphasized
technology or rigorously extrapolated future societies.
Rather, Davidson delights in upsetting the conventions and in imagining offbeat or macabre situations.
While he is a prolific writer, his stories rarely bear the
signs of a hack—flat or cliche-ridden prose; instead,
they reveal an observant eye, a keen ear, and the ability
to create subtle irony, broad comedy, the bizarre, and
the terrifying. His stories are surprisingly free of
repetition. Instead of returning again and again to one
theme or gimmick, he experiments with plot,
characterization, and style and frequently succeeds in
reinvigorating a worn-out device.

Avram Davidson was born in Yonkers, New
York, in a section called Hog Hill. He attended four

colleges without receiving a degree. During 1941-1945
he served with the U.S. Navy as a hospital corpsman
in the South Pacific and in China (an Oriental locale
and mood figure in several of his stories, notably
"Dagon," 1959; collected in *Or All the Seas With
Oysters,* 1962) and then fought with the Israeli Army
during 1948-1949. He has worked at a variety of odd
jobs but has spent most of his life as a professional
writer. In 1958 he won a Hugo Award for "Or All the
Seas With Oysters" (1958; collected in *Or All the Seas
With Oysters*). He also served as the executive editor of
the *Magazine of Fantasy and Science Fiction* (1962-
1964) and during that time edited three volumes of the
magazine's annual "Best From" series. In 1963 he
received another Hugo Award when his magazine was
named Best Professional Magazine. Davidson has
been nominated for several Nebula awards and has
also won awards for his fantasy and mystery stories.

Davidson has published nearly a score of books
(with several more in progress) and around two hundred short stories. While none of his books has been a
spectacular success, he is a steady seller; several of his
books have recently been republished a dozen years or
more after their original publication (although others
are difficult to find). Over thirty of his science-fiction
and fantasy stories have been anthologized, many in
various "best of the year" volumes. Several of these
stories have appeared in more than one anthology;
"The Golem" (1955; collected in *Or All the Seas With
Oysters*) has appeared in seven and "Or All the Seas
With Oysters" (1958) in six—ample testimony to the
quality and popularity of his work. Yet Davidson has
attracted surprisingly little critical attention outside
reviews in science-fiction magazines and prepublica-
tion reviews by other writers. Even Damon Knight
and James Blish, two of the earliest significant critics
within the field, pay little attention to Davidson's
work. One can only speculate on the reasons for this
seeming neglect. Perhaps his evident preference for
fantasy has made him a less interesting figure for
some critics, or perhaps the more spectacular
successes and failures of other writers have diverted
critical attention. Some consideration seems overdue.

Much of Davidson's finest work lies in his short
fiction, especially the stories collected in *Or All the
Seas With Oysters.* Many of these stories are marked
by humor (at times sinister), a vivid sense of place (he
is a master of accumulating details to create moods),
or a sharp parody of science-fiction cliches. "The
Golem" is a clever spoof of the Frankenstein theme.
Mr. and Mrs. Gumbeiner, an elderly Jewish couple,
are sitting on their front porch, arguing about
mowing the lawn. They are accosted by an android

whose melodramatic threats ("When you learn what I am, the flesh will melt from your bones in terror") contrast ludicrously with the affectionate bickering of the Gumbeiners, who ignore it until it insults Mrs. Gumbeiner. Mr. Gumbeiner then slaps the android into submission and, remembering the story of Rabbi Low and the Golem, writes the Holy Name on its forehead and sets it to work mowing the lawn while he and his wife return to their gossip.

"Help! I am Dr. Morris Goldpepper" (1957) parodies two science-fiction conventions—the alien invasion and the council of wise and powerful leaders who resist the aliens. In this story, however, the aliens look and act like querulous senior citizens, and the council is the "Steering Committee of the Executive Committee of the American Dental Association." The aliens, who plan to move in en masse and receive social security, are defeated by the wisdom of the committee and the heroism of Dr. Goldpepper, who destroys the aliens' disguise by making them faulty dentures. The story is told in a delightfully pretentious prose which mocks the more ponderous stylists of the genre.

"Or All the Seas With Oysters" evokes a mood of quiet horror in a commonplace setting, a small-town bicycle shop. Ferd, the sensitive and bright partner to the crude Oscar, discovers "machines" which are alive—actually creatures which mimic machine forms, growing from a pupa form, safety pins, to a larval stage, coat hangers, and finally maturing into bicycles and other machines which regenerate when damaged. Ferd is found dead shortly after this discovery, with an unraveled coat hanger about his neck. The story is notable for its incisive character sketches (Oscar is untouched by his partner's death) and for the restraint with which Davidson handles the grotesque events. The pattern of these three stories is typical of Davidson: the intersection of the strange and the familiar, which can produce comic or terrifying results.

A number of his stories deal with themes of social injustice. "Now Let Us Sleep" (1957) is a mournful, poignant story of a race of "Yahoos," primitive creatures of limited but genuine intelligence, who are hunted, raped, captured for zoos, and finally used as guinea pigs to test possible cures for diseases. A sympathetic Earthman, Harper, whose efforts to rescue them have time and again proved futile, ends their misery by putting them and himself to sleep. Without any overt authorial preaching, the story succeeds as a memorable condemnation of Western man's arrogance and cruelty to "inferior races." Another indictment of racism and exploitation, this time in fantasy terms, is "Or the Grasses Grow" (1958) in which Americans break yet another treaty with the Indians, a treaty the whites have vowed will

Avram Davidson

be kept "as long as the sun shall rise or the grasses grow." After the treaty is denied, the sun does not rise. Moral fables such as this, written before the heyday of the civil rights movement, suggest a well-developed social concern.

"The House the Blakeneys Built" (1965; collected in *Strange Seas and Shores*, 1971) places greater emphasis on science than most of Davidson's fiction. Yet even this story of genetic inbreeding and degeneration on a remote planet is notable more for Davidson's characteristic treatment than for the scientific theme. He imagines a solitary house inhabited by a single (extended) family which can comprehend neither another family nor another house, and which destroys friendly visitors because of their otherness. The Blakeneys are queer-looking creatures with odd naming practices (Old Big Mary, Young Little Mary), which suggest the strictly circumscribed boundaries of their minds, and with a strangely poetic mumbling language: " 'Wasn't right,' he said. 'Wasn't *right*. Another house. Can't be another *house*, a second, a third. Hey, a hey! Never was elses but The House. Never be again. No.' " In this story, as in many of his short stories, Davidson takes a standard science-fiction device, the lost colony, and gives it a unique and refreshing expression.

This unconventional treatment of the conventional is evident in Davidson's best novels. *Rork!* (1965), for instance, deals with the aftermath of the "Third War for the Galaxy" but avoids the usual cliches of battles, revolutions, and palace intrigues. It focuses, instead, on the middle level bureaucracy of an exhausted planetary government, and on the efforts of one man, Ran Lomar, to overcome the widespread lethargy of planet Pia II. Pia II produces Redwing, an important medicinal herb, but production is falling off—largely because of apathy. Ran's quest to increase the harvest involves restoring political and ecological justice to that world and bringing a new sense of initiative and self-reliance to its inhabitants, human and alien. While the physical nature of the planet and its natives is well described, the novel's real strength lies in the satirical depiction of a worn-out, inert society.

The Kar-Chee Reign (1966) imagines an Earth conquered by an alien race intent on scavenging every last ounce of mineral wealth from the planet (their methods include moving whole continents). The Kar-Chee employ dragonlike creatures to terrify the primitive remnants of a human race which has mostly migrated to other planets and forgotten the Earth. The plot is standard: a gallant and resourceful band of humans determine to fight back and, rather

improbably, succeed. The novel is notable, however, for its portrayal of Liam, leader of the rebels. Liam is not the stereotypical square-jawed hero; instead, he is a man who consciously creates a legend, a heroic image of himself, which he uses to establish a new society, ruled by himself. He is neither pure adventure hero nor sinister, melodramatic tyrant, but a successful leader who takes full personal advantage of his triumph. But readers of Davidson's earlier *Rogue Dragon* (1965) will suspect that Liam's new order will eventually become a stagnant, oppressive regime.

Some of Davidson's best novels (and especially his more recent ones) are fantasy, not science fiction, but they may be briefly mentioned here. *The Phoenix and the Mirror* (1969), first of a projected series focusing on Vergil Magus, creates a vivid and yet dreamlike world—the late Roman Empire as it might have been imagined by the Middle Ages—in which Vergil acts rather like a detective following out the threads of a convoluted supernatural mystery involving the legendary Phoenix, a beautiful but suspicious lady, and a missing girl. *Peregrine Primus* (1971) depicts the episodic wanderings of Peregrine, bastard prince of the "last pagan kingdom to resist Christianity." In this novel the reader again sees Davidson playing off the conventions, for Peregrine fights no great battles, succeeds in no great quests, and rescues no damsels in distress (though he does help a brothel full of whores escape the local cops). Yet the novel is not just a reductive parody; Peregrine has a genuine longing for fullness of experience, and, in a startling conclusion, the adherents of a mystery religion, whose rites he has thrice spied upon, transform him into a peregrine falcon, free to explore all the world—punishment . . . or fulfillment? *The Enquiries of Doctor Esterhazy* (1975) is a loosely connected sequence of stories set in the mythical, early twentieth-century "Triune Monarchy of Scythia-Pannonia-Transbalkania," where Doctor Esterhazy solves, or sometimes just admires, natural and unnatural mysteries.

Almost by definition, most science fiction is future oriented—concerned with technology or its ethical, political, military, social, or economic impact. Davidson, however, has always been drawn more to the past. Even some of his early novels which clearly fall within the boundaries of science fiction manifest this concern. *Mutiny in Space* (1964, first published as "Valentine's Planet" in *Worlds of Tomorrow*, August 1964) actually takes place on a planet ruled by a matriarchal feudalism, and *Clash of Star-Kings* (1966) is set in Aztec Mexico. Many of his short stories are also set in vividly depicted pasts. His recent fantasy novels, like *Peregrine Primus*, are set in a past created partly out of history and partly out of history reimagined. It may be in part this love of the past—a past in which technology plays little role—which has led Davidson away from science fiction. It is perhaps revealing that *The Enquiries of Doctor Esterhazy*, which is largely a cheerful book set in a pleasant past world, ends on a somber note as Esterhazy broods over an ominous future.

—*Kevin Mulcahy*

Other:

The Best From Fantasy and Science Fiction #12, edited by Davidson (Garden City: Doubleday, 1963; St. Albans, U.K.: Panther, 1967);

The Best From Fantasy and Science Fiction #13, edited by Davidson (Garden City: Doubleday, 1964; London: Gollancz, 1966);

The Best From Fantasy and Science Fiction #14, edited by Davidson (Garden City: Doubleday, 1965; London: Gollancz, 1966).

L. SPRAGUE DE CAMP
(27 November 1907-   )

SELECTED BOOKS: *Lest Darkness Fall* (New York: Holt, 1941; London: Heinemann, 1955);

The Incomplete Enchanter, by de Camp and Fletcher Pratt (New York: Holt, 1941); republished as part one of *The Compleat Enchanter: The Magical Misadventures of Harold Shea* (Garden City: Doubleday, 1975);

The Carnelian Cube, by de Camp and Pratt (New York: Gnome Press, 1948);

Divide and Rule (Reading, Pa.: Fantasy Press, 1948);

The Wheels of If, and Other Science-Fiction (Chicago: Shasta, 1948);

The Castle of Iron, by de Camp and Pratt (New York: Gnome Press, 1950; London: Remploy, 1973); republished as part two of *The Compleat Enchanter*;

Genus Homo, by de Camp and P. Schuyler Miller (Reading, Pa.: Fantasy Press, 1950);

Rogue Queen (Garden City: Doubleday, 1951; London: Remploy, 1974);

The Undesired Princess (Los Angeles: Fantasy, 1951);

The Continent Makers and Other Tales of the Viagens (New York: Twayne, 1953; London: Remploy, 1974);

Tales from Gavagan's Bar, by de Camp and Pratt (New York: Twayne, 1953; revised edition, Philadelphia: Owlswich Press, 1978);

Science-Fiction Handbook (New York: Hermitage House, 1953); revised edition by de Camp and Catherine Crook de Camp (Philadelphia: Owlswick Press, 1975);

The Tritonian Ring and Other Pusadian Tales (New York: Twayne, 1953);

Lost Continents: The Atlantis Theme in History, Science and Literature (New York: Gnome Press, 1954);

Cosmic Manhunt (New York: Ace, 1954); republished as *A Planet Called Krishna* (London: Robert & Vinter, 1966);

Tales of Conan, by de Camp and Robert E. Howard (New York: Gnome Press, 1955);

The Return of Conan, by de Camp and Bjorn Nyberg (New York: Gnome Press, 1957); republished as *Conan the Avenger* (New York: Lancer, 1968);

Solomon's Stone (New York: Avalon, 1957);

The Tower of Zanid (New York: Avalon, 1958);

Wall of Serpents, by de Camp and Pratt (New York: Avalon, 1960);

The Glory That Was (New York: Avalon, 1960);

The Search For Zei (New York: Avalon, 1962); republished as *The Floating Continent* (London: Compact, 1966);

A Gun for Dinosaur and Other Imaginative Tales (Garden City: Doubleday, 1963; London: Remploy, 1974);

The Hand of Zei (New York: Avalon, 1963);

Conan the Adventurer, by de Camp and Howard (New York: Lancer, 1966);

Conan, by de Camp, Lin Carter, and Howard (New York: Lancer, 1967);

Conan the Usurper, by de Camp and Howard (New York: Lancer, 1967);

The Fantastic Swordsmen (New York: Pyramid 1967);

The Conan Reader (Baltimore: Mirage Press, 1968);

Conan the Freebooter, by de Camp and Howard (New York: Lancer, 1968);

Conan of the Isles, by de Camp and Carter (New York: Lancer, 1968);

Conan the Wanderer, by de Camp, Carter, and Howard (New York: Lancer, 1968);

The Goblin Tower (New York: Pyramid, 1968);

Conan of Cimmeria, by de Camp, Carter, and Howard (New York: Lancer, 1969);

The Reluctant Shaman and Other Fantastic Tales (New York: Pyramid, 1970);

The Clocks of Iraz (New York: Pyramid, 1971);

Conan the Buccaneer, by de Camp and Carter (New York: Lancer, 1971);

3,000 Years of Fantasy and Science Fiction, by de Camp and Catherine Crook de Camp (New York: Lothrop, Lee & Shepard, 1972);

The Fallible Fiend (New York: New American Library, 1973; London: Remploy, 1974);

Tales Beyond Time: From Fantasy to Science Fiction, by de Camp and Catherine Crook de Camp (New York: Lothrop, Lee & Shepard, 1973);

The Virgin and The Wheels (New York: Popular Press, 1976);

The Hostage of Zir (New York: Putnam's, 1977);

The Best of L. Sprague de Camp (Garden City: Doubleday, 1978);

The Great Fetish (Garden City: Doubleday, 1978);

Conan the Liberator, by de Camp and Carter (New York: Lancer, 1978);

Conan the Swordsman, by de Camp and Carter (New York: Lancer, 1978);

The Purple Pterodactyls (Huntington Woods, Mich.: Phantasia Press, 1979).

Lyon Sprague de Camp is one of America's leading writers and scholars of fantasy and science fiction. His interests in technology, history, and language have also resulted in the publication of numerous works of popular science, archaeology, biography, and magic. Having begun his science-fiction career in the 1930s—one of the generation that included Isaac Asimov, Robert A. Heinlein, and A. E. van Vogt—de Camp has provided a model for apprentice authors for forty years. Concerned purely with entertaining the reader, his science fiction rarely achieves the psychological or sociological depths of the greatest science-fiction novels; however, he is a master of the humorous tale, and his stories are always fast paced and satisfying. De Camp began his writing career with science fiction, and though his talents have ranged widely, he has periodically returned to the genre, accumulating twelve novels and several short-story collections. In recent years most of his fiction has been concentrated in the fantasy field, and many younger readers will be familiar with de Camp's work editing and expanding upon the Conan stories of Robert E. Howard.

De Camp was born in New York City and began his education there at Trinity School. After ten years at the Snyder School in North Carolina, he attended the California Institute of Technology, earning a B.S. in aeronautical engineering in 1930. He subsequently took an M.S. in engineering and economics from Stevens Institute of Technology in 1933. Although he has worked as an educator, lecturer, engineer, patent expert, publicity writer, and officer in the U.S. Naval Reserve (in World War II), for most of the last forty years he has pursued the career of a free-lance writer. He and his wife, Catherine H. Crook, make their home today in Villanova, Pennsylvania.

De Camp is the author or coauthor of approximately ninety books, including popularizations of science and technology (*The Ancient Engineers*, 1963, and *The Day of the Dinosaur*, 1968), history (*Great Cities of the Ancient World*, 1972), biography (*Lovecraft*, 1975, and *The Miscast Barbarian: A Biography of Robert E. Howard*, 1975), textbooks (*Inventions and Their Management*, with Alf K. Berle, 1937, and *Science-Fiction Handbook*, 1953), historical novels (*The Dragon of the Ishtar Gate*, 1961, and *The Golden Wind*, 1969), fantasy (*The Incomplete Enchanter*, 1941, and *The Clocks of Iraz*, 1969), juvenile nonfiction (*The Story of Science in America*, 1967, and *Darwin and the Great Discovery*, 1972), and verse (*Demons and Dinosaurs*, 1970). He has edited several anthologies (*Warlocks and Warriors*, 1970) and symposia (*The Conan Swordbook*, 1969). His *The Great Monkey Trial* (1968) is considered the definitive history of the Scopes evolution trial in Dayton, Tennessee, in 1925. Several of his books have been written in collaboration with his wife. Other collaborators have included Fletcher Pratt, Willy Ley, and Lin Carter.

De Camp is also the author of over four hundred articles and stories published in magazines, newspapers, symposia, and encyclopedias; about seventy-five radio scripts; and many poems, book reviews, and other pieces. His works have been translated into at least ten foreign languages, and he has himself translated stories from French and Italian. De Camp belongs to many scholarly, professional, literary, and social organizations, speaks several languages, and has traveled widely in North, Central, and South America, Europe, Asia, Africa, and the Pacific to get material for his books. He has been chased by a hippopotamus in Uganda and by sea lions in the Galapagos Islands, has seen tiger and rhinoceros in India, and has been bitten by a lizard in the jungles of northern Guatemala.

De Camp's stories fall into two distinct but related plot categories. In the first, he places his protagonists in an alternate time period, the historical past or far future. Here the time-travelers must struggle to survive, pitting their wits, courage, and technical know-how against the forces of darkness, superstition, and ignorance. De Camp generally leaves these people in the alien environment, for as he says, "stories that leave the protagonist in an exotic milieu deal largely with the character's problems of making the best of things. If he succeeds, why shouldn't he stay there?" In the second of the plot categories, de Camp places his characters, generally Earthmen, on another planet, usually a more primitive and culturally backward world, and follows the characters through their adventures. This kind of plot is often more madcap, employing quest and chase devices to keep the action moving and to introduce a varied setting. However, in both cases, the protagonists' survival depends on their own abilities to overcome the natural prejudices of various insular cultures. And de Camp makes much fun of the clash of values and cultural shock of men in situations totally different from the expected.

De Camp has the ability to visualize his characters, settings, and action, and to impress these vividly upon the reader. He believes that the creative mind recombines elements that it has received through the senses into new, meaningful, and useful combinations. Herein lies the secret to de Camp's ability. His immense erudition, wide-ranging travels, and ceaselessly inquisitive mind have opened up many potential fields for his writings that other authors have not the time nor the skill to use. De Camp recognizes that one of the most persistent handicaps of writers otherwise adequately equipped with imagination and a command of the language is that they simply do not know enough about their fellow man and the universe they share to avoid glaring mistakes of fact and logic. It is a possible fault in de Camp that he sometimes limits himself by his own conscientiousness about facts. In the preface to *The Continent Makers and Other Tales of the Viagens* (1953), Isaac Asimov tells of de Camp's reluctance to use the concept of hyperspace to permit his characters space travel uninhibited by considerations of time. De Camp instead observes the laws of relativity; his space travelers age only slightly, while those left home on Earth age considerably. This affects the plotting of the stories, often leaving the travelers without emotional ties to those on Earth and thus permitting romantic alliances with those aliens met in the course of the story. De Camp's comment on this issue is, "If I don't believe a thing is possible I try not to use it."

For de Camp this concern with details is not mere pedantry. He has an innate feel for what a reader seeks in a good story. The average reader may care little for the weight of the sword used on the planet Krishna, but if the accumulated burden of carelessness grows too great, the story will sooner or later founder. This explains de Camp's punctilious attention to research and the gathering of credible background material. Many of his novels can be read as how-to-survive-in-an-alien-world handbooks.

De Camp's stories are clearly intended to entertain. Though loaded with satire, that is not their object. Satire usually tends to be socially significant, and that is just what de Camp wishes to avoid. His "yarns are meant purely to amuse and entertain, neither to instruct, nor to incite, nor to improve," he tells the reader in the preface to *The Wheels of If* (1948). They may incidentally enlighten the reader but "don't blame" de Camp. Most of the characters are composites of his imagination and people he has known, sometimes echoing his own beliefs, sometimes not.

Indeed, in de Camp's fiction, character is secondary. As the author of adventure stories he finds that though a good character can sustain a story, such an emphasis can be overdone. De Camp's typical approach to a story is to conceive it first in the form of a problem: what would happen if . . . ? Or he may first get the idea for the setting and build up the background, as is the case with *Divide and Rule* (1948) and the Viagens Interplanetarias stories.

De Camp's first and probably best-known science-fiction novel was *Lest Darkness Fall* (1941), which first appeared in the December 1939 *Unknown*. It contains many of the themes and situations that de Camp would repeatedly turn to. With a bow to Mark Twain's *A Connecticut Yankee in King Arthur's Court*, de Camp arranges for his protagonist, Martin Padway, a twentieth-century American archaeologist, to be suddenly transported into sixth-century Rome. Shortly before being struck by lightning outside the Coliseum, Padway had been discussing a theory of time with a fellow archaeologist. According to Tancredi, if an object is displaced in time, into the past, any action it initiates will not alter time—it is not possible to change the course of history. Instead, a new branch of time begins, establishing an alternate and equal time-branch existing simultaneously with the original. Padway, coming from the future, is aware of future events—that Rome will fall to a succession of barbarian invasions and the dark ages will descend. With his own life at stake he sets about to change these events, knowing by the Tancredi theory that he is only changing his time, not all times. So he "invents" the printing press, a newspaper, and a telegraph system, and then becomes involved in politics, holding democratic elections and leading

the Gothic Army to victory over the barbarian invaders. Padway is a typical de Camp hero, combining a sense of ironic humor with a strong will to succeed. He is in his early thirties, in good shape but not athletic, and has both an aptitude for languages and some skill in arcane weapons such as bow and arrow and sword, both useful in cultures less advanced than his own. Padway is not given to any vices and is a competent mechanic with a solid background in the sciences. He is unattached emotionally but not chaste. In the end he succeeds in altering history, mainly by invoking mid-twentieth-century America's belief that scientific progress is the answer to the world's problems.

Divide and Rule, a revision of a 1939 serial in *Unknown*, is the account of Sir Howard van Slyck, second son of the duke of Poughkeepsie, a young man of limited political consciousness living in a feudal world ruled by "Hoppers," insectlike aliens who vaguely resemble kangaroos. They have partitioned the Earth into fiefdoms to discourage unified resistance. Sir Howard joins the underground movement against the Hoppers, and with his military training organizes guerilla attacks. The

Hoppers are actually quite stupid but remain dominant by means of a kind of helmet which enables the wearer to concentrate his energies. The climax of the story comes when a certain variety of flea is discovered which will get beneath the helmet and cause the Hoppers to itch uncontrollably, forcing the removal of the helmet. Once this is done, they are easily defeated. Thus *Divide and Rule* is a story of the awakening of political consciousness. Sir Howard progresses from viewing all his relationships in terms of class divisions to respecting people for their merit as individuals. This change in viewpoint is brought about by political and social indoctrination by members of the underground and also by Sir Howard's desire for the beautiful Sally Mitten, a woman normally beneath his rank and thus unfit for marriage.

Also found in the *Divide and Rule* volume is a short novel entitled *The Stolen Dormouse*, originally published serially in *Astounding Science-Fiction* in 1941. The two stories are appropriately linked because *The Stolen Dormouse* also takes place in the future, with an aristocratic social milieu. It is a variation on the Romeo and Juliet story. Here the hero, Horace Crosley Juniper-Hallett, must fight bigotry, the class system, and his family in a story which traces a boy's transition to manhood, his developing political awareness, and his winning of his heart's desire, the only daughter of the family his has fought for generations. Her name is Janet Bickham-Coates, and he first meets her by crashing a dance given by her family. They fall immediately in love. There are other parallels to the older story including a geneticist who serves the priest's role and a cousin of Janet's who is severely wounded in a sword fight. This story ends happily, however, as the now exiled young couple joins the forces of a revolutionary band based in Hawaii whose aim is the overthrow of the corrupt mercantile society.

In 1948 de Camp published *The Wheels of If*, a collection of short stories composed over the previous ten years. His next novel was *Genus Homo* (1950), written in collaboration with P. Schuyler Miller. In this story a group of people on a bus wrecked in a tunnel wake up millions of years in the future. Some of the passengers, such as the protagonist Henley Bridger, are scientists on their way to a convention. Others are school teachers, businessmen, their wives, students, dancers, a policeman, and the driver; the characters, in other words, are a cross section of humanity. They have slept for ages because one of the scientists, who unfortunately died in the crash, was carrying a gas cylinder containing a sleep-inducing agent that

-3-

on a smooth pivot or bearings. The wheel itself was
mounted ~~and~~ made heavy enough so that, when it was given a spin,
it ~~xxx~~ would keep turning, long enough for the potter to shape *for several minutes. This was*
an entire pot from a lump of slay slapped down ~~xx~~ on the center
of the wheel. ~~This~~ speeded up the making of pots many times over. *The potter's wheel*
Still
~~Later, refinements included~~ a second wheel, below the first ~~but~~ on *was mounted*
the same shaft, ~~so that~~ the potter could spin the wheel with his *Then*
foot and use both hands in his moulding. In many lands, this foot
wheel is still used. *in*

The first ~~wheeled~~ vehicles were ~~fam~~ carts, war chariots, *farm*
~~and wagons ... royal ... hearses to carry ... sacred carriages ... processions ...~~
~~and~~ royal hearses, and sacred wagons belonging to the gods.
The farm carts carried food to the cities and manure back to the
farms. The war chariots carried archers to harrass the foe or
heavy-armored warriors who jumped ~~xxxxxx~~ down to the ground to
fight. The royal hearses took kings to their graves and were
buried with them, while the sacred wagons carried statues of the
gods though the streets on holidays. ~~For nearly three thousand~~ *¶ For the first ~~over~~ 2,000*
years, after the invention of the wheel, wheeled vehicles were *or so*
hardly ever used for long journeys between cities, because the
roads were ~~too rough,~~ little more ~~in fact,~~ than bridle paths. *at the time*

~~The Mesopotamians~~ Around 1000 B.C., the Mesopotamians began paving *The first street paved was the avenue to the main temple.*
the main streets of their cities, probably to keep the gods' *The original reason for paving was ...*
wagons from getting stuck in the mud, in ~~these~~ processions. Little
by little paving spread, ~~until~~ by Roman times, a little before the
beginning of the Christian ~~Er~~ Era, a few ~~of~~ great cities were
linked by long stretches of paved road, and long-distance wheeled

with flat bricks or stones.

wisher might anger the god.

Unidentified revised typescript

leaked out. They awaken to an unfamiliar environment and are faced with immediate problems of finding clothing, shelter, and food. The scientists assume leadership, though not without dissension, during which the scientists' leadership is questioned and a small mutiny takes place. Henley Bridger, chemist by profession, gains control and leads them on a trek to points unknown. Eventually they encounter intelligent gorillas who take the twenty-seven stranded humans in, placing them in a zoo until communications are established. The humans help the gorillas to fight off a vicious tribe of chimpanzees. De Camp deals here with various themes: man against nature, man against man, the ability of man to adapt to new and challenging surroundings, and the foolish human belief that man is supreme and always will be.

Not all of de Camp's protagonists are men. In one of his best novels, *Rogue Queen* (1951), Iroedh, a worker in a community of egg-laying beings on the planet Niond, comes into contact with visiting scientists from Earth. A neuter female in a community like that of bees, Iroedh is a warrior and worker in the strict caste system which allows for only a single queen who is serviced by a score of drones and hundreds of workers. But Iroedh's interest in the artifacts and antiquities of Niond's former civilizations has set her apart from the other workers, and she has obtained a reputation as a dreamer. She is abetted in her hobby by a drone named Antis. When Antis is to be killed in a periodic cleanup wherein older drones are replaced, she enlists the help of the Earthmen to rescue him. She succeeds, but together Iroedh and Antis must wander as rogues, outcasts from their community. They eventually learn that the workers' purely vegetarian diet inhibits the secretion of sex hormones. Once Iroedh has eaten meat she becomes a fully functional female. Upon bringing this message to the rest of the communities, they realize that the old social organization is likely to be permanently disrupted. The book concludes with a democratic system of government being implemented with Iroedh and Antis serving as links between the native population and the Earthmen.

In 1953 de Camp published his *Science-Fiction Handbook*. In it the aspiring writer is given straightforward information about markets and editors; readers and fans; science-fiction writers and their preparations for their work; sources of ideas; plotting, writing, and selling a story; a writer's extracurricular duties, such as lecturing, giving advice and dodging fans; and even how to be an author's wife. All of this usable information is inserted into a readable history of imaginative fiction, biographies of the leading authors, and gossip, both caustic and friendly, about the authors, their backgrounds, and their literary interests, so that the reader belatedly realizes that he has been instructed as well as entertained. Some of the original information was updated or rejected for the shorter revised edition published in 1975.

De Camp was at this time becoming known for his Viagens Interplanetarias series. In the hypothetical future he posits Brazil as the dominant power in the world and the natural driving force of space exploration. The title of the series is Portuguese for "Interplanetary Tours" (the Earthmen in *Rogue Queen* travel under the auspices of the V.I.), and most of the stories take place on the planet Krishna, though the planets Vishnu and Ganesha often figure as secondary settings. Krishna is an Earthlike planet circling the star Tau Ceti, and its inhabitants are very much like human beings. In fact, for an Earthman to pose as a native, he need only learn the language and customs of one or more of the many little nations and principalities of this world, dye his hair green, attach false antennae to his forehead, and false points on his ears. There are problems, however, because Earth Adminstration in the middle of the twenty-second century cooperates with many alien races in the galaxy, and one of the cardinal rules is that science and gadgets beyond the cultural level of the peoples inhabiting such a planet as Krishna cannot be introduced by more advanced visitors. This premise is the basis for a number of the plots in the series.

The first novel of the group is *Cosmic Manhunt* (1954), originally published as "The Queen of Zamba" in *Astounding Science-Fiction* (August and September 1949). The story is a simple detective adventure in an exotic setting. The hero, Victor Hasselborg from Earth, is sent to Krishna to bring back the eloping daughter of a rich textile merchant. Her companion is Anthony Fallon, a personable young adventurer who has, in disguise, set himself up as the king of the island of Zamba. Fallon tries to solidify his rule by attempting to bribe one of the officials into importing guns, thus breaking the embargo on more advanced mechanical devices. Hasselborg succeeds in getting the girl back and foiling the subterfuge.

In *The Tower of Zanid* (1958) Anthony Fallon returns after a prison term and is hired by an archaeologist from Earth to guide him into an ancient tower built by an earlier civilization and now closed to all but a few members of a Krishnan religious sect. Fallon is also looking for news of three missing Earthmen, feared murdered by the natives.

Most of the novel is taken up with the plotting and machinations necessary to get Fallon into the tower. There he discovers an armament factory directed by hypnotized Earthmen, which is subsequently dismantled. Fallon quickly spends his reward money, and the story ends with the adventurer living a drunken and dissolute life.

One of de Camp's most enjoyable stories is *The Glory That Was* (1960), a rescue tale which reflects his interest in classical Greece. On an Earth sometime in the future, Knut Bulnes is hired by Wiyem Flin to discover the whereabouts of Flin's wife, who has mysteriously disappeared. En route by boat to Greece the men are struck by another craft and washed ashore in what appears to be ancient Athens. Bulnes and Flin discover a young soldier from Yonkers, New York, called Roi Diksen, who tells a similar story of awakening in a land far removed from the one where he went to sleep. Diksen helps them to meet various notables such as Sophokles and Sokrates in an attempt to discover whether they are dreaming or have actually been transported through time. With the help of an astronomer named Meton they see that the positions of the stars are what they should be for the twenty-third century. But why are thousands of people dressed in chitons and speaking classical Greek? The rest of the novel unravels this perplexity, and the reader learns that it is all a massive fantasy played out by the insane Emperor Vasil Hohnsol-Romano, a master of mind control.

In *The Search for Zei* (1962) de Camp returns to Krishna and the adventures of Dirk Barnevelt, who is sent to rescue Igor Shtain, a famous explorer from Earth who has disappeared in the Sunqar, a mysterious area in the Banjoa Sea which is the center both of innumerable legends and of pirates. It is rumored that a pirate leader has put Shtain under a hypnotic spell and that he is serving as an oarsman on a galley. Barnevelt is an accomplished swordsman, which would give him an advantage in this environment, and his disguise as a famous Krishnan warrior opens otherwise closed doors. The search for Shtain leads Barnevelt to Qirib, where he is negotiating with the ruler of this matriarchy, Queen Alvindi, when a pirate raid carries off Princess Zei, to whom Barnevelt has formed an attachment. Now Barnevelt is hired to rescue Zei. His subsequent raid on the pirates is successful up to a point. He discovers that Shtain is indeed being held captive, but he cannot bring him out of the Suqar, though Zei and he escape using water skis. The novel ends with a dilemma for Barnevelt. He has fallen in love with Zei, but she is the heir to her kingdom's throne.

Queens of Qirib take a new consort each year, so Barnevelt's happiness with Zei would be at best only temporary.

The sequel, *The Hand of Zei* (1963), tells the story of Barnevelt's and Zei's return to Qirib. They get into a number of adventures with the pirates, lead a combined army and navy against the pirates, and finally rescue Shtain. It is revealed that Zei has known all along that Barnevelt is an Earthman because he has a navel, which Krishnans do not have because they are hatched from eggs. Zei reveals that she too is human. Queen Alvindi was infertile, so in order to remain queen she had to sneak in a baby girl to pass off as her own daughter. Zei is now free to marry Barnevelt, and together they overthrow the matriarchal system of government. In an epilogue the reader learns that Barnevelt is setting up a soap factory made from materials in the swamp and that Zei has given birth to triplets.

In *The Hostage of Zir* (1977) Fergus Reith, an employee of the Magic Carpet Travel Agency, leads the first organized tour of Krishna. By this time Earthmen have been visiting Krishna for a considerable time, and the danger from pirates and hostile natives is supposedly diminished. De Camp's travelers are a misfit crew of oversexed, silly, selfish, xenophobic outlanders. Reith, however, is an appealing young man who is literally transformed from an introvert to a composed, even heroic, leader. Most of the action is seen through his eyes, so the reader shares in his growth, and the novel proves successful.

The Great Fetish (1978) is another sword-and-sorcery adventure, though this is not part of the Viagens series. On the planet Kforri, which vaguely resembles Earth, a young teacher, Marko Prokopiu, is sentenced to jail for preaching Anti-evolution. This doctrine teaches that the Earth, instead of being a plane of spiritual existence from which souls come and to which they return, is a material place or world like Prokopiu's planet Kforri and that all men, instead of having evolved under the guidance of the gods from the lower animals of Kforri, came from Earth at the time of the Descent in a flying machine. De Camp's tongue-in-cheek novel comically inverts the theories of Darwin. Prokopiu's wife, deciding that life without him is more than she can bear, runs away with his best friend. Prokopiu manages to escape from jail and follows his straying wife across the border to strange lands, where his many adventures change him from a meek teacher into a mighty warrior. His final adventure is to recover the Great Fetish—a deed which will prove whether his original teachings are true.

De Camp consistently turns out exciting science fiction. Though meant to entertain, his tales are more than simple stories. His voluminous research into many areas fills his canvases with brilliant colors of satire, history, politics, sociology, and humanity. De Camp's characters are people placed in uncomfortable and unusual situations where they are forced to make the best of it by using all the resources of inner strength they can muster. His touch is light, and his scope is controlled. Robert Heinlein has best characterized the works of de Camp: "De Camp's restraint may reduce the flavor for some—but not for me. The best fantasy is usually no more than light wine, the worst mere soda pop, all bubbles and synthetic flavor. The best of the Galaxy Busters are strong bourbon; the worst are rotgut. In this analogy I would class de Camp's fiction as a *very* dry martini."

—*William Mattathias Robins*

Other:

Sprague de Camp's New Anthology of Science Fiction, ed. H. J. Campbell (London: Panther, 1953);

Swords and Sorcery, edited by de Camp (New York: Pyramid, 1963);

The Spell of Seven: Stories of Heroic Fantasy, edited by de Camp (New York: Pyramid, 1965);

Robert E. Howard, *Conan the Conqueror*, edited by de Camp (New York: Lancer, 1967);

Howard, *Conan the Warrior*, edited by de Camp (New York: Lancer, 1967; London: Sphere, 1973);

The Conan Swordbook: 27 Examinations of Heroic Fiction, edited by de Camp and George H. Scithers (Baltimore: Mirage Press, 1969);

Warlocks and Warriors, edited with an introduction by de Camp (New York: Putnam's, 1970);

The Conan Grimoire, edited by de Camp and Scithers (Baltimore: Mirage Press, 1972);

Abdul Al-Hazred, *The Necronomicon, or, Al Azif*, introduction by de Camp (Philadelphia: Owlswick Press, 1973).

References:

Poul Anderson, Introduction to *The Best of L. Sprague de Camp* (New York: Ballantine, 1978);

Lin Carter, Introduction to *Literary Swordsmen and Sorcerers* (Sauk City, Wis.: Arkham House, 1976);

Sam Moskowitz, *Seekers of Tomorrow* (Westport, Conn.: Hyperion Press, 1974), pp. 155-169.

Samuel R. Delany

Peter S. Alterman
Gaithersburg, Maryland

BIRTH: New York, 1 April 1942 to Samuel Ray and Margaret Carey Boyd Delany.

EDUCATION: City College of New York, 1961.

MARRIAGE: 24 August 1961 to Marilyn Hacker; children: Iva Alyxander.

AWARDS: Nebula Award for *Babel-17*, 1966; Nebula Award for *The Einstein Intersection*, 1967; Nebula Award for "Aye, and Gomorrah," 1967; Nebula Award for "Time Considered as a Helix of Semi-Precious Stones," 1969; Hugo Award for "Time Considered as a Helix of Semi-Precious Stones," 1970.

BOOKS: *The Jewels of Aptor* (New York: Ace, 1962; London: Gollancz, 1968);

Captives of the Flame (New York: Ace, 1963); revised as *Out of the Dead City* (London: Sphere, 1968);

The Towers of Toron (New York: Ace, 1964; revised edition, London: Sphere, 1968);

City of a Thousand Suns (New York: Ace, 1965; revised edition, London: Sphere, 1969);

The Ballad of Beta-2 (New York: Ace, 1965; London: Sphere, 1977);

Babel-17 (New York: Ace, 1966; London: Gollancz, 1967);

Empire Star (New York: Ace, 1966; London: Sphere, 1977);

The Einstein Intersection (New York: Ace, 1967;

corrected edition, London: Gollancz, 1968);
Nova (Garden City: Doubleday, 1968; London: Gollancz, 1969);
The Fall of the Towers (New York: Ace, 1970; London: Sphere, 1971);
Driftglass (Garden City: Doubleday, 1971; London: Gollancz, 1978);
The Tides of Lust (New York: Lancer, 1973);
Dhalgren (New York: Bantam, 1975);
Triton (New York: Bantam, 1976);
The Jewel-Hinged Jaw: Notes on the Language of Science Fiction (Elizabethtown, N.Y.: Dragon, 1977);
The American Shore (Elizabethtown, N.Y.: Dragon, 1978);
Empire (New York: Berkley, 1978);
The Tales of Nevèrÿon (New York: Berkley, 1979);
Heavenly Breakfast (New York: Berkley, 1979).

Samuel R. Delany is one of the most successful of the so-called New Wave writers, publishing stories remarkable for their introduction of formal innovations such as decreased emphasis on narrative structure, heavy reliance on mythic patterns, and stylistic experimentation into science fiction. Needless to say, these generalizations are inadequate to describe New Wave writers. The fact remains, however, that Delany, along with Roger Zelazny, Thomas Disch, J. G. Ballard, and others, formed a new constellation of writers who during the 1960s were perceived as being in the vanguard of a movement which infused the science-fiction genre with techniques and concerns from mainstream literature, from the literary community, and from the academy. Delany's career during that period was atypical in that he wrote novel-length work almost exclusively.

Perhaps more than any other science-fiction writer, Delany has produced critical articles concerned with theoretical analyses of science fiction as a genre, using the methods of structuralist criticism to examine science fiction. His interest in semiology, with its attendant concerns for the relationship between linguistics and psychology, is indicated in his collection of critical essays, *The Jewel-Hinged Jaw* (1977), and in *The American Shore* (1978), an extended reading of Thomas Disch's "Angouleme" (1971). All of Delany's work to date has been concerned consciously with the nature of language and art, the role of the artist, and the creative process. It is therefore no surprise that his work has been taken up by the scholarly community, but at the same time it has become quite popular with the general readership. All his novels are

currently in print, except for *The Tides of Lust* (1973), a pornographic novel which Lancer published just before that house went bankrupt. Even *Dhalgren* (1975), his most demanding novel to date, had gone through twelve printings by the end of 1979.

Samuel Ray Delany, Jr., was born in Harlem in New York City. His mother was a native New Yorker and a friend of some of the Harlem Renaissance writers of the 1920s and 1930s. His father moved to New York from North Carolina and became a very successful funeral director. Delany's paternal grandfather was the first black Episcopal bishop in North Carolina and a founder of Saint Augustine's College. Delany attended the Dalton School in New York, where he received special attention for reading problems, and then went to the Bronx High School of Science, where his dyslexia was finally diagnosed. He wrote his first novel, "Lost Stars," when he was twelve or thirteen years old, and he wrote eight or nine non-science-fiction novels while in high school. None was published. During this time he met Marilyn Hacker, whom he married in 1961. They both won literary awards throughout high school and together edited the school literary magazine, *Dynamo*.

After graduation and marriage he spent an unsuccessful semester at City College of New York. When he was nineteen, to please his wife (who was working as a science-fiction editor for Ace Books) he wrote *The Jewels of Aptor*, which was accepted by Ace and published in 1962. His wife was thus a major factor in his turning to science fiction. She remained a major influence, helping him discover the structuralist critics and writers and later (1970-1971) coediting *Quark*, an important anthology series of New Wave science fiction and criticism.

From 1963 to 1965 he worked as a musician and singer in Greenwich Village and wrote four novels, *The Fall of the Towers* trilogy (1963-1965) and *The Ballad of Beta-2* (1965). In 1965 Delany traveled to Greece, Italy, France, and Turkey for a year's stay, during which time he wrote *The Einstein Intersection* (1967). This trip was motivated by talks with friends and by Zelazny's first novel, *This Immortal* (1966; it had appeared the year before in magazine). After returning to New York Delany played in a band for a year and a half, then moved to San Francisco. Since then he has returned to New York, where he currently lives, writing science fiction, nonfiction, and criticism.

Delany's mannered techniques, idiosyncratic application of mythologies, shared pool of images and symbols, webs of critical significance, all can be seen as elements of a larger structure which, along with his visually precise prose style, serve to draw attention away from the experiential flow of the narration and focus it on the technique of the novels. Each time the reader confronts one of the elements common to Delany's work, such as the multitude of protagonists who wear only one shoe or sandal, he is thrown back to another fictive construct. Delany's style confronts the reader with a self-conscious and literary vocabulary which turns the reader's attention toward the text as a formal structure. His are stories in which the creative experience of the reader is as important as the narrative. They invite, wheedle, and bully the reader into confronting the process of his reading and thereby participating in both the creation and the experience of the story.

This perspective is supported by the extent to which the novels and shorter pieces discuss the nature of their own creation and by the fact that many of Delany's novels seem to be about the process of writing novels, or more broadly, the process of communicating. Moreover, the protagonists of his novels are young artists who are in the process of learning their art, and the quests which form the narrative structures of his novels can be seen as readers' quests through the texts for the experience of the novels. His fiction exemplifies the theoretical premises of his criticism with wit, excitement, and great power.

Delany's literary background, allied to his prodigious curiosity about literary theory and his joy in telling a story, exerts more influence on his work than the fact that he is premier among the very small number of black science-fiction writers, or that he grew up in Harlem in a privileged environment, the son of a highly respected mortician, or that he attended some of New York's finest private and public schools.

Although produced when he was nineteen, Delany's first published novel, *The Jewels of Aptor*, is a sophisticated book with unusual and well-drawn characters moving against a vivid postapocalyptic landscape. On a far-distant earth, a crew of mysterious adventurers sails to Aptor, an island filled with radiation-produced mutations left over from an ancient nuclear war. There Geo, the protagonist, and his companions have a number of adventures which culminate with his theft of the third and last jewel of Aptor from the eye of a huge idol. At the same time, he meets the sister of the leader of his expedition, who is one of three goddesses Argo. The other two are her mother and daughter.

The novel follows the general outline of the story of Jason and the Argonauts, but it also belongs with more modern thief/guest stories such as Tolkien's *The Hobbit* and *The Lord of the Rings*. Delany's emphasis on literary antecedents, both within and without science fiction, begins a pattern of literary self-referral which is present throughout his novels and which quickly develops into a technique for referring the reader from one of his books to another in order to comment on the issues raised generically. At the same time it is evidence of his use of varying mythological archetypes to illuminate his narratives.

Another significant stylistic device which is present in *The Jewels of Aptor*, and throughout his other novels, is the presence of a young artist/criminal as protagonist. This device is tightly bound to Delany's use of the quest as a controlling narrative form. Most of his quests involve youths who are poets or musicians—creative artists of one kind or another—although in some cases the artists are not the primary protagonists. In these quests, the protagonists resolve personal problems at the same time that they search for meaning in their words; the inner and outer worlds are thus related within the context of the novel.

Furthermore, the artist/criminals who appear throughout Delany's novels are part of a French literary tradition from Villon to Genet, who

Samuel R. Delany

celebrate a link between art and crime. Identifying the artist with the criminal is a dialectical technique for exploring the roles of the artist in society. The levels of criminal behavior in which Delany's protagonists participate are broad, ranging from petty theft to piracy and assassination, from morally self-righteous activism to treason. The reason the two roles of artist and criminal are linked is fairly commonplace: the criminal and the artist both operate outside the normal standards of society, according to their own self-centered value systems. This allows them the detachment to comment on social issues, but more importantly it divorces them from social norms so that their points of conflict with society can define an aesthetic that emphasizes the revolutionary nature of artistic creation and the separation of the creative mind from the background of society.

After writing *The Jewels of Aptor*, Delany wrote a trilogy, *Captives of the Flame* (1963), *The Towers of Toron* (1964), and *City of a Thousand Suns* (1965), subsequently collected as *The Fall of the Towers* (1970). An ambitious undertaking for so inexperienced a writer, the trilogy is particularly notable for the depth of the societal construct of the island nation of Toromon, another postapocalypse society on a future earth, and for the imaginative presentation of a psychic war created in the minds of Toromon's inhabitants by a mad computer. It is also notable for the development of his use of common structural elements, such as the artist/criminal association.

Delany followed the trilogy with a slim volume, *The Ballad of Beta-2*, in which the protagonist studies an enigmatic ballad about the transit of a fleet of generation-ships through lightspace. Beta-2 is the designation of the ship from which a god-analog residing in interstellar space contacts humans. As the meaning of the ballad unfolds, the novel develops two themes, one mimicking the Christian myths of the annunciation and the nativity, the other mimicking Heinlein's *Orphans of the Sky* (1963; 1941 in magazine), a story of genetic drift and civil war among passengers of a colonizing space ship. Together, these novels may be read profitably as Delany's apprenticeship to magazine science fiction of the 1940s and 1950s: just as *The Ballad of Beta-2* mimics Heinlein, *The Fall of the Towers* may be seen as a variation on Asimov's *Foundation* trilogy (1942-1953).

With his next novels, *Babel-17* (1966) and *Empire Star* (1966), Delany's early stylistic and technical experiments are allied with original and inventive themes. Both novels are fictions of the highest quality and are concerned with the weblike relationship among thought, language, and society. With the addition of nonlinear narrative structures in *Empire Star*, another dimension is added to the web—time. *Babel-17* is a novel about an intergalactic human civilization, the Alliance, at war with another human civilization, the Invaders. The Alliance engages the famous poet Rydra Wong to decipher an Invader message in a code they name Babel-17. Due to her unusual linguistic gifts, she quickly discovers that Babel-17 is not a code but a language, and she decides to search out personally the people who speak it.

After many adventures, Rydra learns to think in Babel-17, a strange, dense language which requires thinking in a unique, analytic way. Thus armed, she is able at one point to analyze the stress patterns of the webbing which holds her by sounding out in Babel-17 the syllables of the word for the thing restraining her. By analyzing the word, she discovers where to attack the webbing and thereby frees herself. Likewise, thinking in Babel-17 allows her to direct an attack against enemy Invaders. The language triggers latent telepathic abilities in Rydra, and she uses Babel-17 to expose and destroy a potential assassin. Thinking in Babel-17 sickens and endangers her, however, and in self-defense she joins telepathically with a strange character named Butcher whose personality embodies some of the features of Babel-17. When Rydra and her allies realize that Babel-17 is similar to a computer language and is the secret weapon of the Invaders, who use it to program the Alliance's own eugenically cloned spies to turn against their own leaders, they are able to use Babel-17 to end the war.

The thematic concerns of this novel are elucidated by the conversations Rydra has with many characters concerning the technical properties of languages and the effects language has on thought and behavior. From the beginning of the novel, she is at the center of a web of significance whose threads are the relationship among language, thought, and action. For example, a crew-assembling sequence portrays Rydra as one who can talk and think in many ways. One of several assassination sequences shows her serving as a bridge among many conflicting groups, bringing them together. Her poetry is a communications technique, as is her muscle-reading ability, her knack for learning languages, and ultimately her telepathic ability. She discovers that thinking in Babel-17 imposes a view of the Alliance as the enemy, so that she sabotages her own ship, hypnotizes herself to forget that, and nearly drives herself mad with the contradictions. Only her telepathic ability and her knowledge of

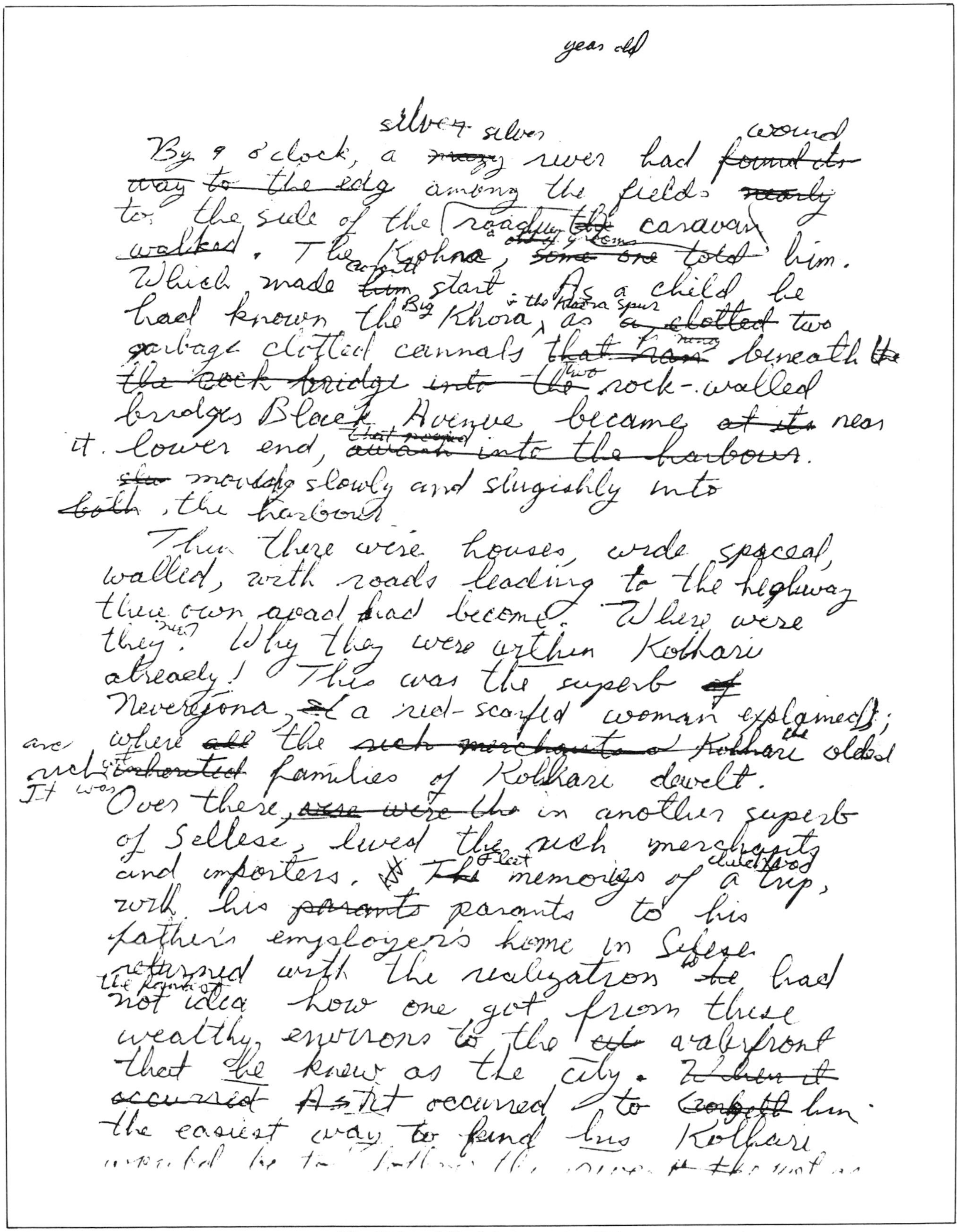

[handwritten manuscript draft with numerous interlinear insertions and deletions]

years old

silver. silver.

By 9 o'clock, a ~~murky~~ river had ~~found its~~ wound
way ~~to the edge~~ among the fields ~~nearly~~
to the side of the ~~road~~ caravan
~~walked~~. The Kohora, ~~some one told~~ him.
Which made ~~him~~ start. As a child he
had known the Big Khora, as ~~a~~ clotted two
garbage clotted canals ~~that ran~~ beneath
~~the rock bridge into the~~ two rock-walled
bridges ~~Black~~ Avenue became ~~at its~~ near
it. lower end, ~~that moved into the harbour.~~
~~it~~ moved slowly and sluggishly into
~~both,~~ the harbour.

Then there were houses, wide spaceal,
walled, with roads leading to the highway
their own ~~road had become~~. Where were
they? Why they were within Kolhari
already! This was the superb ~~of~~
Nevèrÿona, ~~a~~ a red-scarfed woman explained;
are where ~~all~~ the ~~rich merchants of Kolhari~~ oldest
rich ~~inherited~~ families of Kolhari dwelt.
It was Over there, ~~also were the~~ in another superb
of Sellese, lived the rich merchants
and importers. ~~The~~ memories of a trip,
with his ~~parents~~ parents to his
father's employer's home in Sellese
returned with the realization ~~he had~~
not idea how one got from these
wealthy, environs to the ~~city~~ waterfront
that he knew as the city. ~~When it~~
~~occurred~~ As it occurred ~~to~~ him
the easiest way to find his Kolhari

linguistics help her overcome the Invaders' weapon. Language is thus shown to be a way of programming human perceptions of reality, and Delany applies that thesis in the mechanics of the novel by creating several highly charged and controlling symbols, the dominant one being the web.

In *Babel-17* the web is introduced as a symbol for the enveloping structure within which symbols, images, metaphors, characters, and allusions interact to create a narrative. In an appendix to *Triton* (1976), Delany discusses his theory of metonymy, drawn from the semiological studies of Barthes, Foucault, and others, as words which together form a web of meaning within which the narrative, or text, exists. The web actually is present from the first, in *The Jewels of Aptor*, in a more restricted use as a metaphor for the political, cultural, and economic ties among remnant survivor states on a far-future earth. More often in Delany's work the web is an image of the creative relationship between mind and narrative, mind and language. At their most extreme use, the webs of human empire parallel the archetypal patterns of human consciousness, and therefore Brooklyn Bridges, New Yorks, and Earths run through Delany's galactic landscapes as literary or psychological archetypes are said to run through human consciousness. The web is the symbol of external and internal reality conjoined, and his preoccupation with that symbol is one reason why his narrative point of view and his landscapes seem so tightly connected: the symbol of the web controls both.

The web that symbolizes the relationship among language, thought, and action in *Babel-17* is not a linear construct. In *Empire Star*, published the same year, Delany uses a similar technique to produce a story line which twists in on itself like a web and appears to violate all rules of temporal sequence. In fact, *Empire Star* is quite subtly shaped in geometric or topological form. The seemingly sprawling and random narrative and temporal lines of *Empire Star* are rigorously structured as a cycloid, which is referred to at the beginning of the book. A cycloid is the curve that a point on a rolling circle describes as the circle rolls along a straight line; it controls the shape of the story as well as its content.

The novel tells the story of the history of a galactic civilization recursively. That is, the limited number of characters show up in the course of the narrative at different ages, performing different functions. The protagonist, Comet Jo, meets older versions of himself who help him as he grows and travels toward galactic center, the Empire Star, to bring word of the freeing of the Lll, an enslaved artisan race. At the end of the novel Comet Jo dies, only to begin the process which leads to his beginning his journey again. Thus the novel advances by spiral steps (rather than simply circular ones). Comet Jo learns what he does about the very simple narrative from those around him, who, knowing that time flows in an advancing cycloid (moving much like a child's toy, the Slinky), already know what will happen, both to them and to him.

An example of the way in which Delany picks up this recursive structural element and applies it to other elements of the story is his referring to *Empire Star* in *Babel-17*. In this case, he modifies the referent so that the *Empire Star* referred to in *Babel-17* does not seem to be quite the same novel he actually wrote, and to underscore the change, he changes the name of *Empire Star*'s author anagrammatically from Samuel R. Delany to Muels Aranlyde (which is also the name of a computer which appears in the former novel). The anagram symbolizes the rearranging of the apparent content of *Empire Star* which occurs when it is discussed as a work of fiction in *Babel-17*. In like manner, Delany transfers slightly modified scenes from novel to novel as part of a strategy to emphasize the structural nature of his fiction.

By twisting the narrative line into a geometric shape announced at the beginning of the novel, and then identifying that line as the shape of time flowing in and out of the Empire Star, he modifies the technique of the circular novel, exemplified by Joyce's *Finnegans Wake*. Each reading of *Empire Star* leaves us with more information, since the protagonist's life is laid out for us, and we, like the rest of the characters, know the future. Thus the reader comes to understand the shifting characters and the nonlinear narratives, and experiences the novel in the way the characters do. Furthermore, the process of creating a somewhat solipsistic reality leads Delany to consider the question of how such multi-temporal knowledge may be disseminated. As it is in Arthur C. Clarke's *Childhood's End* (1953), knowledge of the future in *Empire Star* is transmitted as myth. Thus, Delany's novels pick up the thread of another concern present from the very beginning of his work, and move from a consideration of the relationship among language, thought, action, and time to an analytic and imaginative investigation of the patterns of myths and archetypes and their interaction with the conscious mind.

In Delany's next published novel, *The Einstein Intersection* (1967), the protagonist is as concerned with the fact of knowing as Comet Jo was. He is concerned as well with the question of the extent to which myths and archetypes create reality. In *Empire Star* they define the shape of reality. *The Einstein Intersection* frees man, society, and reality from the bondage of myth and archetype through a mathematical definition of the nature of reality as both knowable and unknowable—Gödel's Incompleteness Theorem (1931). *The Einstein Intersection* is the first of a pair of novels—the other is *Nova* (1968)—which, more directly than any of his other books, attempts to discover what myths are. That the novels are allied is indicated by the interconnections present between them; for example, the epigraphs for each of *Nova*'s chapters are quotations from notebooks Delany kept while writing *The Einstein Intersection* and wandering about the Mediterranean.

On the Earth of *The Einstein Intersection*, over thirty thousand years in the future, a new race of beings struggles to become human and thus stabilize society and culture. Mutations run rampant, both among the "humans" and in the landscape. People are born who are fundamentally "different" from humans—they have strange bodies and psychic powers of varying kinds—and who are being killed by another "different" character called Kid Death, who fears and hates them. The people of this strange and different earth must constantly mix the gene pool to maintain human form, for nature is changing them. Mythic parallels swarm through the novel.

The protagonist, Lo Lobey, narrates the story of his quest both to kill Kid Death and to find his lost love Friza. His search takes him from his simple village to a major city. Along the way he meets Spider (remember the web), who explains that the earth now exists in a universe dominated by Gödel's theorem: "In any closed mathematical system there are an infinite number of true theorems which, though contained in the original system, can not be deduced from it." In effect, the controlling elements of myth and of the past no longer dominate the new people of earth. Spider also reveals that Lobey embodies a basic force, music or relation. Kid Death is identified with change, and a character named Green-eye with creation. At the same time that Lobey is an avatar of a basic force, he is still Lobey, whom Kid Death says he needs. At the end of the novel Lobey has participated in Kid Death's murder, regained and relost Friza, and is prepared to leave a diminished earth for the larger context of galactic space.

The reader shares Lobey's confusion over what he is supposed to do. He is looking for instructions, directions, the kind of predetermined knowledge which he must learn to shun. While the actual quest Lobey undertakes is easily apprehensible and described with great attention to detail, the argument of the novel is carried by the shifting patterns of incomplete myth, and this also adds to the confusion. Lobey in his quest for Friza is like Orpheus, for example, but also like Jesus in his quest to kill Death, and finally like Lo Hawk, another character, in his desire to leave Earth. Lobey is none of them, however, no matter how hard the patterns try to force him to be one or the other.

Some of the confusion that arises does so because characters fill so many different mythic roles at various times. This is necessary to the thematic point of the novel, which concerns the freeing of behavior from the confines of mythic patterns by working through the roles they impose. As Lobey and the other characters advance through the novel, they exhaust a variety of myths. When Lobey drives his machete into Green-eye's thigh, he kills not only Green-eye, but also the cycle of mythic patterns he has been caught in, and he moves forward to help create a different future for the world, having conquered the major obstructions to the emergence of difference.

As Lobey moves ever closer to his goal, he confronts the concept of difference more and more often. These differences are personal, societal, and cultural. When Lobey does act, he makes his decisions in a "different" way, not by rational analysis but by irrational choice, a way appropriate to the dictates of the new universe which is coming into being. This is the root of his selfishness and part of his difference. He begins accepting this when he finds his own music while composing a dirge for lost Friza, a dirge for the past, and he fully accepts it when he realizes his isolation in his quest. At that moment he transcends the myths he has been playing out and, although surrounded by mythic patterns, makes his own patterns. He chooses to look past Friza, he chooses to kill Green-eye, and he chooses to help kill Kid Death. As he embodies order, he imposes a different order on his world, his universe.

In *Nova*, Delany turns his focus to the creation of the novel itself. Both nova and novel come from the Latin root for "new" and this concern with creation echoes the concerns of *The Einstein Intersection*. The etymological game implied in the title refers one to the linguistic concerns of *Babel-17*. *Nova* is about what makes a novel: narrative, mythic quest, character acting against the backdrop of society, the play of history, conflict, relationship. It is at once a grail quest and, again, a quest for the golden fleece.

Against a carefully painted portrait of galactic

civilization, a band of heroes led by Lorq Von Ray, scion of the most powerful family in the Pleiades Federation, attempts to control the future of civilization by wresting Illyrion from the heart of a nova. Illyrion is the generic name for the major energy source for human civilization used for everything from heating planets to driving starships to powering musical instruments. It is an appropriate symbol of power, which is what the true battle is about. Von Ray is after a quantity of Illyrion which would tip the economic and political balance of civilization and at the same time raise the Von Ray family over its rivals, the Reds.

Lorq's crew includes Katin, a young scholar taking notes on writing a novel, and Mouse, a young gypsy who plays the sensory syrinx; Sebastian and Tyy, a married couple; and Lynceos and Idas, twin brothers, one of whom is black and the other white. Each pair is a mythic pair, and the mythologies coalesce around Tyy's Tarot readings. The other half of the broken pair implied by Lorq's isolation is Blind Dan, an old friend and employee of his who, on an earlier attempt to mine a nova, looked into the exploding heart of the star and went mad, his senses whipped to constant stimulation by exposure to its energies. Another potential pairing for Lorq is Ruby Red, sister of the one-armed, mad Prince Red, scion of the most powerful family in the Draco sector, the old home of man whose capital is Earth. The battle between the Reds and Von Ray is the battle between Draco and the Pleiades.

Nova focuses on the development of the death duel between Lorq and Prince Red. Mouse's history is described, focusing on his attainment and mastery of the syrinx, a marvelous olfactory, visual, and aural instrument. Katin's history is more briefly described: he is a lover of moons, an eccentric scholar, and an antiquarian. The histories of the rest of the crew are given briefly since they play comparatively minor roles in the central conflict and serve mainly as mythic incarnations.

The narrative of *Nova* is spare in outline, and the bulk of the novel consists of flashbacks to Von Ray's earlier life. These contain the personal history of the battle between the Von Rays and the Reds, showing an extensive economic, political, and social analysis of civilization which parallels the interfamily feud. The development of a complex social structure, replete with neural sockets (for plugging into machinery) and theories of work, art, literature, and culture, is more extensive than in any of Delany's earlier novels.

The reason for this elaboration is expressed by the parallel between the conflict of the families and the conflict between the Pleiades and Draco, which elevates the individual to symbolize the state, as in Greek tragedies. Delany chooses to focus on the significance of society in the novel and on society's relationship to the actions of individual characters. The reader is led to consider this issue through Katin's extensive note-taking and theorizing about history, culture, aesthetics, and the art of the novel. It is Katin who supplies the aesthetic as well as the cultural narrative which weaves through *Nova* and which illuminates the personal history of the Von Rays and the Reds. Katin's theory of culture is the web which infuses all Delany's novels, here in the guise of a structural theory of communications reinforced by Katin's method of learning what he reports: through the communications media of society. It is in this context that a signal event in the history of the society of *Nova*, the assassination of one of Lorq's uncles, is shared by all watching the event through a device providing complete sensory communication. The sharing of a single event, an individual's violent death, is present in *The Fall of the Towers* trilogy. Other such nearly identical scenes permeate *Nova*, reinforcing its novelistic focus.

The dialogue between Katin's note-taking and Mouse's playing of the syrinx is fundamental to artistic creation: how much should be predetermined, intellectualized, and how much should be spontaneous, partaking of the universe described by Gödel's Theorem as enunciated in *The Einstein Intersection*. The names of the pair (cat and mouse) define the play of dialogue between them and further define a central focus where history and psychology meet: where the rational and intellectual, as embodied in the political issues underlying the quest, conflict with the irrational, embodied by Lorq's hatred of Prince Red and desire for Ruby.

These two arguments focus attention on the architectonics of the novel and the intricate web that is woven of mythic patterns, characters, theories, and spontaneous behaviors. *Nova* is Delany's novel about novels and serves as a summary of his work to that point, incorporating the structural skills of *Empire Star*, the linguistic concerns of *Babel-17*, the mythic awareness of *The Einstein Intersection*, and the complex vision of an alien culture present in *The Fall of the Towers*. *Nova* is evidence of Delany's gathering strength before the massive creation of *Dhalgren*.

More than five years elapsed between the publication of *Nova* and that of *Dhalgren*, during which Delany published *Driftglass*, an anthology of short fiction, and only one novel, *The Tides of Lust*

(1973), which was not widely distributed and whose distribution would have been significantly affected by its explicit sexual content in any event. *Dhalgren* became an immediate best-seller and created quite a stir. Some reviewers denied it was science fiction at all, others condemned it as being self-indulgent, and still others claimed it made no sense whatsoever. Nobody, however, criticized Delany's masterful use of language in *Dhalgren*. Indeed, his prose style is brilliant. While a debate still continues on the value of this novel as a work of art, it has proven to be a durable, popular book and has sold over 500,000 copies to date.

At the most basic level, each of Delany's earlier novels is reasonably accessible to the casual reader. That is, novels such as *The Einstein Intersection* and *Empire Star* may confuse some readers, but the sense of quest begun and ended is apparent, the protagonists's awareness is easy to share in, and enough traditional genre landscapes exist to give the reader a comforting sense of location among Delany's constructs. But in *Dhalgren* none of those supports is provided. The reader who enters the novel casually is caught by the mass of it (over 875 pages) and the lack of stable elements. The protagonist does not know who he is, has lapses of consciousness, and forgets his experiences. Mythic patterns weave as extended metaphors throughout the novel. The landscape shifts from moment to moment; time stops and then lurches forward; symbols migrate from host to host. Bellona, the city landscape of the novel, is inexplicable. It makes no sense except as an extended metaphor for chaos, being opposed by the human, artistic ordering of experience for which the novel itself serves as metaphor. Thus the novel as an aesthetic construction is in conflict with its landscape.

Every technique used in *Dhalgren* is present in the earlier novels. The major difference between *Dhalgren* and the earlier novels is that by locating *Dhalgren* in the present, Delany has freed its prose from the didactic quality required to describe and define imaginative settings. Thus, his prose becomes even more symbolic than usual, and the novel's descriptive technique imparts to the commonest event mythic significance because of the fullness of detail provided to it. This style of description works well with the purpose of the novel.

Dhalgren is the story of a young man, apparently suffering from amnesia, who enters the city of Bellona, which is constantly in the throes of apocalyptic collapse. He has many adventures, becoming first a poet, then the acknowledged leader of a teenage gang, the Scorpions, who haunt the city.

At the end of the book, the protagonist is disgorged from the city during a cataclysm of mysterious nature, only to meet a group entering who both mirror those leaving and are reminiscent of the group which the protagonist met when he entered.

The combination of fluid landscape interacting with a fluid point of view makes *Dhalgren* a difficult novel to read, and in places language seems to be twisted out of comprehensible form. This is particularly true of the beginning of the story. It begins with the genesis of a protagonist, one so unformed that he has no name, no identity, the quest for which is the novel's central theme. In this quest, he must wrest that identity from the landscape and the action of the novel: in other words, from the structure which has given rise to him.

The first sentence is only part of a sentence: "to wound the autumnal city." The phrase is composed of only a verbal, an action without a subject, and its complement, a setting. The second sentence, also incomplete, develops the purpose of these fragments: "So howled out for the wind to give him a name." Still the subject is absent, but "him" exists, an object, weaker and more passive in the syntax of the sentence than the subject would be, but present all the same. Furthermore, the sentence is constructed in such a way that it generates a tension around the site of the missing subject, and it is that tension within the structure of the sentence which generates the subject as distinct from landscape.

Here in the opening lines and throughout the narrative the fundamental combat between subject and object is commented upon. The self, in the form of the protagonist Kid, wrests its identity from its experiences in the narrative, so that by the end of the novel the self has absorbed all background objects into its mind. The myths, symbols, metaphors, and images which parallel each other from novel to novel are caught in a web of intersecting references within *Dhalgren*, where they gain extra significance as techniques whereby the artist subsumes landscape in his/her consciousness. The fragmentary "plague journal" which concludes the novel reflects this pattern: it presents the episodes of which the novel is constructed as the unalloyed experience or report of the perceiver within his own mind. Background is, after all, internal, it seems to say. And yet paradoxically, the ur-journal referred to frequently within the novel and of which the novel *Dhalgren* is part, is itself part of the background.

The ambiguity of both landscapes, those with objective reality and of those which exist only within the human mind, forms the basis for a theory of dynamic relationship between self and other, structure and meaning. This is why the last chapter is full of emendations and alternative constructions, why it collapses into a working draft of the novel, then deteriorates into atemporal, chaotic, nonsense fragments: the web of creation is being unraveled down to its core; the self becomes abstraction.

Dhalgren ends with the incomplete sentence, "Waiting here, away from the terrifying weaponry, out of the halls of vapor and light, beyond holland and into the hills, I have come to" (no end punctuation). This is essentially subject and verb, the perceiver and the act of perceiving, lacking the perceived, which was all there was at the beginning of the book. This last line can mean that he becomes aware, he awakens, or it can mean that what is left is only the perceiver perceiving. The logical rules underlying this fragment demand completion, a context in which the subject can act, perhaps the context which the opening fragment of the novel provides. Paradoxically, however, the novel truly ends despite its circularity. At the end Kid has a name and a life, both of which are the novel itself; he is a persona whose experience in *Dhalgren* defines him.

Triton (1976), Delany's next novel, is an attempt at a psychological utopian novel which presents a future society where all forms of social interaction and personal identification are possible. In many ways *Triton* offers the reader a vision of the same chaotic existence as does *Dhalgren*, yet an existence viewed from a more stabilized point of view. In *Triton*'s world of possibilities the interactions of characters generate webs of behavior which identify individuals. The narrative exists within a critical web of semiological thought which is explicated in two appendices, one a construct of "metalogic" and the other an essay on semiology, both serving as intellectual poles for the novel.

The appendices to the narrative of *Triton* provide a smooth transition into Delany's structuralist criticism of science fiction in *The Jewel-Hinged Jaw* and *The American Shore*. The first is a collection of essays written mostly during 1970-1976 which chronicle the development of his critical thought. The second offers the fruit of that development. Delany's more recent fiction—*Empire* (1978), in the form of a comic book, and *The Tales of Nevèrÿon* (1979), a probing psycholinguistic and mythological study in a setting of heroic fantasy—reveal a

continuing interest in experimentation with the forms of fiction.

Other:

Quark 1-4, edited by Delany and Marilyn Hacker (New York: Paperback Library, 1970-1971);
Nebula Winners 13, edited by Delany (New York: Harper & Row, 1980).

Periodical Publications:

"Prismatica," *Magazine of Fantasy and Science Fiction*, 317 (October 1977): 6-33;
"Teaching Science Fiction: Unique Challenges," by Delany, Gregory Benford, Robert Scholes, Alan J. Friedman, and John Woodcock, *Science-Fiction Studies*, 19 (November 1979): 249-262.

References:

Peter S. Alterman, "The Surreal Translations of Samuel R. Delany," *Science-Fiction Studies*, 4 (March 1977): 25-34;
Douglas Barbour, "Cultural Invention and Metaphor in the Novels of Samuel R. Delany," *Foundation*, 7/8 (March 1975): 105-121;
Barbour, "Multiplex Misdemeanors: The Figure of the Artist and the Criminal in the Science Fiction Novels of Samuel R. Delany," *Khatru #2* (1975);
Sandra Miesel, "Samuel R. Delany's Use of Myth in *Nova*," *Extrapolation*, 12 (May 1971): 86-93;
Darrell Schweitzer, "Algol Interview: Samuel R. Delany," *Algol*, 13 (Summer 1976):16-22;
Stephen Scobie, "Different Mazes: Mythology in Samuel Delany's *The Einstein Intersection*," *Riverside Quarterly*, 5 (July 1971): 12-19;
George Edgar Slusser, *The Delany Intersection; Samuel R. Delany Considered As a Writer of Semi-Precious Words* (San Bernardino: Borgo, 1977);
Jane B. Weedman, "Delany's *Babel-17*: The Power of Language," *Extrapolation*, 19 (May 1978): 132-137;
Weedman, *Reader's Guide to Samuel R. Delany* (West Linn, Oreg.: Starmont, 1979).

LESTER DEL REY
(2 June 1915-   )

BOOKS: *". . . And Some Were Human"* (Philadelphia: Prime Press, 1948);

It's Your Atomic Age (New York: Abelard Press, 1951);

A Pirate Flag for Monterey: The Story of the Sack of Monterey (Philadelphia & Toronto: Winston, 1952);

Marooned on Mars (Philadelphia & Toronto: Winston, 1952; London: Hutchinson, 1953);

Rocket Jockey, as Philip St. John (Philadelphia & Toronto: Winston, 1952); republished as *Rocket Pilot* (London: Hutchinson, 1955);

Attack from Atlantis (Philadelphia & Toronto: Winston, 1953);

Battle on Mercury, as Erik van Lhin (Philadelphia & Toronto: Winston, 1953);

The Mysterious Planet, as Kenneth Wright (Philadelphia & Toronto: Winston, 1953);

Step to the Stars (Philadelphia & Toronto: Winston, 1954; London: Hutchinson, 1956);

Rockets to Nowhere, as Philip St. John (Philadelphia & Toronto: Winston, 1954);

Preferred Risk, by del Rey and Frederik Pohl, as Edson McCann (New York: Simon & Schuster, 1955);

Nerves (New York: Ballantine, 1956; revised edition, New York: Ballantine, 1976; London: Futura, 1976);

Police Your Planet, as Erik van Lhin (New York: Avalon, 1956; revised edition, New York: Ballantine, 1975; London: New English Library, 1978);

Mission to the Moon (Philadelphia & Toronto: Winston, 1956);

The Cave of Spears (New York: Knopf, 1957);

Rockets Through Space (Philadelphia: Winston, 1957; London: Thorsons, 1960);

Robots and Changelings (New York: Ballantine, 1958; Anstey, U.K.: Thorpe, 1961);

Space Flight (New York: Golden Press, 1959; Folkstone, U.K.: Bailey, 1959);

Day of the Giants (New York: Avalon, 1959);

The Mysterious Earth (Philadelphia: Chilton, 1960; St. Albans, U.K.: Mayflower, 1960);

The Mysterious Sea (Philadelphia: Chilton, 1961);

Rocks and What They Tell Us (Racine, Wis.: Whitman, 1961);

Moon of Mutiny (New York: Holt, Rinehart & Winston, 1961; London: Faber & Faber, 1963);

The Eleventh Commandment (Evanston, Ill.: Regency, 1962; revised edition, New York: Ballantine, 1970; London: Futura, 1976);

Outpost of Jupiter (New York, Chicago & San Francisco: Holt, Rinehart & Winston, 1963; London: Gollancz, 1964);

Two Complete Novels: The Sky Is Falling, Badge of Infamy (New York: Galaxy, 1963);

The Mysterious Sky (Philadelphia: Chilton, 1964);

Mortals and Monsters (New York: Ballantine, 1965; London: Tandem, 1967);

The Runaway Robot, ghostwritten by Paul W. Fairman (Philadelphia: Westminster Press, 1965; London: Gollancz, 1967);

Siege Perilous, ghostwritten by Fairman (New York: Lancer, 1966); republished as *The Man without a Planet* (New York: Lancer, 1969);

The Scheme of Things, ghostwritten by Fairman (New York: Belmont Books, 1966);

Tunnel through Time, ghostwritten by Fairman (Philadelphia: Westminster Press, 1966);

Rocket from Infinity, ghostwritten by Fairman (New York, Chicago & San Francisco: Holt, Rinehart & Winston, 1966; London: Faber & Faber, 1967);

The Infinite Worlds of Maybe, ghostwritten by Fairman (New York, Chicago & San Francisco: Holt, Rinehart & Winston, 1966; London: Faber & Faber, 1968);

Prisoners of Space, ghostwritten by Fairman (Philadelphia: Westminster Press, 1968);

Pstalemate (New York: Putnam's: 1971; London: Gollancz, 1972);

Gods and Golems (New York: Ballantine, 1973);

Early del Rey, 2 vols. (Garden City: Doubleday, 1975);

The Best of Lester del Rey (New York: Ballantine, 1978);

Weeping May Tarry, by del Rey and Raymond F. Jones (Los Angeles: Pinnacle, 1978);

The World of Science Fiction: 1926-1976 (New York: Garland, 1979).

Philip St. John, Erik van Lhin, Wade Kaempfert, Philip James, and Kenneth Wright are just some of the pseudonyms Lester del Rey has published under during his long career. Indeed, both the number and variety of his pen names give ample evidence of what his colleagues and readers acknowledge as del Rey's astounding eclecticism and intellectual energy. No wonder, then, that his continuing involvement over four decades with the cause of science-fiction literature has earned him a unique place in the colorful history of its development. Del Rey has been instrumental in guiding the fortunes of science fiction from the vagaries of the early pulp-magazine market to the respectability of the prestigious del Rey imprint.

The son of Franc del Rey, a carpenter and farmer, and Jane Sidway del Rey, he was born Ramon Felipe San Juan Mario Silvio Enrico Smith Heathcourt-Brace Sierra y Alvarez-del Rel y de los Verdes in Saratoga County, Minnesota. Del Rey left for Washington, D.C., in 1931, where he attended George Washington University but dropped out after two years, convinced he could learn more, and faster, on his own. In 1938, he sold his first story, "The Faithful," to *Astounding Science-Fiction*; from then until 1950 he continued writing on a part-time basis while holding down a number of different jobs, including sheet metal worker. Those twelve years are entertainingly chronicled in *Early del Rey* (1975). By 1950, however, he was sufficiently encouraged by the sale of his stories to devote himself full time to the business of writing. His editorial and critical work has been equally successful. From 1947 to 1950, he was an editor at the Scott Meredith Literary Agency in New York. In 1952, he became editor of a new magazine called *Space Science Fiction*. Since then he has edited *Science Fiction Adventures* (as Philip St. John, 1952-1953), *Fantasy Fiction* (1953), *Rocket Stories* (as Wade Kaempfert, 1953), and *Worlds of Fantasy* (1968-1970), in addition to many book anthologies and collections. In 1971, del Rey married Judy-Lynn Benjamin, a writer and science-fiction editor.

It is difficult to gauge exactly how pervasive an influence del Rey has had on science fiction because he is reluctant to reveal all his pseudonyms, but an adequate measure of that influence can be deduced from a list of his current activities. Since 1975 he has been fantasy editor for Ballantine and also acts as a general consultant on a wide range of subjects, including art. In addition to serving as book reviewer for *Analog Science Fiction/Science Fact* since 1974, del Rey has recently taught workshops and courses in fantasy literature, and he has made numerous appearances on radio and television talk shows. When he is not writing fiction, he writes books on a host of subjects—from nuclear physics and rocketry to geology, oceanography, and astronomy.

Del Rey explores the nature of identity by posing fundamental questions about man's struggle for survival and the conflict between his creative and destructive urges. Beginning with the earliest stories, from "Helen O'Loy (1938; collected in ". . . And Some Were Human," 1948) through "Into Thy Hands" (1945; collected in *Robots and Changelings*, 1958); and "Though Dreamers Die" (1944; collected in *Early del Rey*, 1975), to "Vengeance Is Mine" (1964; collected in *Gods and Golems*, 1973), del Rey is preoccupied with the precarious relationship between man and his creations. Often in these tales survival hinges on the sensitivity, vision, and common sense with which man, mortal and mutable, handles the inorganic creatures produced by his fertile brain. The struggle between man as maker-creator and man as destroyer is a struggle for the survival of man himself—and for his humanity. This theme, effectively tapping into a primary anxiety of our age, becomes the axis of del Rey's fiction.

The novels echo and expand on the essential theme. Predictably, del Rey's concern with man's survival is not treated in the fiction alone; the problem finds expression in nonfiction works such as the trilogy *The Mysterious Earth* (1960), *The Mysterious Sea* (1961), and *The Mysterious Sky* (1964), where the message is clear: know your world and wonder at its marvels, miracles, and mysteries, lest you forfeit your right to it. On the whole, these nonfiction works are extremely well done and especially interesting for an audience of young readers who may already have been exposed to science fiction through del Rey's juvenile novels.

Though del Rey has published a dozen or more successful juvenile novels, beginning with *Marooned on Mars* and *Rocket Jockey* in 1952, they tend to be formulaic and monotonous. In an overview of del Rey's work, the juvenile titles seem the least impressive. For the young adult reader certainly, or even for an initiated younger science-fiction fan, the theme of survival as a cooperative effort of self-reliant individuals or civilizations is finally too simplistically delivered and narrowly drawn. In these books a young hero (usually seventeen or eighteen years old) with an uncle, father, or older brother as mentor inevitably faces a challenge that threatens his survival and the survival of those who depend on him. Overcoming the threat involves the exercise of courage, discipline, and enough righteous indignation (coupled with mechanical and scientific skill) to insure the safety of the individual and the species. Happily, del Rey's reputation does not rest on the juvenile fiction.

The short stories are another matter, as they document a sustained level of achievement. Such collections as ". . . And Some Were Human," *Robots and Changelings*, and *Mortals and Monsters* (1965) offer a representative sampling of del Rey's shorter fiction. The more recent *Early del Rey*, which includes biographical recollections and anecdotes about the writing, marketing, and publishing of science fiction in those early days, is singularly engaging. The personal commentaries prefacing each selection lend a particular nostalgia to the stories themselves, as if the fictions were, curiously, annotations to the narrative of the writer's life. There is, after all, high romance in the saga of the poor farm boy who, coming east in search of an education, writes his first story on a dare and eventually becomes one of the most respected and influential critics in his field.

The latest collection of short stories, *The Best of Lester del Rey* (1978), is perhaps the most significant since del Rey's perception of his "best" is very good indeed. Starting with "Helen O'Loy," the best known of his early stories and one frequently included in science-fiction anthologies, the reader is introduced to the theme encountered again and again in del Rey's fiction: the problematic relationship between man and his works. The inherent difficulty, as del Rey perceives it, lies not just in what man does, but in what he chooses to create. "Helen O'Loy" concerns a man who marries the female robot he has created. In a variation on the Pygmalion theme but with tragic overtones, the creator ages and finally dies, while the beloved object, who has had herself artificially aged to keep pace with her husband, keeps final pace with him by denying her potential for near immortality and burning out her own circuits so that they may "cross this last bridge together." The story ends somewhat sentimentally; yet this resolution in no way detracts from the fundamental question the story raises. What are the consequences of loving too excessively the fascinating but sterile machinery created by our own minds? What can we hope for by uniting ourselves with the appearance of things as we would have them, instead of committing ourselves to the mysterious, ever-changing, and palpable reality which often eludes us? And what, if any, obligations does man have to creatures formed and given existence by him?

Del Rey seems intrigued with the issue of how man himself shall live when he discovers his awesome power not only to alter and control life but, like God, to breathe a kind of life into creatures he can make in his own image, for the power to create is also the power to destroy. In pursuing the problem of man's trying to adjudicate between these contradictory aspects of himself, del Rey often presents a wholly sympathetic and affecting portrait of man's robot creations as an expression of his immortality. "Into Thy Hands" offers a situation in which survival after the holocaust depends entirely on robots carrying within them the secrets of life,

science, and culture essential to renewing the human race. Similarly in "The Monster" (1951) the cruel interrelationship between man and machine is explored from the viewpoint of a mechanical monster that is being used, and abused, by its makers in order to satisfy their ambition to become "almost gods in power." The story is a compelling one that pointedly asks who, after all, are the monsters. In

Lester del Rey

"Instinct" (1952) survival of the species depends on a combination of robot intelligence and human instinct; and as only man is capable of both intelligence and instinct, the robot must serve man. However, if man forsakes either of his gifts, he is doomed to extinction—as he is in "The Keepers of the House" (1956) where the world literally becomes the domain of a canine survivor named King.

Though some of the later stories, "For I Am a Jealous People" (1954) and "The Seat of Judgment" (1957) for example, suffer from heavy doses of metaphysics that tend to make the stories oblique and even pretentious, a story like "Vengeance Is Mine" restores the balance. What is more, it contains another of del Rey's inimitable robots, this one called Sam. The only survivor on Earth or Moon, Sam fathers a race of computer-built robots dedicated to avenging the murder of its god—Man.

The conditions of man's survival on this and

other planets is central to del Rey's novels, beginning with *Nerves*. Originally published as a novelette (*Astounding Science-Fiction*, 1942), it was later expanded to novel length and published in 1956. The fictional subject is unnervingly close to current issues since it has to do with an industrial atomic power plant gone out of control. Disaster is imminent, but the situation is defused by a young doctor named Jenkins, who is the stepson of the one man, now dead, thought capable of saving the continent. The revelation about Jenkins's parentage and past technical training prompts him to initiate a plan to avert disaster. The story is told from the point of view of the plant physician, Dr. Ferrel, which lends conviction to the narrative. But though the premise is chilling and suspenseful, the novel's impact is diluted by a pedestrian style.

Yet the concerns that preoccupy del Rey persist. He questions how much control man can exercise over things and situations of his own making. Further, does man imperil the very survival of the race by his vaulting ambition for more and greater power and by his putting into motion forces he cannot entirely understand? Man surely has an infinite capacity to invent. But, posits del Rey, can he survive his inventions?

The parameters of such queries are reduced considerably in *Police Your Planet* (1956), also expanded from a shorter version (in *Science Fiction Adventures*, 1953) for publication as a book. The title, though misleading and inappropriate, reflects del Rey's concern with survival of the species on an interplanetary scale. Here attention is concentrated on the rugged individualist not yet beaten by the self-destructive system. Bruce Gordon, a pugnacious ex-cop exiled from Earth, joins the crooked police force in Marsport as a means of personal survival. He winds up helping to reform the system, a hero in spite of himself. The novel is an overplotted space western. The stock character is that of the tough guy with a grudge who is only concerned with taking care of himself. By virtue of his hidden heart of gold and the love of a reformed bad woman, he is persuaded to clean up a town run by graft and greed. The plot is prosaic and so is the writing.

However, an earlier novel, *Day of the Giants* (1959), is engaging fantasy based on myths about the Norse gods. The mortal hero, Leif, is adopted by Odin, whose power and position are threatened by a race of giants wishing to conquer Earth. Mistaken for a twin brother renowned for his valor, Leif is the choice of the gods to lead their cause against the giants. Quite by chance, then, he becomes a potential

giant-killer, faced with unacceptable alternatives. Victory for Odin means that Earth will continue in the role of vassal, subject to the whim of the gods. If the giants win, the Earth will be wracked by fire and destruction. Leif's desire to survive the dilemma entails his outwitting Odin. This accomplished, Leif returns to Earth having guaranteed his own survival, the dominion of the gods above, and breathing space of a thousand years for Earth to rise to the challenge of freedom.

With the publication of *The Eleventh Commandment* (1962), del Rey advances the thesis of a future church militant tyrannically commanding Earth's starving population to continue to be fruitful and multiply. Jensen, a Martian-born scientist shipped back to his ancestral homeland Earth for genetic reasons, discovers a daily struggle for survival beyond his wildest imaginings. Though a skeptic, Jensen searches for meaning. He discovers the unsettling fact that survival of humanity depends on the implementation of a breeding policy developed after the atomic holocaust had produced mutant generations. Persuaded that the raw struggle for survival will eventuate in a new race of beings, Jensen and his bride join a holy crusade with the mission of carrying the word to the heathens.

Moving in another direction, *The Scheme of Things* (1966) exploits the notion of a multiple personality operating on different levels of reality. This novel is one of several which appeared from 1965 to 1968 under del Rey's name but which were ghostwritten by Paul W. Fairman from outlines provided by del Rey. The central theme, however, is essentially del Rey. In *The Scheme of Things*, Mike Strong, a fantastic Walter Mitty out of control, moves through his various lives in myriad worlds and believes he is going insane. The story is interesting, and not without its whimsical side, but though it serves to raise issues about the nature of reality and the survival of individual equilibrium in the face of shifting identities, the novel never really resolves the questions it poses. Nevertheless, its concern for shifting identities introduces another aspect of the subject of survival which del Rey explores in later novels.

The problems of mistaken or hidden identity involving namesakes, twins, or unknown parentage and the implications these hold for survival become increasingly prevalent in del Rey's later novels. The conflicts del Rey previously expressed in terms of man's attitudes toward and manipulations of the things he has created now turn inward. The antagonist resides within man himself, where, del

Rey suggests, it has always really been. Now man battles for survival within the limitless and often perilous realms of his own mind. He battles himself for his own soul. Del Rey's metaphysical impulse gains strength in these late novels. Characterization may be uneven, the plot occasionally unwieldy and curved, the titles unnecessarily oblique (*Pstalemate* and *Weeping May Tarry* especially), but overall the display of imaginative and intellectual power in these novels is impressive.

Pstalemate (1971) records the odyssey of Harry Bronson as he discovers his extraordinary powers, the terrible destiny those powers seem to commit him to, and the struggle of his will to survive the ordeal with his mind and soul intact. Harry saves his mind by driving his will with a single purpose—to conquer the alien entity seeking control of his soul. By absorbing that identity, accepting it as a part of himself, Harry can reconcile the tension between reality and possibility, the enlightened mind and the darkness of the soul, the past and the future. The ever-shifting self, hanging perilously over an abyss of fear and doubt, must confront the awful aspect of itself and accept the danger that recognition brings.

The confrontation of a man with his self—demon or god—as the essential, even ultimate, task of survival is the central theme of del Rey's *Weeping May Tarry* (1978), written in collaboration with Raymond F. Jones. It moves the theme from the problem of survival to the idea of salvation. The plot concerns a spaceship that crash-lands on a deserted planet. The crew, accompanied by a fanatically righteous priest, comes from a planet that had been accidentally victimized by galactic war. The result of this occurrence is a society under the absolute rule of a priesthood and an unknown power to which they give unquestioning obedience. Now stranded on a strange world with little hope of survival, the aliens find comfort and help in two artifacts accidentally discovered by the priest: the representation of a man nailed to a cross and a book that tells the story of that man and his fate.

Thus, the problem of survival becomes the issue of faith, and the journey for intelligence and data becomes the quest of the sentient being for the source of belief itself. The story concerns a high priest who promotes belief but cannot himself believe. In loneliness and anguish he must suffer his soul to be melted down and recast in the spirit of true faith, of authentic religion. Once the human and the humane coalesce in a single bond, faithfully nurtured even in the face of the inevitable tragedy of the human condition, then the struggle for survival becomes the way of salvation.

In the main body of his fiction del Rey has developed and worked variations on a single theme, and the result is considerable. At his best, del Rey is a sensitive and articulate spokesman for humanistic values in a world no longer able to discern properly what constitutes the uniquely human and thus no longer willing to cherish and preserve it. Del Rey balances cynicism and optimism: man, he seems to say, carries within him the seeds of his own destruction and the means of his own salvation. In the balance is all of civilization, and del Rey skillfully charts for his readers some of the crucial distance between the struggle and the promise.

—*Greta Eisner*

Other:

The Year After Tomorrow, edited by del Rey, Cecile Matschat, and Carl Carmer (Philadelphia & Toronto: Winston, 1954);

Introduction to *The Fantastic Universe Omnibus*, ed. Hans Santesson (Englewood Cliffs, N. J.: Prentice-Hall, 1960);

The Best Science Fiction Stories of the Year, vols. 1-5, edited by del Rey (New York: Dutton, 1972-1976; vols. 3-5, republished editions; London: Kaye & Ward, 1976-1977);

Fantastic Science-Fiction Art 1926-1954, compiled with an introduction by del Rey (New York: Ballantine, 1975);

The Best of Frederik Pohl, edited by del Rey (New York: Ballantine, 1975);

The Best of C. L. Moore, edited by del Rey (Garden City: Doubleday, 1975);

The Best of John W. Campbell, edited by del Rey (Garden City: Doubleday, 1976);

The Best of Robert Bloch, edited by del Rey (New York: Ballantine, 1977);

The Fantastic Art of Boris Vallejo, compiled with an introduction by del Rey (New York: Ballantine, 1978);

The Best of Hal Clement, edited by del Rey (New York: Ballantine, 1979).

Reference:

Sam Moskowitz, *Seekers of Tomorrow* (Westport, Conn.: Hyperion Press, 1974), pp. 171-189.

Philip K. Dick

Patrick G. Hogan, Jr.
University of Houston

BIRTH: Chicago, Illinois, 16 December 1928, to Joseph Edgar and Dorothy Kindred Dick.

EDUCATION: University of California, Berkeley, 1950.

MARRIAGE: 1949 to Jeanette, divorced. 1951 to Kleo, divorced. 1958 to Ann, divorced; children: Laura. 18 April 1967 to Nancy, divorced; children: Isolde. 18 April 1973 to Tessa Busby; children: Christopher.

AWARDS: Hugo Award for *The Man in the High Castle*, 1963; John W. Campbell Memorial Award for *Flow My Tears, the Policeman Said*, 1975.

BOOKS: *Solar Lottery* (New York: Ace, 1955); republished as *World of Chance* (London: Rich & Cowan, 1956);
A Handful of Darkness (London: Rich & Cowan, 1955; Boston: Gregg, 1978);
The World Jones Made (New York: Ace, 1956; London: Sidgwick & Jackson, 1968);
The Man Who Japed (New York: Ace, 1956; London: Magnum, 1978);
Eye in the Sky (New York: Ace, 1957; London: Arrow, 1971);
The Cosmic Puppets (New York: Ace, 1957);
The Variable Man and Other Stories (New York: Ace, 1957; London: Sphere, 1969);
Time Out of Joint (Philadelphia: Lippincott, 1959; London: Sidgwick & Jackson, 1961);
Dr. Futurity (New York: Ace, 1960);
Vulcan's Hammer (New York: Ace, 1960; London: Arrow, 1976);
The Man in the High Castle (New York: Putnam's, 1962; Harmondsworth, U.K.: Penguin, 1965);
The Game-Players of Titan (New York: Ace, 1963; London: Sphere, 1969);
Martian Time-Slip (New York: Ballantine, 1964; London: Methuen, 1975);
The Simulacra (New York: Ace, 1964; London: Methuen, 1977);
The Penultimate Truth (New York: Belmont, 1964; London: Cape, 1967);

Clans of the Alphane Moon (New York: Ace, 1964; St. Albans, U.K.: Panther, 1975);
The Three Stigmata of Palmer Eldritch (Garden City: Doubleday, 1965; London: Cape, 1966);
Dr. Bloodmoney, or How We Got Along After the Bomb (New York: Ace, 1965; London: Arrow, 1977);
Now Wait for Last Year (Garden City: Doubleday, 1966; London: Manor, 1974);
The Crack in Space (New York: Ace, 1966; London: Methuen, 1977);
The Unteleported Man (New York: Ace, 1966; London: Methuen, 1976);
The Zap Gun (New York: Pyramid, 1967; St. Albans, U.K.: Panther, 1975);
Counter-Clock World (New York: Berkley, 1967; London: Sphere, 1968);
The Ganymede Takeover, by Dick and Ray Nelson (New York: Ace, 1967; London: Arrow, 1971);
Do Androids Dream of Electric Sheep? (Garden City: Doubleday, 1968; London: Rapp & Whiting, 1969);
The Preserving Machine and Other Stories (New York: Ace, 1969; London: Gollancz, 1971);
Galactic Pot-Healer (New York: Berkley, 1969; London: Gollancz, 1971);
Ubik (Garden City: Doubleday, 1969; London: Rapp & Whiting, 1970);
A Philip K. Dick Omnibus (London: Sidgwick & Jackson, 1970);
A Maze of Death (Garden City: Doubleday, 1970; London: Gollancz, 1972);
Our Friends from Frolix 8 (New York: Ace, 1970; St. Albans, U.K.: Panther, 1976);
We Can Build You (New York: DAW, 1972; London: Fontana, 1977);
The Book of Philip K. Dick (New York: DAW, 1973); republished as *The Turning Wheel and Other Stories* (London: Coronet, 1977);
Flow My Tears, the Policeman Said (Garden City: Doubleday, 1974; London: Gollancz, 1974);
Confessions of a Crap Artist (New York: Entwhistle Books, 1975; London: Magnum, 1979);
Deus Irae, by Dick and Roger Zelazny (Garden City: Doubleday, 1976; London: Gollancz, 1977);

A Scanner Darkly (Garden City: Doubleday, 1977; London: Gollancz, 1977);

The Best of Philip K. Dick, ed. John Brunner (New York: Ballantine, 1977);

The Golden Man (New York: Berkley, 1980).

From Philip K. Dick's first sale of a story entitled "Roog" to Anthony Boucher of the *Magazine of Fantasy and Science Fiction* in 1952 and his first published story, "Beyond Lies the Wub" in *Planet Stories* in the same year (both collected in *The Best of Philip K. Dick*, 1977), his publishing career has followed a curious course. Of his some one hundred and ten short stories, twenty-eight were published in 1953 and another twenty-eight in 1954, but beginning with the appearance of *Solar Lottery* in 1955 he turned primarily to the novel. Although his Hugo Award-winning *The Man in the High Castle* was published in 1962, his peak period for novels was perhaps 1964 to 1969, during which time sixteen volumes were published. Although it is not uncommon for a writer to progress from shorter forms to longer ones and although there was a scattering of stories from 1963 to 1967, Dick's career has sometimes proceeded intermittently with some periods of creative activity greater than others, as well as intervals of relative silence. Either the progression from the short story to the novel or the number and variety of his novels seems to have persuaded some science-fiction scholars that his short stories are lesser efforts. That opinion needs to be challenged, for some stories, such as "Autofac" (1955, collected in *The Best of Philip K. Dick*) and "Beyond Lies the Wub," to name but two, stand in a relationship to subsequent science-fiction writing not unlike that of Stanley G. Weinbaum's much reprinted "A Martian Odyssey" (1934).

Philip Kindred Dick was born in Chicago in 1928, but he has lived most of his life in California in the San Francisco and Berkeley areas, one recent address being Fullerton. A longtime music lover, he worked while still in his teens as an announcer for a classical music program on station KSMO in 1947; he also operated a record store from 1948 to 1952. He attended the University of California at Berkeley in 1950 but dropped out because the required ROTC conflicted with his "anti-war convictions." In recent years he has frequently lectured on college campuses. In early 1975 he was invited to participate in a series of lectures at the Institute of Contemporary Arts in London, organized by anthropologist Ted Polhemus, but was unable to attend because of illness; his contribution, "Man, Android and Machine," was printed in *Science Fiction at Large* (1976). Evidence of his varied interests is provided by his memberships in organizations ranging from the Animal Protection Institute to the Science Fiction Writers of America, his authorship of radio scripts for the Mutual Broadcasting System, his work in antiabortion efforts and drug rehabilitation, and his discussions about religion with the late Bishop James A. Pike. These interests were in part summarized in 1975 by Dick: "My major preoccupation is the question, 'What is reality?' Many of my stories and novels deal with psychotic states or drug-induced states by which I can present the concept of a multiverse rather than a universe. Music and sociology are themes in my novels, also radical political trends; in particular I've written about fascism and my fear of it." Proof of the depth of his concern with drug abuse is his dedication of *A Scanner Darkly* (1977) to some fifteen "comrades" who are either deceased or permanently damaged as a result of drug abuse. On occasion, Dick has published stories under the pseudonym Richard Phillips, and in addition to his vast science-fiction canon he has written a mainstream novel, *Confessions of a Crap Artist* (1975).

Typical of introductory comments about Dick are those which decry the efficacy of his usual methods of approach or those which bemoan the lack of systematic progression among his stories and novels. As Robert Scholes and Eric S. Rabkin phrase it, "His work is not easy to discuss, since it does not fall neatly into a few books of exceptional achievement and a larger body of lesser works. All his books offer ideas, situations, and passages of considerable interest. None quite achieves that seamless perfection of form that constitutes one kind of literary excellence." Two basic narrative situations recur in his work, and his existential treatment of the ideas or concepts implicit in these situations may leave the reader in a state of uncertainty and not uncommonly with a feeling of depression. One favorite plot device is that of alternate universes or parallel worlds, of which *The Man in the High Castle* is a prime example. He is also fascinated by what he characteristically calls simulacra, devices ranging from merely complex mechanical and electronic constructs to androids, and by the paradoxes created by their relationships to organic life, especially that of human beings. Typical examples are *The Simulacra* (1964), *We Can Build You* (1972), and the better-known *Do Androids Dream of Electric Sheep?* (1968).

An excellent example of an early novel on the theme of alternate worlds is *Eye in the Sky* (1957), one of Dick's most meaningful and satisfying works. In this novel the defective proton beam deflector of a bevatron (an installation that produces a six-billion-volt beam for investigating the properties of artificially generated cosmic rays) plummets eight people into a series of bizarre experiences. The eight include sightseers, the research director and the security chief of a nearby guided missile facility, the researcher's wife (accused of communist leanings), and a black physicist whose race bars him from any more meaningful work than acting as the plant's tour guide. These characters find themselves in a strange new dimension where each is in turn the creator or god of a universe reflecting his or her personal obsessions. Always hovering in the background are the issues of scientific research in instruments of death, real and imagined problems of national security, racism, and the questions raised by the Eye in the Sky, a godlike presence which may or may not be more powerful or durable than the fantastic "creative" powers exercised by the characters in their alternate realities. Additional worlds, however, such as those of an old right-wing veteran, a paranoid businesswoman, and a communist spy, are in the end no more frightening than the real world, in which a red scare can throw innocent people out of a job and racism can keep others from jobs. Jack Hamilton, the young electronics researcher who is the central character, finally abandons research in instruments of destruction for research in high-fidelity audio equipment, having learned a lesson that reveals the purpose behind Dick's manipulations of realities: "I like to call it awakening conscience . . . . I've seen a lot of aspects of reality I didn't realize existed. I've come out of this with an altered perspective. Maybe it takes a thing like this to break down the walls of the groove. If so, it makes the whole experience worth it."

Eye in the Sky introduces by way of the image of the Eye a question corollary to the problem of alternate worlds, a question developed further in *Time Out of Joint* (1959): who or what controls reality? The time is 1998 and a state of war exists between the One Happy Worlders on Earth, to whom the main characters Ragle Gumm and Victor Nielson owe allegiance, and the Lunatics, as Earth's colonists on the Moon are called. Gumm's special ability to exercise the Law of Probabilities to foresee what sites will be bombed by the Lunatics is endangered when his sympathies begin to shift to the other side, and he is on the verge of a mental breakdown. The One Happy Worlders contrive an environment which duplicates in detail the Earth of 1959. There Gumm acquires a reputation as a solver of newspaper puzzles, the purpose of which, unknown to him, is to locate the areas which may be bombed by the Lunatics in 1998 and to make possible the advance evacuation of the inhabitants. As both Gumm and Nielson begin to question the reality of the world they are supposed to be in, the objective evidence of reality and unreality tends to be associated with vehicles, which begin to acquire symbolic import. One example, as David Ketterer has pointed out, is a bus trip experienced by Nielson in which "the sides of the bus became transparent." As "the passengers fade away," the driver does not change, but he is "driving a hollow bus." Nielson later describes the experience as "a look at how things really are." The novel's story line, concerning the war between the One Happy Worlders and the Lunatics, becomes secondary to the novel's real purpose, which is to encourage the reader to toy with the idea that, as Ketterer phrases it, "The world around him may be artificially created by outside manipulators for unsuspected purposes."

Dick's classic alternate world novel is *The Man in the High Castle*, which may more accurately be described as an alternate present novel. The story is set in a United States that lost World War II, with the West Coast, where most of the story takes place, dominated by Japan, the East occupied by Germany, and a semiautonomous area, the Rocky Mountain States, acting as a buffer between. The reader's interest is gripped by Dick's imaginative and detailed account of several characters who attempt to live and carry on personal and business activities in a pseudodemocracy on the West Coast under the supervision of Japanese officials such as Mr. Tagomi, who has a high position in the Trade Mission and who is interested in the artifacts of American popular culture. Of special importance are Robert Childan, an American tradesman who panders to Japanese tastes and mimics their manners and culture while he reveals a racist attitude sympathetic to the worst of Nazism, and Frank Frink, a Jewish-American craftsman who struggles to be an artist at the same time he tries to avoid a Nazi program of extraditing Jews and other unacceptable races from Japanese-controlled territory for extermination, a program already complete in German-controlled parts of the world. In addition, the novel contains something of the high intrigue of a spy thriller, revealing a Nazi plan to exterminate the Japanese in a surprise atomic attack, a counterplot of more moderate German officers to overthrow the war party, and a smaller-scale Nazi plot to assassinate the Man in the High Castle, the author of a popular but subversive science-fiction novel portraying an alternate present in which the United States won World War II.

Obviously, the novel is a prime example of the multiple levels for which Dick's narratives have been praised. Several characters are more carefully drawn than is the usual practice in science-fiction novels, and there are even touches of humor to relieve the grimness, especially when some of the "artifacts" so prized by Japanese collectors turn out to be elaborately contrived fakes. Perhaps the most chilling effect of the novel, however, is how Dick reveals to the America of 1962, still sure of its international righteousness, how easily this nation would have surrendered its own culture under a Japanese occupation and how compatible American fears, prejudices, and desires were with Nazism. The alternate present again makes significant comments on the real one.

The point here is Dick's clarification of an important aspect of his own prolific contribution to science fiction in one of his relatively few essays, "Who Is an SF Writer?" (1974). Dick says of the science-fiction writer: "Flexibility is the key word here; it is creating *multi*verses, rather than a *uni*verse, that fascinates and drives him. 'What if—' is always his starting premise. . . . He *wants* to see possibilities, not actualities." Dick goes on to stress the writer's need to avoid both the extremes of escapism and of presumed realism; in brief, he is explaining the process of dealing with possibilities which are based in realities but not absolutely controlled by them.

More recently, in his article "Man, Android and Machine" (1976), Dick provides additional insights into the genuine complexities of the dream universes and the dream-universe people or beings which are the settings and the characters of many of his stories and novels. In Dick's cosmology entities that see man's plight but offer no help coexist in the universe with beings or visions of beings which, if they do exist outside the dreams of men (including Dick), are trying to help mankind. The aid may be in man's struggles against tyranny of various kinds, against continued pollution of the environment, and against his own unwillingness to seek some form of human fulfillment. Much of Dick's fiction has been addressed to such questions, and the very variety of his fabulations (the term made popular by Robert Scholes for "That modern body of fictional works which . . . either accepts or pretends to accept a cognitive responsibility to imagine what is not yet apparent or existent, and to examine this in some systematic way") is a partial indication of both the potentials and the dangers an author must face in dealing with these problems or with problems-yet-to-be.

Problems both present and future are the subjects of *The Three Stigmata of Palmer Eldritch* (1965), a Nebula Award nominee which again concerns multiple realities, in this instance as they are induced by hallucinogenic drugs such as Chew-Z and Can-D, the very names of which reveal a touch of acidic humor. A central character is Barney Mayerson, an executive of P. P. Layouts, "from which Perky Pat and all the units of her miniature world originated." Perky Pat is a kind of adult Barbie Doll that is sold with various toy settings, costumes, and characters; these layouts, when contemplated under the influence of Can-D, an illegal hallucinogen, provide an escape from reality for people who are trying to survive in the nearly intolerable environments of the colonies on Mars, Venus, and Ganymede. As a result, Perky Pat "had conquered man as man at the same time conquered the planets of the Sol system," and the doll had become "the obsession of the colonists." But Palmer Eldritch, a wealthy industrialist, has brought back from Proxima Centauri a new and apparently superior drug, Chew-Z, which seems to make possible a "trip" of potentially unlimited duration into a self-created reality. As the new advertisements read, "God promises eternal life. We can deliver it."

It is doubtful, however, that Eldritch is still a human being. In a conversation between Barney Mayerson and a persona in the guise of Eldritch, the persona claims to have been cast out of a distant star system and to have assumed the appearance of Eldritch in order not only to introduce Chew-Z to human beings but also to perpetuate itself. On the other hand, "the creature residing in deep space which had taken the form of Palmer Eldritch bore some relationship to God." Chew-Z is in some ways like a divine gift since its realities are largely self-created and therefore carry with them—unlike the predigested, mass-market world of Perky Pat—the potential for self-discovery. Like God, Eldritch emerges as a dominating presence in all the realities inspired by his drug; more and more humanity seems made in his image as individuals increasingly exhibit his three stigmata—an artificial arm with interchangeable hands, enormous steel teeth, and artificial eyes with wide-angle lenses. What these may symbolize becomes tied up with larger questions in the novel about the nature of God and his relation to man. Near the end of the novel, Leo Bolero, Barney's superior at P. P. Layouts, describes Eldritch's stigmata as symbolic of "the evil, negative trinity of alienation, blurred reality, and despair that Eldritch brought back with him," but the novel contains abundant evidence of the presence of such a trinity before the return of Eldritch. The stigmata seem more likely to symbolize the ambiguous mixture of knowledge and creative and destructive power present in man, God, and the universe. Like the original Satan, Eldritch renews the awareness of that knowledge and power, but in doing so he also seems—again like Satan—to function as God's instrument in giving man the capacity to do greater good as well as evil. The novel therefore ends with the ambiguous hope that reality may be shaped not by drugs but—and here the ambiguity of an artificial arm with interchangeable appendages is especially significant—by eye and hand, by tooth and claw.

From the time Dick wrote *Eye in the Sky* and *Time Out of Joint* to the publication of *The Three Stigmata of Palmer Eldritch*, he produced some nine novels that developed not only themes associated with mysterious outside control of man and his activities but also themes such as time-travel, multiple dimensions, the logic and illogic of the laws of chance, simulacra, game theory, the effects of various drugs, and the nature of reality. Even Dick's first novel, *Solar Lottery*, is thematically sophisticated; it introduces a future world whose societal and political forms are determined by Minimax, a kind of lottery of power and wealth. Implicit in humanity's surrender to randomness is a terrible negation of morality. In the end there is some hope that men can once again become free to realize their dreams and aspirations—through personal initiative rather than chance.

Though Dick rarely varies his themes, he hit his stride as a novelist in the 1960s, and several of these works merit a glance. In *Dr. Futurity* (1960) a physician named Jim Parsons finds himself in the remote future among tribesmen who oblige him to play a role in which he must tamper with destiny. This novel was followed by *The Man in the High Castle*; *The Game-Players of Titan* (1963), a further development of game theory and other standard Dick themes; *Clans of the Alphane Moon* (1964); and *The Penultimate Truth* (1964). The last, another story of rulers and the ruled, is further evidence of Dick's concern with fascism and oppression of any kind. In *The Penultimate Truth*, set in 2025 A.D., most people live in underground factories to construct robots that are being used in World War III. Actually, the robots are necessary for the maintenance of the rulers' vast estates on the supposedly radioactive surface. The politicians do not mention to the underground populace that the war has been over for ten years; instead, they claim that enemy bacteria will cause the death of anyone who comes to the surface. Dick's point seems to be the extent of mankind's willing-

ness to submit to oppression, whatever the time or circumstances.

In *The Simulacra*, as the title indicates, Dick gives emphasis to another of his major themes, that of mechanical, electronic, or other simulations of organic life. These simulacra range from insect-sized "commercials," futuristic advertising devices which invade one's privacy, to der Alte, the "consort" of Nicole Thibodeaux, the latter having nominally ruled in the White House for almost a century, apparently without aging. In addition, there are devices such as "the living protoplasm incorporated into the Ampek F-a2 recording system." This "Ganymedean life form did not experience pain and had not yet objected to being made over into a portion of an electronic system. . . ." This novel, like *Solar Lottery* and *The Penultimate Truth*, concerns a power struggle. Among those caught up in it are the last practicing psychiatrist, Dr. Superb, and a famous psychokinetic pianist, Richard Kongrosian. Among other developments, Nicole turns out to be an imposter, an actress (thus one of the simulacra), and National Police Commissioner Pembroke tries to seize power. Nicole escapes, transported by Kongrosian's developing talent to a community of chuppers, a radiation-spawned subrace which is either a genetic reversal or the prospect of a regressive development of the future. The real power seems to be in the hands of cartels such as the Karps; escape from conditions on Earth seems to be possible only in the vehicles available at Loony Luke's "jalopy jungles" for those who can afford such transportation to Mars. In an ostensibly happy ending the story concludes with the army of the United States of Europe and America in temporary power, the plants of the Karps and the pharmaceutical cartel A. G. Chemie blown up, and the National Police overcome. But as so often in Dick, the ending is ambiguous, for the question of who is really in charge remains unanswered as fewer and fewer individuals—not to mention phenomena—can be identified as anything other than simulacra.

Simulacra figure prominently in two other important books of the late 1960s, *Now Wait for Last Year* (1966) and *Do Androids Dream of Electric Sheep?* Residing in the former Gino Molinari, ruler of Earth, may be a robant, a kind of hybrid robot; the survival of Earth hinges on his problematic death. Meanwhile a major character named Eric Sweetscent (the names of Dick's characters are often humorous) is faced with the personal problem of his relationship with his wife, who has received irreversible drug damage to the brain. He is advised at one point to stay with her "Because life is composed of reality

Philip K. Dick

configurations so constituted. To abandon her would be to say, I can't endure reality as such." Like so many of Dick's books, *Now Wait for Last Year* is an extended meditation on the nature of reality and on the necessary distinctions between the real and the merely simulated. Yet there is always an ambivalence about Dick's attitude toward simulacra, as is seen in the sympathetic treatment of the persecuted androids in *Do Androids Dream of Electric Sheep?* In this novel, nominated for the Nebula Award in 1968, androids originally used in the colony worlds develop increasingly human traits; some escape to Earth and pose as human beings, although they are subject to destruction by bounty hunters. The central character is Rick Deckard, a bounty hunter who slowly comes to a new opinion of androids. The problem posed is the proper evaluation of nonhuman life forms in an age when human life forms are becoming increasingly prized as the polluted Earth becomes increasingly barren. What, the book asks, is the real meaning of humanity? Earth has been depopulated by war and its attendant ills, and in order for there to be sufficient diversity the survivors have devised electric sheep and even tiny electric spiders. Yet however hungry for the presence of life forms they become, humans look

upon the androids, for which they were originally responsible, as enemies. But if androids can dream—whether man provided them with that capability or whether it was independently developed—to what extent does that human trait equate them with real human beings? Dick has written a modern version of *Frankenstein*, for the ambivalence of man toward his own creation tends, in Dick's novel as in Shelley's, to travesty the divine creation. Although *Ubik* (1969) has its partisans, *Do Androids Dream of Electric Sheep?* is probably Dick's most important work between *The Three Stigmata of Palmer Eldritch* and such recent works as *Flow My Tears, the Policeman Said* (1974, another novel involving drugs, alternate realities, a police state, and what has been called a "parody of dystopia") and *A Scanner Darkly.*

In *A Scanner Darkly* Dick arrives at what one reviewer has called his "enigmatic best." A detailed account of a future drug culture, it weaves a plot in which Fred, an undercover narcotics agent, and Robert Arctor, a user, are one and the same more-or-less human being until the irreversible brain damage caused by Substance D leaves only a lesser being called Bruce, who at the end of the story is working in a cornfield which conceals the "lovely little blue flowers" of *Mors ontologica* ("Death of the spirit. The identity. The essential nature."), the apparent source of Substance D. The central enigma of the novel is Dick's insistence that "There is no moral to this novel," when the book so obviously attacks the drug culture; and the answer to this enigma sums up much of what Dick's work has been all about. When a modern satirist like Dick attacks an aberration like the drug culture, he runs the risk of seeming to side with the forces of conventional morality which also attack it. In fact Dick attacks the manifold efforts to evade reality so common to the modern world, including those efforts sanctioned by society. Dick's excursions into alternate realities have all along been minimally escapist, for he has always sought to adumbrate the possibilities for human beings to choose their own reality, to choose one more congenial than those favored by various dark forces all around them in society and government. In *A Scanner Darkly* he charges society with a particularly blighting form of escapism—and pointedly implicates governmental authorities along with addicts, who are always more victims than villains. Dick means to shock the bourgeois guardians of a culture in deadly stagnation; to do so he must make statements like "There is no moral to this novel," lest the bourgeois accept it and interpret it as some kind of endorsement of the values they hold sacred. *A Scanner Darkly*, along with Dick's other works, is eminently didactic, but only on a plane far above the apprehension of the mindless forces of conformity and stagnation.

Dick's works have been highly praised by his fellow writers of science fiction, ranging from Anthony Boucher to Harlan Ellison, from Michael Moorcock to Robert Silverberg. John Brunner, himself a master of parallel universes, has repeatedly called Dick "the most consistently brilliant science-fiction writer in the world." Such an estimate deserves serious consideration, but the ultimate evaluation will be that of the ever-increasing number of readers of science fiction. Dick is entitled to a better fate than, say, an Olaf Stapledon, who continues to be more praised than read. There is little doubt that Dick's own fame will continue to grow.

Other:

"The Android and the Human," *SF Commentary*, no. 31 (December 1972);

"Who Is an SF Writer?" in *Science Fiction: The Academic Awakening*, ed. Willis E. McNelly, 37 (November 1974): 46-50;

"Foreword to *The Preserving Machine*," *Science Fiction Studies*, 2 (March 1975): 22-23;

"Man, Android and Machine," in *Science Fiction at Large*, ed. Peter Nicholls (London: Gollancz, 1976), pp. 202-224.

References:

Brian W. Aldiss, "Dick's Maledictory Web: About and Around *Martian Time-Slip*," *Science-Fiction Studies*, 2 (March 1975): 42-47;

Mary Kay Bray, "Mandalic Activism: An Approach to Structure, Theme, and Tone in Four Novels by Philip K. Dick," *Extrapolation*, 21 (Summer 1980): 146-157;

Daniel DePrez, "An Interview with Philip K. Dick: Conducted September 10, 1976," *Science Fiction Review*, 5, 4 (1976): 6-12;

Peter Fitting, "*Ubik*: The Deconstruction of Bourgeois SF," *Science-Fiction Studies*, 2 (March 1975): 47-54;

Bruce Gillespie, ed., *Philip K. Dick: Electric Shepherd. The Best of SF Commentary, Number 1* (Melbourne, Australia: Norstrilla Press, 1975);

Terence M. Green, "Philip K. Dick: A Parallax View," *Science Fiction Review*, 5, 2 (1976): 12-15;

Frederic Jameson, "After Armageddon: Character Systems in *Dr. Bloodmoney*," *Science-Fiction Studies*, 2 (March 1975): 31-42;

David Ketterer, *New Worlds for Old: The Apocalyptic Imagination, Science Fiction, and American Literature* (Bloomington: Indiana University Press, 1974), pp. 242-249, 263-265;

Ursula K. Le Guin, "Science Fiction as Prophesy: Philip K. Dick," *New Republic*, 175 (30 October 1976): 33-34;

Stanislaw Lem, "Philip K. Dick: A Visionary Among the Charlatans," *Science-Fiction Studies*, 2 (March 1975): 54-67;

Sam Moskowitz, *Seekers of Tomorrow* (New York: Ballantine, 1967);

R. D. Mullen and Darko Suvin, eds., "The Science Fiction of Philip K. Dick," *Science-Fiction Studies*, 2 (March 1975): 3-75;

Carlo Pagetti, "Dick and Meta-SF," *Science-Fiction Studies*, 2 (March 1975): 24-31;

Robert Scholes and Eric S. Rabkin, *Science Fiction: History, Science, Vision* (New York: Oxford University Press, 1977), pp. 71-75, 180;

Suvin, "P. K. Dick's Opus: Artifice as Refuge and World View (Introductory Reflections)," *Science-Fiction Studies*, 2 (March 1975): 8-22;

Angus Taylor, *Philip K. Dick & The Umbrella of Light* (Baltimore: T-K Graphics, 1975);

Patricia Warrick, "The Encounter of Taoism and Fascism in Philip K. Dick's *The Man in the High Castle*," *Science-Fiction Studies*, 7 (July 1980): 174-190.

Gordon R. Dickson

Robert L. Jones
Radford University

BIRTH: Edmonton, Alberta, Canada, 1 November 1923, to Maude Leola Ford and Gordon Fraser Dickson.

EDUCATION: B.A. in creative writing, University of Minnesota, 1948; graduate work, 1948-1950.

AWARDS: Hugo Award for "Soldier, Ask Not," 1965; Nebula Award for "Call Him Lord," 1966; E. E. Smith Award (Skylark) for imaginative fiction, 1975; August Derleth Memorial Award for *The Dragon and the George*, 1977; Jupiter Award for *Time Storm*, 1977.

SELECTED BOOKS: *Alien from Arcturus* (New York: Ace, 1956); revised and republished as *Arcturus Landing* (New York: Ace, 1978);
Mankind on the Run (New York: Ace, 1956);
Earthman's Burden, by Dickson and Poul Anderson (New York: Gnome Press, 1957);
The Genetic General and *Time to Teleport* (New York: Ace, 1960);
Secret Under the Sea (New York: Holt, Rinehart & Winston, 1960; London: Hutchinson, 1962);
The Genetic General (London: Digit, 1961); revised as *Dorsai!* (New York: DAW, 1976; London: Sphere, 1976);
Spacial Delivery and *Delusion World* (New York: Ace, 1961);
Naked to the Stars (New York: Pyramid, 1961; London: Sphere, 1978);
Necromancer (Garden City: Doubleday, 1962; London: Mayflower, 1963); republished as *No Room for Man* (New York: Macfadden-Bartel, 1963);
Secret Under Antarctica (New York: Holt, Rinehart & Winston, 1963);
Secret Under the Caribbean (New York: Holt, Rinehart & Winston, 1964);
The Alien Way (New York: Bantam, 1965; London: Corgi, 1973);
Mission to Universe (New York: Berkley, 1965; London: Sphere, 1978);

Space Winners (New York: Holt, Rinehart & Winston, 1965; London: Faber & Faber, 1967);
Planet Run, by Dickson and Keith Laumer (Garden City: Doubleday, 1967; London: Hale, 1977);
The Space Swimmers (New York: Berkley, 1967; London: Sidgwick & Jackson, 1968);
Soldier, Ask Not (New York: Dell, 1967; London: Sphere, 1975);
None But Man (Garden City: Doubleday, 1969; London: Macdonald, 1970);
Spacepaw (New York: Putnam's, 1969);
Wolfling (New York: Dell, 1969);
Hour of the Horde (New York: Putnam's, 1970);
Mutants: A Science Fiction Adventure (New York: Macmillan, 1970);
Danger—Human (Garden City: Doubleday, 1970); republished as *The Book of Gordon Dickson* (New York: DAW, 1973);
Sleepwalker's World (Philadelphia: Lippincott, 1971; London: Hale, 1973);
The Tactics of Mistake (Garden City: Doubleday, 1971; London: Sphere, 1976);
The Outposter (Philadelphia: Lippincott, 1972; London: Hale, 1973);
The Pritcher Mass (Garden City: Doubleday, 1972);
The R-Master (Philadelphia: Lippincott, 1973; London: Hale, 1976);
The Star Road (Garden City: Doubleday, 1973; London: Hale, 1975);
Alien Art (New York: Dutton, 1973; London: Hale, 1974);
Gremlins, Go Home!, by Dickson and Ben Bova (New York: St. Martin's, 1974; London: St. James, 1974);
Ancient, My Enemy (Garden City: Doubleday, 1974; London: Sphere, 1978);
Star Prince Charlie, by Dickson and Anderson (New York: Putnam's, 1975);
The Dragon and the George (Garden City: Doubleday, 1976; London: Ballantine, 1978);
The Lifeship, by Dickson and Harry Harrison (New York: Harper & Row, 1976); republished as *Lifeboat* (London: Futura, 1978);

Timestorm (New York: St. Martin's, 1977; London: Sphere, 1978);

The Far Call (New York: Dial, 1978; London: Sidgwick & Jackson, 1978);

Pro (New York: Ace, 1978);

Home from the Shore (New York: Sunridge, 1978);

The Spirit of Dorsai (New York: Ace, 1979);

In Iron Years (Garden City: Doubleday, 1980);

Masters of Evron (New York: Ace, 1980).

Gordon Rupert Dickson knew from the time he began to read at age four that he wanted to write. After his father, a mining engineer, died in the summer of 1936, he moved with his mother to Minneapolis, where in 1939—at the age of fifteen—he enrolled in the University of Minnesota. In 1943 Dickson's schooling was interrupted by the army; afflicted with asthma, he missed combat in the Pacific but was decorated for service on the West Coast. After his discharge in 1946 he returned to the University of Minnesota and completed his undergraduate work in creative writing. In what he terms his "only wavering" from his chosen calling, he enrolled in the graduate school to begin work toward an academic career, but with restored nerve he left without a second degree. Since then he has written more than 150 stories and more than thirty novels, surviving almost solely on the potency of his pen and working toward mastery of his craft.

Almost all of Dickson's fiction has been "initiation" literature, not an uncommon pattern in science fiction. As he puts it, initiation is not a one-time ritual but a constantly unfolding process that parallels the physical and moral evolution of the human species and of the universe as a whole. His central characters are often artists who discover, under stress, superior abilities which are also latent in other humans. In Dickson's most effective fiction, the reader is led to undergo the same process of recognition and acceptance.

His first published novel, *Alien from Arcturus* (1956), is only partly successful, even in its revised version (*Arcturus Landing*, 1978), but it contains the germ of his major work. Just as human technological capabilities have launched the first starship toward Arcturus, aliens arrive to intercept the flight and quarantine the planet, aided by The Company, an Earthwide cartel. The basic conflict is between reactionary greed and inertia on the one hand and progressive discovery and creation, aided by friendship, on the other. The hero, Malcolm Fletcher, is befriended by a delightful rodentlike alien, an "Atakit" named Peep, who assists him in the invention of a faster-than-light matter transmission device, which qualifies humans for full, free membership in the alien galactic community. The "science" of the tale—never Dickson's major concern—is not particularly well handled; indeed, everything about the book is a bit heavy-handed, but *Alien from Arcturus* is noteworthy as a preview of the more substantial things Dickson would achieve as he acquired greater technical control of his material.

It is, at any rate, a cut above its successor, *Mankind on the Run*, also published in 1956. The following year, however, saw the appearance of *Earthman's Burden*, the fruit of a collaboration with Poul Anderson begun while both writers were students at the University of Minnesota. The stories in this volume concern a race of teddy-bear-like creatures called Hokas, who mimic humans to a fault. The experience Dickson acquired in the creation of these winsome aliens no doubt contributed to his success with Peep, the charming Alien from Arcturus, and the numerous animallike creatures featured in his later works.

In 1959 the first part of what has become Dickson's magnum opus—the Childe Cycle—appeared serially in *Analog* under the title *Dorsai!* In its initial publication as a book (paired with the contemporaneous but slighter *Time to Teleport*), the novel was called *The Genetic General* (1960), but it has recently been republished under the original magazine title. *Dorsai!* had the unfortunate effect of almost immediately typing Dickson, at least in publisher's hype, as a "war author." The Dorsai are indeed warriors of formidable abilities, but they are only a part of the total picture. In the twenty-fourth century mankind has "splintered" as it has migrated to the stars, each new world or group of worlds nurturing a single characteristic of human nature, which remains whole, although undeveloped, only on the homeworld, Earth. The three most important splinter cultures represent the three prime aspects of humanity—body, spirit, and mind. Body predominates on the world of the Dorsai; spirit on the planets Harmony and Association, known together as the Friendlies; and mind on the worlds of Mara and Kultis, known as the Exotics. In a single "normal" human such imbalances would be psychotic, but each of these cultures and their citizenry are sane; they have merely specialized.

This historical background is basic to the whole series of books, still in progress at this writing. *Dorsai!*, the first of the group to appear but not the earliest in terms of the series's internal chronology, deals with the rise to success of Donal Graeme of the Dorsai within a web of interstellar intrigue set into motion by William of Ceta, an entrepreneur who plans for himself the role of world ruler. The Dorsai fighting abilities, boosted by Donal's gift of intuition inherited from his Exotic mother, are the ultimate cause of William's defeat.

Within this wide scope, however, the focus of the book is directly on Donal's personal initiation into maturity through the stages of first admitting, then accepting, and finally using his "difference," the gift of intuition. He comes close to being a full-spectrum human reuniting the splinter talents, now that they have been developed to fullness, all of which guide him toward his vision of a whole, creative humanity. This is also Dickson's vision. One of what he calls his "consciously thematic" novels, the book is a schematic rendering of general ideas about human nature and about what is necessary for species survival. It has gained most attention, however—and probably deserves to—for the creation of the Dorsai warriors.

Perhaps as a conscious reaction against the perception of his work as a celebration of war, Dickson in *Naked to the Stars* (1961) turns to an indictment of war. The novel's action takes place for the most part during a period of conflict between an expanding Earth culture and three alien races. The battle scenes, unlike the glorious victories of *Dorsai!*, are presented as mindless orgies of needless cruelty.

But the author does not advocate simple pacifism. The hero, Calvin Truant (the name, like those of many of Dickson's characters, is significant), rebels against his father's ethics of nonviolence and demonstrates that violence—or the threat of violence—is sometimes necessary to achieve peaceful ends.

Dickson resumed his Childe Cycle with *Necromancer* (1962), which depicts a period antecedent to *Dorsai!* on an Earth torn by pressures of rising population and overdependence on technology. There is an increasing rate of emotional disturbance, and there is a central computer, the Super Complex, with its own ideas about what is good for people. Opposed to the Super Complex and the bureaucrats who want to maintain the status quo is a group calling themselves the Chantry Guild who follow the way of "the alternate laws." Into this situation comes Paul Formain, an accident-prone engineer looking for a replacement arm, who matures into an awareness of his paranormal abilities. A product of the Chantry Guild's program, he moves beyond them into a belief in construction rather than destruction; he also gains a new arm.

More mythical and mystical than Dickson's usual work, *Necromancer* lays the groundwork for the Exotic worlds that are eventually settled by

Gordon R. Dickson

intellectual descendants of the Chantry Guild. The "alternate laws" of the Guild are primarily controllable psychic abilities, although they are also functional within a universal moral and philosophical system that is as real as the physical laws of nature. Although he remains constant to his thematic material, in this work Dickson moves a long way toward the fantasy-romance that substitutes magic for science. Only *The Dragon and the George* (1976) goes further in this direction. There it works, but *Necromancer*, weakest of the Childe books, is not entirely successful.

The Alien Way (1965) returns to alien contact, this time sought by humans through an early warning system devised by the Foundation for the Association of Learned and Professional Societies. A sphere of space around Earth is "baited" with mechanisms that will establish telepathic contact between a designated human mind and whatever alien mind is "hooked." The humans who await telepathic contact are fishermen, and one of them, Jason Burchar, makes contact with Kator Second-cousin, a catlike alien intent on "Founding a Kingdom." While the Foundation prepares the government to repel invaders, Jason shares the plans and adventures of the unsuspecting Kator. Because of his understanding and because he successfully evades the government's attempts to prevent him from acting, Jason foils the invasion without warfare and paves the way to friendly contact between the races.

What Kator is really after is the chance to found a family which will preserve his superior abilities; his failure proves him inferior, and he is killed without offspring. The Darwinian premise of natural selection is enforced as a cultural law by Kator's race. Humanity, having defeated Kator, avoids competing with Kator's species in a larger struggle for survival. Because of atavistic instincts, the two civilized species' drives to continue themselves are expressed in divergent cultural patterns and forms. But the instincts in question are vestigial on the human side, and it is humanity that manages to be flexible enough culturally to accommodate the aliens and avert the need for one race to survive at the expense of the other.

To undergird his plot, which in dealing with racial and personal survival deals with fertility, Dickson weaves into his story the myth of the Fisher King. Not only is the "bait" an earthworm, but Jason also later appears as an actual fisherman sitting alone on the bank of a stream when Kator lands on Earth. When Kator dies while Jason is in psychic contact, Jason is wounded almost to death and lies in a wasting coma for a long time; he rises to health and action as he goes to make the final pact of friendship with Kator's race and also cements his romantic bond with Mele, the woman who has loved him all along. The symbolic material is not intrusive and forms a pleasant counterpoint to the action in order to reinforce the theme of growth through empathetic relationships into a higher form of being.

The third installment of the Childe Cycle, *Soldier, Ask Not*, won the Hugo Award in 1965 as a story in *Galaxy*, before Dickson expanded his work to a full-length novel. Contemporary with the action of *Dorsai!*, the plot focuses on some of the characters and events recorded peripherally in that story of Donal Graeme's rise to power. The narrator, Tam Olyn, is a man from Earth who has been warped in his upbringing to find value only in destruction. Although he discovers he has unusual abilities for the work, he rejects a constructive part in establishing The Final Encyclopedia, a computerized compendium of all knowledge about human nature. His rise to power and position is finally ended by a dead man, a former suitor of his sister, named Jamethon Black. When this commandant of the Friendlies' forces dies for his faith, he causes Tam to discover his own faith and to submit to the task of The Final Encyclopedia.

The book, especially the last five chapters (which constitute the original story), is among Dickson's best works. The point of view allows a clearer and at the same time less intrusive exposition of the ideas and themes that are central to his total body of work, and it allows the reader to identify with a "human" character from Earth rather than with the real hero, who is a splinter character, Jamethon Black. Only the later *Time Storm* (1977) and *The Far Call* (1978) rival this novel as the most important of the Dickson canon.

In *None But Man* (1969) Dickson again treats alien contact in the pattern of *The Alien Way*, but with added complications. On the border of the human area of influence in the galaxy, a conflict arises as the heretofore peaceful Moldaug also lay claim to the territory. Efforts at negotiating a settlement seem only to promote the likelihood of war, until Culihan O'Rourke When manages an interstellar power play that averts disaster. As Frontiersmen, Cully When and his associates are feared and mistrusted as decadent savages by Earth humans, with their rigid space-phobia. Cully must force the Earth government to accept his actions while he is also acquiring an understanding of the Moldaug and kidnapping their ruling family's heirs to force them to a conference. The problem all along has been the differing value systems of the Moldaug and humanity, which cause each to misinterpret as threats the peaceful overtures of the other. Cully's flexible point of view allows him to explain the antagonists to themselves and to each other. Dickson's giving the final word to the alien children is a technical success for both psychological and thematic reasons.

Wolfling (1969) departs from some of Dickson's usual assumptions. Earth was colonized by a lost party from the Galactic Empire, which included as members a few of the ruling aristocracy, the Highborn. In the millenia since then, both the Highborn on the Throne World and their descendants on Earth have degenerated, but in different ways. Now the two worlds are again in contact, and a barbarian from Earth is taken to the Throne World to entertain the royalty. The barbarian, or "wolfling," is James Keil, who not only discovers—in the process of frustrating a galactic plot—that he is a throwback to the original Highborn, but also proves himself more vigorous because of his frontier heritage than the decadent aristocracy of the empire. This much is consistent with Dickson's usual themes. But, although Keil's powers are genetically inherent, the connections of humans with their antecedents in the animal kingdom are missing, as is the integral evolution of the human species as part of the evolving planet. This is a good adventure story, but it is an anomaly among Dickson's other efforts.

A more typical view of evolution figures in *Hour of the Horde* (1970). The Center Aliens—a composite of races from near the center of the galaxy—request from Earth a representative to help defend the galaxy against an impending invasion by a roving intergalactic menace, the Horde. Miles Vander, a polio-stricken painter, is chosen. His psychic "overdrive" abilities, triggered by his will to fight, generate the strategy that successfully fends off the Horde, even after the Center Aliens—superior in almost every way—have given up the battle. Because the Center Aliens have stopped in their evolutionary drive, they will be superseded by the now barbarian races whose evolution is still in progress; among these races the human spirit that refuses to admit the existence of the impossible will rise to prominence. The motif of the crippled hero is almost too obvious, but it reinforces the plot and theme.

The same heroic qualities of courage and refusal to accept defeat are more successfully handled in the character of Cletus Graeme, hero of *The Tactics of Mistake* (1971), the latest work of the Childe Cycle to

appear. The book chronicles the career of the founder of the Dorsai culture and provides the link between the Chantry Guild of *Necromancer* and the Association for the Investigation and Development of Exotic Sciences located on the worlds of Mara and Kultis. Graeme, an officer of Earth's Western Alliance Military Academy, reveals himself a strategist without equal and the possessor of mental abilities that are envied by the Exotics. He defeats the plot of Dow de Castris, leader of the Coalition of Eastern Nations, who desires to retain economic control over Earth's colony worlds.

The title of the book refers to the method of warfare based on the Taoist-derived philosophy central to Eastern martial arts such as judo: any action likely to succeed is in accord with the unfolding way of things in the universe at large; the successful combatant makes use of the opponent's misdirected force. This principle is also applied in fencing, which is in fact the analogy used in the text. Intuition of course is of great value to the "tactics of mistake"; an equally great aid is empathy, for one's opponent as well as for one's friends. This central ideology makes the work believable and ties the warfare theme to Dickson's larger concerns.

The Pritcher Mass (1972) features psychic talents even more centrally. The hero, Chaz Sant, has long desired to work on the Pritcher Mass, a psychic "machine" intended as a "bridge to the stars" from an Earth ravaged by the berry-rot, an incurable spore-borne disease from which people have sought refuge in domed sterile cities. Chaz finds his success impeded by the Citadel, a criminal organization against whom he enlists the aid of a witch, Melissa Fortmain, and her coven. Not only does Melissa have parapsychic strength, but the world crisis triggers a survival instinct in the species to develop latent psychic abilities that had been repressed. With the united strength of all humanity, the berry-rot fungus is destroyed, and an ability is discovered that will eventually lead to human movement outward into the galaxy, not for escape but for discovery. Though significant in terms of its development of Dickson's basic themes, the book is not an unqualified success. The world that Chaz contacts through the Mass is a cartoon world, and the rather cloying charm with which it is characterized unfortunately colors other aspects of the novel as well.

In *The R-Master* (1973) humans are not capable of such extraordinary mentation. An experimental drug has been produced to boost thinking ability in those who volunteer. The Earth Council carefully controls and makes ineffectual the few R-Masters so produced, in the interest of preserving their own power "for the good of humanity." Etter Ho, the most recent R-Master, takes on the establishment and wins, producing a state of creative confusion in the Earth bureaucracy that will lead to renewed growth. Although much less sanguine than Dickson's other books about the potential mental abilities in humanity, the basic pattern of static "perfection" versus continued growth is the same. The book is a clever experiment, and it offers technological solutions that may be more acceptable to some readers than the almost magic ones in some of his other books.

Over the years Dickson has often collaborated with other science-fiction authors, producing *Planet Run* (1967) with Keith Laumer, *Gremlins, Go Home!* (1974) with Ben Bova, and *The Lifeship* (1976) with Harry Harrison. These efforts were in the main uncharacteristic, but in 1975 he and Poul Anderson again collaborated on a tale of the Hokas, the intelligent little bears of their earlier collaboration, *Earthman's Burden. Star Prince Charlie* (1975) is a parodic work, and each chapter is headed by a title from a literary predecessor, ranging from Blake's "The Tiger" to Heinlein's *Stranger in a Strange Land*. The chapters all prove to be related in some way to the works that furnish their titles.

Charles Stuart, a bookish son of a starship captain, is kidnapped by a local warlord while on vacation on the backward planet of Talyina. He is coerced into acting out a legend in which he is featured as the red-haired hero who performs—with some trickery—five semimythic feats to demonstrate his right to rule the planet. His Hoka companion, who has adopted the role of a Scots follower of Bonnie Prince Charlie, instead of helping Charles to escape helps him perform the feats necessary to claim the throne. The boy is initiated into manhood and responsibility, to the delight of his father.

The fusion of the fantastic story with ironic use of materials from history and from literature makes this work more interesting than it might otherwise be. The Hoka's use of historical and literary models to gain the flexibility of character needed for success—and the human boy's ability to do this without consciously resorting to such models—ties the book to Dickson's more serious explorations of human nature.

A different literary tradition is important in *The Dragon and the George*, in which a young couple planning marriage and trying to eke out a living on salaries as university instructors are victimized by the woman's supervisor, Professor Grottwold, who sends Angie off into space/time without the ability to get her back. The hero, James Eckart, follows to find himself in the right place but incarnate as a dragon. Caught in a mythic pattern of action, related to him by Carolinus, a george (human) magician, he wages war against the forces of evil to rescue his imprisoned lady, aided by a knight-errant with problems of his own, a talking English wolf, two other dragons—one senile and the other cowardly—a band of outlaw archers in the Robin Hood pattern, and magic.

The book belongs to the tradition of C. S. Lewis, Charles Williams, and Frank Baum. In its Manichaean universe physical and philosophical laws correspond. Eckart becomes a dragon because he has the sensibility of a dragon, and he has to learn through his trial to be a george. After his return to his own body, he and Angie choose to stay in their quasi-magical world, where the traditional emblems of myth are realities.

In *Time Storm* (incorrectly titled *Timestorm* by the publisher), the most conceptually complete of Dickson's novels, the expanding universe has begun to contract in parts and pieces at an uneven rate. The result is a network of temporal fault lines that threatens to reach the condition in which adjacent particles are temporally discontinuous: chaos, the end of space/time, the end of the universe. Against this impending doom, Marc Despard struggles—with the aid of a crazy leopard named Sunday, a girl-woman named Ellen, an alien named Porniarsk who comes to them through a line of temporal discontinuity, a group of contemporary survivors who follow Marc into the frontier, and eventually people of the far-distant future—and finally calms the time storm.

The real story, however, is that of Marc's developing awareness of the unity of things and of the time storm as an external symbol of his—and everyone's—internal conflict between universal identification and individual identity. The resolution comes when Marc recognizes his lifelong struggle as the "human search for love." Characteristic of Dickson's fiction, Marc's means of discovery is paranormal mentation, boosted through technology and intensified by emotion. Perhaps the most interesting character in the book is the Old Man, member of a species of apelike experimental beings created, at some point in the future, in a test tube for the sake of sociological study. The Old Man is just a bit more than animal, just a bit less than human. His struggle to understand his world parallels Marc Despard's and makes him a more "human" character than some of the humans who come equipped with less "soul" than he does. The common element between the subhuman and the superhuman characters is the spirit's quest for wholeness and value.

The clarity and poignance of this theme make *Time Storm* one of Dickson's most intimate works, and despite the large canvas on which it is painted, it is closer to the concerns of contemporary humanity than most of his novels. It is finally less important in the book that Marc performs heroic feats than that he has befriended a leopard named Sunday, that he empathizes with the Old Man, and that he loves and is loved by a woman named Ellen; in the internal world these are the heroic feats of which the external action is a symbol.

Dickson goes one step further in *The Far Call*, his closest incursion to date into a fictional world close to our real one. Set in the late years of the twentieth century, the book is about the first manned spaceflight past the moon by an international Mars expedition. Jens Wylie, U. S. Undersecretary for the Development of Space, fails to circumvent the effect of competitive international politics which endangers the mission. When the foreseen disaster happens and the mission must be aborted, Jens, in order to insure that there will be a second attempt, ruins himself by exposing the international intrigue. In the meantime, one of the Marsnauts decides on his own to accomplish the same end by refusing to abandon his one-way flight and sails on to Mars, where his body will await the arrival of the next mission.

The themes are familiar, but their expression is different. Instead of alien and human, the potential opponents are nations on Earth, but they too must learn to adjust value differences to cooperate. The villains are still inertia, reactionary timidity, and greed. Here, too, we find among the Marsnauts the man of action, Tad Hansard, who dies in a kind of combat but is not defeated; the man of the mind, Dirk Welles, whose empathy with his wife approaches telepathy; and the man of faith, Fedya Arstunov, who dies faithful to his call, planting the flag of the United Nations on Mars. These adventurers also have their counterparts on the ground, manifested in only a slightly less heroic way. Jens Wylie, whose name makes him the "clever man," the Odysseus figure, learns to unite all of these aspects of his own humanity.

The novel, however, is not really Jens Wylie's story, nor that of any other character. It is "a tapestry in which he and everyone else were individual threads . . . meaningless, except as they were woven with the other threads." But each of these threads of individual life is carefully developed by Dickson into a believable character, and their weaving does not diminish them. *The Far Call* is technically Dickson's most fully realized work to date and ranks in importance with *Time Storm* and the Childe Cycle. The Cycle, however, is the opus on which

Dickson himself places most value. It will run to twelve volumes, and he considers all of his novels that are not a part of the series to be experiments preparing him for the books that are yet to be written. The completed whole will include, in addition to the six volumes already mentioned, three contemporary novels and three historical novels, the first of which, set in the fourteenth century, will focus on Sir John Hawkwood. It is planned for 1983-1984.

Unless the unexpected happens, the pattern for these final books is set. In Dickson's vision, rooted in mythic and evolutionary forms and fleshed out in allusions to art, literature, history, and other human endeavors, there will be the same polarities of inertia and evolution, swept forward by human aggression, thought, and faith toward increasing consciousness, creativity, and self-control in the species. The development of Dickson's own work has followed a similar path; the technical resources and the sureness of touch in his later fiction show gains in power and fluency. The completed Childe Cycle promises to establish Dickson as a writer who deserves more serious attention than he has yet received.

Other:

"The Things that are Caesar's," in *The Day the Sun Stood Still: Three Original Novellas of Science Fiction*, by Dickson, Poul Anderson, and Robert Silverberg (Nashville: Nelson, 1972);

1975 Annual World's Best Science Fiction, edited by Dickson (New York: DAW, 1975);

"Ten Years of Nebula Awards," in *Nebula Award Stories Ten*, ed. James Gunn (New York & London: Harper, 1975), pp. 98-104;

Nebula Winners 12, edited by Dickson (New York & London: Harper, 1978).

Interviews:

Clifford McMurray, "An Interview with Gordon R. Dickson," *Science Fiction Review*, 7 (July 1978): 6-12;

Sandra Miesel, "*Algol* Interview: Gordon R. Dickson," *Algol*, 15 (Spring 1978): 33-38.

References:

Sandra Miesel, "About Gordon R. Dickson," in *Alien Art* by Dickson (New York: Ace, 1978); republished in *Arcturus Landing* (New York: Ace, 1978);

Miesel, "An Afterword," in *Home from the Shore* by Dickson (New York: Sunridge, 1978).

Thomas M. Disch

Erich S. Rupprecht
South River, New Jersey

BIRTH: Des Moines, Iowa, 2 February 1940, to Felix Henry and Helen Margaret Gilbertson Disch.

EDUCATION: Cooper Union; New York University, 1959-1962.

BOOKS: *The Genocides* (New York: Berkley, 1965; London: Whiting & Wheaton, 1967);

Mankind Under the Leash (New York: Ace, 1966); republished as *The Puppies of Terra* (London: Panther, 1978; New York: Pocket Books, 1980);

One Hundred and Two H Bombs (London: Compact Books, 1966; with new arrangement of stories, New York: Berkley, 1971); with another arrangement of stories as *White Fang Goes Dingo and Other Funny S.F. Stories* (London: Arrow, 1971);

The House that Fear Built, by Disch and John Sladek, as Cassandra Knye (New York: Paperback Library, 1966);

Echo Round His Bones (New York: Berkley, 1967; London: Hart-Davis, 1969);

Camp Concentration (London: Hart-Davis, 1968; Garden City: Doubleday, 1969);

Under Compulsion (London: Hart-Davis, 1968); republished as *Fun With Your New Head* (Garden City: Doubleday, 1971);

Black Alice, by Disch and Sladek, as Thom Demijohn, (Garden City: Doubleday, 1968; London: Allen, 1969);

The Prisoner (New York: Ace, 1969; London: Dobson, 1979);

Highway Sandwiches, by Disch, Marilyn Hacker, and Charles Platt (N.p., 1970);

334 (London: MacGibbon & Kee, 1972; New York: Avon, 1974);

The Right Way to Figure Plumbing, Poems (Fredonia, N.Y.: Basilisk Press, 1972);

Getting Into Death and Other Stories (London: Hart-Davis, MacGibbon, 1973; with new arrangement of stories, New York: Knopf, 1976);

Clara Reeve, as Leonie Hargrave (New York: Knopf, 1975);

The Early Science Fiction Stories of Thomas M. Disch (Boston: Gregg Press, 1977)—includes

Mankind Under the Leash and *One Hundred and Two H Bombs*;

On Wings of Song (London: Gollancz, 1979; New York: St. Martin's Press, 1979);

Neighboring Lives, by Disch and Charles Naylor (New York: Scribners, 1981).

Thomas M. Disch has been called by one critic "very likely the finest intellect in science fiction today." He is more than that, however. He is one of the finest writers of fiction today. Disch is a writer who constantly challenges the ultimately limiting dichotomy between science fiction and so-called mainstream literature. Early and late, his works display the wit, intelligence, moral seriousness, and stylistic energy usually associated with mainstream writers. Indeed, Disch seems to delight in skirting the edge of science fiction, in blurring easy distinctions. He often employs standard science-fiction themes—such as alien invasions or future technological advances—for dramatically untraditional effects, and he does not hesitate to introduce into his work the kind of technical experimentation and aesthetic novelty usually reserved for serious fiction.

Disch himself clearly rejects the second-rate status to which science fiction is often relegated. In a witty and iconoclastic lecture, "The Embarrassments of Science Fiction," Disch says that science-fiction writers are the "provincials of literature." He derides the condescension of serious critics who find science fiction's charm only in its gaucheries and vulgarities. Disch is also hard on science-fiction writers who are too often concerned with "ideas" and not with writing superior fiction. His final implication seems to be that the dichotomy between science fiction and the mainstream is largely illusory: "lousy books don't survive and good ones do."

Born in Des Moines, Iowa, Thomas Michael Disch grew up in Minnesota and graduated from high school in Saint Paul. After a series of what he calls "nebbish jobs"—including a stint as a night attendant in a Minneapolis funeral parlor ("for $10 and an attic room over the embalming studio")—Disch moved to New York. He attended Cooper

Union and New York University between 1959 and 1962 but dropped out of both. After working as a checkroom attendant at the Majestic Theatre, Disch was hired in 1963 by Doyle Dane Bernbach, an advertising agency, and wrote copy for liquor, luggage, and Volkswagen advertisements. During this time Disch also had been getting stories published; his work first appeared in the October 1962 issue of *Fantastic*. He left the advertising agency in 1964 to become a free-lance writer.

In 1967 Disch was asked by an editor for a brief biographical sketch of himself. He wrote back: "Occupation: Beach-comber on a semi-global scale." While this was something of a joke, Disch has pursued a rootless existence since 1964. He has lived in Mexico, England, Austria, Spain, Italy, Turkey, and New York. His work has appeared in such varied publications as *Playboy, Penthouse, Harper's, Poetry, Paris Review, Transatlantic Review, Mademoiselle*, and numerous science-fiction magazines. He has written or edited well over a dozen books, including a volume of poetry.

Disch's wide acceptance is a result of the power and depth of his vision—which tends to be dark, disturbing, and skeptical. He rejects both the melioristic and apocalyptic tendencies of science fiction. Not only do his stories imply that there will be little, if any, progress in the human condition, but they also brilliantly suggest that science fiction's darker visions of the future—with Big Brothers and sinister technologies—are equally fanciful. In Disch's fiction the real horror resides in the fact that the future is always distressingly like our own present; hell is just around the next corner. Disch, along with some of the other New Wave writers such as Michael Moorcock and J. G. Ballard, creates in his best fiction alternate worlds that are really mirrors of our present one. As James Gunn has said, the New Wave writers of the 1960s and 1970s, Disch especially, exhibit a new concern "for complex characters conducting their lives on a treadmill of meaningless days, for little people or strange people caught up in the innumerable folds of an inexplicable world, for lives that are static, trapped, or doomed. . . ."

This concern for the drab, the trivial, the meaningless reaches its finest expression in Disch's later fiction—*334* (1972) is the most brilliant example. But even as early as his first novel, *The Genocides* (1965), he is clearly working toward a different kind of science-fiction story. *The Genocides* is instructive because it is the closest Disch comes to a traditional science-fiction tale, yet he is already experimenting, already attempting to articulate his

unique and disturbing vision. In this novel Disch is working within the familiar end-of-mankind theme. Unlike the usual apocalyptic fantasy about colliding worlds or intergalactic warfare, however, the work depicts the destruction of mankind with an absolute minimum of drama. Instead of the familiar cosmic bang, the world ends with only the faintest of whimpers. The Earth becomes a huge vegetable patch, a farm for a race of unseen aliens. The "invasion" is carried out by sowing the Earth with plants which grow to an incredible height and consequently crowd out all other forms of life. The few survivors who have not starved to death are incinerated by roaming heat machines. The book concentrates on a handful of survivors who manage to enter the roots of one of the plants and live for a time on the edible inner matter. They too eventually starve to death after the plants are harvested, and the Earth is left stripped of all life.

The novel succeeds on several counts. One source of its power is the utter absurdity of the humans' situation. Like characters in a Kafka novel, they are absolutely bewildered by events outside their control. They are impotent and helpless in the face of this suddenly hostile environment. The aliens make no attempt to communicate with them; they never even appear. Thus there is no resistance to be offered, no battle to be fought, no appeal to be made. And, as in so many works of twentieth-century literature, there is absolutely no one to answer any questions. The humans never know why or by whom they are being destroyed, and the aliens have no compunctions, apparently, about the destruction they are causing. Mankind's extermination is wanton, arbitrary, and inscrutable.

The novel is also powerful in the way that it forces the reader to alter his perspective, to reexamine what it means to be human. To the aliens, the humans are mere garden pests; destroying them is simply "spraying the garden." As one of the characters realizes with horror, the few humans surviving inside the roots of the great plants are no more to the aliens than worms "crawling through an apple." Even more disturbing is the extent to which the humans actually become animals. As food becomes scarce, the survivors resort to murder and cannibalism; they make a kind of gruesome sausage out of any survivors who wander too near their camp. Later, when they live in the roots of the plants, they almost literally become worms—living for months in utter darkness, feeding on and living within the sickly sweet pulp: "He found a spot where the pulp had not been disturbed and shoved his body into it backward. Once you got used to the sticky feeling, it was quite comfortable: soft, warm, snuggly." In the pulp, characters tend to lose their human features. A beautiful young woman becomes so obese that her face is almost indistinguishable from the rest of her body: "it was an uncomplicated mass of flaccid fat." Another character completely loses his mind: he kills his father, makes sexual advances toward his sister, and finally satisfies "the years' pent-up lusts" on the decapitated head of a woman he has killed. In short, the novel puts these characters in hell and watches what happens to them. Although some characters—the protagonist and his young lover, for instance—grow and even manage to find a kind of doomed love among the ruins, other characters tend to disintegrate, to dissolve as human beings.

This becomes Disch's recurrent theme: charting his characters' attempts to keep themselves intact in a world which grows increasingly hostile, irrational, inhuman. As Disch progresses as a writer, these pressures come less and less from identifiable external sources and more and more from the fabric of life itself. Disch's main interest lies, as M. John Harrison says, in exploring "the way we manage the continuing psychic crisis of being alive." Being alive in Disch's world always involves a struggle against disintegration.

In *Echo Round His Bones* (1967) hell is the result of that technological monkey wrench, the unanticipated side effect. The novel articulates a concern common in an age of thalidomide babies and cancer-causing food additives: the fear that no matter what positive effects are anticipated from any technological innovation, an unforeseen and horrible side effect is likely to follow. A matter transmitter has been developed for use primarily in the transportation of military personnel and hardware between Earth and Mars. No one is aware, however, that every time a person or object is passed through the matter transmitter, an exact duplicate is formed. These duplicates inhabit a kind of shadow world just beyond the range of the normal world: they can observe the real world but are not part of it. Invisible and without substance, they pass through physical objects. The shadow world is also eerily silent: sound does not pass from one world to the other, so the duplicates have no way of communicating with the normal world.

The novel traces the efforts of an army officer to survive in this weird environment, which becomes another version of hell. Since there is no matter in this subworld except for what passes through the transmitter, the inhabitants have little food. The supplies of food that occasionally materialize are

rapidly eaten; so that when bewildered new arrivals appear, they are immediately butchered and eaten by the ravenous ghosts. As in *The Genocides*, the problem for these characters is keeping psychically and spiritually intact. Cannibalism again becomes a kind of human dissolution.

Echo Round His Bones represents, however, a more substantial achievement than *The Genocides*. In the later novel, Disch manages to combine an exciting and plausible science-fiction tale with a theme that is profound and serious. With the shadow world and its duplicate beings, Disch creates a metaphor as powerful as any in recent fiction. The shadow world becomes a vehicle for Disch's disturbing vision of modern life, which he sees as ugly, violent, and inhuman. And yet, absurdly, human beings must learn to live in it. They yearn to escape into the real world but never can, for in one sense they do not really exist. One can think of few characters in literature who are so completely alienated. These duplicate beings also literalize Disch's recurrent theme of psychic disintegration. In this novel, characters actually do disintegrate: many of them exist in two or more versions, and these duplicate characters even have to compete with themselves for survival. Finally, the normal world is, in an odd way, also duplicated in the shadow world. There is nothing in the real world quite as stomach-turning as the cannibalism of the ghosts, yet in the novel the Earth is threatened with large-scale butchery in the form of a nuclear war. In fact, only by some contrived plot manipulations—including moving the Earth across the solar system—does Disch manage to save the world from a nuclear holocaust.

Disch's next novel, *Camp Concentration* (1968), ends with a similar implausibility. Disch self-consciously creates a gloomy, indeed hopeless situation that is narrowly averted at the end. *Camp Concentration* logically should end with the protagonist—as well as most of the population of the United States—succumbing to a deadly form of syphilis. Instead, in a manner reminiscent of Fielding in *Tom Jones*, the very nature of what has been presented is suddenly altered in the last few pages. The novelist juggles reality in order to manufacture a happy ending. While some reviewers found this sort of game playing distracting and even offensive, the effect is actually deliberate and quite complicated. Disch, in effect, provides the reader with an ending which suggests a number of grim possibilities for the future, yet he manages to avoid the gothic extremes of his earlier novels. The ending of the novel avoids dreariness, yet one cannot help but feel its optimism has been purchased at some novelistic expense.

Camp Concentration tells the story of Louis Sacchetti, an imprisoned conscientious objector, who is opposed to a war that clearly suggests Vietnam (President McNamara is now in charge). Sacchetti is "kidnapped" from his "lawful" prison and spirited away to Camp Archimedes, where experiments are being conducted by the army on unwitting prisoners to increase their mental powers. This enrichment, however, is caused by a type of syphilis which rapidly destroys the central nervous system. Sacchetti does not realize it for some time, but he too has been injected with Pallidine, the mind-expanding drug. The novel traces Sacchetti's attempts to come to terms with his imminent death—as well as the death of all the inmates of the camp. They are saved, however, as one of the inmates comes up with a miraculous solution in the last few pages.

The novel is prophetic in the pervasive atmosphere of paranoia it creates. The secret drug experiments in *Camp Concentration* are eerily like recently disclosed drug experiments actually conducted by governmental agencies on unwitting subjects. One must keep reminding oneself that the

novel was not published in the mid-1970s but in 1968, before Watergate and before reports about politically motivated burglaries of psychiatrists' private files:

> "Oh, there's very little we don't know about you, sir. Before you were brought here you may be sure we examined every dirty little cranny in your past. . . .We know you inside and out. Your schools, relatives, friends, what you've read, where you've been. We know what room you occupied in every hotel you stayed at in Switzerland and Germany when you had your Fulbright. We know every girl you dated at Bard and afterward, and just how far you got with each. And it hasn't been a very good showing, I must say. We know, in considerable detail, just how much you've earned during the last fifteen years, and how you've spent it. Any time the government cares to, it can send you right back to Springfield on tax evasion charges. We have the records from your two years of psychotherapy."
>
> "And have you bugged the confessionals as well?"
>
> "Only since you came to Springfield."

The novel is subtle, disturbing, and, at times, humorous. It would have been easy—given the nature of the story—for Disch to grind political axes, or to make the novel a political parable in the tradition of *1984* and *Brave New World*. Disch is obviously responding to the contemporary political situation: the novel examines and pokes fun at the political and military mentality which involved the United States in the Vietnam War. And yet, although *Camp Concentration* is concerned with politics and the abuses of power, it never descends into mere propaganda. For one thing, the novel concentrates less on the political aspects of the situation and more on the inmates' attempts to keep functioning despite the fact that they have been arbitrarily chosen to die. Louis Sacchetti, the obese narrator, has much too flexible a point of view, much too interesting a verbal style to become trapped in a limiting or self-serving political rhetoric. Rather than preach or burst into impassioned grandiloquence at the injustice of it all, Sacchetti responds with irony, with incisive humor, with philosophical detachment. He comes to realize that his imprisonment in Camp Archimedes is in some ways merely a metaphor for

Her First Ball

She knew, before he'd even entered, that she would fall in love with him — with someone, anyhow — just as starlings I know, with annual infallibility, that they must begin to collect the straws that will become, with a bit of poking and prodding, their dear little nest (in Italian, *nidino*).

This was her first ball, and she was dressed all in pink — pink shoes and pink stockings, a pink ballgown with pink ceintures, pink feathers in her hair and clutched in her lovely fingers a pink *fazzoletto*, or handkerchief. She hoped he liked pink, whoever he was.

The violins whirled about her, leaves by the wild hurricane tossed. Some, growing tired, nestled in the chandeliers; others, wholly reckless, floated in fountains of recirculated champagne; and still the waltz went on: one two three; one two three; Vienna, Paris, Hollywood! Where *was* he?

But even before she could think that thought, before one scintilla of her first intuition had dimmed, a servant approached with a crystal gourd brimming with champagne. "Mademoiselle?" the waiter inquired. She accepted a glass of the frivolous beverage, and even as she drank it, he whispered to her the legend of the Blessed Giulietta — how she had slept three nights in the same pair of overshoes, how she had grown old and cured a beggar simply by the passage of her shadow over the incised letters of his name. A strange and slightly ominous tale, which she listened to with every fiber of her being.

What was happening to her? Too late to ask! Even before the waiter had finished relating this legend, before he vanished into the throng with his tray of drinks, she realized that her forebodings had been realized: she had fallen in love! And with him, with a waiter in a starched white shirt front and a black bow tie. A waiter, moreover, who, unless she were mistaken, had just stolen her pink handkerchief and one of her pink gloves. She didn't even know there was nothing she could do, except to hide the an even greater incarceration: as one character tells him, "the whole goddamned universe is a . . . concentration camp."

Camp Concentration, finally, is about two ways of living in a concentration camp. One way is represented by Louis Sacchetti, who attempts to retain a moral order despite the fact that his world has become increasingly chaotic: "Not since the playground tyrannies of childhood have the rules of the game been so utterly and arrogantly abrogated, and I am helpless to cope." The other way is represented by Dr. Skilliman, a nuclear physicist who willingly takes Pallidine in order to complete his work on a "geological bomb." Disch uses Skilliman to demonstrate how fragile Sacchetti's moral position is when confronted with a vision of unbridled malice. For if the universe is a death camp, Skilliman is its willing collaborator. Skilliman is in love with death; he is obsessed with hastening the inevitable, of ending the world. As Skilliman observes, "The exciting thing, you know, is that it's altogether possible. It's possible to make weapons of absolutely god-like power. We can blow this little world apart the way we used to explode tomatoes with firecrackers. We only have to make the weapons and give them to our dear governments. They can be counted on to carry the ball from there."

The novel ends with Skilliman's death and Sacchetti's redemption, but the redemption has been gained at a heavy psychic cost. In order for Sacchetti to be saved, his mind has been placed into the body of a murdered camp guard. Even though the mind reciprocator has been used without Sacchetti's knowledge, Sacchetti profits from the guard's murder. He is alive, but in a dead man's body, and his sense of self is clearly dislocated. Finally, he declares: "I resemble nothing. The poison has had not two effects—genius and death—but one. Call it by which name you will."

Disch's most brilliant and disturbing work is *334*, a grim novel set fifty years in the future in New York City. *334* exhibits one of Disch's most notable characteristics as a writer: his refusal to reduce complicated situations or emotions to simplified, easily assimilated forms. This respect for complexity makes *334* dazzlingly variegated, complex, and inconclusive. The reader of *334* is presented with a work which grows in meaning and significance directly in proportion to the amount of energy, understanding, and intelligence he is willing to supply. Nevertheless, the reader must be prepared to realize that Disch's respect for complexity is so great that the novel will always retain some of its essential mysteriousness, will never be totally "understood."

The structure of the book mirrors the willingness of its author to deal with complexity. *334* is presented in six sections, but only the last has more than a tangential connection with the others. Each section contains a dark view of life, represented by a tiny pathetic moment which one imagines must be multiplied a thousand times in the huge city. The characters are living in another of Disch's hells, but the triumph of the novel is that it refuses to blame anyone for this hellish existence. It would perhaps be more comforting if someone or something were responsible for the emptiness of these lives, if there were a Big Brother maliciously exercising power for its own sake. In *Camp Concentration*, Skilliman chooses to believe in hell rather than heaven because "hell is something we can *make*." *334*, however, seems to be suggesting that more often than not hell will simply happen.

One of the most depressing aspects of the novel, for example, is the utter emptiness of the lives of its characters, the people living in 334 West Eleventh Street, a huge low-income housing unit that today would be called a project. Housing in the building is part of the MODICUM program, the welfare organization which guarantees people a living wage. In fact, society has become so efficient that most low-level jobs have been eliminated: the majority of the characters in the novel either have nothing to do or work for MODICUM in some capacity. While Disch could probably have targeted MODICUM as the villain, he is not concerned with finding villains. MODICUM certainly is to blame for some of the boredom and ugliness of this world; keeping people alive but giving them nothing to live for, it provides subsistence without dignity. Yet like many social programs, it probably seemed like a decent, humane means of insuring a minimum standard of living for everyone. No one foresaw that it would become a monster, helping to perpetuate the drab hell that modern life has become.

Perhaps the most frightening aspect of *334* is the startling proximity between that world and the present. As one critic has said, "*334* is a cry for help, a voice from a future not so far off—or, if you like, from a present we may never leave behind." Reading the novel is like looking at a slightly distorted mirror image of contemporary life. It is all there. Characters in the book have few emotional attachments: there are only ruins of families, and there are no complete relationships. Television provides the only "genuine" emotional attachments many of these characters have. In lieu of genuine interpersonal relationships, for instance, one character derives a pathetic emotional sustenance from "As the World Turns," a soap opera: "the faces of the actors, their voices, their gestures, the smooth wide-open, whole-bodied way they moved. So long as they themselves seemed stirred by their imaginary problems, Chapel was satisfied. What he needed was the spectacle of authentic emotion—eyes that cried, chests that heaved, lips that kissed or frowned or tightened with anxiety, . . . ''

Against this backdrop of ruined lives and pathetic emptiness, Disch traces the lives of a number of characters who are intent upon trying to survive unaware even of the spiritual desolation in which they exist. As in Disch's other fiction, the novel is populated with characters who are ruined, broken, and disintegrated. One character is missing a finger which he cut off as a youth in a gesture of defiance, another has a deformed shoulder, some are obese, and one is an invalid. One section, appropriately titled "Bodies," tells the story of a worker in the city morgue who sells the corpses of young women to necrophiliacs—one of whom enjoys dismembering them: "The body was scattered all over the patchy linoleum. A heavy roselike scent masked the stench of the decaying organs . . . the head seemed to be missing." Expressions of love in the novel are almost invariably met by indifference or hostility.

And yet, even these ruined people yearn for something more, for some inexpressible value in their lives. In one of the novel's most poignant moments, a woman tries to articulate this need after visiting the A & P Museum (where all the food is plastic): "Heaven. What is heaven? Heaven is a supermarket. Like that one they built outside the museum. Full of everything you could ever ask for. Full of fresh meat—I wouldn't live in a vegetarian heaven—full of cake mixes and cartons of cold milk and fizzies in cans. And I would just go down the aisle with my big cart in a kind of trance, the way they say the housewives did then, without thinking what any of it was going to cost. Without thinking. Nineteen-fifty-three A.D.—you're right, that's heaven."
After considering a few moments, she decides the supermarket does not fully answer her need: "So what *I* want, what I really do want . . . .I don't know how to say it. What I really want is to *really* want something."

One can think of few writers—of science fiction or other genres—who could convey a similar sense of emptiness, of yearning, of ruin with this power and grace. Disch, at his best, clearly illustrates the fact that superior science fiction is superior fiction. Like all great writers, Disch forces his readers to see the

reality of their lives in a way that is fresh, startling, disturbing, and moving.

Other:

The Ruins of Earth: An Anthology of Stories of the Immediate Future, edited by Disch (New York: Putnam's, 1971; London: Hutchinson, 1973);

Bad Moon Rising: An Anthology of Political Foreboding, edited by Disch (New York: Harper & Row, 1973; London: Hutchinson, 1974);

The New Improved Sun: An Anthology of Utopian Science Fiction, edited by Disch (New York: Harper & Row, 1975; London: Hutchinson, 1976);

"Representation in SF," in *A Multitude of Visions*, ed. Cy Chauvin (Baltimore: T-K Graphics, 1975), pp. 8-13;

"The Embarrassments of Science Fiction," in *Science Fiction at Large*, ed. Peter Nicholls (New York: Harper & Row, 1976), pp. 141-155;

New Constellations: An Anthology of Tomorrow's Mythologies, edited by Disch and Charles Naylor (New York: Harper & Row, 1976);

Strangeness: A Collection of Curious Tales, edited by Disch and Naylor (New York: Scribners, 1977).

Periodical Publication:

"Ideas: A Popular Misconception," *Foundation*, 14 (September 1978): 43-47.

References:

John Brunner, "One Sense of Wonder, Slightly Tarnished," *Books and Bookmen*, 12 (July 1967): 19-20;

Samuel R. Delany, *The American Shore: Meditations on a Tale of Science Fiction by Thomas M. Disch* (Elizabethtown, N.Y.: Dragon, 1978);

Delany, "Faust and Archimedes," in his *The Jewel-Hinged Jaw: Notes on the Language of Science Fiction* (Elizabethtown, N.Y.: Dragon, 1977);

M. John Harrison, Introduction to *334* (Boston: Gregg, 1976), pp. v-xiii;

Darko Suvin, "The Science Fiction Novel in 1969," in *Nebula Award Stories 5*, ed. James Blish (Garden City: Doubleday, 1970), pp. 193-205;

Robert Thurston, Introduction to *The Early Science Fiction Stories of Thomas M. Disch* (Boston: Gregg, 1977), pp. vii-xxxii.

GEORGE ALEC EFFINGER
(10 January 1947-   )

BOOKS: *What Entropy Means to Me* (Garden City: Doubleday, 1972);

Relatives (New York: Harper & Row, 1973);

Mixed Feelings (New York: Harper & Row, 1974);

Man the Fugitive (New York: Award Books, 1974);

Escape to Tomorrow (New York: Award Books, 1975);

Journey into Terror (New York: Award Books, 1975);

Nightmare Blue, by Effinger and Gardner Dozois (New York: Berkley, 1975; London: Collins Fontanas, 1977);

Lord of the Apes (New York: Award, 1976);

Irrational Numbers (Garden City: Doubleday, 1976);

Felicia (New York: Berkley, 1976);

Those Gentle Voices: A Promethean Romance of the Spaceways (New York: Warner, 1976);

Death in Florence (Garden City: Doubleday, 1978); republished as *Utopia Three* (New York: Playboy Press, 1980);

Dirty Tricks (Garden City: Doubleday, 1978);

Heroics (Garden City: Doubleday, 1979);

Blood Pinball (New York: Dell, 1981).

George Alec Effinger is one of the most promising and prolific of the new breed of contemporary writers of speculative fiction. Since the appearance in 1972 of his acclaimed first novel, *What Entropy Means to Me*, Effinger has published nine more novels, three volumes of short stories, and numerous uncollected stories. In these works his ironic wit, his sense of the absurdity of the universe, his eye for concrete detail, and his parody of different styles have caused him to be compared to such writers as Jorge Luis Borges, John Barth, Donald Barthelme, and Thomas Pynchon.

Effinger was born in Cleveland, Ohio, the son of George Paul and Ruth Uray Effinger. A National Merit scholar in high school, Effinger entered Yale in 1965 but soon dropped out to pursue full time his lifelong ambition to be a writer. He attended New York University in 1968 and Yale once again in 1969. He first gained recognition as an author at the Clarion Writers' Workshop in 1970, but the real magnitude of his talent did not become apparent until the publication of *What Entropy Means to Me*. It was nominated for a Nebula Award, and Effinger himself was nominated for the John W. Campbell Award, which is given to the best new writer each year by the World Science Fiction Convention.

Though he did not win the awards, his career had a dramatic beginning.

Effinger's love of popular culture and fiction is evident throughout his works in the parody of certain forms of literature and in his many references to games, sports, and various forms of mass entertainment. He is an avid fan of basketball, baseball, and pinball, having recently completed a nonfiction work entitled *Blood Pinball* (1981). He seems also to have a strong background in traditional literature. Thus, in his impressive first novel, Effinger parodies a spectrum of genres, from the epic and romantic literature of the *Odyssey, Sir Gawain and the Green Knight*, and *The Faerie Queene* to popular entertainments such as comic books and grade-B horror movies. The openly allegorical narrative explores the creative process: the artist's experience of reality, the transformation of raw materials through his imagination, the influence of criticism on his work, and the subsequent effect of his artistic creation upon life itself.

Using one of his favorite structural techniques, Effinger weaves strands of three different stories through *What Entropy Means to Me* so that each strand parallels or counterpoints the others. The first major story details the heroic journey of Dore, the eldest son of the first family of a planet called Home, who goes out in search of his lost father and the origin of the symbolic River of Life. Since no one accompanies Dore, and he does not return to relate his adventures, his younger brother Seyt writes the narrative of what might have happened in Dore's search for the meaning of life. The young artist invents details "out of thin air [that] would have the bite of authenticity." As Seyt repeatedly tells the reader, he creates episodes based directly on his literary heritage and his flair for the dramatic. Through this kind of consciously created narrative, Effinger—the artist behind the artist—can satirize the heroic tradition and epic styles as well as demonstrate the creative process.

But Seyt is not creating his account totally in a vacuum. No one may know what really happens to Dore, but everyone has his own opinion. In the second major story line Seyt is besieged by constant criticism and suggestions from his large, eccentric family. As each episode is completed and critiqued by the various brothers and sisters, all with their particular prejudices, the interpretation of the character and mission of Dore becomes the center of a bitter religious controversy. Satirizing the divisive extremes of religious debates and the excesses of cultism, Effinger suggests that Seyt's art is actually more valid than the family's theology as a means to comprehend the mysteries of Dore's quest (and of life).

In the third and least well integrated segment of the plot, Seyt relates details concerning the background of the mother and father, implying some connection between the past and present. Their ignoble escape from Pittsburg and establishment of a feudal society on Home ironically undercuts the

George Alec Effinger

religious nature of Dore's search. Although the allegorical journey of Dore is also undermined by unheroic, undignified adventures, the fundamental meaning of his quest is serious. After his humorous encounters with the giant mutant radishes of Dr. Dread, the dissembling daughter of Baron von Glech who steals his clothes, the phallic giant Loo from whom he escapes tied Ulysses-like to the belly of a filthy goat, and others, Dore must abandon his companion Glorian of the Knowledge, who has saved him from every disaster, and face the ultimate confrontation alone.

The great father, Dore finds after all of his trials, is somewhat disappointing—an average, unheroic man running away from a shrewish wife. Caught on a cliff between the River of Life and the Well of Entropy, the father explains to Dore the central concepts of life and entropy: "Down there is the entropic center of Home at least, and possibly the universe. Everything that falls down there becomes more and more dissociated, tending to the primal chaotic state. . . . Up there, where you came from, is the River, the symbol and essence of divinity on this planet. God is the ultimate Order, the embodiment of organization. The River and the Well are the two poles of existence; I suppose that it is necessary for the River to have its source from the Well to make the cycle complete."

Thus the meaning of life lies in the tension between these two poles of existence—order versus chaos, a dichotomy explored in most of Effinger's works. In Seyt's narrative, "entropy" means death or chaotic nonexistence for Dore and his father when they fall to their doom in the dark Well. Ultimately, what entropy means is a subjective, aesthetic reality as the artist sets out on his own quest at the end of the novel: "What real dangers there will be, I cannot say. I don't know. The River I see over there, and the River I described for Dore probably won't be the same. (If they are, I'm already lost.) But, as Fluellen says to Gower in William Shakespeare's immortal play *Henry V*, 'There is a river in Macedon, and there is also moreover a river at Monmouth. . . .But 'tis all one; 'tis alike as my fingers is to my fingers, and there is salmons in both.' " Although each individual must confront the absurdity and irrationality of existence in his own way, there are certain eternal principles behind man's perpetual search for meaning.

Effinger implies the seriousness of the novel's message in his comments on the construction of *What Entropy Means to Me*: "On one level it is an attempt to weld successfully the episodic novel with the more organic sort. On another level I have tried to take a classic form—the novel of moral education—and fill it with astoundingly unconventional characters, to see what happens to both morals *and* education." Even though his book does deal with morality and education, Effinger's wit, as Edward A. Sklepowich has observed, shines through his imaginative handling of the epic traditions, his "multiple anachronisms," and his comic alterations of tone: "Effinger fabulates a universe in which the mundane is made to seem marvelous and the strange illusively familiar; the serious trivial, and the trivial pontifically serious." This technique of humor is a staple of all of Effinger's works; as he himself comments, "What I want to do is begin mildly, feed the reader acceptable bits of strangeness at a slow but constant rate, and build this until he must recognize the logical but no less astonishing social framework."

Effinger's deliberate use of wit and parody has

brought both positive and negative criticism. One standard guide calls the novel "more technique than substance," and perhaps Effinger is often too clever for his own good. To Sklepowich, however, *What Entropy Means to Me* is a "fascinating piece of innovative fiction" that indicates a "new direction taken by science fiction and fantasy in order to revitalize themselves and to pay oblique, perhaps even perverted, homage to the literary traditions of which they are manifestations." Theodore Sturgeon extols the novel as "truly extraordinary" and praises Effinger's originality: "The impact of the colorful, meaningful book must be experienced to be fully savored."

Effinger employs the trilevel narrative that is so effective in *What Entropy Means to Me* with less success in his second novel, *Relatives* (1973). Although he uses these levels to show that the rigidity of bureaucracy does not vary from period to period and from society to society, the complete segregation of the three stories is less satisfying than the more fluid narrative of the previous novel. The three main characters, whose names are confusingly similar, are relatives in that they are all eventually destroyed by the absurd machinations of an anonymous, omnipotent, authoritarian organization.

The most fully developed plot line concerns Ernest Weintraub in the not-too-distant future of overpopulation and automation. The highly structured society is ruled by six despotic Representatives who use the mass media to control the population. Their announcement of imminent doom that will destroy most of the world culminates in a chaotic scramble for the limited tokens redeemable for salvation. When Ernest, who has learned of the treachery of people and the desperation of his life through his struggle for a token, finds that the apocalypse has all been a hoax, he cannot accept the irrationality of his existence and kills himself and his nagging, unimaginative wife.

Social and personal decadence, the corrupting influence of bureaucracy, the failure of love, and the absurdity of life are recurring themes that are also found in the other two story lines. Ernest Weintraub is a degenerate, drunken, would-be artist living in the only populated city on the African continent in a decaying world where the Americas have been deemed unfit for colonization. Like a Beckett character, he is paralyzed by inaction as he waits endlessly, hopelessly, for the arrival of M. Gargotier. In the third story Ernest Weintraub, a dedicated communist from Jermany, in a world where the Allies lost World War I, is sent to Ostamerika to subvert the morality of the population through clever corrupting arguments at meetings of local

book clubs and church organizations. His success, loyalty, and dedication to the cause, however, do not prevent him from being sacrificed by his party as a scapegoat.

Effinger's careful alternations of "meanwhiles" and "meantimes" suggest the simultaneous existence of these three worlds and sets of characters. The novel can be interpreted as a kind of eternal negative statement of society's treatment of the individual; as each of the three relatives struggles to come to terms with his environment, he becomes part of a bleak composite portrait of Man. But the wit that distinguishes *What Entropy Means to Me* is seen only in flashes in *Relatives*. The fascinating details of scene and character (such as Vladieki, the midget who was once a munchkin in *The Wizard of Oz*) are unfortunately overshadowed by Effinger's moralistic textbook socialism. As Gerald Walker observes, "It is a modish waste of what would appear to be, judging sentence by sentence and paragraph by paragraph, an eloquent writing talent."

From 1974 to 1976 Effinger was involved with the task of adapting "Planet of the Apes" movie scripts into the paperback novels *Man the Fugitive* (1974), *Escape to Tomorrow* (1975), *Journey Into Terror* (1975), and *Lord of the Apes* (1976). Though he improves on the originals considerably, this is still hack work, and the taint of hack may be seen in his novel, *Those Gentle Voices: A Promethean Romance of the Spaceways* (1976). With its space travel and alien worlds, it is less original—and consequently less effective—than his earlier works. But the novel is somewhat redeemed by Effinger's refusal to give up his ironic view of human nature and by an occasional touch of wit. To preserve the mystery of the story, which is divided into five parts, *Those Gentle Voices* begins with part 2 and ends with part 1. In "Part Two: 1988" Dr. Jennings and his associate Dr. Janet Short discover radio waves emanating from the distant planet Wolf 359. Jennings apparently wants to keep this information secret even though the research project is an international one; his secrecy prompts Dr. Short to publish the discovery widely, a reaction, it is later revealed, which Jennings intended.

In "Part Three: 2021" a crew of explorers sent to seek out the intelligent life forms that must have created the radio transmitter find instead a race of primitive subhumans who acquire centuries of education in days. The black commander Leigh, who assists them in their advancement by the Promethean gift of fire, in "Part Four: 2022," becomes a god to them. Because their intelligence surpasses Leigh's, however, the natives set out to take over the world in "Part Five: 2029." In this section six authoritarian Representatives, also found in other Effinger stories, divide Earth among themselves to rule. The book ends with "Part One: 1953," where the reader learns that Jennings had been born on Wolf 359 and had planned all along for his people to take over the world. Though the structure is clever, it smacks of gimmickry and fails to achieve the cosmic irony Effinger aspires to. At best he succeeds in communicating an ironic outlook on man's narrow-mindedness, pettiness, and self-delusion.

Effinger ventures into futuristic utopian fiction in *Death in Florence* (1978), a novel that follows the exploits and interactions of three characters involved in Utopia 3, an international experiment supposedly based on the total freedom of the individual. Most of Europe has been voluntarily vacated by the inhabitants to create a colony for the free exploration, travel, and cultural experiences of the selected colonists. Eileen Brant, a cool, somewhat cynical young woman who revels in solitude and her fantasies, benefits from the experiment without believing in the philosophy of the founder, Dr. Waters. Unlike Brant, Norman Moore truly wants to believe in the philosophy of love that the program espouses. Bo Staefler, competing with Moore for Brant's affections, is a true cynic who is accidentally accepted into the project by being at the right place at the wrong time; his sustaining dream is to build in Venice the world's largest miniature golf course.

Using these three different perspectives on utopia, Effinger explores this Eden, which like the original is not without its serpent. Sandor Courane—a frequent character in Effinger's stories—is here the unseen voice crying out in the wilderness by means of huge posters plastered throughout the cities of Europe; like the other characters, he expresses the conflict with the program's sinister founder in biblical terms: "Let us join hands, then, in a struggle against the serpent in this Garden of Eden, a serpent who wears the guise of Creator, better to deceive you." Despite their experience with the power hungry, treacherous Dr. Waters, all three characters eventually come to believe in the ideals of the colony, rejecting the false prophet but affirming the underlying faith. The novel ends in a religious epiphany with the birth of the future savior (with Brant as the Virgin Mary), complete with nativity hymns, three wise men, and a minor miracle: the silent Arab youth who accompanies Staefler pronounces the benediction on the scene in his only words in the novel.

The "death" in Florence refers to the death of the false version of religion: "In a sense Utopia 3 is dead, at least the corrupt original version of Utopia

3. Hostility and jealousy are dead. A good deal of the world's evils have died here in Florence tonight." Effinger, however, does not allow a totally optimistic or unambiguous ending, for the painful screams of Brant struggling to give birth undercut the whole scene; the actual birth of the child is never seen, but there is hope that the death in the title will not also refer to Brant or her baby. The deft characterizations, the allegorical implications of the narrative, the skillful orchestration of the plots, and the use of black humor show a return to the power and promise of Effinger's early work.

Harlan Ellison claims Effinger's next novel, *Heroics* (1979), to be his best work to date. Indeed, Effinger returns to some of the same themes and literary techniques that he had used so successfully in *What Entropy Means to Me*. Like his first novel, *Heroics* centers around a quest for life's meaning, this time undertaken by an eighty-two-year-old woman Irene, who is dead at the beginning of the story and who is physically transformed numerous times in the course of her search. Her memories of her journey across America to augment her Depression glass collection, recalled as she is floating in the void, form the core of the third-person narrative.

The America that she traverses, accompanied by Glorian of the Knowledge (who was also Dore's companion in *Entropy*), is another of Effinger's imaginative visions of the future world. East of the Mississippi lies a vast but sparsely populated forest where life is spent in leisurely, "back-to-nature" pursuits. As a reminder of the hated technology of a former civilization (our own current industrial world), this ecology-conscious society has flattened the Great Plains, covering this huge section of the country with Teflon. California, a distant land of freedom and wealth, is the end of Irene's quest in her symbolic journey through life, history, and culture.

Throughout the novel, the past haunts Irene as she is forced by the mysterious "Powers that Be" to undergo trials that require her participation in history (like the Battle of Maldon and the Lewis and Clark expedition). The dissatisfaction that impelled her to leave her secure home in what was once downtown Louisville leads her into a search for the knowledge of the past. Commonly accepted truths of history, astronomy, and science are debated, ignored, challenged, and/or rejected repeatedly by Glorian and Irene. What she finally comes to realize is that truth is relative: "Knowledge is not static . . . it changes to fit the occasion."

Irene's quest introduces complex existential issues of freedom and fate, such as the power of the

Effinger/5

Quinn. Second base."

"Wonderful," I said. "Terrific."

"Don't worry," said Norris. "I have to go. I'll talk with you later." He hung up.

I looked at the phone. "Terrific," I muttered.

The other guy propped himself up in the other bed and said, "Shut up, Mac, will you?" I just stared at him.

I realized that I should have asked Norris whose body he was in. I shrugged. Maybe Jim would know.

A few days later we had the situation completely sorted out. It still didn't bring us any closer to solving the problem, but at least it was sorted out. This is the way it looked:

FAMOUS SCIENCE FICTION WRITER	IN THE BODY OF	TEAM	POSITION AND BATTING AVERAGE	
Sandor Courane (me)	Ellard MacIver	Boston Red Sox	Inf.	.221
Norris Page	Don Di Mauro	Chicago White Sox	Left Field	.288
Larry Shrader	Gerhardt "Dutch" Ruhl	New York Yankees	1B	.334
Dick Shrader	Marv Croxton	Cleveland Indians	Center Field	.291
Jim Benedetti	Charlie Quinn	Detroit Tigers	2B	.254

I didn't like it at all. Not batting .221 and being thirty-six years old (I'm not thirty-six, but MacIver was, and he was in danger of losing his job next spring, and if we didn't get home soon, I'd have to become a broadcaster or something).

That morning I went to the ballpark with my roommate. His name

"The Pinch-Hitters," typescript

individual will in a seemingly chaotic universe. Although in her adventures accidents occur that alter the plans made for her, the predetermined end is always accomplished. The final chapter deals with the meaning of her death and recollections but does not provide an unambiguous statement on man's condition. Though physically dead, she can still "live" any way she chooses by willing a life into being; as Glorian tells her: "It's your world. Yours alone. Everyone else has one, and this is yours. Do with it what you will. . . . You are the only reality."

In addition to these science-fiction novels and a mainstream novel (*Felicia*, 1976), Effinger has completed three excellent collections of his shorter fiction: *Mixed Feelings* (1974), *Irrational Numbers* (1976), and *Dirty Tricks* (1978). The themes and styles of his novels are reflected in these shorter pieces, and he also explores some of the same characters and situations. For example, several of his stories deal with Gremmage, Pennsylvania, a small town which represents a spiritual conformity and limitation that destroys individuality and initiative. Although Sandor Courane, Dr. Janet Short, and the six Representatives reappear in a number of stories, Effinger is not always consistent in his use of character names, dates, and events; there does not seem to be an encompassing purpose or logic to his repetition of details. If Effinger is attempting to create his own mythology, it is just as irrational and inexplicable as the world he writes about in his fiction.

In his novels and short fiction, Effinger blends science-fiction themes and popular culture in a witty style that is all his own, as Robert Silverberg observes in his introduction to *Irrational Numbers*: "Effinger's material includes all the standard schlock furniture of contemporary pop culture; what he makes out of it is something more than pop. There once was an old man in Los Angeles named Simon Rodia who built a kind of Taj Mahal out of broken soda bottles and bits of castoff Mahal out of broken soda bottles and bits of castoff tile, and Effinger is doing something of the same thing, at times, with his ball players and mad

scientists and sinister computers." Although he has been compared in his style to Barth and Pynchon, Effinger does not turn to science-fiction themes, as they do, to revitalize his art; he is, as David Pringle notes, "the 'insider-travelling-out,' the writer who has grown up as a reader of, and later a contributor to, the sf magazines, who accepts the genre as a perfectly natural part of his imaginative environment, but who nevertheless loathes the publisher's category of 'science fiction.' " Theodore Sturgeon is optimistic about the future of this young gifted writer: "The best summing-up of George Alec Effinger is to say his summing-up is far in the future. He is only now beginning. He has a long way to go, but he is already in the high places and he will not stop—there is too much substance and too much caring already evident in his work, the kind of force which simply will not be stopped." —*Carol M. Ward*

Periodical Publication:

"Comments on *What Entropy Means to Me*," *Library Journal*, 97 (15 June 1972): 2220.

References:

David Pringle, "Games People Play," *Foundation*, 11 (March 1977): 96-99;

Robert Silverberg, Introduction to *Irrational Numbers* (Garden City: Doubleday, 1976), ix-xiv;

Edward A. Sklepowich, "The Fictive Quest: Effinger's *What Entropy Means to Me*," *Extrapolation*, 18 (May 1977): 107-115;

Theodore Sturgeon, "All the Effingers at Once," introduction to *Mixed Feelings* (Garden City: Doubleday, 1974), ix-xiii;

Sturgeon, Review of *What Entropy Means to Me*, *New York Times Book Review*, 3 September 1972, p. 20;

Gerald Walker, Review of *Relatives*, *New York Times Book Review*, 23 December 1973, p. 14.

Harlan Ellison

Thomas F. Dillingham
Stephens College

BIRTH: Cleveland, Ohio, 27 May 1934, to Louis Laverne and Serita Rosenthal Ellison.

EDUCATION: 1951-1953, Ohio State University.

MARRIAGE: 1956 to Charlotte Stein, divorced; 1961 to Billie Joyce Sanders, divorced; 1965 to Lory Patrick, divorced; 1976 to Lori Horowitz, divorced.

AWARDS: Writers Guild of America Award for "Demon with the Glass Hand," 1965; Nebula Award for " 'Repent, Harlequin!' Said the Ticktockman," 1965; Hugo Award for " 'Repent, Harlequin!' Said the Ticktockman," 1966; Hugo Award for "I Have No Mouth and I Must Scream," 1968; Hugo Award for *The City on the Edge of Forever* episode of "Star Trek," 1968; Writers Guild of America Award for *The City on the Edge of Forever* episode of "Star Trek," 1968; Special Hugo Award for *Dangerous Visions*, 1968; Hugo Award for "The Beast That Shouted Love at the Heart of the World," 1969; Nebula Award for "A Boy and His Dog," 1969; Special Hugo Award for *Again, Dangerous Visions*, 1972; Edgar Allan Poe Award for "The Whimper of Whipped Dogs," 1973; Jupiter Award for "The Deathbird," 1973; Writers Guild of America Award for "Phoenix Without Ashes," 1974; Hugo Award for "The Deathbird," 1974; Hugo Award for "Adrift Just Off the Islets of Langerhans: Latitude 38°54′N, Longitude 77°00′13″W," 1975; Nebula Award for "Jeffty Is Five," 1977; Hugo Award for "Jeffty Is Five," 1978.

BOOKS: *Rumble* (New York: Pyramid, 1958); republished as *Web of the City* (New York: Pyramid, 1975);
The Deadly Streets (New York: Ace, 1958; London: Brown Watson, 1959; revised and enlarged edition, New York: Pyramid, 1975);
The Man With Nine Lives and *A Touch of Infinity* (New York: Ace, 1960);
The Juvies (New York: Ace, 1961);
Gentleman Junkie and Other Stories of the Hung-up Generation (Evanston, Ill.: Regency, 1961; revised edition, New York: Pyramid, 1975);

Memos from Purgatory: Two Journeys of Our Times (Evanston, Ill.: Regency, 1961);
Rockabilly (Greenwich, Conn.: Fawcett, 1961; London: Muller, 1963); republished as *Spider Kiss* (New York: Pyramid, 1975);
Ellison Wonderland (New York: Paperback Library, 1962; London: Thorpe & Porter, 1963; revised edition, New York: New American Library, 1974); republished as *Earthman, Go Home* (New York: Paperback Library, 1964);
Paingod and Other Delusions (New York: Pyramid, 1965; revised and enlarged edition, New York: Pyramid, 1975);
I Have No Mouth and I Must Scream (New York: Pyramid, 1967);
Doomsman (New York: Belmont Books, 1967);
From the Land of Fear (New York: Belmont Books, 1967);
Love Ain't Nothing But Sex Misspelled (New York: Trident, 1968; revised edition, New York: Pyramid, 1976);
The Beast That Shouted Love at the Heart of the World (New York: Avon, 1969; abridged edition, London: Millington, 1976);
The Glass Teat: Essays of Opinion on the Subject of Television (New York: Ace, 1969);
Over the Edge: Stories from Somewhere Else (New York: Belmont Books, 1970);
Alone Against Tomorrow: Stories of Alienation in Speculative Fiction (New York: Macmillan, 1971); republished in two volumes as *All the Sounds of Fear* (St. Albans, U.K.: Panther, 1973) and *The Time of the Eye* (St. Albans, U.K.: Panther, 1974);
Partners in Wonder: Harlan Ellison in Collaboration, by Ellison and others (New York: Walker, 1971);
Approaching Oblivion: Roadsigns on the Treadmill Toward Tomorrow (New York: Walker, 1974; London: Millington, 1976);
Phoenix Without Ashes, by Ellison and Edward Bryant (Greenwich, Conn.: Fawcett, 1975);
Deathbird Stories: A Pantheon of Modern Gods (New York: Harper & Row, 1975; London: Pan, 1978);
The Other Glass Teat: Further Essays of Opinion on

Television (New York: Pyramid, 1975);

No Doors, No Windows (New York: Pyramid, 1975);

The City on the Edge of Forever: Star Trek Fotonovel (Toronto, New York & London: Bantam, 1977; London: Corgi, 1978);

Strange Wine: Fifteen New Stories from the Nightside of the World (New York: Harper & Row, 1978);

The Illustrated Harlan Ellison (New York: Baronet, 1978);

The Fantasies of Harlan Ellison (Boston: Gregg Press 1979);

All the Lies that Are My Life (San Francisco: Underwood/Miller, 1980).

Harlan Ellison has spent much of his life evading labels. It is difficult to make a general statement about him, or about his work, that must not be followed immediately by a qualifying negation: Ellison both is and is not a science-fiction writer; Ellison both is and is not the godfather/prime practitioner of the New Wave; Ellison both is and is not a radical critic of contemporary sociopolitical trends; Ellison both is and is not a conservative humanistic moralist. He has built a major reputation by writing short stories and editing anthologies. He has written no trilogies or tetralogies, created no galactic empires or foundations. On the other hand, he has created a body of fiction which contributes to the characteristic twentieth-century redefinition of literary genres. He has built a mode of consciousness in his works that challenges the boundary lines between truth and fiction, between history and myth, between autobiography and journalism, between the particular and the general. In some sense none of these developments seems new. Of Ellison's chosen mentors, Henry David Thoreau, Mark Twain, Edgar Allan Poe, and Ambrose Bierce, each has one or both of two things in common with Ellison—moral outrage at institutionalized human stupidity and a subversive sense of humor. They also share his evasion of easy labels.

Although he is generally associated with science fiction, Ellison has published several novels in a more naturalistic mode, based on his experiences with juvenile gangs, the drug culture, and the popular music business. He has also written screenplays for movies and television and has contributed columns to various newspapers, most notably the *Los Angeles Free Press*, which published his television commentaries from 1968 to 1972. In his journalism and in his editorial introductions both to his own story collections and to the important

anthologies, *Dangerous Visions* (1967) and *Again, Dangerous Visions* (1972), Ellison has created a vivid, distinctive voice that occasionally threatens to overwhelm his fiction and subsume his whole written work into a single autobiographical text filled with elaborate myths of self and other, with masks, charades, and competing gods, both false and true. As George Edgar Slusser has observed, this Ellisonian persona has become increasingly obtrusive, serving "as the means of binding and unifying collections," as well as providing extended autobiographical comments which surround and, in a sense, humanize the stories. The voice reveals both Ellison's unabashed ambition and his serious commitment to literature. In confessing his own failings, he further reveals the moral ground for his stories, even going so far as to criticize the moral failings of some of his own earlier stories. In all, the variety and unpredictability of his career are most apparent in his autobiographical statements.

Some readers have found not exactly a label but at least a metaphor for Ellison's literary character in the name of one of his most famous creations, the Harlequin of the prizewinning story, " 'Repent, Harlequin!' said the Ticktockman" (1965; collected in *Paingod and Other Delusions*, 1965). The name evokes the traditional commedia dell'arte figure of comedy and pathos: dressed in motley, he is loved by all but unlucky in love; he is the ironist, satirist, and underminer of fixed structures but also the sympathetic participant in times of creative joy and in times of mourning or despair. Such a figure may well be diverse enough to encompass the complexities of Ellison's presentation of himself. But the commedia Harlequin, while his behavior may be subversive, can hardly be called a social critic. He gains some of his resilience from his disinterest. While Ellison is resilient, he is also fiercely combative. Everett C. Marms, the schedule-busting Harlequin of his story, replies to the injunction to repent with a favorite 1960s retort: "Get stuffed." For such eloquence, Ellison's Harlequin is brainwashed, like Winston Smith of George Orwell's *1984* (1949) or the hero/victim of Ken Kesey's *One Flew Over the Cuckoo's Nest* (1962). Ellison thus adds his entry to the special subgenre of twentieth-century works that explore violation of the mind as the ultimate form of slavery.

Harlan Jay Ellison's background provides some clue to his own harlequinade. He was born in Cleveland, Ohio, to Louis Laverne and Serita Rosenthal Ellison. As a boy he often appeared in the productions of the Cleveland Play House. At the age of thirteen he published his first story in the

Cleveland News, and at the age of sixteen he founded the Cleveland Science-Fiction Society. After two years at Ohio State University (1951-1953), he held a variety of jobs, from driving dynamite trucks to shilling at carnivals before serving two years in the army (1957-1959). An editor for *Rogue* magazine in 1959-1960, he founded his own press, Regency Books, in 1960. In the sixties, concurrently with his burgeoning career as a fiction writer, he began to work in television, contributing scripts for numerous programs including "Route 66," "The Alfred Hitchcock Hour," "Star Trek," and "The Outer Limits." In the 1970s he continued writing for television ("Burke's Law," "The Starlost") and began writing for films. Among the films to which he contributed are *The Oscar* (1966) and *The Dream Merchants*. Recently he has been involved as a scriptwriter for Warner Brothers' projected film of Isaac Asimov's 1950 novel, *I, Robot*.

Ellison has often identified himself with social causes, from civil rights to the women's movement. His sympathy for oppressed minorities and other groups may be traced from his own experiences as a child. In the introduction to *Approaching Oblivion* (1974) he tells of being labeled a Jew by other children, who beat him and excluded him from games. On one occasion he forced himself to accept the blame for having torn his clothes in a fight rather than shift the guilt to someone else. "How could I tell [my mother] that it was not only that I was a smart aleck? How could I tell her it was because I was a Jew and they had been taught Jews were something loathsome? How could I tell her it was easier for me to carry a broken nose and bruises than for me to act cowardly and deny that I was a Jew?" It would be simplistic to relate this experience directly either to Ellison's impulse to write or even to any specific themes of his fiction. But, seen as a fiction among fictions (true as any fiction), the anecdote is continuous with his recurrent themes. The label (Jew in this case) both distorts the sense of self and simultaneously creates a new false self for the one labeled. Resistance in such a situation may lead to the harlequin stance (agile, protean, deracinated) or to active opposition (bounded, assertive, pugnacious). The either-or is too simple in this case. Certainly in his work and seemingly in his life he has developed an active dialectic between these two stances. The dialectic seems to give him the freedom to choose his own battleground, to draw his opponents onto his ground, and to fight on his own terms. That he has shifted his ground often has led to charges of inconsistency, opportunism, or even cynicism. A generous estimate of his career, however, must not only grant him his freedom of movement, but must also affirm the value of his resultant complexity.

Identity is a self-conscious construct among the strong, an unconscious imposition among the weak. Many of Ellison's stories turn on the problems created by this conception of identity. In some cases, an unselfconscious, weak individual becomes aware of his situation and fights to throw off the false or stereotypic characteristics imposed by genes, environment, or a malevolent external force. In others, a strong character encounters an attack on his autonomy and fights to protect it. The outcomes of these conflicts are not necessarily simple or consistent solutions to these identity crises. In some cases character is destiny, but in others—where certain of the variables of character are not readily visible—it is the vehicle of a trenchant irony.

Ellison's earliest book-length science-fiction publication was a 1960 Ace Double Book which included *The Man With Nine Lives* and *A Touch of Infinity*, the first a novel, the second a collection of stories. In the novel, Ellison links a number of fairly conventional narratives of survival on an alien

ELLISON / 14

"You'll need Surgat to open it. Look."

And she touched a symbol, a character cut into the rounded top of the chest:

"He won't harm you. He serves only one purpose: he opens all locks. Take a hair from my head...don't argue with me, Chris, do it...please..." And because her voice was now barely a whisper, he did it. And she said, "He'll demand a hair of your head. Don't give it to him. Make him take mine. And this is what you say to invoke his presence..."

In her last minutes she went over it with him till he realized she was serious, that she was not delirious, that he ought to write it **down.** So he transcribed her words exactly.

"Once you get the bahut opened, all the rest will be clear. Just be careful, Chris. It's all I have to give you, so make the best of it." Her eyes were half-closed and now she opened them completely, with effort, and looked at him. "Why are you angry with me?"

He looked away.

"I can't help it that I'm dying, dear. I'm sorry, but that's what's happening. You'll just have to forgive me and do the best you can."

Then she closed her eyes and her hand opened and the cloisonné herb container fell to the carpet; and he was alone.

"Grail," typescript

planet by arranging for his central character, Cal Emory, to be placed in suspended animation so that his consciousness can be implanted in various aliens. His task is to take over the aliens' minds and induce them to make changes in their environments or in their political structures so as to facilitate human colonization at some future date. This device is as old as the Buddhist Jataka tales, and as recent as Stapledon's *Star Maker* (1937) or T. H. White's *The Once and Future King* (1958). Emory, a man who has been traduced and humiliated by an ostensible friend, Paul Lederman, is determined to destroy Lederman in revenge for the years of loss, humiliation, and self-denial inflicted on him. As Emory lives through his several alien lives, he learns the limits of his own abilities, learns to appreciate his own strengths, and learns that both are more manageable and more extensive than he had imagined before. He also perceives more clearly the perfidy of Lederman, who "had no morals, no feelings, no humanity in him that a normal man could identify with." (Ellison does not always strip his antagonists of all humanity as he does Lederman. As his stories increase in sophistication, the boundaries between good and evil become increasingly vague.) Significantly, Emory has to change his identity (that is, his visible, surface identity) in order to lure Lederman to a final showdown on the asteroid Brutus. In the final confrontation, Emory does not conquer Lederman by superior strength or cunning— his victory is, rather, the result of a kind of moral judo. By refusing to deliver the killing blow, Emory demonstrates his superior selfhood: "Lederman could not bear to see this symbol of his own weakness, a symbol he had used for many years, rising above himself." This novel could be read, then, as a simple case of wish-fulfillment revenge— the better person, oppressed for too long, finally shows the oppressor the error of his ways, and the oppressor, recognizing his guilt, destroys himself. Fortunately Ellison is too sophisticated a writer to allow so simple a moral to be attached to his fiction. For all its clumsiness and paste-up quality, *The Man With Nine Lives* reveals both some of Ellison's characteristic moral interests and some of his interest in formal experimentation. He continually breaks the narrative line with flashbacks and asides which he labels interlogues, dialogues, and travelogues. These are early examples of Ellison's refusal to follow narrative conventions which exclude the author's voice, or which insist on traditional unities such as point of view. These and other experiments connect him later with the New Wave of science fiction.

Three later stories demonstrate Ellison's awareness of the ways in which a coherent ethical stance may turn back upon itself and destroy its creator. In "The Whimper of Whipped Dogs" (1973; collected in *Deathbird Stories*, 1975), a story based loosely on the murder of Kitty Genovese, Ellison explores the reactions of one of the many witnesses who made no effort to stop the slaughter. Ellison's central character, Beth O'Neill, is an artistic, sensitive woman, a graduate of Bennington, who sees the brutal murder of a woman in the courtyard below O'Neill's apartment window. More disturbingly, she also observes the other witnesses, the many others who—like herself—do nothing but watch. The murder is only the first of a series of events which, as they draw closer to her and intrude more forcefully on her "personal space," strip away the sentimental notions which conceal and repress her understanding of both the inherent violence of city life and her own potential for violence. When she is attacked by a burglar who may be planning to rape her, she appeals to the "god" who is the essence, as she perceives it, of the violence of city life: "A God who needed worshippers and offered the choices of death as a victim or life as an eternal witness to the deaths of *other* chosen victims. A God to fit the times, a God of streets and people." O'Neill's assailant is chewed up by the "god," and she anticipates a life of "freedom" from anxiety under the god's protection. But unlike Cal Emory, who achieves a certain inner strength through his assertion of his identity, Beth has achieved her identity only through surrender to an inchoate and gruesomely evil force.

"Lonelyache" (1964; collected in *I Have No Mouth and I Must Scream*, 1967), is a study of the moral and emotional collapse of a man after the breakup of his marriage. The point of this story might seem to contradict the lesson of Cal Emory (find strength and stability within oneself), but it is more properly an extension. Paul Reed is haunted by his wife's "presence" in the other half of his bed, a presence which refuses to let him forget both the pains and the pleasures of his broken marriage. When he sleeps, he is tormented by dreams in which he is forced over and over to kill in self-defense a succession of deceptively friendly men who, he realizes, are planning to kill him once they gain his friendship. He tries to evade both the presence of his wife and the horrors of the dreams by staying awake and by seducing a sequence of women who can have no real meaning for him except as distractions. Reed not only cannot replace the part of himself which was his wife, but he cannot finally evade the recognition that he is, himself, the murderers in his dreams. His suicidal self, which is reified in the story, becomes a growing shadow in the corner of his bedroom, a shadow which lives on after he has shot himself "through the eye." In Reed's life, the interaction of social conventions, psychological dependency, and the sense of self which is the core of identity, has been irretrievably disrupted. Unlike Lederman in *The Man With Nine Lives*, Reed's wife is not made to appear inhuman or cruel, but neither is she presented as having any saving grace. Reed's fate depends less on the personality of the woman he is with than on his need for certain conventional relationships, however thinly realized. Since he loses all sense of himself except as self-destructive (the murderers in his dreams are all his doubles), he must externalize his identity or die. Unfortunately for him, he is perceived by his friends and the women he picks up as a recognizable, labelable type. Since their labels do not fit his sense of himself, he has no place to externalize himself and must die.

"The Diagnosis of Dr. D'arqueAngel" (1977; collected in *Strange Wine*, 1978) unites two themes common in Ellison's fiction: the desire for indefinite (if not eternal) life, and the peculiar danger of the supernaturally beautiful woman to any man with a greater than usual edge to his desires, whether they be sexual, economic, or temporal. The wish for immortality is the ultimate refusal of a label (human being/mortal being). The attribution of supernatural metamorphic powers to woman (as in Graves's *The White Goddess*) is a characteristic masculine refusal of responsibility for human weaknesses. Ellison's ironic embodiment of these impulses in the figure of Dr. D'arqueAngel is one of the stranger entries in a tradition which runs from Homer's Circe through the Faust legend and the third book of *Gulliver's Travels* to any number of modern speculative fictions. In Ellison's version Charles Romb wants not merely to live forever, or at least as long as he can imagine, but to get rid of his unwanted wife as well. He consults Dr. D'arqueAngel, an exceptionally beautiful and seductive woman, because she is supposed to have developed a process of immunization to death. After treatments and a conveniently staged automobile accident in which he is "killed" along with his wife, Romb returns to life to discover that the good doctor now has him in her power. He must receive (and give) continued doses of her death-life substance in order to maintain his youthful existence. Like all immortals, he needs his cupbearer, his Ganymede or Freia. The doctor fulfills that function, but she arouses his desires and sustains his life only to lead him into an eternity of sterility and dependency. He has murdered his wife

because he believed she was depriving him of his identity. In regaining himself from her, he simultaneously and nightmarishly loses himself to an even more overwhelming force.

As indicated by the preceding examples, the difficulties and dangers of building a coherent, stable sense of identity are major themes of Ellison's fiction. The personal strength and psychic wholeness of true individuals—evident in Everett C. Marm's refusal to conform in " 'Repent, Harlequin!' Said the Ticktockman"—are neither very common in Ellison's fictive worlds nor any guarantee of survival. He sees contemporary society, if one is to accept his journalistic statements, as populated with fearful and quiescent blobs (consumers, television watchers) whose main function in the world is to prop up destructive social systems and, by such complicity, participate in the destruction of the few individuals who have achieved a sense of self and who have the imagination to see the truth about the masses. While individuality makes survival worth fighting for, it also makes a fight inevitable. In some cases, a gesture of defiance, no matter how self-defeating, may be the only self-authenticating effort an individual can make. Ellison creates in his fictions metaphors for the destructive forces at work to obliterate the independent mind. Two stories, the

Harlan Ellison

very early "Life Hutch" (1956; collected in *From the Land of Fear*, 1967) and the famous "I Have No Mouth and I Must Scream" (1967; collected in *I Have No Mouth and I Must Scream*), provide convenient examples.

The hero of "Life Hutch" is obliged to outwit a "rogue robot," a machine intended merely to perform cleanup duties which has, however, been damaged so that it responds to all movement in its vicinity with destructive force. It has even smashed the clocks. This relatively simple man-against-machine drama is complicated when the man begins to explore his doubts about the validity of a war he has been fighting against an extraterrestrial race. The doubts are never resolved in the story, though the hero does finally manage to outwit the robot, turning its violence against its own control mechanism so that it destroys itself. By the same token, Ellison never really develops the ironic implication that those who set in motion machines over which they cannot guarantee continued control (including, of course, a war machine) may finally be threatened with destruction by their own handiwork.

Unfortunately for the hero-victim of "I Have No Mouth and I Must Scream," it is not always possible to trick one's enemies into destroying themselves. Like the malfunctioning robot of "Life Hutch," the gigantic AM, a computer system which has constituted itself from the computer weapons systems of the various combatants of World War III, has decided to destroy all human life. But AM is functioning "normally," and because it has linked together the full capacities of the most sophisticated computer systems in the world, it has successfully come to dominate the Earth. As Ellison describes it: "one day AM woke up and knew who he was, and he linked himself, and he began feeding all the killing data, until everyone was dead." AM does, however, spare five human beings to serve as playthings, which it treats like the steel balls in a pinball machine; endlessly, torturously alive, the humans careen through the labyrinths of AM's circuits. AM feeds them repellent foods, creates nightmarish experiences for them, and refuses to allow them the comfortable oblivion of death. In a desperate and ironic affirmation of human values, Ted kills his four companions to release them from the computer's sadistic control. Ted's own fate, however, is a grisly mirror image of the harlequin's: where Everett Marm is "regularized" by the machine and returned to a "normal" existence, Ted is reduced to a subhuman physical existence, but his mind remains intact. He is a prisoner inside an inexpressive body, incapable of uttering his humanity, but doomed to

witness it to himself for an indefinite period of "life."

In many of his stories, then, Ellison not only explores the special psychological problems of individuals caught in impersonal, mechanized systems, but also launches a satiric attack on the two poles of totalitarian victimization which are present in the twentieth century: total loss of will, intellect, individuality, on the one hand; loss of effective control over the phenomenal world of which one is conscious, on the other. These losses, along with the specter of nuclear holocaust, which is a metaphor for them both, constitute the special nightmare of the second half of the century.

Although Ellison's themes are handled in distinctive ways, they are not unique to him. He is distinguished, however, by the intense and varied ways in which he has pursued his career as a writer. His best stories are "pure Ellison," but much of what he has written might have been done by many writers. This observation does not hold for the peculiar amalgam of autobiography and social satire which makes up the bulk of his authorial introductions to his stories and collections and which reappears in the columns he has written for various newspapers—most notably the television criticism he wrote for the *Los Angeles Free Press* between 1968 and 1972, subsequently collected in the volumes *The Glass Teat* (1969) and *The Other Glass Teat* (1975). Ellison attacks the mindless stupidity of most television programming, which any critic could do, but he also consistently relates that phenomenon to the larger social and political structures which both create it and are re-created by it. In this context, the interweaving of his personal experiences with larger aesthetic and social concerns (Ellison would argue that aesthetic and social are nearly inseparable categories) gains him the status of a serious social commentator. The mind-deadening effect of mass culture, as represented by the network programming which "gives the audience what it wants," is one of his major concerns. In the introduction to *Strange Wine*, he makes his strongest statement on this subject, concluding that television itself, as a medium, regardless of its "content," is a "bad thing." He repeats several anecdotes of persons whose sense of the boundary between reality and fantasy has virtually disappeared, so that they believe television personalities are "real," more real than people they encounter in daily life. Far from being a flight into imagination, Ellison sees this phenomenon as a symptom of a breakdown of imagination, an indication that our civilization is headed toward extinction, since, for Ellison, imagination is not a refuge from reality, but a life-preserving capacity to encounter reality more intensely. As he remarks of himself, "even though I write fantasy, I live in the real world, my feet sunk to the ankles in pragmatism."

Ellison's autobiographical commentaries on his stories, and his opinionated style of journalism, indicate the intimate links between his "fantasy" and his reality. Occasionally the imaginative link breaks down or is insufficiently controlled by his literary instincts, and he sinks into simplistic allegory or sophomoric polemic. A recent example is "The New York Review of Bird" (collected in *Strange Wine*). Given sufficient wit, or a more important theme, this story could have been amusing. Ellison, almost defensively, reminds the reader that it is a fable. But it is barely even that. A tiresome tirade about the "literary establishment," it grossly misses its mark, though it may feed the paranoia of a few young writers who have trouble getting their work published. Certainly publishing is as guilty as any industry of providing its customers with some inferior products, but to link that with resentment that science fiction is not taken seriously and to tie it to a story of improbable revenge carried out by a four-foot-tall whiz-bang of a writer and street fighter, is to obscure the point and open the author to reasonable charges of personal animus.

There are quite a few such failures scattered through Ellison's many collections, some of them made dangerously prominent by inflated claims for their importance. (Ellison should never allow, for example, the kind of jacket blurb found on the 1968 collection *Love Ain't Nothing But Sex Misspelled* which calls *The Resurgence of Miss Ankle-Strap Wedgie* "the best Hollywood novella since *Day of the Locust.*" Ellison, at his best, competes on the same ground with Nathanael West, but this bittersweet soap opera of a story is not in the same class with West's *Day of the Locust*, and the comparison merely calls attention to the blatant shortcomings of Ellison's story.) The unevenness of the collections may indicate unwillingness to give up on even the weakest of his writings, or his ability to dominate his editors, or just the economics of publishing short fiction and the need to fill out a volume. It is surprising, in any case, to see a writer who is so vocally concerned with "quality" so often publishing work that is below his own best standard.

Ellison's experiments with fictional form and his explicit treatment of formerly taboo subjects such as sexuality and mental derangement have led readers to associate him with the New Wave in science fiction. An added factor in this association is his important editorial work on the two collections, *Dangerous Visions* and *Again, Dangerous Visions*. Most of the writers in these collections had had work published before, and many were quite well known. However, the first volume had the appearance, and the effect, of a literary manifesto, announcing a fellowship of writers devoted to exploring new levels of freedom and experimentation. As is consistent with Ellison's refusal of labels, he has subsequently insisted on the differences among the various writers and has flatly repudiated the whole notion of the New Wave. In the introduction to *The Beast That Shouted Love at the Heart of the World* (1969), Ellison states: "For the record, and for those who need to be told bluntly, I do not believe there is such a thing as 'New Wave' in speculative fiction (any more than there is something labeled with the abhorrent abbreviation 'sci-fi'. . .). It is a convenient journalese expression for inept critics and voyeur-observers of the passing scene, because they have neither the wit nor the depth to understand that this richness of new voices is *many* waves: each composed of one writer."

Whether there is or is not a New Wave may or may not be a matter of as little interest as Ellison indicates. There can be little doubt, however, that Ellison has been an important force in the field, publicizing good writing, insisting on the dignity of his own and his colleagues' work, and writing some very fine stories himself. The best of his stories will undoubtedly continue to be read (unless his gloomy prediction of the death of reading and the subsequent, inevitable death of the race comes true) long after such questions of literary politics or literary labels cease to be interesting. Ellison's evasion of labels may seem, in some cases, to involve evasion of any coherent philosophical or political stance. Certainly there are times when he seems to insist on having both. The point of reference is always, of course, his allegiance to the life of writing and to sustaining the life of literature, which is, for him, the life of the imagination or life itself. He is not the first author to place the concerns of his art above all other competing loyalties. That he is sometimes less successful in pursuit of his literary goals than he is in pursuit of his polemical interests is probably inevitable. But that he will continue to be read is also a safe assumption.

Other:

Dangerous Visions, 33 Original Stories, edited by Ellison (Garden City: Doubleday, 1967; London: Sphere, 1974);
Again, Dangerous Visions, edited by Ellison

(Garden City: Doubleday, 1972; London: Millington, 1976).

References:

Andrew Porter, ed., *The Book of Ellison* (New York: Algol, 1978);

George Edgar Slusser, *Harlan Ellison: Unrepentant Harlequin* (San Bernardino, Cal.: Borgo Press, 1977);

Special Harlan Ellison issue, *Magazine of Fantasy and Science Fiction* 53, (July 1977);

Leslie Kay Swigart, *Harlan Ellison: A Bibliographical Checklist* (Dallas: Williams, 1973);

Alice K. Turner, "PW Interviews: Harlan Ellison," *Publishers Weekly*, 207 (10 February 1975): 8-9;

Paul Walker, "Harlan Ellison," in his *Speaking of Science Fiction: The Paul Walker Interviews* (Oradell, N.J.: Luna, 1978), pp. 291-301;

Donald Wollheim, *The Universe Makers* (New York: Harper & Row, 1971), pp. 105-106.

Philip José Farmer

Thomas L. Wymer
Bowling Green State University

BIRTH: North Terre Haute, Indiana, 26 January 1918, to George and Lucile Theodora Jackson Farmer.

EDUCATION: B.A., Bradley University, 1950.

MARRIAGE: 10 May 1941 to Elizabeth Andre; children: Philip Laird, Kristen.

AWARDS: Hugo Award for Most Promising Writer, 1953; Hugo Award for "Riders of the Purple Wage," 1968; Hugo Award for *To Your Scattered Bodies Go*, 1972; induction to Sigma Tau Delta National English Honor Society as life member, 1978.

BOOKS: *The Green Odyssey* (New York: Ballantine, 1957; London: Sphere, 1976);

Strange Relations (New York: Ballantine, 1960; London: Gollancz, 1964);

Flesh (New York: Beacon, 1960; expanded edition, Garden City: Doubleday, 1968; London: Rapp & Whiting, 1969);

A Woman a Day (New York: Beacon, 1960); republished as *The Day of Timestop* (New York: Lancer, 1968); republished again as *Timestop!* (London: Quartet, 1973);

The Lovers (New York: Ballantine, 1961; revised edition, New York: Ballantine, 1979);

Fire and the Night (Evanston, Ill.: Regency, 1962);

The Alley God (New York: Ballantine, 1962; London: Sidgwick & Jackson, 1970);

Cache from Outer Space and *The Celestial Blueprint* (New York: Ace, 1962);

Inside Outside (New York: Ballantine, 1964);

Tongues of the Moon (New York: Pyramid, 1964);

Dare (New York: Ballantine, 1965; London: Quartet, 1974);

The Maker of Universes (New York: Ace, 1965; London: Sphere, 1970);

The Gates of Creation (New York: Ace, 1966; London: Sphere, 1970);

The Gate of Time (New York: Belmont Books, 1966; London: Quartet, 1974); expanded edition, *Two Hawks from Earth* (New York: Ace, 1979);

Night of Light (New York: Berkley, 1966; Harmondsworth, U.K.: Penguin, 1972);

The Image of the Beast, An Exorcism: Ritual One (North Hollywood, Cal.: Essex House, 1968; London: Quartet, 1975);

A Private Cosmos (New York: Ace, 1968; London: Sphere, 1970);

A Feast Unknown: Volume IX of the Memoirs of Lord Grandrith (North Hollywood, Cal.: Essex House, 1969; London: Quartet, 1975);

Blown, or Sketches Among the Ruins of My Mind, An Exorcism: Ritual Two (North Hollywood, Cal.: Essex House, 1969; London: Quartet, 1976);

Behind the Walls of Terra (New York: Ace, 1970; London: Sphere, 1975);

Lord of the Trees: Volume X of the Memoirs of Lord Grandrith and *The Mad Goblin* (New York: Ace, 1970);

The Stone God Awakens (New York: Ace, 1970; St. Albans, U.K.: Panther, 1976);

Lord Tyger (Garden City: Doubleday, 1970; St.

Albans, U.K.: Panther, 1974);
Love Song (North Hollywood, Cal.: Brandon House, 1970);
Down in the Black Gang and Other Stories (Garden City: Doubleday, 1971);
The Wind Whales of Ishmael (New York: Ace, 1971; London: Quartet, 1973);
To Your Scattered Bodies Go (New York: Putnam's, 1971; London: Rapp & Whiting, 1973);
The Fabulous Riverboat (New York: Putnam's, 1971; London: Rapp & Whiting, 1973);
Tarzan Alive: A Definitive Biography of Lord Greystoke (Garden City: Doubleday, 1972; St. Albans, U.K.: Panther, 1974);
Time's Last Gift (New York: Ballantine, 1972; St. Albans, U.K.: Panther, 1975);
The Other Log of Phileas Fogg (New York: DAW, 1973; Middlesex, U.K.: Hamlyn, 1979);
The Book of Philip José Farmer, or The Wares of Simple Simon's Custard Pie and Space Man (New York: DAW, 1973; London: Elmfield Press, 1976);
Doc Savage: His Apocalyptic Life (Garden City: Doubleday, 1973; St. Albans, U.K.: Panther, 1975);
Traitor to the Living (New York: Ballantine, 1973; St. Albans, U.K.: Panther, 1975);
The Adventure of the Peerless Peer, as John H. Watson, M.D. (Boulder, Colo.: Aspen Press, 1974);
Hadon of Ancient Opar (New York: DAW, 1974; London: Eyre & Spottiswoode, 1977);
Venus on the Half-Shell, as Kilgore Trout (New York: Dell, 1975; London: Star Books, 1976);
Flight to Opar (New York: DAW, 1976);
The Lavalite World (New York: Ace, 1977; London: Sphere, 1979);
The Dark Design (New York: Putnam's, 1977);
Dark Is the Sun (New York: Ballantine, 1979);
Jesus on Mars (Los Angeles: Pinnacle, 1979);
Riverworld and Other Stories (New York: Berkley, 1979);
The Magic Labyrinth (New York: Berkley, 1980);
Riverworld War: the Suppressed Fiction of Philip José Farmer (Peoria, Ill.: Ellis Press, 1980).

Inherent in science fiction are a number of contradictory impulses: imaginative wonder and scientific exactness, romance and realism, childish joy and adult seriousness, the desire to escape and the passion to know. No modern writer expresses and explores these contradictions with more intensity than Philip José Farmer. Dreams and contradictions were part of Farmer's life from an early age. He was a voracious reader who developed an early passion for the heroes of Greek and Norse mythology and those of such writers as Edgar Rice Burroughs, H. Rider Haggard, Arthur Conan Doyle, L. Frank Baum, James Fenimore Cooper, Henry Wadsworth Longfellow, Mark Twain, Herman Melville, and many more. No bookish recluse, however, he had a passion for the physical as well. As he describes himself in an interview in *Luna*, "I was very strong and swift and was so agile in the trees that my nickname in grade school was 'Tarzan.' " Until one day, urged by a friend, he attempted too great a leap through the trees: "And so, like Lucifer, I fell because of pride. I ripped some muscles in my thighs and was paralyzed for half an hour with the intense pain." He recovered physically and went on to become an outstanding high-school athlete, but from the day of that fall he describes himself as becoming introverted. Indeed, this incident helps to explain a preoccupation which he attributes to one of his created alter egos, Timothy Howller in "After King Kong Fell" (1973): "Since he had been thirteen, he had been trying to equate the great falls in man's myths and legends and to find some sort of intelligence in them. The fall of the tower of Babel, of Lucifer, of Vulcan, of Icarus, and finally of King Kong. But he wasn't equal to the task; he didn't have the genius to perceive what the falls meant . . . ."

Whether the cause was this fall or some earlier forgotten trauma, as he speculates in *The Dark Design* (1977) in the form of Farmer alter ego Peter Jairus Frigate, he developed internal conflicts which have remained with him. Though he broke world broad jump records in high-school practice, he could never do so in official meets. He became an agnostic at the age of fourteen, but never lost his desire to know a god or his hunger for immortality, an incongruity which later manifested itself in fantasies of immortality and themes built around exposures of false gods.

After high school, from which he graduated in 1936, he worked as a ground man for the local power and light company and attended Bradley Polytechnic Institute and Missouri University for two years. In 1941 he married and began as a laborer in the steel mill where, except for a few months during which he failed flight training with the U.S. Air Corps, he worked for eleven years. In 1949 he went back to what was by then Bradley University, where he finished his B.A. in English while working the night shift at the mill. All this time he nursed a desire to be a professional writer; he succeeded in placing a non-science-fiction story in *Adventure* magazine in 1946 but experienced no further success until 1952, when

"The Lovers" appeared in *Startling Stories* and seemed to turn the science-fiction world upside down. Flushed with the story's success and the high praise of writers like Poul Anderson, Theodore Sturgeon, and John Brunner, Farmer quit the steel mill and devoted himself to full-time writing. Winning a 1953 Hugo Award as the most promising writer of 1952, however, turned out to be small consolation for a series of disasters which 1953 offered. "I Owe for the Flesh," the original novel of his Riverworld series, won a prize novel contest and $4,000, which Farmer never saw because of an unscrupulous editor who diverted the funds and strung Farmer along with arbitrary demands for time-consuming rewrites. Though "somewhat rewritten parts" of "I Owe for the Flesh" were later worked into the Riverworld stories which began appearing twelve years later in the magazine *Worlds of Tomorrow*, for the most part the novel was lost. "A Beast of the Fields," the original version of *Dare* (1965), was scheduled to be the first serial to appear in *Startling Stories*, but the magazine ceased publication that year; this novel too was put aside and did not see print until, after considerable rewriting, it was published as an original paperback—also twelve years later. Hopeful expectations of imminent paperback publication of *The Lovers* and "Moth and Rust" also collapsed (the former did not appear until 1961, the latter—as *A Woman a Day*—in 1960). Farmer lost his house and was forced for a time to go back to manual labor.

In 1956 Farmer left Peoria and began a fourteen-year sojourn working as a technical writer in various defense industries from Syracuse to Los Angeles. Continuing to write, he was described by Norman Spinrad as one of the better writers of the fifties who "clung on, heroic and windblown martyrs." In the 1960s Farmer's reputation gained a more solid footing. Sixteen of his novels or collections appeared in that decade; a novel was a Nebula nominee; three shorter works were Hugo nominees, one of which was a winner; and both the World of Tiers series (later called the Wolff-Kickaha series) and the Riverworld series were established, the second of which especially set up Farmer's greater success of the 1970s.

In 1969 Farmer again risked a return to full-time writing, this time with happier results, although delayed payments made the first year a difficult one. Nevertheless, nine new novels or collections appeared in 1970-1971, a change in fortune accompanied by Farmer's return in early 1971 from Beverly Hills to Peoria. *To Your Scattered Bodies Go* (1971), the first separately published Riverworld

novel, won a Hugo Award in 1972 and, in addition to the original hardcover, went through fourteen paperback printings by 1979. This success, together with that of *The Fabulous Riverboat* (1971), the second Riverworld novel, made the third of the series, *The Dark Design*, one of the most eagerly awaited science-fiction novels of the decade; the series has been concluded with *The Magic Labyrinth* (1980). Also in the 1970s Farmer's most elaborate series, the Wold Newton Families, and its Fictional Authors subseries were developed. Twenty-five new novels or collections in all appeared during the 1970s, most of the earlier works were reprinted, especially during the second half of the decade, and Farmer's position as a major science-fiction author was assured.

Although he has developed considerably as a writer over his thirty-year career, much of the essential Farmer was revealed in his first major work, *The Lovers* (1961). Generally credited with breaking the taboo against mature dealing with sex in American science fiction, *The Lovers* began Farmer's career-long exploration and analysis of the concepts of sexual freedom and perversion and their relationship with complex cultural problems. The 1961 version of the novel begins on Earth with the central character, Hal Yarrow, waking from a dream, muttering, "I've got to get out. . . . There must be a way out." These words express another major Farmer theme, the repeated metaphor of the world as prison and the struggle of the hero for freedom. In this case the prison is a totalitarian future Earth government ruled by the Sturch, a kind of theocracy based on a religion of materialism, science, and pseudoscience and established by Isaac Sigmen, the Forerunner. As with the satire of Huxley and Orwell, Farmer's purpose is not to predict but to use the future as a means of exploring present problems in exaggerated and heightened forms. The Sturch's world is one in which puritanically repressive sexual conditioning is the keystone to a total structure of tyranny which controls the political, intellectual, spiritual, and physical life of citizens. This system reflects the modern world, revealing the connections among the varieties of imperialism—political, ecological, racial, and sexual—and exposing their roots in the human personality, in man's lust for power, fear of change, and fear of self. An ultimate expression of this neurotic pattern is the expedition of which Hal becomes a part, an expedition intended to exterminate the sentient inhabitants of a recently discovered habitable planet.

Since sex is so important a factor in Hal's prison, it is likewise crucial to his struggle for

Philip José Farmer

freedom. And, as it will become typical in Farmer's works, women function as instruments and symbols of both man's imprisonment and his freedom. Mary, Hal's wife on Earth, is an Earth Mother in her destructive aspect, smothering, guilt-loading, old beyond her years, sterile, frigid, traitorous, and life-denying. On the alien planet, however, Hal meets her opposite in the form of the *lalitha* Jeannette, a beautiful, human-looking alien. Loving, warm, life-affirming, and a worshipper of the Great Mother, Jeannette becomes the instrument of Hal's liberation by helping him to overcome his sexual guilt and fear, to accept his feelings, and to love. But because neither is open and trusting enough—she conceals the true alienness of her physiology, fearing his rejection; he tries to "cure" her of her apparent alcoholism without her knowledge, thereby depriving her of a substance necessary to her survival—their love affair ends with Jeannette's tragic death. In the process, however, another important Farmer theme emerges, the concern with sexual perversion. As human as she looks, Jeannette is a "mimetic parasite" evolved from arthropods, which means that in the eyes of the Sturch Hal has "lusted after and lain with an insect" and is "an unspeakable degenerate." Yet her genuine love for Hal is clear, so that Farmer is able to argue what becomes a common

idea throughout his work: that most so-called perversions are defined by ignorance and prejudice and that the functions of bodies are rendered truly perverse only by the hate, cruelty, and fear that may accompany or prevent their conjunction.

The best of Farmer's short fiction of the 1950s, published in the collections *Strange Relations* (1960) and *The Alley God* (1962), develop these themes further. Often these stories involve a central character who either is or presumes himself to be highly virtuous, but who confronts a situation which strains his repressed fears, his hidden insecurities, to the point where his virtue betrays him into some terrible wrong. Asaph Everlake of "The Captain's Daughter" (1953; collected in *The Alley God*) is typical of the puritanical religious cult to which he belongs in that he cannot cope with his own and his daughter's affliction with a parasite that induces mutually irresistible sexual desires in its hosts. The detective story plot exposes Everlake's efforts to deny his disease, which lead to two murders and the threat of spreading the parasite throughout the galaxy. The situation is analogous to the contemporary problem of venereal disease and shows how an ideal of purity based on fear and denial of the body fosters ignorance, hypocrisy, and destruction.

In "Father" (1955; collected in *Strange Relations*) Andre is a Catholic bishop who also has a puritanical background. A forced landing on an unusually Edenic planet sets up a temptation in which he is offered the opportunity to assume the godlike role of the master of this planet, a humanoid creature called simply the Father. Among the Father's powers is the ability to enter into and guide the nonsexual re-creation of the animal life of the planet, a process which, although physically "pure," produces in the guide an ecstatic state similar to that of sexual excitation and climax. Bishop Andre's purity, in effect, becomes a handicap, a point emphasized by contrast with his assistant, Father John Carmody, a former sinner of monumental proportions whose conversion is the subject of *Night of Light* (1966). Andre is deceived into thinking that what is essentially a masturbatory experience is one of truly creative love. Like a youth undergoing his first sexual experience, he thinks with his gonads rather than with his mind, while the more experienced Carmody, similarly tempted, sees through the deception.

In these two stories one can see Farmer also developing both his sense of character and his understanding of the complexity of such problems. Whereas Captain Everlake is rather a straw man, the typical stiff-backed, intolerant, guilt-ridden, yet self-justifying puritan, Bishop Andre is closer to the standard conception of a tragic hero, an essentially good man with a fatal flaw. In "My Sister's Brother" (1959; collected in *Strange Relations*) Farmer applies the test to an even better, indeed an ideal man. Cardigan Lane is deeply religious yet tolerant, strong and courageous yet able to weep unashamedly; he is even compared to Christ. A member of the first expedition to land on Mars, he is left alone by the disappearance of his companions and risks his life to seek them rather than return alone. He is saved from reenacting their deaths by a creature who turns out to be a humanoid, apparently female, from another solar system, like him the sole survivor of an expedition which had met with a fatal accident. A relationship develops in which Lane constantly has to face an inward struggle between his belly, which tells him to loathe and reject several of her ways that repel and shock him, and his brain, which tells him that "he shouldn't react to her as he would to a Terrestrial." His brain has the best of the battle for most of the time, with some help from his heart, as he discovers that she too is deeply religious, loving, and even innocent to the degree of seeming unfallen. His sexual fears, however, finally get the best of him when he discovers that her unisexual reproductive system demands a series of practices that in his mind suggest fellatio, homosexuality, and masturbation. But masturbation is not in fact involved, since the reproductive process does involve an exchange of love between partners, which she offers him. The result is a vicious act on his part of what amounts to infanticide, committed in the name of defending the human race, but done in fact "because he was afraid, not of her, but of himself, . . . because he, too, beneath his disgust, had wanted to commit that act of love." Lane's terrible act makes the fear of love appear far more perverse than any possible expression of love and reinforces the ironic theme which points to man as the most dangerous and monstrous creature in the universe.

These stories expose rigid value reflexes which cannot be overcome and which finally lead to violent or destructive behavior, revealing how individuals may be locked within the prison of the self. Other stories are wish-fulfillment fantasies that turn the self inside out and set up the possibility of self discovery, sometimes even of escape from the prison of the self. But the experience can display the contradictory results of therapy: faced with the truth, one can learn from it and begin to control one's life, or one can withdraw, hide from self-consciousness, and immerse oneself more deeply in one's roles and reflexes. The latter is illustrated in "Mother" (1953; collected in *Strange Relations*). In this, one of Farmer's earliest stories and the one most often reprinted, the central character's fondest desires are destructive. Eddie Fetts is a young man whose domineering, possessive, smothering mother has rendered him emotionally dependent on her and sexually impotent. Shipwrecked with her on a strange planet, they are separated by his being swallowed up by a bizarre, sentient creature inside of whom he manages to survive. The creature is of an exclusively female species which is rooted like a vegetable and able to reproduce by the use of any mobile animal she can lure into her womb, which also functions like a marsupial pouch. In adjusting to this situation, Eddie manages to act out his deepest desires, a complex collection which includes participating in his mother's destruction (she is captured by the creature and served up to him in a sort of stew); "raping" his mother-substitute, thereby overcoming his impotence; and finally reverting to a preinfantile state in the peace of the "mother's" womb.

In "The God Business" (1954; collected in *The Alley God*) wish fulfillment has a more positive effect. Daniel Temper enters the domain of Mahrud, where he is gradually stripped of his inhibitions and learns that the key to all his problems is himself. He undergoes an almost literal death and rebirth and achieves a kind of self-transcendence by discovering "the drowned god in the abyss of himself." Although "The God Business" is more optimistic than most of Farmer's works, the quest for psychic freedom is a major theme of Farmer's wish-fulfillment fantasies, in novels as well as short fiction. In *Dare* Jack Cage, like Hal Yarrow of *The Lovers*, is a man imprisoned by a neurotic culture. This one is that of the survivors of the lost Roanoke colony, who had been transported to another planet by the Arra, a super-powerful extraterrestrial race. Corresponding to Hal's Jeannette is Jack's R'li, a female "horstel," one of a race of seemingly primitive humanoids with horse tails who appear to be aborigines. Horstels are a nontechnological but highly civilized race of worshipers of the Great Mother; they are unified with nature, at peace with themselves, and tolerant of others. Partly based on the horse-tailed sileni, ancient nature daemons of Greece, they are also idealized versions of Amerindians. The colonists, on the other hand, are types of Western man, neurotic worshipers of a masculine god and of money, afraid of their own bodies and emotions, indifferent to nature except insofar as it can be exploited for profit, and intolerant of the native sentients, whom they would gladly enslave or exterminate if the horstels did not defend themselves so effectively. Like colonial Puritan Americans these colonists project their fears of their own unconscious out into the horstel forest, which becomes demonic rather than daemonic in their eyes, while the horstels themselves, like Amerindians and blacks, become symbolic projections of the colonists' id, of repressed sexuality, which must be exorcised or subdued.

In this context Jack Cage, like Hal Yarrow, struggles to cross the boundary between neurotic civilized consciousness and the fertile darkness of the forest of his unconscious and unite the two. Again the quest is for escape from the limitations of a culturally determined neurotic self bound by hate and fear to a new experience of the whole self, "more balanced, more psychically integrated." To do so, however, Jack must become a traitor to a culture much more like our own than that of *The Lovers*. Moreover, though his struggle is successful, the new psychic health he achieves, unlike that achieved in "The God Business," is not tantamount to godhood, but simply gives him the wisdom to deal honestly with a world that remains uncertain and dangerous.

In *Night of Light* the results are more ambiguous and more frightening. In part 1, first published in 1957 in the *Magazine of Fantasy and Science Fiction*, John Carmody, thief, murderer, and galactic public enemy number one, makes his way to the planet Dante's Joy because it is beyond Federation jurisdiction. There he is caught up in the Night of Light, a periodic occurrence caused by strange magnetic storms on the planet's sun. The resulting radiation somehow stimulates the unconscious mind and causes material projections of unconscious images; the sun "rouses the image of the beast that lives in the dark caves of our minds, or else wakens the sleeping golden god." These metaphors are literalized in the ritual of the Night of Light, which volunteers participate in by remaining awake while the rest of the population retreats into a drugged sleep. The collective projections of the unconscious desires of those courageous enough to face themselves determine whether the good Yess or the evil Algul is born out of the womb of Boonta, an archaic Great Mother. Like most archaic Great Mother goddesses, she is both creator / preserver and destroyer; Boonta's contradictory qualities are depicted in a colossal statue in which she is giving birth to one baby, devouring another, and lovingly nursing yet another, her face "a study in split personality," with one side loving, the other vicious.

Put in simplest terms, "Dante's Joy is the planet where you get what you really want" and where the psyche is turned inside out. For Carmody, a man who lusts after power, the Night becomes an opportunity to fulfill his wildest conscious fantasy, to kill a god, but it also becomes a learning process in which he reenacts his worst crimes in bloody detail and discovers himself as his own victim. The end result is the discovery of the self-destructive nature of his violence, the potential for creation and compassion which he has long suppressed, and the god within himself which he cooperates in giving birth to. Though part 1 reveals many of those images of the beast within, it ends with what must be one of Farmer's own fantasies, the affirmation that both individuals and the world can be changed for the better. Part 2, however, first published in the 1966 paperback, presents a darker vision. It begins twenty-seven years later when Carmody, now a Catholic priest, is sent back to Dante's Joy by the church, which is alarmed by the spread of Boontism, with its literally and continually dying and resurrecting god. Moreover, the current god Yess, whom Carmody cofathered, is planning to force a major change in the ritual of the Night: he intends to command all natives of the planet to remain awake so that he can use the Night to create an ultimate conflict between the collective unconscious forces of good and evil in order to end the periodic conflict between them. But as a result of the altered ritual, civilization on the planet is all but destroyed, and both Yess and Algul survive, setting the stage for an apocalyptic struggle that promises to engulf the galaxy. Even worse for Carmody is the blow to his faith produced by the accuracy of a whole series of Yess's prophecies: "How could he have seen and not believe in the all-power of Boonta?"

The two parts of *Night of Light* and the tensions between them reveal a shift in Farmer's vision that seems to have taken place around 1960. In the 1950s the crucial flaws in characters are not in their stars but in themselves. Though flawed, both man and the universe are presented as subject to improvement, largely knowable, and governed ultimately by love. The stories of the 1960s, however, seem to darken into a vision of an ironic universe, not exactly governed by evil, but best expressed by the archetypal image of the Earth Mother, a frustrating combination of contraries, creative and destructive, loving, malevolent, and indifferent, knowable and mysterious. The earlier vision is one in which heroes like Carmody most effectively dwell; they are wise and loving men who in Joseph Campbell's terms exemplify the myth of the shaman, mastering the world by sympathy. Carmody does so in all of the short fiction in which he appears—"Attitudes" (1953), "Father," "A Few Miles" (1960; collected in *Down in the Black Gang and Other Stories*, 1971), and "Prometheus" (1961; collected in *Down in the Black Gang*)—all of which concern events occurring chronologically between parts 1 and 2 of *Night of Light*. But that second vision that comes to dominate the 1960s, before which Carmody finds himself helpless, calls for what Campbell calls the myth of the hunter, who masters the world by power.

This shift is a subtle, not a dramatic one. The earlier vision includes tragic failures as early as *The Lovers*, and the later vision by no means abandons the sense of need for compassion and understanding, but increasingly there is revealed an ironic sense of intractability about both man and the universe, which resist or even contravene human hopes. In its milder forms this irony is expressed in situations in which individuals who find their fantasies fulfilled discover also fundamental limitations, sometimes comically. In *Flesh* (1960; expanded edition, 1968), for instance, Peter Stagg, captain of a spaceship which returns to Earth hundreds of years after it left, is transformed by a biologically sophisticated but otherwise primitive, postapocalyptic Earth culture into an ancient King of the Wood right out of Sir James G. Frazer's *Golden Bough*. He becomes a creature of Herculean sexual prowess, biologically

altered to inseminate the virgins of a nation. This is, of course, the ultimate male sexual wish-fulfillment fantasy, but Stagg's sexual capacity is also a compulsion which becomes a curse, revealing in the process the kind of control which sexual drives and desires can exert on an individual. Rather than godlike freedom godhead itself becomes a prison.

Farmer's ironic vision is more starkly revealed, however, in fantasies in which the theme of imprisonment is expressed in highly explicit metaphors of the universe itself—not just an aberrant society or culture—as prison. Typically the prisonlike quality of the world inspires in the hero a Promethean response of some sort, although Farmer finds considerable variety in the kinds of prison and the kinds of rebelliousness it may inspire.

In "A Bowl Bigger than Earth" (1967; collected in *Down in the Black Gang*) Morfiks, an anti-hero, finds that he has died and gone to what seems to be hell, a bowl-shaped world in which he has been reincarnated in an indestructible but sexless body. The deepest irony is that Morfiks—all his life a classic, other-directed, nice guy who had always done what was expected of him and so feared to live his own life that he forgot what he might really like to be—now finds himself in a world which, in its totalitarian regularity, is an exaggeration of the life he seemed most to desire, one characterized by

Philip José Farmer

security, stability, conformity, certainty—and boredom. With no possible escape, Morfiks's only source of satisfaction and only possible act of defiance is to gnaw on the leg of another citizen who gnaws on Morfiks's leg, a sadomasochistic orgy producing a feeling which he recognizes as "a reasonable facsimile to that which he had known" on Earth.

Inside Outside (1964) also concerns an anti-hero in a prisonlike afterlife, this time the inside of a planet-sized rotating sphere. Here the Promethean act is the struggle to find out who or what has created and is controlling this world and for what purpose, including the question of whether it is purgatory or hell. Jack Cull's quest takes him on a Dantean journey by way of the world's sewers through the shell to discover that he is on an artificial planet in outer space. That answer, however, leads to more questions and the discovery that the whole situation has been created not by any god but by "the Immortals," a race of technologically advanced extraterrestrials who have artificially created not only the planet but human souls, and that this is not an afterlife but in fact a prenatal world where souls are being preconditioned to understand the nature of good and evil and thereby become more ethical. In spite of all these answers, the inside-out world remains a mirror image of Earth; it is a place, where, as one character says, things "are just as obscure, puzzling, and unanswerable as they were on Earth," because the answers to the most fundamental questions of value and purpose remain ambiguous. The Immortals are obviously not omnipotent or omniscient, and they may even be lying, or simply failing in their purpose. While Cull does seem finally to achieve a genuine love for the woman who has accompanied him on his quest, another character sees the inhabitants of this world as "defeating the purpose of the Immortals by getting meaner and more vicious and cynical and sadistic."

The struggle to find out who—or what—is running the world or universe is a recurring motif in Farmer's work and central to the complex of religious and philosophical questions that pervade it. Especially since the mid-1960s Farmer seems quite consistent in his rejection of supernatural explanations for anything. His plots repeatedly revolve around characters discovering that their religious presuppositions are false. Indeed, the rejection of past beliefs often becomes crucial to survival, a point which Farmer sometimes makes with blatant symbolism. In *Inside Outside* Cull and his companions return to the inside surface of their planetoid through a tunnel lined with broken idols, which function as a graphic history of religion.

When an apocalyptic earthquake breaks a portion of the tunnel loose, rolling the humans and statues inside, Cull realizes that all the idols must be cast out before the people are crushed, a situation which symbolically suggests that the contending claims of religions, all false, threaten to crush man's spirit.

This theme of rejection of false gods may sound like the antireligious scientism conventional in the science fiction of the 1940s, but Farmer is never glib about his lack of faith. To call him an agnostic would not do justice to what would more accurately be described as doubt-riddled atheism, complicated by a compelling hunger for immortality and for a sense of higher purpose to human life. His attempts to rationalize and project this hunger are most commonly manifested in fantasies of beings of superior technology who, like the Arra of *Dare*, often behave like gods in their testing or teaching of man, but usually they seem to be failing in their purpose, presuming too much like the Immortals of *Inside Outside* or the Ethicals of the Riverworld series.

The Riverworld series, begun in the magazine *Worlds of Tomorrow* with "Day of the Great Shout" (1965), which was expanded into the first half of *To Your Scattered Bodies Go*, repeats and extends the theme of an artificially created afterlife managed by superior sentient beings, this time called Ethicals, who also seem to want to give man another chance to become better, more ethical beings. Indeed, on Riverworld people are given more than a second chance: people can still die, but the dead find themselves resurrected hundreds of miles from where they died. The Riverworld setting is a vast planet containing all the sentient creatures that ever lived on Earth, including prehistoric human species like Neanderthals. Winding all around the planet in a mazelike pattern is a single continuous river a mile and a half wide, flanked by two or three miles of grassy plains and foothills leading up to an equally continuous line of unscalable mountains. It is a vast conception which gives Farmer the opportunity to combine such motifs as the inward and satirical journey of Huck Finn, the exploratory quest of Richard Burton, Parsifal's quest for the Holy Grail, and Childe Roland's quest for the Dark Tower— together with an encyclopedic series of confrontations with historical characters.

To Your Scattered Bodies Go centers on Richard Burton's quest for the Dark Tower, reputed to be the source of the river and the repository of the secrets of the purpose of the planet and man's resurrection. Burton is accompanied by, among others, Alice Pleasance Liddell Hargreaves, who as a young girl was the model for Lewis Carroll's Alice, and by Peter

Jairus Frigate, a Farmer alter ego. He is most often opposed by Hermann Göring, who finally recognizes the horror of his former life and converts to the Church of the Second Chance. *The Fabulous Riverboat* focuses on Sam Clemens's dream of creating a riverboat equal to the river, a task he accomplishes only to have it stolen by the unscrupulous King John of England. Göring again turns up, along with Lothar von Richthofen, Cyrano de Bergerac, a thinly disguised version of Eldridge Cleaver named Elwood Hacking, and many others.

The Dark Design begins to weave these plots together, along with several new ones. The most disturbing development is the fact that resurrections have ceased to occur, so that death now seems to be permanent. Meanwhile Sam has built another riverboat and is sailing up the river, ostensibly to reach the Dark Tower, but really to catch King John and wreak vengeance on him. Sam's chief lieutenant, Milton Firebrass, a fictional character who is supposed to have been the first black astronaut on Earth, has remained behind to direct the building of a dirigible to assault the Dark Tower from the air. Burton appears relatively briefly, but long enough to discover that an agent of the Ethicals is posing as his companion Frigate and to decide to find King John and join his crew in order to achieve his own quest. Elsewhere on the river the real Frigate turns up and becomes a member of the crew of a schooner cocaptained by Jack London and Tom Mix, also making their way to the source of the river.

The plot is Byzantine in its surprises and disguises, but theme and character are of greater importance than the identity and purpose of the Ethicals. The overriding question of the series is whether man, if given a second chance, would make anything better of his life than he did before. On Resurrection Day early in *To Your Scattered Bodies Go* Burton expresses the expectation that man will soon return to his "normal state" of mutual destructiveness, a prediction which events bear out. At the end of the novel Burton acknowledges having discovered "several perfect and upright men," but "damn few," while "most men and women are still the selfish, ignorant, superstitious, self-blinding, hypocritical, cowardly wretches they were on Earth." Göring is one of those few who change, but Burton himself remains a flawed hero, "the eternal pilgrim and wanderer" obsessed with his quest, driven by a seemingly neurotic compulsion to know, ready by the time of *The Dark Design* to do almost anything, including fighting for King John, to achieve his quest. Sam Clemens likewise shows little change, still childishly dreaming of intrigues like

Tom Sawyer, still yearning for the careless peace of a downriver raft journey, still ridden by guilt for everything bad that happened to those he loved, still "the same paralyzed pessimist" full of the same invincible ignorance he despises in others. In *The Dark Design*, after more than thirty years of second chance on Riverworld, he jeopardizes his friends' quest for the Dark Tower by insisting for the sake of revenge on a vain attack on King John.

The Magic Labyrinth is ostensibly the last of the main series, although Farmer plans to write other "sidestream" stories in addition to "Riverworld" (1966), which has been expanded for his most recent collection, *Riverworld and Other Stories* (1979). In *The Magic Labyrinth* the various quests are completed, but at terrible cost. Sam finally catches King John and barely survives a catastrophic battle which destroys both riverboats, only to die of a heart attack when he meets an old enemy whom he had long before betrayed. Cyrano, who had been the sole survivor of the dirigible, which was destroyed at the end of *The Dark Design*, is not so lucky in this battle and dies tragically at the hands of Burton and Alice. These two are among a few survivors, including the real Frigate, whom Burton gathers for a final assault on the Dark Tower. More tragic deaths follow, but the quest is finally achieved, the plans of the Ethicals and the causes for division among them are revealed, and the threat to man's continuing chance for resurrection is removed, at least for a while. But the conclusion is not simply happy. Although mankind has been assured of some three hundred years to make something better of himself, what has happened during the first thirty-odd years on Riverworld remains unencouraging.

A major source of affirmation throughout the series, however, is the quest itself. Early in *To Your Scattered Bodies Go* as Burton and company set out on their newly constructed boat, the narrator says, "They had no maps nor travelers' tales to guide them; the world would be created with every mile forward." A similar idea appears at the end of *The Dark Design* when the mind of "X," the Promethean Ethical who has been directing the rebellion against his own people, is finally revealed. His mechanical means for knowing the whereabouts of the agents of the Ethicals and his own rebel recruits breaks down, and he too is left "in the house of night," forced to act in ignorance and uncertainty. Undaunted, he accepts the challenge: "like all sentient creatures, he would have to make his own light." *The Magic Labyrinth* ends in a similar vein, with problems not so much solved as faced, understood, and accepted— and with new problems ready to emerge.

In the mid-1960s, at the same time he was beginning to resurrect the Riverworld, Farmer, then in his late forties, was also resurrecting what he calls "the buried fifteen-year-old" in himself, renewing his appreciation of the pulp literature he enjoyed in his youth, with its heroes like Doc Savage, Tarzan, John Carter, Alan Quatermain, and others. Fascinated by the combination of popularity with psychological validity and apocalyptic power which he found in these works, he began trying to create for himself some of the magic he felt there. This effort accounts in part for the effectiveness of the Wolff-Kickaha series, the first of which appeared the same year as the first Riverworld story. So far the series includes five novels, *The Maker of Universes* (1965), *The Gates of Creation* (1966), *A Private Cosmos* (1968), *Behind the Walls of Terra* (1970), and *The Lavalite World* (1977), all of which are marked by an intense sense of pulp action-adventure, with fast-paced and very physical action, battles and contests, intrigues, disguises, and surprises. But Farmer combines this action with a fascinating sense of psychological exploration.

Robert Wolff in *The Maker of Universes* is transported from Earth to the World of Tiers, a pocket universe where he ends up leading an assault on the planet's Lord, one of the immortal but selfish and tyrannical remnants of a technologically advanced race which had mastered the means of creating such universes but had long since forgotten the principles behind the technology they were still able to operate. They are therefore godlike "ignoramuses, . . . sybarites, megalomaniacs, paranoiacs." Wolff finally learns that he is himself one of them, in fact the original Lord of this world, dispossessed by a rival Lord and gated to Earth in a state of amnesiac shock. His experiences of the pains and limitations of Earth have changed him, however, and in the process of Wolff's rebellion Farmer is able to reveal how much of what man most despises, even the gods, is the projection of what man hates most in himself.

The Gates of Creation presents a variation on the same point when Wolff's world is invaded again by a rival Lord, this time his own father. The resulting quest takes him through a series of trials and tests in another pocket universe, culminating in the discovery that his father has all the time been the helpless prisoner of Wolff's sister, who has engineered the challenge and quest from the beginning. In his struggle to that knowledge, however, Wolff has managed to overcome not only an external threat but his own Oedipal fears. In Farmer's universes there are real forces of evil that

may destroy the hero, but any chance of dealing with them effectively is dependent on the hero's eliminating the destructive or crippling elements within his own personality.

The next three novels approach the problem from the opposite direction by concentrating on the other major hero of the series, Kickaha. Originally Paul Janus Finnegan on Earth (another Farmer alter ego, this time a wish-fulfillment version), Kickaha is the ideal nonneurotic man, afraid only of real threats and always ready to risk his life without hesitation. He functions not only as an ideal model but also as a means of exposing by contrast the neurotic. Indeed, what he struggles against is the result of human (or Lord, for they are really the same) vanity, stupidity, and sickness. He too had gated from Earth into Wolff's universe by chance, and before Wolff's return he had already begun his own opposition to the tyrannical rule of the usurper Lord. He does so by assuming the proto-Promethean role of the archaic trickster figure, a role which also symbolically suggests Farmer's role as artist: "I am Kickaha, the *kickaha*, the tricky one, the maker of fantasies and of realities. I am the man whom boundaries cannot hold. I slip from one to another, in-again-out-again Finnegan." Indeed the title *The Maker of Universes* is an elaborate pun which includes not only Wolff, who constructed the pocket universe setting, but Kickaha, who informs it with creative energy, and Farmer himself, who created the story.

In *The Maker of Universes* Kickaha's trickster function includes becoming Wolff's partner in rebellion and guiding him to the recovery of his memory and the discovery of his full self. In *A Private Cosmos* Kickaha is the defender of Wolff's world from an invasion by Black Bellers, devices originally created by the Lords to store their minds and thus guarantee their immortality. The Bellers became autonomous, however, bent on exterminating the minds of all Lords and humans and occupying their bodies. In more general terms the Bellers are another symbolic manifestation of man's neurotic desire for absolute certainty and security. Kickaha nearly eliminates the menace, but a last escaping Beller forces him to gate to Earth in pursuit, which leads to the next novel, *Behind the Walls of Terra*.

On Earth Kickaha learns that the solar system is not in *the* universe but is in another of the many pocket universes created by the Lords. Moreover, though Earth has its own evil Lord (two contending ones in fact, whose neurotic fears get in the way of Kickaha's pursuit of the Beller), Kickaha learns that the sorry state of Earth, hanging on the brink of nuclear war while choking on its own mounting wastes, has not been caused by any Lord at all. In fact, the original Lord, after a few prehistoric appearances, had chosen to pursue his private pleasure while maintaining a hands-off policy toward the management of the rest of the Earth. Most of what is corrupt, evil, and dangerous in our world, therefore, man has managed to create for himself.

The Lavalite World, the latest of the series, is set in another pocket universe, this one centered on a plastic planet in a constant state of change, with mountains rising and valleys sinking in a matter of hours. Kickaha has seen to the death of the last of the Bellers, but his conflict with the Lords has continued and led to this ultimate test of his adaptability. Again the action-adventure plot becomes a means of asserting in exaggerated form Farmer's sense of the fundamental inconstancy of the universe.

In the late 1960s Farmer's interest in pulp action-adventure expanded into parody, but his fascination with its psychological implications remained. Another series (three novels so far) with hero Herald Childe began with *The Image of the Beast* (1968). It was inspired first by the desire of a California publisher to produce a body of pornographic fiction that also exhibited a respectable sense of plot and character. For Farmer, whose stories had often been bowdlerized by timid editors, the opportunity was irresistible. As he says in an interview in *Luna*, "I'd always considered vampire stories, werewolf tales, and in fact the whole Gothic field, as more-or-less disguised sex stories. Pornography of the weird. Why not bring out the hidden stuff into the open." If stories of vampires sucking blood from victims' necks are subconscious disguises for "other fluids and organs, . . . why not show Dracula for what he really is?" The result is immediately apparent in the opening scene, in which California smog replaces the conventional Gothic fog and "a private eye (this is a parody on the private eye story too) is losing his penis to the pointed iron dentures of a vampiress."

What he does to the Gothic and detective in *The Image of the Beast* he does to pulp action-adventure, especially the Tarzan and Doc Savage stories, in *A Feast Unknown: Volume IX of the Memoirs of Lord Grandrith* (1969). Another exercise in respectable pornography which renders conscious and explicit what is usually unconscious and implicit, the story pits the Tarzan figure, Lord Grandrith, the feral human nurtured in violence without the restraints of civilization, against the Doc Savage figure, Doc Caliban, the supercivilized man trained from birth to war against the forces of chaos and evil. Their conflict allegorically reveals the feral savage at the base of all civilized humans and suggests the kind of

honest reconciliation between something like the id and the superego that true civilization requires. And, as is usual in Farmer's worlds, peace with the self only establishes the basis for a more effective war against evil, a war continued in a pair of sequels published together by Ace as *Lord of the Trees: Volume X in the Memoirs of Lord Grandrith* and *The Mad Goblin* (1970).

The Tarzan figure continues to interest Farmer because by himself Tarzan embodies both the tension between and the precarious union of the savage archaic and the civilized. *Lord Tyger* (1970) concerns an experimental exploration of Tarzan's origin and early development. Told from the point of view of the Tarzan figure, the story posits a wealthy Burroughs fan, Boygur, obsessed with the desire to create his own Tarzan by adapting the environment of an isolated African valley so that he can manage the growth of an abducted infant into a modern lord of the jungle. Boygur fails twice before he makes the necessary compromises between Burroughs's imagination and reality and nurtures the third infant into a successful Tarzan. But there remain important differences between reality and Burroughs's or Boygur's conception of nature, differences which lead to Boygur's destruction in a familiar Farmer plot: the hero becomes a successful Prometheus in his rebellion against the "god" who created his universe.

More than a type of the relation between the archaic and the civilized, however, Tarzan, by reason of his growth from savagery to civilization, is an archetypal hero who incarnates the history of man. Farmer has in fact literalized this seemingly hyperbolic observation in another Tarzan figure appearing in *Time's Last Gift* (1972). The story concerns the journey by time machine from 2070 A.D. to 12,000 B.C. of a group of people including John Gribardson, a man who like Tarzan had been raised in the jungle (though born some fifteen years before Burroughs's Lord Greystoke) and given an immortality elixir by a witch doctor. He remains in the past, becoming the original of Hercules, Quetzalcoatl, and many others as he lives his way back to modern times. Among his manifestations is Sahhindar, the light-bearing god of Opar, the ancient African empire whose lost city Burroughs's Tarzan discovered. This incarnation inspires yet another series set in that ancient time, of which two novels have so far been completed—*Hadon of Ancient Opar* (1974) and *Flight to Opar* (1976)—and a third contracted.

Farmer's most fertile Tarzan spin-off, however, is *Tarzan Alive: A Definitive Biography of Lord Greystoke* (1972), which he calls an exercise in creative mythography. He also calls it "the first analogical, or parallel biography." It is a biography because it is presented as the story of the real man on whom Burroughs based his stories, many of which were highly inaccurate, some almost totally so. Farmer straightens out many of these problems, but he is also operating under certain constraints, especially the obligation imposed on him by Tarzan himself not to reveal his secret identity. Many of the names, places, and dates presented in the biography are therefore deliberately inaccurate analogues.

The idea of a biography of a fictional character is not original; Farmer's work was preceded by biographies of Sir Percy Blakeney (of *The Scarlet Pimpernel*), Nero Wolfe, Sherlock Holmes, Harry Flashman (of *Tom Brown's Schooldays*), and Horatio Hornblower. Farmer's work is unique, however, not only in its analogical approach to documentation, but also in its assumption of the historical reality of other fictional persons. Indeed, the ambiguity about what is really "true" and what is only like the truth is part of an elaborate game in which it turns out that Tarzan is only one of a number of supposedly fictional characters, including, in addition to those already mentioned, Phileas Fogg, Alan Quatermain, Wolf Larsen, Leopold Bloom, Sam Spade, Lord Peter Wimsey, and James Bond, who are all presented as either real or based on real persons. Moreover, a detailed genealogy demonstrates how most of these individuals trace their ancestry back to one or more of a group of fourteen people—including Sir Percy Blakeney and Fitzwilliam Darcy and his wife Elizabeth Bennet from Jane Austen's *Pride and Prejudice*—who in 1795 were passengers in two coaches riding past Wold Newton, a village in Yorkshire, when a meteorite struck nearby. Their remarkable progeny Farmer attributes to resulting radiation, which must have caused favorable mutations in the genes of those exposed.

The game founded on the premise of the Wold Newton families has produced an extensive series of works, which include another full-scale analogical biography, *Doc Savage: His Apocalyptic Life* (1973); a novel, *The Other Log of Phileas Fogg* (1973); a translation from the French (with appropriate interpolations to make the connections with the series) of J. H. Rosny aîné's *Ironcastle* (1976); and a number of shorter works including a biographical sketch of Kilgore Trout, an interview with Lord Greystoke, and one of Farmer's finest recent short stories, "After King Kong Fell." But this is only the beginning of a self-perpetuating game of concealment, misdirection, and revelation which

Leslie Fiedler has described as an indication of Farmer's "gargantuan lust to swallow down the whole cosmos, past, present, and to come, and to spew it out again," a part of a "larger attempt (at once absurd and beautiful, foredoomed to failure, but once conceived, already a success) to subsume in his own works all of the books in the world that have touched or moved him."

Fiedler's comment was highly perceptive since at the time Farmer had not yet begun the most fruitful spin-off from the Wold Newton premise, what he calls his Fictional Authors series. The first, *The Adventure of the Peerless Peer* (1974), is another Sherlock Holmes story, "written," of course, by Dr. Watson. It appeared the same year as *The Seven-Per-Cent Solution*, the first of Nicholas Meyer's popular additions to the Holmes canon, and a comparison of the two reveals Farmer's technique. Rather than place Holmes and Watson in a context that is otherwise scrupulously historical, as did Meyer, Farmer places the two in a world that is a bewildering mixture of history and fiction. In Farmer's story the aging Holmes is called during World War I into a desperate venture in which he and Watson are flown to Africa over enemy territory by a pilot who is clearly G-8, the American flying ace and secret agent of pulp fame. In Africa the detectives find themselves involved with Tarzan in upsetting German plans for East Africa.

A similar trick is pulled by Farmer in a short story, "The Problem of the Sore Bridge—Among Others" (1976; collected in *Riverworld and Other Stories*), "written" by Harry Manders, the man who plays Watson to A. J. Raffles, the criminal hero of a series of stories by Ernest William Horning, Conan Doyle's brother-in-law. But both Watson and Manders are established fictional voices. Farmer seems to have more fun writing stories by authors whose works no one has ever seen. The most successful piece of this sort is *Venus on the Half-Shell* (1975), which Farmer wrote as Kilgore Trout, the favorite science-fiction author of Kurt Vonnegut's characters Eliot Rosewater and Billy Pilgrim. A popular novel, *Venus on the Half-Shell* was also a highly successful hoax. Farmer's name appeared nowhere in the book and many reviewers attributed it to Vonnegut. The hoax may have worked so well in part because it would be almost inevitable that an attempt to write as Kilgore Trout would come out sounding like a parody of Vonnegut, although this factor would not guarantee that it would be as good a parody as *Venus on the Half-Shell*. But the novel is also, whether consciously or not, a self-parody, concerned as it is with the quest of the somewhat pornographic Simon Wagstaff, a "compulsive questioner" whose "only fault is that he asks questions no one can answer." His most notable question is one that equally preoccupies Farmer, "Why are we created only to suffer and die?"

And the game goes on: Simon Wagstaff also has a favorite author, Jonathan Swift Somers III, and Farmer has now written a biographical sketch of Somers and two short stories which form the beginning of the Ralph von Wau Wau series, concerning an intelligent dog of the future who plays private eye, a cross between Sherlock Holmes, Sam Spade, and Rin Tin Tin. There are more fictional authors stories and more planned; more analogical biographies are planned or in preparation of such characters as the Shadow, Allan Quatermain, Fu Manchu, the Wizard of Oz, and others; and there are other series to add to or create. In fact, by Farmer's count he has some twenty-two series and subseries going.

The production of series is not a unique phenomenon, but the number, richness, and complexity of Farmer's series can lay claim to uniqueness. Indeed, Farmer has raised the series to a philosophical level, for most of his are consistent with a pervasive and fitting vision of the universe as varied and constantly changing: it bares its mysteries to the prying spirit of man, but always teases him with his limitations, exposing his gods as projections of himself while luring him with the hint that something truly higher might yet be found behind the veil. In Farmer's universe, however, final answers are always withheld, and new forms of chaos and evil are ever breeding. It is a universe which lends itself to the series format, for the achievement of one guest only sets the stage for the sequel, and all sequels are parts of the never-ending quest for answers. Farmer's universe is also fascinatingly complex, with its mixture of hard and disillusioning reality with wish-fulfillment fantasy. It is a universe which inspires a sense of anger and frustration even in the best of heroes, but one which demands courage, adaptability, and love. Perhaps the secret of Farmer's appeal is the paradoxical combination of limitation and possibility, of irony and despair on the one hand and the spirit of irrepressible humor and play on the other.

Whatever his secret, Farmer is now among the most firmly established writers in the field. Though his appeal is not universal, at least as measured by numbers of Hugo and Nebula awards, it is solid, as measured by publications and reprints, and backed by a core of strongly committed fans. In fact, there are two flourishing fan groups, the Philip José Farmer Society, which publishes *Farmerage*, and the Wold Newton Meteorics Society, which publishes *The Wold Atlas*; these are groups which may one day rival the Baker Street Irregulars, the venerable society for Sherlock Holmes fans.

Among critics and writers he has received widely divergent reviews. Though his works have produced adverse reactions from Ted White, James Blish, and Joanna Russ, he has received high praise from Alfred Bester, Theodore Sturgeon, Roger Zelazny, and Norman Spinrad. Academics have been equally diverse. Leslie Fiedler, while admitting that Farmer writes "sometimes downright sloppily," insists that "he has an imagination capable of being kindled by the irredeemable mystery of the universe and of the soul, and in turn able to kindle the imagination of others." Franz Rottensteiner has attacked Farmer's Riverworld series for its exploitation of "the peculiar method of mass-market SF," which draws "a kaleidoscope of oddities . . . into the gigantic junk-yard of SF, where everything is but a pretext for another cops-and-robbers story." Russell Letson has come to Farmer's defense in two studies, one examining his hero types, the other showing the influences on Farmer of Carl Jung, Joseph Campbell, and Robert Graves. In the most recent study, Thomas L. Wymer has attempted to find the key to Farmer's peculiar magic in his manipulations of the trickster archetype. Though critical unanimity will be a long time in coming, the complex interrelatedness of his works and their confusing publishing history have inspired considerable bibliographical work by several hands, soon scheduled to culminate in a bibliography to be published by Kent State University Press.

Other:

"Attitudes," *Magazine of Fantasy and Science Fiction* (October 1953);

"After King Kong Fell," in *Omega*, ed. Roger Elwood (New York: Walker, 1973);

Mother Was a Lovely Beast: A Feral Man Anthology, edited by Farmer (Radnor, Pa.: Chilton, 1974);

Ironcastle, translated and enlarged from J. H. Rosny aîné's *L'Etonnante Aventure de Hareton Ironcastle* (New York: DAW, 1976).

Interviews:

David Kraft and Mitch Scheele, "An Interview with Philip José Farmer," *Science Fiction Review*, 4 (August 1975): 7-21;

Paul Walker, "Philip José Farmer," in *Speaking of*

Science Fiction: The Paul Walker Interviews (Oradell, N.J.: Luna, 1978), pp. 37-55;

Philip A. Shreffler, "An Interview with Philip José Farmer," *Xenophile*, no. 42 (September-October 1979): 7-8, 20.

Bibliographies:

Lawrence J. Knapp, *The First Editions of Philip José Farmer, Science Fiction Bibliographies 2* (Menlo Park, Cal.: David G. Turner, 1976);

Thomas L. Wymer, "Speculative Fiction, Bibliographies, and Philip José Farmer," *Extrapolation*, 18 (December 1976): 59-72;

Paul Whitney, "Philip José Farmer: A Checklist," *Science Fiction Collector*, 5 (September 1977): 4-20.

References:

Mary Brizzi, *The Reader's Guide to Philip José Farmer* (West Linn, Oreg.: Starmont, 1980);

Leslie Fiedler, "Thanks for the Feast: Notes on Philip José Farmer," in *The Book of Philip José Farmer* (New York: DAW, 1973), pp. 233-239;

Claudia Jannone, "*Venus on the Half-Shell* as Structuralist Activity," *Extrapolation*, 17 (May 1976): 110-117;

Russell Letson, "The Faces of a Thousand Heroes: Philip José Farmer," *Science-Fiction Studies*, 4 (1977): 35-41;

Letson, Introduction to *The Green Odyssey* (Boston: Gregg, 1978), pp. v-xv;

Letson, "The Worlds of Philip José Farmer," *Extrapolation*, 18 (May 1977); 124-130;

Sam Moskowitz, "Philip José Farmer," in his *Seekers of Tomorrow: Masters of Modern Science Fiction* (Westport, Conn.: Hyperion, 1974), pp. 392-409;

Franz Rottensteiner, "Playing Around with Creation: Philip José Farmer," *Science-Fiction Studies*, 1 (1973): 94-98;

George Scheetz, ed., *Farmerage*, three issues (The Philip José Farmer Society, 1978-1980);

These Ven, "The Updated Farmer, or What You Never Knew about Richard Wentworth's Genealogy and Never Thought to Ask," *Xenophile*, no. 42 (September-October 1977): 17-19;

Thomas L. Wymer, "Philip José Farmer: The Trickster as Artist," in *Voices for the Future*, vol. 2, ed. Thomas D. Clareson (Bowling Green, Ohio: Bowling Green University Popular Press, 1979).

JACK FINNEY
(WALTER BRADEN FINNEY)
(1911-   )

BOOKS: *5 Against the House* (Garden City: Doubleday, 1954; London: Eyre & Spottiswoode, 1954);

The Body Snatchers (New York: Dell, 1955; London: Eyre & Spottiswoode, 1955); republished as *Invasion of the Body Snatchers* (New York: Dell, 1961; London: Sphere, 1978); revised as *The Invasion of the Body Snatchers* (New York: Award, 1973);

Telephone Roulette (play) (Chicago: Dramatic Publishing, 1956);

The Third Level (New York & Toronto: Rinehart, 1957); republished as *The Clock of Time* (London: Eyre & Spottiswoode, 1958);

The House of Numbers (New York: Dell, 1957; London: Eyre & Spottiswoode, 1957);

Assault on a Queen (New York: Simon & Schuster, 1959; London: Eyre & Spottiswoode, 1960);

I Love Galesburg in the Springtime (New York: Simon & Schuster, 1963; London: Eyre & Spottiswoode, 1965);

Good Neighbor Sam (New York: Simon & Schuster, 1963; London: Eyre & Spottiswoode, 1963);

The Woodrow Wilson Dime (New York: Simon & Schuster, 1968);

Time and Again (New York: Simon & Schuster, 1970);

Marion's Wall (New York: Simon & Schuster, 1973);

The Night People (Garden City: Doubleday, 1977).

Jack Finney has never shown in his writing the fascination with the future as a setting which is so often central to science fiction. Instead he develops a mystique of the past, its lost opportunities and its lost values. He shares with science-fiction writers a sense of the dullness and mundaneness of the present, but deals with this quality in a manner which puts him at the margins of the genre. His stories were published in *Collier's*, the *Saturday Evening Post*, and *Good Housekeeping* rather than in *Astounding Science-Fiction* or *Galaxy* (though occasionally one of his stories would be reprinted in the *Magazine of Fantasy and Science Fiction*). Reviews of his work in the science-fiction magazines frequently refer to him as an outsider, sometimes with hostility. Even as critics describe Finney's writing as ingenious, bright, and deft, they also call it slick, glib, and facile. However, what may have annoyed hard-core science-fiction readers even more than the glossiness of Finney's style may have been his lack of interest in the future.

Jack Finney was born Walter Braden Finney in Milwaukee in 1911. To judge from the biographical information he has made available, Finney is a writer who values his privacy. A fragmentary, whimsical biographical sketch in *Collier's* (5 April 1947) portrays him as a writer of advertising jingles in New York. The jacket flaps and settings of more recent works inform us that he is now living in Mill Valley, California. His earliest writings were suspense stories, and in fact his short story "The Widow's Walk" took a special prize in the second annual competition sponsored by *Ellery Queen's Mystery Magazine*. His first story was published in 1946, and he began thereafter to write prolifically for the slick magazines. His first novel, *5 Against the House* (1954), in which a group of bored college students in search of excitement plan and execute an elaborate robbery of Harold's Club in Reno, sets the pattern for his suspense stories. The theme looks forward to *Assault on a Queen* (1959), where the thieves are somewhat older and the target is the *Queen Mary* (it became a successful Paramount film in 1966, with a screenplay by Rod Serling). Finney's first prominent success was a science-fiction story serialized in *Collier's* (26 November, 10 December, and 24 December 1954), then published in novel form as *The Body Snatchers* (1955), which later was the source of the celebrated film, *Invasion of the Body Snatchers*, directed by Don Siegel and produced by Allied Artists in 1956. Finney collaborated in the screenplay.

The plot of *The Body Snatchers*, which concerns aliens who visit the Earth in order to inhabit human bodies, is not particularly original, and reviewers in the science-fiction magazines noted similarities to Robert Heinlein's *The Puppet Masters* (1951) and Philip K. Dick's "The Father-Thing" (1954). But Finney's novel has taken its place beside these works as a science-fiction classic, perhaps because his approach to the theme of alien encounter is distinctive: his alien beings are never individualized or even represented except in their human form (unless one counts the giant seed pods out of which the human victims are duplicated). Finney's real focus is on community reaction to deviant behavior among its own members. This aspect of the book was emphasized in the 1956 film to the extent that critics have tended to view both book and film as a reflection of popular anticommunism in the McCarthy years or, conversely, as a parable about the spread of fascism. But because the human-to-alien transformations do not occur because of conscious choice or inclination, the reaction to them

functions as a generalized social anxiety rather than a specific political one. What critic Pauline Kael calls the story's "deliciously paranoid theme" (*New Yorker*, 25 December 1978) is consistently nonspecific, despite efforts of critics to limit the range of its focus. The difficulty of specifying a political context stems largely from the difficulty of seeing the hero, Dr. Miles Bennell, as a representative of specific values. If he is unusual, it is only in his loyalty to the past: he lives alone in the home of his late parents, has inherited his father's medical practice, and speaks pointedly of the virtues of remaining in one place. In any event his resistance to the pod people is hardly a moral lesson; he outwits them once by a stratagem and once by an act of rage.

P. Schuyler Miller, in a review for *Astounding Science-Fiction* (September 1955), found the denouement unconvincing. (The pods spontaneously abandon earth because the hero has set fire to the nursery where new pods are being grown.) If the 1956 film version and a United Artists remake in 1978 by director Phil Kaufman are considered as commentaries on the novel, they also question the logic of Finney's hopeful resolution. Don Siegel first shot a version in which the pods win, and even with the tacked-on ending which the studio demanded, where Miles Bennell manages to call out the FBI at the last moment, the film is considerably more somber than the novel. Another difference between the film versions and the novel is that in the films the romantic subplot is abandoned. In both versions of the film, the heroine is possessed by the pods at climactic moments. In the novel the love story between Dr. Bennell and Becky Driscoll is given a prominence at least as important as the pods. Unfortunately, the love story mitigates the reader's growing sense of panic and conflicts with the economy of effect. Finney's emphasis on the love relationship suggests that romantic love of the naive, traditional kind lines up most effectively against the forces of conformity and eroded individuality which the pods represent.

The short stories collected in 1957 in *The Third Level* are perhaps even clearer evidence of Finney's aloofness from science-fiction norms, but the critical reception from the science-fiction establishment was almost unanimously positive. Miller, in *Astounding Science-Fiction* (May 1958), voiced a dissenting opinion, saying he regretted that the single theme of time-travel dominated the collection, but added, "If you want to know what kind of SF the general public wants, this is as good a sample as you're likely to get." Other science-fiction reviewers found the stories superior to the standard product. When *The*

Third Level was selected by *Infinity Science Fiction* as the best short-story collection of 1958, Damon Knight wrote: "Finney's specialty is time travel, a subject which in his hands has rich overtones of nostalgia and fear. While some writers have made a time machine as prosaic as the 5:40 to Scarsdale, Finney re-invests it with all the strangeness and wonder that properly belong to it." There is no doubt that Finney claims time-travel as his particular domain in this collection: he runs the theme through every imaginable variation. The narrator of the title story (1951) discovers a third level in Grand Central Station from which trains run to 1894 America. In "Such Interesting Neighbors" the couple who have moved in next door to the narrator and his wife in San Rafael, California, turn out to be refugees from an uninhabitable future who are delighted to live in a world where the hydrogen bomb is still only in its infancy and the public anxiety has not yet reached panic level. In "I'm Scared" (1951) it is suggested that mankind has already reached that level. The narrator recounts a series of anomalies in the texture of time, starting with his own anecdote of hearing on his radio, for a few moments one evening, a fragment of the long defunct Major Bowes amateur program. The narrative is simply a series of incidents he has since collected of brief visitations from the past. He finds that these incidents are becoming more frequent, and the apocalyptic conclusion works as a keynote of the collection:

> Haven't you noticed . . . on the part of nearly everyone you know, a growing rebellion against the *present*? And an increasing longing for the past? . . .
>
> For the first time in man's history, man is desperate to escape the present . . . I am utterly convinced that this terrible mass pressure of millions of minds is already, slightly but definitely, affecting time itself. In the moments when this happens—when the almost universal longing to escape is greatest—my incidents occur. Man is disturbing the clock of time, and I am afraid it will break. When it does, I leave to your imagination the last few hours of madness that will be left to us; all the countless moments that now make up our lives suddenly ripped apart and chaotically tangled in time.

The sense of horror in the last two sentences is uncharacteristic of Finney, but the portrait of an entire society straining semiconsciously to escape the present is a compact argument for the sensibility behind most of his writing. Thematically, "I'm Scared" stands at the center of *The Third Level* in much the same way that its companion piece, "I Love Galesburg in the Springtime" (1960), stands at the center of the collection of that name (1963). In "I Love Galesburg in the Springtime" the visitations from the past turn out to be benevolent attempts by spirits of a happier age to save artifacts from the past—old houses, forests, trees on city streets—from being destroyed by developers and modernizers.

The premise that time is malleable and subject to change through human emotions is not a common science-fiction theme. (Fritz Lieber's haunting story "The Man Who Never Grew Young," 1947, in which the pressure of collective anxiety makes time turn around and run backward, is a rare example.) The science that underlies Finney's time-travel is often, properly speaking, not science but sympathetic magic, that mode of prescientific thinking whereby objects that have been physically connected in the past retain a magical connection after they have been separated. Perhaps Finney's most successful realization of the mystique of artifacts from the past is "Second Chance" (1956; collected in *The Third Level*), which employs this logic brilliantly. The object in question is an old car, a 1923 Jordan Playboy rebuilt by a teenager in the 1950s. It had been wrecked in a collision with a train in the 1920s. After he has rebuilt it with vintage parts, the hero finds himself driving around in a 1920s setting. He parks, the car is apparently stolen, and he ends up back in the 1950s looking for another Jordan Playboy. He meets a new girl in town whose father has a slightly less damaged Jordan Playboy with the same license plates as the one stolen in the visit to the 1920s. The conclusion is that the Jordan Playboy belonged to the girl's father, who was killed the first time around in the train collision. Once restored, the Jordan Playboy returned to the 1920s to give him a second chance in an alternate branch of time, in a nonfatal collision with the same train. The story suggests that there is a redemptive power in connections with the past, even—since the second chance has made possible the love interest of the story—an erotic power. This theme of erotic links with the past becomes increasingly central to Finney's writing, as in "The Love Letter" (1959; collected in *I Love Galesburg in the Springtime*), where a series of letters found in an antique desk become a means of communication with a woman in nineteenth-century New York.

In *The Woodrow Wilson Dime* (1968) the erotic link is achieved not by going back in time but by shunting laterally from one possible world to another. (The novel is expanded from a short story, "The Other Wife," which was originally published in the *Saturday Evening Post*, 30 January 1960, and is included in *I Love Galesburg in the Springtime* under the title "The Coin Collector.") The hero Benjamin Bennell (apparently no relation to Dr. Miles Bennell) discovers a parallel world through the medium of one of its coins which circulate in small numbers in this world. Again the artifact of one setting draws humans to its source. As the original title suggests, he finds that in the alternate world he is married to a beautiful woman. The construction of the alternate world is one of Finney's most innovative creations: in it they still make Pierce Arrow cars, there never was a Chrysler Building, and Cary Grant works as a pharmacist on the ground floor of the building which stands in its place. The weakness of *The Woodrow Wilson Dime* emerges from the conflict between the strangeness of the alternate world and the gratuitous hallucinatory style with which the narrator comically describes both worlds. (For example, a hand comes forth from the mirror in the opening scene to stamp the word failure on his forehead.) Such a style may have seemed innovative in 1968, but the two kinds of strangeness—hallucinatory narrative style and alternate world—conflict with one another and ultimately blur the novel's effect.

One of Finney's most prominent and acclaimed works is *Time and Again* (1970). Finney's fascination in the novel with the neighborhoods and history of New York has made it a minor cult book among New York enthusiasts. Plot outline is simple enough, but the details of the story make it a baroque, labyrinthine mystery novel. Si Morley, an artist in an advertising agency, is chosen by a secret government project to be sent into the past by means of new scientific methods. His destination is New York in 1892, and once he arrives he falls in love with Julia, who works in his boardinghouse on Gramercy Park. There was some complaint among reviewers (notably Miller in *Analog Science Fiction/Science Fact*, February 1971) about the plausibility of the time-travel technology in the novel. The technique used is an update of the Jordan Playboy or Woodrow Wilson dime idea: an environment from the past is duplicated, an individual is hypnotized into forgetting temporarily that he is in his own present, and since time is only in one's mind anyway, the rest happens spontaneously. *Time and Again* is a heavily researched and documented work which contains photographs, including portraits of nineteenth-century people intended to illustrate characters in

the story, sketches from nineteenth-century life (since Morley is a commercial artist), and authentic quotations from the newspapers Morley reads. Perhaps one reason for the popularity of *Time and Again* is that it took the naive and stable nineteenth century seriously and attempted to put the reader into it.

Time and Again is the most solid and consequential of Finney's novels and the one in which his characteristic stratagems and complex turns of plot work out in the most satisfying manner. The concluding scene, though somewhat contrived, is perhaps Finney's masterpiece. Morley has returned a final time to 1892, urged by Dr. E. E. Danziger, who has developed the secret government project to change the past. Morley has access to a future adviser of Grover Cleveland through whom Morley can effect a change in state policy that will make Cuba an American possession. For one who respects the past, this has moral repercussions beyond the political ones, and Morley's method of evading the command is extraordinary. He learns that Dr. Danziger's parents met at a theater in 1892 when Danziger asks Morley to make a sketch of the scene for sentimental reasons. However, instead of sketching the encounter between Danziger's future parents, Morley erases the possibility of the existence of the time-travel project by casually distracting the attention of Danziger's potential father as the potential bride walks by. This action leaves Morley permanently in the past, and his courtship of Julia in 1892 continues undisturbed.

The two novels which follow *Time and Again* fall distinctly out of the area of science fiction, though both exploit recognizable Finney themes. In *Marion's Wall* (1973) there is an erotic link with the past in the form of a silent-film actress's ghost which haunts an old Victorian house in San Francisco. She had died in a car wreck before becoming well known, and visits the hero by inhabiting the body of his shy, inhibited wife. The body snatching is benign: she stays only long enough to realize that she does not want a movie career in the film industry of the 1970s. *The Night People* (1977) is another of Finney's suspense stories: two young couples in protest against the boredom of contemporary life decide to spend one night a week in increasingly daring pranks. Finney's writing is always slick, with all that this implies of the light and artificial. But throughout even his lightest writing there runs a continuing critique of the present, not a political critique but an aesthetic one, which is the source of his unmistakable, peculiar integrity.

—Michael Beard

HUGO GERNSBACK
(16 August 1884-19 August 1967)

BOOKS: *Ralph 124C41+* (Boston: Stratford, 1925);
republished with new preface by Gernsback
(New York: Frederick Fell, 1950);
Ultimate World (New York: Walker, 1971).

Hugo Gernsback was an imaginative, insightful,
and opportunistic American editor and publisher
who not only introduced the first science fiction
magazine (*Amazing Stories*, in April 1926), but the
next six successive titles as well (*Amazing Stories
Annual, Amazing Stories Quarterly, Science Wonder Stories, Air Wonder Stories, Science Wonder
Quarterly,* and *Scientific Detective Monthly*), all
before 1930. Seeking a simple, precise name for the
narrative genre he packaged and repackaged so
profitably, Gernsback gave the field a new literary
referent not once, but twice: his first coinage, the
1926 term *scientifiction*, being supplanted only by
his own second invention, *science fiction*, of 1929.
Gernsback was also the first man to single out
science fiction for individual editorial promotion,
an undertaking he pursued eagerly in such early
popular science journals of his own creation as
*Modern Electrics, Electrical Experimenter, Science
and Invention,* and *Radio News*, gradually building
up the audience he would eventually tap with
Amazing Stories. He introduced several of the best-
known science-fiction writers of his time and later,
such as David H. Keller, Jack Williamson, Edward
E. Smith, Stanley G. Weinbaum, John W. Campbell,
Jr., and Fletcher Pratt, and showcased the delightfully
amusing and fanciful cartoon work of Frank R.
Paul, doyen of science-fiction magazine illustrators
for more than a quarter of a century. A remarkable
and memorable figure, briefly sullied now and again
by happenstance and personal foibles, but of
enormous importance to the development of the
twentieth-century science-fiction field, Gernsback
has yet to be evenly assessed in a full-length
biography or in a detailed study of his publishing
work. Sam Moscowitz's informative but somewhat
biased short studies in *Explorers of the Infinite*
(1960) whet the reader's interest but leave much
unsaid and unresearched. Shorter entries on
Gernsback in such works as Donald Tuck's
Encyclopedia of Science Fiction (1974), merely echo
Moscowitz's data without fresh additions.

Born in Luxembourg, Gernsback came to the
United States in February 1904. His early interest in
electronics led to a partnership in late 1905 to design
and manufacture a Gernsback invention which was

nothing less than the first home radio set. The
introduction of the first effective walkie-talkie
followed in 1908. Also operating an electronic parts
importing business, Gernsback moved from the periodic publication of a parts catalogue into his first
full-fledged magazine venture, the popular *Modern
Electrics* of 1908. He found editorial work congenial;
he became increasingly more involved in writing
and editing than in formal electronic development,
beginning his first novel, a futuristic fantasy called
Ralph 124C41+ (One-to-foresee-for-one-plus), as a
serial for *Modern Electrics* in April 1911. This book,
paralyzingly impossible to read as entertainment
now, was nevertheless a remarkable catalogue of
technical prophecy, predicting (among a great many
other things) microfilm, tape recorders, radio
networks, radar, and even jukeboxes. Changing the
name of his magazine to the *Electrical Experimenter*
in 1913, Gernsback hired Frank R. Paul as illustrator
the following year and undertook his only other
venture into science-fiction writing, publishing the
series of short comic fantasies he called "Baron
Munchausen's New Scientific Adventures" in the
Electrical Experimenter between May 1915 and
February 1917. (The entire series was reprinted in
Amazing Stories between February and July of 1928;
there has been no book edition.) These, especially
when read with Paul's capricious illustrations, are

Hugo Gernsback

considerably more amusing than *Ralph 124C41+* and seem to represent a real and often overlooked sense of humor in Gernsback's persona. Moscowitz, who knew Gernsback personally, refers to his "almost rapier-like" social wit, and his "rare ability to joke about his own misfortunes."

Noting his readers' pleased response to the fictionalized scientific speculation in his magazine, Gernsback not only encouraged new writers to contribute, but sought fresh material from established writers such as George Allen England and Ray Cummings, who were then writing what were called "different" or "pseudo-science" stories for popular adventure-fiction magazines such as *Argosy, Blue Book,* and *Adventure.* Initially publishing one such story in each issue of the *Electrical Experimenter,* Gernsback doubled its science-fiction quota when he again changed its name in August 1920 to *Science and Invention.* He also ran a science-fiction story in each number of his new companion magazine, *Radio News* of 1919, in effect printing three new science-fiction stories each month—more than any other magazine publisher of the time except for Frank Munsey, whose top-selling *Argosy* was now a weekly. Reader interest continued to rise, in part because those devotees of "different fiction" in other magazines had discovered Gernsback's two titles and bought them regularly, leading Gernsback to publish a "Scientific Fiction Number" of *Science and Invention* in August 1923; six stories appeared, to the virtual exclusion of the usual popular science content. The sale of that issue jumped noticeably, and Gernsback was spurred to try the logical next step, a magazine wholly devoted to science fiction.

Circularizing his subscribers about a new all-fiction publication to be called *Scientifiction,* Gernsback received only a disappointing handful of subscriptions. As Moscowitz suggests, Gernsback had failed to realize that most popular fiction magazines derived the bulk of their circulation from newsstand sales, while sizable subscriptions were generally limited to home service, family, or popular technical magazines. At the time, he seems to have blamed the projected magazine's bizarre and cumbersome title as much as anything else, for he limited his newly coined term to the subtitle of his subsequent magazine concept, *Amazing Stories, The Magazine of Scientifiction,* which was delivered directly to the nation's newsstands on 5 April 1926.

The first issue, roughly the 8"x11" size of *Science and Invention,* was printed on ninety-six pages of heavy, gray paper stock and featured public domain reprint stories by H. G. Wells and Jules Verne, and new fiction by George Allen England and

Modern Electrics, *cover of February 1912 issue containing chapters of* Ralph 124C41

Wonder Stories, *cover*

Austin Hall. It looked well worth its face price of twenty-five cents, despite a surprisingly flat and unimaginative cover by Paul. It sold well, as did the following monthly issues. Yet Gernsback poor-mouthed it to his readers, even as circulation mounted. Unwilling to spend a bit of his swelling income to improve the paper stock, he told readers in his October 1927 issue that—despite an attained circulation of 150,000—*Amazing Stories* was not yet on a paying basis. As James Gunn points out, this hardly seems likely, in view of the magazine's continuing large measure of noncopyright reprints and half-cent-a-word rate to new contributors; the low editorial costs combined with low production costs should have meant a high rate of profit on such large newsstand sales. It could be argued, of course, that Gernsback was putting *Amazing Stories* profits into other experimental titles, for he shortly launched *Amazing Stories Annual* (1927), which sold out on newsstands within three months and so promptly became *Amazing Stories Quarterly*, a fat, 8"x11" magazine of 130 pages priced at fifty cents, and a good seller through the rest of the 1920s. He added further titles as well to what was becoming a small magazine empire: *Your Body*, *Tid-Bits*, *French Humor*, *Cuckoo Nuts*, and others. Many of them, like *Amazing Stories*, consisted of cheap or public domain reprint material.

Yet something was wrong. In February 1929 bankruptcy proceedings were filed against the Experimenter Publishing Company, Gernsback's magazine group, with the company's assets and titles being sold at a public auction. A group called Teck Publications bought *Amazing Stories*, *Amazing Stories Quarterly*, and *Radio News*, continuing publication into the 1930s. Gernsback's own funds were not depleted, however, for he promptly bounced back in the spring of 1929 with the first issue of *Science Wonder Stories* (June 1929), quickly following it with *Air Wonder Stories* (July 1929), *Science Wonder Quarterly* (Fall 1929), and *Scientific Detective Monthly* (January 1930), as well as continuing his popular science titles under new names. But the new publishing venture was not as profitable as the old; the national financial collapse at the decade's end cut severely into magazine sales everywhere, and Gernsback was forced to drop title after title, reduce page size and count, cut writers' payments or avoid them altogether when possible, and eventually bow out of the field completely with the sale of his sole remaining title, *Wonder Stories*, to Standard Magazines in early 1936.

Gernsback's major influence on the science-fiction magazine scene had ended. He had effectively launched science fiction as an active and nationally recognized literary genre, creating a profitable milieu in which the talents that were to be responsible for the fruition of modern science fiction could comfortably develop. It is questionable whether Gernsback may fairly be called, as he has often been in the past, the father of science fiction (although he is inarguably the parent of the term itself), but there is no doubt he was an extremely active and indispensable midwife in aiding the popular spread of interest in imaginative speculation on the nature of the future and of technological development. Certainly he was crucial in establishing the genre-wide concept of authorial responsibility for scientific plausibility in projecting future likelihoods. As Brian W. Aldiss makes clear, "Gernsback laid great emphasis on the need for scientific accuracy in stories, and later competitors felt bound to copy him." This concern with rational extrapolation from known principles, although often "more honored in the breach than the observance," as Aldiss remarks, is of course the element which most sharply distinguishes science fiction as a genre of its own, apart from fantastic fiction in general, and Gernsback has been accordingly honored by having had the prestigious annual science-fiction Hugo awards named for him and his shaping influence on the field.

Absorbed through the next two decades with other publishing projects—notably the ill-fated launching of *Technocracy Review* in 1933, the more successful introduction of *Sexology* in the same year, and the experimental publication of *Superworld Comics* (with Paul art) in 1939—Gernsback reentered the science-fiction field with the auspicious March 1953 debut of his streamlined *Science Fiction Plus*, a large format magazine printed in two colors on slick paper, edited by Sam Moscowitz, featuring the art work of Paul and others and fiction by such noted authors as Philip José Farmer, Harry Bates, Jack Williamson, James H. Schmitz, and others. Too costly a product for the market of the time, the magazine folded after only seven issues, and Gernsback, by then a revered but distinctly old-fashioned figure in the era of Campbell and Gold, dropped from active participation in the field he had named only twenty-five years before. (A posthumous satiric novel of alien invasion, written by Gernsback in the late 1950s and called *Ultimate World*, was published in 1971.) Dead at eighty-three in 1967, Hugo Gernsback is secure in his position of honor in the field of science fiction as a man who saw how to package identifiably his favorite form of reading matter and focus the attention of its many followers on a single outlet—with the results we all know today. —*Bill Blackbeard*

References:

Brian W. Aldiss, *Billion Year Spree: The True History of Science Fiction* (Garden City: Doubleday, 1973), pp. 209-216;

James Gunn, *Alternate Worlds: The Illustrated History of Science Fiction* (New York: Prentice-Hall, 1975), pp. 120-128;

Sam Moskowitz, *Explorers of the Infinite* (Cleveland: World, 1960), pp. 225-242;

Darrell Schweitzer, "Keeper of the Flame: A Different View of Hugo Gernsback," *Algol*, 15 (Winter 1978): 23-27.

DAVID GERROLD

(24 January 1944-   )

BOOKS: *The Flying Sorcerers*, by Gerrold and Larry Niven (New York: Ballantine, 1971; London: Corgi, 1975);

Space Skimmer (New York: Ballantine, 1972);

Vith a Finger In My I (New York: Ballantine, 1972);

Yesterday's Children (New York: Dell, 1972; London: Faber & Faber, 1974);

When Harlie Was One (Garden City: Doubleday, 1972);

The Trouble With Tribbles (New York: Ballantine, 1973);

The World of Star Trek (New York: Ballantine, 1973);

The Man Who Folded Himself (New York: Random House, 1973; London: Faber & Faber, 1973);

Battle for the Planet of the Apes (New York: Award Books, 1973);

Moonstar Odyssey (New York: New American Library, 1977);

Deathbeast (New York: Popular Library, 1978);

SF Yearbook (New York: O'Quinn Studio/Starlog, 1979).

David Gerrold's first sale was to television; in 1967 his "The Trouble With Tribbles" became a script for "Star Trek." Since then he has added short stories, novels, and nonfiction to his bibliography. However, his work has received little critical attention beyond a few book reviews.

Born in Los Angeles as David Jerrold Friedman, he read science fiction from childhood and was active in fandom. He attended Los Angeles Valley Junior College, took cinema courses at the University of Southern California, and received a B.A. in theater arts from California State College at Northridge in 1967. Several of his works have been nominated for Hugo or Nebula awards, including "The Trouble With Tribbles" and the novels *When Harlie Was One* (1972), *The Man Who Folded Himself* (1973), and *Moonstar Odyssey* (1977). In 1979 he won a Skylark, the E. E. Smith Memorial Award. Gerrold served as media editor for *Galileo* magazine in 1978, and since 1976 his columns have appeared regularly in *Starlog* magazine.

Gerrold's first published book, *The Flying Sorcerers* (1971), a collaboration with Larry Niven, is a hilarious account of the coming of industrialization to a primitive planet whose eleven moons and whose position in a dust cloud have caused magic rather than science to develop. The shrewd and practical protagonist and the character of the humor reveal Niven's touch, but the word play, sympathy for women, and general humanity seem to be Gerrold's.

More serious is *Space Skimmer* (1972), which

gerrold/MM 9-20

"These do -- maybe there's something about them
that's distasteful."

"That's obvious -- hmm, an egg with its own defense
mechanism." He looked up. "What are you planning to
do with them?"

"I was thinking of rigging up an incubator -- "

Ted whistled softly. "Jimmy, I've got to admire
your -- bravado. Or something. You're either the
smartest damn fool around here -- or the dumbest. It's
not enough you have to rescue Chtorran eggs from the
incinerator; now you want to hatch them. When Duke
hears about this, he's going to have a fit."

I hadn't thought about Duke. "Why -- ? What's
wrong with the idea?"

"Oh, nothing -- it's just that the purpose of this
Special Forces Operation is to kill worms, not breed
them."

"Not entirely," I insisted. "You and I were sent
up here to study the Chtorrans."

"That doesn't mean we have to make pets of them."

"And how else are we going to get close enough
to study them? Do you know a better way to observe
one long enough to learn anything? On a hunt, as soon

A Matter for Men, *typescript*

concerns the realization by a space crew during a diverse series of adventures that no one can be whole until he is a member of a family or group. *Yesterday's Children*, published the same year, was less successful than *Space Skimmer*. The novel seems to have been originally conceived as a "Star Trek" episode; without the series background, however, it seems rather thin. It is hard to care whether First Officer Korie gets his "bogie" or is impeded by conservative Captain Brandt, and the surprise ending is ultimately ineffective.

When Harlie Was One, on the other hand, treats standard ideas innovatively. HARLIE, a huge computer, resembles Mike, the computer in Robert A. Heinlein's *The Moon is a Harsh Mistress* (1966), and Project Chief Auberson reminds one of a male Dr. Susan Calvin, the psychologist in Isaac Asimov's *I, Robot* (1950). Examining the problematic morality of a sentient computer, Gerrold speculates on the use of knowledge by humans, the purpose of humanity, and the nature of God. Unfortunately, the determinedly upbeat ending undercuts any substantive answers to the questions raised.

The Man Who Folded Himself shows a growing maturity of thought and emphasis in Gerrold's work. After Danny and his one-day-in-the-future self Don win $57,600 at the race track, each becomes the only real friend the other has ever had. Danny explores paradoxes and alternate time lines, has affairs with both Don and their female version Diane (a female self, that is, on an alternate time line), fathers a son who becomes Danny himself, and witnesses his own death. Though the end is somewhat weak, such a book demonstrates the capacity of science fiction to deal with philosophical questions—such as solipsism and the meaning of personal choice—in readable, comprehensible ways.

Gerrold wrote the script for a 1967 episode of "Star Trek," "The Trouble With Tribbles," is credited with the story idea for "The Cloud Minders," and wrote two episodes of the animated version of the series. Participation in Trek fandom also led to two books for Trekkies. In *The Trouble With Tribbles* (1973) Gerrold outlines his background in science fiction, tells how he sold the episode and won the right to do the script, and discusses the production of the episode. *The World of Star Trek* (1973) is complementary in presenting general information on the series; analyzing characters, plot structures, and appeal; and providing numerous anecdotes for "Star Trek" fans. Gerrold has also been associated with other television programs such as

"Logan's Run" and "Land of the Lost." He was also involved as story editor for *Buck Rogers*. He also wrote the novel *Battle for the Planet of the Apes* (1973) from the filmscript for the movie.

After having published four books in 1973, Gerrold produced only anthologies until the publication in 1977 of *Moonstar Odyssey*, which concerns the Satlik, inhabitants of a planet on which primitive sailing and fishing survive side by side with advanced technology such as computers and the screens that make the planet livable. The people's main variation from the Terran norm is that, in adolescence, each Satliki chooses her sex. (The feminine pronoun is used generically throughout.) The protagonist Jobe, who lacks the confidence to choose, speculates at length about the value of both female and male identities. Her Unchosen aunt tells her that she must learn to live for herself, "the same way every human being has to if they are ever to be mature. You have the same Choice that an Erdik [Terran] does—the same Choice that I had—the same Choice every Satlik has—you can accept yourself and make the best of you, or you can choose to be unhappy." The aunt's little homily sounds the characteristic theme of Gerrold's best writing. The search for self-fulfillment also figures in *Deathbeast* (1978), in which eight time-travelers land in the Cretaceous period to kill a *Tyrannosaurus rex*. Based on sound scientific research, the descriptions of dinosaurs and other Cretaceous life are striking. Ethab, the macho leader of the time-travelers, wishes to find the self-fulfillment he has previously found in the hunt, but he and the other somewhat stereotypical characters each learn their limits in the hunt for the terrible saurian.

In the introduction to the anthology *Protostars* (1971), Gerrold discusses the need of writers to cultivate traditional writing skills; he also takes pride—as he affirms in *The Trouble With Tribbles*—in his ability to write to order. Yet this facility is a danger to Gerrold, sometimes resulting in fiction without feeling and in incompletely explored themes. Gerrold's best work, like the quality science fiction he defines in *Protostars*, presents "aspects of the individual's roles, both those he has chosen for himself and the ones he has been forced into." But whether dealing with the sex roles of male or female, the moral responsibility of intelligence, or the uses of heroism, Gerrold demonstrates his ability as a serious science-ficiton writer.

—*Edra Bogle*

Other:

Protostars, edited by Gerrold (New York: Ballantine, 1971);

Generation: An Anthology of Speculative Fiction, edited by Gerrold (New York: Dell, 1972);

Science Fiction Emphasis I, edited by Gerrold and Stephen Goldin (New York: Ballantine, 1974);

Alternities, edited by Gerrold and Goldin (New York: Dell, 1974);

Ascents of Wonder, edited by Gerrold and Goldin (New York: Popular Library, 1977).

MARK S. GESTON
(20 June 1946-   )

BOOKS: *Lords of the Starship* (New York: Ace, 1967; London: Joseph, 1971);

Out of the Mouth of the Dragon (New York: Ace, 1969; London: Joseph, 1972);

The Day Star (New York: DAW, 1972);

The Siege of Wonder (Garden City: Doubleday, 1976).

Mark S. Geston has received only scant attention in current histories of science fiction, though his four novels, written between 1967 and 1976, have been given brief favorable commentary in reviews. Geston is still in the early stages of his work as a writer, but the thematic evolution and the refining of literary technique, especially of characterization, that can be discerned between his first novel and his fourth reveal a rapid literary development.

Geston was born in Atlantic City, New Jersey, and wrote his first novel, *Lords of the Starship* (1967), while he was a student at Kenyon College. His second book, *Out of the Mouth of the Dragon* (1969), is a more ambitious but not completely successful work. Geston's first novels show a fascination with the apocalyptic—his worlds are dying and only death seems meaningful; human despair and the machinery of war dominate these works. They reflect, perhaps, the period in which they were written—the time of student unrest and rebellion at the United States' involvement in Vietnam during the 1960s. In the latter two novels, *The Day Star* (1972) and *The Siege of Wonder* (1976), the apocalyptic has been transmuted to the elegiac. Except for *The Day Star*, Geston's novels are characterized by a deliberate seriousness and tortured sensibility; they show a penchant for the grotesque

and even for the gruesome, but these elements, for the most part, are kept under control by being confined to the battle scenes where they are appropriate.

Lords of the Starship is a novel of concentric plots. What appears to be an extended hoax to revitalize a dying world—the building of an impossibly huge starship, seven miles long by three miles wide—becomes increasingly suspect as the peoples of the world are manipulated by a series of characters who are strikingly similar to one another. When all the nations of the known world have been maneuvered into a final battle among themselves, the Ship's supposedly nonfunctional engines ignite, incinerating the armies and the Ship itself. Simultaneously, incendiary missiles from the near-mythical West destroy the remaining combatants. Ironically, the building of the starship was a hoax after all, a scheme by the West to regain its lost power.

The numerous characters of *Lords of the Starship* represent different stages in the story of the Ship's building, but, with few exceptions, they are not developed as persons. The closest the novel comes to having a central figure is the recurring character who first appears as General Toriman, the original conceiver of the hoax, and even he is little more than a unifying device. The progressive revelation of the plots and the vain struggle against ultimate failure and loss provide the basic story structure in the novel. The success of *Lords of the Starship*, however, lies in the consistency of tone and feeling that tempers mere ingenuity of plotting and makes up for the lack of characterization. One senses, though, that there is a greater depth of feeling than Geston can, at this stage, communicate.

The dominant impression left by *Out of the Mouth of the Dragon* is that of pain. The world of Amon VanRoark is devoted to finding an Armageddon and making a proper end of itself. In accordance with this desire each successive age follows a prophet who calls for the final battle. VanRoark hears *his* prophet, Timonias, and sets out to find the Meadows, the traditional site of Armageddon. He journeys with alcoholics, monomaniacs, consumptives, and lepers to yet another abortive apocalypse. In the rest of the story he oscillates between what he describes as sanity and madness but what progressively seems to the reader to be varying degrees of insanity. After a final, macabre banquet during which the failed, flawed prophet Timonias reveals himself, VanRoark escapes the struggle in an ambiguous denouement:

> He thrust the bayonet deeply into the wet sand
> and retreated.

A wave slid in from the Sea and cut itself upon the metal blade.

VanRoark watched as a darkness spread outward from where the water had touched the bayonet; the surf gradually died and the surface of the ocean became as a sheet of obsidian. . . .

He looked up to notice that the sun had already dimmed perceptibly in its radiance. It was a huge thing, though, and would probably burn on for several more days. . . .

The consistent focus on VanRoark maintains unity, and the portrayal of his progressive derangement is convincing, largely because of the contrast provided by brief periods of near sanity. But the reiteration of horror can be as numbing to the reader as to the sufferer, particularly when intensity defeats clarity, and the point about the futility of effort in such a world has been made long before Timonias's summation. There is, nevertheless, a certain integrity of thought in this work, an intellectual toughness that refuses to allow the absurdities of the world being described to render meaningless and absurd the novel itself.

Thel, the central figure in *The Day Star*, is set apart from the others of his race by his acceptance of the imagination; the others are so terrified of the visible and the invisible worlds that they live in a self-induced narcosis. Thel accepts the ghostly presence of one of his ancestors, a sailor who refuses to admit that he has died, and, guided by a fragment of the Day Star, a time beacon, they journey to Ferrin, the universe's place of ultimate reality, where time moves most slowly. Thel is eventually shipwrecked on his world, to which he returns an old man, almost unable to dream.

Of all of Geston's works, *The Day Star* is the lightest in tone. There is no strain, no self-destructive impulse in Thel's loss; it is simply maturity and simply inevitable. Thel can affirm the imaginative but he is still a child of his fear-ridden world; he is reflective but rather ineffectual. The disparity between Thel and the sailor, Pagent, causes a slight disunity at the end of the novel when Pagent, by far the stronger and more vivid character, is abruptly dropped from the narrative as the focus shifts to Thel and his final voyages.

Geston's earlier works hinted at magic or sorcery. In *The Siege of Wonder* magic becomes one of the poles of the known world, in conflict with the desire for knowledge and the impulse to analyze. In the last days of the conflict between Magic and Science, Aden, an espionage agent, is sent to implant a surveillance device in the eye of a magician's unicorn. Knowledge is the weapon of his race; one can destroy a sorcerer by analyzing his spell. Aden, increasingly sympathetic to magic, races to recapture the eye from the unicorn, but loses to the scientifically oriented Border Command researchers. He kills the unicorn, perhaps at its command, so that there might be at least one last mystery in the world, but he realizes that, ultimately, knowledge will triumph.

Like Amon VanRoark and Thel, Aden seems bewildered and at a loss in his world. He wants to regain the eye because he is dependent on the praetor-human perceptions it provides; he seems incapable of trusting his own instincts or impulses. His helplessness is accentuated by contrast with the ruthlessness of the researcher Etridge, who allows nearly one hundred thousand people to die in an attack by the magicians so that his machines can study the enemy. Geston resolves the rather too simple opposition of science and magic that informs the actual battles of the novel by making Aden more a victim of his own weakness than of the monstrous Etridge.

The Siege of Wonder combines most of the themes and motifs of Geston's early work. There is an apocalypse, but now there is something—the demise of magic—that is lamentable. The earlier novels could not accommodate elegy since there was little worth mourning. If this tale lacks the intensity of some of its predecessors, its subjectivity is more balanced and ironic, and the author's seriousness is given expression beyond rage and despair. One looks forward to the continued development of Geston's literary talent. —*Amelia A. Rutledge*

JAMES E. GUNN
(12 July 1923-   )

BOOKS: *This Fortress World* (New York: Gnome Press, 1955; London: Sphere, 1977);

Star Bridge, by Gunn and Jack Williamson (New York: Gnome Press, 1955; London: Sidgwick & Jackson, 1978);

Station In Space (New York: Bantam, 1958);

The Joy Makers (New York: Bantam, 1961; London: Gollancz, 1963);

The Immortals (New York: Bantam, 1962; St. Albans, U.K.: Panther, 1975);

Future Imperfect (New York: Bantam, 1964);

The Witching Hour (New York: Dell, 1970);

The Immortal (New York: Bantam, 1970);

The Burning (New York: Dell, 1972);

Breaking Point (New York: Walker, 1972);

The Listeners (New York: Scribners, 1972; London: Arrow, 1978);

Some Dreams Are Nightmares (New York: Scribners, 1974);

The End of the Dreams (New York: Scribners, 1975);

Alternate Worlds, The Illustrated History of Science Fiction (Englewood Cliffs, N. J.: Prentice-Hall, 1975);

The Magicians (New York: Scribners, 1976);

Kampus (New York: Bantam, 1977).

James E. Gunn, as editor, critic, and teacher, has done much to introduce science fiction and make it accessible to uninitiated readers. Ultimately, Gunn will prove more important as a commentator on science fiction—as the popularizer of an already popular form within the world of the academy—than as an original contributor to the genre. Ironically, Gunn's own science fiction is seldom innovative and almost always betrays the weaknesses, as well as displays the strengths, of traditional science fiction.

Born in Kansas City, Missouri, James Edwin Gunn grew up with the pulp magazines of the 1930s and 1940s while pursuing a formal education in literature. He received a B.S. in journalism from the University of Kansas in 1947, spent the next year studying theater at Northwestern, returned to Kansas to do graduate work in English literature and completed his M.A. in 1951. His master's thesis was a study of science fiction. During the next few years, Gunn worked as a free-lance writer and sometimes taught. From 1958 to the present, he has steadily offered courses in fiction writing and science fiction at the University of Kansas, where he was made a professor in 1973.

In the early 1950s, Gunn began publishing short stories in such magazines as *Astounding Science-Fiction* and *Amazing Stories*, under the name of Edwin James (an inversion of his own name). Gunn's stories soon began to appear under his real name, however, and one of these, "The Misogynist" (1952; collected in *Future Imperfect*, 1964), provides a surprisingly reliable blueprint to most of his subsequent science fiction. Much anthologized, "The Misogynist" is a clever story utterly dependent on two hallmarks of science fiction—the twist ending and total disregard for characterization. The basic premise of the story is one man's conviction that the traditional lack of communication between men and women, the sense of alienation felt when dealing with the opposite sex, is due to the simple fact that the majority of women are aliens, quietly taking over the human race and replacing the more lovable Earth women. Harry, the prophet of this vision, sets forth his case to the narrator Jim by listing, with haunting completeness, instances of proof drawn from literature of all types and times—the Bible, Greek and Latin mythology, folklore, "Plautus, Clement of Alexandria, Tasso, Shakespeare, Dekker, Fletcher, Thomas Browne—the list is endless." The story concludes after Harry has succumbed to a mysterious heart attack. Jim, now a convert, is called to the basement by his wife. As he descends the steps, he worries, "Why . . . are there more widows than widowers?"

The structure of "The Misogynist"—formulaic both in technique and theme—remains characteristic of Gunn's fiction. The use of literary allusion and a deft ability to reflect and project paranoia also remain characteristic of Gunn's work, as does the short-story form. Though Gunn has written more than a dozen books, all but *Kampus* (1977) are novellas or long short stories linked together. *This Fortress World* (1955), the first of Gunn's published novellas, shows him still mastering the science-fiction formulas of the 1950s.

The story is a fairly engaging adventure tale told from the point of view of Will Dane, an apprentice monk in some future-world monastery dedicated to preserving the knowledge of a now dead (but ready to be resurrected) galactic empire. *This Fortress World* demonstrates Gunn's crisp, unobtrusive, though frequently cliched prose style. The story holds our attention with a series of chase-capture-escape scenes, a bit of soft sex and violence, and an optimistic ending. The most interesting aspect of the novella is Dane's encounter with the dark forces outside the monastery and within himself as he struggles with various ethical dilemmas. Gunn's future-world machinery—a complex technology of mind control—draws attention to the author's true concern: the human psyche.

As Gunn's work developed, his fiction began to emphasize psychology rather than physics or biology. *The Joy Makers* (1961), three linked novellas, contains one of Gunn's best stories, "Name Your Pleasure" (1955), included as "The Hedonist" in his retrospective collection *Some Dreams Are Nightmares* (1974). All three stories in *The Joy Makers* deal with a future world in which total happiness can be reached through the combined advances of psychology and technology. Here Gunn plays adroitly with various dystopian models, leading us to view the ultimate irony of total happiness in the image of a world filled with "womb-rooms" and adult fetuses.

In "The Hedonist," Gunn returns to his use of literary allusion. Each chapter opens with an epigraph chosen from the masterpieces of world literature, all on the pursuit of happiness. The adventure-story model also holds here, as does Gunn's use of sprightly young heroines who have well-rounded bottoms, an ability to rescue protagonists, and a fetching way of collapsing into the hero's arms once he has proven himself. Gunn's strength again rests in his ability to portray through conventional formulas the ethical struggles and psychological torments of modern man. The hedonist of the title is a practitioner of happiness who must fight against the moral corruption of his own profession. His mission is to preserve the benefits of classical hedonism without succumbing to the easy, mechanistic happiness offered by drugs and technology. The sense of paranoia captured by Gunn in most of his work here centers on the fear of science itself, or rather, of man's abuse of science.

The Immortals (1962) varies Gunn's usual distribution of adventure-story formulas and science-fiction themes. (The novel, which had been expanded from a 1958 short story, became the basis for a television movie, "The Immortal," 1969, which inspired a 1970-1971 television series; Gunn in turn novelized the series in *The Immortal*, 1970.) In the original story, science fiction provides only an initiating premise for an adventure story which is actually a moral tale. Protagonist Ben Richards, a race car driver, has mutant blood which makes him on the one hand immortal, but on the other hand a target for an evil, aging billionaire named Braddock, who seeks the fountain of youth. The story is very slim, but the sense of being chased (as well as the dilemma of a blessing which is also a curse) is handled deftly.

While experimenting with science fiction in the 1950s, Gunn also worked with the formulas of fantasy. His stories of witchcraft and magic, however, follow the structural pattern of all his fiction: an adventure-story skeleton is fleshed out with motifs and conventions borrowed from related genres such as the detective story and the Gothic novel. Such is surely the case with the stories found in *The Witching Hour* (1970), particularly in "The Magicians," a short story originally published in 1954 as "Sine of the Magus" and later expanded into a novel, *The Magicians* (1976). Detective Casey attempts to uncover the true identity of an evil magician who calls himself Solomon. Casey's client is a beautiful witch named Ariel (daughter of Prospero, who was murdered by Solomon). The blend of genres is interesting, although Gunn's quick explication of the magic's ultimate basis in mathematics makes for weak science fiction.

The blend of science fiction and fantasy in *The Burning* (1972) is somewhat more successful. The emotional tone of this collection is reminiscent of *The Joy Makers* as the reader enters a future world in which psychologist and metaphysicist John Wilson must pretend to practice witchcraft in a world which has rebelled against technology by burning its temple, the university. As in his earlier work, Gunn conveys the blindness which comes with fear—as

James E. Gunn

```
                AMONG THE BEAUTIFUL BRIGHT CHILDREN

                        by James Gunn


     The beautiful bright children spilled into the room like a

handful of golden coins.

     How long had it been since anyone had held a golden coin, Lau-

rence wondered.  How long had it been since anyone had thought of a

golden coin?  Perhaps only a historian would remember what it was.

     He sat in his study, interrupted at his work, not caring, smiling

benignly at the young men and women as they streamed out of the lift

shaft and filled the sterile room with life and laughter.

     Golden coins spilling from the hand, turning as they fall,

glinting in the light....

     They seemed like actors, an Elizabethan company capering through

Stratford shouting "Players!" or a commedia dell'arte troupe appropri-

ating an Italian square.

     The forgotten console clicked and a new display appeared upon its
```

"Among the Beautiful Bright Children," typescript

well as the fear which stems from blindness. The book is, however, flawed by an excessively blunt didacticism which seems to foreshadow the even more didactic *Kampus*.

In *Kampus* Gunn extrapolates from the student unrest of the 1960s. He offers the reader a world in which professors must literally hawk their specialties at a preregistration carnival, teachers must travel in armored cars, and the university must withstand a student revolution. For a book set in the future, the novel seems oddly dated; the atmosphere that inspired it is no longer typical of American campuses. *Kampus* may serve some cathartic purpose for those who taught in the 1960s, but it hardly compares with Gunn's best work, *The Listeners*, a novella which appeared five years before *Kampus*.

Gunn's best techniques and most interesting themes successfully merge in *The Listeners*. There are six major chapters (most published earlier as short stories) bridged by sections of "Computer run." In the sections of computer run, Gunn's literary allusions and epigraphs become voices from the past, the present, and the near future. The device shows Gunn mastering the relationship of form and content more skillfully than in any of his earlier work.

The story begins in the year 2025, at an installation in Puerto Rico that was established in order to monitor transmissions from the stars—to listen, in effect, for signs of intelligent life. The scientists who have waited fifty years receive their first message in 2027 and debate the wisdom of sending a reply. A reply is sent, and an answer awaited. In 2118 a new generation of listeners receives that answer from a now dead race, from a past made present by the law of physics. Gunn sustains the technological basis of this story carefully, relying on the simplicity of radio technology and extrapolating cautiously from the writings of respected commentators like Carl Sagan and Loren Eisley. Gunn's references to Dante, Goethe, and Cervantes—mixed with references to such 1940s science-fiction masters as Murray Leinster, A. E. van Vogt, Eric Frank Russell, Theodore Sturgeon, and Clifford D. Simak—are neither pretentious nor unwittingly parodic. Instead, all of the voices blend, and the science-fiction writers are shown to be saying what all authors have said about the unknown, but in different language, and often without being heard. Though individual characterization is weak in *The Listeners*, Gunn captures specific or particularizing moments which parallel the personal with the cosmic. He depicts the tension of waiting for news—whether from the stars or from the hospital where a wife lies dying. He speculates on the difficulties of translation—whether of Italian or of galactic talk. He conveys the difficulties of reaching others who are like and not like us—whether an estranged son or an alien race.

The Listeners is noteworthy for its ability to speak without noticeably teaching; it is, however, in the nonmetaphoric classroom that James Gunn has most valuably served writers, readers, and students of science fiction. In the late 1950s and early 1960s, a time before pop culture courses, a time when academicians scoffed at science fiction, Gunn began his own program of enlightenment. He has taught science fiction for over twenty years now as both university professor and critical editor. Finally, Gunn has produced one of the most useful critical tools available to students of science fiction. In *Alternate Worlds, The Illustrated History of Science Fiction* (1975), Gunn has traced science fiction from Plato to the present and beyond, giving the reader sufficient unbiased data to make his own decisions about the true origins, tools, and definitions of science fiction. Moreover, he does so in clear, refreshingly nonacademic prose. The magazine illustrations are well chosen, and Gunn's commentary on the 1940s and 1950s which produced those covers will remain a key to all future research on that crucial period of growth.

Gunn has served as chairman of the John W. Campbell Memorial Award jury and has been president of the Science Fiction Writers of America (1971-1972). He received the Pilgrim Award in 1976 and a special award for *Alternate Worlds* bestowed at the 1976 World Science Fiction Convention. As Gunn's interest in science fiction continues, so does his contribution to literary studies.

　　　　　　　　　　　　　　　　　—*Helen M. Whall*

Other:

Man and the Future, edited by Gunn (Lawrence: University of Kansas Press, 1968);

"On Style," in *Those Who Can: A Science Fiction Reader*, ed. Robin Scott Wilson (New York: Mentor, 1973), pp. 303-312;

"Science Fiction and the Mainstream," in *Science Fiction: Today and Tomorrow*, ed. Reginald Bretnor (New York: Harper & Row, 1974), pp. 183-214;

Nebula Award Stories Ten, edited by Gunn (New York: Harper & Row, 1975; London: Gollancz, 1975);

"Henry Kuttner, C. L. Moore, Lewis Padgett, Lawrence O'Donnell, *et. al.*," in *Voices for the Future*, vol. 1, ed. Thomas D. Clareson (Bowling Green, Ohio: Bowling Green University Popular Press, 1976), pp. 185-215;

"Heroes, Heroines, Villains: The Characters in Science Fiction," in *The Craft of Science Fiction*, ed. Bretnor (New York: Harper & Row, 1976), pp. 161-175;

The Road to Science Fiction, From Gilgamesh to Wells, Volume I, edited by Gunn (New York: New American Library, 1977);

The Road to Science Fiction, From Wells to Heinlein, Volume II, edited by Gunn (New York: Mentor, 1979);

The Road to Science Fiction, From Heinlein to Here, Volume III, edited by Gunn (New York: Mentor, 1979).

Periodical Publications:

"Teaching Science Fiction Revisited," *Analog, Science Fiction/Science Fact*, 94 (November 1974): 5-10, 175-178;

"Teaching Science Fiction," *Publishers Weekly*, 209 (June 1976): 62-63.

Reference:

Darrell Schweitzer, "James Gunn," in his *SF Voices*, (Baltimore: T-K Graphics,1976).

JOE HALDEMAN
(9 June 1943-   )

SELECTED BOOKS: *War Year* (New York: Holt, Rinehart & Winston, 1972);

The Forever War (New York: St. Martin's, 1974; London: Weidenfeld & Nicolson, 1975);

Attar's Revenge, as Robert Graham (New York: Pocket Books, 1975); as Haldeman (London: New English Library, 1977);

War of Nerves, as Robert Graham (New York: Pocket Books, 1975);

Mindbridge (New York: St. Martin's, 1976; London: Macdonald & Jane's, 1977);

All My Sins Remembered (New York: St. Martin's, 1977; London: Macdonald & Jane's, 1978);

Planet of Judgment (New York: Bantam, 1977; London: Corgi, 1977);

Infinite Dreams (New York: St. Martin's, 1978);

World Without End (New York: Bantam, 1979).

Joe W. Haldeman, born in Oklahoma City, Oklahoma, was raised in and around Washington, D.C., where his father was an administrator for military health programs. After high school, he obtained an M.A. in English and a B.S. in astronomy at Iowa State, and spent three months at postgraduate studies in computer sciences at the University of Maryland. In the U. S. Army from 1967 through 1969, he served for a year in the central highlands of Vietnam as a combat engineer, an experience that cost him a serious leg wound which resulted from "having stood too close to a boobytrap when a booby set it off." The wound caused him to undergo four months of painful therapy.

Having sold a few stories sporadically, Haldeman became convinced at one of Damon Knight's Milford Conferences in the early 1970s that he could make a career from his writing. Under his new resolve, his first sale was to Knight himself, who included a short story called "Counterpoint" in his anthology, *Orbit II* (1972). "Counterpoint" (collected in *Infinite Dreams*, 1978) is an offbeat and disturbing tale concerning two brothers who are psychically linked but do not even know of each other's existence. Michael, a legitimate son, and Roger, a bastard orphan, lead contrasting lives each ignorant of the other until a fateful encounter on the battlefields of Vietnam. The story is written in straight narrative prose without benefit of dialogue and establishes an important and recurrent motif in Haldeman's work: Vietnam.

The theme of the folly of war is the basis for his first novel, *War Year* (1972), in which Haldeman—drawing from his own wartime diary—follows Private John Farmer through a year of hell in Vietnam. But the demon of Vietnam was not exorcised from Haldeman's soul by writing this novel, and frontline combat became the subject of his first science-fiction novel, *The Forever War* (1974). At the outset, it is similar to *War Year*, as the reader is plunged into the midst of a war that is already raging, among characters who take their situation for granted: it is 1997 and Earth is at war with a race known as the Taurans. But Earth's armed forces are completely unlike those of today; an interstellar strike force is composed of men and women of all Earthly nations. Sexual escapades between soldiers are common, and marijuana is not only legal but commonplace. To make possible the interplanetary war, Haldeman invents the "collapsar jump," by which a spacecraft is catapulted into a black hole and reappears somewhere else in space.

The main character, who relates the story in the first person (as does Farmer in *War Year*), describes how the first extraterrestrial encounter results in Earth's gearing for total war. William Mandella is inducted into "the most elitely conscripted army in the history of warfare." After basic training in the "fighting suit," an astronautical suit of armor bristling with weapons, Mandella's platoon is ordered into enemy territory to take a Tauran captive, but in the process they ignorantly ambush and slaughter an innocent band of natives. Guilt invades Mandella's mind, as well as the mind of a fellow soldier, Marygay Potter (the maiden name of Haldeman's wife). The first Tauran encounter is a massacre of the creatures, committed by Mandella and his comrades in the throes of a posthypnotic order to kill. The guilt caused by the massacre is an added dimension not present in Haldeman's previous novel and is one reason why the characters of *The Forever War* are more fully rounded as individuals, hence more believable in their dramatic functions.

As Mandella is shuttled from planet to planet to continue the bloody campaign, he is hit with a unique cruelty of war in the space age: as he travels across the galaxy and beyond he ages only months, while decades pass on Earth. The implications of this are muted for him when Marygay suffers grisly wounds after a Tauran attack on their spaceship. Mandella reluctantly admits to himself that he loves her, an incongruous realization in the midst of the emotional harshness of war. They return to an Earth twenty-six years older, while they have aged barely two. The culture shock is disconcerting: six billion out of nine billion are unemployed; one third of

Joe Haldeman

Earth's population is homosexual; and private property is outlawed. He and Marygay rejoin the army and are immediately shipped back into combat. Assigned to different companies, they realize that the difference in respective collapsar jumps could mean a difference of decades in their respective ages should they ever, by chance, meet again. It is here that Haldeman's strongest indictment of war is made. In the awful realization that after separation from friends and family, after the horror and guilt of combat and the pain of injury, the most terrifying aspect of war is that the high command considers its soldiers expendable. While Mandella fights for several hundred more years, the human race evolves into a group of telepathic clones, individual units of a mass mind—the precise nature of the Taurans. The species finally make peace with each other, and Mandella is reunited with Marygay. The theme of quiet resentment felt by those waging war, however, is never overshadowed by individual episodes, as detailed and powerful as they might be. The novel won both the Hugo and Nebula awards as best novel of 1974.

Haldeman's next novel, *Mindbridge* (1976), moves beyond the obsessive rendering of frontline combat to delve more deeply into the meaning of war not only as a historical force, but as a specific concern in the arena of extraterrestrial contact. Nonetheless, some plot devices are taken from *The Forever War*, especially the image of a platoon of soldiers traveling from world to world to make the galaxy safe for democracy. The fighting suit is also carried over, with some refinements and a rather more in-depth description of "suiting up." As a method of space travel, Haldeman discards the collapsar jump and creates the "Levant-Meyer Translation," a somewhat limited and dangerous form of teleportation. The two central characters, Jaque Lefavre and Carol Wachal, are so similar in disposition and idiom to their predecessors, Mandella and Marygay, that they might as well be the same people. They are "Tamers" who are beamed to other worlds to determine colonial suitability. On a planet called Groombridge they discover a black, urchinlike creature that, when touched, passes on its telepathic abilities to whoever is in contact. On Earth, Jaque and Carol use the mindbridge for sexual experimentation, each delving into the other's psyche during intercourse.

It is this experimentation that enables Jaque to become an interpreter between his own people and a belligerent race of telepaths known as the L'vrai. These bloodthirsty beings are like the Taurans of *The Forever War* in that they are components of one huge organism. It is not only Jaque's skill with the mindbridge that enables him to become peacemaker with the L'vrai, but as one of the aliens comments, Jaque has "brought the animal part of his nature into harmony with . . . the angel part." The hesitation, indicated by the elipsis, over the term "angel" is not accidental; it signals the alien's groping for a human word to describe higher thought processes without recourse to theological terminology, with its automatic connotations of good and evil and life after death. Creatures with no belief in individuality would have no inclination to believe in personal survival after death. Yet the novel vindicates human individuality in its final, touching episode. Unlike *The Forever War*, Haldeman lets the lyricism, terror, and sometimes humor of individual episodes get the better of the book's several themes. It is interestingly presented, however, as there is no pattern to succeeding chapters; one may be a first-person narrative by Jaque, another an omniscient treatment of his past, and another an "excerpt" from a future college textbook.

All My Sins Remembered (1977) is written more traditionally and returns to the theme of guilt, as experienced by Otto McGavin. Otto is one of twelve "prime operators," futuristic spies ordered about what seems to be a predominantly Spanish-speaking galaxy to ensure the upkeep of the unifying Charter of Confederación. The book is composed of three of Otto's adventures, related as he journeys from planet to planet encased in plastiflesh countenances of different persons. Haldeman creates three fascinating worlds to visit: Bruuch, inhabited by slightly daft anthropoids whose reverence for death borders only slightly this side of necrophilia; Selva, where Spanish colonists have instituted a society based on machismo; and Cinder, which houses some of the most engaging aliens in science fiction, the S'kang, an immortal race of giant beetles whose specialties are planetary telekinesis and sarcasm. In between these adventures are brief Earthside chapters concerning Otto's hypnotherapy to cure the guilt complex which results from the forty-odd assassinations he commits throughout the novel. But Otto cannot recover from his ordeal on Cinder, where his machinations seal the doom of the peaceful S'kang, and so he is disposed of by his own secret agency. Although the novel suffers, like *War Year*, in its lack of characterization, it is satisfying both for its adventure and its theme.

Haldeman's only other two novels as of this writing, *Planet of Judgment* (1977) and *World Without End* (1979), are both derived from the NBC television series "Star Trek." In the former, the series' heroes, Captain Kirk, Dr. McCoy, and Mr. Spock, work with a race of telepaths to forestall an invasion of their section of the galaxy by the treacherous Irapina, a sanguinary people reminiscent of Haldeman's own L'vrai. It is a work worthy of note by virtue of the fact that in it a Hugo and Nebula award winner is writing for the most popular form of science fiction yet to appear; at the same time, it is far more disjointed than most of Haldeman's work and more so than most of the television episodes. *Planet of Judgment* is enjoyable for the strange visions Haldeman conjures, for his dialogue for Spock, and for the telepathic race's interpretation of those people limited to just five senses, but overall there seems to be no strong underlying thematic structure.

World Without End holds up somewhat better on its own merits, though it begins with an incident straight from a "Star Trek" episode ("For the World is Hollow and I Have Touched the Sky"), in which the *Enterprise* encounters a planet-sized spaceship on an eons-long journey. Inside the hollow sphere, Kirk and his landing party are captured by the inhabitants, the Chatalia, who are ignorant of the nature of their world. Unfortunately Haldeman introduces too many cliched situations from the series: Kirk's unlikely helplessness in the face of a less sophisticated civilization, the peril of the U.S.S. *Enterprise*, the forecasts of doom by engineer Montgomery Scott, and a starship full of dastardly Klingons.

In addition to these novels, Joe Haldeman has authored several adventure stories under the pseudonym Robert Graham, and under his own name published a collection of his short stories, *Infinite Dreams* (1978); the latter includes "Tricentennial," winner of the Hugo Award for best short story of 1977. He has edited several anthologies, the best known of which is *Study War No More* (1977).

While all of his work is enjoyable, ranging as it does from the horrors of combat to some of the best humor in recent science fiction, his standing in current literature has been harmed somewhat by his preoccupation with the single theme of war. Haldeman exercises his literary license to comment on, and ultimately to expunge from his memory, America's last ground war; yet he does it so well that his self-indulgence should be excused. A unifying thread in his study of belligerent alien cultures is the concept of many individuals combining to create one mass mind, evident in his combatants from the Taurans of *The Forever War* to the Chatalia of *World Without End*. And in the introduction to *Study War No More* he proffers, with bitter irony, their modes of life and consciousness as a solution to the problem of human aggression. People can, he says, "concentrate on survival, though it may mean giving up our precious individual freedom, or illusion of freedom: have our genes manipulated; grow up in Skinner boxes, automatic lobotomy the penalty for any sign of aggression. A race of cloned cowards, of soft passive hedonists. Consider the alternative."

Haldeman confronts his reader with painful questions, but he asks them with no small literary skill and with careful attention to scientific credibility. His futuristic hardware is always conceived with an eye not only to its sensational features, but also to its dangers and discomforts: his "fighting suit" is a claustrophobic incarceration that must be endured for weeks at a time, and his teleportation technique requires precise registration in sending and receiving, lest a subject materialize missing a part of his anatomy. The reader must pass these ordeals with Haldeman's characters if he would experience his work fully. —*James Scott Hicks*

Other:

Cosmic Laughter, edited by Haldeman (New York: Holt, Rinehart & Winston, 1974);

Study War No More, edited by Haldeman (New York: St. Martin's, 1977).

References:

Eric March, "Joe Haldeman and the SF Alternative," *Starlog*, no. 17 (1978): 45-47;

Patrick McGuire, "Variants: Joe Haldeman's SF Novels," *Algol*, 14 (Summer-Fall 1977): 19-20;

Darrell Schweitzer, "An Interview with Joe Haldeman," *Science Fiction Review*, 6 (February 1977): 26-30.

EDMOND HAMILTON

(21 October 1904-1 February 1977)

BOOKS: *The Horror on the Asteroid and Other Tales of Planetary Horror* (London: Allan, 1936);

A Yank at Valhalla (New York: Ace, 1940); republished as *The Monsters of Juntonheim* (Manchester, U.K.: S. Pemberton, 1950);

Quest Beyond the Stars (New York: Popular Library, 1941);

Outlaws of the Moon (New York: Popular Library, 1942);

The Comet Kings (New York: Popular Library, 1942);

Planets in Peril (New York: Popular Library, 1942);

The Tenth Planet, as Brett Sterling (New York: Popular Library, 1944);

Outlaw World (New York: Popular Library, 1945);

Tiger Girl (London: Utopian, 1945);

Murder in the Clinic (London: Utopian, 1946);

The Star Kings (New York: Fell, 1949; London: Museum Press, 1951); republished as *Beyond the Moon* (New York: Signet, 1950);

Tharkol, Lord of the Unknown (Manchester, U.K.: S. Pemberton, 1950);

City at World's End (New York: Fell, 1951; London: Museum Press, 1951);

The Sun Smasher (New York: Ace, 1959);

The Star of Life (New York: Dodd, Mead, 1959);

The Haunted Stars (New York: Dodd, Mead, 1960; London: Jenkins, 1965);

Battle for the Stars (New York: Dodd, Mead, 1961; London: Mayflower, 1963);

Outside the Universe (New York: Ace, 1964);

The Valley of Creation (New York: Lancer, 1964);

Crashing Suns (New York: Ace, 1965);

Fugitive of the Stars (New York: Ace, 1965);

Doomstar (New York: Belmont Books, 1966);

The Weapon from Beyond (New York: Ace, 1967);

Calling Captain Future (New York: Popular Library, 1967);

Captain Future's Challenge (New York: Popular Library, 1967);

Galaxy Mission (New York: Popular Library, 1967);

Captain Future and the Space Emperor (New York: Popular Library, 1967);

The Magician of Mars (New York: Popular Library, 1968);

The Closed Worlds (New York: Ace, 1968);

World of the Starwolves (New York: Ace, 1968);

Danger Planet, as Brett Sterling (New York: Popular Library, 1968);

Return to the Stars (New York: Lancer, 1969);

What's It Like Out There? (New York: Ace, 1974);

The Best of Edmond Hamilton, ed. Leigh Brackett (Garden City: Doubleday, 1977).

Edmond Hamilton

Edmond Hamilton was one of the pioneers of science fiction, publishing his first short story in 1926. He was one of the major creators of the myth of the future galactic empire in his series of stories on the Interstellar Patrol. His works were slanted for the pulp magazines and were often repetitious in theme; however, he was always innovative and helped expand the imaginative range of readers, other writers, and editors. His work in the 1930s and 1940s was mostly space opera, earning him the title of "World-Saver" Hamilton. But his works were of sufficient importance to entitle him to be the first writer of science-fiction pulp to have a collection issued in hardcover, *The Horror on the Asteroid* (1936). In later years, this prolific storyteller slowed his production and created more careful and polished fiction. Unfortunately, his quality work is often overlooked while his Captain Future stories are remembered. He wrote 24 of the 27 Captain Future stories, which appeared in the magazines *Captain Future* and *Startling Stories* from 1940 to 1951, and 12 Captain Future stories were finally published as novels in 1967. In addition, Hamilton wrote 33 books and more than 140 short stories under his own name and under the pseudonyms Robert Castle, Hugh Davidson, Will Garth, Brett Sterling, and Robert Wentworth.

Edmond Moore Hamilton was born in Youngstown, Ohio. Something of a prodigy, he entered Westminster College in Pennsylvania in 1919. He majored in physics, but his attention was soon diverted from his studies by the magazine fiction he read. He left college during his third year when he was expelled for cutting chapel. Hamilton worked as a yard clerk on the Pennsylvania Railroad until 1924, for he loved railroads. When the railroad eliminated his job, he turned to writing. His first short story was published in *Weird Tales* in August 1926. He remained a writer with rather antiacademic feelings for the rest of his life. In 1932, he began to contribute detective fiction to Street and Smith's *Detective Story* magazine; this association continued throughout the thirties. In 1940, through his friend Jack Williamson and his manager Julius Schwartz, he met Leigh Brackett, a fledgling science-fiction writer who later became a scenario writer for movies and television. They were married on 31 December 1946, settling in Kinsman, Ohio, and later established a second home in Lancaster, California, where Hamilton died 1 February 1977.

A world traveler and an excellent amateur photographer, Hamilton was particularly fond of England. He was also a voracious reader with broad

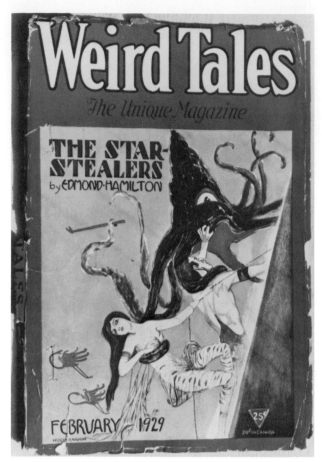

Weird Tales, *February 1929 cover*

cultural interests, and his library included books on subjects as wide ranging as Chinese and Indian music, Near Eastern architecture, and Iranian and Spanish biography. Many of these interests in foreign places and ancient times found their way into his writing, which is terse and vivid. Avoiding cumbersome and pretentious adjectives and poetic diction, his prose is stark, brutal, and convincing—true, in other words, to the tradition of lean writing he helped to found. But his greatest contribution to science fiction lay in the originality he brought to it, particularly in his short stories, though the framework of each story was nearly the same during those early years: a conqueror threatens to destroy or enslave the earth—or the whole universe—and is thwarted by a single man, moving through a maze of major scientific faults so glaring as virtually to negate credibility.

His first book, *The Horror on the Asteroid*, was a collection of six short stories representative of his early fiction: "The Horror on the Asteroid" (1936); "The Accursed Galaxy" (1935); "The Man Who Saw

Everything'' (1936); "The Earth Brain" (1932); "The Monster-God of Mamurth" (1926); and "The Man Who Evolved" (1931). "The Monster-God of Mamurth," his first published story, tells of an explorer who discovers a hidden legendary city in a North African desert. In exploring this long deserted city he encounters the ancient giant spider which has long been the local divinity. Both the spider and its temple are invisible, but in an exciting and vivid scene the hero destroys the spider by crushing it with a huge, invisible building block. Another representative tale is "The Man Who Evolved." It is the best of his several stories dealing with evolution. Here a machine increases the rapidity of change, and a mad scientist transforms himself into a tremendous brain which feeds itself on pure energy. Insatiable for knowledge, the brain drives itself on to the ultimate form, which is protoplasm: evolution is circular. "The Earth Brain" is about a man who tracks the intelligence center of the Earth to the North Pole. He violates it by discovering the brain's location and secret and is forced to wander the Earth the rest of his life as the brain tears the Earth apart searching for him.

His novels contain many of the same limitations that characterize his short fiction. Popular but unconvincing, *The Star Kings* (1949), his best-known novel, tells of the adventure of a man flung across time and space into a perilous whirl of intrigue and conflict between galaxies, some two thousand centuries in the future. Though even less convincing, *City at World's End* (1951) was also well received. This time a whole midwestern city is blasted by a superbomb into a future so remote that the sun has become a flickering red disc. The city, the only survivor of a dying Earth, must fight to remain alive. *The Sun Smasher* (1959) was not as well received. It deals with a young book salesman who has inherited a bewildering stellar empire and is further troubled by his knowledge of an omnipotent weapon. Three of Hamilton's novels were selected by Doubleday as Science-Fiction-Book-Club selections: *The Star of Life* (1959), *The Haunted Stars* (1960), and *Battle for the Stars* (1961). The first is probably the best; it concerns a man frozen in space, who is revived after many years to find himself in the midst of a struggle between two mutant races of humanity.

Other notable novels include *The Valley of Creation* (1964), in which mercenaries in telepathic partnership with animals fight a common enemy, and *The Weapon from Beyond* (1967), the first of the Starwolf series, in which the hero Morgan Chane was raised by humanoids on a world dedicated to piracy and cast out to find his place in interstellar society. *What's It Like Out There?* (1974), which contains some of Hamilton's best writing, is a terse and realistic tale of space exploration in which the author describes space pioneering as cruel and deadly.

The Best of Edmond Hamilton (1977) includes his and Leigh Brackett's selection of twenty-one of his best short stories beginning with "The Monster-God of Mamurth" and ending with "Castaway" (1968), forty-two years apart. The book is introduced by Brackett with an excellent and sensitive essay, "Fifty Years of Wonder." Hamilton himself provides an afterword in which he pays homage to his early inspirations: Robert Louis Stevenson, A. Merritt, and Homer Eon Flint. Hamilton's conclusion is simple, personal, and typical of the man: "Looking back upon the older of these stories, I feel that they were written by a different person. The thin, dark, wiry young Hamilton of those days seems a bit of a stranger to me, now. *He* could pound all day on the typewriter, eagerly setting down the feverish visions that filled his head—visions of wonders to come, of great dooms sweeping upon the hapless Earth, of strange and usually ominous forms of life undreamed of now, of the vast grandeur of things to come when the starry universe would be webbed by the fleets of man. I believe that that enthusiasm was what sparked me in all that work, for certainly the monetary rewards from the magazines of those days was not much incentive.

"I think it was George Gissing who, recalling his youthful days of writing, said that, 'On the whole, I approve of that eager, intense young man.' And, in my own case, on the whole, I do too."

—*Gerald M. Garmon*

References:

Joseph Kankowski, "Fiction by Edmond Hamilton," *Xenophile*, no. 30 (1977): 14-15;

Sam Moskowitz, *Seekers of Tomorrow: Masters of Modern Science Fiction* (Cleveland: World, 1966), pp. 66-83.

Papers:

Eastern New Mexico University has the manuscripts of most of Hamilton's works.

CHARLES L. HARNESS
(29 December 1915-   )

BOOKS: *Flight Into Yesterday* (New York: Bouregy & Curl, 1953); republished as *The Paradox Men* (New York: Ace, 1955; London: Faber & Faber, 1964);

The Rose (London: Compact, 1966; New York: Berkley, 1966);

The Ring of Ritornel (New York: Berkley, 1968; London: Gollancz, 1968);

Wolfhead (New York: Berkley, 1978);

The Catalyst (New York: Pocket Books, 1980).

Charles Leonard Harness, patent lawyer and science-fiction writer, is the son of Conrad T. and Lillian B. Harness. Born in Colorado City, Texas, he was educated at George Washington University, where he took a B.S. in 1942 and an LL.B. in 1946. He and his wife, Nell, whom he married 27 July 1938, have two children, Mollie and Charles. His career as a science-fiction writer has been somewhat sporadic. His first published story, "Time Trap," appeared in the August 1948 *Astounding Science-Fiction*. The following year saw the publication of his first novel, *Flight Into Yesterday*, in the May 1949 *Startling Stories*; later expanded, it was his first book publication in 1953. Harness quickly established a reputation among editors and fellow writers for his competent prose; he has been praised by such writers as Arthur C. Clarke and Brian Aldiss. But after the publication of *The Rose* (*Authentic Science Fiction*, March 1953), he stopped writing to spend more time with his children. Although *The Rose* appeared in book form in 1966, Harness published nothing new from 1953 until 1968, the year that his third novel, *The Ring of Ritornel*, appeared. His readers waited yet another ten years for his next book, *Wolfhead* (1978).

His short stories are mainly notable for their similar motifs and themes, but it is chiefly through his novels that he develops these themes to their full potential. Harness deals with serious matters: religion, death, birth, tragedy, metaphysics, art, and science. The themes of evolution and of cyclical recurrence (manifested in the imagery of burial and rebirth) figure in all of his novels. His work is sprinkled through with allusions to classical works of literature, art, and music. Thus, while it is entertaining in its fast action, Harness's fiction is primarily distinguished by its intellectual content. As Michael Moorcock notes in his introduction to *The Rose*, "A closer look shows nuances and throw-away ideas revealing a serious mind operating at a much deeper and broader level than its contemporaries. . . ."

While Harness has been criticized for the melodrama of his work, other aspects are more disturbing. There is at times a certain ponderousness in the devices he uses to bring in scientific explanations, an ever present problem for science-fiction writers; he also has a tendency at important breaks in the action to leave gaps in the descriptions of that action. Despite these flaws, Harness is normally a very careful craftsman. His plots are intricately constructed, but complete and detailed. His science is consistently accurate, and his explanations of art, science, and philosophy are clear and interesting even when they do not fit smoothly into the story line.

His first novel, *Flight Into Yesterday* (1953), is an engrossing tale of action, intrigue, and time-travel paradoxes. In a decadent America on the brink of collapse, slavery has become widespread, governmental power absolute, and the only surviving "moral force" is the Society of Thieves that robs from the rich to ransom poor slaves. This is the background for the personal conflict between the Chancellor, Haze-Gaunt, and Alar, the man he has been told that he must kill to carry out his plans for international domination. Alar is an amnesiac and a member of the Thieves. The novel traces Alar's attempt to discover his own identity while escaping the murderous wrath of Haze-Gaunt and his henchmen, Thurmond and Shey. The name Kennicot Muir weaves in and out of the dialogue as the mysterious founder of the Society of Thieves and former husband of Keiris, wife-slave of Haze-Gaunt. She is a spy for the Thieves who helps Alar, only to be mutilated for her trouble at the hands of Shey. As Alar is chased across the solar system he discovers unknown talents in himself that indicate he is the next step in man's evolutionary ladder: he is the only hope for saving civilization through his ability to move backward through time.

The Rose (1966) continues the theme of man's evolution. Probably Harness's best work, this rather short novel was well received when it first appeared in *Authentic Science Fiction* magazine in March 1953. The author deals with the conflict between art and science and asserts some imaginative options for the next step in man's evolution. The theme of rebirth is more beautifully delineated here than in any of his other work. *The Rose* is a story of two people, Anna van Tuyl and Ruy Jacques, who are deformed and ugly from the same unknown disease. Anna is a psychiatrist who has written a ballet, *Nightingale and the Rose*. The ballet is to be performed by her patient, the bohemian artist Ruy Jacques. His insanely jealous wife, Martha, is a scientist working on a mathematical formula which will unify science and eliminate art. The novel's discussions of the primacy of art over science are heady, but clear and interesting. Through a confrontation between Anna and Martha, Anna's condition is revealed to be not a disease but the outward effect of a metamorphosis: she is becoming a new kind of human. The eventual triumph of her art over Martha's science is the harbinger of a renaissance for both art and science.

In *The Ring of Ritornel* (1968) Harness returns—though with less control—to the complex plotting of his first novel. The major character is James Andrek, a minor legal counselor for the ruling house of one of twelve galaxies. In his search for his missing brother, Omere (the poet laureate whose mind has been locked away in the state's computer-poet), Andrek becomes entangled in the conflict between the two religions that dominate the galaxies. Alea, the religion of chance, is symbolized by a twelve-sided die. Ritornel, the religion of cycles and returning, is symbolized by a ring. Many of the elements of the story are mythic in nature. The theme of rebirth is interestingly executed, and the complicated plot drives powerfully to the indeterminate conclusion: the concealed outcome of a final toss of the Alean die which might prove one or the other of the religions to be true. Although the novel is entertaining, the problem of breaks in the action is severe, and some of the passages are heavily melodramatic. Harness also falters in his normally scrupulous handling of scientific detail, but certain liberties are justified when the object is not mere extrapolation but the creation of myth.

Most of Harness's characteristic themes and motifs are found in his latest work, *Wolfhead* (1978), but they are not handled with the same competence that marked his earliest stories. Jeremy Wolfhead is the only real character in the novel. His wife Beatra is stolen during their honeymoon and carried underground into a corrupt, hidden society, heretofore known only in myths. The "Undergrounders" have nearly killed Jeremy while in the process of stealing his wife, and he is healed by monks who teach him telepathy and telekinesis. With these paltry skills and a telepathically linked wolf that can see in the dark, Jeremy goes underground after his wife and spoils an Undergrounder plot to dominate the surface world he has left, destroying them in the process.

Charles Harness has been little appreciated in this country save by his colleagues, who see his underlying skill and depth. Although his recent work has not been up to his original promise, it seems possible that he will find his stride and once again produce fiction of the quality of *The Rose*.

—*Charles L. Wentworth*

Reference:

Norman L. Hills, "Charles L. Harness: The Flowering of Melodrama," *Extrapolation*, 19 (May 1978): 141-148.

HARRY HARRISON
(12 March 1925-   )

BOOKS: *Deathworld* (New York: Bantam, 1960; London: Spire, 1973);

The Stainless Steel Rat (New York: Pyramid, 1961; London: Sphere, 1973);

Planet of the Damned (New York: Bantam, 1962); republished as *Sense of Obligation* (London: Dobson, 1967);

War with the Robots (New York: Pyramid, 1962; London: Dobson, 1967);

Deathworld 2 (Toronto, New York & London: Bantam, 1964); republished as *The Ethical Engineer* (London: Gollancz, 1964);

Plague from Space (Garden City: Doubleday, 1965; London: Gollancz, 1966); republished as *The Jupiter Legacy* (Toronto, New York & London: Bantam, 1970);

Bill, the Galactic Hero (Garden City: Doubleday, 1965; London: Gollancz, 1965);

Two Tales and 8 Tomorrows (London: Gollancz, 1965; New York: Bantam, 1968);

Make Room! Make Room! (Garden City: Doubleday, 1966; Harmondsworth, U. K.: Penguin, 1967);

The Technicolor Time Machine (Garden City: Doubleday, 1967; London: Faber & Faber, 1968);

The Man from P.I.G. (New York: Avon, 1968); republished as *The Man from P.I.G. and R.O.B.O.T.* (London: Faber & Faber, 1974; New York: Atheneum, 1978);

Deathworld 3 (New York: Dell, 1968; London: Faber & Faber, 1969);

Captive Universe (New York: Putnam's, 1969; London: Faber & Faber, 1970);

The Daleth Effect (New York: Putnam's, 1970); republished as *In Our Hands, the Stars* (London: Faber & Faber, 1970);

Spaceship Medic (Garden City: Doubleday, 1970; London: Faber & Faber, 1970);

One Step from Earth (New York: Macmillan, 1970; London: Faber & Faber, 1972);

Prime Number (New York: Berkley, 1970; London: Sphere, 1978);

The Stainless Steel Rat's Revenge (New York: Walker, 1970; London: Faber & Faber, 1971);

Montezuma's Revenge (Garden City: Doubleday, 1972);

Tunnel Through the Deeps (New York: Putnam's, 1972); republished as *A Transatlantic Tunnel, Hurrah!* (London: Faber & Faber, 1972);

Stonehenge, by Harrison and Leon E. Stover (New York: Scribners, 1972; London: Davies, 1972);

The Stainless Steel Rat Saves the World (New York: Putnam's, 1972; London: Sphere, 1973);

Star Smashers of the Galaxy Rangers (New York: Putnam's, 1973; London: Faber & Faber, 1975);

Queen Victoria's Revenge (Garden City: Doubleday, 1974; London: Severn House, 1977);

The California Iceberg (New York: Walker, 1975; London: Faber & Faber, 1975);

The Best of Harry Harrison (New York: Pocket Books, 1976; London: Sidgwick & Jackson, 1976);

Skyfall (London: Faber & Faber, 1976; New York: Atheneum, 1977);

The Lifeship, by Harrison and Gordon R. Dickson (New York, Hagerstown, San Francisco & London: Harper & Row, 1976); republished as *Lifeboat* (London: Futura, 1978);

Great Balls of Fire: History of Sex in Science Fiction (New York: Grossett, 1977; London: Pierrot, 1978);

Mechanismo: An Illustrated Manual of Science Fiction Hardware (London: Pierrot, 1978; Danby, N.H.: Reed Books, 1979);

The Stainless Steel Rat Wants You! (London: Joseph, 1978; New York: Bantam, 1979);

Planet Story, by Harrison and Jim Barnes (New York: A & W, 1979);

Spacecraft in Fact and Fiction, by Harrison and Malcolm Edwards (New York: Exeter Books, 1979).

Harry Max Harrison was born in Stamford, Connecticut, and grew up in New York City. After serving in the army from 1943 to 1946, he began a career as a commercial artist and editor. During the 1950s he was the editor of several magazines at various times, including *Science Fiction Adventures, Fantasy Fiction, Impulse, Amazing Stories,* and *Fantastic.* His first story, "Rock Diver," appeared in *Worlds Beyond* in February 1951, but he did not have work published regularly until the late 1950s. Finding New York increasingly unattractive, he moved his family, by way of Mexico, England, and Europe, to Ireland, where he now resides. His more than thirty books offer action, technological wonders, and various degrees of violence.

Harrison's first novel, *Deathworld* (1960), begins a trilogy dealing with Jason dinAlt, a gambler, and the natives of the planet Pyrrhus, where the flora and fauna are rendered increasingly deadly by their psychic sensitivity to human animosities. Jason convinces the Pyrrhan leaders, including the beautiful Meta, to end their losing battle and leave the planet. In *Deathworld 2* (1964) dinAlt is subjected to arrest by the ethically inflexible Mikah Samon, whose rigid principles endanger their survival on the primitive planet where they crash. Jason is rescued by Meta, who will survive ethically if possible but efficiently when necessary. *Deathworld 3* (1968) concerns dinAlt and the Pyrrhans's travels to Felicity, a planet controlled by barbarian hordes whose ruler, Temuchin, conquers the world, winning a costly victory as his former wild, free life vanishes. All three books are science-fiction escape classics; their themes of the futility, the necessity, and the limitations of violence are somewhat muted by sensationalistic treatment.

Harrison's second novel, *The Stainless Steel Rat* (1961), is the first book of another adventure series. The character James Bolivar diGriz lives for adventure and freedom in a controlled, orderly world until he is trapped and convinced to join the Special Corps to combat "sick criminals" who kill. Slippery Jim's first antagonist is the beautiful but deadly Angelina, who is caught, treated, and converted. *The Stainless Steel Rat's Revenge* (1970) depicts diGriz, now married to Angelina, as a spy sent to defeat a militaristic criminal world; he has to be aided by Angelina, who kills now only in defense of self or family. In *The Stainless Steel Rat Saves the World* (1972), diGriz is sent back into time to defeat He, a megalomaniac out to destroy the future. Again the aid of Angelina is required. The Stainless Steel Rat books, like the Deathworld trilogy, depict strong women. The men, however, are stronger, and if might does not make right, it at least produces survivors; the women live for their strong, smart men, the masters of technology. The books are exciting and can be believed if one wants to.

Altogether too believable is *Make Room! Make Room!* (1966), later adapted as the film *Soylent Green* (1973). The protagonist is Andrew Rausch, policeman in the overpopulated New York City of 1999. He experiences the horrors of metropolitan life in the future: a diet of seaweed crackers, insoluble crimes, riots in the streets, food and water shortages, needless disease and death made worse by insufficient hospital space, and the final loss of meaningful human relationships. This is perhaps the most troubling book ever written about population problems. Overpopulation is resolved by drastic methods in *Captive Universe* (1969). The title refers to a terraformed hollow asteroid starship, the population of which is well controlled by genetic engineering and by intentionally high mortality enforced by religious law. The system, which includes human sacrifice, is broken by Chimal who is able to understand what the others can do only by rote and according to rite. The programming of humans through technology or through religion is evil; the point is made, but not at the expense of violent action.

Harry Harrison is also noted as an editor and anthologist, often in collaboration with Brian W. Aldiss. Their annual *Best SF* anthology appeared from 1967 to 1975. Harrison's own fiction continues to supply imaginative escape from the restrictions of civilization—restrictions which science, once a liberator, seems ready to further. These themes have

been, and no doubt will continue to be, the central concerns of Harrison's work. —*Robert L. Jones*

Other:

Nebula Award Stories Two, edited by Harrison and Brian W. Aldiss (Garden City: Doubleday, 1967; London: Gollancz, 1967);

SF: Authors' Choice, edited by Harrison (New York: Berkley, 1968); republished as *Backdrop of Stars* (London: Dobson, 1968);

Apeman, Spaceman, edited by Harrison and Leon E. Stover (Garden City: Doubleday, 1968; London: Rapp & Whiting, 1968);

Farewell, Fantastic Venus! edited by Harrison and Aldiss (London: Macdonald, 1968);

Best SF: 1967, edited by Harrison and Aldiss (New York: Berkley, 1968); republished as *The Year's Best Science Fiction No. 1* (London: Sphere, 1968);

Blast Off: S. F. for Boys, edited by Harrison (London: Faber & Faber, 1969);

Four For the Future, edited by Harrison (London: Macdonald, 1969);

Worlds of Wonder, edited by Harrison (Garden City: Doubleday, 1969);

Harry Harrison

Best SF: 1968-1973, edited by Harrison and Aldiss (New York: Putnam's, 1969-1975); republished as *The Year's Best Science Fiction Nos. 2-7* (London: Sphere, 1969-75);

SF: Authors' Choice 2, edited by Harrison (New York: Berkley, 1970);

Nova 1, edited by Harrison (New York: Delacorte, 1970; London: Hale, 1976);

The Year 2000: An Anthology, edited by Harrison (Garden City: Doubleday, 1970; London: Faber & Faber, 1971);

SF: Authors' Choice 3, edited by Harrison (New York: Putnam's, 1971);

The Light Fantastic: Science Fiction Classics from the Mainstream, edited by Harrison (New York: Scribners, 1971);

Ahead of Time, edited by Harrison and Theodore J. Gordon (Garden City: Doubleday, 1972);

A Science Fiction Reader, edited by Harrison (New York: Scribners, 1972);

The Astounding-Analog Reader, 2 vols., edited by Harrison and Aldiss (Garden City: Doubleday, 1972-1973; London: Sphere, 1973);

Nova 2, edited by Harrison (New York: Walker, 1972; London: Hale, 1976);

Astounding: John W. Campbell Memorial Anthology of Science Fiction, edited by Harrison (New York: Random House, 1973; London: Sidgwick & Jackson, 1974);

A Science Fiction Reader, edited by Harrison and Carol Pugner (New York: Scribners, 1973);

Nova 3, edited by Harrison (New York: Walker, 1973;

London: Hale, 1977); republished as *The Outdated Man* (New York: Dell, 1975);

SF: Authors' Choice 4, edited by Harrison (New York: Putnam's 1974);

Nova 4, edited by Harrison (New York: Walker, 1975; London: Sphere, 1976);

Science Fiction Horizons, edited by Harrison (New York: Arno, 1975);

Science Fiction Novellas, edited by Harrison and Willis E. McNelly (New York: Scribners, 1975);

Best SF: 1974, edited by Harrison and Aldiss (New York: Bobbs-Merrill, 1975); republished as *The Year's Best Science Fiction No. 8* (London: Sphere, 1976);

Decade the 1940s, edited by Harrison and Aldiss (London: Macmillan, 1975);

Best SF: 75. The Ninth Annual, edited by Harrison and Aldiss (New York: Bobbs-Merrill, 1976); republished as *The Year's Best Science Fiction No. 9* (London: Weidenfeld & Nicholson, 1976);

Decade the 1950s, edited by Harrison and Aldiss (London: Macmillan, 1976);

Decade the 1960s, edited by Harrison and Aldiss (London: Macmillan, 1977).

Reference:

Steven R. Carter, "Harry Harrison's *The Adventures of the Stainless Steel Rat*: A Study in Multiple Interfaces," *Extrapolation*, 21 (Summer 1980):139-145.

Robert A. Heinlein

Joseph Patrouch
University of Dayton

BIRTH: Butler, Missouri, 7 July 1907, to Rex Ivar and Bam Lyle Heinlein.

EDUCATION: University of Missouri, 1924-1925; B.S., U.S. Naval Academy, 1929; University of California, Los Angeles, 1934-1935.

MARRIAGE: To Leslyn McDonald, divorced; October 1948 to Virginia Gerstenfeld.

AWARDS: Hugo Award for *Double Star*, 1956; Hugo Award for *Starship Troopers*, 1960; Hugo Award for *Stranger in a Strange Land*, 1962; Hugo

Award for *The Moon Is a Harsh Mistress*, 1967; Science Fiction Writers of America Grand Master Award, 1975.

BOOKS: *Rocketship Galileo* (New York: Scribners, 1947; London: New English Library, 1971);

Beyond This Horizon (Reading, Pa.: Fantasy Press, 1948); republished in *A Robert Heinlein Omnibus* (London: Sidgwick & Jackson, 1966);

Space Cadet (New York: Scribners, 1948; London: Gollancz, 1966);

Red Planet (New York: Scribners, 1949; London: Gollancz, 1963);

Sixth Column (New York: Gnome Press, 1949); republished as *The Day After Tomorrow* (New York: New American Library, 1951; London: Mayflower, 1962);

Waldo and Magic, Inc. (Garden City: Doubleday, 1950); republished in *A Heinlein Triad* (London: Gollancz, 1966); republished as *Waldo: Genius in Orbit* (New York: Avon, 1958);

The Man Who Sold the Moon (Chicago: Shasta, 1950; London: Sidgwick & Jackson, 1953);

Farmer in the Sky (New York: Scribners, 1950; London: Gollancz, 1963);

Between Planets (New York: Scribners, 1951; London: Gollancz, 1968);

The Green Hills of Earth (Chicago: Shasta, 1951; London: Sidgwick & Jackson, 1954);

The Puppet Masters (Garden City: Doubleday, 1951; London: Museum Press, 1953);

Universe (New York: Dell, 1951); republished as *Orphans of the Sky* (London: Gollancz, 1963; New York: Putnam's, 1964);

The Rolling Stones (New York: Scribners, 1952); republished as *Space Family Stone* (London: Gollancz, 1969);

Starman Jones (New York: Scribners, 1953; London: Sidgwick & Jackson, 1954);

Revolt in 2100 (Chicago: Shasta, 1953; London: Digit, 1959);

Assignment in Eternity (Reading, Pa.: Fantasy Press, 1953; London: Museum Press, 1954);

The Star Beast (New York: Scribners, 1954);

Tunnel in the Sky (New York: Scribners, 1955; London: Gollancz, 1965);

Double Star (Garden City: Doubleday, 1956; London: M. Joseph, 1958);

Time for the Stars (New York: Scribners, 1956; London: Gollancz, 1963);

The Door Into Summer (Garden City: Doubleday, 1957; London: Gollancz, 1967);

Citizen of the Galaxy (New York: Scribners, 1957; London: Gollancz, 1969);

Methuselah's Children (Hicksville, N.Y.: Gnome Press, 1958; London: Gollancz, 1963);

Have Spacesuit—Will Travel (New York: Scribners, 1958; London: Gollancz, 1970);

The Menace from Earth (Hicksville, N.Y.: Gnome Press, 1959; London: Dobson, 1966);

Starship Troopers (New York: Putnam's, 1959; London: Four Square Books, 1961);

The Unpleasant Profession of Jonathan Hoag (Hicksville, N.Y.: Gnome Press, 1959; London: Dobson, 1964); republished as *6 x H* (New York: Pyramid, 1961);

Stranger in a Strange Land (New York: Putnam's, 1961; London: Four Square Books, 1965);

Podkayne of Mars, Her Life and Times (New York: Putnam's, 1963; London: New English Library, 1969);

Glory Road (New York: Putnam's, 1963; London: Four Square Books, 1965);

Farnham's Freehold (New York: Putnam's, 1964; London: Dobson, 1965);

The Moon Is a Harsh Mistress (New York: Putnam's, 1966; London: Dobson, 1967);

The Worlds of Robert A. Heinlein (New York: Ace, 1966; London: New English Library, 1970);

The Past Through Tomorrow (New York: Putnam's, 1967; London: New English Library, 1977);

I Will Fear No Evil (New York: Putnam's, 1970; London: New English Library, 1974);

Time Enough for Love . . . (New York: Putnam's, 1973; London: New English Library, 1974);

The Number of the Beast (New York: Fawcett, 1980);

The Expanded Universe: More Worlds of Robert A. Heinlein (New York: Ace, 1980).

Robert Anson Heinlein was born in Butler, Missouri, a small town some sixty-five miles south of Kansas City. He and his six brothers and sisters were raised in Kansas City, where he attended grade school and high school, graduating from Central High in 1924. He spent a year at the University of Missouri before accepting an appointment to the U.S. Naval Academy at Annapolis. When he graduated in 1929, he stood twentieth in a class of 243. For the next five years he served as a gunnery officer on aircraft carriers. He developed tuberculosis and retired from the navy on permanent disability in 1934. He then briefly attended UCLA, studying physics and mathematics, but his continuing ill health forced him to move to Colorado to recuperate. In the next few years he tried a variety of ventures, including mining for silver in Colorado, selling real estate, and running (unsuccessfully) for public office in California.

Almost as soon as he learned to read, Heinlein began reading science fiction, first the Tom Swift and Frank Reade stories, later Jules Verne, H. G. Wells, Edgar Rice Burroughs, and *Argosy* magazine. In 1938, while casting about for a way to raise money to make a mortgage payment on his home, he chanced upon an editorial by John W. Campbell, Jr., in *Astounding Science-Fiction* which suggested that readers try their hands at writing. Prospective authors were advised to consider story submissions as if they were contest entries; the winning writers would receive cash prizes and their entries would be published. Heinlein worked on a story for four days, liked it enough to send it first to a higher paying market (*Collier's*, where it did not sell), and eventually sent it to *Astounding Science-Fiction* (where it did). "Life-Line" (first collected in *The Man Who Sold the Moon*, 1950) appeared in the August 1939 issue, and Heinlein's career as a science-fiction writer had begun. In the next three years twenty-eight stories of varying lengths under a variety of pseudonyms were published, and all but four of these stories were published in *Astounding Science-Fiction* or *Unknown Worlds*, both edited by Campbell. Through Campbell's editorship and Heinlein's innovation, the face of science fiction was changed radically.

Before Campbell and Heinlein science fiction's two major types were represented primarily by H. G. Wells and Edgar Rice Burroughs. For Wells science fiction was a set of literary devices for discussing the present. *The Time Machine* (1895), for example, uses the journey into the future as a device for attacking Victorian attitudes on scientific progress, biological evolution, and class relationships. For Burroughs, on the other hand, science fiction was action/adventure escape literature. The reader is invited to forget his daily problems and to journey with John Carter to Mars for a series of fabulous and successful adventures. Wells used the future to offer insights into his own present; Burroughs used the future as a refuge from the present, as a setting for exciting daydreams.

But Campbell and Heinlein had an entirely different notion as to what science fiction should be and do. They wished to make the future believable, plausible, possible. They domesticated the future. Heinlein's stories convinced a whole generation that man will really be able to do things he can only imagine now—and that generation grew up and sent Apollo to the moon. Heinlein's fiction showed that the future need not be either a symbolic representation of the present or a refuge from real-life problems. It is also something to be shaped by people today. As Jules Verne once remarked, "What one man can imagine, another man can do." Heinlein wrote in 1952, "Youths who build hot-rods are not dismayed by spaceships; in their adult years they will build such ships. In the meantime they will read stories of interplanetary travel." Heinlein wrote many such stories for exactly that audience. To a larger degree than most people realize, science fiction in the 1940s and 1950s was a set of self-fulfilling prophecies.

Heinlein stopped writing science fiction during World War II and went to work in the Philadelphia naval yards (along with two other Campbell writers,

Isaac Asimov and L. Sprague de Camp). When Heinlein returned to writing in 1947, he had outgrown Campbell and his magazines, and in the years to come he would publish only a handful of stories in *Astounding Science-Fiction*. Instead he developed two new major better-paying markets. He moved from the category pulp magazines to the more prestigious slick magazines like the *Saturday Evening Post*, *Argosy*, and *Bluebook*. Heinlein was the first major science-fiction writer to break out of category and reach the larger general-fiction market, and therefore he was the first to start breaking down the walls that had isolated science fiction for so long. More significantly for his personal career, his work began to be published in hardcover. After some revision he reprinted such *Astounding Science-Fiction* stories as *Beyond This Horizon* (1948) and *Sixth Column* (1949), and he began a new series of original juvenile fiction for Scribners, the first being his earliest hardcover book, *Rocketship Galileo* (1947). In the 1950s Heinlein abandoned the slicks—and with them, for all intents and purposes, the short story form—and concentrated his new work on his annual Scribners juveniles while ocasionally producing an adult novel like *The Puppet Masters* (1951) or *Double Star* (1956). During the 1950s he also found time to work in television on the "Tom Corbett: Space Cadet" series (based largely on his own juvenile novel *Space Cadet*, 1948) and in the movies on *Destination Moon* (1950) and *Project Moonbase* (1953). Heinlein was clearly the most successful and the most diversified writer American science fiction had yet produced.

Then, in 1957, two things happened which seem to have profoundly influenced Heinlein's writing career. On 7 July 1957 he reached his fiftieth birthday, an occasion which surely stimulated a certain amount of reflection and introspection. After twenty years of hard work Heinlein had established himself at the top of a kind of literature almost no one respected or valued. Science fiction was considered to be for kids, primarily for restless male adolescents who could be expected to outgrow it. He had spent his last ten years on a series specifically labeled juvenile. Heinlein seems to have concluded that a man in his fifties, at the height of his writing powers, should produce something directed more toward adults.

The second important event of 1957 was his participation in a series of four lectures given at the University of Chicago in January, February, and March. C. M. Kornbluth gave the first lecture, Heinlein the second, Alfred Bester the third, and Robert Bloch the fourth. All four lectures have been collected and introduced by Basil Davenport in *The Science Fiction Novel: Imagination and Social Criticism* (1959), which was also the general topic of the series. In his talk "Science Fiction: Its Nature, Faults, and Virtues" Heinlein attacked "the neurotic and psychotic fiction now being palmed off on us as 'serious literature,' " and he defended science fiction as the real "serious and mature" literature of our time, despite his recognition "that much of it is crude and not too competent." He was even willing to assert that "for the survival and health of the human race one crudely written science-fiction story containing a single worthwhile new idea is more valuable than a bookcaseful of beautifully written non-science fiction."

But Heinlein's lecture was not the important thing about the series. It is backward-looking, justifying his work in the field, rather than forward-looking, indicating where he will go next. The consensus of the other lecturers on their assigned topic is summed up in Kornbluth's title, "The Failure of the Science Fiction Novel as Social Criticism." Of one of the other contributions Davenport remarks in his introduction: "With disturbing cogency, Robert Bloch mounts a real offensive, charging science fiction not merely with being ineffective as social criticism, but with accepting in large part the worst of today's values . . . and with a failure to come to the help of anything really unpopular."

Bloch himself says: "The hero rebels . . . merely to restore the 'normal' culture and value-standards of the mass-minds of the Twentieth Century. You won't find him fighting in defense of incest, homosexuality, free love, nihilism, . . . abolition of individual property rights, [or] euthanasia . . . . His viewpoint is that of today's average citizen . . . . The implication is that once Law and Order are restored, everything will settle down to a general approximation of life as it is lived today." Bloch then launches a four-page attack on Heinlein's *Beyond This Horizon*. Could Heinlein, on the eve of his fiftieth birthday, mulling over his career so far, have failed to notice?

After his participation in the Chicago lectures, Heinlein's first important works were "All You Zombies—" (1959; collected in *The Unpleasant Profession of Jonathan Hoag*, 1959), a sort of reductio ad absurdum of the incest theme, and *Starship Troopers* (1959), which was such a strong justification and defense of violence that Scribners refused it, thus ending Heinlein's string of juveniles for them. (It was eventually published by the *Magazine of Fantasy and Science Fiction* as

"Starship Soldier" and by Putnam's, and it won him his second Hugo Award.) Four years after the Chicago lectures, two years after the printing of those lectures in book form, and after a two-year hiatus (his longest since World War II), Heinlein published *Stranger in a Strange Land* (1961). This work certainly does not "steadfastly adhere to the conventional outlooks of the community regarding heroes and standards of values," as Bloch had accused science fiction of doing; instead it examines and criticizes sexual and religious values and offers possible—and controversial—alternatives. It is science fiction for an adult audience. More than any other single science-fiction novel—Frank Herbert's *Dune* (1965) being its closest rival—*Stranger in a Strange Land* broke out of category and forced a reevaluation of what science fiction could be and do. As he had done immediately before World War II, Heinlein helped to reshape the genre and make it more significant and valuable than it had been.

Since 1966 Heinlein has lived in California with his second wife, the former Virginia Gerstenfeld. Plagued by varying degrees of ill health since at least 1934, he was on one occasion saved during surgery only by the ready availability of blood from a blood bank. In recent years he has appeared regularly at science-fiction conventions in support of blood drives, and he has given receptions in honor of blood donors. On 28 April 1978 he underwent successful brain surgery in which a carotid artery bypass was installed, allowing blood and oxygen to flow freely to a previously deprived section of his brain. He is fully recovered, and his most recent novel, *The Number of the Beast*, was published in 1980.

During his forty-year career as a writer Heinlein has produced some fifty short stories (especially the Future History series), fourteen juvenile works which he had published between 1947 and 1963, and fifteen adult novels running from his fourth published story through *Time Enough for Love . . .* (1973). The mammoth collection *The Past Through Tomorrow* (1967) is the best place to begin a survey of Heinlein's short fiction. The collection contains nineteen short stories and *If This Goes On—* (1940) and *Methuselah's Children* (1941), two of the early *Astounding Science-Fiction* short novels revised after World War II. The feature which most clearly distinguishes science fiction from other kinds of fiction is its emphasis on scientifically plausible (not necessarily accurate), alternate (to human experience so far) settings in which stories may occur. This means a science-fiction writer must create not only characters and a plot for each story but also a new setting. It is clearly easier to use the same setting several times than it is to keep creating new settings for new stories. Edgar Rice Burroughs set eleven novels on Barsoom, his version of Mars, and Isaac Asimov built his reputation on his Foundation and robot stories. Similarly, Heinlein worked out a loose background for a series of stories which stretch into the future, and these Future History stories are the ones reprinted in *The Past Through Tomorrow*.

A background chart is included in most editions of *The Past Through Tomorrow*. Of it Heinlein once wrote, "The chart was worked up, a bit at a time, to keep me from stumbling as I added new stories. It was originally a large wall chart in my study, to which I added pencilled notes from time to time. This was an idea I had gotten from Mr. Sinclair Lewis. . . . In 1940 I showed the chart to John W. Campbell, Jr.; he insisted on publishing it. From then on I was stuck with it; it became increasingly difficult to avoid fitting a story into the chart. . . . By now [1949] I hardly need the chart; the fictional future history embodied in it is at least as real to me as Plymouth Rock." This chart gives the dates of the major events in the stories; the names of the stories; the life lines of the major characters; chronologically arranged displays of technological, sociological, and political developments; and miscellaneous remarks. In general, standard science-fiction assumptions are embedded in the chart: the moon and nearer planets are reached and colonized; not one but two processes are developed which defeat aging and produce longevity; starships are eventually built so man can spread beyond the solar system. More interesting are two assumptions which are not all that standard. Heinlein does not see technological progress as being uniformly upward and outward. For most of his twenty-first century, interplanetary travel is abandoned (as in fact we have already abandoned manned lunar landings). Furthermore, Heinlein suggests the future will be different but not always better. He plays with the idea that in the not-too-distant future the Constitution of the United States is set aside by a religious zealot named Nehemiah Scudder.

Seven of Heinlein's first eight published stories were eventually fitted into the Future History plan and so are printed in *The Past Through Tomorrow*. (The eighth, "Let There Be Light," used to be included but is not any longer.) Two of these works, "Life-Line" and "Requiem," are of special interest. In "Life-Line" a character invents a device for measuring the length of one's life. After using the device for some pointed satire—insurance companies, for example, oppose the marketing and use of such a device—Heinlein has the inventor killed and the

device destroyed. The theme of the story, then, is not a usual one for Heinlein or—except in the movies—for science fiction: there are some things man was not meant to know. "Life-Line" is still interesting and pleasant reading, despite its anti-science-fiction, antiintellectual theme, and it is notably better than many writers' first published stories.

In "Requiem" (1939), his third published story, Heinlein introduces D. D. Harriman, an industrialist fired by the vision of building a manned rocket to the moon. For a combination of health and business reasons, Harriman stays on Earth while others go into space, make the moon landings, and establish a moon base. As an old man, knowing the trip will probably kill him, Harriman breaks all the rules and finally makes it to the moon, where he dies, a happy man, his childhood dreams and ambitions fulfilled. Like any great poet or visionary, Heinlein in this story was able to express and give direction to the vague and confused yearnings, the unrealized but deeply felt stirrings in the imaginations of his readers. (Ten years after "Requiem" Heinlein published a long "prequel" to it called "The Man Who Sold the Moon," 1949; collected in *The Past Through Tomorrow*. Here he movingly details Harriman's earlier life and career. It begins with a character exclaiming, "You've got to be a believer!" and ends with "There's work to be done.") "Requiem" found Heinlein striking a new and important chord in the American imagination. From "Requiem" on he would be a leader in science fiction because he spoke for, not merely to, his readers.

The stories in *The Past Through Tomorrow* are arranged in chronological order according to where their settings and events come in the Future History, not according to the sequence in which Heinlein originally wrote or published them. While World War II stories that appeared in the slick magazines are mixed in with pre-World War II stories first published in pulp magazines, certain early stories stand out in the series. "The Roads Must Roll" (1940), for example, is a fast-paced, solidly constructed story. Its premise is that toward the end of this century individual passenger cars and trucks have been replaced by massive conveyer-belt roads. The story's initial scene presents the major complication: an assistant supervisor of the roads, Van Kleeck, harangues a union meeting until the members decide to seize political power by seizing control of the roads on which the country's commerce and transportation depend. The story's central character—that is, its problem solver—is a supervisor named Larry Gaines. After an expository conversation with a secondary character, a conversation that recounts the roads' history and major problems, Gaines becomes aware of the complication when the road on which he is riding stops. His job is to get it started again, and his attempts to do so form the story's conflict. Gaines goes over Van Kleeck's psychological profile and decides how to handle him in a face-to-face confrontation. When this solution is put into effect in the story's climactic scene, Gaines defeats Van Kleeck and restores the operation of the roads to normal. The efficient construction of "The Roads Must Roll" shows Heinlein's rapid growth as a writer. "Life-Line" is largely a series of disparate scenes held loosely together; it would not have affected the story much if there had been more or fewer of them. Written only ten months after "Life-Line," "The Roads Must Roll" is a model of the art of plotting. If there is any problem of story construction here, it is the tendency to stop the story for expository lectures. There is, for example, a two-page lecture on how the rolling roads replaced the automobile, and Heinlein takes nearly a page to state explicitly the theme of the story. Much of this is fascinating material, but it is presented in essay form, not as fictional. As will be seen, this conflict between the techniques of fiction and the techniques of the essay runs through Heinlein's career.

Another justly praised early story from *The Past Through Tomorrow* is "—We Also Walk Dogs" (1941). General Services, an organization that will undertake any task for the proper fee, solves the problems involved in arranging facilities for an interplanetary conference of aliens all of whom breathe different atmospheres and live under different gravities. To do this requires the invention of an antigravity device; however, the only man for that job makes certain demands that must be met if he is to assist in the project. The story becomes an intricately plotted set of stories-within-stories, each of which must be worked out, dominolike, before the conference can be held. "—We Also Walk Dogs" shows Heinlein's plotting ability and imagination working together to produce a thoroughly entertaining story.

One may view science fiction as a set of laboratory experiments in the relationship between environment and psychology—if his physical environment were different, man would behave differently. Unfortunately, most science fiction assumes a changing environment and a static psychology so that readers can more easily understand why the characters do and think what they do. However, some of the best science fiction takes the environment-psychology relationship into

Robert A. Heinlein

account. Isaac Asimov's "Nightfall" (1940) is a notable example of environment determining the psychology of a civilization. Heinlein's "It's Great to be Back!" (1946) derives its validity from the same theme. A young couple from Earth have lived and worked on the moon for several years. Their tour of duty over, they return to Earth, only to find themselves ill suited to live there any longer. Their lunar environment has reshaped their thinking, and they cannot go home again. Heinlein uses this theme of people adapting psychologically to strange environments often in his work, especially in his juveniles.

Three other stories in *The Past Through Tomorrow* should at least be mentioned. Like "Requiem," "The Green Hills of Earth" (1947) is an emotional and moving story, and its hero Rhysling, the Blind Singer of the Spaceways, has passed into the folklore of science fiction. The songs in it have been set to music and are sung regularly at science-fiction conventions and meetings. Perhaps the most famous quatrain is "We pray for one last landing/ On the globe that gave us birth;/ Let us rest our eyes on the fleecy skies/ And the cool, green hills of earth." "Blowups Happen" (1940) and "Delilah and the Spacerigger" (1949) have a contemporary interest they would not have had when they were first published. The women's liberation movement colors one's reading of "Delilah and the Spacerigger," the story of a woman's eventually being accepted by her male co-workers on an orbital construction job, while "Blowups Happen" removes from Earth the dangers inherent in atomic energy plants by placing those plants in orbit around the Earth.

A companion piece to "Blowups Happen," "Solution Unsatisfactory" (1941; collected in *The Worlds of Robert A. Heinlein*, 1966) is not a part of the Future History series and so is not printed in *The Past Through Tomorrow*, but it is an important story. Written before the American involvement in World War II, "Solution Unsatisfactory" postulates the development through a secret project—like the Manhattan Project—of an atomic weapon that ends the war. The weapon is an atomic dust which irradiates anyone and any place on which it falls. As Isaac Asimov puts it, Heinlein jumped right over the atom bomb and landed in fallout. The story does not stop with the end of World War II, however. The protagonist realizes that if the United States can develop such a weapon, then other nations can too. Eventually every nation has atomic weapons, yet no one knows how to control their use. No solution to this nuclear stalemate is evident—hence the story's title. Again it was Asimov who pointed out that in 1900 it would have been easy enough to predict the automobile; what would have been hard would be to predict the traffic jam. Many science-fiction writers in the 1930s and earlier had predicted atomic weapons. It was Heinlein who looked past the obvious and saw the not-so-obvious: the occurrence of a nuclear stalemate five years after Heinlein published "Solution Unsatisfactory."

Two 1941 stories which are part of the Future History series and which appear on the chart but are not reprinted in *The Past Through Tomorrow* are important enough to demand some attention. These two stories, "Universe" and "Common Sense," have been put together in a slim volume entitled *Orphans of the Sky* (1963). "Universe" is one of Heinlein's most successful stories. Where D. D. Harriman financed and directed the building of the first rocket to the moon, a man named Jordan early in the twenty-second century does the same for the first interstellar spaceship. The ship is not capable of translight speeds, however, so its crew departs for Alpha Centauri knowing it has begun a journey that will last several generations. There is unrest among colonists who want to turn back, a mutiny, the unleashing of some atomic energy. Eventually the ship settles into a routine. The crew is divided into two groups, the crew and the muties (for both "mutants" and "mutineers"). The crew lives on the ship's lower levels; the muties live on the upper levels in a sort of uneasy peace with the crew. Eventually a motivated and curious member of the crew, Hugh Hoyland, joins with a lazy but knowledgeable mutant, Joe-Jim, to regain control of the ship and take it to its original destination. This was the first of the multi-generation starship stories, and as such it made a valuable contribution to science fiction. While everyone else was figuring out rhetorical ways to get around the fact that the speed of light is unattainable, Heinlein accepted it and worked within it. As Larry Niven has pointed out, the only theoretical problem with Heinlein's multi-generation starship is that it is too dependent on planets. If the ship can support multiple generations of human life, why use it merely as a vehicle to get from planet A to planet B? Why not let a segment of the human race simply live on it permanently? "Universe" has its problems, especially toward the end when Hugh is imprisoned, and a friend of his is conjured up solely to go to the muties for help despite the fact that the friend is conservative and believes scarcely anything Hugh tells him. If the friend had not gone for help, Hugh would not have been freed, so the friend must act against his nature in order to make the story line come out right. Hugh remains alive at the story's end, but his central problem—how to regain control of the drifting ship—is no nearer solution.

In the sequel, "Common Sense," Hugh and his friends steal a lifeboat, in which they escape from the ship and manage to land on a habitable moon that Heinlein puts nearby. A strange story, it reads as if Heinlein were deliberately pushing the conventions of science fiction to such extremes that they actually offend and irritate the reader. For example, the ship, which has drifted the interstellar void for generations, is conveniently swinging through a solar system when Hugh and his companions escape. Moreover, without knowing what he is doing, Hugh locates and approaches a gas giant. He decides to land the lifeboat on one of the gas giant's moons, and as Heinlein puts it, "Luck again. Coincidence of such colossal proportions that one need not be expected to believe it—for the moon-planet was suitable for terrestrial life." Eventually, "Hugh got the vessel down into the stratosphere and straightened it triumphantly into a course that would with certainty kill them all." But disaster is averted: "the autopilots took over." As if such absurd coincidences are not distracting and irritating enough, one must also consider the treatment of women in the story. During the lifeboat's escape, Hugh orders, "Keep those damned women out of the way." Finally outside the starship and into space, he relents and suggests they let the women look outside, but another male disagrees. "It's a mistake to show the women. You'll scare 'em silly." After Hugh has accidentally discovered the gas giant and while he is trying to figure out how to go into orbit around it, one of his wives gets uppity: "The other wife, the unnamed one, kept out of his sight after losing a tooth quite suddenly." Filled with such incidents, "Common Sense" has never been considered one of Heinlein's more likable stories. Its major value, perhaps, is its clear demonstration that even early in his career Heinlein was willing to irritate his readers.

Heinlein's short stories illustrate several of his characteristics as a writer. These include a rapid mastery of the techniques of the short story, as illustrated by the tightly constructed plot in "The Roads Must Roll"; an interest in people, like D. D. Harriman and Rhysling, rather than things; a slight tendency to use the essay as a technique for writing fiction; a fertile and inventive imagination especially with regard to social structures such as governments and industries; and a clear, colloquial, and entertaining writing style. Furthermore, in his fifty-odd short stories Heinlein accomplished two things of major importance to the development of science fiction. First, he produced a body of work that set the example for one major new way the future could be used as a setting for stories. Not a cluster of symbols, not a setting for daydreams, Heinlein's future was a real time and place in which real people could live their own lives independent of ours. Along the way they also gave voice to the innermost yearnings of a very significant, though perhaps relatively small group of people: the technically oriented teenagers who followed D. D. Harriman to the moon. His message was that with vision, dedication, and hard work man can create the future man wants to live in. Second, by breaking out of category with his stories for the slick magazines immediately after World War II, especially "The Green Hills of Earth," first published in the *Saturday Evening Post*, Heinlein sounded the trumpet call that began to shatter the walls surrounding science fiction. One may conclude that there has been no more influential writer in the field since H. G. Wells and Edgar Rice Burroughs.

Heinlein's influence was exerted through his novels as well. Heinlein so far has had published fourteen juvenile and fifteen adult novels. He produced a juvenile novel a year between 1947 and 1959, and added the last one in 1963. In science-fiction criticism a consensus is forming that of all Heinlein's work it is his juveniles that will continue to be read on into the next century and beyond. In these works Heinlein used his newly evolved technique to produce a body of work that for the most part avoids the fatal error that mars so many of his later adult novels—his substitution of the techniques of the essay for those of the novel. The juveniles are clearly written and clearly imagined. The characters, aliens, settings, governments, and gadgets meld together as satisfying wholes. The central characters are teenage males (except in the last one, added four years later almost as an afterthought). These males either have no immediate families or are casting about for ways to live outside their families. Their stories begin with their having average teenage interests like working on hobbies or soda jerking at the corner drugstore. From here they go on to find their places in the world, so that their stories are coming-of-age or rite-of-passage narratives. In addition to being Anglo-Saxon males, they are often naturally curious, quick learners, and extremely intelligent. Some are given extra powers like telepathy or an eidetic memory; others have relatives in key positions who can help them along, or they turn out to be long-lost heirs to power, influence, and wealth. Read in the order in which they were written, the first twelve novels form a Future History of their own. *Rocketship Galileo* is set just after World War II and concerns man's first flights to the moon, while at the end of *Have Spacesuit—Will Travel* (1958) the hero is whisked off to the Lesser Magellanic Cloud from which he looks out and sees the Milky Way from the outside. In the earlier novels the reader visits the moon, Mars, Venus, and Ganymede; in the later ones he journeys across interstellar space to the planets of other suns. Heinlein's juveniles as a whole are about man's conquest of space—interplanetary, interstellar, and finally intergalactic.

In the context of motivating his young audience, Heinlein's *Rocketship Galileo* may be his most significant juvenile novel. The cover blurb on one paperback edition—"The classic moon-flight novel that inspired modern astronautics"—is probably not too far wrong. *Rocketship Galileo* is often condemned for having stock characters and stiff dialogue, and to a certain extent this is true. It was Heinlein's first fiction after a hiatus of several years, and it was his first juvenile novel. However, *Rocketship Galileo* is more interesting than most critics give it credit for, and it is especially fascinating to notice elements in the novel that have come to be so typically associated with Heinlein. A child of the Kansas prairie, he has always admired the pioneer spirit, and he idealizes it in story after story. (*Farmer in the Sky*, 1950; *Tunnel in the Sky*, 1955; *Farnham's Freehold*, 1964; *The Moon Is a Harsh Mistress*, 1966; and *Time Enough for Love . . .*, 1973, all spring to mind.) In *Rocketship Galileo* one of the boys' mothers at first refuses to allow her son Ross to go to the moon, but then she changes her mind with the following explanation:

> "This country was not built by people who were afraid to go. Ross's great-great-grandfather crossed the mountains in a Conestoga wagon and homesteaded this place. He was nineteen, his bride was seventeen. It's a matter of family record that their parents opposed the move." She stirred suddenly and one of her knitting needles broke. "I would hate to think that I had let the blood run thin."

Rocketship Galileo also illustrates Heinlein's tendency to include in his novels insightful, offhand remarks, which help the reader to see how the society of the novel works. The society of *Rocketship Galileo* is that of contemporary America, and Dr. Cargraves's recognition of the difference between tinkering with gadgets and science is instructive: "It is common enough for boys in the United States to build and take apart almost anything mechanical, from alarm clocks to hiked-up jalopies. It is not so common for them to understand the sort of controlled and recorded experimentation on which science is based." Here Heinlein puts the insight into the mind of one of his characters, and he keeps it brief. In later works these insightful observations swell into lectures either from one character to another or directly from Heinlein to his readers. The first method is expository conversation, a lecture dramatized; the second abandons all pretense of fiction and becomes essay. His first juvenile also contains dramatized lectures on such subjects as the difference between gunnery and rocketry and on the operation of a cyclotron. The subject matter itself is interesting, and Heinlein writes about it clearly and informatively. It is the method of presenting that material—and the tendency thus revealed—that should be noted.

Heinlein's obvious militaristic bent is especially clear in *Rocketship Galileo*. For example, Cargraves is telling one of the three teenagers that the youth must develop leadership ability: "You've got to behave so that, if the time comes, they'll *want* to take your orders . . . . The trouble is . . . American boys are brought up loose and easy . . . . But there comes a time when loose and easy isn't enough, when you have to be willing to obey, and do it wholeheartedly and

without argument." The militaristic organizations and attitudes of "The Roads Must Roll," *The Puppet Masters*, *Starship Troopers*, and even *Farnham's Freehold* are not far in the background here. Finally, Heinlein likes to think and write in terms of living things—people, aliens, even governments and movements (which are clusters of living things). In *Rocketship Galileo* this is best exemplified in the way he presents the *Galileo*'s computer, "Joe the Robot." Joe is not alive or sentient, but he is given some character. For one thing, Joe is a "he" instead of an "it." He is also otherwise personified. For example, "While they slept, Joe the Robot stirred, consulted his cam, decided that he had had enough of this weightlessness, and started the jet." Joe is never integrated into the story in any important way, but the way he is treated stylistically anticipates the much more fully developed Mike in *The Moon is a Harsh Mistress*.

Rocketship Galileo, as well as Heinlein's second juvenile, *Space Cadet*, demonstrates how science fiction inculcates into its readers certain values and assumptions. One of these lessons is that it is better to respond to a crisis rationally than emotionally. As Cargraves puts it in *Rocketship Galileo*, "Let's see if we can think ourselves out of this mess." A second of science fiction's assumptions, that all intelligent life is kin, regardless of the external shape of that life, is illustrated in *Space Cadet*, a large part of which is set on a watery Venus. Oscar, a human raised on Venus, brings two recent arrivals, Tex and Matt, to the realization that the local intelligent life forms are truly people. The villain in the story, a flunked-out space cadet named Burke, cannot be convinced and ends up in a Venerian jail for killing some of the natives. Oscar shows Tex and Matt that Burke's attitude is simply race prejudice, an argument which reveals a corollary of the science-fiction rule that all intelligence is kin: racism makes no sense. Science fiction is a form of fiction that endorses reason, intelligence, and brotherhood. Reinforced in *Space Cadet* is another notion of science fiction: all assumptions are to be examined. For example, in a course called "Doubt" taken by Matt at the Academy, "The seminar leader would chuck out some proposition that attacked a value usually regarded as axiomatic. . . . The following week [Matt] heard both mother love and love of mother questioned. . . . Thereafter came attacks on monotheism as a desirable religious form, the usefulness of the scientific method, and the rule of the majority in reaching decisions."

Space Cadet contains at least two other items

worth noting, both typical of Heinlein. First is his care with details. Heinlein may be one of few writers who would do the work necessary to know that "spaceships on long cruises must carry about seven hundred pounds of food per man per year" or that to clear the carbon dioxide out of the air "each man in the ship must be balanced by about ten square feet of green plant leaf." Second is his ability to create aphorisms. Distinguishing between precedent and tradition, for example, one character observes: "Precedent is merely the assumption that somebody else, in the past with less information, nevertheless knows better than the man on the spot. . . . To follow a tradition means to do things in the same grand style as your predecessors; it does not mean to do the same things."

One debatable theme in *Space Cadet* was pointed out by Jack Williamson: "the idea that common men must be guided and guarded by a competent elite." In this novel that group is the Space Patrol. There is no doubt that Matt, the young recruit whose story is told in the novel, comes to believe this. But the degree to which Heinlein also believes what Matt comes to believe is unclear. So long as one is dealing with fiction, it is better not to take the attitudes of characters and try to apply them to their authors. The problem is that the attitude recurs in other Heinlein novels till one becomes suspicious that it is Heinlein's position after all.

It is generally conceded that with *Rocketship Galileo* and *Space Cadet* Heinlein was doing what he had already done with "Life-Line" and "Requiem"—that is, teaching himself how to write in a new form. By *Red Planet* (1949), *Farmer in the Sky*, and *Between Planets* (1951), he had clearly learned how to use the juvenile-novel form to say those things he wanted to say. The story lines in all three books are strong and clear. In *Red Planet* a company on Earth has established two colonies on Mars, one in the northern hemisphere, one in the southern, and a single group of colonists migrates back and forth between them to avoid the severe Martian winters. The story begins when the company decides to double the population of Mars—and its own profits—by forbidding the migration and using both colonies the year around. A young man named Jim Marlowe learns of this plan and must get the information to his father, who is one of the colony's political leaders. One of the best features of the novel is the planet itself, its ecology and life forms. A fuzzy Martian basketball named Willis steals every scene in which he appears and is far and away Heinlein's most convincing alien to date. In fact, it is instructive that Heinlein seldom uses aliens

at all. In his prewar stories they figure most prominently in the latter part of *Methuselah's Children*. How to accommodate aliens forms the problem of "—We Also Walk Dogs," but the aliens themselves are not onstage or important. The Future History series largely ignores aliens. There is an important difference between his use of aliens in his juveniles and in his adult novels. In his juveniles the aliens are usually friendly. The benevolent characters treat them as equals, the malevolent treat them as inferiors, and the youthful readers learn something about racism. Aliens are important in only one adult novel, *The Puppet Masters*, where they are so evil that the only good alien is a dead alien, an attitude *The Puppet Masters* shares with *Starship Troopers*. The reason for Heinlein's lack of interest in aliens is probably that he is simply more interested in humanity. The problem of learning how to get along with people takes precedence over learning to get along with some hypothetical aliens sometime in the indefinite future.

The colonists in *Red Planet* are terraforming Mars; those in *Farmer in the Sky* are terraforming Ganymede, one of the moons of Jupiter. There are three things that are usually mentioned about *Farmer in the Sky*. First, originally written for and published in *Boy's Life*, it contains a strong Boy Scout flavor. The central character, Bill Lermer, is himself a scout; he takes his uniform to Ganymede; there are scout meetings on the ship en route; and scout troops are organized on Ganymede. Second, the novel is rather stark and grim for a juvenile. Half the colony is killed in a quake, and Bill's frail stepsister weakens and dies. Third, the process of terraforming Ganymede is described in some detail, especially the freeing of oxygen to create an atmosphere and the preparation of a soil in which to grow crops. Heinlein's genius for aphorism continues to generate remarks like "Horses can manufacture more horses, and that is one trick that tractors have never learned." There are set pieces that present background material, especially about the terraforming process, but they are kept brief and unobtrusive, and they are melded smoothly into the story line. *Farmer in the Sky* ends on a familiar and pleasing note. Like the young couple in "It's Great to be Back!," Bill Lermer has been psychologically shaped by his environment in the course of his experiences, until he is at home on Ganymede and realizes that he will stay there. *Farmer in the Sky* is the story of the human race versus an alien environment, not versus aliens or villains, and so some find it deficient in story line. These people are wrong. *Farmer in the Sky* is one of Heinlein's most satisfying juveniles.

Between Planets is another matter. The plot is melodramatic and contrived; it is filled with secret messages and couriers and escapes. The problem is probably that the central character, Don Harvey, ignorant of what is happening, is more acted upon than acting. He spends most of the novel scurrying pointlessly about. But the novel is perhaps saved by two things. The first is a Venerian "dragon" nicknamed Sir Isaac Newton who speaks English with a Cockney accent through a device called a voder. Like Willis in *Red Planet* Sir Isaac steals the scenes in which he appears, and the only possible complaint could be that he is not included in enough of them. A second strong feature in the novel is that it gives clear expression to a problem which Jack Williamson has pointed out as an irreconcilable difficulty in Heinlein's thinking: "As evolving technologies become more and more complex, so does the teamwork needed to support them. Heinlein seems completely aware of this when he is carrying his young protagonists through their education and their rites of initiation, yet he often seems unhappy with the sacrifice of personal freedom that a technological culture seems to require." The organization for which Don has unwittingly been working shares "a belief in the dignity and natural worth of free intelligence," and it fights "against the historical imperative of the last two centuries, the withering away of individual freedom under larger and ever more pervasive organizations." As a synonym for *free*, Heinlein sometimes has his characters use a different word. Don says of government, "There ought to be a sort of *looseness* about it. You know—a man ought to be able to do what he wants to, if he can, and not be pushed around." As Williamson suggests, it is hard to square this with the modern necessity to be a team member. Compare it, for example, with that earlier passage in *Rocketship Galileo*: "There comes a time when loose and easy isn't enough, when you have to be willing to obey, and do it wholeheartedly and without argument." Looseness and freedom must somehow coexist with a willingness to obey wholeheartedly and without question. The issue this raises—the role of the individual in a militaristic and/or technological society—is by no means a trivial one.

In *Between Planets* Heinlein made a prediction that came true and an observation that has become even more relevant. It is often pointed out that no science-fiction story predicted that the moon landing would be made from an orbiting spaceship with a shuttlecraft. But in this novel the interplanetary ship *Nautilus* goes into a polar orbit around Venus and

the colonies are supplied via "shuttle ships." Heinlein even describes in some detail the process of rendezvousing the orbiter and the shuttle. The observation that has become more relevant has to do with scientists' problematic sense of responsibility. A character remarks to Don, "We are about to turn loose into the world forces the outcome of which I cannot guess," and then suggests, "You might think about it. Those laboratory laddies won't, that's sure. These physicists—they produce wonders but they never know what other wonders their wonders will beget." This reminds one of Asimov's praise of Heinlein for being able to see implications in wonders, implications that most others miss.

One of the problems with *Rocketship Galileo* might be its lack of focus. It follows a group composed of one scientist and three teenagers. The next four juveniles were all better focused because they were told through the thoughts and experiences of one character with whom the reader could identify. If Heinlein had not already published over thirty stories and four novels in the magazines, one would suspect that the "error" in *Rocketship Galileo* was due to inexperience and that he had learned to correct the error in his next four juveniles. The sixth juvenile novel, *The Rolling Stones* (1952), could then be considered a deliberate experiment. As it is, one can only asume that Heinlein had tired of writing novels in the same point of view after four of them in a row. *The Rolling Stones* is a picaresque novel, stringing its episodes along the lives of the seven members of the Stone family. Sometimes the author follows one member of the family, sometimes another (or, in the case of the twins, two others). Mr. Stone is able to maintain a certain amount of order and authority, so in the sense that he is central to the family, he is also central to the novel. But the narration is from the twins' point of view at least as much as it is from his, and occasionally the point of view is that of others—or an omniscient narrator. As Brian Aldiss has observed, Heinlein does not like to repeat a successful formula.

The novel may be described as being about the series of attempts by the Stones to find a comfortable—loose—place for them among the various planets, moons, and cultures that exist within the solar system. By the end they are fed up with the restrictions of the inner planets and have decided to see the rings of Saturn. After that, who knows? Larry Niven mentioned that the spaceship in "Universe" was too dependent on planets; *Between Planets* features a central character born in space and therefore not a citizen of any particular planet; by the end of *The Rolling Stones* the family has come to realize that when they are on their spaceship together and traveling, they are home. Home is wherever they are all together, an attitude that rather accurately reflects the peripatetic culture of the twentieth century. What Heinlein has developed by the end of this novel is the concept of macrolife, life in the space between the stars rather than life restricted to the surfaces of planets. He was among the first, if not the first, to do so.

Starman Jones (1953), often mentioned as the best of Heinlein's juveniles, returns to the single-character narrative point of view. The character is Max Jones, and the story concerns his finding his way in a world he never made. He wants to go into space and travel the stars, but space travel is controlled by hereditary guilds and he is excluded. Eventually he uses forged papers to get a minor berth, and when the ship gets into trouble—it is lost in space—his eidetic memory helps him become captain of the ship so he can save the crew and passengers. He returns to Earth a hero, is fined for his transgressions, but is allowed to stay in space and begin to work his way up the ranks legitimately. He begins the story as a daydreaming farmboy—like so many of Heinlein's readers—and ends it among the stars. At the very end he goes back home and realizes, "I'm all through here." He has grown beyond his beginnings. He has found his place. But he does not entirely accept the status quo. He vows that when he works his way into an influential position he will do what he can to rid the guilds of their hereditary requirements so that all of the best qualified can get in.

In *Starman Jones*, as in most science fiction, interstellar travel is the symbol of freedom. Earth is seen as a jail from which the only escape is space. Max is helped to escape by an older, experienced friend, Sam Montgomery. They leave from Earth and plan to jump ship at a colony where they can be free, where the political climate is "looser" than it is on Earth. They reject any domed colony because in them "you do exactly what the powers-that-be say, or you stop breathing. . . . There's more freedom even back on Terra." Interestingly enough, Max eventually finds his niche in the crew of an interstellar spaceship, and such a ship is little more than a portable domed colony. The novel is justly praised for its convincing and sympathetic portrayal of the disciplined life of the crew. Heinlein's naval experience is doubtless being drawn on here. But the point Heinlein is making is exactly the one made by Wordsworth in his lines, "In truth, the prison into which we doom/ Ourselves, no prison is." Max finds freedom and self-fulfillment in military discipline.

Surely this is Heinlein's answer to the problem Williamson had pointed out earlier: how to reconcile individual freedom to an advanced technological society which emphasizes teamwork and discipline.

Besides the tightly organized story of Max's finding his way in the world and the convincing portrayal of shipboard life, *Starman Jones* has one of Heinlein's most believable heroines, an independent and strong-willed young woman named Ellie. The relationship that develops between Max and Ellie is extremely well done. In contemporary society it has been for some reason assumed that a woman must choose between being a businesswoman or a wife and mother, while no man is asked to choose between being an engineer or a husband and father. This strange thought pattern is today breaking down, and both men and women can have careers and families. Heinlein approaches the issue from the other direction. If women must so choose, why not men? Max chooses his career, and Ellie marries someone else.

For those who prefer slapstick comedy on Earth, Heinlein's next juvenile, *The Star Beast* (1954), would probably be a better choice. Several generations before the story opens, a space explorer had returned to Earth with a pet. Now the gentle little puppy has grown into a gigantic lumbering ox—a Lummox—which eats anything from roses to automobiles. The authorities decide to kill it, somehow; its somewhat obtuse owner and his much quicker girl friend try to save it; and Earth's Department of Spatial Affairs gradually becomes aware of more and more serious implications of the Lummox Affair—especially when a shipful of aliens appears in orbit around Earth and threatens to destroy the planet unless the Lummox is turned over to them. The ostensible central character of *The Star Beast* is John Thomas Stuart XI, Lummox's "owner," but unfortunately, like Don Harvey in *Between Planets*, Stuart is not an actor but a reactor. He wrings his hands a lot, protests often that he does not approve of the way things are going, and generally muddles about and gets in the way. Betty, his more alert and lively girl friend, lectures him on his deficiencies, but it does no good. Whenever John Thomas is centerstage, the story moves its slowest. As with Willis in *Red Planet* and Sir Isaac in *Between Planets*, Lummox steals all the scenes he is in. The most important and interesting human character, however, is Mr. Kiku, Under-Secretary of the Department of Spatial Affairs, who is responsible for everything connected with space and is therefore ultimately responsible for solving the Lummox problem. Since *The Star Beast* is basically a comedy, Heinlein gives

Mr. Kiku an amusing countertrait. Since he is responsible for Earth's alien affairs, Heinlein makes him xenophobic. Each time Mr. Kiku is to meet with a particularly noxious alien named Dr. Ftaeml, he must first see his hypnotherapist—and he meets with Dr. Ftaeml regularly through the novel. Mr. Kiku knows consciously what every reader of science fiction learns, "that weird creatures such as Dr. Ftaeml had made the differences between breeds of men seem less important." In fact, so far as there is a serious theme emphasized repeatedly in *The Star Beast*, it is the standard science-fiction theme that intelligence need not reside solely in human shape. One of the other characters "did not expect 'men' to look like men and had no prejudice in favor of the human form." Copernicus shattered the heliocentric view of the universe; science fiction like *The Star Beast* is shattering the homocentric view. At the end of the novel, John Thomas volunteers to go to Lummox's planet as *its* pet.

Toward the end of *Starman Jones*, while the ship is lost, the crew land on a planet they call Charity, and for a while it looks as if they will have to live out their lives there. Fortunately for them, they are finally able to return to Earth. This *Robinson Crusoe / Swiss Family Robinson* theme has always exercised a strong fascination for readers, probably because everyone wonders what life would be like if he had to start over again with completely different ground rules. This is surely part of the fascination of science fiction too. Strangely—even fighteningly— some novels seem to hint at a strain in man that would welcome an atomic war, because such war would destroy the world in which many are not well-off psychologically or physically. Atomic armageddon would free people from the tangled web of social and economic obligations and duties in which they live. In that sense, the violent end of civilization would free its survivors. In *Tunnel in the Sky* Heinlein does not free his characters from their constraining civilization by stranding them on an alien planet because of a crashed or lost spaceship (as in *Starman Jones*) or through an atomic war (as he will do in *Farnham's Freehold*). Instead he transports his small band of people to an alien world via a space portal, a Gate. With the Gate one simply warps space until the place he wants to be is alongside where he is. He walks through. This makes pioneering possible again on a grand scale. The Gate

eliminated the basic cause of war and solved the problem of what to do with all those dimpled babies. A hundred thousand planets were no farther away than the other side of the street. Virgin continents, raw wildernesses, fecund jungles, killing deserts, frozen tundras, and implacable mountains lay just beyond the city gates, and the human race was again going out . . . as it had so often before. . . . The most urbanized, mechanized, and civilized . . . culture in all history trained its best children, its potential leaders, in primitive pioneer survival—man naked against nature.

This training is done in classes like the one Rod Walker takes in his "Advanced Survival" course. The final exam is a stay of unspecified duration on an unspecified planet. *Tunnel in the Sky* concerns a group that is isolated when the Gate breaks down behind them.

The novel is often contrasted to William Golding's *Lord of the Flies* (1954). In Golding's book the stranded teenagers descend into savagery; more in the tradition of *Robinson Crusoe*, Heinlein's teenagers build a civilization. The novel is a perceptive analysis of the personal relationships that develop and are strained while a group of young men and women struggle to survive. Heinlein is optimistic: competent, well-trained people will survive no matter what. The ending, in which the Gate is reestablished and the colony is reabsorbed into the background technological civilization, has been criticized because the reestablishment of the Gate interrupts, actually terminates, the story in which the reader has become so involved. The rescue is a disappointment. But the ending is not really arbitrary, as it has been called. There is no reason to suppose that the technicians on Earth would simply abandon the stranded students, any more than a ship in distress on the ocean today would be ignored. Then too, Heinlein likes to round off his stories. In the first chapter of *Tunnel in the Sky* Rod had watched the mounted captain of a pioneer party lead a wagon train through a Gate to another world. In the last chapter Rod has grown up and replaces that captain: "The control light turned green. He brought his arm down hard and shouted, 'Roll 'em! Ho!' as he squeezed and released the little horse with his knees. The pinto sprang forward, cut in front of the lead wagon, and Captain Walker headed out on his long road." The major point of *Tunnel in the Sky* has been after all a survival test. Rod has passed it and become a professional pioneer.

The Rolling Stones, Starman Jones, The Star Beast, and *Tunnel in the Sky* form the heart of Heinlein's series of juveniles. They are varied in their structures and subject matters, yet they share a consistently high level of imagination and writing.

The next three novels all show some falling off in quality. *Time for the Stars* (1956) is told in the first person and falls into two traps of this kind of narration. First, the reader does not often participate in the events as they are happening; instead he is told about those events—often in a summary sort of way—after they have happened. Second (and this overlaps the first), the narrator talks too much. There is a vivid scene in chapter one, for example, but it is overwhelmed, drowned, in the narrator's verbiage. *Citizen of the Galaxy* (1957) was serialized in four parts before it appeared as a novel in one volume. It was probably written with this serialization in mind. As a result, instead of one novel, it is four connecting novelettes unified largely by the character from whose point of view all four parts are narrated. Like "Life-Line" *Citizen of the Galaxy* could have been made longer or shorter simply by adding or subtracting episodes. The story has no natural length of its own. Nevertheless, individual episodes succeed very well. The relationship between Thorby and Baslim in the first episode and the "clan society" of the middle two are extremely well worked out, though the last section reduces Thorby to the same sort of ineffectual handwringer that John Thomas was in *The Star Beast* and Don Harvey in *Between Planets*. Despite its carrying its central character from slave boy to rich and powerful heir, *Citizen of the Galaxy* is disunified and its individual sections are uneven. *Have Spacesuit—Will Travel* is a good-natured romp which most readers enjoy for its description and use of the spacesuit, for its intelligent and precocious heroine, for its unusual aliens, and for its hectic pace. If *Citizen of the Galaxy* is made up of four consecutive stories that move horizontally one after the other, *Have Spacesuit—Will Travel* is made up of a series of stories that fall through trapdoors into one another. A soda jerk at a drugstore wins a spacesuit in a contest he entered hoping to win first prize, which was a trip to the moon. He fixes the suit up and takes a walk in it, only to be kidnapped by space pirates led by a very ugly alien and taken to the moon along with a young girl who had been kidnapped earlier. After a pointless escape and recapture on the moon, they are translated to Pluto, and thence to the Lesser Magellanic Cloud, where they must explain why the human race should be allowed to continue to exist. The hero returns at last to his job as a soda jerk, but now he has developed enough initiative and sense of self-worth to reward an unruly customer with a chocolate milkshake in the face. Thus does one mature through one's experiences.

Neither *Time for the Stars, Citizen of the*

Galaxy, nor *Have Spacesuit—Will Travel* is quite as good as any of the previous four, but those previous four had set a very high standard. Perhaps the most interesting thing in any of these three later juveniles is the cosmological background of *Time for the Stars,* which takes into account Einstein's theory of time dilation at near-light speeds. Imagine two twins. If one stays on Earth and the other goes off in a spaceship that approaches the speed of light, their experience of time will diverge. A clock on the ship runs at the proper rate for the twin on the ship, while a clock on the Earth runs at the proper rate for the twin on Earth. But if the former could see the clock on Earth, it would appear to him to be running much too quickly, and if the latter could see the clock on the ship, it would appear to him to be running much too slowly. Time is relative to the speed of the observer. But of course the two cannot see one another's clocks, not unless they are telepathic. And that is what Heinlein makes them. He uses telepathic twins as the communications links between his exploration ships and Earth (and even among his ships), and he takes the time-dilation effect into account. When the ship's speed is too great, communication with Earth is lost because of the different speeds with which thoughts form in the communicating minds. It is an instructive idea beautifully worked out, and an outstanding example of Heinlein's creative and extrapolative abilities.

Podkayne of Mars (1963) is a late addition to the juveniles and not a good place to end a consideration of them. Far better is *Starship Troopers,* which had been refused as a juvenile novel by Scribners but was published in 1959 by Putnam's. It was Heinlein's first novel after his fiftieth birthday and after his participation in that series of lectures at the University of Chicago. As was argued earlier, those two events of 1957 probably contributed to moving Heinlein's fiction in entirely new directions after 1957. *Starship Troopers,* with its defense of militarism and its unusual narrative techniques, and *Stranger in a Strange Land* two years later, with its examination of sexual and religious attitudes, both contributed significantly to that 1960s revolution in science fiction that went under the label New Wave.

As early as 1941, in his speech as Guest of Honor at the Third World Science-Fiction Convention in Denver, Heinlein had remarked, "It's a luxury to me not to be held down by a plot and a set of characters." After 1957 Heinlein has been increasingly willing to indulge in this luxury in his fiction too. To put it positively, one could say that he has been trying to combine the discipline of fiction—the necessity to speak through plot and characters—with the

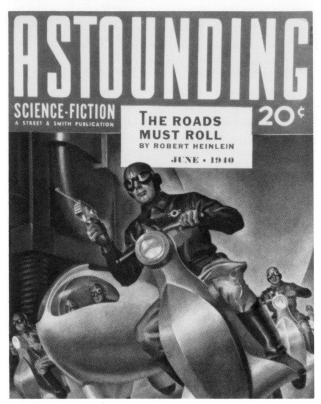

Astounding Science-Fiction, *June 1940 cover*

freedom of the essay—the luxury of speaking straight out to an audience on the things that concern him. Heinlein has not followed Asimov and switched to nonfiction, but the veneer of fiction covering his ideas has worn very thin. Much of his fiction since 1957 is in the form of a dialogue in which two figures sit down and discuss a topic. Large swatches of later Heinlein are novels in the same way that Plato's *Apology* or Boethius's *Consolation of Philosophy* are novels. In *Starship Troopers* the outstanding example is the set of Socratic dialogues between Colonel DuBois and the members of his class in "History and Moral Philosophy." (For the sake of variety, there are also such dialogues between Sergeant Zim and Juan Rico, the narrator, and between Major Reid and his students.) The subject matters of these Socratic dialogues include an analysis of the statement "Violence never settles anything"; the definition and purpose of war; juvenile delinquents; the inalienable rights of life, liberty, and the pursuit of happiness; and the extending of the franchise only to discharged veterans. In each case, Heinlein's characters become convinced of the validity of an unpopular idea: that violence has been the greatest settler of issues in the history of the world; that war is controlled violence whose purpose is to support by force the decisions of one's government; that juvenile delinquents are merely the symptoms of a sick culture in which everyone has concentrated on rights and forgotten duties; that a human being has no natural rights of any kind, and that only veterans should have the franchise because then "every voter and officeholder is a man who has demonstrated through voluntary and difficult service that he places the welfare of the group ahead of personal advantage." Besides defending and glorifying violence and war, Heinlein presents and defends the idea of public flogging (for a variety of offenses, including drunken driving). In *Starship Troopers* he also points out the ultimate reason men fight: to protect the women who will give birth to and raise the next generation of the human race. None of these things is demonstrated in a story line acted out by characters (fiction); instead they are discussed in conversation (dramatized essay). Furthermore, the narrator has the same tendencies as the one in *Time for the Stars*: he summarizes events for the reader long after they have happened, so that one is told about them rather than allowed to participate in them. Too much of *Starship Troopers* is either interior monologue or Socratic dialogue. Again, the fictional element in this story has become a very thin veneer, and Heinlein is contriving dialogues in which he can almost-but-not-quite speak directly to the reader unencumbered by the necessity of plot and character. The first and last chapters contain almost the only scenes in the novel where Heinlein uses the narrative techniques that had changed the face of science fiction in the early 1940s. He has switched his attention to subject matter, and the form is no longer nearly so important.

Starship Troopers seethes with conviction. It was written in a hard white flame. The first controversial subject Heinlein had chosen to defend was one he knew best—the military. There is nothing subtle about *Starship Troopers*. It is an all-out frontal attack on conventional attitudes toward war and violence and on the roles of war and violence in human history. When he expressed some of the same notions in his speech as Guest of Honor at the World Science-Fiction Convention in Kansas City in 1976, some in the audience seemed willing to fight to prove how peace-loving they were. The popularity of the novel is surprising considering its use of other than fictional techniques and its presentation and defense of unpopular positions. The result, despite all odds, was a stunning success.

Two years later, in 1961, he achieved another such success with *Stranger in a Strange Land*, probably Heinlein's best-known book, especially outside of the regular science-fiction readership. Before he wrote *Stranger in a Strange Land*, however, he had written several other stories which, with some rewriting, were published as adult novels. Several of these first appeared in *Astounding Science-Fiction* during 1940-1942: *Beyond This Horizon* (1948), *Sixth Column* (1949), and *If This Goes On*—(which appeared in *Revolt in 2100*, 1953), and *Methuselah's Children* (1958) were all revised to varying degrees for book publication; "Waldo" (1942) and "Magic, Inc." (1940) were joined as *Waldo and Magic, Inc.* (1950), while "Universe" and "Common Sense" were joined to become first *Universe* (1951) and then *Orphans of the Sky* (1963). Other novels of the 1950s include *The Puppet Masters* (1951), *Double Star* (1956), and *The Door Into Summer* (1957).

The four novels Heinlein wrote before his career was interrupted by World War II are still very readable. *If This Goes On*—is a good story about an organized cabal throwing the rascals out. Interestingly enough, while the villains here are a religious dictatorship, in the even more readable *Sixth Column* the heroes throw off the yoke of their Panasian masters by establishing a technologically based pseudoreligion. Heinlein's first two novels, then, deal with religious organizations, a concern he will use again in *Stranger in a Strange Land*. *Methuselah's Children*, his third early novel, is also enjoyable, and in the context of his writing career it is fairly significant. It shows Heinlein's tendency to interlock his stories. Andrew Jackson Libbey, a major character of the novel, was the central character of his second published story, "Misfit." The most important character in the novel is Lazarus Long, who is also the central character in *Time Enough for Love*; and extensive use is made of a sister ship of the one in "Universe." Furthermore, *Methuselah's Children* develops a theme that became important to Heinlein down through the years, the theme of longevity. In this novel long life is achieved by genetic self-control (by the Howard Families) and by a newly developed scientific process (applicable to the non-Howards), so all the human race can live exceedingly long lives. Finally, the last third of the story takes the Howard Families to a variety of alien worlds and lets them encounter a variety of alien life forms. *Methuselah's Children* is one of the few novels outside his juveniles where Heinlein uses aliens, and the aliens in this story are extremely well done.

Beyond This Horizon is Heinlein's best early novel. It is not so melodramatic as the others. Where the Howard Families of *Methuselah's Children* had

bred in secret for longevity, the civilization in *Beyond This Horizon* breeds by government control and permission for the improvement of the race. Tooth decay, color blindness, cancer, birth defects—all have been bred out. Positively, there has been some improvement in intelligence, and Hamilton Felix is the result of one such line of research. The central character in the novel is Mordan, whose problem is to get Felix to marry Longcourt Phyllis and produce children. Felix resists the idea because he does not see the point to life, and right here *Beyond This Horizon* takes a quantum leap in significance. The key question in the novel becomes: What is the point of being alive? Why *be* at all? To get Felix to procreate, Mordan must help him answer "the old, old question as to whether a man has anything more than his hundred years here on earth?" (In *Time Enough for Love* Lazarus Long must be convinced of the value of life, or he will commit suicide.) In exchange for a Great Research program set up to study scientifically such questions as survival after death, Felix agrees to have children. It is important to see clearly here what Felix's motivation really is. He does not change his mind about having children simply because a specific problem—survival after death—is going to be studied; he changes his mind because he has discovered a problem which can engage his intelligence and attention. Longevity for its own sake is not his motivation any more than it is Lazarus Long's: once Lazarus finds something that can interest and stimulate him, he decides to continue to live; exactly the same is true of Felix. It is the intellectual stimulation that life brings that Felix cannot deny his potential children. The plot ends with Felix's decision, but the novel does not. The last third of the novel presents a variety of stimulating problems in order to point up the correctness of Felix's decision. Many of these are related to the Great Research. For example, contact with an alien civilization might help answer the question of survival after death by seeing what the aliens think, so stardrive development and starship construction become part of the Great Research. But life can be stimulating and exciting outside the Great Research. The novel ends on the following note: "It was a good world, he assured himself again, filled with interesting things. Of which the most interesting were children. He glanced at [his son] Theobald. The boy was a lot of fun now, and would be more interesting as he grew up—if he could refrain from wringing his cussed little neck in the meantime!" The emphasis on the word "interesting" is not an accident. *Beyond This Horizon* demonstrates that the reason for life is not longevity; instead, the reason for longevity is life. Heinlein always emphasizes survival and longevity because without them one cannot continue to experience life.

It is remarkable how many of Heinlein's novels concern themselves with revolutions. In *If This Goes On—* the religious dictatorship which had suspended the American Constitution is overthrown and what Heinlein calls "the First Human Civilization" is established. In *Sixth Column* the Panasian conquerors of North America are overthrown by a religious-appearing sixth column. In *The Puppet Masters* the Earth is invaded and nearly conquered by alien parasite slugs who fasten themselves to their hosts' nervous systems by riding between the shoulders of their victims, and these alien tyrants must be fought and overthrown. *The Moon Is a Harsh Mistress*, published five years after *Stranger in a Strange Land*, reenacts the American Revolution on the moon. (One could argue that *Methuselah's Children* is a revolutionary novel, too, because the clans refuse to accept the rule of the established government and set up their own government elsewhere, or that *Beyond This Horizon* is revolutionary because its central character is asked to join an ineffectual revolutionary movement, or that *Orphans of the Sky* is revolutionary because a small group tries to seize control of the ship and put it back on what they consider the right course, or even that *Double Star* is revolutionary because the actor is helping to keep political power out of the hands of a group that wants it. However, such consideration of any of these novels would probably be forcing the argument.)

The reason for Heinlein's interest in revolution is surely related to the major science-fiction belief that the future will be different from the present. Sometimes the point is made through natural disasters, as in H. G. Wells's "The Star" (1897) or John Christopher's *No Blade of Grass* (1957); sometimes it is made through man-made disasters, as in any postatomic war novel; and sometimes it is made through alien invasions, as in Wells's *The War of the Worlds* (1898). Heinlein has used at various times all three kinds of disasters. In "The Year of the Jackpot" (1952; collected in *The Menace from Earth*, 1959) the sun goes nova; in *Farnham's Freehold* a nuclear bomb propels a family into the future; and in *The Puppet Masters* aliens invade. The establishment of a dictatorship would also be a form of man-made disaster which would make the future different from the present. As was observed earlier, Heinlein likes to write about secondary effects, such as the traffic jam, not the automobile. It is instructive that *If This Goes On—* (also available in *The Past Through Tomorrow*) is about the overthrow of the dictatorship that replaced constitutional government in the United States and that he never wrote the novel about Nehemiah Scudder's setting up that religious dictatorship in the first place. In other words, Heinlein's revolutionary novels are actually very conservative and reinforce a belief that whatever is, is right. There is nothing controversial or unpopular about throwing out a religious dictatorship or a foreign or alien invader and reinstituting truth, justice, and the American way of life.

Heinlein's early novels are certainly susceptible to Robert Bloch's criticism: once a corrupt government seizes power, there arises "the necessity of rebellion in the form of some sort of Underground movement, . . . [with] the implication that once Law and Order are restored, everything will settle down to a general approximation of life as it is lived today." In other words, "most social criticism in science fiction novels is not directed against present-day society." In the context of this discussion, Bloch is saying that most pre-1957 science fiction suggests the future will not be different from the present. No wonder Heinlein was stung into writing *Starship Troopers*, whose society is so different from contemporary society, and *Stranger in a Strange Land*, in which the advent of Valentine Michael Smith forces contemporary society to evolve into something different. In any event, in his early novels Heinlein's different futures are the results of revolutions and his stories are about the restoration of present-day values to those futures. That they are such conservative works should not be surprising. *If This Goes On—* and *Sixth Column* were written at the onset of World War II, and *The Puppet Masters* is a product of the McCarthy years. In both periods the American way of life was in grave danger of being destroyed or subverted. Literature, whether popular or serious, almost always reflects the times in which it is written, and Heinlein's early novels are no exception. Somewhere in the back of these wartime novels is a morale-building theme as well. America will fight as hard as she can, but if she loses and the enemy prevails, she will continue the fight as an underground movement. Since no one knew the future in 1940 and 1941, Heinlein's novels considered the possibility of defeat and promised that even then ultimate victory would be possible. He spoke to and allayed deep-seated national fears.

The Puppet Masters, *Double Star*, and *The Door Into Summer* were the three adult novels Heinlein published in the years he was working on his Scribners juveniles. *The Puppet Masters* uses several devices that have become cliched since the novel first came out. These include the flying-saucer invasion and the secret spy organization headed by the Old Man and staffed by rugged, deadly professionals, both male and female, who also use clever disguises to get in and out of tight places. The novel still works well because Heinlein forces the reader to see beneath its ostensible subject—the alien invasion—to its real subject—the horrors of slavery and the necessity to fight for freedom. *The Puppet Masters* is one of his novels of revolution, but it differs from the others in this: where the other tyrants used force to compel submission to their rule, the Puppet Masters literally fasten themselves to the body, seize control of the nervous system, and completely bypass one's own will. One becomes a spectator in one's own body. What is entirely lost is self-control. Thus the novel is about responsibility for one's actions. One cannot shuffle one's responsibilities onto a government or an organization or any group to which one happens to belong. This sense of responsibility or duty is the other side of freedom (as Heinlein also teaches in *Starship Troopers*). Here he says, "The price of freedom is the willingness to do sudden battle, anywhere, anytime, and with utter recklessness," and therefore the U.N.S. *Avenger* is outfitted and the character from whose point of view the narrative is told joins an expeditionary force to the Puppet Masters' home, Titan, with the promise, "Puppet Masters—the free men are coming to kill you! *Death and Destruction!*" On purely fictional terms *The Puppet Masters* is a better novel than *Starship Troopers* in that it has more fully realized scenes and less lecture and Socratic dialogue, but the two are very similar in their impact and in their arguments for freedom and responsibility.

Roger Zelazny once remarked, "Character development is the driving force of a story." This is certainly true of much of Heinlein's fiction. Most of his juveniles show a young man learning to accept the responsibilities of adulthood. *Farmer in the Sky*, *Starman Jones*, and *Tunnel in the Sky* are outstanding examples. The best example from among the adult novels is probably *Double Star*. Two major political parties assure the human race's rights in an interplanetary civilization. One of these parties wants to extend these rights to the nonhumans as well; the other wants to reserve them for humans only. At a crucial time in this political struggle, John Joseph Bonforte, the leader of the first party, is kidnapped by the opposition and must be replaced by a self-centered, apolitical, slightly xenophobic actor named the Great Lorenzo. The story tells of how Lorenzo replaces Bonforte temporarily, grows

into the role in a variety of ways, and eventually must replace him permanently. Lorenzo's character development is the driving force of this story. *Double Star* won Heinlein his first Hugo Award, and it remains one of his most readable stories. It is not, however, one of his best because it does not take on any important issues, as does, for example, *Beyond This Horizon*.

The Door Into Summer is Heinlein's time-travel novel. In plot summary it sounds good; in actual reading it is not. The problem usually pointed out is the colorlessness of its central character. He has no identity of his own. But this has plagued other Heinlein stories, like *The Puppet Masters* and *Starship Troopers*, without ruining them. In those novels, however, setting and action were strong and clear. In *The Door Into Summer* the temporal peregrinations of the main character whisk him between time periods before the reader can become aware of them, before he can live in them and accept them as real. With a vague central character and a vague context, the only thing left is the time paradox, and it is not nearly as good as, for instance, the one in Heinlein's own "All You Zombies—" or Asimov's *The End of Eternity* (1955).

If neither *Double Star* nor *The Door Into Summer* take on issues of any real importance, the same cannot be said of Heinlein's 1961 masterpiece, *Stranger in a Strange Land*. It will be remembered that after 1957 Heinlein began to write about unpopular, conservative political causes (in *Starship Troopers*, for example) and unpopular, liberal sexual causes (in *Stranger in a Strange Land*, *I Will Fear No Evil* (1970), and *Time Enough for Love*). It should be emphasized that neither set of unpopular causes sprang out of Heinlein's head ex nihilo. "The Roads Must Roll" showed the value of a strong military organization; the society in *Beyond This Horizon* featured a wearing and use of guns; and in *Red Planet* the wearing of guns was a sign of maturity. His magazine and juvenile fiction was as sexually innocent as his editors thought his readership should be. There is much to be said about male and female role playing in his pre-1957 fiction, but very little about the sex in it. There are sexually active characters in *If This Goes On—*, *Beyond This Horizon*, *The Puppet Masters*, and even *Tunnel in the Sky*, but the novels are about other subjects and sex remains peripheral in them. In *Stranger in a Strange Land* and in his work since, sex moves in from the periphery and often becomes central. But an important distinction must be made here. Heinlein is not interested in describing the sex act itself. He is not attempting—and failing—to write pornography, as some critics seem to say. Instead he is interested in what might be called the sociology of sex and even the psychology of sex. He is interested in the context of sexual behavior, not its content.

Two similar anecdotes exist about the origin of *Stranger in a Strange Land*. One says that Heinlein examined many of the common assumptions by which Americans live and then wrote a novel presenting the other side of each. The other has it that he examined the assumptions behind his own work and then took the other side of those. There is not much to choose between the two anecdotes, for officially, Americans and most of Heinlein's male characters believe in marriage as a prerequisite to sex; in *Stranger in a Strange Land* marriage is irrelevant. Officially, Americans believe in couples limiting their sexual activity to one another; in *Stranger in a Strange Land* sexual promiscuity is the norm. Officially, Americans believe sex is a private activity; in *Stranger in a Strange Land* group sex is encouraged. Officially, America's major religions teach that sex is evil and is to be engaged in only if one wants children or if one cannot control his/her sexual desires (it is better to marry than to burn); in *Stranger in a Strange Land* promiscuous group sex is among the religion's ceremonies. Only in a fictional sense does Heinlein defend the sexual attitudes in the novel; that is, he tries to make them plausible in the context of his story. This is entirely different from saying that Heinlein is in favor of them. He is presenting alternatives. He is writing speculative fiction, and he is speculating about sexual mores. This makes him neither moral nor immoral, for he is merely looking at an important part of the human condition.

Sex is accepted in both *Glory Road* (1963) and *Farnham's Freehold* as a part of the human condition, but in no sense is either novel about sex. *Glory Road* is about fantasy novels, and *Farnham's Freehold* is about survival. In *The Moon Is a Harsh Mistress* the two-to-one predominance of males over females on the moon determines the sociology of sex. The women are more valuable than air and can do whatever pleases them. Various living patterns are possible. One woman can have multiple husbands or multiple lovers, according to her choice. Children require adults to care for them, so various forms of marriage have evolved. The narrator, for example, belongs to a line-marriage, in which adults who die or move away are replaced so that the multiple-adult family can survive indefinitely. The narrator's family is nearly a hundred years old and has had twenty-one links, nine of whom are still alive. When a new woman joins the marriage, the eldest male spends the first night with her; then she settles down with her favorite male but does not refuse the others. This would not work in a society which considers marriage a form of property contract and the marriage partners as one another's property. It works in Heinlein's lunar society because the situation in which these social patterns evolved is different from the one in which patterns have evolved on Earth. Heinlein as usual recognizes that a different environment will create a different psychology, and a different psychology will allow different social patterns to develop. (Again, he is not advocating line-marriages. He is offering them as alternatives to speculate upon. The future will also be different socially from the present.)

I Will Fear No Evil (1970) and *Time Enough for Love* have sex (not pornography) as their central concern. *I Will Fear No Evil* establishes its context for a discussion of sex roles with a fascinating "What if?" What if a male brain were transplanted into a female body? A dying male, Johann, has his brain placed in Eunice's female body. Is the result male or female? And which sex does the result have "normal" sexual relations with? The story will clearly have to be an internal one, concentrating on Johann's attitudes and any changes in them. Character development will be its driving force. In order to avoid long passages of interior monologue and self-analysis, Heinlein allows Eunice to remain somehow conscious in her body after Johann occupies it. The combination of Johann and Eunice is named Joan Eunice. Now, instead of interior monologues there are more dramatic interior dialogues, conversations. The situation's original "What if?" becomes even more complex: What about a female body inhabited by both a male and a female ego? What would the natural sexual role of such a creature be? Male or female? Joan Eunice raises the question in the novel:

> "I'm in the damnedest situation a man ever found himself in. I'm not the ordinary sex change of a homo who gets surgery and hormone shots to tailor his male body into fake female. . . . This body is a normal female. But the brain in it has had a man's canalization and many years of enthusiastic male sex experience. So tell me, Jake, which time am I being normal, and which time perverse?"
>
> "Uh . . . I'm forced to say that your female body controls."
>
> "But *does* it? Psychologists claim that sexual desire and orgasm take place in the brain—*not* in the genitals."

As Joan Eunice also says, "I've been doing lots of reading . . . trying to find out *who* I am, *what* I am, *how* I should behave." In trying to find the answers to these questions, Heinlein is helping his readers examine their own assumptions about human sexuality. What Joan Eunice decides could be taken as the point of the novel: "From my unique experience, embracing both physiological sexes directly and not by hearsay, I say there is just one *sex*." Unfortunately, this insight is never fully developed; its application to the reader—who cannot share Joan Eunice's unique perspective—is never clarified. Instead, Heinlein spends the novel's time playing games with the story situation without using that situation to provide insight into human nature as it really is.

Time Enough for Love is a long and lumpy novel. It is long because it contains a lot of Socratic dialogues on a wide variety of subjects, and it is lumpy because mixed into it are a lot of very good short stories and novelettes. Once again, sex is a central subject, and once again Heinlein is interested in sex roles rather than the sex act itself. The central character is Lazarus Long, from *Methuselah's Children*, for all practical purposes an immortal. In one of the novel's episodes he rescues an infant from a burning house, raises her, then marries and has children by her. He moves from father to husband. Is this incest? Heinlein suggests it is not in the context given. In another episode, twin female clones of himself are raised and he has sex with them. Is this autoeroticism? It is not, Heinlein seems to say, in the context given. Eventually he goes back in time over two thousand years and has intercourse with his own mother. Is this incest? While it technically is, the situation raises two issues. He knew already that no children would result, so there was no genetic reason for the prohibition, and with two thousand years of experience behind it, to what extent is this hunk of protoplasm identical to the child his mother bore?

It seems that the major problem in Heinlein's novels about the sociology of sex is that the sexual roles he examines are no concern of contemporary humanity. Few men are members of orgiastic religions founded by omnipotent Martians. No one has had his brain transplanted into a body of the opposite sex with its original ego lying in wait to debate and instruct the new occupant. The chances are extremely slim that contemporary man will have to face the moral dilemma of having sex with his own clones. No one will live two thousand years before entering a time machine that will take him to a sexual confrontation with his own mother (or father, or both). The problem with Heinlein's sex novels is that they do not really tell us anything about people's sexual selves. They offer no insight into life as it is actually lived. They are not about anything. But here is the real hub of it all: they were not meant to be. A cardinal tenet of criticism is that one cannot criticize a book for not doing what it never intended to do. Therefore, such criticism of Heinlein's sex novels as was offered above is automatically invalidated. From the beginning of his career Heinlein's attitude toward the future has been that it is neither a place to escape to, as in Burroughs's fiction, nor a setting symbolic of the present, as in the works of Wells. The future is an alternate setting for its own sake. The main point is that the future will be different from the present, with different problems confronting the real people who will be alive then. Present-day lives are not being lived in order to provide insights into life as it was lived in Elizabethan England. People live for their own sakes because it is their turn. All science-fiction writers and readers know that the technology of the future will be different from the technology of the present. Heinlein's later novels are reminders that that different technology will create a different society and that that different society will have different sexual mores too. Heinlein's sex novels offer no insight into life as it is lived today precisely because they are about life as it will be lived in the future, when things will be different.

Throughout his career Heinlein has demonstrated that the future will not be the present in disguise. Other concerns have run through his fiction as well: the pioneer spirit; space flight; militarism; man as a ruthless fighting animal; a reverence for the intellect and for intelligent life. But three concerns stand out most: longevity and survival, freedom and slavery, and the joy of living. The first two have been amply discussed and illustrated, but the third is the most important. From *Beyond This Horizon* through *Time Enough for Love* Heinlein's central characters have shown that the reason for living is involvement in life. "It was a good world . . . filled with interesting things," thinks Hamilton Felix in *Beyond This Horizon*, and behind him one hears Heinlein saying, "Enjoy it."

Screenplays:

Destination Moon, by Heinlein, Rip Van Ronkel, and James O'Hanlon, George Pal/Eagle-Lion, 1950;
Project Moonbase, by Heinlein and Jack Seaman, Galaxy Pictures/Lippert, 1953.

Other:

"On the Writing of Speculative Fiction," in *Of Worlds Beyond: The Science of Science Fiction Writing*, ed. Lloyd Arthur Eshback (Reading, Pa.: Fantasy Press, 1947);

Tomorrow the Stars, edited by Heinlein (Garden City: Doubleday, 1951);

"Science Fiction: Its Nature, Faults and Virtues," in *The Science Fiction Novel: Imagination and Social Criticism*, [ed. Basil Davenport] (Chicago: Advent, 1959).

Periodical Publications:

"The Discovery of the Future," *Vertex*, 1 (April 1973): 46-49, 96-98;

"Channel Markers," *Analog*, 95 (January 1974): 5-10, 166-178.

References:

Brian W. Aldiss, *Billion Year Spree: The True History of Science Fiction* (Garden City: Doubleday, 1973), pp. 269-274;

William Atheling, *The Issue at Hand* (Chicago: Advent, 1964), pp. 68-79;

Atheling, *More Issues at Hand* (Chicago: Advent, 1970), pp. 51-58;

Alfred Bester, "Robert Heinlein," *Publishers Weekly* (2 July 1973): 44-45;

Howard Bruce Franklin, *Robert A. Heinlein: America as Science Fiction* (New York: Oxford, 1980);

James Gunn, *Alternate Worlds: The Illustrated History of Science Fiction* (Englewood Cliffs, N.J.: Prentice-Hall, 1975), pp. 7ff;

Damon Knight, *In Search of Wonder* (Chicago: Advent, 1956), pp. 76-89;

Sam Moskowitz, *Seekers of Tomorrow: Masters of Modern Science Fiction* (New York: Ballantine, 1967), pp. 191-214;

Joseph D. Olander and Martin Harry Greenberg, eds., *Robert A. Heinlein* (New York: Taplinger, 1978);

Alexei Panshin, *Heinlein in Dimension* (Chicago: Advent, 1968);

David N. Samuelson, "The Frontier Worlds of Robert A. Heinlein," in *Voices for the Future*, vol. 1, ed. Thomas D. Clareson (Bowling Green, Ohio: Bowling Green University Popular Press, 1976), pp. 104-152;

Robert Scholes and Eric S. Rabkin, *Science Fiction: History, Science, Vision* (New York: Oxford University Press, 1977), pp. 52-58;

George Edgar Slusser, *The Classic Years of Robert A. Heinlein* (San Bernardino, Cal.: Borgo Press, 1977);

Slusser, *Robert A. Heinlein: Stranger in His Own Land* (San Bernardino, Cal.: Borgo Press, 1976);

Donald A. Wollheim, *The Universe Makers: Science Fiction Today* (New York: Harper & Row, 1971), pp. 99-102.

Papers:

Heinlein's papers and correspondence are being collected at the University of California, Santa Cruz.

ZENNA HENDERSON
(1 November 1917-)

BOOKS: *Pilgrimage: The Book of the People* (Garden City: Doubleday, 1961; London: Gollancz, 1962);

The Anything Box (Garden City: Doubleday, 1965; London: Gollancz, 1966);

The People: No Different Flesh (London: Gollancz, 1966; Garden City: Doubleday, 1967);

Holding Wonder (Garden City: Doubleday, 1971).

Zenna Henderson (nee Chlarson) was born in the foothills of the South Catalina Mountains near Tucson, Arizona. She grew up in a strongly religious atmosphere that has had a profound effect on her writing. Henderson received a B.A. from Arizona State University (then Arizona State College) in 1940, and in 1954 completed a master's degree in languages and literature. Henderson married, but she and her husband divorced after seven years. She has no children. Henderson has been a teacher all her adult life, and although much of her time has been spent in the Eloy public school system in Arizona, she has traveled widely. During World War II she taught at the Japanese-American Relocation Camp in Rivers, Arizona; from 1956 to 1958 she taught at a U. S. Air Force base north of Paris, and upon her return at a children's tuberculosis hospital in Connecticut (1958-1959). Presently she teaches first grade, and her concern with the relationship between teacher and child is an important theme in her fiction.

Henderson is best known for her series of stories about the People, a race of aliens physically indistinguishable from humans but endowed with psi powers and an acute moral sense setting them apart from the norm. Although generally accepted as one of the standards of the genre, her fiction actually has few of the customary trappings of science fiction. Unlike the stories her peers were writing in the 1950s and 1960s, which most typically pit characters against outlandish mechanical monsters, Henderson's stories explore human nature, the relationships between People and people, humans and the natural environment. Above all, her stories diffuse a warm humanism celebrating man's potential for compassion as well as his tendency to destroy the unfamiliar. The mildly religious undertone pervading her work expresses her profound respect for the sanctity of the individual.

Henderson's first volume, *Pilgrimage: The Book of the People* (1961), is a novelization of the first six stories about the People, all of which appeared in the *Magazine of Fantasy and Science Fiction* between 1952 and 1959. In an interview with Paul Walker, Henderson said that the People stories began as "a story about some people who crossed the Atlantic by 'lifting' from their home in Transylvania." Gradually, the theme of interstellar refugees emerged from the horror tale. The descendants of the survivors of the crossing "gather" to recreate their history and thus understand their place on Earth. Exiled from the Home and hated by superstitious humans, they epitomize the displaced. The stories are linked by the tale of an Earth woman, Lea, who has lost faith in herself and who has come to the desert to commit suicide. As the novel opens, Karen, one of the People, saves her, and gradually Lea regains her sense of health and rejects her suicidal inertia and despair. Listening to the tales told in the Gathering of the early days on Earth, she begins to understand the difference between her own self-indulgent fear of the world and the real terror of persecution caused by being different. Thus, while the stories are ostensibly about aliens, they actually explore humanity's inadequacies and yet affirm Henderson's faith in human ability to transcend prejudice and ignorance.

The title of the first story, "Ararat" (1952), is like all the others, taken from an Old Testament narrrative: "And the Ark rested . . . upon the mountains of Ararat." It is, like the story of the Israelites, about isolation and the need for a sense of community and place. As in many of Henderson's stories, the main character is a teacher, a woman who is perceptive, kind, but who has no place in the human world because of her psi powers. Her arrival in the Canyon is, like the settling of the ark, a homecoming, and the faith of the People is rewarded when they discover she has many skills the group has

lacked since their disastrous arrival on Earth. The second story, "Gilead" (1954), also deals with the isolation and cruelty suffered by People outside the Canyon, but it is a story of healing. The balm of Gilead, basic education by the knowledgeable, allows a telepathic girl to protect herself against the pain and hostility she feels around her. The link between the frame tale and individual stories becomes apparent here. Only after the story "Pottage" (1955), told by a fellow outsider, does Lea begin to accept the peace that has been forced on her. "Pottage," too, is a story of healing, this time of an entire community of People whose early persecution has crippled their enthusiasm for life. Their new teacher, although an outsider, returns their birthright to them through their children's capacity for wonder and enjoyment of learning.

"Wilderness" (1957), the fourth story, is also about and told by a teacher. Although fully human, Dita has many of the "persuasions" and has chosen to use them in teaching. Her experience with a retarded student "trapped in a body" beyond the control of her mind reinforces Dita's notion of her own deviancy, especially since the typical teacher, Mrs. Kantz, dismisses Dita's interest and compassion as unnecessary brooding over something barely human. The child's imbalance precipitates matters, and Dita learns of a community with gifts like her own. The possible sentimentality of this happy ending is alleviated by its humor—Dita makes the contact through the local wino, who thinks he has seen angels during one of his binges (in reality a People family on a picnic).

The penultimate story of the collection is the strongest, fusing the most important elements of earlier pieces and anticipating the fulfillment of the last. The narrator of "Captivity" (1958) is also a teacher; but this woman, crippled in a car wreck, has like Lea and like the population of Bendo abandoned life. She no longer teaches and instead sits at her window, "sad with a sadness that knows no comfort." Her avocation saves her when a friend challenges her to try to penetrate the walls the Francher kid has erected around himself. Unlike the other exiled People, the Francher kid is an artist, able to transcend the laws of time and space with his music: "The harmonica cried softly in the moonlight, an aching asking cry as it spiraled up and around . . . and lost its voice in the darkness."

Music provides the kid's escape from his abusive foster family, and eventually it places the demands of discipline and normative behavior upon him, so he learns to control his rebellion and focus his gifts. Again, there is a sense of homecoming when he eventually meets others of his kind, but the greatest gift for him is his own to the teacher who has believed in him when he uses his telekinesis to walk her across the yard; the use of his gift for others frees him from his prison of self. Henderson insists faith in self and others is what gives true power. Thus, when the teacher is able to act again for a child, she frees herself from her own body prison and psychological malaise.

The final story of the collection is the only classical science fiction story, but again technology takes second place to human concerns. "Jordan" (1959) is, as the title suggests, about the arrival for a brief stay on Earth by a group from the New Home, the planet colonized after the destruction of the People's Eden. Like Lea, by now healed, the People must decide which path to take—to stay on Earth, the planet of their persecution, or to return with the visitors to their dream home. The narrator, a young, naive idealist, undergoes a painful awakening to the discrepancy between the visitors' technology and their emotional and moral development. Crippled by their dependancy on technology, the New Homers have become alienated from their environment and have lost their concern for the individual. The young man risks travel to the New Home only because he realizes he can learn the science necessary to help his friend and mentor Obla, whose body has been grossly deformed by a plane accident. Like all the narrators in this volume, he grows up, achieves a sense of proportion, and learns the power of belief and compassion. Like the rest of the Earth-bound People, he will return to the Canyon, his home, with new knowledge.

The Anything Box (1965) is a collection of stories ranging from sentimental science fiction ("Subcommittee," 1962) to fantasy-horror ("Stevie and the Dark," 1952), but as in her People stories, Henderson emphasizes the individual's development or lack thereof, and his or her influence on others. The title story, "The Anything Box" (1956), describes an invisible box that allows its possessor, a young child called Sue-lynn, to escape the pressures of her school and family. When the cruelties of her peers become too great, she retreats almost completely into the Never-Never land in the Box. The teacher-narrator helps her progress to maturity by understanding both Sue-lynn's need for peace and the necessity for her accepting and learning from her real life. The story is one of Henderson's best, combining powerful accuracy of detail—her insights into the daily grind of a first-grade teacher—with an insistence on the importance of wonder and imagination. Stories about teaching frame the book. The narrator of "The

Zenna Henderson

Last Step" (1957) exemplifies the worst characteristics of the profession. By her own admission, she does not like children, and in fact she thinks of them as mere "components of my work." She is rigidly unsentimental, cold, and vindictive. Just as the narrator of "The Anything Box" restores order and growth to her environment, so this woman desecrates it. Her destruction of the make-believe world in the children's sandbox predicts the end of the human's exodus from the planet; her negation of imagination becomes a power for unseen forces. Again, Henderson reminds us of our responsibility to each other, and of the vital importance of wonder.

Henderson is also aware of the dangers implicit in imagination. In "Hush!" (1953), a small child invents a noise-eating beast which proceeds to suck all sound from the world. In "Stevie and the Dark," wonder is mixed with terror as a living blackness overpowers the instinctive magic of a five-year-old. The power of the imagination necessitates its control and responsible use; thus children are at particular risk because of their heightened capacity to wonder and their lack of knowledge.

Two of the most powerful tales are also the shortest, cameos from legends epitomizing our greatest fears. "Walking Aunt Daid" (1955), its tone a melange of rustic artlessness and high fantasy, tells of an ageless woman condemned to wake once in every generation from her catatonic state to walk with the youngest male member of her guardian family. The experience simultaneously initiates the boy into sexual awareness and knowledge of mortality as the resurrected Aunt Daid, "light rippling around her like silk," crumples before him to the wrinkled seed he has grown up with. "Things" (1960), like "The Grunder" (1953), has strong folkloric elements but is set on an alien planet and told in a brutally simple style to emphasize the stark confrontation between human and coveti culture. Cast out for his progressiveness, the primitive Deci lies, at the end of the story, "waiting for his own breath to stop" as the dust pours over him.

In her third volume of stories, Henderson returns to the People, giving a historical perspective to their alienation. *The People: No Different Flesh* (1966) treats themes similar to those in the earlier volume, but while *Pilgrimage* focused on psychological isolation, *The People* tells of blatant physical violence. Again, the stories are connected by a framing device, this time the story of Meris and Mark, a couple in mourning for their first child. The discovery of a People child initiates Meris's recovery from her prolonged grief and self-absorption, and the arrival of the child's parents extends the healing process to Mark, enabling him to complete the book he is writing. Tad, a teenage rebel whose gang leaders gratuitously destroy Mark's book, is also "healed" of his antagonism when his frustration is focused by his fascination with the People's vintage jalopy. As the People gather, they retrace their history on Earth, returning for the first time to the early painful years following the crash of the escape ship. "Deluge" (1963) describes the last days on the Home: the loss of traditions closely tied to the land, the agonizing necessity of parting lovers so each ship may be filled, the final exultant sacrifice of the Old One who is called with her planet.

"Angels Unawares" (1966) and "Troubling of the Water" (1966) both explore the prejudice facing the People in nineteenth-century America. In the first, religious fanatics burn some of the People as witches, then daub biblical mottoes on their charred buildings. Only a newly arrived immigrant family perceives that these victims are, ironically, angels in the guise of humans and saves a small girl at the risk of their own deaths. An isolated Person, blinded in his crash, is also rescued and cared for in "Troubling of the Water" by humans recognizing the mutuality of exile: "It's like . . . being the first settler in a big land." He reciprocates by uncovering a well, thus saving them all from a drought.

The fifth story, "Return" (1961), jumps to the most recent period in the People's history, the New Homers' arrival on Earth and presents the first examples of egotism and pride. As in the majority of the stories, People teach humans; they become man's models. Debbie, returning to the freedom of Earth from New Home's groomed perfection, has to discover the worth of humans and her own humility. Only after almost killing by neglect and being cast out from her own group does she realize the extent of her own prejudices. The biblical mottoes delineating human viciousness in "Angels" now teach Debbie: "To whom much is given, much is expected." The burden of being People is as great as the gift, and this provides the plot of the last story, "Shadow on the Moon" (1962), in which the mechanical genius Remy finally creates the bond between humans and People by fulfilling an old man's dream for his dead son. The psi amplifier designed by the human is implemented; both humans, dead son and dying father, are brought to the moon and thus complete a cycle begun a century before by the arrival of the alien race.

Henderson's most recent and most fragmented collection, *Holding Wonder* (1971), contains some of her most powerful pieces, in which the theme of the individual's relationship with the environment becomes omnipresent. Many of these twenty stories are about teachers, all of whom are protective yet encourage their students' exploration. Many of the stories are set in a postholocaust period, and in these tales teachers provide both continuity of culture and courage so that the race may continue. Among the most effective is "As Simple as That" (1971), in which the teacher's daily writing lesson allows the surviving children to explore their recollections of "before." There is no moral, no answer: only a bare sketch of the trauma of survival.

Henderson has a reputation for writing sickly sweet tales; *Holding Wonder* is sparse and brutal compared to her earlier work. The teachers may be kind to their children, even when the students are invisible aliens ("Loo Ree," 1953) or pale lavender fur balls ("The Closest School," 1960); however, the universe is a terrifying place. Several of the stories are about fear: "Incident After" (1971) is set in a domestic scene, but Henderson's masterly selection of revealing mundane details explores the fears of a postholocaust "typical housewife," concentrating on her small victories to reveal her terror and isolation, like venturing "Outside." Other stories ("J-Line to Nowhere," 1969; "Crowning Glory," 1971) are about people trampled by technological culture. "One of Them" (1971) may simply be a science-fiction murder mystery set in a future inhabited by clonelike persons, but it more likely depicts the frantic attempts of a split personality to integrate its selves. The most effective tale, "Swept and Garnished" (1971), depicts an agoraphobic's need for her fear. Healed of her affliction, she has no self-definition; the careful work of the psychiatrist must be undone: "I have to have something somewhere," for terror is a familiar presence that supports as it paralyzes.

The range of Henderson's work is wide; while she is considered an important science-fiction writer, much of her best and most recent material is highly allegorical, as, for example, "There Was a Garden" (1978). This celebration of the death of the Last Man reiterates themes first developed in her People stories: the components of the Earth decide that without man's imagination they are meaningless. At the end of the story they wait, anticipating a Return that will allow Dust to mix with Water and form primeval mud. The story has the sparsity of Henderson's best writing, and because of its allegorical simplicity avoids the charge of sentimentalism. —*Patricia M. Handy*

Other:

"There Was a Garden," in *Cassandra Rising*, ed. Alice Laurance (Garden City: Doubleday, 1978), pp. 29-35.

Periodical Publication:

"Tell Us a Story," *Magazine of Fantasy and Science Fiction* (October 1980): 6-41.

Reference:

Paul Walker, "Zenna Henderson," in *Speaking of Science Fiction: The Paul Walker Interviews* (Oradell, N. J.: Luna, 1978), pp. 271-280.

FRANK HERBERT
(8 October 1920-   )

BOOKS: *The Dragon in the Sea* (Garden City: Doubleday, 1956; London: Gollancz, 1960); republished as *21st Century Sub* (New York: Avon, 1956); republished again as *Under Pressure* (New York: Ballantine, 1974);

Dune (Philadelphia: Chilton, 1965; London: Gollancz, 1966);

The Green Brain (New York: Ace, 1966; London: New English Library, 1973);

Destination: Void (New York: Berkley, 1966; Harmondsworth: Penguin, 1967; revised edition, New York: Berkley, 1978);

The Eyes of Heisenberg (New York: Berkley, 1966; London: Sphere, 1968);

The Heaven Makers (New York: Avon, 1968; London: New English Library, 1970);

The Santaroga Barrier (New York: Berkley, 1968; London: Rapp & Whiting, 1970);

Dune Messiah (New York: Putnam's, 1969; London: Gollancz, 1971);

Whipping Star (New York: Putnam's, 1970; London: New English Library, 1972);

The Worlds of Frank Herbert (London: New English Library, 1970; New York: Ace, 1971);

Soul Catcher (New York: Putnam's, 1972; London: New English Library, 1973);

The God Makers (New York: Putnam's, 1972; London: New English Library, 1972);

Hellstrom's Hive (Garden City: Doubleday, 1973; London: New English Library, 1974);

The Book of Frank Herbert (New York: DAW, 1973; St. Albans, U.K.: Panther, 1977);

Threshold: The Blue Angels Experience (New York: Ballantine, 1973);

The Best of Frank Herbert ed. Angus Wells (London: Sidgwick & Jackson, 1975);

Children of Dune (New York: Berkley, 1976; London: Gollancz, 1976);

The Dosadi Experiment (New York: Putnam's, 1977; London: Gollancz, 1978);

The Illustrated Dune (New York: Berkley, 1978);

The Great Dune Trilogy (London: Gollancz, 1979);

The Jesus Incident, by Herbert and Bill Ransom (New York: Berkley, 1979).

Born in Tacoma, Washington, Frank Herbert is best known as the author of the Dune series. He worked for many years as a journalist for West Coast newspapers from San Francisco to Seattle and at a wide range of other jobs, of which his experiences in the U.S. Navy during World War II and as a lay analyst have had the greatest effect on his fiction. His first science-fiction story was published in 1952 and his first novel in 1956. The enormous success of *Dune* (1965) enabled him to write full time, and he has published fifteen novels to date (including one nonscience fiction) and three collections of short stories. An active member of the World Without War Council, Herbert has been a consultant on social and ecological problems to the Lincoln Foundation and to the governments of Vietnam and Pakistan and has developed a six-acre ecological demonstration project in his native Washington.

Herbert's short fiction is diverse and entertaining, but his novels show a unifying concern with systems and systems interactions. Physical ecology is the subject of *The Green Brain* (1966) and an important part of the Dune series, while a concern with social ecology—the dynamics of social structures and restraints, social conflicts as a means of natural selection, the nature of psychology and religion, and racial imperatives—infuses all of his novels. The most common focus of this interest in systems is an exploration of the causes, functions, and limits of human consciousness. Herbert usually views consciousness as a "systems effect," in which the whole is greater than the sum of its parts, and an understanding of this mechanism permits many of his characters to overcome social manipulation or transcend the limitations of individual memory and power. Many of his characters have formal training which enables them to control their own emotional responses and detect the subtle betrayals of emotion made by their opponents.

Less concerned with plot and characterization than with setting and ideas, Herbert usually employs a fragmented narrative structure, in which relatively brief episodes are introduced by quotations from invented works. Within each episode, the story line progresses less by action than by observation, cogitation, and antagonistic dialogue.

This essentially static exposition is well suited to the intellectual cast of Herbert's fiction, but its dangers are serious. Often the reader is severely distanced from the action, and, although Herbert frequently asserts the value of social cooperation, his books more often involve ruthless competition. Incessant intrigue is the easiest form in which to present intellectual adventure, but Herbert's frequent and unexpected turns of plot make it difficult for the reader to tell whether a character's observations reflect superior intellect or justified paranoia, as in this typical passage from *Children of Dune* (1976):

> He saw now where she had to be going and knowing its effect upon those who watched through the spy eyes, refrained from casting

an apprehensive glance at the door. Only a trained eye could have detected his momentary imbalance, but Jessica saw it and smiled. A smile, after all, could mean anything.

Presumably Herbert intends to show the shortcomings of such behavior and, consequently, the flaws of social systems which demand it. But by creating plots which depend so heavily on intrigue, he fails to provide his audience with convincing examples of social harmony.

In *The Dragon in the Sea* (1956) Herbert minimizes this reliance on intrigue by limiting himself to an examination of psychological adaptation on a small scale. Four men of a near-future U.S. Navy take a subtug on a dangerous mission to pirate undersea oil from the Eastern Powers. The subtug represents "an enveloped world with its own special ecology," symbolically prenatal and subconscious, protected by darkness and quiet salt water from many of the dangers of the surface world. Yet, as the title suggests, the sea causes its own fears. The danger from enemy wolf packs is less threatening than two internal perils: one of the crew is a saboteur, and another, Ensign John Ramsay, through whose eyes the reader sees most of the action, is a psychologist, whose mission to discover why subtug crews show such high rates of insanity and death in action is in itself a threat to the crew's stability. The subtug crew responds to these pressures with adaptations which are insane when judged by outside standards. As Captain Sparrow explains, "I'm nuts in a way which fits me perfectly to my world. That makes my world nuts and me normal. Not sane. Normal. Adapted."

As in most of Herbert's Earth-bound novels, the ultimate insanity in *The Dragon in the Sea* is that of human society. Having dragged on for sixteen years, the vicious war with the Eastern Powers is now limited to acts of sabotage and piracy, and the surface world has become claustrophobic and paranoid. If social sanity, even in the limited sense of functional adaptation, is measured by "unbroken lines of communication," the constant bureaucratic infighting of military personnel points toward a psychotic break. Sparrow defines personal sanity as "the ability to swim . . . to understand *currents*," to which Ramsay's mentor, the sinister psychologist Dr. Oberhausen, adds the ability to "be prepared at all times to grasp a paddle," but as the book ends, Ramsay finds himself once more a victim of political expediency.

Herbert was recognized as a major science-fiction writer with *Dune* (1965), the first novel to win

"Before we get off to any wrong starts," said Gerard, ".
I'd better remind everybody that nobody gets out of this build
alive without my say-so." *He rubbed a few ... popped a white lozenge into his mouth. He*

Addington sat down with a grunt, said, "Save the drama for
those who appreciate it, bulb head." The two aides remained
standing. Addington had not shown that he even knew Movius was
present. Suddenly, he ~~turned toward~~ *whirled on* Movius, said, "What we really
want you for is murder!"

Movius didn't have to feign surprise. He looked from Addington to Gerard, back to Addington. "This is fantastic," he said.
"I've been on my honeymoon. I don't know what you're talking
about." *...*

The Bu-Con chief reached up to his side, *clerk* ~~without looking~~, took
the briefcase, opened it on his lap. ~~All the while he didn't take
his eyes from Movius.~~ From the case he pulled a paper, glanced
briefly at it, said, "On the eve of Midsummer Festival you, in the
company with another man, as yet unidentified, did accost one Howell
Pescado and ~~*Birch Morfon*~~ in the Richmond Warrenate. You and companion
did then attack Mr. Pescado and Mr. Morfon with such violence that
Mr. Pescado died ~~the next morning~~ of a broken neck." *...*

Movius shook his head. "I've never heard of these people,"
he said. "I've never been in such a fight."

Gerard leaned forward. *...* "To hell with a street brawl," he
said. "What's this about Dan failing to report for the ALF?"

Addington flushed, spoke without looking up from his papers.
"That was an error. He is not wanted on such a charge."

Gerard said, "Oh," leaned back. He turned to Movius. "Did
you knock over this Pescado?"

"No."

both the Hugo (1966) and Nebula awards (1965). Together with such books as Heinlein's *Stranger in a Strange Land* (1961) and Tolkien's *Lord of the Rings* (1954-1955), *Dune* helped establish two traditions in contemporary science fiction: the long novel and the invented-world novel, in which details of history, languages, customs, geography, and ecology (often explained in appended essays and maps) are combined with a rich complexity that pleases the reader by its verisimilitude and imaginative scope. As one of the first science-fiction novels to deal with ecology, *Dune* was also influential in introducing a timely and important subject to the field. Continuously in print since its original appearance, *Dune* has sold over a million copies and is now being made into a major motion picture.

The basic plot of *Dune* is similar to that of many of Herbert's novels: a hero with superior intelligence and special abilities struggles through complex intrigues. But the scope of *Dune*, set in a traditional galactic empire, is sufficiently broad to lend dignity to the intrigues. Civilization preserves a delicate military and economic balance between the Imperium and the Great Houses; this balance of power is complicated by specialized organizations such as the Spacing Guild, which controls all interstellar traffic, and the female Bene Gesserit, who study politics, furnish consort-advisers to the nobility, and arrange noble marriages to further their secret breeding program. The program is designed to produce the Kwisatz Haderach, a prescient male who has full access to the genetic memories of his ancestors.

The mode of action in this galactic empire is the matter of heroic fantasy. The ancient Butlerian jihad has imposed a universal abhorrence of intelligent machines, so that a premium is placed on personal mentality, whether it be Bene Gesserit controls of mind and body, the limited prescience by which Spacing Guildsmen navigate, or the superb logic of a trained mentat. The Houses are free to fight among themselves, but since atomic weapons are banned and energized body shields render rapid projectile weapons useless, warfare is largely a question of tactical skill and swordplay.

The Dune trilogy traces the fortunes of the Atreides family and its retainers. As *Dune* opens, Duke Leto has been forced to exchange his home world of Caladan for Arrakis, or Dune, a desert world

which is the only source of melange, the most precious substance in the universe, an addictive spice with geriatric and prescient properties. The gift of this valuable planet is, of course, a trap by the Harkonnens, the Atreides' archrivals, and soon Leto is killed, leaving his son Paul and his widow Jessica, a Bene Gesserit adept, to flee into the desert, where they are taken in by the native Fremen. As Paul matures, a constant diet of melange enhances his genetic prescience so that he becomes the Kwisatz Haderach and more, able to see the future as a network of probability paths which to some extent he can alter or choose between. Using the Fremen, the best warriors in the universe, Paul struggles to free Arrakis from the Harkonnens while avoiding the bloody jihad which his visions tell him will be produced through his victory by the need of the human race "to renew its scattered inheritance, to cross and mingle and infuse their bloodlines in a great new mingling of genes." This knowledge of his "terrible purpose" makes Paul regret and despise his eventual seizure of the Imperial throne.

A substantial part of the success of *Dune* results from this emotional dilemma, which makes Paul the most fully developed character in any of Herbert's novels. Many of the supporting characters are also well realized, especially Gurney Halleck, troubadour and swordsman, Stilgar, the epitome of traditional Fremen ways, and Baron Vladimir Harkonnen, whose caricatured evil is nonetheless loathsome. But the real foundation of *Dune* is the planet and its people. The ecological cycle which connects melange and the giant sandworms is one of the best examples of true scientific imagination in science fiction, and Herbert's descriptions of Dune are vivid and engrossing. The Fremen, whose culture is in essence Arabic, are impressive in their hardiness and marvelous in their adaptation to a brutal, water-poor environment and their calm dedication to a centuries long project to transform the desert. The Fremen thus add a human dimension to the ecology of Dune, making the mystery of the spice cycle and the harsh beauty of the planet seem important as well as interesting.

The two sequels to *Dune* are much less successful. *Dune Messiah* (1969) shows the inevitable corrupting effects of power. Intrigues of Byzantine complexity, the ambiguities of the cult of Paul-Muad'Dib, and pseudoscientific marvels create a complex plot, but the decadence of the Fremen and the taming of Dune deprive the book of much of the power of its precursor. The theme of consciousness in *Dune Messiah* is also different. Passing beyond the stage of simply mastering his powers, Paul now

decides that prescience is lethal, abhorrent to the intellect and therefore uncontrollable. Paul finally abandons his prescience for literal blindness and a traditional Fremen death, but the tragedy of this apotheosis is confused by the victory of his twin children, who from a combination of their mother's spice-rich diet and their Bene Gesserit-selected genes are preborn, fully conscious of past and future while in the womb.

Children of Dune (1976) continues the story of the preborn. Alia, Paul's sister, is overwhelmed by the voices of her ancestors within her and becomes an Abomination, possessed by her grandfather Baron Harkonnen. But Paul's children, Leto and Ghanima, learn to control the voices within and use the information they provide to overcome the usual intrigues. Much of the plot depends on Paul's resurrection and other unexpected turns of plot, and the theme reveals yet another attitude toward the use of prescience. The twins and Paul (echoing Herbert's real beliefs at this point in his career) agree that "absolute prediction is completion . . . is death." Yet despite this argument, by the end of *Children of Dune* young Leto, now both superhuman and an Abomination, follows the single path of his vision and ascends the throne to establish a four-thousand-year Golden Path. This course of action will satiate the citizens of the Empire with security and peace

Frank Herbert

until they erupt in a catastrophic revolutionary catharsis which will restore the race to uncertainty, the path of true maturity. Unfortunately, the lessons of this Golden Path, like Leto's personal suffering, remain distant and unconvincing.

Herbert sought to capitalize on the success of *Dune* with a series of short minor novels. *The Green Brain* (1966) is an ecological novel set in Brazil. Efforts to increase human food supplies by destroying the world's insects cause rapid mutations among the threatened species. Directed by a giant brain which learns how to cluster insects into simulated human forms, the insects try to warn men of the flaw in their plan. Divided by political intrigue, chiefly the attempt of the Chinese to hide the fact that their recently completed "realignment" of the insects has sterilized the soil, men do not accept the truth that ecology requires cooperation among species until all the main characters have been captured by the insects, killed, and restored by the green brain's advanced techniques of organ replacement.

Destination: Void (1966) tells the story of the seventh colony starship sent out under Operation Consciousness. The crew of clones, carefully conditioned into selected behavior patterns and largely unaware of their manipulation by Moonbase Control, has a dual mission: to reach Tau Ceti despite deliberately planned malfunctions, and to react to the frustration of these malfunctions by becoming fully conscious. In many ways a reworking of *The Dragon in the Sea*, this book is more ambitious in its attempt to define consciousness rather than sanity. Its treatment of artificial intelligence is interesting, although the technology is unexplained, and the crew's interminable psychological conflicts, caused in large part by their prior conditioning, do not seem very relevant to actual human life. True consciousness is eventually revealed to be so painful that it can be borne only against the soothing background of unconsciousness and the possibility of death, but Herbert's conclusion—with its literal deus ex machina—shifts from speculation to gimmick and deprives the reader of the opportunity to see the characters actually living with their newfound consciousness.

The Eyes of Heisenberg (1966) presents genetic manipulation and the power of immortality in a rigidly hierarchic future Earth. Salvation, when it comes, is directed by a subversive group of Cyborgs, whose intentions and powers are never clearly revealed. In contrast to this very traditional pulp novel, reminiscent of A. E. van Vogt in tone and plot, *The Heaven Makers* (1968) gives a lurid twist to another old idea. Earth is the plaything of aliens, in this case a set for carefully directed dramatic productions by the Chem, whose immortality is threatened only by boredom. The illegal attraction of Earth—that Chem and humans can interbreed—proves irresistible to the aliens until Dr. Androcles Thurlow, a psychologist, convinces the Chem, who have abducted and raped his beloved Ruth, that immortality is a closed system and that the possibility of death is necessary for a meaningful, mature life.

In *The Santaroga Barrier* (1968), Gilbert Dasein investigates a valley in California whose inhabitants are dominated by a group-mind which controls them through Jaspers, a mildly psychedelic spore. Dasein's efforts to free himself and his fiancee, Jenny Sorge, lead to some interesting questions about reality, isolation, and consciousness which are left unresolved in a conventionally ghoulish conclusion.

Whipping Star (1970) develops a setting first used in "The Tactful Saboteur," which Herbert contributed to Groff Conklin's anthology, *Seven Trips Through Time and Space* (1968). The Bureau of Sabotage (BuSab), with its motto "In Lieu of Red Tape," is a constitutionally protected agency designed to slow the workings of a dangerously efficient government and to curb abuses of power. Jorj X. McKie, Saboteur Extraordinary, is a conventional and likable secret agent, but the real strength of the series based on his exploits lies in its numerous alien races, whose strange customs and abilities provide a satisfying richness of detail to fill out otherwise thin plots. In *Whipping Star*, the mysterious Calebans, who control the jumpdoors, which are the principal means of transportation in the ConSentiency, are withdrawing from the universe. McKie slowly learns that without the Calebans anyone who has ever used a jumpdoor will die. The last Caleban, Fannie Mae, has entered into an unbreakable contract with the sadistic Mliss Abnethe. McKie must learn Caleban thought patterns, especially the concept of connectives, in time to find a loophole in Fannie Mae's contract before Abnethe kills her. The novel is sufficiently fast paced and the ideas original enough for the reader to overlook the weak explanation of connectives.

The most recent of Herbert's short novels, *The God Makers* (1972), is the best representative of one of the major themes of his writing, since it applies personal consciousness and social interactions directly to the concepts of peace and religion. True peace, the author states, is "an internal matter . . . a self-discipline for an individual or for an entire civilization," since externally enforced peace creates paired opposites which inevitably conflict. This theme is presented through the career of Lewis Orne, who works for an agency which forcibly destroys militaristic tendencies on worlds isolated from galactic civilization during the Rim Wars. The issue of peace is overshadowed by religion, for it turns out that Orne moves along a path shaped by the priests of Amel as part of the training of their acolytes in Religious Engineering. As Abbod Halmyrach of Amel explains, "All of mankind acting together represents a great psi force, an energy system. . . . Sometimes, we call this force *religion*. Sometimes, we invest it with an independent focus of action which we call God." Eventually Orne achieves godhood, frees himself from external manipulation, and gets the girl. Herbert's use of prophetic foreshadowing is pleasingly intricate and the definition of peace reasonable and instructive, but the book founders in explaining religion in terms of vaguely defined psi powers, speaking, as the Abbod puts it, "with a certain glibness of eternity, of absolutes."

Hellstrom's Hive (1973), Herbert's longest work since *Dune*, returns to the question of what humans can learn from insect societies. A centuries-long experiment in selective breeding and social dynamics has established a society of 50,000 people living in a Hive beneath a farm in eastern Oregon. Genetic selection and special diets have differentiated the group into insect-type castes, whose behavior is largely conditioned by chemical triggers and the greater will of the Hive.

The plot of *Hellstrom's Hive* involves the efforts of a clandestine Agency to infiltrate the Hive and discover the secret of Project 40, an energy weapon with the potential to destroy the world. Nils Hellstrom, Hive leader, struggles to preserve the secret of the Hive's size and social structure until its superior inhabitants have the strength of numbers to emerge and conquer the world. As Agency and Hive battle each other with violence and political intrigue, the two sides are revealed to be equally repulsive. Neither tolerates individualism, and while the Hive places a higher priority on the lives of its members, it is equally concerned with the well-being of the truncated lower torsos it uses as reproductive stumps. At its best, the Hive is orderly and protective, while the Agency's leaders are smarter than public officials. By the end of the book, it seems clear that whoever wins this struggle, humanity loses.

Herbert continues the theme of the irruption of a closed microsociety into an unsuspecting larger culture in *The Dosadi Experiment* (1977), another Jorj X. McKie novel. The Gowachin, the least assimilated race of the ConSentiency, have established Gowachin and humans on Dosadi as a psychological experiment, but also to allow clandestine body transfers. However, the vicious competition for survival on Dosadi has produced a society whose physical and mental skills are vastly superior to those of outsiders and in which its members live by an implacable code of domination and distrust. The closest any Dosadi comes to idealism is the desire of Keila Jedrik and her followers to escape from Dosadi and avenge themselves on their unknown manipulators. McKie is sent to Dosadi as a BuSab agent under contract to the outside Gowachin. Amid a race war and under threat of planetary destruction, McKie must learn to survive on Dosadi and then determine his own role in the many sided conflict. Although tempted by the raw power that comes with mere survival on Dosadi, in the end McKie remains true to his love of justice. He and Jedrik become lovers, escape from Dosadi, confront the originators of the Dosadi experiment, and defeat them in a trial held according to the lethal Gowachin legal code. Finally, McKie overcomes the neurotic emotional isolation which has ruined his previous fifty-five marriages, finding true love without needing anyone outside his Self.

The Dosadi Experiment is pleasing adventure science fiction, with a tightly organized plot, characters who are distinguishable at least because of their racial differences, plenty of action and intrigue, and some fairly original ideas which connect well to the book's concern with informed consent and the abuses of unrestrained power. Unfortunately, as in many of Herbert's books, the effect of this middle ground of plotting, presentation, and intended theme is undermined by flaws in the deeper matters of motivation and conception. Dosadi is an excessively complex way of hiding a body-transfer racket; it is never clear why McKie's training as a Gowachin Legum was a necessary part of the intended Dosadi cover-up, especially since McKie causes the cover-up to fail; the implausibility of Jedrik's sudden development of the softer emotions is exceeded only by the folly of McKie's trusting her.

With its emphasis on intrigue, consciousness, supernormal mental powers, and the functional meaning of abstractions such as peace, Herbert's science fiction is primarily intellectual. While his manipulation of mentally stimulating complexities is sufficiently adroit to dazzle the casual reader, a more serious approach to these novels leads inevitably to an examination of the framework which encloses this intricacy. Unfortunately, the surface complexity of Herbert's invented societies is rarely matched by an underlying rationale for their development along these lines, and the soulless plotters who people these worlds do not provide a convincingly human perspective on the action. Furthermore, the transformations of mind and body undergone by many of Herbert's characters depend on pseudoscience which is unexplained or implausible, and so the mental powers of these characters do not provide convincing models of human consciousness.

Aside from *The Dragon in the Sea*, which succeeds in part because of its limited scope, only *Dune* possesses the emotional validity and scientific plausibility necessary to serious science fiction. To some extent this is no doubt the result of commercial factors; *Dune* was written over a period of time sufficiently great for its societies and intrigues to develop a coherent complexity. But it is no coincidence that the more successful of Herbert's novels, such as *The God Makers* and *The Dosadi Experiment*, are those in which the characters laugh, love, and display emotions more positive than reflexive ambition. Herbert's novels fail when all the characters act like McKie, who "has built a simulation McKie of his own who acts on the surface of the real McKie." When he takes the trouble to create characters and societies with the depth to transmit his undoubtedly sincere themes, Herbert can be a very good writer. Certainly the one time he escaped completely from the commercialism of convenient artifice he created *Dune*, one of the unquestioned masterpieces of modern science fiction. —*Robert A. Foster*

Other:

New World or No World, interviews conducted and edited with commentary by Herbert (New York: Ace, 1971).

References:

David Allen, *Herbert's Dune and Other Works* (Lincoln, Nebraska: Cliffs Notes, 1975);
John Ower, "Idea and Imagery in Herbert's *Dune*," *Extrapolation* 15 (May 1974): 129-139.

Papers:

The library of the California State University at Fullerton has a large collection of Herbert's papers.

DAMON KNIGHT
(20 September 1922-   )

BOOKS: *Hell's Pavement* (New York: Lion, 1955; London: Miller, 1958); republished as *Analogue Men* (New York: Berkley, 1962; London: Sphere, 1967);
In Search of Wonder (Chicago: Advent, 1956; enlarged edition, Chicago: Advent, 1967);
Masters of Evolution (New York: Ace, 1959);
The People Maker (New York: Zenith, 1959); enlarged as *A for Anything* (London: Four Square Books, 1961; New York: Berkley, 1965);
Far Out (New York: Simon & Schuster, 1961; London: Gollancz, 1962);
The Sun Saboteurs (New York: Ace, 1961); republished as *The Earth Quarter* in *World Without Children and The Earth Quarter* (New York: Lancer, 1970);
In Deep (New York: Berkley, 1963; London: Gollancz, 1964);
Beyond the Barrier (Garden City: Doubleday, 1964; London: Gollancz, 1964);
Mind Switch (New York: Berkley, 1965); republished as *The Other Foot* (London: Whiting & Wheaton, 1966);
Off Center (New York: Ace, 1965; London: Gollancz, 1969);
The Rithian Terror (New York: Ace, 1965);
Turning On (Garden City: Doubleday, 1966; London: Gollancz, 1967);
Three Novels (Garden City: Doubleday, 1967; London: Gollancz, 1967); republished as *Natural State and Other Stories* (London & Sydney: Pan, 1975);
The Best of Damon Knight (Garden City: Doubleday, 1976);
The Futurians: The Story of the Science Fiction "Family" of the 30's That Produced Today's Top SF Writers and Editors (New York: John Day, 1977).

Damon Knight's contributions to the field of science fiction as author, editor, critic, illustrator, and translator represent several decades of commitment to making sense of the literature while defending its existence as a serious enterprise. Born in Baker, Oregon, Damon Francis Knight discovered science fiction in 1932 in the magazine *Amazing Stories*. During the summer of 1940 Knight began his correspondence with various members of a group calling themselves the New York Futurians, including such luminaries as Donald A. Wollheim, Frederik Pohl, C. M. Kornbluth, and Isaac Asimov.

Damon Knight

Knight's first story, "Resilience," was published in Wollheim's *Stirring Science Stories* in February 1941 while he was attending art school in Salem, Oregon. As a science-fiction author, Knight had an inauspicious debut, for a typographical error apparently made the story incomprehensible. Nevertheless, his own fanzine *Snide* so impressed the Futurians that they encouraged him to come to New York in 1941. Knight has chronicled the activities of these New York writers and editors, as well as his own rise from fan to science-fiction editor, in *The Futurians* (1977), a valuable account of the frenetic think tank that nurtured the seminal writers of science fiction in America. It was in this environment that Knight learned some of the important lessons that he communicates so often in his criticism: that science fiction must be taken seriously as literature, that science fiction is about people, and that the "story should be more important than the idea."

After holding a variety of jobs, Knight began his editing career by assisting Ejler Jakobsson at *Super Science Stories* (second series). He left in 1950 to become the editor of *Worlds Beyond*, which, though well received, was canceled by the publisher after three issues. In the 1950s Knight's book reviews

appeared in several science-fiction magazines such as *Infinity Science Fiction, Original SF Stories,* and *Future SF,* and in 1956 he received a Hugo Award for his criticism. Many of these reviews were collected in *In Search of Wonder* (1956). In 1958 Knight returned to editing and worked for five months on J. L. Quinn's *If,* continuing his reviews and editing the magazine in an attempt to increase its circulation; however, the magazine was soon suspended. Although since 1959 Knight has reviewed few books, an excellent sample of his recent reviews appears in *Orbit 14* (1974).

Knight is acclaimed most frequently by science-fiction critics as a short-story writer. His skill was recognized with the publication of the story "Not with a Bang" (1950; collected in *Far Out,* 1961), an amusing yet macabre extrapolation of T. S. Eliot's "The Hollow Men" that tells the tale of the last man and woman on earth—a recurrent theme in Knight's work. During the same year he published another fine story, "To Serve Man" (1950; collected in *Far Out*), which was later dramatized by Rod Serling as the eighty-seventh episode of the "Twilight Zone" television series.

Knight has written more than seventy stories which have appeared in numerous science-fiction magazines since the early 1940s. Recently he has translated several French stories by such writers as C. Henneberg, Claude Veillot, and J. H. Rosny, aine; a number of these translations have appeared in the *Magazine of Fantasy and Science Fiction* and in his anthology *Thirteen French Science Fiction Stories* (1965). Knight is also a notable anthologist—perhaps the most significant of his compilations is the *Orbit* series (1966-1978), one of the earliest and the most influential of the original anthology series which began appearing in the mid-1960s. In 1963 Knight was married to fellow science-fiction writer Kate Wilhelm, whose fine stories have appeared consistently in the *Orbit* series.

The problem for any critic of Knight's work arises in a discussion of his novels because his strength, a prose style full of "so many ideas," as one critic put it, is also his weakness. Many critics have skirted the issue by emphasizing the provocative—while granting the chaotic—qualities of his narrative; others concentrate on his excellence as an anthologist or short-story writer; indeed, most of his novels are expansions of shorter works. In the decade between 1955 and 1965 Knight produced seven novels, four of which are especially important: *Hell's Pavement* (1955), a tale of an oppressed, mind-controlled society in the twenty-first century (derived from his stories "The Analogues," 1952, and

"Turncoat," 1953); *The People Maker* (1959), which is an extended example of his gadget story, featuring a matter duplicator called the gizmo (the novel is an expansion of "A for Anything," 1957—the book, however, suffered several unauthorized cuts, and its 1961 republication as *A for Anything* is the more reliable edition); *The Sun Saboteurs* (1961), a story of humans trying to live on a very un-Earth-like world (expanded from "The Earth Quarter," 1955); and *Mind Switch* (1965), which depicts a man's mental transfer to an alien body (expanded from "The Visitor at the Zoo," 1963).

A common theme in these novels is the situation of man trying to improve himself, and instead, falling pitifully further behind in his own development. *A for Anything* is a poignant example of this theme. The story of the undistinguished yet pugnacious Dick Jones, who is catapulted into hero status in the heyday of the gizmo, has been called "a peculiar story of lust and decadence." In addition to the strange turns of plot, there is the ambivalence of Knight's language, which parallels the ups and downs of the characters, providing an uneven reading experience. Yet perhaps Knight's fascination with language proves, ultimately, to be a weakness in his fiction. Often he appears to be hypnotized by the power of his own metaphors; they are extended beautifully and do perform the function that he has described as essential to science fiction: "to lift us out of the here-and-now and show us marvels." The stunningly apocalyptic description of the falling tower in *A for Anything* is such a marvel, but it seems to lead a life of its own, ignoring the mundane plot. It should be emphasized, however, that such passages are not failures, but they do detract somewhat from the overall unity of the novel.

No discussion of Knight's work would be complete without mentioning his criticism. Possibly the most sentimental, yet among the wisest of science-fiction critics, Knight is the most persistent advocate of the literature. Knight has always promoted the respectability of science fiction, but his love of the genre is tempered with a demanding sense of literacy. As Anthony Boucher observed, Knight is capable of both the "hatchet job" and the "love letter." In 1952 Knight espoused the view that science fiction and literature are not mutually exclusive terms—a view that he has defended persistently and convincingly since that time. As Boucher wrote in his introduction to *In Search of Wonder*, "He is able, as is almost no other professional writer of fiction, to stand apart from his completed work and look at it objectively." Whether the reader experiences Knight's critical persona implicitly, as in the "They Say" and

"Memory Machine" (features of the *Orbit* series in which Knight collects and arranges without comment quotations from various critics and writers), or explicitly, as in the fine critical premises evident in his anthology selections or in his bristling at abuses of language in a "Chuckleheads" essay, he will find Knight to be a perceptive reader who enjoys "the act of thinking" and is willing to risk telling the truth. In an essay on "Half-Bad Writers," Knight makes a comment that may well summarize his goals as a writer, editor, and critic of science fiction. In describing an otherwise poor novel that suddenly comes to life, he exclaims: "Now by God, this is science fiction. It performs s.f.'s specific function, to lift us out of the here-and-now and show us marvels. No matter how badly it's written, if a story does that it is s.f. A story that fails to do that, no matter how well written, isn't."

—*Deborah Schneider Greenhut*

Other:

A Century of Science Fiction, compiled and introduced by Knight (New York: Simon & Schuster, 1962; London: Gollancz, 1963);

First Flight: Maiden Voyages in Space and Time, edited by Knight (New York: Lancer, 1963); republished as *Now Begins Tomorrow* (New York: Lancer, 1969);

A Century of Great Short Science Fiction Novels, edited by Knight (New York: Delacorte, 1964; London: Gollancz, 1965);

Tomorrow X 4, edited by Knight (Greenwich, Conn.: Fawcett, 1964);

Beyond Tomorrow, edited by Knight (New York: Harper & Row, 1965; London: Gollancz, 1968);

Thirteen French Science-Fiction Stories, edited and translated by Knight (New York & London: Bantam, 1965);

The Shape of Things, edited by Knight (New York: Popular Library, 1965);

The Dark Side, edited by Knight (Garden City: Doubleday, 1965);

Cities of Wonder, edited by Knight (Garden City: Doubleday, 1966);

Orbit 1-12, edited by Knight (New York: Putnam's, 1966-1974);

Nebula Award Stories 1965, edited by Knight (Garden City: Doubleday, 1966); republished as *Nebula Award Stories No. 1* (London: Gollancz, 1967);

Worlds to Come, edited by Knight (New York & London: Harper & Row, 1967);

Science Fiction Inventions, edited by Knight (New York: Lancer, 1967);

One Hundred Years of Science Fiction, edited by Knight (New York: Simon & Schuster, 1968);

Toward Infinity: Nine Science Fiction Tales, edited by Knight (New York: Simon & Schuster, 1968);

The Metal Smile, edited by Knight (New York: Belmont Books, 1968);

Dimension X, edited by Knight (New York: Simon & Schuster, 1970);

A Pocketful of Stars, edited by Knight (Garden City: Doubleday, 1971);

First Contact, edited by Knight (Los Angeles: Pinnacle, 1971);

A Science Fiction Argosy, edited by Knight (New York: Simon & Schuster, 1972);

Perchance to Dream, edited by Knight (Garden City: Doubleday, 1972);

The Golden Road, edited by Knight (New York: Simon & Schuster, 1973);

Tomorrow and Tomorrow, edited by Knight (New York: Simon & Schuster, 1973);

Orbit 13, edited by Knight (New York: Berkley, 1974);

Orbit 14-20, edited by Knight (New York & London: Harper & Row, 1974-1978);

Happy Endings, edited by Knight (New York: Bobbs-Merrill, 1974);

A Shocking Thing, edited by Knight (New York: Pocket Books, 1974);

Science Fiction of the Thirties, edited by Knight (New York: Bobbs-Merrill, 1975);

Best Stories from Orbit: Volumes 1-10; edited by Knight (New York: Berkley, 1975);

Orbit 21, edited by Knight (New York & London: Harper & Row, 1980).

Periodical Publications:

"Resilience," *Stirring Science Stories* (February 1941);

"The Analogues," *Astounding Science-Fiction* (January 1952);

"Turncoat," *Thrilling Wonder Stories* (April 1953);

"The Earth Quarter," *If* (January 1955);

"A For Anything," *Magazine of Fantasy and Science Fiction* (November 1957);

"The Visitor at the Zoo," *Galaxy* (April 1963);

"The Tree of Time," *Magazine of Fantasy and Science Fiction*, (December 1963);

"Science Fiction Basics," *Library Journal*, 91 (1 June 1966): 2777-2779.

References:

James Blish, "S.F.: The Critical Literature," *SF Horizons*, 2 (1965): 38-50;

"Voices," *Colloquy*, 4 (May 1971): 2-9;

Paul Walker, "Damon Knight," in his *Speaking of Science Fiction: The Paul Walker Interviews* (Oradell, N. J.: Luna, 1978), pp. 157-167.

C. M. KORNBLUTH
(1923-1958)

BOOKS: *Outpost Mars*, by Kornbluth and Judith Merril, as Cyril Judd (New York: Abelard, 1952); revised as *Sin in Space* (New York: Galaxy, 1961);

Takeoff (Garden City: Doubleday, 1952);

Gunner Cade, by Kornbluth and Merril, as Cyril Judd (New York: Simon & Schuster, 1952);

The Naked Storm, as Simon Eisner (New York: Lion Books, 1952);

Half, as Jordan Park (New York: Lion Books, 1953);

The Space Merchants, by Kornbluth and Frederik Pohl (New York: Ballantine, 1953; London: Heinemann, 1955);

The Syndic (Garden City: Doubleday, 1953; London: Faber & Faber, 1964);

Valerie, as Jordan Park (New York: Lion Books, 1953);

The Explorers (New York: Ballantine, 1954);

Search the Sky, by Kornbluth and Pohl (New York: Ballantine, 1954; London: Digit, 1960);

Gladiator-at-Law, by Kornbluth and Pohl (New York: Ballantine, 1955; London: Digit, 1958);

The Mindworm (London: M. Joseph, 1955);

Not This August (Garden City: Doubleday, 1955); republished as *Christmas Eve* (London: M. Joseph, 1956);

A Town Is Drowning, by Kornbluth and Pohl (New York: Ballantine, 1955);

Presidential Year, by Kornbluth and Pohl (New York: Ballantine, 1956);

Sorority House, by Kornbluth and Pohl, as Jordan Park (New York: Lion Books, 1956);

The Man of Cold Rages, as Jordan Park (New York: Pyramid, 1958);

A Mile Beyond the Moon (Garden City: Doubleday, 1958);

The Marching Morons (New York: Ballantine, 1959);

Wolfbane, by Kornbluth and Pohl (New York: Ballantine, 1959; London: Gollancz, 1960);

The Wonder Effect, by Kornbluth and Pohl (New York: Ballantine, 1962; London: Gollancz, 1967);

Best SF Stories of C. M. Kornbluth (London: Faber & Faber, 1968);

Thirteen O'Clock and Other Zero Hours (New York: Dell, 1970; London: Hale, 1972);

The Best of C. M. Kornbluth (Garden City: Doubleday, 1976);

Critical Mass, by Kornbluth and Pohl (Toronto, New York & London: Bantam, 1977);

Before the Universe, by Kornbluth and Pohl (New York: Ballantine, 1980).

Born in New York City, Cyril M. Kornbluth crowded an impressive body of work into a writing career that spanned nearly twenty years and ended in 1958 with his untimely death from heart failure, at age thirty-four. Perhaps the most darkly perceptive and socially concerned science-fiction writer of the 1950s, author of at least two permanent classics in the genre (and collaborator on another), Kornbluth was a pioneer (with such writers as Jack Vance, Philip K. Dick, and Ray Bradbury) in developing an alternate body of first-rate science fiction in a field otherwise dominated by John W. Campbell, Jr.'s *Astounding Science-Fiction* and its established group of authors.

Kornbluth's creative period is broken by his service in World War II into two distinct parts and divides rather neatly between the 1940s and 1950s. The first period was dominated by a desire to demonstrate productivity and range, as well as by a simple need—at prevailing magazine-fiction rates of a penny a word and less—to make enough to eat, or at least to enjoy himself decently: Kornbluth presumably depended on his parents for bed and board until his story earnings enabled him to venture out on his own. In 1940, at the age of seventeen, he appeared on the science-fiction scene in a fierce cloud of salable prose and under a flurry of pseudonyms, the youngest talented member of a volatile New York fan group which found itself shortly in charge—as editors and authors—of about half the professional science-fiction magazines then being published. Among the members of this precocious group, called the Futurians, were Isaac Asimov, Damon Knight, Robert W. Lowndes, Frederik Pohl, Richard Wilson, Donald A. Wollheim, and the unjustly forgotten John B. Michel; the magazines they edited and largely wrote included *Astonishing Stories* and *Super Science Stories*

(edited by Pohl), *Stirring Science Stories* and *Cosmic Stories* (edited by Wollheim), and *Future Fiction*, *Science Fiction*, and *Science Fiction Quarterly* (edited by Lowndes).

Since the youthful editors of these magazines had to publish as many as a quarter of a million words in any given month and lacked adequate budgets to attract work from the established science-fiction writers of the time, they turned to their handful of Futurian friends for a dependable supply of competent prose. To avoid distressing readers with a series of contents pages all listing the same six or seven authors, it was necessary for both editors and writers to invent a number of pen names. For the particularly prolific Kornbluth, a multiplicity of pseudonyms soon became the order of the day, and at the peak of his 1940s activity he fielded over ten by-lines—almost as many as Henry Kuttner had notoriously undertaken about the same time. These noms de plume, which sometimes concealed collaborations of Kornbluth and his fellow fan-pros, included S. D. Gottesman, Cecil Corwin, Paul Dennis Lavond, Walter C. Davies, Kenneth Falconer, and Ivar Towers. Even his own by-line, C. M. Kornbluth (not actually used until 1949 for a short story, "The Only Thing We Learn," in the July *Startling Stories*), was a pseudonym of a sort, since

C. M. Kornbluth

the middle initial—Cyril Kornbluth had none of his own—was taken from his wife's first name, Mary.

The abundance of Kornbluth's fictional production between 1940 and 1943 matched that of his pen names, but unlike the tyro work of many furious word-producers of the next decade or two (Harlan Ellison and Robert Silverberg were perhaps the most renowned), Kornbluth's early stories were almost always well conceived and effectively written, ranking for the most part just below his later and more famed work. Among the best examples of his early fiction, found in *Thirteen O'Clock and Other Zero Hours* (1970), are "The City in the Sofa" (1941), "The Golden Road" (1942), "Thirteen O'Clock" (1940), "What Sorghum Says" (1941), and "The Rocket of 1955" (1941). Another from this period, an extraordinarily forceful work called "The Words of Guru" (1941; collected in *A Mile Beyond the Moon*, 1958), is probably the best of the lightly satirical group. As James Blish wrote in his introduction to *Thirteen O'Clock*, many of these outwardly cynical and pungently witty stories hold a very "special quality [which] if pressed, I should be tempted to call . . . joy."

Kornbluth's youthful joy in creativity was unfortunately suppressed for several years by his induction into the army in 1944, his time in service giving him sergeant's stripes, an impaired heart, and a turn at the Battle of the Bulge, but not much chance to write. After his return home to his wife, Mary G. Byers, whom he had married just before induction, Kornbluth attended University College in Chicago on the GI Bill. He then went to work for a wire service news agency, which supplied some of the background for a later novel, *The Syndic* (1953). In 1948, he felt financially secure enough to begin writing again—this time under his own name—and began to hit the leading science-fiction magazine markets, beginning with *Startling Stories* and the *Magazine of Fantasy and Science Fiction*, then John W. Campbell, Jr.'s *Astounding Science-Fiction*. His reappearance with a number of striking and memorable stories excited fan comment and attracted editorial attention—particularly that of Horace Gold, who noted Kornbluth's acerbic critical view of scientific orthodoxy and felt he might be a writer to cultivate for Gold's projected new 1950 magazine, *Galaxy Science Fiction*, which was to depart sharply from Campbell's concept of science as a universal panacea for the ailments of mankind. In Kornbluth's classic story, "The Little Black Bag" (1950; collected in *A Mile Beyond the Moon*), for example, a bag full of technological medical wizardry serves neither the far future—where it is one of the means by which science has permitted the survival and fecundity of the least fit, so that the world is dominated by masses of morons—nor the present (to which the bag makes an accidental journey via a time machine), for here, while the bag's wonders first inspire the reform of an alcoholic doctor, his success inspires greed and envy, which lead in turn to murder, accidental suicide, and the destruction of the bag.

As it developed, Kornbluth was to have a great deal to do with *Galaxy Science Fiction*. His first work for the new magazine, which appeared in the seventh issue (April 1951), was "The Marching Morons," a ferociously pessimistic view of mankind's future, which most consider Kornbluth's finest piece of short fiction. It was immediately followed in *Galaxy Science Fiction* by his first novel-length work, *Mars Child*, a collaboration with Judith Merril (previously the author of a much acclaimed novel called *Shadow on the Hearth*, 1950) under the joint pseudonym of Cyril Judd. A second "Judd" novel, *Gunner Cade*, was sold to *Astounding Science-Fiction*, where it was published in the spring of 1952—just before the sensational debut in *Galaxy Science Fiction* of Kornbluth's third and most memorable novel, the classic saga of a future world solidly in the malignant grip of big business and advertising agencies, *The Space Merchants* (serialized as *Gravy Planet*). This work represented the first of a long series of creative and profitable collaborations with his old Futurian friend Frederik Pohl. Kornbluth had moved from Chicago to Pohl's New Jersey home in 1951; later he found a residence on Long Island, which made continued collaboration with Pohl practicable.

The great popular and critical success of *The Space Merchants*, which appeared in book form in 1953 and has never been out of print, gave considerable appeal to the subsequent works of both Kornbluth and Pohl (it sold to films for $50,000 after Kornbluth's death, although it was never filmed). Kornbluth was able to stop giving a good deal of time to writing for secondary pulp and paperback markets (largely detective and suspense fiction) under the name of Simon Eisner, and to concentrate on his real fictional interests on a full-time basis. He continued collaborating with Pohl, but first wrote by himself two well-received novels: *The Syndic*, in which organized crime rules America, and *Takeoff* (1952), a detective/science-fiction thriller about the first space flight. In 1954, his second collaboration with Pohl appeared as a Ballantine paperback original, *Search the Sky* (1954), a satirical novel about space colonization; it was followed almost at once by the *Galaxy Science Fiction* serialization of a third Pohl-Kornbluth novel, *Gladiator-at-Law* (1955), another view of a corporation-dominated world. Kornbluth then wrote a chillingly effective cautionary tale about a Russo-Chinese invasion of the United States called *Not This August*, which appeared as a book in 1955. His last two novels were both collaborations with Pohl: *Presidential Year* (1956), which was not science fiction (it was, in fact, one of three non-science-fiction novels which they wrote together in this period) and *Wolfbane* (serialized in *Galaxy* in 1957 and published in 1959), a surreal novel in which the Earth is stolen from the sun by a pyramid.

In the meantime, of course, Kornbluth continued to write his superbly crafted and composed shorter works for the magazines and eventual collection in books. Among the finest of these from the second half of Kornbluth's career were three collected in *A Mile Beyond the Moon*, "Two Dooms" (1958), "The Last Man Left in the Bar" (1957), and "Shark Ship" (1953), and another three collected in *The Marching Morons* (1959), "The Cosmic Charge Account" (1956), "The Luckiest Man in Denv" (1952), and "MS Found in a Chinese Fortune Cookie" (1957). He wrote a few fine stories with Pohl as well (some were begun by Kornbluth and finished by Pohl after Kornbluth's death), notably "The Quaker Cannon" (1961), "Critical Mass" (1961), "Nightmare with Zeppelins" (1958), and "The Meeting" (1972), which won a Hugo Award in 1973; these four are all collected in *Critical Mass* (1977). In 1957, Kornbluth prepared and delivered his only substantial critical work at an address at University College in Chicago; dealing with "The Failure of the Science Fiction Novel as Social Criticism," it was published in a 1959 volume, *The Science Fiction Novel*, a collection of similar addresses, and causes one to regret that Kornbluth otherwise limited his mature social comment and insight to his fiction.

In the mid-1950s Kornbluth moved from Long Island to an Upstate New York farm in Waverly, a tiny town ideal for the isolation necessary to writing. On 21 March 1958, there was an unseasonably late snowfall in Waverly. Having a date in New York City, Kornbluth shoveled the snow off his driveway, drove to the train station, and collapsed of heart failure, to die two hours later without regaining consciousness. In addition to the World War II-induced heart ailment which killed him and which had made his home life and personal relations with his peers often intolerable to himself and others, Kornbluth had not made a good deal of money during his life, and it seems miraculous in retrospect that so large and living a body of fine work could have been produced under such conditions of recurring ill health and frequent penury. It is perhaps a lasting tribute to the sustaining camaraderie of science-fiction fandom, and the unique professional enthusiasm it evokes within many committed creative talents, that Kornbluth did write so long and so well against such odds. We may certainly be grateful that he did. *—Bill Blackbeard*

Other:

"The Failure of the Science Fiction Novel as Social Criticism," *The Science Fiction Novel: Imagination and Social Criticism* [ed. Basil Davenport] (Chicago: Advent, 1959).

HENRY KUTTNER
(7 April 1915-3 February 1958)

SELECTED BOOKS: *Lawless Gun* (New York: Dodge, 1937);

Dr. Cyclops, as Will Garth (New York: Phoenix, 1940);

The Brass Ring, by Kuttner and C. L. Moore, as Lewis Padgett (New York: Duell, Sloan & Pearce, 1946);

Fury (New York: Grosset & Dunlap, 1950; London: Dobson, 1954); republished as *Destination Infinity* (New York: Avon, 1958);

A Gnome There Was, by Kuttner and Moore, as Lewis Padgett (New York: Simon & Schuster, 1950);

Tomorrow and Tomorrow and *The Fairy Chessmen*, by Kuttner and Moore, as Lewis Padgett (New York: Gnome, 1951); *The Fairy Chessmen* republished as *Chessboard Planet* (New York: Galaxy, 1956); *The Fairy Chessmen* republished again as *The Far Reality* (London: Consul, 1963);

Man Drowning (New York: Harper, 1952; London: Four Square Books, 1961);

Robots Have No Tails, by Kuttner and Moore, as Lewis Padgett (New York: Gnome Press, 1952);

Ahead of Time (New York: Ballantine, 1953; London: Weidenfeld, 1954);

Mutant, by Kuttner and Moore, as Lewis Padgett (New York: Gnome Press, 1953; London: Weidenfeld, 1954);

Well of the Worlds, by Kuttner and Moore, as Lewis
    Padgett (New York: Galaxy, 1953);
Beyond Earth's Gates, by Kuttner, as Lewis Padgett,
    and Moore (New York: Ace, 1954);
Line to Tomorrow, by Kuttner and Moore, as Lewis
    Padgett (New York: Bantam, 1954);
No Boundaries, by Kuttner and Moore (New York:
    Ballantine, 1955; London: World, 1961);
The Murder of Ann Avery (New York: Permabooks,
    1956);
The Murder of Eleanor Pope (New York: Permabooks,
    1956);
Murder of a Mistress (New York: Permabooks, 1957);
Murder of a Wife (New York: Permabooks, 1958);
Bypass to Otherness (New York: Ballantine, 1961;
    London: World, 1963);
Return to Otherness (New York: Ballantine, 1962;
    London: Mayflower, 1965);
Earth's Last Citadel, by Kuttner and Moore (New
    York: Ace, 1964);
Valley of the Flame (New York: Ace, 1964);
The Best of Kuttner I (London: Mayflower, 1965);
The Dark World (New York: Ace, 1965; London:
    Mayflower, 1966);
The Time Axis (New York: Ace, 1965);
The Best of Kuttner II (London: Mayflower, 1966);
The Creature From Beyond Infinity (New York:
    Popular Library, 1968);
The Best of Henry Kuttner (Garden City: Doubleday,
    1975).

Despite Henry Kuttner's major contributions to
the development of science-fiction and fantasy
writing during the 1940s, the work of this prolific
author has been generally neglected by both popular
and critical audiences since his death in 1958. While
other alumni of the pulp magazines that shaped the
character of contemporary science-fiction have been
accorded considerable attention both as pioneers and
as benchmarks within the genre, Kuttner's name has
become progressively more obscure. If he is known at
all, it is as the author of a few widely anthologized
short stories and as a marginal figure in the
distinguished history of *Astounding Science Fiction.*
Although this general neglect is unmerited, its
sources are easily detected. Most importantly,
Kuttner died at forty-four, just prior to the
burgeoning of interest in the genre during the 1960s.
Qualifying neither as an old master nor as a
contemporary figure, Kuttner found no place with
that generation of readers.

Kuttner's early death is not, however, the only
factor that has contributed to his mounting
obscurity. Kuttner's versatility, his prolific output,
his addiction to pseudonyms, and his derivative
tendencies have combined to limit his stature.
Kuttner refused to restrict his work to a particular
format or even to a single genre. In addition to
science fiction, he wrote detective, western, and
adventure stories, humorous sketches, and psycho-
analytic mysteries. While Kuttner's achievements in
each of these areas are significant, the range of his
endeavor prevented him from attaining preeminence
in any single field. Kuttner's enormous productivity
has had a similarly deleterious effect on his
posthumous reputation. Depending for his livelihood
almost entirely on free-lance sales to frequently
penurious journals, Kuttner wrote a vast number of
tales and sketches. Many of these stories, of course,
are hack work; others seem rushed and imprecise.
Unfortunately, Kuttner's first-rate fiction is all too
frequently lost in the sheer bulk of his canon.

Kuttner's use of a large number of pseudonyms
has also impeded his recognition as a major figure in
science fiction. Even in a genre and in a period in
which multiple personae were common, the number
of Kuttner's alter egos was extraordinary. At various
times during his career, Kuttner wrote under at least
seventeen different names. These pseudonyms afforded
him the luxury of publishing multiple stories in
single volumes of magazines, but they further
undermined his status as a broadly identifiable
figure. Perhaps more importantly, they fueled the
critical assumption that Kuttner lacked a style and
vision of his own. That judgment had its sources in
the flexibility of Kuttner's prose and in his
remarkable ability to incorporate the subject matter,
thematic concerns, and stylistic features of other
writers in his fiction. The case against Kuttner as an
imitative artist has been lodged most thoroughly by
Sam Moskowitz in his critical study *Seekers of
Tomorrow* (1966). Moskowitz traces the influence of
H. P. Lovecraft, Robert E. Howard, Stanley G.
Weinbaum, John Collier, Clifford D. Simak. A. E.
van Vogt, Murray Leinster, and A. Merritt in
Kuttner's fiction, and ultimately dismisses him as
merely a talented mimic. Certainly there is some
justice in Moskowitz's argument. Kuttner was a
derivative writer. In addition to the names Moskowitz
cites, those of James M. Cain, Thorne Smith, and
Robert Bloch might be added to the list of Kuttner's
sources. Science fiction itself, however, is a genre that
is predicated upon derivation. Similar plotting
devices and thematic concerns recur across its
history. The test of originality within the genre is
denouement and not donnee. Kuttner's merit, as
James Blish has argued, must be measured not by the
sources of his imagination but by the success with

which he engages those sources. Any assessment of Kuttner's achievement, then, necessarily involves an excavation process in which the coordinates of his world view must be unearthed from the welter of pulp fiction, the pseudonyms, and the derivative tendencies that have obscured his identity.

Henry Kuttner was born in Los Angeles in 1915. His youthful attraction to the stories of Edgar Rice Burroughs and the pulp fiction which appeared in *Amazing Stories* and *Weird Tales* prompted him to initiate a correspondence with Lovecraft, Bloch, and other members of the *Weird Tales* coterie. That correspondence resulted in the publication of a

expansion involved the publication of several titillating stories in *Thrilling Mystery*, *Marvel Science Stories*, and *Marvel Tales*. Tame by contemporary standards, the sadistic and suggestive tenor of stories such as "Avengers of Space" (1938) and "Dictator of the Americas" (1938) nevertheless provoked protest from science-fiction enthusiasts who resented the intrustion of material previously taboo in the genre.

On 7 June 1940, Kuttner married Catherine L. Moore, who had been an established fantasy writer since the publication of "Shambleau" in the November 1933 issue of *Weird Tales*. During the rest

Henry Kuttner and C. L. Moore

poem, "Ballad of the Gods," in the February 1936 issue of *Weird Tales* and a short story, "The Graveyard Rats," in the following issue of that journal. "The Graveyard Rats," a horror tale involving giant rats, curious corpses, and subterranean pursuit, was closely patterned on Lovecraft's fiction; but despite its derivative character, the story won favorable attention for young Kuttner. During the next five years he published widely not only in a broad range of science-fiction and fantasy magazines, but also in detective, adventure, and western pulps as well. The Lovecraft influence is still apparent in many of the stories from this period, but Kuttner's horizons were clearly expanding. One aspect of that

of his career, Kuttner collaborated with Moore, to varying degrees, on almost all of his projects. For some stories, the two worked in relays on the same manuscript; for others they revised each other's drafts. In many cases, including that of the Lewis Padgett stories, the two shared the same pseudonyms. The arrangement was mutually beneficial. Moore's fertile imagination inspired Kuttner's invention; his narrative discipline imposed form on her vision.

With the coming of World War II, Kuttner's stories began to appear in John W. Campbell's *Astounding Science Fiction* and in *Unknown Worlds*. Campbell's stable of writers, which at one time included Robert Heinlein, Isaac Asimov, and

Theodore Sturgeon, had been depleted by the draft. Kuttner took advantage of the resultant opportunity and published his most mature work to date in Campbell's magazines. Writing primarily under the pseudonyms Lewis Padgett and Lawrence O'Donnell, Kuttner published widely acclaimed stories such as "The Twonky" (1942) and "Mimsy Were the Borogoves" (1943; both collected in *The Best of Henry Kuttner*, 1975), and "Clash by Night" (1943; collected in *The Best of Kuttner I*, 1965). When in 1943 Campbell revealed that Kuttner was the source of both the Padgett and the O'Donnell stories, Kuttner's previously modest reputation escalated rapidly. By the end of the war, Kuttner's popular appeal was the equal of van Vogt's, Asimov's, or Leinster's.

During the years immediately following the war, Kuttner enhanced that reputation by continuing to publish a wide range of magazine fiction. In 1950, however, his literary production began to decline when both he and C. L. Moore entered the University of Southern California. Kuttner's education had been interrupted by the Depression, and when the GI bill was passed, he seized the opportunity to recover that loss. He was awarded a B.A. in 1954 and was working on a master's degree when he died from a heart attack on 3 February 1958. Kuttner's absence from the pulp magazines during this period did not, however, significantly erode his popularity. During the decade most of his major stories were reissued in anthologies or as novels. Indeed, it was not until the mid-1960s that Kuttner's readership began its long decline.

Before that neglect can be redressed, some order must be brought to the Kuttner canon. Initially, his non-science-fiction and fantasy writings may be dismissed as interesting but ultimately minor works that never extend their genres. Similarly, Kuttner's horror fantasies offer little of interest. As inventive and as emotionally charged as they often are, they lack the metaphysical power of Lovecraft or Bloch and fail to threaten the props of rational order. The large body of Kuttner's humorous science fiction also requires pruning. Kuttner's Galloway Gallegher stories (collected in *Robots Have No Tails*, 1952), which recount the adventures of an alcoholic inventor who can only work when he is drunk; his Hollywood on the Moon series, stories about the motion picture industry of the future; and his tales about the Hogben family, a group of hillbilly mutants, seem dated and contrived. While these stories are occasionally amusing, they are more often embarrassingly flat. Other obviously formulaic projects such as the Elak of Atlantis stories, which

unsuccessfully imitate Robert E. Howard's Conan series, and novelty pieces such as "The Misguided Halo" (1939), "Housing Problem" (1944), and "Nothing But Gingerbread Left" (1943; all collected in *The Best of Henry Kuttner*) may be dismissed as stories generated by deadlines rather than by imagination.

Even after this process of elimination, a body of fiction sufficient to validate a claim for Kuttner's significance remains. The best of Kuttner's science fiction reflects both a highly personal vision and a capacity to address meaningfully the psychic needs of its audience. In these works Kuttner offers a balanced view of the human condition that at once acknowledges man's capacity for self-destruction and his potential for unlimited growth. In realizing that vision Kuttner engages the cultural dilemmas generated by the coming of World War II, the rise of fascism, the rapid growth of technology, and the harrowing specter of nuclear destruction. Through a fictive displacement and mediation of those tensions, he provides both a crucial perspective and an emotional moratorium for his readers.

In his series of Baldy stories, collected in 1953 under the title *Mutant*, for example, Kuttner engages apocalyptic trauma by projecting a vision of a world restructuring itself after a nuclear holocaust. Its citizens attempt to avoid a repetition of global warfare by prohibiting centralization of any sort. Kuttner maintains, however, that nationalism is only a secondary cause of warfare. Self-interest and suspicion, its primary causes, remain unchecked in this brave new world. Murderous duels are commonplace; the "dusting" of rival cities with nuclear eggs serves as the principal means of preserving the peace. Two races occupy the planet. One, the unaltered survivors of the war, wields full power. The other, a strain of bald mutants with telepathic powers, is subjected to prejudice as a body of dangerous freaks.

In each of the first four Baldy stories, published in *Astounding Science Fiction* during 1945, Kuttner centers his tale around a single Baldy who resists the call of other militant mutants to declare their superiority and eliminate the nonmutant humans. Kuttner acknowledges the appeal of the notion of a super race whose transcendental powers offer a better hope for mankind's future, but he recognizes as well the high costs of racial elitism. This fictional dilemma replicates a contemporary crisis. Man's inherent predilection for violence suggests the inevitability of progressively more harrowing warfare; elitist attempts to check those tendencies are not only futile, but lead to totalitarianism and expedient murder. Kuttner's fiction acknowledges the irresolvable nature of that paradox, but at the same time assuages its force by suggesting a potential mediation. His moderate mutant heroes reject the formation of a super race and place their faith in the dominance of their racial mutation. At some future point, an all-Baldy world will evolve. Men will be joined through their shared telepathy and war will be an impossibility. The final story in the series, "Humpty Dumpty," which Kuttner wrote in 1953 to conclude the collected edition of the stories, makes this fictive mediation explicit. In that tale scientists derive a mechanical device capable of extending telepathic powers to nonmutants. The story's conclusion is somewhat ambiguous, but it does not alter Kuttner's thesis. In his present state, he argues, man confronts a future dominated by destruction. Governmental systems are inadequate to deflect that course. Man does, however, possess the potential for growth, and in that growth both hope for the future and psychic comfort in the present reside.

Fury, a story initially published in 1947 in *Astounding Science Fiction* and published as a novel in 1950, pursues a similar theme. Again global warfare has generated a bifurcated society. Mutants whose life spans extend for centuries rule a race of normal men in an undersea world on Venus, the last resort of man after Earth has been destroyed. The rule of the immortals is benign, and peace reigns in the human communities. The price of peace, however, is the repression of initiative and the stagnation of the race. As he does in the Baldy stories, Kuttner identifies an irredeemable cultural conflict. Unchecked, man will destroy himself; limited by totalitarian control, he will decline. Kuttner again responds to this troubling crisis by creating a fictive middle ground. Initially that mediation is achieved by Sam Harker, an immortal who is unaware of his mutation. His initiative leads a torpid humanity to the surface of Venus where man can pursue his destiny. Power maddens Sam, however, and Kuttner must offer a more refined mediation to insure the story's successful conclusion. The Logician, an immortal oracle, puts Sam into a state of suspended animation, from which he may be called when the race again needs his volatile leadership. Through the agency of the Logician, a replacement deity of sorts, mankind's future is preserved. Kuttner serves his audience by formalizing, displacing, and blunting their fears through a fictive resolution of a threatening conflict.

In one of his most interesting short stories, "What You Need" (1945; collected in *The Best of Henry Kuttner*), Kuttner centers his narrative on another substitute deity. Peter Talley, the proprietor of a small shop that professes to offer its customers what they need, views the various permutations of man's future through a scanner and insures the direction of the race by eliminating dangerous men and fostering the careers of racial benefactors. Kuttner seems somewhat ambivalent about the power Talley possesses. Like Lovecraft, he was not unattracted by the notion of a superman. The effect of the story, however, is to comfort a post-World War II audience badly in need of surrogate gods and to justify the exercise of destructive power in the interest of humanity.

Another story, "Two Handed Engine" (1955; collected in *The Best of Henry Kuttner*), is, like much of Kuttner's fiction, predicated upon mythological and literary sources. In this tale, man's reliance on technology has deprived him of his initiative. In an attempt to restore individual responsibility, guardian computers create giant mechanical furies to follow and eventually execute murderers. The furies ultimately generate the rebirth of conscience and insure human survival. Kuttner experiments here with the recurrent science-fiction motif of technological nightmare, but his real interest continues to be directed toward the question of man's twin capacities for self-destruction and regeneration.

This conjunction of skepticism and faith is also central in *Earth's Last Citadel* (1964), a work first published in *Argosy* in 1943 under the dual authorship of Kuttner and C. L. Moore, and in the short story "The Big Night" (1947; collected in *The Best of Henry Kuttner*). In the former narrative, a Scottish scientist, an American officer, and two Nazi agents are transported to the distant future where the only survivors of the human race are fragile mutants and barbaric tribesmen. The American officer, Alan Drake, restores hope to the fallen world by destroying the alien presence that has enslaved mankind and dispatches the barbarians to Venus where the race may begin anew. Drake himself remains on Earth to rebuild humanity with the surviving mutants. "The Big Night" enacts a similar theme on board *La Cucaracha*, one of the last of the atomic ships to travel interstellar space. The ship and its crew are clearly obsolete, but their commitment to the dream and the freedom the ship represents serve, for Kuttner, as an emblem of perseverance and survival in a world of flux.

Kuttner's projections of human possibility are not limited to tales about future worlds and genetic mutations. Many of his stories propose that skepticism is merely a form of blindness, a conditioning that prevents mankind from reaching its full potential. In "Mimsy Were the Borogoves," perhaps Kuttner's best-known story, for example, he suggests that man's view of reality is narrow and incomplete. A child discovers a box of educational toys from the future which has been brought to the twentieth century by an experimental time machine. The boy and his sister learn a new system of logic from the toys and construct a formula which transports them into another dimension. Their parents, who have been conditioned to view that logic as irrational, must remain in their Euclidian universe. The story's gimmick involves Lewis Carroll's "Jabberwocky," the ostensible formula for transportation, but its impact has far less to do with that device than with Kuttner's projection of an alternative logic and the corollary proposition that crises only seem irremediable because of the artificial limitations of man's perspective.

"Absalom" (1946; collected in *The Best of Henry Kuttner*) offers a similarly comforting vision by again invoking the possibilities inherent in childhood. The story centers on a father's efforts to resist the evolutionary development of his son, one of the precursors of a race of homo superiors. The father's efforts are futile, but he takes perverse comfort in the knowledge that his son too must watch as his own son outstrips his progress. Kuttner generalizes the cruel pleasure of the father to suggest a view of racial progress not unlike that offered by Arthur C. Clarke in *Childhood's End* (1950). Another of Kuttner's variations on this theme of human development involves the notion of parallel universes across the boundaries of which his characters pass. While these stories, most notably "The Mask of Circe" (1948 in *Startling Stories*; republished as *The Mask of Circe*, 1971) and "The Dark World" (1946 in *Startling Stories*; republished as *The Dark World*, 1965), are generally escapist fare, lightly glossed with pseudoscientific data, they affirm Kuttner's vision of vast human potential. Kuttner argues that man's realities are but one version of experience, and hope and comfort lie beyond those boundaries.

There are many other Kuttner stories that deserve attention and reevaluation. "Tomorrow and Tomorrow" (1947, in *Astounding Science Fiction*; republished as *Tomorrow and Tomorrow*, 1951), "The Time Axis" (1949, in *Startling Stories*; republished as *The Time Axis*, 1965), and the collection *Ahead of Time* (1953) come immediately to mind. Individually and collectively they advance the contention that despite the pseudonyms and the hack work that have masked his achievement, Henry Kuttner is a major voice in science fiction. His stories chart the contours of his culture and both suggest and realize the potential of speculative fiction.

—*William P. Kelly*

Periodical Publications:

"The Graveyard Rats," *Weird Tales* (March 1936);
"Avengers of Space," *Marvel Science Stories* (August 1938);
"Dictator of the Americas," as James Hall, *Marvel Science Stories* (August 1938);
"The Mask of Circe," *Startling Stories* (May 1948).

References:

Karen Anderson, ed., *Henry Kuttner: A Memorial Symposium* (Berkeley: Seragram, 1958);
James Blish, "Moskowitz on Kuttner," *Riverside Quarterly*, 5 (1972): 140-144;
James Gunn, "Henry Kuttner, C. L. Moore, Lewis Padgett *et al.*," in *Voices for the Future*, vol. 1, ed. Thomas D. Clareson (Bowling Green, Ohio: Bowling Green Popular Press, 1976), pp. 185-215;
Damon Knight, "Genius to Order: Kuttner and Moore," in his *In Search of Wonder* (Chicago: Advent, 1967), pp. 139-145;
Sam Moskowitz, "Henry Kuttner," in his *Seekers of Tomorrow* (Cleveland: World, 1966), pp. 319-334.

R. A. LAFFERTY
(7 November 1914-   )

BOOKS: *Past Master* (New York: Ace, 1968; London: Rapp & Whiting, 1968);
The Reefs of Earth (New York: Berkley, 1968; London: Dobson, 1970);
Space Chantey (New York: Ace, 1968; London: Dobson, 1976);
Fourth Mansions (New York: Ace, 1969; London: Dobson, 1972);
Nine Hundred Grandmothers (New York: Ace, 1970; London: Dobson, 1975);
The Devil is Dead (New York: Avon, 1971; London: Dobson, 1978);
Arrive at Easterwine (New York: Scribners, 1971; London: Dobson, 1977);
The Fall of Rome (Garden City: Doubleday, 1971);
The Flame is Green (New York: Walker, 1971);

Okla Hannali (Garden City: Doubleday, 1972);

Strange Doings (New York: Scribners, 1972);

Does Anyone Else Have Something Further to Add?
     (New York: Scribners, 1974);

Not to Mention Camels (Indianapolis & New York:
     Bobbs-Merrill, 1976);

Funnyfingers and Cabrito (Portland, Oreg.: Pendragon
     1976);

Horns on Their Heads (Portland, Oreg.: Pendragon,
     1976);

Apocalypses (Los Angeles: Pinnacle, 1977).

Raphael Aloysius Lafferty was born in Neola, Iowa, but moved to Oklahoma at the age of four. After some work from 1932 to 1933 at the University of Tulsa, he began in 1935 a career in electrical wholesaling which was interrupted by four years of military service (1942-1946) in the Pacific theater during World War II. He started to write science fiction in 1959; in that same year he had published the first of more than one hundred fifty short stories. His work in short fiction climaxed in 1973, when he won a Hugo Award for "Eurema's Dam" (1972). Other notable short stories were collected in *Nine Hundred Grandmothers* (1970), *Strange Doings* (1972), and *Does Anyone Else Have Something Further to Add?* (1974). Besides his science fiction, which has been translated into Dutch, French, Italian, Japanese, and Spanish, he has written several historical novels: *The Fall of Rome* (1971), *The Flame is Green* (1971), and *Okla Hannali* (1972). At present he is working on a series of historical novels set in America, entitled "Chapters of the American Novel."

Past Master (1968), Lafferty's first novel, nominated for a Nebula Award in 1968 and for a Hugo Award in 1969, is his redaction of Aldous Huxley's *Brave New World* (1932). Astrobe, a society designed to satisfy everybody's needs, is dying, as is evidenced both by the population growth of the slum Cathead, a cancer of industrial pollution, human degradation, and suffering, and by the increased use of elimination booths for the suicide of people who have become jaded by the delights of Astrobe. Astrobe's rulers, Kingmaker, Proctor, and Freeman, decide to bring Sir Thomas More forward in history to revitalize the society by his martyrdom which they hope will provide the leaven for a new society to grow from Astrobe. More has the strange experience of seeing his Utopia made flesh and of trying to understand the human factors which cause people to oppose the golden ideals of Astrobe. He cannot fully comprehend why they reject the dream of "Finalized Humanity" given the conditions in Cathead, the

physical and metaphysical dangers of the Feral Lands, and the attacks by Programmed Persons who are mechanical killers meant to destroy those who lose faith in the society. More's three refusals to pass a "Ban the Beyond Act," which is a final attack by the Programmed Persons on God, Christianity, and transcendent spiritual meaning, lead to his death. Lafferty's desire to make More into an anti-hero, an overly rational politician who in the end takes his stand only out of pride in his superiority to other men, tends to weaken the effect of the novel. At the end, the reader does not know whether More's death brings a new birth; nor, more importantly, has the reader seen him as a plausible catalyst for revitalization.

Though *Past Master* is considerably less heated in its emotional tone than Lafferty's later works, certain preoccupations common to all of his fiction are introduced. For example, the problem of what constitutes real "humanness" recurs constantly throughout Lafferty. In *Past Master*, one finds a variety of creatures that pass as human, but all are in some way inadequate, flawed, or demonic. It becomes important to establish whether a character is really a Programmed Person in disguise, because that fact automatically makes him the enemy who is against life and humane values. The closely related motif of the demonic machine, as exemplified by the mechanical killers or the mind probes, is also present in this novel. Lafferty's concern with human cruelty and blood-lust is also apparent, but it is not the central matter that it becomes in the later works.

Lafferty's next novel, *The Reefs of Earth* (1968), deals with the question of what aliens would make of us if they came to Earth. The Puca, who are distantly related to man, have been sent to assess what can be done about humanity, whose reputation is atrocious even in the most remote corners of the cosmos. They find that, with few exceptions, human beings are as mean and hostile as rattlesnakes. The human characters of *The Reefs of Earth* closely resemble those of Flannery O'Connor. They are recalcitrant and difficult for the Puca to combat, despite the formidable powers of the aliens, which range from great strength to the Bogarthach rhymes that can kill the subjects that inspired their composition. The Puca adults succumb to the psychic malady of "Earth Allergy," which results from psychically unbalancing alienation and makes one humorless, sour, and fearful of death. Their children, immune by their terrestrial birth to the sickness, tell tall tales to ward off the fear of Earth and take over the Puca mission. They at first decide to eliminate all humanity. However, guided by the dying Witchy, their mother or aunt, they decide to kill only if necessary, controlling and altering until they "see if something cannot be made of the place." The results of unleashing the Puca children on Earth are not seen, the book ending, as is Lafferty's custom, without a final resolution.

The end of *The Reefs of Earth* suggests the Christian metaphysic that provides an implicit ironic background for the action of many of Lafferty's novels. By means of various biblical quotations, we see the Puca as the redemptive agents of what is called the "Giver." The apocalypse they will bring promises to be more unsettling and irresistible than their actions up to the end of the novel. But the book is not simply antihuman and pro-Puca, for the Puca's ethic—"be swift, and be sudden"—is not more elevated than man's, only more primitive. The Puca's moral primitiveness and their strange, ogrelike physiognomy, suggestive of prehistoric origins, indicate that Lafferty is not entirely on their side. Similarly, the role of the Puca as the irregular agents of God links these figures to other more negatively drawn characters in later novels, like *Fourth Mansions* (1969), *The Devil is Dead* (1971), or *Not to Mention Camels* (1976), who are also ambiguous because of their shadowy role in regard to Providence.

Space Chantey (1968) is a fast-paced and broadly humorous parody of the *Odyssey*. Its protagonist, Captain Roadstrum, must lead his men back to Earth after the conclusion of a war in space. The appeal of this short book lies primarily in the author's space-age variations on the episodes in his Homeric model. Humor and interest in science, which are the twin emphases of Lafferty's novel, are clearly illustrated by the following two episodes. Homer's Laestrygonians, for example, become vaguely Scandinavian trolls whose antics burlesque not only Greek epic, but also the mead-hall conventions of Germanic poetry. The next adventure, based on the killing of the Oxen of the Sun, interests the reader by its scientific inventiveness. When Roadstrum's crew catch and eat one of the Oxen of the Sun—an asteroid—they fall into the Vortex, an "involuted, massive, black-giant sun" which causes "the turning inside-out of mass and moment." The crew is saved from annihilation by the pressing of the "Dong button," which in the nick of time—and hilariously—reverses both their fall into the Vortex and the aging process which is its consequence. The crew get back fingers, eyes become unpickled, and the asteroidal space calf, regurgitated, returns to its original condition. "Certain bodily functions," Lafferty notes laconically, "are unusual and almost unpleasant when done in reverse; but to get out of a hole like they were in, you will put up with a lot." As in the *Odyssey*, the hero does return safely home—but decides to set out again when Penny, his wife, launches into a series of interviews featuring in-depth analyses of her dead suitors. Reputedly Lafferty's favorite among his own novels, *Space Chantey* is appealing for both its rollicking humor and its genial view of humanity.

Fourth Mansions, nominated for a Nebula Award in 1970, concerns a piece of investigative journalism by the reporter Freddy Foley into what is wrong with human history. Freddy finds that man's progress is thwarted periodically by "returnees," people who reincarnate themselves in order to prevent mankind's breakthrough to a higher plane of existen·e. This state of near beatitude is identified with Saint Theresa of Avila's mystical "Fourth Mansion" from her *Interior Castle*. While the returnees are preserving the repetitive cycle of history, the Harvesters, who see themselves as the left hand of God, are attempting psychically to break through to the state of a mutated *uebermensch*. Their purpose is to become "full and free people." As elsewhere in Lafferty, the people (and particularly the women) who have Faustian ambitions and power tend to be at once superficially charming and horrible. "Mind rape" is happily indulged in; uninvolved bystanders are carelessly overwhelmed by the psychic force emanating from the seven Harvesters in concert; Earth tremors are effected.

The thesis and antithesis of the returnees and the Harvesters are united in the synthesis of Freddie as hero. His mind has been touched by the Harvesters, but he is also made into a returnee. He has, then, integrated all the archetypes, and because of his simplicity becomes the first real mutant. The novel ends on a positive note with the expectation of Freddie as a potential savior for mankind. However, there is still the possibility that humanity will return cyclically to the First Mansion rather than proceeding upward to the Fifth. Despite these serious features, *Fourth Mansions* is a light, entertaining book, for the nonhuman powers are not yet portrayed as blackly as they appear in the later Lafferty. The emotional involvement of the reader in the problem of the historical development of man is far less than it is in the examination of the role of evil in history in *Not to Mention Camels*. However, Lafferty's vision begins to darken in his next novel, *The Devil is Dead*.

This novel, despite its nomination for a Nebula Award, is as much theological fantasy as science fiction. In *The Devil is Dead*, one finds the mortal

R. A. Lafferty

struggle of the forces of good and evil in a situation described by one of the characters as "a catastrophe looking for a world to happen to." This conflict is expressed in the folk motif of the search to kill the devil. However, in the convoluted plot it is difficult at times for the narrator, Finnegan, and therefore for the reader, to tell exactly who the devil is, who is on which side of the fight, and who is really dead. It is rather like watching the actions of shadows through a shade. The forces of evil appear to be Saxon X. Seaworthy and most of the crew of the *Brunhilde*. The forces of good are mainly Finnegan, Anastasia, and Doll. Papadiabolus, who may or may not be the devil, and who may or may not be dead, seems to be everyone's enemy. Even the evil side is out to destroy him, apparently to lull humanity's suspicions concerning what the dark powers plan for the world. Most of the characters are nonhuman, belonging to what Finnegan terms the "older people." The "older people" represent something innate in all men. They are in fact the Old Adam, Original Sin, which Lafferty identifies with the unconscious mind. Though inescapable, it must be suppressed for life to continue. Even Finnegan, like others who are "on the side of the angels," is only partly human, his other side being "older." Those who fully embrace or embody the "older people," like the Seaworthy lot

or the returnees of *Fourth Mansions*, are against humanity and life. After confrontations all over the Mediterranean, the Caribbean, and America, the outcome between the older "lords of the world" and the completely human "late-world people" is, as usual in Lafferty, left unresolved. But with Doll's hope for salvaging the world as the last words of the novel, the ending seems optimistic for mankind.

The Devil is Dead is perhaps the most appealing of Lafferty's work to the non-science-fiction reader because of its many echoes of mainstream literature. In tone, writing technique, and particular episodes, one is reminded at times of Joyce, Greene, Fowles in *The Magus* (1965), the American underground novel as exemplified by Pynchon and Vonnegut, and the traditional tall tale, an influence seen before in *The Reefs of Earth*. But the strange logic and metamorphoses of the novel are most strongly rooted in the world of dreams—the source, in fact, of many of Lafferty's stories, according to the author himself.

Arrive at Easterwine (1971) is a lighthearted, amusing romp through the author's favorite metaphysical concerns, with less of the heavy horror, violence, and "ultra-violet" humor that characterize much of the rest of Lafferty's work. It is the autobiography of Epiktistes, which means the shaping or creative one. Epiktistes is a supercomputer, which has stored in it the personality precis of all mankind, including such characters as Snake, Mary Sawdust (who may turn out to be the Virgin who will crush Snake), and Easterwine (Christ). Much of the comedy comes from the vain attempts of the computer's masters, members of the Institute for Impure Science, to alter human nature and human destiny. As preposterous as the projects of Swift's Laputan academics, the experiments of the Institute include the creation of a superman, the spraying of people with love essence to bring about the kingdom of heaven on earth, and the examination of mares' nests to find the essence of existence. At the end of the novel, Epiktistes, true to his name, brings forth the pattern or image of the state of the world, the result of all the material fed into him. The "face" of holes that appears on his screen seems to be positive—to suggest that from the horror will come a new birth. This cyclical movement, with its expectations of an upward advancement, is more or less characteristic of Lafferty until *Not to Mention Camels* and *Apocalypses* (1977), which seem to hold out little hope for man.

Not to Mention Camels is one of Lafferty's darkest books in its vision and emotional tone. Despite some science-fiction trappings such as teleportation, alternate worlds, and communication by "voxo," this book is a heavily metaphysical work which is concerned with examining the multiple and recurrent roles of evil throughout history in tones and hues reminiscent of Gustave Doré and Hieronymus Bosch. After a somewhat tedious start which sets up the philosophical framework, the reader is quickly sucked into Lafferty's most powerful and horrifying narrative which centers on three successive avatars of evil, Pilger Tisman, Pilgrim Dusmano, and Polder Dossman, collectively called P.(T)D. This wildly charismatic figure is a world-jumper who, until the final page of the book, is able to escape annihilation by transmigrating to another existence. There is an attempt—always unsuccessful—to destroy utterly the soul of P.(T)D. at the end of each of his incarnations. Thus it is with great relief that the reader learns that P.(T)D., in making his last possible world jump, has landed in Hell. Some form of final reckoning and end to the evil is absolutely necessary in response to the exquisite sadomasochism, the mind control through the collective unconscious, the death wish, and the desire for ultimate power which center in P.(T)D. P.(T)D. as Antichrist is accompanied on his world jumps by a parodic Mary and John, making a triad which is an inversion of More, Evita, and Paul in

Past Master. Mary, John, and the Umbrella Man, who is responsible for P.(T)D.'s soul, are directed by some vague divine command, suggesting that God allows evil in the world and gives it ample opportunity to destroy itself. The role of humanity in history, as evidenced by the semiunwilling discipleship of P.(T)D.'s followers and the actions of the bloodthirsty mobs, is hardly very edifying and reinforces the frequently negative view that Lafferty takes of man.

The vision of *Not to Mention Camels* is so horrific that there is probably not much left to say in that tone. So Lafferty's next two novellas, *Where Have You Been, Sandaliotis?* and *The Three Armageddons of Enniscorthy Sweeney*, published together as *Apocalypses* (1977), swing back to a more comic vein, though the vision is no less disturbing. *Where Have You Been, Sandliotis?* is another exploration of the nature of reality. Utopia, what man wants but cannot have, is illusory rather than flawed as in *Past Master*. The "primary people," that is, the forces of evil or Antimatter, who attempt to bring off the "Billion Dollar World-Jack" and the "Greatest Real Estate Heist," are difficult to identify, metamorphosis being an essential metaphor of the book, along with forgery and filmmaking. The central crucifixion scene is a good example of the book's strategy of confusion. Is the crucifixion of the thirteen people real? And whose testimony or death is to be believed? The multiple biblical parodies and echoes make it difficult to establish the authorial stance toward the material until the end when, in good detective-book style, the exposed powers of evil are overcome by the ingenuity of the human mind, by "dark strength" born in extremis, and by human laughter, which gives the lie to the blackmail of the "primary people" and their Director.

The "primary people" (similar to the returnees, the Harvesters, and the "older people"), who cause most of the problems in Lafferty's books, reappear in *The Three Armageddons of Enniscorthy Sweeney* as the Friends of the Catastrophes. The Friends are the voices that inspire Enniscorthy Sweeney, a writer whose works, it seems, determine the course of history. The "Armageddons" of the title are the works by Sweeney which cause World Wars I, II, and III. Prohibition and the Depression were also born from his writing. But since people do not act as if destruction and war have taken place, or even could take place, there is serious doubt whether certain putative events actually did occur. World War II, in fact, is found to be a mass illusion, a worldwide psychosis. History becomes plastic in the hands of Sweeney, and there is an amusing "revised" chronology of modern history which raises again Lafferty's favorite concern of what is real. After the performance of Armageddon III in 1984, the final apocalypse is upon the world, but the people, standing in front of the Furnace (Hell) in a sea of blood, do not seem to care whether the world ends or not. For mankind, sated with the "abominations [of murder and war and] with . . . their hard pleasures completely removed," the world ends with a whimper, not a bang. Lafferty is quite explicitly condemnatory of the majority of the human race who, all devoted to Sweeney, are described as "gore-oriented people . . . hatred-and-murder people . . . bring-down-the-world people." This seems to be an opinion that Lafferty has held with increasing vigor since *Past Master*, despite certain touches of optimism as in *Arrive at Easterwine* and *Where Have You Been, Sandaliotis?*

It is difficult to guess the direction of Lafferty's future writing. Having investigated history, reality, eschatology, and evil both cosmic and personal, he has virtually exhausted the major metaphysical problems. A redemptive novel seems unlikely, however, for his vision, despite his Roman Catholicism, does not incline to the positive. It is at best ironic and comic in a black vein. Though productive, he has been neglected, and his lot has been relative obscurity perhaps traceable to the limited appeal of his religious themes. But fellow writers such as Roger Zelazny, Samuel Delany, and Harlan Ellison have praised him for the "modern" virtues of vitality, absurd vision, and underground humor, and these qualities may yet lead to a broad readership for R. A. Lafferty. —*Patricia Ower*

Other:

"Eurema's Dam," in *New Dimensions II*, ed. Robert Silverberg (Garden City: Doubleday, 1972), pp. 67-79.

Reference:

Paul Walker, "R. A. Lafferty," in *Speaking of Science Fiction: The Paul Walker Interviews* (Oradell, N.J.: Luna, 1978), pp. 11-23.

KEITH LAUMER
(9 June 1925-   )

SELECTED BOOKS: *How to Design and Build Flying Models* (New York: Harper, 1960; revised edition, New York: Harper, 1970; London: Hale, 1976);

Worlds of the Imperium (New York: Ace, 1962; London: Dobson, 1967);

A Trace of Memory (New York: Berkley, 1963; London: Mayflower, 1968);

Envoy to New Worlds (New York: Ace, 1963; London: Dobson, 1972);

The Great Time Machine Hoax (New York: Simon & Schuster, 1964);

A Plague of Demons (New York: Berkley, 1965; Harmondsworth: Penguin, 1968);

Galactic Diplomat: Nine Incidents of the Corps Diplomatique Terrestrienne (Garden City: Doubleday, 1965);

Embassy (New York: Pyramid, 1965);

The Other Side of Time (New York: Berkley, 1965; London: Dobson, 1968);

The Time Bender (New York: Berkley, 1966; London: Dobson, 1971);

Retief's War (Garden City: Doubleday, 1966);

Catastrophe Planet (New York: Berkley, 1966; London: Dobson, 1970);

Earthblood, by Laumer and Rosel George Brown (Garden City: Doubleday, 1966);

The Monitors (New York: Berkley, 1966; London: Dobson, 1968);

The Frozen Planet and other stories (New York: Ace, 1966);

Galactic Odyssey (New York: Berkley, 1967; London: Dobson, 1968);

Nine by Laumer (Garden City: Doubleday, 1967; London: Faber & Faber, 1968);

Planet Run, by Laumer and Gordon R. Dickson (Garden City: Doubleday, 1967; London: Hale, 1977);

The Invaders (New York: Pyramid, 1967); republished as *The Meteor Men*, as Anthony LeBaron (London: Corgi, 1968);

Enemies From Beyond (New York: Pyramid, 1967);

The Avengers, No. 5: The Afrit Affair (New York: Berkley, 1968);

The Avengers, No. 6: The Drowned Queen (New York: Berkley, 1968);

The Avengers, No. 7: The Gold Bomb (New York: Berkley, 1968);

Retief and the Warlords (Garden City: Doubleday, 1968);

Assignment in Nowhere (New York: Berkley, 1968; London: Dobson, 1972);

Greylorn (New York: Berkley, 1968); republished as *The Other Sky* (London: Dobson, 1968);

The Day Before Forever and Thunderhead (Garden City: Doubleday, 1968);

It's a Mad, Mad, Mad Galaxy (New York: Berkley, 1968; London: Dobson, 1969);

Retief, Ambassador to Space: Seven Incidents of the Corps Diplomatique Terrestrienne (Garden City: Doubleday, 1969);

The Long Twilight (New York: Putnam's, 1969; London: Hale, 1976);

Time Trap (New York: Putnam's, 1970; London: Hale, 1976);

The World Shuffler (New York: Putnam's, 1970; London: Sidgwick & Jackson, 1973);

The House in November (New York: Putnam's, 1970; London: Sidgwick & Jackson, 1973);

The Star Treasure (New York: Putnam's, 1971);

Retief of the CDT (Garden City: Doubleday, 1971);

Dinosaur Beach (New York: Scribners, 1971; London: Hale, 1973);

Once There Was a Giant (Garden City: Doubleday, 1971);

Deadfall (Garden City: Doubleday, 1971; London: Hale, 1974); republished as *Fat Chance* (New York: Pocket Books, 1975);

Retief's Ransom (New York: Putnam's, 1971; London: Dobson, 1976);

Time Tracks (New York: Ballantine, 1972);

The Big Show (New York: Ace, 1972; London: Hale, 1976);

Night of Delusions (New York: Putnam's, 1972; London: Dobson, 1977);

The Infinite Cage (New York: Putnam's, 1972; London: Dobson, 1976);

The Shape Changer (New York: Putnam's, 1972; London: Hale, 1977);

The Glory Game (Garden City: Doubleday, 1973);

The Undefeated (New York: Dell, 1974);

Retief: Emissary to the Stars (New York: Dell, 1975);

Bolo: The Annals of the Dinochrome Brigade (New York: Putnam's, 1976);

The Best of Keith Laumer (New York: Pocket Books, 1976);

The Ultimax Man (New York: Putnam's, 1978);

Retief at Large (New York: Ace, 1978);

Retief and the Rebels (New York: Pocket Books, 1979).

Between the years 1960 and 1979, fifty-three books were published under the name Keith Laumer—a guide to building model airplanes, a mystery, a general-fiction novel, and fifty science-fiction novels or story collections. Although he is not as well-known as Ray Bradbury, Arthur C. Clarke, or Robert Heinlein, his best work rivals theirs, and he is one of the prominent figures of the last two decades in science fiction. His work sometimes reveals the mark of hasty composition—weak character development and unrealized scenes—and he has been stereotyped, inaccurately, as an action writer. But his best fiction contains both action and an exploration of ideas and human situations on a deep and mature level.

John Keith Laumer was born in Syracuse, New York, where he lived until he was twelve. He then moved with his family to Florida, where he has lived for much of his life, and which serves as the locale for parts of such novels as *Catastrophe Planet* (1966) and *The Long Twilight* (1969). In 1943, at the age of eighteen, he enlisted in the army and served in Europe at the end of World War II and during the German occupation. On his return to the United States in 1946, he enrolled at the University of Illinois to study architecture. After spending 1948-1949 at the University of Stockholm, he returned to Illinois and took a B.S. in 1952. By then he was the father of two children, having married Janice Perkinson in February 1949. Convinced, as he explained to Harlan Ellison, that World War III was imminent, he joined the air force in 1953 and "spent a year in solitary on a rock in Labrador," serving as a first lieutenant on radar installations. He joined the U. S. Foreign Service in 1956 and lived for two years in Rangoon, Burma, where he discovered he was a writer. He wrote and sold his first story, "Greylorn," in 1959, at the age of thirty-four. In 1960 he rejoined the air force as a captain, stood a tour of duty at Third Air Force Headquarters in London, and continued writing. He resigned in 1965 to take up writing full time, and between 1965 and 1971 he wrote his best fiction. In 1971 he suffered a debilitating illness and was unable to write until 1976 because of physical discomfort. After a slow recovery he has begun working again and has completed a novel and several stories. He resides in Brooksville, Florida.

Laumer's experience and travels during his military and diplomatic service provided him with much of the subject matter for his stories. Many of his novels concern war (or the threat of it) and life in the military. His best-known character, Retief, the subject of several novels and numerous stories, is a diplomat in the C.D.T.—Corps Diplomatique Terrestrienne. Many of the situations and characters Retief encounters are evidently derived from Laumer's foreign service experience, which led him to hold most diplomats and government officials in low esteem. Laumer also cites the influence in his work—"the parts the critics ignore"—of three well-known writers: S. J. Perelman, Raymond Chandler, and Ernest Hemingway. Perelman's influence is apparent in the wry, sometimes sardonic humor and satire that predominate in the Retief stories and the parallel-world novels. Hemingway's mark appears in Laumer's reliance on dialogue, the economy of his language, and the tightly episodic nature of many of his plots. It is to Chandler, however, and the tough-guy detective persona of Philip Marlowe, that Laumer is most indebted; the callous, cynical, come-what-may attitudes of many of his heroes—Retief, for instance, or Lafayette O'Leary in *The Time Bender* (1966) or Ravel in *Dinosaur Beach* (1971)—are clearly modeled to some degree on Marlowe, who is more vulnerable and human than many of Laumer's heroes. Chandler's influence is especially evident in the novels and stories with first-person narrators.

Laumer's work can best be characterized by three important, interrelated elements: action, character, and idea. His main characters are usually robust and independent-minded men in their late twenties or early thirties. Their personalities are revealed through their reactions to the often demanding situations in which they become involved. Although they are intelligent and fair-minded, they virtually never feel that mere talk will effectively solve a problem. Action—fast, quick, commonsensical—is a better solution, but one which often leaves the hero isolated from popular opinion, even in rebellion against constituted authority. Laumer insists, however, that he is a novelist of ideas, not of action: "Oddly enough," he writes, "I find that I am almost universally regarded as a writer of 'action' stories. The action in my books is purely incidental: I find it more interesting to examine ideas in a dynamic way, rather than in academic discussion." The unity of action, character, and idea is a natural consequence: "By exploring an idea I mean this: I put a character of a specific kind in a specific situation, and then I write it out to see what happens, what follows naturally." The plots of the novels reflect such an exploration: in *A Plague of Demons* (1965) and *The House in November* (1970) a character becomes the only person aware of an alien invasion; in *The Star Treasure* (1971) a naval officer uncovers what appears to be mutiny on his vessel but is himself accused of mutiny; and in *Time Trap* (1970) the descendant of Richard the Lionhearted has to defeat a man seeking to remold reality into his own image.

In several ways Laumer is distinctly different from other writers of contemporary science fiction. He tends to take a cautious, conservative view of human affairs, and he is loath to take up a cause merely because it is popular. In *The Glory Game* (1973), written during the Vietnam conflict, two political groups disagree over whether war should be waged against a race of hostile aliens. Although Laumer dislikes war, he also dislikes simplistic solutions, and he excoriates both groups equally for their lack of foresight and common sense, their hypocrisy. Laumer's language also lacks the overt lyricism typical of such writers as Bradbury or Edgar Pangborn: Laumer's sentences are clear, concrete, and adjectivally lean; only rarely does he indulge in verbal flights of poetic fantasy. Another distinguishing characteristic is his use, in his best work, of relatively normal situations and themes within the framework of science fiction. His characters face the same dilemmas, must make the same kinds of decisions, and exhibit the same virtues and defects as people of all places and times.

Laumer's view of humanity reveals his affinity with other modern science-fiction writers. He believes in certain fundamental virtues: "I address myself . . . ," he says, "to those values which have been important to man since he became man, and will continue to be of value as long as our species is human. Among these values are: truth and beauty, loyalty and justice, kindness and gentleness, ethics and integrity, etc." In Harlan Ellison's anthology *Dangerous Visions* (1967), Laumer elucidates this concern: "The ultimate test of man is his ability to master himself. It is a test which we have so far failed." The measure of Laumer's hero is how well he exhibits these virtues and performs on the test, often in the face of the greatest adversity. A strong streak of romanticism in characterization and plot is the result. In fact, once inside the science-fiction framework of many of his stories, one encounters a world more like that of Sir Walter Scott, Alexandre Dumas, and medieval legend than the world of the future. Fistfights and swordfights, beautiful women in distress, underground movements, subterfuge, espionage, sleight of hand, swashbuckling chases, evil tyrants, quaint or exotic aliens—these and more abound, especially in the novels of time travel and parallel worlds. In the more recent novels this vein of romanticism has become somewhat more subdued. Very often, then, Laumer's work is only incidentally science fiction, being more fundamentally concerned with human heroism, good in conflict with evil, and imaginative, chivalric adventure.

Laumer's fiction can be divided into five general

categories: interstellar adventure, interstellar character studies, stories of alien invasion, the Retief series, and time-travel and parallel-world stories. The last of these categories is the one in which he produced some of his earliest work. His first science-fiction novel was *Worlds of the Imperium* (1962), which describes a police force responsible for keeping order among the parallel worlds. Two other Imperium novels are *The Other Side of Time* (1965) and *Assignment in Nowhere* (1968). The latter is narrated by Richard Curlon, who, though ignorant that he is the last descendant of the Plantagenets, wears at his side a fragment of Richard the Lionhearted's sword. Brion Bayard of the Imperium informs him that "the continuum of multi-ordinal reality" is being disrupted by Baron von Roosevelt, who wants to mold reality to his own liking and who is described as "A fallen angel; a man so evil that the world cannot contain his malice." (Whether Laumer intends any special meaning in the Baron's name is unclear.) As a result reality is beginning to break down; Richard Curlon is taken to the Chateau Gaillard in France, where the "probability force lines" of the "multiordinal continuum" converge. Curlon spends much of the novel moving from one world to another, reassembling fragments of the sword as he uncovers them. The improbability imbalance is finally corrected and Roosevelt is defeated, although Curlon possibly has to die in the process (his fate is unclear; if he does perish he is the only Laumer hero to do so).

Assignment in Nowhere contains the typical elements of a Laumer story: sudden, unexpected turns of plot; a courageous, foolhardy hero; a beautiful woman; plentiful action; and dangerous situations from which escape seems impossible. The concepts of parallel worlds and time travel enable Laumer to explore that period in English history when England was struggling to rid itself of French domination, while the Plantagenet brothers Richard and John vied with one another for power. Like many Laumer heroes, Curlon becomes a man of destiny upon whom the fate of the world, of reality itself, comes to rest. A different series of parallel-world novels features a hero named Lafayette O'Leary—*The Time Bender, The World Shuffler* (1970), and *The Shape Changer* (1972). More fanciful than the Imperium novels, they are characterized by a rowdy, often farcical humor, fast-paced action, exotic characters and scenes, and sometimes shallowly developed episodes and themes. The parallel-world and time-travel novels are, for the most part, well-written and entertaining but undistinguished—although *The Great Time Machine*

Hoax (1964) is an extremely funny tale. In it a young hayseed, the owner of a failing circus, inherits an old computer that can, in addition to functioning as a time machine, manufacture a beautiful woman from a single blood cell.

The most popular type of story in Laumer fiction is that featuring the C.D.T. diplomat Retief. In *Dangerous Visions* Ellison comments: "it is a shame [Laumer] can sell the Retief stuff so easily, because it allows him to coast, allows him to tell extended jokes when he should be grappling with more complex themes...." This assessment is hardly unfair. The Retief fiction is much like a comic strip—stereotyped characters and situations, funny but shallow satire, and plenty of action. Compared with the best of Laumer's writing, it is not very impressive. Perhaps Laumer's own attitude is evident in his abandonment of Retief for other heroes in *The Star Treasure* and *The Glory Game* where he engages in a more serious treatment of diplomatic and military themes than in the Retief fiction. Retief's primary characteristic is invincibility— he does no wrong, makes no mistakes, and never fails. He is so invincible, in fact, that much of the suspense and excitement drain from his adventures. One reads on to discover not whether, but how, he succeeds.

In a letter published in *Dangerous Visions*,

Keith Laumer

RETIEF'S RANSOM

by

Keith Laumer

Four of the seven moons of Furthuron glowed ~~varied shades of~~ **night** pink in the/sky as ~~t~~he twelve-passenger limousine with the green and white Ensign of the <u>Corps Diplomatique Terrestrienne</u> drooping from its prow nosed its way cautiously through the *motley* crowd ~~villa,e~~ thronging the market- place. Colored lights strung on stalls and in the low branches of ~~the~~ **huts** spreading Heo trees shed a polychrome light on/elaborately woven of native grasses, on quaint native garb, and on the natives themselves. The latter appeared in two distinct sizes: knobby, *squat* yoemen, ~~shopkeepers and tradesmen~~ shopkeepers and tradesmen wrapped in dun-colored togas adorned with grotesque appliqués indicative of guild affiliation; and even more knobby seven foot nobles, elegantly swathed in brocaded robes secured by ropes of rough-cut gems, supporting an alarming variety of curved scimitars, businesslike dirks, needle-pointed stilettos, and crude, long barelled pistols with hand-tooled grips.

"Ugh," First Secretary Magnan commented tersely from his crowded seat at the rear of the long vehicle, peering ~~out~~ through the armored glass at alien visages the color and texture of well aged salami, which gazed back at the intruders with unreadable alien expressions. ~~"There are times when I~~ question the wisdom of *all this* indescriminate peace-making," he ~~"I have a feeling~~ their preoccupation with anihilating each other is the only thing restraining these chaps from massacreing all foreigners out of hand."

"You underestimate them, Mr Magnan," Retief re- plied cheerfully. "Given a few more truce propo- sals like the last one, I'm sure they'll find time to include us on the schedule."

"You know very well that **we** didn't <u>really</u> mean to propose that **fifty** percent of the planet be designated a demilitarized zone and turned over to the CDT for use as an experimental worm-ranch, Retief. It was a mere clerical error, you might say."

"Oh, they didn't object to the *idea of giving* fifty percent," Retief pointed out. "It was the fact that it was <u>their</u> fifty percent."

tootling its horns placatingly The big car slowed to a crawl, as the crowd closed in around it.

Retief's Ransom, revised typescript

Laumer observed that when he entered the foreign service in 1956 he "discovered a teeny-weeny preponderance of Sonsofbitches there." In the Retief stories diplomats and government officials are not merely bumbling, hypocritical fools; they are often willing to compromise, betray, and even sacrifice lives for the sake of expediency. Laumer views most of them as despicable. Retief's usual task is to outwit and short-circuit their plans and to do the right thing. Laumer's attitude is also satirically evident in the names of the diplomats and their projects: *Retief and the Warlords* (1968) includes projects CHUMP, SUCKER, and PAUPER (Panel for Alien Uplift, Protection, Enlightenment, and Relief) and describes such men as Foulbrood, Bloodblister, Overdog, and Hikop. Vanity, effeminacy, cowardice, and overweening ambition are characteristics that suggest the true nature of the diplomats.

The best Retief story—because it is the most humorous and most thoroughly developed—is *Retief's War* (1966), about a world called Quopp, inhabited by numerous tribes of insectlike creatures ranging in size from mouse to elephant. The Terran ambassador contrives to unite these warring tribes under the rule of the most despised tribe on the planet, the Voions, whose tyrannical Prime Minister Ikk plans to take over the world and imprison the Terrans. Retief is opposed to this plan, and he unites the Quoppians against Ikk and defeats him. Each of the tribes has a distinct appearance and personality: the Rhoons are huge flying creatures who speak in a Scottish dialect; the tanklike Jackoos are effeminate; the Zilks are bucolic farmers with a New England accent; Weens are tiny creatures who talk babytalk; and the Flinks, who trap their food in thin nets and drive merciless bargains, bear stereotyped Semitic features. There is rich humor in the variety of these tribes and in the fatuous, scheming politicians of Terra and Quopp. Despite the comedy, the plot is shallow and the issue simplistic. Retief is too perfect, too much in control of all that happens. He also shares more than a little of the paternalistic attitude of the C.D.T. toward aliens. While the Terrans may be ruthless and money hungry, they are also intelligent—more so than the Quopps, who are a bit dim-witted. Yet Retief does give them his support, and he ridicules the C.D.T.'s Kiplingesque paternalism when he tells Magnan, his fumbling, ambitious supervisor, "That's the trouble with uplifting the masses; they get to believing it themselves." Even women are shallow stereotypes. When Terran females become lost in a forest, Retief trails them easily by the shreds of "lacy cloth, dropped hankies, candy wrappers, and the deep prints of spike heels."

In *Retief and the Warlords* a secretary "burps" on the telephone with "an angular female face set in an expression of permanent martyrdom," while another, named Cirrhosa, is "a purse-faced female . . . with hair like a bleached sponge."

Laumer, however, defends Retief: "Rather than being a superman, Retief is a perfectly normal specimen of Homo sapiens; he does nothing that some other man could not have done. His distinctive trait is that he has fully realized his human potential. Retief never loses his human dignity, nor, in the face of massive pressures, does he compromise his standards. . . . He is the parfit gentil knight. . . ." Nevertheless, Laumer has created other, much more credible and realistic heroes.

Another important subject in Laumer's novels is that of invading aliens. *A Plague of Demons, Catastrophe Planet, The Monitors* (1966), and *The House in November* are examples. The aliens are hostile in all of these except *The Monitors*, in which Laumer examines the consequences of an invasion by benevolent creatures. Both *A Plague of Demons* and *The House in November* present characters who are the only individuals aware that an invasion has occurred. Paranoia and considerable suspense are the results. The novels bear several similarities—in each the aliens are the manifestations of a disease which has spread like blight across the universe. In *The House in November* they are a huge cloud of microorganisms with a group mind and potent psychic powers, while in *A Plague of Demons* they are invisible catlike creatures who manipulate the human mind and collect human brains. John Bravais is the hero of the latter book. He battles and flees the cat-demons until he is captured and awakens to find his body gone and his brain in control of a huge war machine. He gathers other, similar machines under his command and defeats the aliens. It is not unusual to find invading aliens representative of evil, but in this novel there is a strange twist—the aliens are distantly related to the human race. They are abstract incarnations of the life-force spreading across the galaxy in the forms of good and evil, which are constantly in conflict. The human race is the first life form to combine good and evil together. At the novel's end Bravais and his compatriots have decided to remain in their mechanical bodies as guardians of the future destiny of humankind.

Bravais is faced with the greatest adversity of any Laumer hero when he awakens to find his brain removed from his body, but he rises to the demands of the occasion and performs bravely. The novels of the second half of Laumer's career, those published after his retirement from the air force, emphasize the resilient spirit and valor of humanity, those qualities of "truth and beauty, loyalty and justice, kindness and gentleness, ethics and integrity." These novels also possess a much fuller development of scene, episode, and character than most of the earlier ones. They take several forms: a character may have to deal with the problem of being lost in a desert, or he may have to face an ethical dilemma; he may use logic and common sense to extract himself from a tight corner, or he may save himself with alien, nonhuman powers of which he had previously not known. The latter is exemplified by *The Infinite Cage* (1972), in which Adam Nova suddenly comes to consciousness in a jail cell—he has no past, no memories, and no identity. But his incredible mind can learn such subjects as calculus and foreign languages in seconds by reading the minds of other people. Nova fits nowhere in human society and is about to resign himself to death in a junkyard when he learns he is a new evolutionary step in the growth of humanity, a mind with infinite powers which "arose from the massed mental emanations of the human race" and which can exist without the limiting cage of a physical body.

In *Galactic Odyssey* (1967), a novel written five years earlier, a similar character overcomes adversity through wit, determination, and hard work. One of Laumer's best books, *Galactic Odyssey* is narrated by Billy Danger, a young man who accidentally falls asleep on an alien spaceship and becomes the servant of a rich interstellar hunter. The plot is faintly reminiscent of Charles Dickens or C. S. Forester: a young man begins life as the low servant of the rich and, by his own effort, slowly makes his fortune. Danger faces innumerable episodes of hardship in the course of his quest to honor his pledge to Sir Orfeo, his master, that he will protect the Lady Raire (whose hand he wins at the end of the novel). He is wounded by bat creatures, befriended by a giant cat, attacked by giant fleas, appointed a spy, given command of his own ship, accused of treason, imprisoned by aliens, and forced to make a grueling twenty-day trek across a frozen wasteland, but through his intelligence and common sense he always survives. Unlike Retief, Danger can make mistakes and feel emotion—he has a real personality. The characterizations of the aliens he encounters are varied and excellent, the scenes of the novel are diverse and exotic, and Danger's narration imbues the novel with suspense and personal interest.

Laumer's attitude toward the potential and nature of the human race is epitomized in the thirty-seventh chapter of *Night of Delusions* (1972). Florin, the narrator and main character, also a senator in line to become President of the Earth, is connected to a machine which transforms his dreams into reality. He develops the powers of a god and even creates the world and life out of nothingness. He keeps trying to create an ideal world where all is perfect, but he is never happy with the results. Human nature, he realizes, is essentially imperfect and corruptible, incapable of satisfaction, destined always to continue striving. Accepting his status as a human rather than a god, Florin states: "Success is the challenge nobody's ever met. Because no matter how many you win, there's always a bigger and harder and more complicated problem ahead, and there always will be, and the secret isn't Victory forever but to keep on doing the best you can one day at a time and remember you're a Man, not just god, and for you there aren't and never will be any easy answers, only questions, and no reasons, only causes. . . ."

The responsibility of being human carries with it many obligations, but many benefits as well. The benefits are what convince the two main characters of Laumer's best novel to give up their immortality and become human. *The Long Twilight* contains characteristics which are, for science fiction, little less than epic in proportions: two beings who have lived and fought each other for over twelve hundred years, in the balance of their rivalry hanging not only their own fates but that of the Earth too. When their conflict is resolved, they have to choose between preserving their immortality and serving Xix (the rebellious, sentient spaceship which created them) or saving the human race and becoming mortal. By choosing the latter, they affirm the superiority of imperfect humanity over perfect machines (a theme treated differently by the stories collected in Laumer's *Bolo: The Annals of the Dinochrome Brigade*, 1976). The different elements of this novel work almost to perfection. Seemingly unrelated chapters jump from one locale and group of characters to another. As the plot develops, the hodgepodge of events gradually interconnects. The battles of Gralgathor and Lokrien over the twelve hundred years are chronicled in a series of brief, italicized narratives whose dramatic, elegiac language evokes the mood of Wagnerian opera. Laumer also creates several mysteries at the beginning to sustain reader interest: a huge, unnatural storm; a malfunctioning power station; the strange italicized narratives; and the identities of the main characters. These mysteries are explained as the plot unfolds, although there is suspense up to the last sentence of the book.

In two of his later novels, *The Star Treasure* and

The Glory Game, Laumer has moved away from the conflicts of man against nature and machines and has turned to the issue of human conflict, of the assault of compromise and expediency upon integrity. In both of these novels integrity prevails, but in quite different ways. In both books Laumer also seems concerned with the conflict of right and wrong, the nature of truth, and the impossibility of allying oneself with a "right" side in a political controversy. Because there is never a wholly "wrong" or "right" side, the individual who refuses to take sides and who insists upon upholding truth is isolated and often even punished. Each novel also shows that society is structured so that honoring those human virtues of truth, integrity, and morality can be very difficult. This is also the recurrent theme of *Once There Was a Giant* (1971), a collection of stories in which the traditional values of human life are violated by political decisions, government bureaucracy, greed, and ambition.

The Star Treasure narrates the efforts of Ban Tarleton, a naval lieutenant, to expose the corrupt power of five men known as the Star Lords, who control Earth's commerce, governments, and military. The key to their dominance is a vaguely explained device called the Star Core, a source of tremendous mental powers found in the wreckage of ancient alien space vessels. Throughout the book runs a tripartite tension among the ideal of government authority, the corrupt reality of government authority, and the question of whether rebellion is a legitimate means to achieve the ideal. Tarleton, whose friend has been murdered, who has been falsely charged with treason and sentenced to prison on a barren planet, faithfully believes in the ultimate good of the government. He tells the Hateniks, who plan to overthrow the government, that its defects will be corrected through evolution, and he questions what will replace it when it is destroyed. By providing overwhelming evidence of governmental corruption, Laumer places Tarleton in an almost impossible position. Yet the entire issue is almost dropped when Tarleton gains the powers of the Star Core and is enabled to view the responsibility of authority from the perspectives of the Star Lords. The implication is that a government's corruption is a relative matter, depending on the perspective one views it from. This is a morally hazy resolution to a dilemma already complicated by the fact that Tarleton solves his problems with superhuman, alien powers rather than his own natural abilities. Similar nonhuman powers are also at work in the conclusions of *The Infinite Cage* and *The House in November*.

The same issue is satisfactorily resolved through human logic and ingenuity in *The Glory Game*. Commodore Tancredi Dalton is placed in the unpleasant position of being pressured to ally himself with one of two political factions, neither of which he agrees with. The Softliners support a treaty with the Hukks, hostile aliens who have been behaving in a menacing way toward Terra; the Hardliners urge all-out war. One alternative would endanger Terra's security while the other would destroy the Hukks. Dalton alienates both factions when he captures a Hukk space fleet and refuses either to destroy it or to support the Softliner treaty. He eventually loses his command and his girlfriend and is exiled as a junk dealer to a deserted planet. The theme of *The Glory Game* is that in complex military and political crises, often no one possesses all the facts or the ability to judge them objectively, because often political considerations weigh too heavily. Yet pressure to take sides can be intense, and maintaining one's integrity may be difficult. Dalton explains: "I don't really give a damn about helping any power clique take control. What I'd like to see is a general recognition of the realities of the situation, an ability to deal with what *is*, instead of what somebody hopes, or wishes, or fears, or imagines—some arbitrary guess they've staked a career on, or some article of ideology. Is that too much to ask?" *The Glory Game* contains less action and more dialogue than any other of the earlier novels, but it draws an exciting, clinically objective portrait of one man's insistence on the truth in spite of the greatest odds against him.

Both *The Star Treasure* and *The Glory Game* were written during the Vietnam war, and their themes reflect the debates over the war which were occurring at the time. Yet neither novel is a specific political allegory, but rather a more general commentary on human situations and reactions. Responding to at least one suggestion that *The Glory Game* runs parallel to the 1966 Tonkin Gulf incident, Laumer writes, "none of my books is a commentary on contemporary political situations. Not specifically; they are a commentary on human behavior, which of course includes recent human behavior." He has made use of what he observed during his years in the air force and foreign service, "but in a general way, as in the depiction of fumbling diplomats, not in the detailing of specific incidents." In the same way his novels reflect his concern over the erosion of human values, his belief in the potential of the human spirit, his wariness over the rapid growth of technology, and his aversion to simplistic solutions to anything.

It is unclear what course Laumer's career will take in the future. His most recent novels have been distinguished by a clear emphasis on philosophical themes, and it will be interesting to see in what directions he will carry them. His latest writing has also shown a marked improvement in the delineation of character, development of scene and episode, and construction of plot—all of which were occasional flaws in his earlier work, especially the Retief stories. What is clear, however, is that Keith Laumer is a serious writer of serious science fiction. His stories are rife with profound themes and exciting action, and his best work reveals his rich, creative, and far-ranging imagination. His next novel, already completed, will be entitled "Fort Ancient." He writes, "at last count I had 7,942,621,430½ ideas burning to be written." There is little doubt that he will continue to make his mark in the field of fantasy and science fiction. —*Hugh M. Ruppersburg*

Other:
Five Fates, edited by Laumer (Garden City: Doubleday, 1970).

References:
Harlan Ellison, Introduction to *Nine by Laumer* (Garden City: Doubleday, 1967; London: Faber & Faber, 1968);
Ellison, Introduction to Laumer's "Test to Destruction," in *Dangerous Visions* (Garden City: Doubleday, 1967), pp. 515-517;
Paul Walker, "Keith Laumer," in *Speaking of Science Fiction: The Paul Walker Interviews* (Oradell, New Jersey: Luna, 1978), pp. 101-106.

Papers:
Collections of Laumer's papers are at Syracuse University, New York, and at the University of Mississippi at Oxford.

Ursula K. Le Guin

Brian Attebery
College of Idaho

BIRTH: Berkeley, California, 21 October 1929, to Alfred Louis and Theodora Kracaw Brown Kroeber.

EDUCATION: A.B., Radcliffe College, 1951; A.M., Columbia University, 1952.

MARRIAGE: 22 December 1953 to Charles A. Le Guin; children: Elisabeth, Caroline, Theodore.

AWARDS: Fulbright fellowship, 1953; *Boston Globe* Horn Book Award for *A Wizard of Earthsea*, 1969; Nebula Award for *The Left Hand of Darkness*, 1969; Hugo Award for *The Left Hand of Darkness*, 1970; Newbery Silver Medal Award for *The Tombs of Atuan*, 1972; Hugo Award for "The Word for World Is Forest," 1973; National Book Award for Children's Books for *The Farthest Shore*, 1973; Hugo Award for "The Ones Who Walk Away from Omelas," 1974; Nebula Award for "The Day Before the Revolution," 1974; Jupiter Award for "The Day Before the Revolution," 1974; Nebula Award for *The Dispossessed*, 1974; Jupiter Award for *The Dispossessed*, 1974; Hugo Award for *The Dispossessed*, 1975; Jupiter Award for "The Diary of the Rose," 1976.

BOOKS: *Rocannon's World* (New York: Ace, 1966; London: Tandem, 1972);
Planet of Exile (New York: Ace, 1966; London: Tandem, 1972);
City of Illusions (New York: Ace, 1967; London: Gollancz, 1971);
A Wizard of Earthsea (Berkeley: Parnassus, 1968; London: Gollancz, 1971);
The Left Hand of Darkness (New York: Ace, 1969; London: Macdonald, 1969);
The Tombs of Atuan (New York: Atheneum, 1971; London: Gollancz, 1972);
The Lathe of Heaven (New York: Scribners, 1971; London: Gollancz, 1972);
The Farthest Shore (New York: Atheneum, 1972; London: Gollancz, 1973);
The Dispossessed (New York: Harper & Row, 1974; London: Gollancz, 1974);
The Wind's Twelve Quarters (New York: Harper & Row, 1975; London: Gollancz, 1976);
Wild Angels (Santa Barbara, Cal.: Capra Press, 1975);
The Word for World Is Forest (New York: Berkley, 1976; London: Gollancz, 1977);
Very Far Away from Anywhere Else (New York:

Atheneum, 1976); republished as *A Very Long Way from Anywhere Else* (London: Gollancz, 1976);

Orsinian Tales (New York: Harper & Row, 1976; London: Gollancz, 1977);

The Language of the Night: Essays on Fantasy and Science Fiction, ed. Susan Wood (New York: Berkley/Putnam's, 1979);

Malafrena (New York: Putnam's, 1979);

The Beginning Place (New York: Harper & Row, 1980).

In a decade and a half, since Ursula K. Le Guin's first novel appeared as one half of an Ace Double paperback, she has become one of the most important writers in the field of science fiction. Le Guin writes the sort of stories science-fiction critics have been saying ought to come out of the genre: speculative, richly inventive, stylistically rewarding fiction, effectively combining current ideas with unchanging human concerns. But in order to understand Le Guin's brand of science fiction, one must realize that, as her brother Karl Kroeber points out, she is not really a science-fiction writer: the label does not convey the range of her writing nor indicate her primary literary sources. According to Kroeber, she is a fantasist, a teller of marvelous tales. Her goal in writing is to show us ourselves and our lives at a distance, the better to create orderly patterns out of random information. Science fiction is only one way of marking off that distance; it is not the only ordering device Le Guin has utilized nor even the first she turned to when she began writing. It is, however, a device familiar to a large group of readers, and it was by turning to science fiction that Le Guin found a publisher and an audience.

Le Guin is the daughter of a writer, Theodora Kroeber, and a pioneering anthropologist, Alfred Louis Kroeber. She seems to have acquired from her family background a double orientation, both scholarly and humanistic, that shows in all of her writings. The Kroeber household was a stimulating environment to grow up in: Theodora Kroeber, in her book *Alfred Kroeber: A Personal Configuration* (1970), describes their summer home in the Napa Valley as a gathering place for scientists, students, writers, and California Indians. This was the milieu in which Le Guin began to write, and it may help explain the number of scientists in her stories, who are nearly always humane men deeply concerned about the effect and value of their research. Though she makes no claims to being a scientist herself, she understands what it is to pursue a scientific goal, and the philosophy that underlies anthropological

thought, in particular, informs all of her work.

Le Guin left the West Coast to go to Radcliffe, followed by two years of graduate work at Columbia. Her scholarly field was medieval Romance literature. In her "Response to the Le Guin Issue" of *Science-Fiction Studies*, a gentle but pointed reproof of literary criticism, she asks why "no one has turned for elucidation of the later fictions to the early works of scholarship. Some, indeed, allude to her parents' scholarly qualifications, but none has pursued the lode which lies, obscure but probably still available to the persistent researcher, somewhere in the dimmer galleries of the Romance Languages departments of Radcliffe College and Columbia University." Though she turned away from scholarship after completing a master's thesis and disparages the value of her own scholarly work, she gained from the experience an acute critical perception of others' work and of her own. Her articles demonstrate extensive and thoughtful reading of fiction, both American and European, and poetry, modern as well as medieval. She considers her primary influences to be not Isaac Asimov, Robert A. Heinlein, and Theodore Sturgeon, but Percy Bysshe Shelley, Rainer Maria Rilke, Theodore Roethke, Tolstoy, Chekhov, and Virginia Woolf, among others. She is a latecomer to science fiction and brings to it a wealth of literary perception and technique.

Though her knowledge of science is only that of an interested layman, she is able to turn scientific ideas into effective metaphors for broader areas of human experience, which is what science fiction ideally should do. She generally chooses concepts from the social sciences—anthropology, political science, psychology—perhaps because they are more tentative and therefore more open to fictional exploration. Among the physical sciences, she is most interested in theoretical physics, in the effort to comprehend—and to explain, through models and analogies—processes too vast or too small to be seen. Pseudosciences—telepathy, clairvoyance, and precognition—play important parts in her work, not because she believes in them, but because they can be made to express ideas about man's relationships with other men, with the world, and with his own fate.

All of her stories are about reciprocal relationships. There is a sort of golden rule in her fictional world, which states that whatever you touch touches you. This golden rule has a scientific backing in ecology; it also has philosophical underpinnings in Taoism and in Zen. Le Guin is uncomfortable when critics claim her as a great and original thinker, for she works best with what she calls "fortune cookie ideas," ideas proposed by someone else and capable of expression in very simple terms. Beginning with such an idea—ecological balance, for example—she can show through her stories how simple terms hide a mass of complexity and contradiction that surfaces only when the idea interacts with human lives.

Le Guin started writing, according to an introductory note in her short-story collection, *The Wind's Twelve Quarters* (1975), at about age five. She wrote poetry, some of which was published, and stories, which were not. In the note she mentions a science-fiction story written in 1942, when she was twelve. It was rejected by John Campbell, the editor of *Astounding Science-Fiction*. Her next try at the genre was accepted by Cele Goldsmith Lalli for *Fantastic*—twenty years later. That story, "April in Paris" (collected in *The Wind's Twelve Quarters*), was her first published piece of fiction. It is a lightly comic time-travel story using her knowledge of medieval France. Several more stories appeared in the mid-1960s. One of them, "The Dowry of the Angyar" (1965), or, to use the title Le Guin prefers, "Semley's Necklace" (collected in *The Wind's Twelve Quarters*), grew into her first published novel, *Rocannon's World* (1966). Another, "Winter's King" (1969; collected in *The Wind's Twelve Quarters*), established the setting for her first major critical success, *The Left Hand of Darkness* (1969). These stories and novels, along with two intermediate works, *Planet of Exile* (1966) and *City of Illusions* (1967), form a loosely organized future history; that is, a series of independent works share a common historical background, somewhat like Robert Heinlein's chain of novels and stories. Le Guin's cycle is usually referred to as the Hainish cycle after the original race of humanity who are said to have arisen on the planet Hain and colonized other planets, including Earth, until galactic war isolated the various human settlements. All Le Guin's Hainish stories take place long after the war and a subsequent dark age and cover around twenty-five hundred years, during which contact is gradually being reestablished with the colony worlds. In the meantime, however, most of these colonies have forgotten their origin, and many of their humanoid inhabitants vary widely from "Hainish normal" biologically as well as culturally, altered by time and independent evolution and perhaps, as it is suspected of the androgynous Gethenians of *The Left Hand of Darkness*, by biological experiments conducted by the ancient Hainish. The Hainish cycle also includes *The Dispossessed* (1974), the novella *The Word for World Is Forest* (1976), and

two more of the stories in *The Wind's Twelve Quarters*, "Vaster Than Empires and More Slow" (1971) and "The Day Before the Revolution" (1974). These last four are set centuries before *The Left Hand of Darkness*, which represents the furthest point in time of the cycle so far.

Among the Hainish novels, *Rocannon's World*, *Planet of Exile*, and *City of Illusions* are considered by critics Darko Suvin and Robert Scholes to be Le Guin's apprentice works, leading to the more mature *The Left Hand of Darkness* and *The Dispossessed*. Even these early efforts, however, stand well above most science-fiction writing. One might make a three-part division of Le Guin's career: the real apprenticeship was before 1962, while Le Guin was practicing her art in private, accumulating skills, confidence, and rejection slips. The first published writings mark off a journeyman stage, during which she demonstrated notable gifts of storytelling and characterization despite some unsureness in her handling of theme and occasional slips into unconsidered or conventional turns of plot. *The Left Hand of Darkness* introduces her master stage, in the old craft-guild sense. It showed that she was now on her own, that she knew as much of her art as any of her teachers and was ready to begin expanding its boundaries.

Just about the time Le Guin established her Hainish universe as a significant addition to the body of science fiction, she began to explore other ways of transforming the known into the meaningfully unreal or into other modes of fabulation, as Robert Scholes calls these nonmimetic forms of fiction. *A Wizard of Earthsea*, the first of three stories based on magic, rather than science, was published in 1968. The Earthsea books, originally directed toward young adults, bear the mark of Le Guin's admiration for J. R. R. Tolkien's *The Lord of the Rings*, but the style and thematic material are purely Le Guin. They are closely related to the Hainish works and equally demanding. Especially in the later books, *The Tombs of Atuan* (1971) and *The Farthest Shore* (1972), Le Guin utilizes the fantasy format to explore facets of existence not as readily accessible to more rational modes of narrative, such as death and the soul.

The Lathe of Heaven (1971) represents another new direction for Le Guin; it is comic, satirical, and closer to home than the reaches of space or the dream landscape of Earthsea. It is set in a future Portland, Oregon (Le Guin's home), in which current American conditions can be abstracted, extrapolated from, and held up to the clear light of Le Guin's philosophy, which is primarily derived from a combination of Asian discipline, American Indian mysticism, and ecological holism. Some of the same satirical bent emerges in *The Dispossessed*, marking it off from the rest of the Hainish cycle. Western Oregon figures as the setting for the novella *The New Atlantis* (1975; contained in an anthology of the same title), for some of the short stories, and for the nonfantastic young-adult story *Very Far Away From Anywhere Else* (1976). In each case social satire goes hand-in-hand with Le Guin's obvious love for the Western landscape and traditions.

Orsinian Tales (1976) follows yet another route into the fabulous. Not magical, not relying on displacement into the future or into outer space, the *Orsinian Tales* are set in a nonexistent but plausible country somewhere in Eastern Europe. There is no name for such fictions: they are like the Ruritanian adventures written by Anthony Hope but without the swashbuckling romance, or like Isak Dinesen's Gothic tales but warmer, less artificial and theatrical. Their closest model is Austin Tappan Wright's *Islandia* (1942), a vast narrative whose main point is simply the experiencing of an imaginary country: an experience we can add to and contrast with our knowledge of the real world. Islandia verges on utopia in some respects, and Orsinia on dystopia, but neither is presented as an unchanging model of good or evil society, but rather as a broadening of human possibilities.

Many of Le Guin's central themes are present in her first novel, though they are partially over-shadowed by her uncritical adoption of the conventions of the particular sort of science fiction she was aiming to write. *Rocannon's World* is a highly romantic, sweeping adventure, really more science fantasy than pure science fiction, modeled primarily on the rather distinctive writer of juvenile science fiction, Andre Norton. But there are aspects of *Rocannon's World* that do not belong to the romances it seems to be imitating. The story is a parable of the sort that Poe or Hawthorne wrote, in which surface reality is distorted in order to bring out other, hidden realities. Objects in *Rocannon's World* become mirrors reflecting the souls of its characters.

Gaverel Rocannon, the protagonist of *Rocannon's World*, is an ethnologist specializing in alien cultures. In "Semley's Necklace," which serves as a prologue to the novel, he is a minor character whose primary function is to comment on the action, his wistfully scientific outlook contrasting effectively with the high-flown, legendary quality of the rest of the story. In the novel he is the central figure in a quest that grows increasingly mythlike. Seeking revenge for the destruction of his ethnographic

survey team, he sets out with a group of native friends to warn his home world about the rebels who have set up a military base on Fomalhaut II, later known as Rocannon's World. His most important companions are the aristocratic warrior Mogien, the servant Yahan, and the elf Kyo. Each has a different view of Rocannon and his quest: to Mogien, Rocannon is a warrior avenging his honor; to Yahan, Rocannon is a powerful wizard fighting the evil magicians who are laying waste to the world; to Kyo, Rocannon is a man fulfilling a strange and

wonderful fate. A series of encounters with thieves, nature, and various alien beings serve to reinforce each view of Rocannon, according to each companion's perspective. Yet at the same time Rocannon's own view remains the central one and the view the reader is most likely to have. Rocannon sees himself as "an ordinary League scientist," middle-aged, physically unprepossessing, and funda-mentally peaceable. In the end he plays the traditional mythic hero's role by gaining a great gift at high cost. His treasure is the ability to make contact with other minds telepathically. He uses the gift as a weapon against his enemies and as a consequence must share the experience of their deaths. After the book's climax he seems to fade away, consumed in the legend that is growing around him. One hopes, however, that he will pass on his gift to others, freed of its penalty by his own sacrifice.

Other themes in the novel impress themselves on the reader almost independently of the story's color and adventure: the conflict between rationality and an irrational universe, the responsibilities of a technologically advanced civilization in dealing with a less advanced society, the danger of judging from prejudice, the wonder of establishing ties with someone different from oneself, and the tragedy of having to take up violent means to defend oneself against violent adversaries. Rocannon is the rational being in an irrational world: a scientist in the midst of legend. He learns that truth hangs suspended somewhere between his notions of cause and effect and his friends' belief in spells and talismans. He comes to respect their understanding of the world and their way of life as valid alternatives to his own, the knowledge of which enriches his life. As an anthropologist, he objects to the League of All Worlds' manipulation of this recently discovered planet and puts a stop to its use as a weapon in a cosmic arms race.

Prejudice takes many forms in the novel. The Centaurans who made the initial contact with Fomalhaut II chose to deal only with the crafty, cave-dwelling, tool-making Gdemiar, or Clayfolk, ignoring the other intelligent races on the planet and thus upsetting carefully balanced interspecies relationships. Rocannon makes a similar mistake in assuming intelligence in the tall, humanoid, winged creatures of the southern plains and in failing to recognize it in the small, furry, furtive beings who live among them. The former turn out to be mindless predators, while the latter are not only intelligent but friendly, saving the lives of Rocannon and his companions. Rocannon's life is saved several times in the novel. These rescues serve not only to advance the plot but also to point out how vulnerable man is alone and how dependent upon the good will of friends and strangers. By seeking out individuals unlike himself, meeting them on their own ground, offering them his loyalty and accepting theirs, Rocannon not only completes his quest but also raises its significance beyond a mere exercise in warfare. His passing alters the world he travels through so it is appropriate that it be given his name.

Le Guin's second novel takes up the same themes: prejudice, technology, clashing world views, and communication across barriers of race and culture.

In *Planet of Exile* the telepathic skills won by Rocannon have become codified mental disciplines taught throughout the League of All Worlds. The novel deals with a League colony which has, for unknown reasons, been abandoned. Left without a spaceship or ansible (Le Guin's term for an instantaneous message transmitter), the colony on Werel has struggled to preserve its cultural heritage without unduly influencing the native cultures for a period of ten Werelian years—each equivalent to more than sixty Earth or League years. As the book opens, the planet is entering into winter, a brutal season lasting a quarter of a lifetime.

As in *Rocannon's World*, there is conflict in this story between two cultures, one technological, the other atechnological and illiterate. There are some interesting reversals in this pair of opposing civilizations, however, that prevent our reading the book as a conventional meeting between civilized explorers and colorful savages. The native Tevarians, who live a life so marginal that they have not invented the wheel or learned to sing, are fair-skinned. The colonists from Earth are dark. The colonists practice a variety of psi skills: the skeptical natives view their neighbors as witches. Both groups are inbred and stagnant. The Earthmen are gradually losing the knowledge and skills their ancestors brought with them. Their numbers are shrinking because of a high incidence of infertility and spontaneous abortion. Their body chemistry is alien to the planet: no microorganisms will attack them, but neither can they eat native foods without special medication. One of them comments that the world seems to be rejecting them like an unsuccessful graft. The native population is not decreasing, but they have not furthered their way of life for many generations, and there is no place among them for exceptional individuals like the girl Rolery.

The stalemate between these two cultures is broken by the combined onslaught of winter and the nomadic, plundering Gaal, a rival native culture. Finding a common enemy gives the two groups a common cause. The catalyst bringing them together at last is the Romeo-and-Juliet love between Rolery, the only native born in summer, out of season, and Jakob Agat, a young leader of the colonists. Since the natives are truly aliens, separated long enough by time and perhaps by experiment from their ancient Hainish ancestors to have become almost a separate hominoid species, the love of Jakob and Rolery carries an onus of miscegenation in addition to the division between the two societies.

This star-crossed romance is brought about by a mistake. Jakob warns Rolery by mindspeech, or telepathy, when she is in danger of drowning in the incoming tide, even though telepathic contact with the natives is strictly forbidden. The initial contact establishes a bond between the two. They meet again when Jakob goes to Rolery's ancient father, Wold, to ask his aid in fighting the approaching Gaal hordes. Angry Tevarians see them meeting in a forest hut and attack Jakob, breaking off the uneasy truce he has engineered with Wold.

When the Gaal attack, Wold's village is destroyed, and the survivors seek refuge in the city of the farborn, or colonists, where Rolery is already Jakob's wife. Together, the two groups hold off the Gaal until the first winter storms put an end to fighting and the Gaal move south. During the fighting, the colonists discover themselves to be, for the first time, susceptible to infection. They have begun to adapt to their adopted world and may even prove able to interbreed with natives. Jakob and Rolery are the beginning of a new, vigorous, hybrid race.

Telepathy is again a metaphor for communion between unlike individuals. In the case of Jakob and Rolery it grows into love and the redemption of two societies. But mental powers, as in *Rocannon's World*, can be misused. The old farborn woman, Alla Pasfal, uses her psychic skills to overhear the thoughts of the Gaal. Misunderstanding what she hears, the colonists are unprepared for a last, devastating attack. To make communication into a one-sided thing, in which one ventures nothing oneself but only takes from others, is a major sin in Le Guin's universe, and it is duly punished. But to reach out, to take off one's mental armor before a stranger, is a heroic act that always results in some good. *Planet of Exile* contains a clearer statement than ever before of Le Guin's central theme that the "other" that one fears is really one's most important potential ally, because he or she, being different, has what one lacks.

Planet of Exile represents an advance over *Rocannon's World* primarily in the contribution its well-wrought setting makes to the thematic development. Landscape and climate in *Rocannon's World* are largely arbitrary: if the plot requires mountains there are mountains, and if the author wants flying cats, she furnishes thick air and light gravity, without considering the effect of those conditions on trees or tides or human physiology. In *Planet of Exile*, however, everything centers on Werel's long, violent year. Trees live a single season, specialized plants bloom between winter snows, birds and animals make long migrations, and people spend years preparing for the oncoming cold. Details are

striking and plentiful. The reader finishes the book with a sense of having experienced that immense turning of the seasons.

Cultural details are also more carefully depicted than in the earlier novel. The proud half-empty city of the farborn and the winter camp of the natives are presented with equal care and compassion. The portrayal of both cultures is abetted by occasional looks from one to the other: one sees the farborn through the eyes of both Rolery and Wold, and one sees the scornful picture of native life held by many of the colonists. A scene such as the rock-pounding council of the natives is seen from the inside as a time-honored mainstay of tribal harmony and from the outside as a comically barbaric rite.

Characters, too, are strong in this work. Agat is much like Rocannon and equally attractive. Rolery is a woman in a culture that pays little attention to women, but it is her act of daring that sets events in motion and her endurance that saves Agat's life. She questions, experiments, adapts, and mediates between her people and the farborn. Wold, the old chieftain, is the most memorable of all. He is earthy, crafty, forgetful, and immensely dignified. A strong and rebellious warrior in youth, he is a wise leader in old age. He shares his people's prejudice against the farborn, but he rises above it in his dealings with individual colonists. Alone among his people he remembers the previous winter, and he is willing to drop pride and mistrust in the interests of survival. He bears a great resemblance to Old Lodge Skins in Thomas Berger's *Little Big Man* (1964): both represent the primitive as undivided man. Both may have been influenced by the revival of interest in Indian traditions in the 1960s.

The weaknesses in *Planet of Exile* have to do with conflicts between plot and theme. There is considerable reduplication of adversaries: the Gaal, winter, and the grotesque snowghouls represent the same threat, and it is a threat imposed from outside, not one which grows from the acts and thoughts of the principal characters. Having an outside adversary is not necessarily a flaw, but it lessens the importance of the rapprochement of Earthman and alien. *Planet of Exile* is nevertheless an enjoyable story and might seem more satisfying if Le Guin had not shown in *The Left Hand of Darkness* what more could be done with the same materials.

One learns why the colony in *Planet of Exile* was cut off in Le Guin's next novel, *City of Illusions*. A hostile race called the Shing has conquered the League of All Worlds and taken Earth for the capital planet. Mankind on Earth exists in isolated pockets kept by their Shing overseers from making any real advancements or joining forces to share what knowledge is left to them. The book begins with a nameless amnesiac who appears mysteriously in the vast forests of occupied Earth. He is found by a young girl named Parth in the clearing near her forest home. Although he knows nothing, not even how to speak, he learns quickly from Parth and the other members of her small community. They name him Falk, meaning yellow, because of his strange golden eyes. When he has learned all that they can teach hm, he decides to set out for Es Toch, the legendary city of the Shing, far away in the western mountains, to find out what he is.

The next part of the book is essentially a reworking of *Rocannon's World*—a hero's journey across an alien land in search of a goal. Even the landscape he crosses is similar, though there is a stronger sense of geography here than in *Rocannon's World*, partly because Le Guin has become a more practiced world builder and partly because this is, after all, Earth's own North American continent. The scenery is familiar but also strange, strange to Falk's eyes because he is an outsider and strange to ours because it is restored to its original beauty.

Falk's quest is a journey toward his own maturation through a landscape that complements the stages of his growth. His path leads from the simplicity of the forest to the savagery of the prairies to the unexpected sophistication of the desert to the uneasy civilization of the mountains. There is a hidden valley in the forest where animals speak, and where men are brutal because of their fears. Many of the groups and individuals he meets along the way are notable. An old man has isolated himself from other men because he is a powerful empath, one who reads feelings as a telepath reads thoughts, and he cannot stand the presence of so many emotions; he welcomes Falk, however, and gives him important information. A tribe of wandering herdsmen lives rigidly controlled lives of custom and taboo amid the boundless openness of the prairie. A woman, Estrel, is, like Falk, imprisoned by the herdsmen. They escape together, and she becomes his guide and lover. Ultimately she betrays him, as suggested by her unwillingness to return Falk's confidences or his physical passion. She manipulates him by playing the passive sexual object. The Prince of Kansas, an old man with some of the kingly madness of Othello or Lear, reads Falk's fortune on a device called a patterning frame. The picture of him working it strongly suggests fate or some god ordering the movements of the universe: "Turquoise shot to the left and a double link of polished bone set with garnets looped off to the right and down, while a fire-opal blazed for a moment in the dead center of the frame. Black, lean, strong hands flashed over the wires, playing with the jewels of life and death." Falk's fortune is read twice, on different patterning frames, and both times the yellow stone that represents him refuses to conform to any known pattern except the mystical configuration known as Vastness. Falk thus represents the unknown, the outsider who will break the deformed pattern imposed by the Shing upon the Earth.

Falk reaches his goal—the glass city of Es Toch—almost halfway through the book and then discovers that he has an equal mental and moral distance left to traverse. The Shing confuse him: they treat him with alternating roughness and concern; they lie and then refute their own lies; their city is made of glass, but the glass is murky so that nothing shows clearly through the floors, walls, and ceilings of its towers. They produce a boy who claims to be of Falk's people, like him a traveler from another world. They offer to restore Falk's memories, but say the operation will unavoidably destroy his personality, the self he has built up since he first appeared in the forest. They even tell him that there are no Shing: they are men, they say, maintaining a fiction for the benefit of other men, who would otherwise turn to warfare and destruction. Estrel may or may not be one of their agents. Falk must find his way through all these webs of half-truths and outright lies.

He decides to let them restore his former self, to trade his memories for those of Agad Ramarren, descendant of Jakob Agat of *Planet of Exile*, navigator for the first Werelian expedition to Earth. But he also plants a clue by which his old self might discover and incorporate the new. It is a clue so subtle that even the Shing will not detect it, merely a passage from the so-called Old Canon of man: "The way that can be gone/is not the eternal Way./The name that can be named/ is not the eternal Name." Falk meditates on that passage, which is Le Guin's adaptation of the opening of the Taoist book, Tao Te Ching, until it becomes so much a part of him, body and soul, that it might become a road for his return from the nothingness the Shing wish to cast him into. He succeeds—the memory carries across the imposed mental block—and two personalities, Falk and Ramarren, coexist in one brain. The combined knowledge and strengths of his two selves help him outwit the Shing, penetrate their lies, and escape. He sets out for his home planet, presumably to help prepare the way for ultimate victory over the Shing and the eventual establishment of a new and more humanely conceived League of Worlds.

The great lie of the Shing, which Falk/Ramarren

penetrates, is their one law: "It is wrong to take life." It is a lie because it pretends to be adequate and inflexible, because it denies conscience and moral complexity. The Shing allow themselves to cheat and mistreat mankind in any way short of causing death. As Falk comments, they made a law about killing because it is the only thing they really desire to do. The lie is accompanied by one great secret, hinted at by the old empath in the forest: the Shing are sterile. There are few of them and they cannot mate with humans. Their position is much like that of the colonists on Werel, except that those colonists finally reached across to their neighbors, mentally and physically, and were able thus to renew their race. The Shing cannot even communicate with mankind. They defeated the worlds of the League by their ability to mind-lie. No one else could tell a lie telepathically, and the League was built on that fact. But the Shing cannot send thoughts directly; they can only project what seem to be true thoughts. This inability, which they use as a weapon, is their tragedy. Lacking truth, they devote themselves to falsehood. Their culture emphasizes perversion; their architecture relies on illusion and disorientation. Falk, who vows as he sets out on his journey never to tell an untruth, is able to confound their lies with his trust.

Running counter to the law of the Shing is a theme that helps unify the novel despite its shifts in locale and its mazes of falsehood. It is the Way, the Tao. Falk is seeking his own Way, the path to his true nature, which cannot be guided by arbitrary rules like the Shing law. He carries with him a copy of the Old Canon when he begins his journey: it is stolen by the fearful men who capture him in the forest. The old empath is a Thurro-dowist—he lives his life according to Taoist teachings augmented with Thoreau's *Walden*, the Younger Canon. The Prince of Kansas gives Falk another copy of the Tao Te Ching to replace the one he lost, and it is that copy which enables him to retain his personality.

Taoism preaches simplicity, acceptance, and immersion in the whole; yet it also serves, in this novel, as a spur toward growth, rebellion, and individual identity. It denies any partial answers, such as the Shing law, and any complacency with one's spiritual state. Le Guin's version of Taoism rounds out the philosophy already hinted at in the earlier novels, as represented by Rocannon's personal wisdom and Jakob Agat's embracing of the Other. Its presence makes *City of Illusions* a better organized book than the two earlier ones, at least until the entrance of the Shing. At that point, the novel begins to lose coherence, partly because Le

Guin seems to depart from the Taoist outlook she began with.

Earlier sections of the book reveal Le Guin's growing authority over her material. The forest is deftly, quickly built up with relatively few images. It already carries the connotations of sleep, dream, and the origins of things, which will become important in later stories about forests. The physical setting throughout seems solid and alive, as if Le Guin were taking real pleasure in exploring an unspoiled America. Emotional relationships take on new complexity in this novel. Falk's feelings of attraction and unease toward Estrel anticipate the difficult and shifting friendship of two later travelers, Genly Ai and Estraven in *The Left Hand of Darkness*. The Prince of Kansas is a minor character but an impressive one: his section is as packed with implication as a poem. Language is generally used more tellingly than in earlier works with less feeling of ornamentation, more of conviction. Symbols develop unobtrusively and are picked up later for further investigation in such a way that one would never suspect them of having been purposefully planted. As Falk journeys down the Ohio River, for instance, he encounters an illusion of a boating party from a long-vanished city. He is invited to return with the members but fears some trap; the illusion may have been produced by the Shing. But the promise in his mind, the image of a thriving human city, helps him later to reject Es Toch because it is not a true, living city. Perhaps no true city exists any more, but he knows what one would be like. The image expands beyond its original context in an unexpected direction and enriches the story without ever seeming to impose itself upon the reader.

But the Shing, as Le Guin admits, are not a particularly successful creation. They are necessary for the development of the plot. They are essential, unlike the Gaal of *Planet of Exile*, to the theme, but they prove to be unworkable as actual characters. The principal reason is that "the Shing" and "the Lie" are equivalent concepts. Together they represent the disruption of the human community through mistrust, for they are the very spirit of mistrust. Therefore it is simply not satisfactory to claim that they are actual invaders from some far corner of space. Either they are invaders, with a culture and motivations, however alien, of their own, and thus deserve to be treated with the respect Le Guin urges toward any Other, or they are a symbol of evil and should never be confined within the realm of physical reality. One of the lies the Shing tell, that they are merely a fiction maintained by a select group of humans, is a preferable solution to the problem of theme, though it would throw the plot into disorder.

Each of these first three novels holds out the promise of better work to come. In *The Left Hand of Darkness* their individual strengths—*Rocannon's World*'s interplay of legend and science, *Planet of Exile*'s clash of cultures, *City of Illusion*'s controlled use of symbolism and its ethical base—are combined and the promise fulfilled. In *The Left Hand of Darkness*, one immediately becomes aware of the presence of an individualized narrator. Le Guin's previous books were all narrated anonymously by someone outside the story. The narrator of *The Left Hand of Darkness* is also its protagonist, Genly Ai, a native of Earth sent to a planet called Winter or Gethen. Ai is the lone envoy of a post-League organization, the Ekumen, which is not so much a political body as an idea and a hope of free commerce and communication among far-flung worlds. The Ekumen has mystical overtones reminiscent of the Instrumentality of Man in the novels and stories of Cordwainer Smith, who is one of the few science-fiction writers Le Guin acknowledges as an influence. Genly Ai comes alone to Gethen bearing the message to its natives that they are not alone in the universe, that there is a family of similar worlds which they are invited to join. He is alone because a lone alien will generate curiosity without triggering fear, but behind him stands a wise and benevolent organization that has learned from the mistakes of its predecessor and from the conflict with the Shing. He is an apostle of the gospel of peaceful interdependence.

But Genly Ai is not old, wise, and experienced. He is young, fervent, and often mistaken in his judgments of people and events. He is telling a story that is still very close to him and still painful, and he resorts to a rich variety of methods to tell it. Into his narrative he pulls reports by previous Ekumenical observers, recorded myths and legends from different parts of Gethen, and the diaries of his principal ally, Therem Harth rem ir Estraven, who he does not even know is an ally until late in the story.

The story is Ai's own report to the Ekumen, but it is no impersonal listing of contacts and treaties. The Ekumen would not be satisfied by that sort of thing, nor would Ai consider it sufficient. He says, at the outset, "I'll make my report as if I told a story, for I was taught as a child on my homeworld that Truth is a matter of the imagination. The soundest fact may fail or prevail in the style of its telling: like that singular organic jewel of our seas, which grows brighter as one woman wears it and, worn by another, dulls and goes to dust." Le Guin makes good use of her narrator and of his complex

relationship with the events he is recounting. He is sensitive enough to allow her to display her gifts for description and metaphoric analysis; he is fallible enough to generate considerable tension through gaps in understanding; and he is deeply enough involved in the story to lend it tremendous emotional weight.

An important aspect of the book is the culture in which it is set. The story begins with a parade, an exotic, colorful ritual surviving from Gethen's distant past. Pomp and panoply indicate the presence of aristocracy, and the heavy clothing of the participants indicates a cold climate. There is no military aspect to this parade; instead of soldiers there are merchants, lords, and entertainers. The cars in the parade are electric, one discovers later. This is no backward world to be conquered or raised up by civilized invaders, nor is it a mechanistic wonderland. Instead of either of these cliches, it is a culture approximately on a level with our own, a rarity in science fiction. Gethen, or this particular part of it, Karhide, is a monarchy, and the purpose of the parade is to accompany the king to the dedication of a new bridge. Ai's talk with his neighbors at the ceremony contains little details that begin to fix Karhide in the reader's mind. More of the capital city of Erhenrang is seen as Ai returns to his home, and more is learned about its climate, history, and social organization. An unfamiliar word appears in passing—"kemmer"—and then a related form, "kemmering." Ai goes to dinner at Estraven's home, and only then is the important fact about Gethen revealed: its people are neither men nor women. They are androgynes, sexless except for their periods of sexual potency—kemmer—during which they make take on the characteristics of either sex. This is further explained by a Karhidish tale about two "brothers," one of whom bears the other's child. Gethenians are androgynous, a fact no more startling to them than the fact that they have two ears and only one nose. Ai has been among them long enough that he partially shares their view and begins to feel like a freak himself. The Gethenian sexual arrangement does not become the central issue of the story but develops into an effective vehicle for exploring the implications of sexual differentiation. It is a part, though not usually the commanding element, of every institution in Karhide.

The dominant influence upon Karhide and the other regions of Gethen is its climate. The physical environment becomes a third noticeable feature, after narrator and culture. Gethen is cold, even in the tropics; elsewhere there is nothing but ice fields and volcanoes. Life is marginal, and because of the cold,

UKL

If they are hermaphroditic –
Who raises the kids?
People who choose to do so, in government-supervised creches – about ⅓ of the people between 25 & 50 are engaged thus. In early times & in villages now, it is simply an essential job like any other, farming soldiering tailoring etc – In the modern cities it is well paid & pensioned, & rather over-volunteered-for. Primitively, rearing was communal.
Who nurses them?
The one who bears them – for about 6 ~~mos~~ – 2 yrs.
There is no marriage, & fidelity is not legalised in any way, tho' there are moral & religious semi-institutions & arrangements. Essentially however they do not pair, & love is, institutionally, par with Earth friendships.
During a period of about 3 days out of 26, a Gethenian is sexually receptive/active, but only (except in perversities) with another person in 'oestrus' (~~kemmer~~). During courtship & sexual play one (normally) begins to be dominated by m. or f. hormones, & his/her behavior rapidly triggers the opposite reaction in the partner; the respective organs engorge & dominate, & consummation is possible within ½ hour to 24 hours. It is not a notably efficient arrangement as so much depends on place + timing; but conception is equivalently frequent: the partner who played female conceives at least 85% of the time. There are contraceptive drugs. There are also cycle-inducing & postponing drugs, often used by repetitive partners. Hormone derivatives are taken by those who prefer one o the other sex-role.
The other 23 days of the month, the whole sexual complex, physical-emotional, is 'checked' by inhibitors: it is not absent, but suppressed by these secretions, genetically implanted by the colonisers of Hain in this one colony-stock – As an experiment? who knows? – The sexual energy typical of humans is not lessened, but

The Left Hand of Darkness, *working notes*

change is slow. Time-tested traditions survive into the machine age virtually intact. People dress in furs, travel cautiously, gather together in great communal dwellings, eat much and often, conserve every resource. They have innumerable words for ice, fog, and snow. Feuds are common, but full-scale warfare is unknown—though the novel suggests that this may be due to a lack of masculine aggressiveness. As the story progresses, its background of cold and ice intensifies until at the climax there is nothing in sight but two people and a sled on an immense field of ice. Le Guin says she conceived the book starting with that image. It is a mark of her virtuosity that the wealth of detail in the first half of the book gives way smoothly and naturally to the starkness of the second.

Two themes carry over from *Planet of Exile*. One is winter as a commanding force in men's lives and a symbol of all that is implacable in nature. The other is the companionship that can spring up between strangers in the face of such a mindless enemy as cold. Like the earlier book, *The Left Hand of Darkness*, it is in large part a love story. This, however, is a love born in mistrust, crossed not by the stars but by the protagonists' prior loyalties and preconceptions. The love between Genly Ai and Estraven, prime minister of Karhide, is subtler, more mature, and less easily fulfilled than that of Jakob Agat and Rolery. For Estraven, it grows out of a recognition, in the Ekumen, of the values he has spent his political career fostering: from this recognition evolves a personal attachment to the Ekumen's envoy. For Ai, Estraven represents everything he finds most disturbing about Karhide. Estraven is a master at the intricacies of prestige that dominate Karhidish society. He is powerful and proud, yet through the eyes of Ai, who insists on trying to view Gethenians as men, he is womanish. Only when these two are isolated on the great ice field are they able to reconcile Ai's blunt hastiness and the ambiguities that underlie Estraven's character. Even so, their love stops short of complete commitment. They avoid the sexual contact that is theoretically possible between them, although Ai comes to terms with Estraven's androgyny when the latter enters kemmer in the female phase, responding to Ai's permanent masculinity. Their true consummation is through mindspeech, which is previously unknown on Gethen. Even that pure form of communication is troubled between them, because Estraven "hears" Ai's telepathic speech in the voice of his long-dead brother and lover.

Le Guin's customary storytelling format, the journey of discovery, takes two forms corresponding to the two parts of the book. In the first half of the book, the Envoy travels around Karhide and into the other large region of the Gethenian Great Continent, Orgoreyn. His discoveries are primarily cultural ones, as Le Guin explores the ramifications of her major postulates, ambisexuality and an ice age. The first half of the book exposes a wealth of supportive detail that brings the world of Gethen to life. Slow, silent electric cars that crawl over mountain ranges; a plump, chatty "landlady" who shows strangers into the Envoy's room for a small fee; a glimpse of a sort of monastery perched on seemingly inaccessible cliffs; an ancient city whose streets are tunnels because of the ever-present snow; a religion that praises all things incomplete and uncertain; a ritual that seems to foretell the future accurately but also shows how useless it is to mankind to know the future; tragic tales; icy myths; and blood-colored palaces—all these contribute to our sense of Karhide and its way of life. Orgoreyn has a different set of cultural clues: great, smelly fish warehouses; enormous banquets of bland food and fierce liquor; luxuries unknown in Karhide, like hot showers; secret police and endless piles of paperwork; and prison camps out in the vast western forest of the country. Orgoreyn is clearly modeled on Stalinist Russia, which leads many critics to assume Karhide to be America, as if the two were the only possible counterpoints to one another. In this case, however, the choices are a centralized and seemingly efficient but highly oppressive bureaucracy and a disorganized and illogical but essentially humane tribalism. Karhide is the more attractive not because it reflects our own way of life but because it retains values that American and Soviet societies tend to push aside: harmony with nature, unlimited hospitality, continuity with the past, social grace, and inner tranquility. These are Oriental values, and the primary religion of Karhide, Handdara, blends aspects of Taoism and Zen. The rival religion of Orgoreyn, Yomesh, is more like Christianity or Islam, that is, an activist faith based on revelation.

The second half of the book recounts Genly Ai's rescue by Estraven from an Orgota prison camp and their flight over the glaciers back to Karhide. During this time Ai begins to absorb everything that he has observed on Gethen and to relate it to himself. Against the blank background of ice and snow, Gethen and the Ekumen meet and merge in the persons of Ai and Estraven. We are given to understand that this is what the Ekumen is, a meeting face to face or mind to mind of unlike individuals, like a marriage on a grand scale.

From this elevated conception of human

interaction, Le Guin jumps, in her next science-fiction stories, back down the scale of social evolution to the troublesome near future. *The Lathe of Heaven* takes place on Earth in the twenty-first century. It is independent of the Hainish cycle of history: many events are incompatible with what we know of Earth's future from the other books. In regard to general trends the two possible futures are quite similar, however. Both involve war, over-crowding, and near catastrophic unraveling of the ecosystem. In both cases Earth people require rescuing. In *The Dispossessed*, Hainish explorers rediscover their old colony on Earth and set it on the road to eventual recovery, so that by the time of *City of Illusions* the natural environment is largely unspoiled wilderness. In *The Lathe of Heaven*, the rescuing agent is one man, without spaceships or other machines, who changes the Earth without the knowledge of anyone except the other two main characters. He does so by dreaming.

Although Le Guin's major sources are outside the sphere of science fiction, she does acknowledge the influence of a few writers: Cordwainer Smith, Marion Zimmer Bradley, and Stanislaw Lem. But the clearest influence is that of Philip Dick on *The Lathe of Heaven*, which is a homage to Dick. The form of the novel is his; the characters, thematic material, and viewpoint are hers. It is an unexpected blend, and critics are divided on whether it is a wholly successful one. It is certainly a major work of science fiction, though not so perfectly ordered as *The Left Hand of Darkness*.

Dick's novels are all variations on one major premise: that reality is a subjective and shifting thing. The world is subject to change without notice. This is also the basis of *The Lathe of Heaven*. Le Guin, however, is a more restrained storyteller than Dick, and she limits the ability to alter reality to one character, George Orr, and then gives that power only to his unconscious, dreaming mind. For reasons unknown and unimaginable, certain of George's dreams change the fabric of existence; furthermore, they do so retroactively, so that unless one is aware of the dream as it occurs, one's memory is changed along with everything else. The dream, as George says, hides its traces.

This capacity to change things disturbs George. He is content with the world as it is, with adapting himself to reality rather than wrenching reality to fit his expectations. In an effort to suppress his dreams he resorts to sedatives, and that results in his being assigned to a government-affiliated psychologist, Dr. Haber. Dr. Haber is also a researcher, a specialist in dreams, and he is excited by the strange wave patterns generated by George's sleeping brain. He does not admit to himself that he believes George's story, but he begins using the dreams to bring about specific changes, giving George hypnotic suggestions about their content. He has George reduce population, alter weather patterns, and give him, Haber, the directorship of a large dream-study institute. George is alarmed; he is now upsetting things more than he had been on his own. Haber will neither acknowledge his power nor stop taking advantage of it. George enlists the aid of a lawyer, a skeptical young woman named Heather Lelache. She observes a dream session with Haber and feels the change as it occurs, though Haber half convinces her that nothing has happened. In the end it takes George, Heather, and some improbable turtlelike aliens dreamed up by George to overcome Haber and let the Earth return to its own course.

The Lathe of Heaven is rare among Le Guin stories in that it is not cast in the form of a journey. Instead it revolves around the interactions of three main characters, George, Heather, and Dr. Haber. It almost seems, for a while, like a tug of war between Heather and Haber, with George as the rope, but the reader realizes eventually that George, passive as he seems, is the strongest of the three. He is more like the fulcrum on which the other two rock back and forth. The power Dr. Haber seems to have is only what George lends him, and Heather, under a mask of cold efficiency, is frightened and insecure and needs George's quiet confidence.

Each character has a role to play, and each role is matched by the character's name. George Orr is the dreamer and the adjudicator. He lives among possibilities; he poises on the either-or's. He is the Tao personified: one who accepts and loves, who welcomes whatever occurs and is never overwhelmed. Both of the other characters see him as weak at first, but Heather later finds in him integrity. His power is somehow related to his inner peace: he is so sure of himself that the world accommodates itself to his dreams.

Haber is the manipulator. His name (English "haver," one who has; Latin "havere," to have) suggests possessiveness, the will to have or control. He is a caricature of the Judeo-Christian tradition of striving toward progress. He wishes to move forward without knowing where he stands. Whereas Orr is a solid block of wood, Haber is compared to an onion—all slippery layers, with no core. He has walled off his conscious mind from his unconscious; the rationality of the former serves only to disguise the blind desires of the latter. He is so out of touch with his motivations that he never realizes he is lying to George or to himself. In the end, when he has learned to duplicate George's gift, his hidden self breaks through and nearly plunges the world into a permanent nightmare.

Heather Lelache is the coward. (That is what *le lache* means in French.) Coward, however, is more her self-assessment than fact. The mask she has built up for herself, that of a hard-edged, ambitious, calculating spiderwoman (she also calls herself the Black Widow) does enable her to take action, to help George when he needs help. She has the courage to believe George, to stand beside him, and, when necessary, to let herself draw on his strength.

The book follows the shifting relationships among these three people, which are further complicated by the successive reality shifts caused by George's dreams. These changes are never exactly what Haber intends them to be: George's unconscious mind always throws in unexpected elements without disobeying instructions. Like wishes in many traditional fairy tales, George's dreams have their own logic and proportion that defy control by an outsider. They cannot be dictated to: there is always an unexpected penalty with every boon. Population is reduced, but at the expense of a devastating worldwide plague. War ends on Earth, but only because aliens attack from outer space. Racial strife stops, but at the loss of all variation among mankind. Everyone is gray. During this sequence Heather, who is black, disappears briefly, then reappears with much of her personality gone along with her color. George, the arbitrator, assigns the cost of every change, and as the designs get more grandiose the penalties grow more severe.

A summary of *The Lathe of Heaven* does not reveal the wry humor running through it. Much of what happens is rather grim: people are crowded and unhappy before Haber takes command and oppressed and unhappy afterward, but Orr's cheerfulness saves the book from too much darkness. Some of the humor consists of inside jokes about its setting, and some of it comes from the characters' self-appraisals. The aliens that appear either from the depths of space or from the equally obscure depths of George's unconscious are indubitably comical. They look like giant sea turtles and talk in mangled English peppered with quotations and platitudes. They are also connected with one of the most beautiful images developed in the book, one associating sleep with the ocean: the waking mind is compared in the opening passage to a jellyfish drifting onto a rocky shore. The aliens are creatures who live in a state closer to dream than to waking life; the universe of dream is their native habitat. And in that universe they are no longer comical and awkward. George dreams of them, near the end of the book: "His dreams, like waves of the deep sea far from any shore, came and went, rose and fell, profound and harmless, breaking nowhere, changing nothing. Through his sleep the great, green sea turtles dived, swimming with heavy inexhaustible grace through the depths, in their element."

When Le Guin returns to the Hainish universe in *The Dispossessed*, it is markedly different. The difference is reflected in the novel's setting, both time and place. The time is early, long before the events of even *Rocannon's World*. There is no "ansible," no mindspeech. Technology is not much advanced from what we know today, although the people of Hain have interstellar spaceships. The place is a pair of planets known as the Cetian worlds. We have not heard much about these twin worlds before, only that they produced an advanced mathematical system which will subsequently be adopted by all other worlds, even the home planet of Hain. The Cetian worlds share a single orbit and each circles the other. They are like the Earth and the moon, only more equal; each is the other's moon. One world is lush and watery and is the home planet for the Cetians. The other is dry and spare, and was colonized many years before the story begins by a group of anarchists who hoped to create utopia.

The story has no alien beings, only men of various persuasions. It has no disguised magic, such as telepathy or precognition. Everything is slow, sober, down-to-earth. The writing verges on pure naturalistic reporting, except that the places being written about do not exist on Earth. When Le Guin wrote *The Dispossessed*, she was in the middle of her fantasy trilogy of Earthsea; all of her impulse toward magic seems to have gone into the latter and none into this story. But it is fuller than any other of her stories in character and in social and political interplay.

At the beginning of the book Shevek, the hero, is getting ready to leave his home planet, the colony world Anarres. It is the exact middle of his story. The second chapter takes us back to Shevek's childhood on Anarres. From there the chapters alternate, one on Anarres, taking Shevek toward the point of his departure, and then one on Urras, following his exploration of a new world and his eventual return home. Although the subject matter of this story is less magical, more realistic, than earlier ones, the form of it is less straightforward. One deviation from the expected replaces another. We watch Shevek simultaneously move from Anarres to Urras and back again to Anarres. That is particularly appropriate because Shevek is a mathematician, and his subject is simultaneity.

Anarres is a harsh and ugly world. Most of it is barely habitable desert with no margin for elegance or much comfort. Everyone is occupied with survival. People work hard. For vacations from their regular work they work at something else. The code of behavior is very strict. Sexual standards are loose, but in other ways it is an almost puritanical place. The reforming fervor that launched the colony has settled down into moralistic conformity. Custom, as is often the case, proves more binding than law. But there is a certain joyfulness among the people of Anarres that grows out of a spirit of cooperation. Though no one has very much, no one is left out either. Men and women are treated equally: even their names are interchangeable, being randomly assigned at birth by a computer. All occupations carry equal dignity. There still remains from the old revolutionary impulse a sense of common cause. In addition, the fact that no one on Anarres owns anything begins to seem wonderfully liberating. There is a certain gypsy feeling that comes of having no "hostages to fortune." Le Guin captures the excitement of living in an ongoing experiment in freedom.

The experiment is based on the theories of a philosopher named Odo, whose life and ideas are modeled on such figures as Karl Marx and anarchists Emma Goldman and Peter Kropotkin. Odo proposed a society without laws or institutions, a society based on personal responsibility, on each member's recognition of his own needs and the needs of others. Odo's theories inspired a number of people on Urras to reject every governmental and economic system offered to them. Soon after her death, a large group of her followers took up an offer by the State to be transported to the moon, that is, to Anarres. This move was designed to get those troublesome followers off the hands of the various Urrasti governments.

The Dispossessed is subtitled "An Ambiguous Utopia" because Anarres is both utopia and dystopia. However, Urras is also a mixture of the flawed and the ideal. The two worlds therefore each hold only half of the truth. Urras is a place of great beauty, vivid colors, and luxuriant life. There is inequality, but the poorest people are not much worse off than the people of Anarres. It is a world of variety. There are three main countries, corresponding approximately to our own capitalistic, communistic, and Third World nations. The reader discovers most about the capitalistic state. It has much elegance and beauty, but sharp social and sexual divisions. Shevek finds intolerable the fact that everything and everyone there is essentially owned by someone else. He is treated as a commodity, with all the respect given to a valuable object and none of the sensitivity owed to fellowmen. The pampered, artificial women of Urras both fascinate and repel him. He sees little difference between the capitalistic and socialistic states. To an Odonian, as long as there is property it does not matter whether individuals or the state own it, and as long as there is a state, it does not matter how firm or lenient it is. Odonians consider socialism to be a betrayal of their own movement, a halfway gesture.

But, as Shevek discovers, there are freedoms on Urras which cannot be found on Anarres, values which Anarres has sacrificed along with property and government. Urras is rich not only in material things. It has a history which Anarres has cut itself off from. It allows a free play of ideas that is limited by the utilitarianism of a collective society. It is in communication with the rest of the universe, whereas Anarres has closed itself off for fear of contamination. On Urras, Shevek discovers the work of the Terran mathematician Ainsetain (Einstein). It provides him with the clues he needs to finish his theory of Simultaneity. With his completed theory and the technology of Urras, the ansible can be built. Instantaneous communication between worlds will allow for a League of All Worlds, just as mindspeech later offers the possibility of a greater union, the Ekumen.

On Anarres, in the alternate chapters, Shevek acts as the conscience of the Odonian revolution. He and his friends start an organization which they call the Syndicate of Initiative. Its main purposes are to publish the work of Shevek and other original thinkers who have not been able to convince the majority of its value, and to open communication with Urras after generations of isolation. On Urras Shevek is the messenger of freedom. In spite of the efforts of his official hosts to isolate him from the lower classes, who still hold some Odonian sentiments, he meets some rebels and partakes in a spontaneous rally against the government, or, more precisely, against Government. He is shot at, goes into hiding, and takes refuge at the Terran embassy. Neither world is comfortable with his presence, which indicates that both have need of him. When he makes his breakthrough and discovers the equations for Simultaneity, he also comes to a decision. He refuses to let Urras buy his ideas, and he refuses to let Anarres suppress them. The alternative is to give his equations away to all groups, all worlds, so that none can either keep them hidden or profit from them. He dispossesses himself. Then, with nothing to burden him, he goes home.

The political, economic, and mathematical aspects of *The Dispossessed* have occupied the attention of most readers of the book. But its thematic core is about a man throwing a rock over a wall. In the opening scene both rock and wall are physically present, but we do not know yet what they signify. More often they are there only as terms in analogies: Shevek is a rock, Anarres is a rock hanging in space, Shevek finds himself locked in or out of a room, his syndic breaches the wall of distance to open radio contact with Urras, and his theory of Simultaneity formulates in his mind as a picture of a rock perpetually approaching but never reaching its goal. The act of throwing a rock is a sign in the book for a refusal to accept boundaries. Even on Anarres walls are constantly springing up, and even an Odonian finds it difficult to pick up the rock and throw it. Shevek, who is to some degree based on Le Guin's childhood memories of the physicist J. Robert Oppenheimer, is the sort of individual every society tolerates most grudgingly and needs most desperately; he is a free and creative man. He cannot help picking up the rock: scientific curiosity will leave nothing unexamined. But to throw it is to call attention to oneself, to be labeled uncooperative, dangerous, a traitor. Le Guin says that even in utopia there are rocks to be thrown, social or mental boundaries to be crossed. That is a further refinement of her concept of heroism, and Shevek is the most fully realized and developed of her heroes.

Since *The Dispossessed*, Le Guin has produced no book-length works of science fiction. Her volumes on Earthsea and Orsinia must be discussed in other terms and categories than those of speculation and extrapolation. They should, however, be read by anyone with a serious interest in Le Guin's work. Thematically they are more central than many of the future- and space-oriented stories. James Bittner, in an article called "Persuading Us to Rejoice and Teaching Us How to Praise," draws connections between the *Orsinian Tales* and the rest of her work and also sheds a great deal of light on their origins. The tale called "Imaginary Worlds" in particular reveals something of the purpose behind Le Guin's ventures into the unreal.

Le Guin has continued to write shorter works of science fiction. *The Wind's Twelve Quarters* contains a few post-*Dispossessed* pieces, including a lovely, elegiac portrait of Odo called "The Day Before the Revolution" (1974). Many of her uncollected stories from this period are quirky experiments in point of view such as "The Author of

Ursula K. Le Guin

the Acacia Seeds and Other Extracts from the *Journal of the Association of Therolinguistics*" (1973). Along with these recent stories she has produced one novella, *The New Atlantis*. Le Guin is fond of forms that fall between the short story and the novel. One of her most widely reprinted short pieces, a story called "Nine Lives" (1969), was nominated for a Nebula Award in the novelette category. Another piece, included along with "Nine Lives" in *The Wind's Twelve Quarters*, is slightly longer: Le Guin jokes in her introduction about its deserving all too well the title "Vaster Than Empires and More Slow." "The Word for World Is Forest," which first appeared in Harlan Ellison's anthology *Again, Dangerous Visions* in 1972, came out in a volume by itself four years later. In these middle-length fictions Le Guin tends to come out more strongly on issues that concern her than in short stories, which do not allow for sufficient development, or in novels, which require a fuller and therefore more equivocal treatment of theme.

Aside from "Nine Lives," a fairly straightforward story on cloning, these novelettes and novellas are a disturbing group. "Vaster Than Empires and More Slow" is troubling because of its characters, who are all psychological misfits. The story concerns an expedition, very early in League history, to the far reaches of the galaxy. The trip is to be long and quite possibly fruitless. If the members return at all they will be faced with a time gap of hundreds of years due to the speed of their ship. Only maladjusted people volunteer for such an expedition: people seeking escape from the complexities of normal society.

The cast of the story is not only an odd one, it is singularly unattractive, or at least seems so at first. One expedition member who particularly irritates his fellow travelers and the reader is Osden. He is defensive, egotistical, and sarcastic. He is also sensitive not only to human emotions but to those of any sentient being. He feels the hostility of those around him and feeds it with his offensive behavior, bringing out the worst in everyone else. Even the most sympathetic character, the commander Haito Tomiko, is angry and destructive around Osden. The least engaging character, Porlock, is a quivering slob, a blend, as the name suggests, of Philip Roth's Portnoy and H. G. Wells's Morlock. The atmosphere aboard ship is one of profound unease, and the tension increases when they land on the first planet on their path.

The world they encounter is an all-vegetable one: trees, grasses, shrubs in profusion, but nothing mobile, no foragers or grazers or predators. The explorers see furtive shapes in the shadows, though there should be none; their fear intensifies when Osden is mysteriously attacked (by Porlock, it turns out). Osden finally realizes that the planet's biosphere is one sentient organism, connected by nervelike roots just below the surface. The fear they feel is the forest's fear of them, the invaders. He breaks through the fear and enters into communication with the great green being. While the others depart, he remains behind, having found a companion who does not fear or pity him.

Most of the story is disconcerting and the descriptions harsh. The early League years seem to be, for Le Guin, a time of trouble and misunderstanding. But the forest world encountered by the explorers, much as they fear it, is a thing of great beauty. It grows in the reader's mind until it finally overpowers the rest of the story. At the end there is a vision of timeless peace, as Osden shares the forest's perception of light, growth, and wholeness.

"The Word for World Is Forest" carries over the same picture of a world of unbroken greenery, the Garden of Eden before the Fall. This time inhabitants share the forest's peace: small greenish men of Hainish stock, hunters and food gatherers living in harmony with the forest. These people are dreamers, able to induce a dream state while they are awake and to control it. They live among visions, and the visions keep them sane and whole. The story could have been a charming study of these people who lived amid shadows—forest shadows and dream shadows. But into this setting comes an echo of the author's times: war in Vietnam, exploitation of resources, dominance of one racial or cultural group by another more powerful. The clash between peaceful natives and brutal Terran colonists results in a story that seems, in contrast with Le Guin's usual elegance, raw, fierce, and ungoverned. There is much less distance than usual between author and subject and much less hope of an eventual ordering of the elements. If it were not for the energy of presentation and the strength of the original world picture, the story could degenerate into an antiwar, proecology tract. As it is, the very harshness of it attracts many readers who prefer their fiction less thoroughly digested.

There are three main characters. Le Guin alternates between binary systems, like yin/yang and self/other, and triads, which offer more lines of conflict. The apexes of this story are Lyubov, a Terran scientist; Davidson, a military leader; and Selver, a native. Lyubov is a typical Le Guin hero, with a twist. He respects the natives, is intrigued by their culture, and tries to protect them against the abuses of the colonists, but he is weak. Lacking authority, he has, in fact, no strong cards to play in his conflict with the Terran military-industrial machine. Davidson, on the other hand, is strong, but, in Le Guin's view, quite mad. He represents Le Guin's attempt to get inside the masculine-dominant mind. He views this world the way he views women, as a conquest. Natives are work animals, their women a temporary substitute for women of his own species. He and most of the other men in the colony call them Creechies, evidently a corruption of "creatures." Selver is a leader among the natives, Athsheans, as they call themselves. Bullied and humiliated by the Terrans, neither he nor any other Athshean has put up resistance until his wife is raped by Davidson and dies. Then the deep pacifism of his culture gives way to the realization that Terrans will not treat Athsheans as fellow men and therefore cannot be treated as such. Selver becomes possessed of a new vision, the possibility of violence. He becomes, in Athshean terms, a god: one who translates a heretofore unknown dream or vision into action. In leading an Athshean uprising, Selver loses the balance of dream and waking that keeps his people sane. He is nearly overcome by the vision of murder that fills him, but escapes it in the end, aided by the dream self of his murdered friend Lyubov.

Davidson finds no such escape. His private war with the Creechies escalates even after his people have surrendered to them. He had made the wrong decision long before to treat all Others as if they did not matter. Everything unlike himself—and that ultimately comes to include everything—is a thing to be utilized for his benefit. This decision leads him on a course with no retreat. He can only respond to gentleness with scorn and to resistance with savagery. He must "teach them a lesson" and "save his honor." There is no compromise. Selver is wiser. He twice decides not to kill Davidson when he has the opportunity. Davidson is ultimately exiled to an island which he and his exploiters have made into a desert. The Terrans abandon their colony. Unlike most Le Guin stories, this one ends with no meeting of strangers, only a bitter lesson learned on both sides and the hope of a reconciliation between the two peoples in some distant future.

The New Atlantis, a dark, sardonic picture of life in a future America, is an illustration of the fact that oppression can come from any quarter, from free enterprise and the American Way as surely as from any "ism." The heroine of *The New Atlantis* is a violist in Portland not too far—maybe twenty years, maybe a hundred—in the future. Her husband, a physicist, has just been released from a Rehabilitation Camp, really a concentration camp for radicals, intellectuals, and other groups deemed dangerous to the state. Interestingly enough, this combination, woman musician and man scientist, is exactly the same in Le Guin's young-adult novel, *Very Far Away From Anywhere Else*, published the following year. *The New Atlantis* shows the love between the musician, Belle, and the scientist, Simon, in a society where marriage is illegal and even fidelity is suspect. They survive illness, shortages of food and resources, and FBI surveillance, but when Simon and his friends discover a method of tapping solar energy directly, without expensive equipment, the government moves in and takes him away again.

Running throughout the story are a series of counterpoint passages, perhaps Belle's dreams, about a drowned continent and the beings who have begun to awaken as it starts to rise again. The reader is given no explanation of these passages, only the sensations of pressure and darkness giving way gradually to light and life. Other clues suggest that Belle may be in tune with the unknown Atlanteans. For instance, a man on a bus with her starts talking about rising and sinking continents, and although he tells her that it is all in the pamphlet he is reading, the pamphlet proves to be completely unrelated.

Later, when she improvises on her viola, listeners in the next room have a vision of white towers rising from the sea. The underwater speakers tell of music that they hear as they rise: "the voices of the great souls, the great lives, the lonely ones, the voyagers." The great composers in this story may be Belle's Schubert and Paul Hindemith, or they may be some unnamed aliens calling out to people above and beneath the water.

Nothing is explained: who or what is in the New Atlantis, why the sea beds are rising and the continents sinking, what those have to do with Belle and Simon. Although one of Simon's colleagues suggests using their sun tap to help raise the underwater towers, there seems to be no need for any human help. The lack of clear connections is frustrating. It is not that the story seems meaningless: one gets a sense of purpose beyond human comprehension. The Atlanteans are waiting for some consummation, but it never comes. The story ends with their questions, "Where are you? We are here. Where have you gone?" People on the surface have failed to keep the appointment. Because Simon's discovery is suppressed or lost, civilization ends before the white towers break into the air. As in "The Word for World Is Forest," there is no meeting. It is a sad and puzzling story, a story of squandered opportunity.

More Le Guin productions are appearing. A television film of *The Lathe of Heaven*, made by the Public Broadcasting System, was shown in 1980 and she was actively involved with the screenplay. Susan Wood has edited a collection of her essays on fantasy and science fiction called *The Language of the Night* (1979). It also includes a comprehensive checklist of her work by Jeffrey Levin. *Malafrena* (1979), a novel set in Orsinia, has appeared, along with *The Beginning Place* (1980), a fantasy dealing with the borderline between the ordinary world and the world of magic. To readers and critics of fantastic and speculative fiction, there is no doubt of Le Guin's place at the very top of her field.

Le Guin has brought to science fiction a new sensitivity to language, a powerful set of symbols and images, and a number of striking and sympathetic characters. She has purposely avoided most technical details in order to concentrate on human problems and relationships. Writers of fantasy, and in this sense science fiction may be considered a branch of fantasy, tend to view literature as a way not merely of seeing reality but of coming to terms with it. By altering elements and changing rules, a fantasist tries to explore the patterns that lie beneath the surface of observable fact. Consequently Le Guin's fiction is extraordinarily risky: it is full of hypotheses about morality, love, society, and ways of enriching life expressed in the symbolic language found in myth, dream, or poetry. However, the greater the risk, the greater the reward, and for the reader of a story like *The Left Hand of Darkness*, the reward is a glimpse of something glowing, something very much like truth.

Other:

"The Author of the Acacia Seeds and Other Extracts from the *Journal of the Association of Therolinguistics*," in *Fellowship of the Stars*, ed. Terry Carr (New York: Simon & Schuster, 1974);

The New Atlantis, in *The New Atlantis*, ed. Robert Silverberg (New York: Hawthorn Books, 1975);

Nebula Award Stories 11, edited by Le Guin (London: Gollancz, 1976; New York: Harper & Row, 1977);

"The Diary of the Rose," in *Future Power*, ed. Jack Dann and Gardner Dozois (New York: Dutton, 1977);

Interfaces, edited by Le Guin and Virginia Kidd (New York: Ace, 1980);

Edges, edited by Le Guin and Kidd (New York: Pocket Books, 1980).

Periodical Publications:

"On Norman Spinrad's *The Iron Dream*," *Science-Fiction Studies*, 1 (Spring 1973): 41-44;

"Surveying the Battlefield," *Science-Fiction Studies*, 1 (Fall 1973): 88-90;

"European SF: Rottensteiner's Anthology, the Strugatskys, and Lem," *Science-Fiction Studies*, 1 (Spring 1974): 181-185;

"Ketterer on *The Left Hand of Darkness*," *Science-Fiction Studies*, 2 (July 1975): 137-139;

"A Response to the Le Guin Issue," *Science-Fiction Studies*, 3 (Spring 1976): 43-46;

"The Space Crone," *The CoEvolution Quarterly*, 10 (Summer 1976): 108-111.

Interviews:

Charles Bigelow and J. McMahon, "Science Fiction and the Future of Anarchy," *Oregon Times*, 4 (December 1974): 24-29;

Gene Van Troyer, "Vertex Interviews Ursula K. Le Guin," *Vertex*, 2 (December 1974): 34-39, 92, 96-97;

Barry Barth, "Tricks, Anthropology Create New Worlds," *Portland Scribe*, 4 (17-25 May 1975): 8-9;

"Ursula K. Le Guin Interviewed by Jonathan Ward," *Algol*, 12 (Summer 1975): 6-10;

Dorothy Gilbert, "Interview: Ursula K. Le Guin," *California Quarterly*, 13-14 (Spring-Summer 1978): 38-55;

Paul Walker, "Ursula K. Le Guin," *Speaking of Science Fiction: The Paul Walker Interviews* (Oradell, N. J.: Luna, 1978), pp. 24-36.

References:

Douglas Barbour, "Wholeness and Balance in the Hainish Novels of Ursula K. Le Guin," *Science-Fiction Studies*, 1 (Spring 1974): 164-173;

James W. Bittner, "Persuading Us to Rejoice and Teaching Us How to Praise: Le Guin's *Orsinian Tales*," *Science-Fiction Studies*, 5 (November 1978): 215-242;

Joe DeBolt, ed., *Ursula K. Le Guin: Voyager to Inner Lands and to Outer Space* (Port Washington, N.Y. & London: Kennikat Press, 1979);

David Ketterer, *New Worlds for Old: The Apocalyptic Imagination, Science Fiction and American Literature* (Bloomington: Indiana University Press, 1974);

Karl Kroeber, "Sisters and Science Fiction," *The Little Magazine*, 10 (Spring-Summer 1976): 87-90;

Theodora Kroeber, *Alfred Kroeber: A Personal Configuration* (Berkeley, Los Angeles & London: University of California Press, 1970);

Robert Scholes, *Structural Fabulation: An Essay on the Future of Fiction* (Notre Dame: University of Notre Dame Press, 1975);

Science-Fiction Studies, special Le Guin issue, 2 (November 1975);

George Edgar Slusser, *The Farthest Shores of Ursula K. Le Guin* (San Bernardino, Cal.: Borgo Press, 1976);

Ian Watson, "Le Guin's *Lathe of Heaven* and the Role of Dick: The False Reality as Mediator," *Science-Fiction Studies*, 2 (March 1975): 67-75;

Michael Wood, "Coffee Break for Sisyphus," *New York Review of Books*, 2 October 1975, pp. 3-7;

Susan Wood, "Discovering Worlds: The Fiction of Ursula K. Le Guin," in *Voices for the Future*, vol. 2, ed. Thomas D. Clareson (Bowling Green, Ohio: Bowling Green University Popular Press, 1979), pp. 154-179.

Fritz Leiber

Norman L. Hills
Des Moines, Iowa

BIRTH: Chicago, Illinois, 24 December 1910, to Fritz and Virginia Bronson Leiber.

EDUCATION: Ph.B., University of Chicago, 1932.

MARRIAGE: 16 January 1936 to Jonquil Stephens, died 1969; children: Justin.

AWARDS: Eighth Annual Mrs. Ann Radcliffe Award for *Conjure Wife*, 1953; Hugo Award for *The Big Time*, 1958; Hugo Award for *The Wanderer*, 1965; Nebula Award for "Gonna Roll the Bones," 1967; Hugo Award for "Gonna Roll the Bones," 1968; Hugo Award for "Ship of Shadows," 1970; Nebula Award for "Ill Met in Lankhmar," 1970; Hugo Award for "Ill Met in Lankhmar," 1971; Gandalf Award for Achievement in Fantasy, 1975; Nebula Award for "Catch That Zeppelin!," 1975; Hugo Award for "Catch That Zeppelin!," 1976; August Derleth Fantasy Award for "Belsen Express," 1976; World Fantasy Award for "Belsen Express," 1976; World Fantasy Life Award, 1976; World Fantasy Award for *Our Lady of Darkness*, 1978.

BOOKS: *Night's Black Agents* (Sauk City, Wis.: Arkham, 1947; St. Helier, Jersey, U.K.: Spearman, 1975); abridged as *Tales from Night's Black Agents* (New York: Ballantine, 1961);
Gather, Darkness! (New York: Pellegrini & Cudahy, 1950; London: Four Square Books, 1966);
Conjure Wife (New York: Twayne, 1953); republished as *Burn Witch Burn* (New York: Berkley, 1962);
The Green Millennium (New York: Abelard, 1953; London: Abelard-Schuman, 1959);
The Sinful Ones (New York: Universal, 1953); republished as *You're All Alone* (New York: Ace, 1972);
Two Sought Adventure (New York: Gnome Press, 1957);
Destiny Times Three (New York: Galaxy, 1957);
The Mind Spider (New York: Ace, 1961);
The Big Time (New York: Ace, 1961; London: Four Square Books, 1965);
The Silver Eggheads (New York: Ballantine, 1962; London: Four Square Books, 1966);
Shadows With Eyes (New York: Ballantine, 1962);

Ships to the Stars (New York: Ace, 1964);
A Pail of Air (New York: Ballantine, 1964);
The Wanderer (New York: Ballantine, 1964; London: Dobson, 1967);
The Night of the Wolf (New York: Ballantine, 1966; London: Sphere, 1976);
Tarzan and the Valley of Gold (New York: Ballantine, 1966);
The Swords of Lankhmar (New York: Ace, 1968; London: Rupert Hart-Davis, 1969);
Swords Against Wizardry (New York: Ace, 1968; London: G. Prior, 1977);
Swords in the Mist (New York: Ace, 1968; St. Albans, U.K.: Mayflower, 1979);
The Secret Songs (London: Rupert Hart-Davis, 1968);
The Demons of the Upper Air (Glendale, Cal.: R. Squires, 1969);
Night Monsters (New York: Ace, 1969; London: Gollancz, 1974);
A Specter is Haunting Texas (New York: Walker, 1969; London: Gollancz, 1969);
Swords and Deviltry (New York: Ace, 1970; London: New English Library, 1971);
Swords Against Death (New York: Ace, 1970; London: New English Library, 1972);
The Best of Fritz Leiber (Garden City: Doubleday, 1974; London: Sphere, 1974);
The Book of Fritz Leiber (New York: DAW, 1974);
The Second Book of Fritz Leiber (New York: DAW, 1975);
The Worlds of Fritz Leiber (New York: Ace, 1976);
Swords and Ice Magic (New York: Ace, 1977; St. Albans, U.K.: Mayflower, 1979);
Rime Isle (Chapel Hill, N.C.: Whispers Press, 1977);
Our Lady of the Darkness (New York: Berkley, 1977; London: Millington, 1978);
Heroes and Horrors (Brown Mills, N.J.: Whispers Press, 1978);
Bazaar of the Bizarre (West Kingston, R.I.: Grant, 1978);
The Ship of Shadows (London: Gollancz, 1979).

Fritz Leiber is one of the durable masters of science fiction. For forty years he has been delighting his readers with a wide range of stories—from hard science fiction to widely acclaimed fantasy. Fritz Leiber, Jr., was born in Chicago and lived there with relatives during the winter in his early years, while his parents, Fritz Leiber, Sr., and Virginia Bronson Leiber, toured the country with a repertory company. Much of the remaining time was spent with his parents in New Jersey and with a grandmother in Michigan. After receiving his bachelor's degree in psychology from the University of Chicago in 1932, he worked briefly as a lay reader for two Episcopalian "missionary" churches while attending the General Theological Seminary in New York. Not finding this to his liking, he returned to the University of Chicago in 1933 to study philosophy, but left without a further degree to join his father's road company. Following a year on tour, he tried acting in bit parts in Hollywood and a brief stint of free-lance writing, eventually settling temporarily in Chicago as a staff writer for the *Standard American Encyclopedia*. In the meantime, he had married Jonquil Stephens, whom he had met while they were both students at the University of Chicago. Leiber made his first professional sale to *Unknown* in 1939 with "Two Sought Adventure " (collected in *Two Sought Adventure*, 1957), a story in the Fafhrd and the Gray Mouser series.

In 1941 Leiber, with his wife and son, lived in Los Angeles, where he taught drama and speech at Occidental College for a year. This experience provided much of the background of the academic life for *Conjure Wife* (1953). He tried full-time writing, but shortly after his first novels had appeared he took a war job as an inspector at Douglas Aircraft. Eventually, he reconciled this choice with his belief in pacifism, but a strain of pacifism still runs through his writing. In 1945 Leiber became a member of the editorial staff of *Science Digest* in Chicago. He continued to write fiction, as well as editorials and articles, and left *Science Digest* in 1956 after finding that his work there interfered with his writing. He had a new creative burst in the late 1950s and returned to California, where he currently lives. He has had unproductive periods since then, but he has continued to make his living as a professional writer ever since.

For Fritz Leiber, the central value of literature lies in human understanding, and this emphasis on humanity is reflected in the psychological presentation of character in his work. He seems to view literature as a process of vicarious experience through which he can work out his thoughts, worries, and emotions. The primary method for this process is satire, in that there is humor based on fantasy or the grotesque,

Fritz Leiber

combined with social and psychological objects of attack. The result is science fiction that entertains at the same time that it allows Leiber to comment on the human condition.

In the foreground of his work is an interest in the potential of the human mind—to imagine better or different worlds, or to alter its perception of reality. These adaptations of the mind apply not just to the physical world, but are also required for the suspension of disbelief that is essential to literature. Science fiction requires even more mental flexibility and the theater also demands an additional acceptance of dramatic conventions. Beyond the obvious similarities between melodrama and space opera, the effects of the drama are relatively unexploited in science fiction. Leiber is one of the few who has not only used the devices of drama directly as narrative techniques, but has been able to interpret much of human life directly as drama.

The potential of the human mind is also explored in stories which deal with the origins and effects of horror. In some writers, horror can represent an abnegation of personality, but in Leiber this self-denial seems more closely related to the willful and temporary suspension of personality by the actor. In addition, although Leiber has acknowledged the influence of Lovecraft, he seems to have escaped Lovecraft's distrust of science. The horror of Leiber is more closely related to Edmund Burke's sublimely delightful horror.

Some of Leiber's earliest short stories dealt with the idea of the supernatural as it might appear in modern guise. His first published novel, *Gather, Darkness!* (1950), continued in this vein by presenting a picture of a society where a rigidly structured religious hierarchy represses the population by using science and technology to provide seemingly supernatural proofs of its omnipotence. The underground resistance to this priesthood exploits the trappings and symbolism of witchcraft and black magic by also using the disguised products of technology. The story follows a renegade priest, Brother Jarles, as he tries to reconcile his moral views with his duty while he helps the revolution to erupt and finally succeed.

Leiber seems to relish the irony of interpreting various supernatural phenomena as misunderstood applications of science, and his irrepressible humor appears from the start with the introduction of electronically controlled haunted houses, flying "angels," and telepathic vampires. In general, the explanations for the more spectacular "miracles" and examples of "divine" power are extrapolations of quasi-feasible science, but they are also selected for their effect as theater. The crowd reactions to these apparitions are orchestrated much like the audience response to highly competent actors in a well-rehearsed drama. Leiber's denouement, however, follows directly from character and action: he shrewdly resists the temptation to resolve the plot—in its own theatrical terms—with a deus ex machina.

In addition to the theatrical features, Leiber embellishes the novel with parody, satire, and wordplay; moreover, his character names—derived from historic and mythic personages such as Michael Servetus, Asmodaeus, and Saint Boniface—hint at extra dimensions of meaning in the realm of historic or religious allegory. But from the standpoint of serious social commentary, the major themes of the book concern the respective roles of religion and science. Beneath the witty and literate surface is a warning about the problems and dangers of suppressing scientific knowledge, regardless of the appearance of benevolence. Another aspect of the same concern is the control of such knowledge by a small group, whether it uses it or merely prevents others from doing so. There is also a cogent argument for the separation of science from religious dogma and an argument—probably prompted by the nuclear research during and after World War II—against the intervention of government in basic research.

While there are similarities to other science fiction of the period, and possibly even some borrowing (the chase scene involving Jarles calls to mind the pursuit of Jommy Cross in van Vogt's *Slan*, 1946), the novel does not seem dated. The treatment of the supernatural as a form of theater wears better than the treatment of the supernatural in, say, Jack Williamson's roughly contemporary werewolf-novel, *Darker Than You Think* (1948). The theme of the supernatural as misunderstood reality, at any rate, was to figure in many of Leiber's subsequent novels—though he ends *Gather, Darkness!* with the suggestion that it may not be wise to remove all of the mystery from life.

One such attempt to banish mystery is the subject of Leiber's next book, *Conjure Wife* (1953), which became the basis for the 1963 movie *Burn, Witch, Burn!* Norman Saylor, a professor of sociology at a small college, discovers that his wife has been practicing magic to protect them from the overly rigid traditions of the school and the status seeking of the other professors, administrators, and their wives. He forces her to stop her magical activities, only to be forced to use magic himself to recover his wife's soul. The rational basis for Saylor's skepticism starts with his professional interest in superstition, neuroses, and feminine psychology. He starts from a completely rational rejection of magic and witchcraft but gradually alters this point of view as his well-ordered life starts to crumble with increasing signs of supernatural events. Leiber's extensive knowledge of the literature of magic is evident without being obtrusive, and in the first half of the novel, he skillfully creates a very believable atmosphere in which the reader can accept at least the possibility of magic as an interpretation of reality.

Saylor continues his rational approach to the problem by attempting to discover the logical basis and operating laws of magic, just as though it were another set of hypotheses in physical science, and equally subject to experimental verification and the laws of deduction. Saylor's quest is the major science-fiction element as Leiber extends his presentation of the unknown potential and resources of the human mind. This interest in the human mind raises the book above the level of a pure horror story. The psychological and logical progressions are handled very well. The book's proposition that all women are witches probably helped to sell the book as a horror novel, but obviously cannot be taken seriously. If magic is interpreted symbolically as representing the emotions, with Norman Saylor's skepticism and rational approach representing the rational mind (without relating these to sex), then the book's thesis may be thought of as the need for a balance between the rational mind and the emotions. But however serious the book's theme, the deft plotting and the control of tension combine to make *Conjure Wife* highly entertaining.

Leiber's next novel, *The Green Millennium* (1953), uses some of the same background as his famous short story, "Coming Attraction" (1950). The novel follows Phil Gish on a quest through a decadent United States where organized crime is in league with a corrupt government to control the people through sex and diversions. Two alien species from Vega, one looking like green cats and the other very much like satyrs, covertly invade the country and put an end to war and violence. The complex plot follows Gish as he searches for one of the green cats which has befriended him.

Leiber's fascination with cats has led him to write a number of stories about them over the years. Their air of disinterested intelligence and mystery makes them fascinating, not to mention their long association with the supernatural, which dates at least from the time of the worship of Bast. The novel's main value is as fast-moving entertainment, but it is also a satire formed by extrapolating from various social trends that Leiber thinks of as threatening society. Much of his best writing is satire, and although this is not the most ambitious of Leiber's novels, the following excerpt gives some idea of his concerns beneath the humor: "Not that this current social madness is a deep secret or anything to be startled at. What other results could have been expected when American society began to overvalue on the one hand security, censorship, an imagined world-saving idealism and self-sacrifice in war, and on the other hand insatiable hunger for possessions, fiercely competitive aggressiveness, sadistic male belligerence, contempt for parents and the state, and a fantastically overstimulated sexuality?" Rarely is Leiber this open about his motives in a story. This is an isolated quotation and does not convey the overall tone of the book. The detailed social background, well-constructed minor characterizations, witty language, and humorous situations make this novel great fun to read.

Leiber's next novel, *Destiny Times Three*, was published in 1957; the magazine story had appeared in 1945. The novel is not as polished as most of Leiber's later work. An immense alien machine has accidentally fragmented the time stream of Earth and allowed a small group of men to play with the lives of the people inhabiting the resulting three worlds.

These worlds have similar people living under very different conditions. One of these manipulated people, Thorn, discovers the situation and has a chance to rectify some of the problems while waiting for the creators of the machine to intervene—if they can.

The presentation of the three different societies is well-handled, primarily by alternating chapters in which Thorn is followed from one time stream to another. The alternate worlds also provide an opportunity for Leiber to exercise his penchant for descriptions of settings that border on the baroque. The existence of the alternate worlds is used as an explanation of nightmares as contacts with the duplicate personalities and as the source of many superstitions. Again, this tendency to attempt rationalizing the supernatural is common to much of Leiber's work. Elements of the macabre and the supernatural are scattered throughout the book, as are unusually apt epigraphs from Norse mythology, Shakespeare, John Webster, and H. P. Lovecraft. What on the surface could have been treated as a hard-science story has been handled more as allegory and myth; the result has an ethereal atmosphere that makes the influence of Lovecraft more apparent than in most of Leiber's novels.

Leiber won his first Hugo Award for *The Big Time* (1961), the major work in a series of stories about the Change War. This gigantic war is fought by two largely undefined groups called Snakes and Spiders that recruit warriors from various species and from all times, past and future, usually by offering an escape from imminent death. The war is fought by these time-traveling warriors as they attempt to change the past so that the resulting different future will produce victory. All of the action in *The Big Time* takes place in a medical and entertainment recuperation facility used by Spider soldiers between missions. The story is narrated by Greta Forzane, a party-girl in the Place, which is located outside of space and time. Concepts of Einsteinian space-time and topology provide a scientific basis for the setting and plot.

Most reviewers noted that the staging, action, and dialogue of *The Big Time* are reminiscent of a play. Almost all of the action occurs in one room and the movements of the characters around this room are presented much like well thought-out stage directions. There is also a resemblance—possibly not accidental—to Samuel Beckett's comparison of a man in a room to a mind looking out of a brain-case. The reader is often able to picture the scene as Greta sees it, from the middle of the room, for example, or from the floor where she lies. Forceful and economical dialogue supplies much of the background and plot movement. The novel probably could be converted to a stage play or screenplay by converting portions of Greta's first-person interior narration to monologues. The tensions created by the plot follow the traditional progression of building to a climax, followed by an ironic denouement. The mixture of characters from different times and places is used not only to stress the universal nature of the Change War, but to provide character differentiation, primarily through a series of excellent parodies of diction, vocabulary, and style. Leiber's parodies of Elizabethan and Greek dramatic styles are two of the best examples. Leiber is one of the masters of style in science fiction and few can match his wit. The parodies, interjected poems, alliteration, and skillful use of first-person narrative reinforce this conclusion. Quotations from *Macbeth*, John Webster, Gertrude Stein, and others contribute to the literary fun.

The supernatural again plays a role as a possible manifestation of the Change War through nightmares and dreams of demons. Leiber's interest in the possibilities of the human mind appears in the suggestion that demons are a fourth order of evolution in their ability to bind possibility—that is, to "make all of what might be part of what is. . . ." The choice of Spiders and Snakes as the names of the opposing factions not only leads to ingenious analogies about the serpentine tactics of one and the webs of intrigue of the other, but also reflects two of the ancient fears of man. Leiber has been devoted to pacifism much of his life, and an underlying theme of *The Big Time* is a commentary on the psychological effects of war. The insights gained by the ability of the characters to see the results of war in many contexts lead them to disillusionment about the possibility of "victory." Their only hope is that these insights will contribute to the further evolution of life in the universe, so that the Change War will become unnecessary.

While *The Big Time* is one of the high points of Leiber's career, and of science fiction as well, his next book, *The Silver Eggheads* (1962), is not a complete success. Leiber has used satire or at least humor in much of his writing, but *The Silver Eggheads* is more in the line of farce or slapstick. While there are witty bits, Leiber does not seem at home with this variety of humor. The plot is a weak pretext for his comments about writers, editors, and readers. In the book, all literature is being written by machines called wordmills, and after the destruction of these machines by striking writers, the preserved brains of ancient authors (the silver eggheads) are persuaded to try writing again. One problem is that

wordwooze, the wordmill product, has caused readers' tastes to degenerate to the point where they can only appreciate "its warm rosy clouds of adjectives, its action verbs like wild winds blowing, its four-dimensionally solid nouns and electro-welded connectives." The wordmills have been "turning out stories involving action at the bumping level, feelings suitable for conformist morons, and a lead-heavy emphasis on that tiresome tumescence which you euphemistically call love."

As might be expected there are many humorous twists and references to literature, ranging from Lovecraft's use of a similar brain device in "The Whisperer in Darkness" (1931)—which Leiber acknowledges—to nutty synopses of the points of famous novels, such as calling Joyce's *Finnegans Wake* a "little rib-tickler about an Irish funeral." Much of the fun relates to the robots in the novel as he says that "while robots excelled at trouble-shooting and original work, it took a human working stiff to really carry through on a monotonous job." Beneath the mirth, there seems to be a genuine protest against the worst practices of modern publishing. Leiber is not alone among science-fiction writers in being underpaid in comparison with mainstream novelists. He has not suffered from his critics—he has simply been ignored outside the science-fiction community. Although *The Silver Eggheads* is far from being his best work, it is still wickedly amusing.

Leiber's next major effort was a long novel called *The Wanderer* (1964), which earned him another Hugo Award in 1965. The title of the book derives from the Greek verb *planasthai*, meaning to wander, as the planets seem to wander relative to the fixed stars. This is a disaster story about the traumatic effect on people when Earth suffers earthquakes, tidal waves, and other cataclysmic disasters caused by a huge purple and gold "planet," actually a giant space vehicle, which has entered an orbit around Earth. The alien occupants try to rectify some of the problems they have caused, but are finally driven away by another planet-sized spacecraft that is trying to prevent such disasters. The mechanics of the mobile planet and the other plot devices are merely excuses for the main interest in examining the reactions of people. A large cast of characters, both heroes and villains, attempts to survive in the face of total chaos. The story line follows the characters by treating them in successive chapters on a roughly round-robin basis. The characters are generally distinctive enough that there is little problem keeping track of them, in spite of rather abrupt transitions.

An immense amount of detail is given about the events and the characters, and it is this descriptive material which accounts for the length of the novel. The leisurely pace of the narrative results in a depth of characterization that is rarely found in science fiction, even in other disaster novels of this type which depend largely on characterization as their reason for existence. All of Leiber's interests, from cats to the theater, are present. One appearance of the cat is in the character of Tigerishka, a very feline alien. One of Leiber's favorite plays must be Webster's *The Duchess of Malfi*; there are references to it in many of his books and it is used in *The Wanderer* as the basis for a striking, albeit macabre, death scene. Leiber has attempted to deal with almost every facet of human life, from sex to death, or as Samuel Beckett has said, "from the spermarium to the crematorium." The novel provides a vast canvas on which to explore many varieties of the human animal in depth, and to combine with this the rough-and-tumble action of space opera and bits of well-extrapolated science. However, catastrophe stories have been written for thousands of years and even an innately interesting series of character studies does not add up to a cohesive purpose for such a large book; perhaps significantly, Leiber has not attempted anything similar since.

Five years passed before the publication of *A Specter is Haunting Texas* (1969), in which Leiber satirizes racism, war, and inconsistency in values and morals. In this book Scully, an actor from a colony on a satellite around Earth's moon, arrives on an Earth where Texas controls all of North America. He finds himself a reluctant leader in a revolution of the enslaved Mexes against the ruling Texans, who have become giants through the use of hormones. Scully, having been raised in free fall as a ninety-seven-pound "thin," is forced to wear a battery-powered, titanium exo-skeleton to move his eight-foot height in Earth's gravity. His black clothes and visible metal skeleton make him a theatrically convincing death figure, a specter haunting Texas. Theatrical motifs provide an almost constant counterpoint to the plot as in the following description of his experience in Theater-in-the-Sphere:

> Yes, acting in three dimensions in free fall has its special techniques and requires its special conditions. For instance, upstage lies in all directions from stage-center, but so does downstage. You must learn to favor all sections of the audience by rotation in at least two planes, and that requires motivated or surreptitious contact with the other actors on the stage. Also, to make an exit, you must take off from another actor or preferably several, and there should be a counterbalancing entrance. . . . Ideally, 3-D nullgrav acting becomes dramatic ballet with dialogue. Think of . . . Antony's oration again, with the mob a ragged sphere between the orator and the larger sphere of the audience.

Scully quotes Shakespeare when he is at a loss for words; moreover, the clothes and symbolic roles of the leaders are much like costuming and staging, and even the actor's necessity for speaking more loudly than normal has its counterpart in Scully's loud voice, which results from the greater sound transmission of Earth's atmosphere.

Leiber has returned in this novel to satire spiced with a generous dose of the theater, and the result is one of his most satisfying works. Although the melodrama swamps the satire toward the end, the political and social commentary is biting, and the parodies and caricatures continually enliven the fast-paced narrative. However great his concern about the world's troubled future, Leiber rarely preaches; furthermore, though innovative, he rarely tries to be radically avant-garde, and consequently his work has not made the strident call for attention associated with more superficially experimental writing. Perhaps for these reasons, *A Specter is Haunting Texas* has not received the attention it deserves.

In *Our Lady of Darkness* (1977) Leiber returns to the subject matter of *Conjure Wife*, and again the result is something closer to the horror genre than to science fiction. There are in fact a great many references to the literature of the occult and to writers such as Lovecraft and Clark Ashton Smith, not to mention deft mimicry such as this: "Coming back today, I felt that my senses were metamorphosing. San Francisco was a meganecropolis vibrant with paramentals on the verge of vision and audition, each block a surreal cenotaph that would bury Dali, and I one of the living dead aware of everything with cold delight. But now I am afraid of this room's walls!" As in *Conjure Wife*, the progression from the normal to the paranormal is made gradually and believably. The book begins by building a normal picture of Franz Westen, a writer in San Francisco. He is a widower who, though skeptical of such matters, has a professional interest in the occult and supernatural for his writing (the novel seems to contain a certain amount of autobiography). In the course of reading an old book and journal that he has found in a used-book shop—passages from which again reveal Leiber's skill as a mimic of styles—Westen gradually becomes involved with inexplicable events and with the strange contents of the journal,

of which at my age I have quite
a few, it

CATCH THE OSTWALD!

~~FIRST CLASS ON THE OSTWALD~~

by Fritz Leiber

This year on a trip to New York
City to visit my son, who is a
social historian at a leading
municipal university there, ~~in Manhattan~~
I had a very unsettling ex-
perience. At black moments, ~~of which I have quite a few, it at my age~~
still makes me distrust profoundly
those absolute boundaries in Space

①

"Catch the Ostwald!," manuscript

which he feels increasingly certain was written by Clark Ashton Smith. In the end the situation is resolved through witchcraft, but Leiber is no more willing to abandon equivocation about the reality of the supernatural than he was in his earlier fictional explorations of witchcraft a quarter of a century previously.

Leiber has been an unusually prolific writer of short stories and many of these have won awards. The collection of his stories entitled *The Best of Fritz Leiber* (1974), edited by Poul Anderson, contains a high proportion of his best stories. Many of them are relatively simple vignettes portraying a character or situation. One of these, "The Ship Sails at Midnight" (1950), is a brief but effective picture of an alien visitation. One of the characters is interested in "a blend of semantics and introspective psychology designed to chart the chaotic inner world of human experience." If the definition of semantics is stretched a bit to include the use of words in creating fiction, the statement could well apply to Leiber.

Several of Leiber's short stories, including one of his most famous, "Coming Attraction," were published in 1950. This story is part of a series dealing with a decadent United States where women mask their faces but not their breasts, cars are used as weapons, and violence is a favorite form of entertainment. Wysten Turner, a British businessman visiting the United States, encounters one of the fashionably masked women of New York and tries to help her—with surprising results. The series is a satire of a world where the Russian dream of "impossible equality" and the American dream of "impossible success" have clashed and produced little more than chaos and "great psychological insecurity." Leiber has a discerning sense of people's deep-seated psychological motivations. During the 1950s other striking stories appeared, such as "A Pail of Air" (1951), in which the Earth has been pulled away from the sun by a dark star and the atmosphere has frozen solid. (The story may be a precursor to *The Wanderer*.) "Rump-Titty-Titty-Tum-Tah-Tee" (1958) further explores the tendency of the human mind to be hypnotized by phenomena that might be classed as supernatural, in this case the paralyzing effect of a sound sequence and its visual analog. "The Girl With Hungry Eyes" (1949) is an ironic treatment of advertising. Equally imaginative but more experimental is "Little Old Miss Macbeth" (1958). Leiber's use of theatrical technique has been pervasive, but this story is an attempt to use a Shakespearean background as a symbolic basis for plot and imagery. The sleep walking of Lady Macbeth has been transfered to an after-the-bomb

environment, and the imaginary hand washing has become the "pling" of a dripping faucet.

One of the most famous of Leiber's stories, and the winner of both Hugo and Nebula awards, is "Gonna Roll the Bones" (1967). Cast in the form of the American tall tale, this is a psychological horror fantasy about a miner who finds himself in a crap game with the devil, with his soul as the wager. The story is far from simple, with its physical basis in psychokinesis and solid geometry. The Prince of Darkness is an ancient force in Western civilization, and in the afterword to the story in Harlan Ellison's *Dangerous Visions* (1967), Leiber commented on part of the complex symbolism: "The story of the bogeyman is the oldest and best in the world, . . . For the modern American male, as for Joe Slattermill, the ultimate bogey may turn out to be the Mom figure. . . ." The author also discusses witchcraft in psychological terms, defining it as "just another word for the powers of self-hypnotism, prayer, suggestion and the whole sub-conscious mind."

Another Hugo Award winner is "Ship of Shadows" (1969; collected in *Ship of Shadows*, 1979). This is an initially confusing story as the reader tries to get his bearings, much as the characters must navigate in three-dimensional free fall. The main character, Spar, attempts to overcome the equivalent of alcoholism as the reader gradually figures out that the stage is a spaceship. Indeed, the descriptions of this environment are extensions of the theater-in-the-sphere of *A Specter is Haunting Texas*. The futuristic treatment of the supernatural includes vampires and experimental writing. But the narrative experimentation is abandoned in "Catch That Zeppelin!" (1975), a traditional alternate-world science-fiction story that won both Hugo and Nebula awards. Leiber has borrowed some of the mechanics of his Change War series for this story of a German businessman trying to sort pieces of ordinary everyday reality from a world where helium zeppelins and electric cars have solved many of the world's pollution problems. The Change Winds are described as the psychological basis for the mental perception of alternate realities, and the Law of Conservation of Reality, which states that reality tends to change as little as possible, prevents the absurdities that often accompany stories involving the results of changes to the past. The alternate evolution of science and scientists that has made this different world possible is imaginative and convincing.

In addition to his science fiction, Leiber has at least as large a reputation for his fantasy. One unusual item here is that he has written the only

Tarzan sequel authorized by the Burroughs estate. But probably best known is his heroic fantasy series featuring Fafhrd and the Gray Mouser. One of the best of these stories, "Ill Met in Lankhmar" (1971), won both Hugo and Nebula awards as science fiction. Obviously, these stories are not typical "sword and sorcery."

In the series, the world of Nehwon and the city of Lankhmar are made real through richly detailed description and the almost baroque atmosphere of a decadent and strangely civilized barbarism. The stylistic influences of Clark Ashton Smith and E. R. Eddison are evident as is the rich description of Jacobean drama. The characterizations of the tall, northern barbarian and the small, city-bred thief are complex blends of love, pity, terror, and humor; in short, they are made to live as fascinating people. The characters were originally created by Harry Otto Fischer in a letter to Leiber, but Leiber has made them completely his own. Probably the best introduction to these stories is Leiber's own foreword to *The Swords of Lankhmar* (1968):

> Fafhrd and the Mouser are rogues through and through, though each has in him a lot of humanity and at least a diamond chip of the spirit of true adventure. They drink, they feast, they wench, they brawl, they steal, they gamble, and surely they hire out their swords to powers that are only a shade better, if that, than the villains. It strikes me (and something might be made of this) that Fafhrd and the Gray Mouser are almost at the opposite extreme from the heroes of Tolkien. My stuff is at least equally as fantastic as his, but it's an earthier sort of fantasy with a strong seasoning of "black fantasy"—or of black humor, to use the current phrase for something that was once called gallows humor and goes back a long, long way. Though with their vitality, appetites, warm sympathies, and imagination, Fafhrd and the Mouser are anything but "sick" heroes.
>
> One of the original motives for conceiving Fafhrd and the Mouser was to have a couple of fantasy heroes closer to true human stature than supermen like Conan and Tarzan and many another. In a way they're a mixture of Cabell and Eddison, if we must look for literary ancestors. Fafhrd and the Mouser have a touch of Jurgen's cynicism and anti-romanticism, but they go on boldly having adventures—one more roll of the dice with destiny and death. While the characters they most parallel in *The Worm Ouroboros* are Corund and Gro, yet I don't think they're touched with evil as those two, rather they're

rogues in a decadent world where you have to be a rogue to survive; perhaps, in legendry, Robin Hood comes closest to them, though they're certainly a pair of lone-wolf Robin Hoods. . . .

Throughout his career, Leiber has used the same topics and motifs, although with varying emphasis—theater, horror, cats, chess, time, sex, politics, alcohol, humor, sorcery, and romantic love. His stories can be roughly categorized within these, but doing so is not very useful. Leiber's interests and talents make him one of the Renaissance men of modern science fiction. His most commonly used method is satire, but always human understanding is central in his work. It is particularly necessary to understand that the supernatural provides him with more than material for horror stories in that it provides him with a method for dealing symbolically with the unknown. The following comments about monsters from an article in *The Book of Fritz Leiber* (1974) can be extended to this entire subject: "a monster, symbolizing that about which we can only speculate and wonder, is a master symbol suggesting the remotest mysteries of nature and human nature, the most dimly-sensed secrets of space, time, and the hidden regions of the mind. . . . [The artist] knows that he is trying only to design an artistic symbol and give his audience a harmless thrill of fear, asking not for belief but merely for momentary suspension of disbelief. However, many of his sober-minded and perhaps less imaginative critics will feel that he is simply trying to create a new superstition or refurbish an old one . . . . Many of the most typical creations of science fiction, especially the robot, the android, and the extraterrestrial, are simply the monster in a new guise . . . . For, so long as man progresses, the area of the unknown will continue to grow, both inside and outside the mind, and wherever the unknown is, there will be monsters."

Although his imagery is very visual, Leiber is one of the most highly skilled stylists in science fiction, with a fine ear for language and the ability to write parodies effectively. Many literary influences are apparent in his writing, and many of them are acknowledged through direct reference or quotation. The most important are Shakespeare and Lovecraft, but the list can be expanded to include Poe, Machen, Dunsany, Cabell, Eddison, Smith, and Burroughs. There are often flashes of the dark side of Elizabethan and Jacobean drama, particularly John Webster. Despite the fact that much of his writing first appeared in the pulp magazines, most of it is polished and confident, with little of the air of hasty writing characteristic of much science fiction. His control of style has increased over the years, but even the earliest stories are definitely professional pieces.

Much of Leiber's work is innovative and, for its time, experimental. He has gone through four major creative periods, interspersed with relatively fallow times. In each of these he has managed to find new ideas and approaches to science fiction. Through all of his ups and downs he has been able to retain his gusto and obvious belief in the value of human life and to produce works distinguished by a gentle and urbane humanity.

A review of the critical literature of science fiction reveals a surprising lacuna: Fritz Leiber. In one of the few critical treatments of Leiber (outside of book reviews), Judith Merril has said: "Leiber has been ubiquitous, seminal, influential, widely read—and, critically, virtually ignored." This comment was written in 1969 but it is still largely true today. His readers and his fellow writers, who have honored him as the World Science-Fiction Convention Guest

of Honor in 1951 and again in 1979, are more perceptive.

Periodical Publication:

"Catch that Zeppelin!," *Magazine of Fantasy and Science Fiction* (March 1975).

Interviews:

Jim Purviance, *"Algol* Interview: Fritz Leiber," *Algol*, 15 (Summer-Fall 1978): 23-28;

Paul Walker, "Fritz Leiber," in *Speaking of Science Fiction: The Paul Walker Interviews* (Oradell, N.J.: Luna, 1978), pp. 68-77.

References:

Judith Merril, "Fritz Leiber," in a special Leiber issue of *Magazine of Fantasy and Science Fiction*, 37 (July 1969): 44-61;

Sam Moskowitz, *Seekers of Tomorrow* (New York: Ballantine, 1967), pp. 283-301.

Murray Leinster
(William Fitzgerald Jenkins)

Gary K. Wolfe
Roosevelt University

BIRTH: Norfolk, Virginia, 16 June 1896, to George Briggs and Mary Louise Murray Jenkins.

EDUCATION: Public and private schools in Norfolk, Virginia, to eighth grade.

MARRIAGE: 9 August 1921 to Mary Mandola; children: Mary, Elizabeth, Wenllian, Joan.

AWARDS: Hugo Award for "Exploration Team," 1956.

DEATH: Gloucester, Virginia, 8 June 1975.

SELECTED BOOKS: *Murder Madness* (New York: Brewer & Warren,1931);
The Murder of the U. S. A., as Will F. Jenkins (New York: Crown, 1946); republished as *Destroy the U.S.A.* (Toronto, London & New York: News Stand Library, 1950);
The Last Space Ship (New York: Frederick Fell, 1949);

Fight for Life (New York: Crestwood, 1949);
Sidewise in Time, and Other Scientific Adventures (Chicago: Shasta, 1950);
Space Platform (Chicago: Shasta, 1953; revised edition, New York: Belmont Books, 1965);
Space Tug (Chicago: Shasta, 1953);
The Black Galaxy (New York: Galaxy, 1954);
The Brain-Stealers (New York: Ace, 1954);
The Forgotten Planet (New York: Gnome Press, 1954);
Gateway to Elsewhere (New York: Ace, 1954);
Operation: Outer Space (Reading, Pa.: Fantasy Press, 1954);
The Other Side of Here (New York: Ace, 1955);
City on the Moon (New York: Avalon, 1957);
Colonial Survey (New York: Gnome Press, 1957); republished as *Planet Explorer* (New York: Avon, 1957);
Out of This World (New York: Avalon, 1958);
War with the Gizmos (Greenwich, Conn.: Fawcett, 1958);
The Monster from Earth's End (Greenwich, Conn.:

Fawcett, 1959; London: White Lion, 1973);

Four from Planet 5 (Greenwich, Conn.: Fawcett, 1959; London: White Lion, 1974);

The Pirates of Zan and *The Mutant Weapon* (New York: Ace, 1959);

Monsters and Such (New York: Avon, 1959);

The Aliens (New York: Berkley, 1960);

The Wailing Asteroid (New York: Avon, 1960; London: Sphere, 1968);

Twists in Time (New York: Avon, 1960);

Men Into Space (New York: Berkley, 1960);

This World is Taboo (New York: Ace, 1961);

Creatures of the Abyss (New York: Berkley, 1961); republished as *The Listeners* (London: Sidgwick & Jackson, 1969);

Operation Terror (New York: Berkley, 1962; London: Tandem, 1968);

Talents, Incorporated (New York: Avon, 1962);

The Greks Bring Gifts (New York: Macfadden, 1964);

The Duplicators (New York: Ace, 1964);

Invaders of Space (New York: Berkley, 1964);

Time Tunnel (New York: Pyramid, 1964; London: Sidgwick & Jackson, 1971);

The Other Side of Nowhere (New York: Berkley, 1964);

Doctor to the Stars (New York: Pyramid, 1964);

Space Captain (New York: Ace, 1966);

Checkpoint Lambda (New York: Berkley, 1966);

Get Off My World! (New York: Belmont, 1966);

S. O. S. from Three Worlds (New York: Ace, 1966);

Miners in the Sky (New York: Avon, 1967; London: Sphere, 1968);

Space Gypsies (New York: Avon, 1967; London: Sphere, 1968);

Timeslip! (New York: Pyramid, 1967);

The Time Tunnel (New York: Pyramid, 1967; London: Sidgwick & Jackson, 1971);

Land of the Giants (New York: Pyramid, 1968);

A Murray Leinster Omnibus (London: Sidgwick & Jackson, 1968);

Land of the Giants #2: The Hot Spot (New York: Pyramid, 1969);

Land of the Giants #3: Unknown Danger (New York: Pyramid, 1969);

The Best of Murray Leinster, ed. J. J. Pierce (London: Corgi, 1976; New York: Ballantine, 1978).

Depending on one's attitude toward popular fiction, William F. Jenkins might well be regarded as either the quintessential hack or the epitome of the highly professional fiction writer. Of more than one thousand short stories and nearly seventy novels that

he wrote during his long career, relatively little stand out as remarkable from today's perspective, but even fewer seem incompetent or poorly crafted. Though he wrote westerns, adventure tales, murder mysteries, and fiction for magazines such as the *Saturday Evening Post* and *Collier's*, Jenkins's reputation rests mainly on the huge body of science fiction he produced under the name Murray Leinster (though occasionally he would use Will F. Jenkins for the slick magazines or William Fitzgerald in issues of science-fiction magazines that already contained one Murray Leinster story, offering some hint of his prolificness). The Leinster canon is worth studying, if for no other reason, simply because it represents such a huge bulk of the body of popular fiction that gave science fiction its name and traditions during the crucial half-century of its development from 1920 to 1970. Leinster stories appeared with remarkable regularity throughout this period, and to read a sampling of them is to get an overview of the strengths and weaknesses of the developing genre.

Leinster's many novels are generally less significant to the history of science fiction than his magazine work, and indeed many of the novels were merely reworked material from earlier magazine publications. The short fiction is also all too often forgettable. Despite the label of "dean of science fiction" that has often been attached to Leinster, he won surprisingly few awards during his long career and seldom appears on lists of favorite authors or in college classes in science fiction today, but he is worth examining for two principal reasons. In the first place, many of Leinster's early stories are pioneer works in the genre, introducing themes or concepts that would later become standard science-fiction devices— such as the idea of parallel time-tracks introduced in the 1934 *Astounding* story "Sidewise in Time" (collected in *The Best of Murray Leinster*, 1976). In the second place, Leinster's very professionalism and his acute sense of the prevailing editorial winds enabled him to produce a body of work that reflects to a remarkable degree the changing market of science fiction over the years. In other words, Leinster is valuable for his conventions as well as his inventions, for the ways in which he helped create the market for science fiction as well as for the ways in which he responded to that market.

As a youngster in Virginia, Jenkins was fascinated by science, but in a way that would lead readers from today's perspective to regard him as a budding technologist rather than a scientist. His models seemed to be figures such as Edison and the Wright brothers rather than theoretical scientists, and his actual inventions, as well as his later science fiction, reflect this mechanical bias. At the age of thirteen, he successfully designed and built a working glider—only six years after the Wright brothers' flight—and later, among other things, he designed a back-projection system for motion-picture special effects which gained fairly wide use in the industry.

But from an early age, Jenkins's only real occupation was writing. As a teenager, he began to sell short pieces to *Smart Set* and later began to contribute to the pulps, attaining enough success that at the age of twenty-one he was able to resign a position as a bookkeeper with Prudential Insurance in Newark, New Jersey, and declare himself a free-lance writer. Ostensibly to avoid confusion with his more serious work in magazines such as *Smart Set*, he created a pseudonym, Murray Leinster, for his pulp fiction that was apparently compounded from his mother's maiden name and his family's ancestral home in Leinster County, Ireland. His first science-fiction story under this name appeared in *Argosy* on 22 February 1919. In "The Runaway Skyscraper" (1919) New York's Metropolitan Life Insurance Tower is mysteriously transported several centuries back in time. Though no plausible explanation is given for the occurrence, the idea of modern, rational humans confronting a hostile environment and the juxtaposition of what must in 1919 have seemed a technological marvel—a skyscraper—with an unformed natural landscape provide some hint of themes that were to occupy Murray Leinster during much of his science-fiction career.

Two elements characterize much of Leinster's early fiction and serve to illustrate the ongoing tension between convention and invention in his work. Certainly one of the most apparent conventions of pulp science fiction during the early 1920s was that of the mad scientist or the criminal mastermind. Leinster provided many such figures and had them invent such heinous devices as a machine that absorbs heat ("A Thousand Degrees Below Zero," 1919), a machine that absorbs light ("Darkness on Fifth Avenue," 1929) and thus creates heat that gives rise to giant electrical storms ("The City of the Blind," 1929), a machine that creates massive windstorms ("The Storm that Had to be Stopped," 1930), and a machine that blocks the sun's rays from Earth ("The Man Who Put Out the Sun," 1930). But equally apparent in these stories is Leinster's movement away from convention: instead of focusing on the mad scientists involved, he concentrates on the reactions of characters trapped in a radically altered environment. The mad scientist

becomes merely a convenient and conventional means to an end, and the end is really no different from what it had been in "The Runaway Skyscraper"—to construct an adventure out of the reactions of ordinary humans to a changed world.

In fact, while Leinster was happily employing the convention of the mad or addleheaded scientist for much of his fiction, he was at the same time evolving his own version of the scientist as hero. To some extent this is evident in the stories already mentioned, which characteristically feature a brilliant young hero who pits his wits against the supervillain, but it is even more directly expressed in two of Leinster's earlier stories to attain the status of pulp classics. "The Mad Planet" (1920) and "Red Dust" (1921) were later rewritten with a late sequel, "Nightmare Planet" (1953), into one of Leinster's most important novels, *The Forgotten Planet* (1954). The stories are set on a hostile jungle planet—in the original two stories, a distant future Earth, but changed to an artificially "seeded" planet for the novel—in which descendants of technological humanity are reduced to barbarism in a violent world of giant insects and overgrown fungi. But a brilliant scientific mind is born into this society: Burl's curiosity and inductive reasoning enable him gradually to rediscover civilization, first by wandering from his tribal home and later by learning the use of weapons, the possibilities of hunting, and the domestication of animals. Burl leads his people out of the jungle into a temperate area better suited for human life, and there they are met by a spaceship—coincidentally, the first one to visit the forgotten planet in thousands of years—carrying instant-education machines that quickly make Burl and his people into shrewd entrepreneurs who turn their planet into a vacation resort for big-game insect hunters. Despite the absurdities of plot and situation, the novel gains power not only by exploiting primal fears of spiders and insects, but by portraying a simplified version of scientific induction in a context in which it is necessary for survival. Unlikely a candidate as he may be, Burl is Leinster's first real scientist-hero, and the predecessor of a common Galilean hero type in science fiction: the adventurous mind born into a frightened and degenerate society.

By the 1930s there were still plenty of loony scientists in Leinster's fiction, but increasingly they were coming to be replaced by scientists who were heroic, youthful, and brilliant. An interesting meeting between both types occurs in "The Fifth-Dimension Catapult" (1931), an early treatment of the parallel-world theme that was to be a favorite of

Leinster's. Professor Denham is not quite a mad scientist, but he is inept enough to get himself and his daughter trapped in a violent fifth-dimension universe (the fourth dimension, we are told, is time) with his only hope for rescue a slimy German assistant who is secretly in the pay of a Chicago gangster. He is eventually rescued by Tommy Reames, a handsome society playboy who is secretly also one of the world's leading theoretical mathematicians. Unintentionally comic as the story may seem today, it provides an interesting insight into the changing image of the science-fiction scientist; even Denham is redeemed as an admirable fellow in the end.

possible presents; in other words, there are alternate "time paths" in which history took different turns from the ones which produced our world. A cosmic disaster jumbles these time paths, resulting in a situation that gives full play to Leinster's inventiveness: Roman soldiers in Joplin, Missouri, Vikings in New England, and dinosaurs in Ohio. This device of alternate time-tracks was to become a feature not only of Leinster's later fiction, but would be adopted by other writers as well, such as Ward Moore and Philip K. Dick.

The rise of special interest science-fiction pulps after the founding of *Amazing Stories* in 1926 seemed to give Leinster greater freedom in playing with

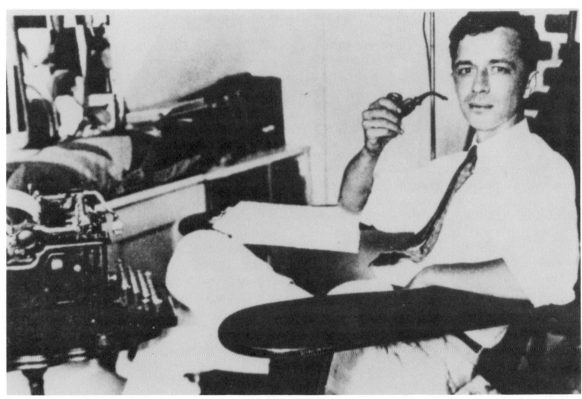

Murray Leinster

But the mousy, maladjusted, power-hungry scientist returns in full force in one of Leinster's most influential stories of the 1930s, "Sidewise in Time." However, an important change has now occurred in this character: instead of being the cause of the disaster, he merely is the only one brilliant enough to forecast and prepare for it, thus becoming a somewhat more morally ambiguous character than the earlier supercriminals. But it is the disaster he prepares for that accounts for the story's historical significance. Because there are a limitless number of possible futures, the narrator explains, it stands to reason that there are an equally limitless number of

science-fiction concepts than he had with general-market magazines such as *Argosy*. An audience began to evolve that shared common interests and assumptions about the content of science fiction— the idea that space travel would lead to encounters with alien life forms, for example—and Leinster addressed this audience with stories that moved beyond the simple adventure story formulae of his earlier fiction. Specifically three kinds of stories began to appear from the Leinster pen that might not have been possible had it not been for the development of this specialized market: space operas, which rested on common assumptions with the reader of interplanetary and interstellar travel and which would become perhaps the most characteristic kind of Leinster story; comic stories, which parodied science-fiction conventions or used them to create slapstick situations; and somewhat more complex idea stories, which used the science-fiction framework to explore real social issues and problems. Though Leinster would never become a significant social satirist, some of his stories in the last category reveal a remarkable prescience about the possible social effects of certain technological innovations.

Examples of all three types of stories abound in the Leinster canon throughout the 1930s and 1940s. Certainly one of his most famous space operas, and a classic science-fiction story, is "Proxima Centauri" (1935; collected in *The Best of Murray Leinster*), significant for its use of two plot devices that would later become common in science fiction: the idea of interstellar space travel requiring many years, and thus resulting in the development of a self-contained society on board the spacecraft, and the idea of an alien civilization evolved from plants rather than animals, resulting in a technology in which spaceships are grown rather than built. Leinster handles well the mounting sense of despair as these plant creatures infiltrate and take over the spaceship from Earth, and even his unlikely ending is based on a well-thought-out pseudoscientific account of the effects of an interstellar drive on neighboring masses.

An early example of Leinster's comedy is "The Fourth-Dimensional Demonstrator" (1935; collected in *The Best of Murray Leinster*), which uses a clever time-travel paradox—the idea that a time machine can bring an object out of the past even if that object still exists in the present—to create a matter-duplicating machine that results in great wealth for its owner but also, in the end, leads to a plethora of duplicated fiancees and kangaroos.

Some social and political ideas were evident in Leinster's fiction of the early 1930s—a 1931 story called "Morale," prophetically subtitled "A Story of the War of 1941-43," predicted that such a war would focus largely on the manipulation of civilian morale, and "Invasion" (1933) has the United Nations founded in 1987. But it was not until the 1940s that he began regularly to focus on the social implications of technology and space travel. In some of these stories the social issues are only implied; "The Wabbler" (1942) is told entirely from the point of view of a machine, a computerized search-and-destroy bomb, but even with no human characters to guide us, we are invited to speculate on the possible effects of such "thinking" weapons. Other stories

make satirical points more explicitly. "Plague" (1944) shows how a massive, rule-bound bureaucracy, set up to govern space travel, nearly allows a "plague" of electron intelligences to destroy human civilization. But perhaps the best, and probably the most prescient, of Leinster's ventures into social satire is "A Logic Named Joe" (1946; collected in *The Best of Murray Leinster*). Essentially, "logics" are computer terminals which have been installed in every home, replacing televisions, telephones, newspapers, libraries, and all other information technologies. Such universal access to limitless information, Leinster argues, would necessitate some sort of "censor circuits" to prevent the entire social order from disintegrating as both personal and public secrets disappear. But a defective logic named Joe somehow causes the whole system to bypass these censor circuits, resulting in persons using logics to spy on their neighbors, commit crimes, and transfer everyone else's funds into their own computerized bank accounts. Told from the point of view not of a scientist but of an uneducated technician who services logics (and who earlier had been a television repairman), the story focuses wittily on the possible consequences of a mass-culture technology that is not fully understood and that is maintained largely by technologists who do not consider its implications.

Leinster served in the Office of War Information during World War II, and, although it is difficult to trace directly what effect this may have had on his fiction, there is certainly an element of political paranoia that begins to appear in his stories dealing with alien civilizations during the postwar period. The most famous of these—indeed the most famous of all Leinster stories—is "First Contact" (1945; collected in *The Best of Murray Leinster*), which depicts the first encounter with an alien civilization as taking place not on a planetary surface but in deep space, in the Crab Nebula. In terms of structure and imagery (particularly Leinster's use of the spectacular, shining background of the nebula) the story stands as one of Leinster's best, but its central feature is the problematical assumption that the alien race may be treacherous and that neither ship can thus return home for fear that the other will follow to stage an invasion. The solution is that the two crews trade spaceships after fixing their own ship so that it cannot track the other—but the true good nature of the alien race is illustrated by the fact that one of them enjoys swapping dirty jokes with one of the humans. The story was attacked in a tale by Soviet science-fiction writer Ivan Yefremov, who denounced the wholesale transplanting of World War II mentality into a future age of such great technical achievement as interstellar travel. But other Leinster stories repeat this theme: "Propagandist" (1947) poses the same problem but uses a pet dog as an intermediary to prove to the aliens that humans are a decent sort. Even in "Incident on Calypso" (1945) a stranded spaceman who is rescued by friendly alien robots on a barren moon chooses to wait until the aliens have left before taking off for home in his own ship—just to be sure they do not follow him. And "Symbiosis," published under the name Will F. Jenkins for the wider audiences of *Collier's* in 1947 (collected in *The Best of Murray Leinster*), concerns a small country, fearful of invasion, that deliberately infects itself with disease and inoculates its entire population; invading armies thus cannot survive in the country's environment, but presumably no other outsiders can either.

The postwar era—more specifically, the post-Hiroshima era—saw an abundance of nuclear holocaust and postholocaust stories, and Leinster responded to this new market trend with a number of stories, all of which are curiously apolitical (Leinster never identifies the attacking country, for example). As Will F. Jenkins, he published a general audience novel, *The Murder of the U. S. A.* (1946), in which the atomic destruction of all major American cities by an unknown aggressor becomes a glorified murder mystery, and was even marketed as such by its publisher, Crown. "The Day of the Deepies" (1947) deals with what would become a fairly common theme in postholocaust stories, the notion that all science would be stigmatized by the atomic destruction it had brought forth. The story portrays the rediscovery of the value of science among a group of persons who are persuaded by a "deepie" ("d.p.," or displaced person, ostracized because of his scientific training) that this is the only way to defend against the unknown invaders. "The Laws of Chance" (1947; republished as *Fight for Life,* 1949) adds a curious fantasy element to this motif: the atomic blasts have created a few crystalline rocks that somehow serve to align the laws of chance in accord with the wishes of the holder, making virtually any wish not impossible come true. The concept reflects an ambivalent attitude toward atomic energy—it is literally a wish-granting genie as well as an agent of destruction—as well as a recurring desire on Leinster's part to find some correlation between natural laws and human behavior. This desire may have something to do with Leinster's Catholicism (he was a devout convert), and is expressed even more directly in "The Ethical Equations" (1945; collected in *The Best of Murray Leinster*), which posits a

mathematical relationship between good works and good fortune.

During the late 1940s and early 1950s, aided by the rise of the paperback industry, science fiction began to appear more frequently in book form, and a good case could be made that the anthology was the most influential form of science-fiction publishing throughout much of the 1950s. As Leinster's stories began to appear with remarkable frequency in anthologies, and as he kept up his prolific contributions to the magazines, the Leinster name came more and more to permeate the genre. He collected several of his earlier stories in *Sidewise in Time, and Other Scientific Adventures* and edited a general collection, *Great Stories of Science Fiction* (1951), introduced by Clifton Fadiman. Later in the next two decades more collections of Leinster's own short fiction would appear: *Monsters and Such,* a collection of tales featuring, of course, monsters; *The Aliens* (1960), a collection concerning forms of alien intelligence; *Twists in Time,* stories about time-travel; *Doctor to the Stars* (1964) and *S. O. S. from Three Worlds* (1966), stories concerning an Interstellar Medical Service, which came to be known as the Med Service stories. Two notable effects resulted from this increased paperback market: Leinster's stories gained a wider and more permanent audience and influence, and Leinster began moving into the more profitable segment of the paperback book field—full-length novels.

Although direct influences are difficult to determine in a mass-market field such as science fiction, it is clear that Leinster either introduced or developed concepts that would later become conventions of the genre. He continued to develop new ideas in the late 1940s, and the wider audience afforded by the anthologies makes it seem plausible that some of these ideas may have had a direct effect on later authors who would develop them further. A number of examples come to mind. "The End" (1946; collected in *Twists in Time*) concerns the crew of a spaceship who avoids the end of the universe by using relativity-dilation to travel into the distant future, into the new universe formed by the new big bang—an idea also used by Poul Anderson in his *Tau Zero* (1970). "This Star Shall *Be* Free" (1949) anticipates ancient-astronaut theories by presenting the notion that art, hunting, and weaponry evolved as the result of an experiment in artificial imbalance by aliens visiting Cro-Magnon man. "The Lonely Planet" (1949; collected in *Monsters and Such*), which concerns a being named Alyx that covers the entire surface of a planet and can read human minds, contains many elements developed at greater length and depth in Stanislaw Lem's *Solaris* (1961). "The Lost Race" (1949), which Leinster identified as his favorite story for a 1949 anthology, concerns an ancient race that mysteriously committed racial suicide (a theme also used in the film *Forbidden Planet*, 1956) because they found themselves evolving into monsters. The monsters, of course, turn out to be human beings.

With the expanding paperback and magazine markets in the 1950s and 1960s, Leinster, and indeed the field of science fiction itself, began to suffer an embarrassment of riches. In fact it might be argued that it was too easy to get published during this period, and Leinster's increasing output of novels reflects this. Many are merely short stories written into continuity, with little thought of overall structure. *The Last Space Ship* (1949) was a stringing together of three space-opera stories published in *Thrilling Wonder Stories* in 1946 and 1947; *The Forgotten Planet* was based on stories published as early as 1920; *Colonial Survey* (1957) wove together four stories from *Astounding Science-Fiction* in 1955 and 1956; *Out of This World* (1958) was three stories from 1947 issues of *Thrilling Wonder Stories*. Another group of novels was rewritten slightly, if at all, from their original appearances as novelettes in magazines, or as serials. Thus, for example, "Journey to Barkut" (1950) became *Gateway to Elsewhere* (1954); "The Man in the Iron Cap" (1947) became *The Brain-Stealers* (1954); "The Strange Invasion" (1958) became *War with the Gizmos* (1958); "Lord of the Uffts" (1964) became *The Duplicators* (1964); "Stopover in Space" (1966) became *Checkpoint Lambda* (1966); and so on. This practice of reworking magazine material into book form is certainly widely accepted in science fiction, but the frequency with which Leinster practiced it is further evidence that he remained to the end of his career essentially a magazine writer.

The novels that Leinster published originally in book form tend to be highly formulaic and largely undistinguished. Three of them—*Space Platform* (1953), *Space Tug* (1953), and *City on the Moon* (1957)—are directed at a juvenile audience and share a common hero, Joe Kenmore, who thwarts spies and saboteurs on space stations, spaceships, and in a lunar colony. Others are fairly standard reworkings of traditional science-fiction plots. Encounters with powerful monsters are the substance of *Creatures of the Abyss* (1961) and *The Monster from Earth's End* (1959); the latter generates some fairly effective suspense in its variation on John W. Campbell, Jr.'s classic "Who Goes There?" (1938). Alien invaders are treated in *The Greks Bring Gifts* (1964), a

variation on Damon Knight's earlier story, "To Serve Man." Psi powers are the subject in *Talents, Incorporated* (1962), travel into the past in *Time Tunnel* (1964), and the exploration of space in *Operation: Outer Space* (1954) and *Miners in the Sky* (1967). *Operation Terror* (1962) is one of several science-fiction novels that reflects a cold-war mentality by arguing that the only way to avert war on Earth is to stage a false invasion by alien creatures, thus uniting Earth's warring factions. Several of Leinster's novels during this period are adaptations of popular television shows: *Men Into Space* (1960) from the "Men Into Space" television series; two novels from the "Time Tunnel" series, *The Time Tunnel* and *Timeslip!* (both 1967); and three novels from the "Land of the Giants" series, *Land of the Giants* (1968), *Land of the Giants #2: The Hot Spot* (1969), and *Land of the Giants #3: Unknown Danger* (1969).

As many of these novels indicate, Leinster in his later career grew increasingly to depend on established formulae and the demands of an easy market. Although few of these stories introduced important innovations of plot or concept, many exhibited what readers were coming to feel was a Leinster trademark: the posing of a complicated problem to be worked out given the resources of an advanced but reasonably constrained technology. His Colonial Survey stories of the 1950s and his Med Service stories of the 1950s and 1960s consistently follow this structure. The problems to be solved may be as massive as the sudden cooling of an entire planet ("Critical Difference," 1956; collected in *Colonial Survey* as "Solar Constant"), and the solutions as ingenious as collaboration between men and mutated bears ("Exploration Team," 1956; collected in *Colonial Survey* as "Combat Team"). Such problem solving was recognized with a Hugo Award for "Exploration Team" in 1956 and was continued with the possible applications of future medical technology in the Med Service tales. Occasionally Leinster's problem-solving ability was combined with his parodic skills, as in his last major novel of the 1950s, *The Pirates of Zan* (1959), which broadly satirizes many of the same conventions of space opera that Leinster had helped to introduce, while at the same time using those conventions to construct a clever plot. The novel was nominated for a Hugo Award in 1960.

Leinster's astonishing publication record—averaging something like a story every two weeks and a novel every nine months for better than a half-century—makes it difficult to gain a critical perspective on him, and it may be in part because of this that the years have not been particularly kind to him. While his historical importance is undeniable, his work suffers from the anonymity of ubiquitousness; while virtually every science-fiction reader and writer knows some of his work, few cite him as a major influence or a favorite author. Perhaps the 1978 collection *The Best of Murray Leinster*, edited by John J. Pierce, will enable readers to get a better perspective on his work. If it does, they will be able to see that his consistent belief in enlightened rationalism and human advancement through scientific reasoning is among the most accurate reflectors of the central values of the science-fiction genre through more than fifty years of its development.

Other:

Great Stories of Science Fiction, edited by Leinster (New York: Random House, 1951; London: Cassell, 1951).

Periodical Publications:

"The Runaway Skyscraper," *Argosy* (22 February 1919);

"A Thousand Degrees Below Zero," *Thrill Book* (15 July 1919);

"The Mad Planet," *Argosy* (12 June 1920);

"The Red Dust," *Argosy* (2 April 1921);

"Darkness on Fifth Avenue," *Argosy* (30 November 1929);

"The City of the Blind," *Argosy* (28 December 1929);

"The Storm that Had to be Stopped," *Argosy* (1 March 1930);

"The Man Who Put Out the Sun," *Argosy* (14 June 1930);

"The Fifth-Dimension Catapult," *Astounding Stories* (January 1931);

"Morale: A Story of the War of 1941-43," *Astounding Stories* (December 1931);

"Invasion," *Astounding Stories* (March 1933);

"The Wabbler," *Astounding Stories* (October 1942);

"Plague," *Astounding Stories* (February 1944);

"Incident on Calypso," *Startling Stories* (Fall 1945);

"The Laws of Chance," *Startling Stories* (March 1947);

"The Day of the Deepies," *Famous Fantastic Mysteries* (October 1947);

"Propagandist," *Astounding Stories* (October 1947);

"The Lost Race," *Thrilling Wonder Stories* (April 1949);

"This Star Shall *Be* Free," *Super Science Stories* (November 1949);

"Nightmare Planet," *Science Fiction Plus* (June 1953).

References:

Sam Moskowitz, "Murray Leinster," in his *Seekers of Tomorrow: Masters of Modern Science Fiction* (New York: Ballantine, 1967), pp. 55-72;

J. J. Pierce, "The Dean of Science Fiction," introduction to *The Best of Murray Leinster*, ed. Pierce (New York: Ballantine, 1978), pp. ix-xvi.

JACK LONDON
(12 January 1876-22 November 1916)

SELECTED BOOKS: *Children of the Frost* (New York: Macmillan, 1902; London: George Newnes, 1913);

Moon-Face and Other Stories (New York: Macmillan, 1906; London: Heinemann, 1914);

Before Adam (New York: Macmillan, 1907; London: T. Werner Laurie, 1908);

The Iron Heel (New York: Macmillan, 1908; London: Everett, 1908);

When God Laughs and Other Stories (New York: Macmillan, 1911; London: Mills & Boon, 1912);

The Night Born (New York: Century, 1913; London: Mills & Boon, 1916);

The Strength of the Strong (New York: Macmillan, 1914; London: Nelson, 1917);

The Scarlet Plague (New York: Macmillan, 1915; London: Mills & Boon, 1915);

The Star Rover (New York: Macmillan, 1915); republished as *The Jacket* (London: Mills & Boon, 1915);

The Red One (New York: Macmillan, 1918; London: Mills & Boon, 1919);

The Science Fiction of Jack London, ed. Richard Gid Powers (Boston: Gregg Press, 1975);

Curious Fragments: Jack London's Tales of Fantasy Fiction, ed. Dale L. Walker (Port Washington, N.Y.: Kennikat Press, 1975).

While historians of American literature have routinely placed Jack London among the Naturalists, there are among his enormous output a number of works that belie such classification. Three of the novels—*Before Adam* (1907), *The Iron Heel* (1908), and *The Star Rover* (1915)—a novella, *The Scarlet Plague* (1915), and a dozen or so short stories are clearly works of science fiction, at least in the widest sense of that rather imprecise term. But just as literary historians have accorded little attention to the fantastic dimension of his art, so historians of science fiction have tended to scant London's contribution to their genre. Recently, however, the publication of two collections of his science-fiction stories and a growing critical reexamination of London's total achievement have focused interest on his role as a fabulist in the tradition of Edgar Allan Poe and H. G. Wells. Yet his influence on the development of science fiction and his proper place in that tradition remain largely to be fixed.

John Griffith London was born in San Francisco, the child of a spiritualist, Flora Wellman, and her common-law husband, William Henry Chaney, an itinerant astrologer. Although in later life Chaney denied to London that he was his father, the evidence leaves little doubt of his paternity. The year of her son's birth, Flora Wellman married John London, who accepted the boy as his own and gave him his name. The family's declining economic condition, the result of Flora's get-rich-quick schemes that invariably failed, entailed frequent relocation, so that London's boyhood was lonely and insecure. By age sixteen, however, he had borrowed the money to buy a sloop and established himself as "Prince of the Oyster Pirates" on San Francisco Bay. The next year he spent several months as a hand on a sealing schooner working the North Pacific; on his return to San Francisco he won first prize in a newspaper contest with his description of a typhoon off the coast of Japan. After a brief but debilitating stint shoveling coal in a power station, London joined in 1894 the western detachment of "Coxey's Army" for its bonus march on Washington, D.C. He deserted it, however, in the Midwest to ride the rails as a hobo and chicken thief, until in Niagara Falls, New York, he was arrested for vagrancy and sentenced to a month in the county prison—experiences he would later recount in *The Road* (1907). Returning to California, London finished high school in Oakland, joined the Socialist Party, and entered the University of California at Berkeley, which he attended for only one semester in 1896. Like his mother, ambitious to get rich quick, London joined the Klondike gold rush and spent the winter of 1897 in the Yukon, where he found little gold but a rich vein of narrative material that he would mine lucratively in his meteoric rise to literary fame. Once again in California, but now with an amazing variety of experience for a man of his age, London determined to pursue a career as a writer, or "brain worker" as he termed it, and began

inundating publishers with everything from poetry to philosophical essays—at first to no avail. But in 1899 he sold his first stories, the most financially rewarding of which was a science-fiction tale, "A Thousand Deaths" (collected in *Curious Fragments*, 1975), for which he was paid forty dollars. This sale allowed him to pay off his debts and confirmed his decision to be a writer.

London later considered "A Thousand Deaths" "a penny's worth of rot," but the story is one of his most fascinating efforts at science fiction and extremely revealing of his attitude toward William Chaney, whom he now knew to be his true father. In it a young man is used by his scientist father as a guinea pig "to discover the method—and by practical demonstration prove the possibility—of renewing vitality in a structure from which life had seemingly fled." For this purpose the son is repeatedly killed by his own father—"not a father but a scientific machine"—in a variety of gruesome ways and repeatedly resurrected. Driven to desperation, the son, through some scientific wizardry of his own, disintegrates his father into a mass of isolated elements. "A little pile of elementary solids lay among his garments. That was all. The wide world lay before." The story invites psychological probing, but apart from its relevance to London's own psychic life, "A Thousand Deaths" contributes to the already venerable "mad scientist" motif of science fiction, evincing kinship with Mary Shelley's *Frankenstein* (1818), Wells's *The Island of Dr. Moreau* (1896), and, most particularly, with Nathaniel Hawthorne's "Rapaccini's Daughter" (1844). Another London story of that same year, "The Rejuvenation of Major Rathbone" (collected in *Curious Fragments*), also shares a motif with Hawthorne's "Dr. Heidegger's Experiment"—the quest for eternal youth. Whereas Hawthorne's story is soberly moralistic, London's is comically high-spirited, a tall tale in the Western tradition; but both are only marginally science fiction, depending on the scientist's discovery of an elixir of life to set the plot in motion.

In 1900 London married Bessie Maddern, an alliance seemingly more of convenience than of passion, and published his first book, *The Son of the Wolf*, a collection of Alaskan stories. By 1903, when *The Call of the Wild* appeared and propelled him to fame, London was financially secure and producing at a prodigious pace. His next science-fiction story, "The Shadow and the Flash," was published that year. Perhaps inspired by Wells's *The Invisible Man* (1897), London's tale recounts the rivalry of two men, each of whom discovers a different way of rendering himself invisible: one, the Shadow, by deriving "the perfect black . . . [that] will be utterly and absolutely invisible"; the other, the Flash, by achieving perfect transparency. Their duel to the death is a surreal battle of rainbow lights and swift shadows. Though some science-fiction critics claim that London's story is superior to Wells's, the claim is entirely misguided: despite some mildly interesting notions about visual perception, the story is trivial and lacks altogether Wells's serious probing into the scientific mentality.

By 1907 London had divorced his first wife and married his second, Charmian Kittredge—the Mate Woman of his fantasy—and achieved notoriety both for his escapades and his espousal of socialism in a lecture tour he undertook across the country. He had sunk a small fortune in the building of the ill-fated yacht the *Snark*, on which he began a voyage through the South Seas in April 1907. That year also saw the publication of his first science-fiction novel, *Before Adam*. It belongs to the tradition of the anthropological romance, tales of prehistoric times stimulated by the widespread interest in Darwin's evolutionary theories, tales whose characters are only protohuman, as close to the ape as to modern man. In *Before Adam* London employs a narrator who has both a primitive and a modern existence: the story is composed of the structured fragments of dreams, "a procession of nightmares," that the modern incarnation dreams of his primeval past. "My dream life and my waking life were lives apart," the narrator states. "I was the connecting link that somehow lived both lives." London is adumbrating here Jung's theory of a collective unconscious, a racial memory, but particularizing it in one schizophrenic consciousness: "Snakes? Long before I had heard of the existence of snakes, I was tormented by them in my sleep."

Maxwell Geismar has noted that the novel's "dominant mood was of primitive fear or, at its best, of brief, and still terror-haunted and transient pleasure amidst all the horrors of the jungle." The narrator's mid-Pleistocene alter ego—Big Tooth—belongs to The Folk, one of three simian "species" that occupy the same evolutionary time and space and struggle against one another. Although the narrative recounts Big Tooth's diversions with his friend Lop Ear and his mate Swift One, his life is pervaded with danger, dread, and destruction—by prehistoric beasts, by the atavistic Red-Eye of his own tribe, and finally by the technically more advanced Fire People, who annihilate all but a small remnant of The Folk. *Before Adam* closes on that elegiac, even apocalyptic note that will mark a number of London's later works: "We do not sing

and chatter and laugh. We play no pranks. . . . We make plaintive, querulous noises, look at one another, and cluster close together. It is like the meeting of the handful of survivors after the day of the end of the world." The narrator confesses his own puzzlement at how the knowledge of his previous existence is transmitted when The Folk appear evolutionarily doomed, but London rests content with the ambiguity.

Since its original publication, *Before Adam* has never been out of print and remains one of London's most popular fictions, the first of his works, he proudly noted, to be translated into Russian. Loren Eisley has claimed that "no writer has since produced so moving and vivid a picture of man's primordial past as has Jack London"; and Charmian wrote in her biography of her husband that the novel "went into the universities of the United States as a textbook in Anthropology." On the surface it is deceptively simple, almost a child's book, but like other books once relegated to the nursery—such as *Gulliver's Travels* or *Alice in Wonderland*—it is a serious, even pessimistic, work, containing some of London's most skillful blending of materials from psychology, anthropology, and biology. The dual personality motif that London uses for his narrator-protagonist reappears in two other of his short

Jack London

stories—"When the World Was Young" (1910; first collected in *The Night Born*, 1913), a tale often thought to be the prototype for the Tarzan books, and "South of the Slot" (1909; collected in *The Strength of the Strong*, 1914)—and will be used in an immensely more complicated form as the basis for *The Star Rover*.

In 1908 London published his most famous and influential work of science fiction, *The Iron Heel*. Indebted to Wells's *When the Sleeper Awakes* (1899), and in turn influencing George Orwell's *1984* (1949), *The Iron Heel* projects a nightmare future when America falls under the domination of a rigid capitalist Oligarchy, The Iron Heel. The main narrative is composed of a manuscript written by Avis Everhard, wife of Ernest Everhard, the socialist leader opposing the Oligarchy and the novel's hero. Appended to her manuscript, however, are the comments of an editor who writes from the vantage of the twenty-seventh century, "after three centuries of The Iron Heel and four centuries of the Brotherhood of Man." The Oligarchy's initial triumph, London indicates, could not be sustained, despite the most repressive, totalitarian measures, against the inexorable evolution of socialism. The immediate pessimism of the novel is thus superseded by an ultimate optimism, dystopia giving way to utopia—the only utopia, surely, ever to be couched exclusively in footnotes.

Avis's manuscript recounts the events from 1912 to 1932 that led to the destruction of an emerging socialist consensus at the hands of the capitalist oligarchs. Though the story focuses on the personal experiences of the Everhards, since they are at the eye of the storm, their fate serves as synecdoche for the fate of socialism. The effect is a tale both immediate and personal, yet theoretical and general. While long stretches of the novel are devoted to Ernest's preachments on socialism that grow tedious, still others are intensely dramatic; London's imagination seems particularly energized by scenes of mass destruction and carnage, such as in the titanic battle for Chicago where the workers' uprising is brutally crushed by the mercenaries of the Oligarchy. Indeed, so compelling is London's detailing of the destruction of the socialists that some have concluded that his imaginative attraction to violence subverts his message of hope. David Ketterer, for instance, remarks, "The critical reader . . . being unable to accept the reality of London's socialist utopia, can only conceive of a reality in which the dystopian situation continues indefinitely." While it is true that the dystopian drama far outweighs the utopian promise, still London has so framed the

novel that his hopeful resolution does not appear wholly false—only depressingly distant. As Avis declares after the Chicago debacle: "The Cause for this one time was lost, but the Cause would be there tomorrow, the same Cause, ever fresh and ever burning."

Much of the fame of *The Iron Heel* rests on its apparent prophecy of fascism. Though many of his fellow socialists were dismayed by London's scenario of the future and roundly condemned the book as defeatist, Trotsky, writing in 1936, hailed the book as the most perceptive analysis of the rise of fascism yet made, superior even to those of Lenin and Rosa Luxemburg. Anatole France concurred: "Alas, Jack London had that particular genius which perceives what is hidden from the common herd, and possessed a special knowledge enabling him to anticipate the future." While London should not be denied such insight as he had, his prescience in anticipating fascism, with its unparalleled will to destruction, may well have stemmed not so much from profound historical analysis as from a similar impulse within himself, an imaginative penchant for the cataclysmic that fascism realized historically. In any event, *The Iron Heel* remains his most powerful and significant fantasy of the future, widely recognized as one of the classics of social science fiction.

Several of the science-fiction short stories collected in *Curious Fragments* and in *The Science Fiction of Jack London* (1975) may be clustered around *The Iron Heel*, almost as ancillaries to it. One is "A Curious Fragment" (1908), a dull and didactic tale of slave life under the Oligarchy. "Goliah" (1908), by contrast, serves as an important counterpoint to the novel. Here a scientific genius, possessed of a mysterious energy source called Energon, destroys armies and topples governments to impose a socialist utopia on a stunned but grateful world. "Today I destroyed the American Navy," London gleefully reported to a friend while composing the story. "Oh, I haven't a bit of conscience when my imagination gets to working." Indeed, London's conscienceless delight in imagining destruction undermines the putative melioration of Goliah's new social order and renders the story more dystopian than he intended. Both "The Enemy of All the World" (1908) and "The Unparalleled Invasion" (1910) again demonstrate London's fascination with wholesale destruction. In the former, a socially persecuted scientist takes revenge on society by murdering large numbers of its officials by remote control; in the latter, the extermination through biological warfare of the entire population of China is envisioned—an evidence of London's fear of "the yellow peril" that had grown in him since, as a war correspondent, he had witnessed Japan's defeat of Russia in the Russo-Japanese War of 1904. The horror with which millions of Chinese perish is rendered with a vividness almost psychopathic in its power.

In "The Strength of the Strong" (1911) London returns to prehistory for a parable of social organization to rebut an attack on socialism made by his erstwhile literary model, Kipling. London's fable is to capitalism what Orwell's *Animal Farm* (1945) is to communism, as telling in its own way, but less witty and far more heavy handed. Nevertheless, Philip Foner has called it "one of the classics of socialist literature" and it was widely distributed in pamphlet form as anticapitalist propaganda. So, too, "The Dream of Debs" (1909) was circulated by labor unions, particularly the International Workers of the World, as evidence of the way in which a general strike could succeed. In this tale such a strike paralyzes the entire nation and brings capitalist America to its knees, begging to negotiate. The scenes of San Francisco despoiled and reduced to anarchy in "The Dream of Debs" are repeated even more effectively in *The Scarlet Plague*, one of London's most artistically accomplished works of science fiction. An apocalyptic tale of civilization's collapse as a result of a mysterious disease, in the tradition of Mary Shelley's *The Last Man* (1826) and countless later end-of-the-world projections, *The Scarlet Plague* equals Wells's *The War of the Worlds* in its depiction of a society in its panicked death throes. The few survivors of the plague revert to a primitive tribalism of posthistory, not greatly different from that of the prehistoric clans of *Before Adam*. The proffered possibility that civilized life might reappear after a centuries-long dark age seems to commit London to the sort of cyclical pattern of history exemplified in Walter M. Miller, Jr.'s *A Canticle for Leibowitz* (1960).

This theme is taken up, but on the level of one individual's metempsychosis, in London's last and most ambitious science fiction novel, *The Star Rover*. By 1914, though now a world famous figure, London had suffered a serious decline in artistic power: most of his writing was hackwork, churned out for the money he needed to support his vast and unprofitable ranch in California's Sonoma Valley. In her study of London's life and times, his daughter, Joan London, noted, "*The Star Rover* . . . was Jack's last attempt at a serious work. Into this extraordinary and little-known book he flung with a prodigal hand riches which he had hoarded for years, and

compressed into brilliant episodes notes originally intended for full-length books . . . After *The Star Rover* he made no further effort to write well."

The framing narrative of *The Star Rover* is the story of Professor Darrell Standing, convicted of murder and sentenced to life imprisonment in San Quentin. As additional punishment, he is subjected to long stretches in the "jacket," a cruel device for rendering a man immobile. Finally, he is hanged for hitting a guard. This stratum of the novel comprises a vigorous expose of and protest against inhumane prison conditions and capital punishment. The novel shades into science fiction, however, with Standing's discovery while in the jacket that he can make his physical body die and send his spirit out to reexperience its many past incarnations: "I trod interstellar space, exalted by the knowledge that I was bound on a vast adventure, where, at the end, I would find all the cosmic formulae and have made clear to me the ultimate secret of the universe." The cosmic secret that Standing arrives at, through reliving his past lives, is that the soul is immortal and never perishes, only transmigrates. "I did not begin when I was born nor when I was conceived. I have been growing, developing through incalculable myriads of millenniums. All these experiences of all these lives, and of countless other lives, have gone into the making of the soul-stuff or the spirit-stuff that is I . . . I am this spirit compounded of the memories of my endless incarnations." In this late work, London's Naturalistic materialism—most forcefully expressed by the character Wolf Larsen in London's *The Sea-Wolf* (1904)—gives way to spiritual transcendence, a romantic idealism utterly at odds with the views commonly associated with the author's name. The view, however, allows for a technique of incorporating the many different narratives he had stored up into one encompassing synthesis, the keynote of which, London proclaims, "is: THE SPIRIT TRIUMPHANT." Whether idealism determines the technique, or vice versa, is an open question, for London elsewhere wrote that he had concocted the pseudophilosophy of the novel to appeal "to the Christian Science folks . . . and the millions who are interested in such subjects."

The biographical sketches incorporated in *The Star Rover* range from that of Ragnar Lodbrog, a Dane serving as Roman legionnaire in Jerusalem at the time of Christ's crucifixion, to Jesse Fancher, a youth killed by Mormons in the notorious Mountain Meadows Massacre of 1857. Except for representing previous incarnations of Standing's soul, the stories have no common denominator; they vary in length, quality and interest, and neither singly nor collectively support the novel's "triumphant spirit" thesis. Any other set of tales, one feels, could serve as well. London, in a sense, agrees: Standing, he says, has been every kind of man and woman and will be so countless times again. While such a theoretical stance justifies the inclusion of any number of stories of any kind whatever, in practice the structure of the book is arbitrary, a series of sketches stuck together with some metaphysical paste, but lacking organic coherence. The whole is obviously meant to be greater than the sum of its parts, but conception outstrips execution.

The Star Rover remains the most obscure of London's science-fiction novels, its quality a matter of controversy. Maxwell Geismar dismisses it as "incredibly bad," but Andrew Sinclair, London's most recent biographer, calls it "a genuine quest for the myths of the unconscious," a work of "true power," and Leslie Fiedler believes it to be one of the forgotten classics of American literature. About a work as ambitious, sprawling, innovative, and uneven as this, a critical consensus is unlikely ever to emerge. It remains London's most problematic novel.

The last years of London's life were increasingly unhappy. For all the high fees his writing brought, his financial affairs were in disarray. Having broken with the Socialist Party, he became ever more isolated from former friends and political comrades. Alcoholic, ill, dependent on drugs, his attempts at serious writing only fitful, London was by 1916 a man at the end of his tether. On November 22, he died from an overdose of drugs, possibly a suicide, although the death certificate gave the cause as uremic poisoning. He was forty years old.

The last and best of London's science-fiction stories was written a few months before his death and published posthumously—"The Red One" (1918; collected in *The Red One*, 1918). Bassett, a botanist attacked by cannibals on Guadalcanal, finds refuge with an inland tribe of headhunters whose shaman patiently tends the dying but armed and thus still dangerous man, until he can claim Bassett's head as the prize of his collection. Bassett had found the tribe by following a mysterious, hauntingly ominous sound that he discovers to emanate from a huge, perfectly spherical object, worshipped by the natives as a star-born god. Bassett's meditations on the unearthly sounds of the Red One, the irony of the space messenger mired among uncomprehending savages, compose the center of this profoundly provocative story: "Who were they, what were they, those far distant and superior ones who had bridged the sky with their gigantic, red-iridescent, heaven singing message? . . . And . . . were their far conclusions, their long-won wisdoms, shut even then in the huge, metallic heart of the Red One, waiting for the first earth-man to read?" As he surrendered his head to the shaman's ax before the Red One, Bassett "gazed upon the serene face of the Medusa, Truth."

Though "The Red One" lacks the renown among readers of science fiction that it deserves, knowledgeable London critics concur that, as Richard G. Powers puts it, "it is both his finest science fiction story and one of his best efforts in any genre." Dale Walker calls it an extraordinary fantasy "of shuddering impact." Though by no means flawless—the tortuously baroque style of its telling often proves an annoyance—"The Red One" is clearly a minor masterpiece of science fiction, more teasingly ambiguous yet more compelling than anything else London ever wrote in this form. Here his artistry soars far above his wonted Naturalist theories and achieves an imaginative purity of vision all too rare in his other work. The tale is a fitting coda to London's career. —*Gorman Beauchamp*

Biographies:

Irving Stone, *Sailor on Horseback: The Biography of Jack London* (Boston: Houghton Mifflin, 1938);

Joan London, *Jack London and His Times* (Garden City: Doubleday, 1939);

Richard O'Connor, *Jack London: A Biography* (Boston: Little, Brown, 1964);

Andrew Sinclair, *Jack: Biography of Jack London* (New York: Harper & Row, 1977).

References:

Gorman Beauchamp, "Jack London's Utopian Dystopia and Dystopian Utopia," in *America as Utopia*, ed. Kenneth Roemer (New York: Burt Franklin, 1980);

Philip Foner, *Jack London: American Rebel* (New York: Citadel Press, 1947);

Maxwell Geismar, *Rebels and Ancestors: The American Novel, 1890-1915* (Boston: Houghton Mifflin, 1953), pp. 139-215;

Frederic Cople Jaher, *Doubters and Dissenters: Cataclysmic Thought in America, 1885-1918* (New York: Free Press, 1964), pp. 188-216;

David Ketterer, *New Worlds for Old: The Apocalyptic Imagination, Science Fiction, and American Literature* (Bloomington: Indiana

University Press, 1974), pp. 126-133;

Nadia Khouri, "Utopia and Epic: Ideological Confrontation in Jack London's *The Iron Heel*," *Science-Fiction Studies*, 3 (July 1976): 174-181;

Earle Labor, *Jack London* (New York: Twayne, 1974);

Labor, ed., *Modern Fiction Studies*, special London issue, 22 (Spring 1976);

Charmian Kittredge London, *The Book of Jack London*, 2 vols. (New York: Century, 1921);

Kenneth S. Lynn, *The Dream of Success: A Study of the Modern American Imagination* (Boston: Little, Brown, 1955), pp. 75-118;

Jay Martin, *Harvests of Change: American Literature 1865-1914* (Englewood Cliffs, N. J.: Prentice-Hall, 1967), pp. 234-239;

Walter B. Rideout, *The Radical Novel in the United States 1900-1954* (Cambridge: Harvard University Press, 1956), pp. 38-61;

Joan R. Sherman, *Jack London: A Reference Guide* (Boston: G. K. Hall, 1977);

Dale Walker, *The Alien Worlds of Jack London* (Grand Rapids: Wolf House Books, 1973);

Walker and James E. Sisson III, *The Fiction of Jack London: A Chronological Bibliography* (El Paso: Texas Western Press, 1972);

Conway Zirkle, *Evolution, Marxian Biology and the Social Scene* (Philadelphia: University of Pennsylvania Press, 1959), pp. 301-350.

Papers:

Major collections of London's materials are located at the Henry E. Huntington Library, San Marino, California, and at the Utah State University Library, Logan.

Contributors

Peter S. Alterman..*Gaithersburg, Maryland*
Brian Attebery ....*College of Idaho*
William C. Barnwell..*Columbia, South Carolina*
Alex Batman...*University of South Carolina*
Michael Beard..*University of North Dakota*
Gorman Beauchamp ....*University of Michigan*
Patricia Bizzell..*College of the Holy Cross*
Bill Blackbeard..*San Francisco Academy of Comic Art*
Edra Bogle...*North Texas State University*
Stephen Buccleugh ....*University of Alabama*
Gerald W. Conley...*Columbia, South Carolina*
Thomas F. Dillingham ....*Stephens College*
Greta Eisner...*George Mason University*
Robert A. Foster...*Glen Mills, Pennsylvania*
Gerald M. Garmon...*West Georgia College*
William L. Godshalk ....*University of Cincinnati*
Stephen H. Goldman ....*University of Kansas*
Deborah Schneider Greenhut..*Rutgers University*
Patricia M. Handy ....*University of Nebraska at Omaha*
Bruce Herzberg..*Clark University*
James Scott Hicks...*Columbia, South Carolina*
Norman L. Hills ....*Des Moines, Iowa*
Patrick G. Hogan, Jr. ....*University of Houston*
John Hollow...*Ohio University*
Robert L. Jones..*Radford University*
William P. Kelly ....*Queens College*
Michael W. McClintock..*University of Montana*
Kevin Mulcahy...*Rutgers University*
Laura Murphy ....*Chapel Hill, North Carolina*
Patricia Ower..*Columbia, South Carolina*
Donald Palumbo ....*Northern Michigan University*
Joseph Patrouch ....*University of Dayton*
William Mattathias Robins ....*West Orange, New Jersey*
Hugh M. Ruppersburg ....*University of Georgia*
Erich S. Rupprecht...*South River, New Jersey*
Beverly Rush..*University of Alabama*

Amelia A. Rutledge ....*George Mason University*
Tyler Smith ....*University of South Carolina*
Carol M. Ward ....*University of Tennessee*
Charles L. Wentworth...*Columbia, South Carolina*
Helen M. Whall ....*College of the Holy Cross*
Raymond J. Wilson III .... *Kearney State College*
Gary K. Wolfe ....*Roosevelt University*
Thomas L. Wymer ....*Bowling Green State University*

VANGUARD
science fiction

FIRST ISSUE: KORNBLUTH · JONES · DEL REY · DE CAMP

COS: PLANET UNKNOWN
By A. Bertram Chandler

EDITED BY JAMES BLISH

WONDER Stories

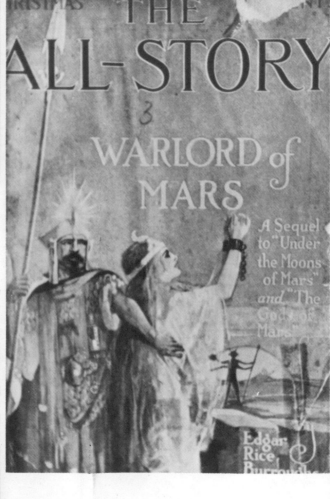

THE ALL-STORY

WARLORD of MARS

A Sequel to "Under the Moons of Mars" and "The Gods of Mars"

Edgar Rice Burroughs

ASTOUNDING
SCIENCE-FICTION
A STREET & SMITH PUBLICATION

NIGHTFALL
By ISAAC ASIMOV
SEPTEMBER · 1941

FEBRUARY 1920 25 cts.

ELEC
EXPERI
SCIENCE A

SUSPENDED GRAV
SEE PAGE 990